S0-AZO-003

KING
OF PARIS

A NOVEL BY

Guy Endore

19 56

SIMON AND SCHUSTER
New York

ALL RIGHTS RESERVED
INCLUDING THE RIGHT OF REPRODUCTION
IN WHOLE OR IN PART IN ANY FORM
© 1956 BY GUY ENDORE
PUBLISHED BY SIMON AND SCHUSTER, INC.
ROCKEFELLER CENTER, 630 FIFTH AVENUE
NEW YORK 20, N. Y.

W

LIBRARY OF CONGRESS CATALOG CARD NUMBER: 56-9908
MANUFACTURED IN THE UNITED STATES OF AMERICA

TO

Marcia and Gita, my daughters

And my thanks to the library staff of the University of California in Los Angeles for providing me with many hard-to-find books, and to Mary Clarke for friendly discussions and help on the manuscript, and to Joseph Mischel (*zichrono livracha*, may his memory be a blessing) for his invaluable encouragement and stimulation.

Le livre de la vie est le livre suprême
Qu'on ne peut ni fermer, ni rouvrir à son choix;
Le passage attachant ne s'y lit pas deux fois,
Mais le feuillet fatal se tourne de lui-même;
On voudrait revenir à la page où l'on aime
Et le page où l'on meurt est déjà sous vos doigts.

—Verse written in an album by
Alphonse de Lamartine

∾ CONTENTS ∾

PROLOGUE

The Secret That Every Man Takes to His Grave

HE WAS ONE of those men who live ten lives while the rest of us are struggling through one.

What an experience it must have been to have known him in person. In the flesh. In his towering mass of warm flesh, never tired and never cold, six feet three in his stockinged feet. Laughing at all his enemies, shrugging off their scorn and their ridicule, saying, "What do you expect of me? I'm once and for all simply incapable of hate. Rage? Yes, I can be enraged. Because rage is brief. But hate? No, I can't hate. Hate endures." (And this in spite of the fact that he wrote *The Count of Monte Cristo*, classic novel of implacable hatred.)

He fought, according to his own count, at least thirteen duels. The result of his momentary rages, of course. And one of these duels has the distinction of being perhaps the shortest on record.

"Pistols!" cried Dumas. "I insist on pistols!"

"Swords!" countered Jules Janin, the well-known critic and novelist. "Am I not the injured party? Have I not the right to the choice of weapons? Very well then: I say swords!"

"You must be mad!" Dumas exclaimed. "Don't you know that I'm a genius with the sword? I command every one of the 12,210 combinations of the eight positions. Pistols—or you are as good as dead."

"Do you question my ability with a pistol?" Janin protested. "Why, I can snuff out a candle at thirty paces. You're finished if you put a pistol in my hand. No. It must be swords."

Such mutual magnanimity proved irresistible. Touched by a common generous impulse, critic and author fell into each other's arms and wept.

Dumas' duels. Ah, yes, Dumas' duels. It will take us this whole book to have our say on them. For *there* is the essence of the man. If you had to express Alexandre Dumas in one word, that word could not be anything else but "duel." Not only in his life but also

1

in his novels and his plays, men are forever crying to each other, "*En garde!* Defend yourself!"

And yet on more than one occasion Dumas evaded a fight. Particularly in the case of his bitterest enemy, Eugène de Mirecourt, who publicly and repeatedly insulted Dumas in the grossest terms. This would have been Dumas' most sensational duel—if he had fought it. But he didn't.

Dumas' reputation as a man of courage, already long under suspicion, was then definitely finished. When he produced his *Clichy Barrier*, a melodrama based on France's last desperate effort to hold up the capture of Paris after Napoleon's massive defeat at Leipzig, and thought to clinch the success of his play by firing off real cannons on stage and unfurling authentic battle-scarred flags, the most timid critic of Paris did not hesitate to write: "Dumas' drama at the Théâtre National last night displayed such fulsome evidence of the author's patriotism that one can only wonder that he didn't pay his beloved France the supreme compliment of writing it in some other language."

Clichy Barrier closed quickly when this deadly comment became the joke of the town. The real cannons and the real flags were returned to the armory.

What then? Swords? Pistols?

No. Dumas, broke again, borrowed some cash from his moneylender Hirschler and took the young critic to lunch at the Frères Provençaux, the city's most expensive restaurant. "One thing is certain," Dumas assured him. "You will never lack for a job. A David critic who can kill my Goliath of a five-act play with a single sentence is always sure of a place on a Paris paper."

Duel? What for? Aren't authors and public and critics already engaged in a sufficiently deadly duel? As for the fate of his play—well, too bad. But then he was already busy with another one and didn't have time to weep over what was already in the past. *Clichy Barrier* was his forty-eighth or maybe his fifty-eighth play and he was still to write some forty or fifty more. And at that speed there's little time to be wasted in regrets. Indeed, Dumas wrote his plays—between novels—at such a rate that once when a play got lost in manuscript he actually forgot the whole thing.

Frédéric Lemaître, the great star, had been so anxious to have this particular play that Dumas had sent the manuscript to him, tied in a blue ribbon, before having the usual copies made. But every time Dumas suggested that they get a cast together and read the play in preparation for production, Lemaître found some new excuse.

The truth was that Lemaître had mislaid the play and didn't dare tell Dumas. And thus months passed and piled up gradually into years, and eventually Dumas put the matter out of his mind.

Then one day Lemaître went to see Dumas. "Remember the play you wrote specially for me?"

"Yes, yes, of course!" Dumas cried. "Well, shall we get to it finally?"

"Certainly," said Lemaître. "That is, if you can read this. I can't." And he handed Dumas a mass of papers so weather-beaten as to be absolutely illegible. Only the blue ribbon had somehow retained its color. "I don't know how it happened, but your play got stored in our attic. There was a leak in the roof right above it. If it weren't for the fact that we are now in the process of moving, this thing would never have been found at all."

"No matter," said Dumas. "It will all come back to me. Just re-mind me of the plot."

"You expect me to remember the plot?" Lemaître cried.

"Just a hint is all I need," said Dumas. "One hint and the whole thing will probably come back to me."

"I'm sorry," said Lemaître, "but the play disappeared the day you sent it to me. I never even got to read it. Can you ever forgive me?"

"Forgive you?" Dumas smiled. "Perhaps I ought to thank you. You may have saved me from another failure like *Clichy Barrier*." And he calmly tossed the indecipherable manuscript into the fire-place.

Such was this man. No wonder that even after he lost his reputa-tion because of his refusal to fight Eugène de Mirecourt, he re-mained in a sense as popular as ever. Perhaps because he was a figure—that is to say, a person so easily recognized that he was like a landmark in Paris. And perhaps because he was a genuine char-acter—that is to say, a person completely himself, modeled after no one else.

And also because he never underplayed himself.

He was not one of your closed-box types. You need have no fear of wounding his sensibilities by addressing him directly. His warm smile and his ready handshake never failed. His paw was big and friendly. Naturally he was incapable of hate: where would hate have managed to lodge itself in all that solid, radiant warmth?

You would have thought that in return people could no more hate him than they could hate a St. Bernard dog. But you would be wrong. He was hated. And not cordially either. Because you could not possibly hate him cordially. Anyone owning a heart, the organ of cordiality, must have liked and forgiven the man.

Michelet, the French historian, for example, being shown how great chunks had been torn out of his *History of the French Revolution* and dressed up as novels under Dumas' name, went to pick a bone with Dumas; but he was so charmed by the man that he wrote to him afterward: "You're not a man. You're a force of nature!"

And Dumas replied in one of his magazine articles: "My dear Michelet, admit that historians are better the more their works read like novels, while novels are best the more they read like history."

No, the correct style for those who wanted to hate Dumas was to pity him. With a smile of tolerance, to be sure. This was an attitude so indicative of one's own superiority that it was a pleasure to assume it. Then Dumas became "that good old blackamoor!" And one would gladly have patted his crinkly hair and forgiven him his clowning and his crudity.

Of course the ordinary run of people continued to read and to love his best books and his best plays, and they forgave him the others, for even when he tired you Dumas never exhausted or annoyed you. His wine was often mixed with too much water, but it was never tepid or turgid or off taste.

And the publishers continued to publish him because Dumas always had the good sense to borrow so heavily from them that they were forced to keep pushing his works so as to balance their accounts.

The Goncourt brothers, those two writers who collaborated so consistently and who lived such closely linked lives that it was said that one of them would sometimes scratch the other without having been told that he itched, or even where he itched, and that both of them got along on one shared breath—these Goncourt brothers, seeing Dumas once at the evenings of the Princess Mathilde Bonaparte, described him thus in their common diary (well, yes, they kept a common diary, though it is not true that they snuggled up in one nightgown to write it):

Dumas is a kind of a giant with the hair of a Negro, the salt beginning to mix with the pepper, and with little blue eyes buried in his flesh like those of a hippopotamus, clear and mischievous; and an enormous moon face, exactly the way the cartoonists love to draw him. No doubt about it: there's a magnetism that radiates from him. A kind of mesmerism. You sense at once the showman of freaks and prodigies; the vendor of wonders; the traveling salesman for the Arabian Nights. He talks volubly and, it must be admitted, engagingly; but what holds you is not brilliance, nor mordancy, nor color; it is an endless array of facts, astounding facts, facts that he keeps dredging up in a pleasantly hoarse voice from a memory that is like a bottomless ocean.

Nadar, the ubiquitous photographer of Paris (whose advertisement of himself in the nacelle of a gas balloon was eventually plastered on every blank wall of the city), could not have produced a better portrait of the man.

An American Negro, a free Negro, William Wells Brown, came all the way from the United States hoping to induce Alexandre Dumas to journey to America and lecture in behalf of the abolition of slavery. But Brown found it next to impossible to secure an interview. Dumas was perpetually surrounded by people, especially by girls who were always besieging him for a part in his next play, and he answered none of Brown's many notes.

Dumas simply didn't write letters. "I often sit down to write a letter," he used to explain, "but I always end up by selling it as an article or a story. After all, I'm too well paid for whatever I may write to fold it up and mail it off to a single reader when I can just as well have ten thousand readers and some cash in the bargain."

To which argument no one has ever been able to find an adequate answer.

Just as no one has ever been able to answer his reason for refusing to use punctuation marks in his manuscripts. This resulted from a printer's once changing the position of one of his commas.

"Ah," said Dumas, "so you know how to punctuate?"

"Of course, Monsieur. Every printer has to learn how to punctuate correctly."

From that day on, despite the hundreds of thousands of manuscript pages he wrote, Dumas was never guilty of a single punctuation mark, neither comma nor period, neither question mark nor dash.

"These are matters that every printer knows," Dumas would always say. "Let me take care of the words. Let him handle the punctuation. With both of us doing our best we'll have a fine book."

Well, this man Brown happened one evening to be in a Parisian theater waiting for the curtain to rise when he noticed the whole audience giving their attention to a commotion that was taking place in one of the boxes. He saw a stout man, dressed in a startling costume of deep black velvet, with white vest and white kid gloves, entering a box and taking his place there along with a flock of pretty girls. He sat looking like a pasha in his harem, and a very pleased pasha at that. He was a great black-and-white rock against which a surf of femininity dashed itself into a spray of silk and velvet. Or to put it perhaps better: he looked like a huge bumblebee about to devastate a bouquet of sweet-smelling flowers. There was something about it that was both immoral and disgusting, and yet, somehow, you had to smile.

Everyone whispered the name of Alexandre Dumas.

Brown rose immediately, with the determination that this time the man would not elude him. He pushed his way into the box. The rumor that Dumas had African blood in his veins was confirmed the moment you laid eyes on him: he had kinky hair, a pudgy nose in a swarthy face, thick lips smiling over brilliantly white but chunky, crooked teeth, and nothing in his face attempting to belie his origin except a pair of blue eyes, clear as polar ice.

Over the heads of the giggling girls Brown managed to reach Dumas' ear. He extended to him the invitation which he had put into his many letters.

Dumas burst into hearty laughter. "Go to America?" he cried. "My dear ladies, salute this brave man! He has managed, at the risk of his life, to escape from the slave barracoons of the Carolinas, and now what do you think? He does me the honor of assuming that I am as brave as he is, and that I will go back to America with him!"

"I am not a slave," Brown corrected rather stiffly. "I didn't escape. I am a free man of color."

"You pay me a great compliment, Monsieur," Dumas declared. "But really, there's a limit to my manhood. I am not so foolhardy as to go to America, where every cotton planter will drool at the thought of putting chains on my ankles, a cangue around my neck, and driving my two hundred and ninety pounds of muscle off to his cotton or rice fields. Brrr. Just the thought of a bastinado on my sensitive feet, Monsieur! No, no. Spare me. Indeed, I marvel that you, having escaped alive, contemplate returning."

"You are picturing the condition in the South, sir. There's no slavery in the North. Not in Boston, which is the Athens of our culture."

"Yes. But *la loi de Lynch*, you have that, don't you? Didn't they lynch that man Lovejoy? Yes, that poor fellow, an editor like myself, was murdered for no more than what I would have shouted had I been in your country: freedom! For I cannot forget your great Washington, your Jefferson and your Paine, who made the revolution in America and whose deeds then inspired a similar movement in our own country. Don't forget, Monsieur, that this right hand shook that of General Lafayette and received from him a commission in the army that overthrew our king, Charles X, in 1830."

"But, Monsieur Dumas," Brown exclaimed, "that's precisely what America has yearned to hear from you ever since we published your first book, *Progress and Democracy!*"

"Yes. My *Gaule et France*."

"Yes, sir."

"Really you do tempt me, Monsieur Brown. But no. It's unthinkable. You see my grandfather was the Marquis de la Pailleterie. And I myself am entitled to display the arms of the family, although like my father I use the name of my Negro grandmother, Dumas." And unceremoniously pushing aside the girls around him, Dumas described and illustrated with great waving gestures the three eagles of his escutcheon whose beaks and talons held various

armorial devices as well as the motto: *"Deus dedit, Deus dabit"*—
meaning, "God has given, God will give"— "which would be a pre-
sumptuous statement," Dumas explained, "if God had not so obviously countersigned it." And with a laugh Dumas put his arms
around two girls.

Brown, dazzled and lost, conjectured that perhaps Dumas, despite his proudly proclaimed democratic principles, still cherished
his aristocratic birth and was afraid that in the fierce leveling atmosphere of America he would not receive his due as a member of
the nobility of France. Brown said, "America will be glad to show
you all the honors due your marquisate, Monsieur Dumas. I assure
you Americans are very partial to titles of aristocracy in spite of
our equalitarianism."

"You misunderstand me," Dumas said. "My father fought through
the entire French Revolution—on the side of the people, of course—
rising from a common soldier to become a full general. It was his
misfortune to divine Napoleon's secret ambition to place himself
on the throne of France. This my father had to oppose, and Napoleon broke him. No, no, we Dumas scorn inherited honors. But I
did want to show you that I am not the type of man who would
submit to being insulted."

"But who proposes to insult you, sir?"

"Why, the Americans!"

"Not at all!" Brown cried, bridling.

"Let us be clear," said Dumas. "Is it not true that in your country
even a fraction of black blood makes a man a Negro?"

"That is indeed our cutaneous prejudice," Brown admitted, "but
it is subscribed to mainly in the South."

"Well, don't you see, then, that though I take pride in my African
blood and cannot concede that any reference to it constitutes an
insult, yet I would be obliged to interpret as such any remarks or
looks that seem to take exception to or derive humor from my
appearance? A trip to America would mean a hundred duels for
me. I can see that clearly. Of course I would win ninety-nine out
of a hundred, because I was trained by Grisiers, the world's greatest
master of the dueling sword, and in the matter of firearms I am
only to be compared to those squirrel hunters who never kill except
with a bullet through the squirrel's eye, so as not to damage his

pelt. But winning ninety-nine duels is just one short of what is required for life and limb. And my schedule of work calls for another hundred and fifty novels, which I must write before I have covered the entire range of human history so that everyone may make himself familiar with the whole story of man's civilization merely by amusing himself—that is to say, by reading my novels."

At this moment an usher came to the Dumas box and, with many pardons for his intrusion, begged Monsieur Dumas to observe that the raising of the curtain was being delayed because the actors did not feel themselves equipped to compete with Dumas for the attention of the audience.

Dumas apologized and promised that he would efface himself. But as the usher left he continued to talk: "If you wish to do your black compatriots a service," he said, "then note that man below, the tall man sitting bolt upright, dressed all in mouse-gray."

"I see him," Brown said. "Who is he?"

"That is Granier de Cassagnac, an editor and writer, whose name sounds like the crunching of pebbles, and whose heart is as hard as rock. He is the inveterate enemy of the colored man. He fought Schoelcher when it came to the question of freeing the slaves of our French sugar islands in the West Indies. Go and insult him, and force him to a duel and kill him. You will be doing your race a great service. And France too. For he will yet destroy our country. But I warn you. He is as deadly as your American rattlesnake. He practices with the *épée* two hours a day, and every week goes target shooting. He has already been responsible for many deaths. It was he, I am sure, who organized the duel that I fought with Gaillardet. He is certainly responsible for the killing of Dujarier in a duel. He is full of deadly tricks."

The traditional three knocks sounded and the curtain rose.

"Sh-sh!" said Dumas so loudly that it frightened people sitting high up in the gallery.

Brown never again got close enough to Dumas to exchange any words. But his description of the author conforms to that of others who had met him: the amiable giant, the engaging clown, the sparkling wit, as well as his addiction to the company of the other sex.

And of course the subject of dueling. Always the subject of dueling. As for himself, Brown took good care not to get mixed up in any duel with Granier de Cassagnac. After some further brief glimpses of the author—once at Tortoni's, where he saw him passing out free theater tickets to a knot of squealing girls, and another time driving by in an open barouche in the midst of loud company—Brown returned safely to America.

What an opportunity this man Brown missed when Dumas proposed to him that he should provoke Granier de Cassagnac to a duel! What an opportunity to ask Dumas: "Why don't *you?* What's stopping you from provoking him to a duel and killing him? After all, you're the unbeatable Dumas, aren't you?"

This was of course the core of the matter: that this unbeatable Dumas whose every page of writing glitters with the clash of swords; that this unbeatable Dumas who for years posed as France's authority on every phase of the subject of dueling; that this unbeatable man who, you might say, made his fame and fortune from duels (paper duels, to be sure) should have ducked a physical encounter with Eugène de Mirecourt and instead sued him for libel in the most humdrum way—*that* was the ugly fact in Dumas' life. The literary and artistic world of Europe and America gasped—and then rocked with laughter.

Dumas' reputation was done for. The hero had become the clown. It is at this stage that whatever dirty joke happened to be circulating immediately got itself attached to the name of Dumas. Nineteenth-century gossip swarms with Dumas jokes. So that, whether true or not, it was Dumas who, being a guest one evening in a terribly crowded salon, permitted himself one of the rudest of human noises and excused himself by saying, "Sorry. Stuffy, isn't it? Just had to let in a little fresh air," et cetera, et cetera, *ad nauseam.*

Not that I wish to give the impression that Dumas was incapable of a salty wit of his own, of the same type as that displayed by Balzac in his *Contes Drôlatiques.* This was after all part and parcel of the Romantic movement in literature, a kind of thumbing of one's nose at the purist pretensions of the classicists: the Gallic, the Gothic side of France, revolting against the Latin. But it is one thing to be salacious and quite another to be a buffoon.

Thus it was that my first impression of how wonderful it would have been to have known this man in the flesh became, on further study, corrupted with the fear that it might on the contrary have been quite embarrassing. And yet already the man had captured me. Already I loved him and felt that, if only I studied on, I would find the explanation for his conduct.

But Dumas isn't so easy to know, even though you will run into his name everywhere, in all the periodicals, in all the memoirs, in all the collections of letters of the mid-nineteenth century, for he knew everyone and everyone knew him. Still, as clearly as you may be able to picture Dumas—for example, on a rainy afternoon in Paris, running for a cab along the Boulevard des Italiens, his gold chains, his jewel-studded fobs, his prized order of Nizam bouncing furiously on his generous belly, while he brandishes his sword cane and yells, as he himself phrased it, "like a sow with a breach presentation"; as sharply as you may envisage every detail of him, as, wet to the skin, with muddy shoes and trousers, and swearing Dantesque imprecations at all the tribe of coachmen, he sets off for the nearest public bath to clean himself up, the real man still somehow escapes you. No, not even the six huge volumes of his autobiography give you the feeling that you have got to the bottom of this personality.

The Countess Dash, who was a real enough countess but took the name of her dog for a nom de plume when circumstances forced her to earn her living with her pen (how well she knew that it was going to be a dog's life!), told Dumas the truth about his memoirs: "Despite the three thousand pages you've filled with words, you've managed to leave out the most interesting parts of your life."

Dumas shrugged. "Is that my fault? Don't you realize that nowadays even little girls are taught to read?"

Countess Dash burst into laughter right in Dumas' face, for she couldn't believe, not for one moment, that it was for the sake of keeping blushes away from the pure cheeks of little girls that Dumas had omitted some of the most important events of his life.

Dumas' son, the second Alexandre Dumas to figure in the history of literature, the man who wrote *The Lady of the Camellias,* generally called *Camille* in America, was more honest about it when, in his reply to a professor at the University of Edinburgh who had written to him for an account of his life, he stated: "Autobiographies are meaningless because no man dares put into writing the most significant facts of his life."

When I ran across that sentence in my studies on Dumas I suddenly had the eerie feeling that perhaps father and son were both thinking of the same significant event. Plutarch says somewhere that every man has had at least one experience that he would sooner die than reveal. And Voltaire has expressed the same thought this way: "In every confession there is a crime that is never confessed."

This secret that every man takes to his grave, could it, in this case, be the selfsame secret that both father and son had taken with them? Then how could anyone possibly hope to discover it at this late date? And yet, perhaps I may have done just that.

And quite by chance, too. Because I was consulting Pierre Larousse's vast masterpiece, his *Universal Dictionary of the Nineteenth Century*, not for his articles on the two Dumas, which are brief and contain nothing new, but in order to fill out my picture of the Paris of those days. And it is there, in Larousse, that I stumbled onto what to me seems the clue to the man.

CHAPTER ONE

"Duel after the Masquerade Ball"

PARIS, in the mid-nineteenth century, was already in the process of changing from a medieval city to a modern one. Baron Haussmann, it is true, had not yet torn open the town with his huge slashes which, it was said, were aimed at preventing the Parisians from ever again building barricades against the authorities, and thus, surrounded by the old boulevards, the ancient streets still twisted and turned every which way and like as not ended in blind alleys. But changes there were. For one thing the city was no longer lighted by candlelight as it had been for several centuries—one lantern by royal decree at every street corner, and another lantern (by still another royal decree proclaimed some fifty years later) midway in between. In those days, when the candles had burned out, which was about midnight, the city was given over to ruffians, and honest people avoided the out-of-doors. Parisians of those days were frugal, and the candles were lighted only on the three weeks of the month that did not have a good moon. For half a century the royal lanterns were in use only during the dark months from November until February. Those were, by the way, the lampposts on which mobs hanged aristocrats, to the terrible cry of *"À la lanterne!"*—a cry that caused the disappearance of the too easily recognized aristocratic wig and breeches and gave us our modern styles.

How different was Paris in the middle of the nineteenth century when she was lighted by 13,910 gas jets, each jet made of porcelain and pierced with thirty tiny holes. Lights that burned no matter what the month, or what the moon, and were not extinguished until dawn. And the practice of hanging aristocrats had meanwhile gone quite out of style. There wouldn't have been enough aristocrats in any case.

Truly Paris was becoming *"la ville lumière,"* and it was also destined to acquire a huge sewer, a real cloaca maxima, indeed that very same celebrated sewer which figures in Victor Hugo's *Les Misérables,* and against which that author was to fulminate in some wonderful paragraphs predicting the downfall of France because

13

this sewer would rob the fields of their most valuable fertilizer—night soil—a fertilizer to which, Hugo declared, Chinese philosophers wrote ecstatic poems because it had kept the soil of China fertile and its population virile for five thousand years. But the sewer was built all the same and the picturesque scavengers and their donkeys who used to gather the ordure of Paris became the victims of progress, Chinese philosophers and Victor Hugo notwithstanding.

Anyhow, there was now a sewer. And of course the railroads. They sprouted out from Paris in all directions, and Dumas commented: "You arrive. True. You reach your destination. That much can't be contradicted. But have you traveled? No. You have merely had your body transported, no more and no less than one might have shipped a corpse." And he himself continued to prefer the horse-drawn diligences wherever they could still be found, which was rarer and rarer as time went on.

He loved to be able to inspect dreamy wayside villages, note every old building, every stream and every field. And when there was a rise and the pace of the horses relaxed, he loved to get out and walk beside the stagecoach, often gun in hand. And if no game warden showed, then he would take an occasional shot at a rabbit or a partridge, which he would share with his fellow passengers later at some inn.

More than anything else he loved old inns where one stopped to change horses and where each time, as a new postilion entered the scene, Dumas could pump him for information about local people and local events. And what scenes too when diligence would meet diligence on the road and the two postilions would argue as to whether to switch horses and thus enable each postilion to return all the sooner to his station with his horses.

And then at night, to sit beside the fire in some good hostelry where an innkeeper's wife who was a character in her own right could be wheedled out of the secret of her special crawfish soup, a recipe which Dumas would hoard away against the time in his old age when he would publish his enormous *Grand Dictionnaire de Cuisine.*

That, yes, that he called traveling. Time wasn't wasted. One lived. One met people. One had adventures. And Dumas wrote about it all in such a way that years later tourists could use his travel books as Baedekers that were more exciting than Baedeker and in many cases more reliable.

For he who brought to life again the cloak and dagger of old France was himself in some respects the last representative of a world that was soon to die. A world that lived faster, perhaps precisely because it lived at a slower pace.

You may skip the following description of Paris in the middle of the nineteenth century if you like. But in truth, if it hadn't been for that curious condition of Paris which someone has called "vertical democracy," this story could never have happened exactly as it did.

In Paris the old buildings, the old private residences, were gradually transformed into apartment houses to accommodate the growing population, and for many years the rule was that the more steps you had to climb, the cheaper the apartment. Later came the era of speculative building, new suburbs were opened up, and the whole feeling of Paris changed. But for many years it was true, and often said, that those who lived beneath you deemed themselves above you.

On the first floor, amidst crushing luxury, lived the wealthy bankers, along with those aristocrats who had been clever enough to follow the intricate dance from revolution to empire, from Bourbon to Bonaparte and back again, with little quick change-steps in between when the republics took over. On the second floor dwelt prosperous merchants and magistrates who understood a thing or two. On the third floor were the humbler ranks of the *bourgeoisie*, actresses in vogue, retired officers living on their pensions, and so forth. Above them, in ever smaller rooms with ever more moderately priced furniture, were the little shopkeepers, the musicians who had won conservatory prizes, and the kept women of the intermediate variety, also such professors who had managed to marry an income of a modest nature.

Thus on the staircase of these houses every class rubbed up against every other class in a most democratic sort of friction, which gave a special flavor to Parisian life, and especially to Parisian novels.

It was the architect Mansard who had shown the landlords of Paris how to get an extra rental floor by turning the garrets formerly used as storage or as sleeping quarters for the most wretched refuse of society into habitable apartments by breaking the angle of the roof and punching out dormer windows. Working girls found these rooms overlooking the roofs of Paris suited to their slender earnings. They put pretty little curtains in the windows, and flower pots on the sills, and suddenly all Paris discovered that wherever you raised your eyes you might see a pretty girl framed by lacy curtains and underlined by red geraniums or orange nasturtiums.

Yes, thus did the students and artists of Paris discover Bohemia: it was up in the air. And a whole literature, a whole philosophy of life, arose from this discovery, which to be sure was far from being in strict accord with the truth, for actually these working girls labored from morn to midnight at sweatshop wages and were therefore only too willing to earn a free meal along with some little joy, by adding the hours of the night to their working time. And furthermore, in summer, there, directly under the roof, one was in a veritable Turkish bath. While in winter one well nigh froze to death.

Nevertheless this was Bohemia. And here Dumas, when quite young and newly come to Paris, discovered a pretty seamstress by the name of Catherine Lebay and fathered from her a son who grew up to be the author of *The Lady of the Camellias*, in some respects a more famous writer than his father.

It was finding so many various subjects so interestingly discussed in Larousse's great dictionary that led me to continue my research in this vast amalgam of information, where, for example, you may learn that the first rapid-transit system for Paris was conceived by a man named Omnes, who thought to perpetuate his name by calling the special vehicle he designed *Omnibus*, which is really a clever pun on his own name since in Latin that signifies *for everyone*. But alas it was not his name that was to be given immortality, but only that last meaningless syllable, *bus*.

Oh, you will find everything in this Larousse dictionary—for example, the fact that the Omnibus company stabled six thousand horses in its Parisian stables and kept them so clean that rewards could be posted for anyone who would discover a fly there. And that the speed of a bus was about six miles an hour and each team of horses could be worked for a total of fifteen miles a day.

Is it actually so surprising, then, that I should find my clue to the Dumas mystery under the word "Duel" in volume D of this great dictionary? After all, it was Larousse's idea to gather together in one work everything that might be of interest to a man of the nineteenth century, and he therefore gave himself and his collaborators all the leeway they wanted. For which reason you will find here a long article on tightrope dancing in which the encyclopedist argues that tightrope dancing being more difficult than ordinary dancing and in addition dangerous, he cannot see why it should be deemed a lesser art and relegated to circuses and other cheap forms of entertainment. Why, he asks, should a dancer who dances on the floor and never risks her neck be paid huge sums, while a dancer who has to use far more skill to balance herself on a rope is paid a miserly wage?

Imagine the editors of our staid *Encyclopaedia Britannica* finding room for such an excursus!

This Pierre Larousse was himself a striking figure, a typical product of France in the nineteenth century—that is to say, a character altogether his own: independent, fearless, hard-working, concentrated, determined to know everything there was to know. Such ambitions are to be found only in a century that could still believe in the basic values of courage and application, in the leadership of reason and talent, in the glow of a dawn that seemed to promise a world society of science and enlightenment. Who today would dream the dream of a Bartholdi: to plant at the gate of the New World a gigantic copper lady with a lamp upraised? Who today would say, like Balzac, I shall be greater than Napoleon: he failed to conquer the world with his sword. I shall conquer it with my pen!

What a time it was! Even pygmies were consumed with an ambition to walk like giants. The brain of man seemed to be on fire. Every heart was bursting with a desire to achieve. Man pitted his enthusiasm against the mystery of God, the immensity of space, the wonder of nature, the stubbornness of matter, as if by an intoxication for work, as if by a passion for truth one could sweep aside the Himalayas and guide mankind into a fresh world of new glories.

It seemed as if God had never been so lavish with talent. The competition among writers, musicians, painters was furious. The Salon of Paris began to find the old square hall of the Louvre too small as the number of selected paintings rose to nearly two thousand, and the exhibit had to transfer itself to the Tuileries. And there the battle for the public's attention had reached the feverish pitch of the so-called *coup de pistolet* painting, the pistol-shot canvas whose purpose was primarily to startle, to make sure of at least one thing: that, whether praised or damned, the artist was not going to be ignored.

Among the pistol-shot paintings of one year's salon was Gérôme's "Duel after the Masquerade Ball." At a time when other artists were still seeking to overwhelm by the size of their canvases and the grandeur or terror of their subject, with vast crowds of horses, camels, elephants and people agitating themselves all over the scene, Gérôme's little oil was cleverly designed not to rock the spectator like an eruption from a volcano, but to imprint on his mind a single idea which would stay with him and haunt him.

This pistol-shot technique was not limited to painters or to paintings. Larousse was visiting this exhibit in the company of Pierre Joseph Proudhon, the great philosophical anarchist, and with Jules Verne, the stockbroker, and his mistress Louise Michel. They were all pistol-shot characters, all determined to make of their lives a bullet that would find its mark in the brain and heart of man.

Pierre Larousse had come to Paris so poor in cash and so rich in his ambition to master all knowledge that he had to limit himself for eight years to a single meal a day, and that meal limited to one dish. Moreover, he lived in a house so cheap that it was practically made of paper, and all cooking had to be forbidden because of the danger of fire. Nevertheless, since Larousse could not afford to go to a restaurant, he cooked his sole article of diet in his room. He thought that onion soup would come nearest to nourishing him at the least expense, because it was closest to the famous black soup on which the Spartans lived (the recipe for which Madame Dacier, the famous translator of Greek classics, claimed to have rediscovered). For this purpose Larousse had his mother send him a crock of butter every month, product of the single cow she kept. He bought every week a huge loaf of heavy army bread. Onions and charcoal were cheap.

So that no one should know of his breaking of the rule against cooking, Larousse determined on two o'clock in the morning as the hour when the odor of boiling onions would be least likely to be noticed. And thus each night, at this ungodly hour, famished by many hours of work in the Sainte Geneviève library, he would open his trunk, take out his hidden supplies and prepare his solitary meal.

Then, after many years of study, he began to issue those quotation-studded, well-organized little textbooks, those solid grammars and intransigent spelling books that sold wherever the French language was spoken and which in time made him a multimillionaire.

Nor were his friends any less determined in their assault on the fortress of man. Pierre Joseph Proudhon was the son of a blacksmith who early in life launched those three words that the mid-nineteenth century considered the most dangerous three words ever uttered—*property is theft*—three words that kept Proudhon in a boiling caldron of controversy all his life and whose power to rouse men has never ceased. Larousse loved and venerated the philosopher, and years later when he began to compile his great dictionary he proudly displayed a letter from Proudhon, who had just received the first volume A, had immediately looked up the word *Anarchy* and found the text under that word everything he could ask for in accuracy and lucidity.

Jules Verne, too, admired Proudhon. Verne was then a tall red-headed fellow, full of fun, hating his career of stockbroker and anxious to distinguish himself in some other field. One evening, leaving a gay Bohemian party, he slid down the banister and landed so softly that he was surprised to discover that his landing place was the big belly of a huge man.

"I trust I haven't disturbed your digestion," Jules Verne apologized.

"Young man," thundered the giant, but without anger in his voice, "you have just now ruined the finest omelet in the style of Nantes that man ever tucked under his vest."

"That's impossible!" Verne declared.

"Why impossible?"

"Because Nantes is three hundred and ninety-six kilometers from Paris, and you couldn't possibly have dined this evening on the finest omelet in the style of Nantes and be here in Paris already."

"But who says I dined in Nantes? All I say is I ate an omelet in that style."

"No. You said the finest omelet, and I say that's impossible, because I'm from Nantes, and there's no one in Paris knows how to make the finest omelet in the style of Nantes."

"Do you?"

"Of course I do."

"Then you owe me that finest of all omelets. Here's my card. I shall expect you to make up for this omelet which you have totally ruined." And he tapped his belly and went up the stairs.

The card read: Alexandre Dumas.

And that's how Verne met Dumas and one day, after an omelet, said to him, "I want to put geography, countries, continents, the whole globe and the stars into novels, just as you have decided to cover all history with your books."

"Why not?" Dumas asked. And he repeated the advice he often gave to young writers. "If you write a page a day it will take you a year to write a novel. If you write two pages a day you will turn out two novels a year. Three pages a day gives you three novels a year. You see that the whole thing is mathematical."

"Stockbrokerage is entirely mathematical too," said Verne.

"Precisely," said Dumas.

And so Verne, though his stock business entitled him to live on a lower floor, lived in a garret, and every morning got up at five o'clock and wrote until the stock market was about to open, when he put on his dark business suit and his fine cylinder hat and went to his office. He had no success. That is, in writing. For years he labored and produced nothing. But he continued to have faith in the mathematics of Alexandre Dumas, and in time, long after the period we are describing, he was to write *Five Weeks in a Balloon* and thus to originate what has since become known as science fiction. Years later he was to write his masterpiece, *Twenty Thousand Leagues under the Sea* (as the result of a suggestion from Louise Michel), in which the hero is a multimillionaire anarchist, Captain Nemo, who knows and can do everything and is obviously modeled after no one else but Pierre Larousse.

As for Louise Michel, she was still years away from the Communard uprising in Paris which was to make her famous (or infamous) and which was to put her on trial for her life and result in her exile to the tropical prisons of New Caledonia.

These four of Dumas' friends were strolling and talking their way from one work of art to another in the exhibit when they noticed a crowd gathered around a painting. They stopped at the periphery and saw that at the center of the group was Alexandre Dumas. The painting was the little canvas by Gérôme, "Duel after the Masquerade Ball."

One lady was saying, "But, Monsieur Dumas, I can't understand that you should say the painting isn't dramatic. Imagine! Two men are engaged in a duel for life and death while still dressed in their *costume de bal.*"

And another spectator said, "Really? You don't think the painting is beautiful?"

"As for that, yes," Dumas said. "It is very beautiful."

"But you don't find the idea dramatic?"

"I don't say the idea is not dramatic," Dumas corrected. "Naturally a duel is always dramatic. Whatever the cause, whatever the result, to reduce the clash of human beings to the sharpened point of a sword reaching for the life blood of the human heart—that is something intensely dramatic. And at the same time something intensely French, this transposition of an argument from the field of words to the terrain of steel and the vital organs of the human body. It is the very essence of drama. It is the drama of man's existence, as every Frenchman of courage and honor understands it, for it means, or it should mean: Gentleman, I am no idle chatterer; I am a man of serious purpose, who takes life as something serious and important, and I will answer with my life for everything I say and everything I do. This is what has made France rise above nations where each individual does not similarly hold himself on perpetual trial."

There was silence for a moment, and perhaps—who knows?—someone may have had it on the tip of his tongue to ask, "And you, Monsieur Dumas, why did you evade a duel with . . ." But then a lady said, "And still you say this painting is not dramatic."

"Let me be very clear," said Dumas. "I distinguish between the painting itself and the idea of the painting. The idea is dramatic because a duel is dramatic. Any duel is dramatic. And in particular the idea of a duel after a masquerade ball is dramatic. But this painting isn't dramatic."

"But I find it most startling," said a lady. "I have been here three times already and each time there has been a crowd around this painting."

"Then let me make still another distinction," Dumas said. "The idea is dramatic, and the execution here is dramatic. It is the painting itself that is not dramatic."

"I don't understand how you can say that, Monsieur Dumas."

"The reason I can say it, Madame, is that I can prove it."

"Then please do."

It was the kind of moment that Dumas relished, and yet he seemed to hesitate for a moment. Then he said, "With Madame's permission, may I say that the painter has undoubtedly got hold here of a very dramatic idea, and that he undoubtedly has had the talent to exploit that idea, but he did not have the genius to make the scene completely realistic."

"It seems to me, Monsieur, that, on the contrary, the scene is terribly realistic."

"Well, let us analyze," Dumas replied. "Let us take it detail by detail. Temperature first. Every painting that represents a real scene must include the temperature of that scene since there is no scene on earth that does not have a temperature. Right?"

"Of course. There is always some temperature or other."

"Good. So we see here that there is a light blanket of snow on the ground. And the snow is not melting. Ergo, it is cold indeed."

"Below freezing," said the lady.

"*Madame est savante*," said Dumas with a slight inclination of the head. "*Donc, il fait froid.* And moreover it is close to dawn, which, as we know, is always the chilliest part of the night. Through the bare trees of what is possibly the Bois de Boulogne or possibly the Bois de Vincennes you can see the sky of a new day, but an ugly day, a cold, cheerless day with the promise of more snow."

"On the atmospheric side, then, Monsieur, you've got to admit the painting is very well done, if it can say all that so clearly."

"Very well done," Dumas went on, infuriating and mystifying at once with this curious mélange of praise and blame. "And just notice too the excellence of this foreground scene: the duel with the participants in their medieval and Renaissance costumes, and then the shock, the shiver, as one raises one's eyes to this level and sees in the distance two modern coaches waiting, their drivers huddled, impassive, wrapped to their noses in their heavy carricks, and the horses, half frozen, as if in a coma from the cold. All that is very good. One feels it. That's not atelier. That's the real out-doors."

"So, then, you admit—"

"Wait! Let us continue our examination of this painting. I'll admit that such a duel might have taken place, immediately upon leaving a *bal masqué*, because of some outrageous remarks, some repeated provocation, some unforgivable insult, some . . . I don't know what, but something between two people that exploded to a climax in the last hours of the *bal*, so that Pierrot, Harlequin, this man in the dress of an Indian, this Duke de Guise, all would adjourn to the Bois de Boulogne in carriages to settle this matter in the only way possible: with blood."

"Yes. Then I fail to see your objection . . ."

"Please, Madame, allow me to develop my argument."

"Your pardon. I shan't interrupt again."

"I say then: I admit the basic premise. I even go further: I develop it for you. What is a masquerade ball? Why did man invent such a thing? Is it not because life itself imposes too many restrictions and a safety valve must be provided? Think of the Roman Saturnalia, celebrated each year by the master becoming the slave, the slave becoming the master, society turned topsy-turvy, so that for the other fifty-one weeks of the year the master might feel safer amidst a society in which there was much injustice and oppression.

"What is the purpose of these fantastic costumes, these masks? Is it not so that for a few moments we need not be ourselves, or rather so that finally we may be truly ourselves? It's the anonymity that does it. To be oneself unknown among people who are unknown throws all social restraints to the ground, flat like the walls of Jericho, and one can escape from oneself at last. All these gaudy costumes are only for the purpose of showing that after all there are but two basic characters on earth: male and female. And now, if ever, both sides have the opportunity to be frank, to be ribald, to be coarse. And to be true. Do you follow me?"

The crowd, breathless, nodded, and it was obvious that Dumas was improving on the picture, leaping beyond its frame to include a whole world of past, present and future, such as only the art of writing can do.

"Go on, Monsieur, please," someone said.

"Good. I accept then that the disputants, roused to a pitch of fury, would not tarry for the cumbersome code of sending seconds to each other, but would call upon the nearest men to act as seconds, would not even take time to go home for a change of costume, but would proceed at once to the field of honor. I say I will accept all that which is subsumed in the premise of the painting. But I ask you this: did they go to this ball in the dead of winter without a cloak, a paletot, a cape? And when they left for their duel, did they not stop to don their cloaks? And if it was a public ball, say at the Opéra, would they not want to redeem their outer greatcoats, or whatever they wore, from the *vestiaire*?" Dumas paused and then said, "I see that Madame is smiling. Have I made a blunder?"

"I'm afraid so, Monsieur. For it is obvious to me that they did stop for their coats, but upon coming to the spot where the duel was to be held, they left their cloaks in the carriages."

"The principals, yes, Madame, for they wanted their arms free, their bodies unencumbered by any heavy cloth. But the seconds? Would they too take off their coats in such iron weather? No, Madame, I will not accept that, and neither will you. May I explain to you why these characters, in mid-winter, wear nothing but their flimsy costumes? It is because these costumes are so colorful to paint that the painter preferred to sacrifice reality rather than to hamper his palette and darken his canvas with drab colors."

From the approving murmurs of the audience it was plain that Dumas had scored. The lady who had smiled before now said, "You have a small point there."

"We won't quarrel as to the size of the point, Madame," said Dumas. "Besides, I am far from finished. But before leaving this particular matter, we may offer the observation that to our mind the painting would have been perhaps more striking and more powerful had the costumes been only glimpsed underneath the coats, so that the spectator would have divined the drama instead of having it thrust right at him."

"True," said a voice.

"Yes, the scene might have been even more stark, more frightening. Isn't it part of the art of painting to invite the spectator into the canvas to play a role there with his own intelligence and imagination?"

"Yes. I agree."

"And now, for a moment, let us consider the various actors in this tragedy. Let us take Pierrot, to begin with. This Pierrot is really first-rate. No doubt of it. Drawing, coloring, pose, everything. His lifeblood, welling up from the place where the sword has thrust home, stains his costume and drops to the snow, and his pretty white suit will now clearly be of no further use to him except as a shroud. He has crumpled into the arms of his second, the Duke de Guise. A black domino, clasping his head in despair, kneels beside the dying man. Another dressed in doge's costume, or perhaps a magician's robe with what I take to be cabalistic symbols on it, is evidently a doctor and seeks in vain to stem the flow of blood from the chest.

"All this is very correctly done. Yes, even to the froth of blood due to air escaping from the wounded lung and whipping the blood as it passes. I have myself in such a case seen a candle flame shiver in the air that whistled out of a man when the sword that had given the fatal thrust was withdrawn from the victim's chest."

"Like in your *Queen Margot*, where Cocannos—"

"Thank you, my dear lady," said Dumas. "Yes, I used that incident there."

"I remember it too," said a young man. "It sent thrills up and down my spine."

Others chimed in, recalling the famous moment in that drama. Dumas smiled, pleased. Then he went on: "Yes, Pierrot dies correctly, his powdered face in agony, his head with its skull cap fallen upon his chest, his mouth making one last and sorry effort to pull in a breath of air, and his naked arm, as you see, still holding his sword, a powerfully muscled arm, but now obviously drained of life and will."

"It is very moving," someone said.

"Yes." Dumas sighed. "It is very moving indeed. But now we come to a puzzle. See the two figures leaving the field of battle. Who can they be but the victor and his second? One of them is dressed in a Harlequin costume that fits him like the tights of a ballet dancer, outlining an athletic figure. He is putting an arm on the shoulder of the Indian, a Mohican in a buffalo robe, with feathers in his hair and a necklace of bears' claws around his throat. If I may interpret, it seems as if Harlequin were saying to Mohican, 'I'm sorry. I didn't mean to kill him. But he had only himself to blame. He shouldn't have continued to provoke me.' While the Mohican has turned away as if in disgust at this spectacle of what calls itself civilization and is yet at bottom more cruel than savagery. One can almost hear him saying: 'We savages would have smoked the pipe of peace.'"

"Yes, yes! That's exactly what he is saying. One can read it in his walk, in everything."

"Yes," said Dumas. "Unfortunately."

"What do you mean, unfortunately? This is an achievement of painting, to express all that merely in the way a man turns away from a scene."

"Yes, that is what is so unfortunate," Dumas insisted.

"But that's the height of art!" a lady exclaimed. "What talent! What genius!"

"Talent, perhaps," Dumas said. "But genius, no. Definitely not."

"And why not, may I ask?"

"Because, Madame, you see, that Mohican has no right to such thoughts. He is not really a Mohican at all. He's not an Indian. He's not a savage. He's a Parisian like yourself, my dear lady. He's a man who rented a costume yesterday, a costume for this ball, and in a few hours he will send his servant to return the costume to the store where he rented it, and he will be back in his office where he sells and buys railroad shares."

"Oh!"

"Yes. And he has no right to suggest such thoughts to you or to me."

"I think I begin to see Monsieur's objections. It is too well done, this painting."

"Precisely. The painter fell victim to his own masquerade. He sacrificed his good sense to his own cleverness. And that's why we stand here and admire. Whereas we should be standing here and shuddering. This tragedy ought to cause fingers of ice to go crawling up and down our spines. Tomorrow all these characters will have to come out of the romantic trance in which they are trapped for the moment and resume their humdrum occupations. The doge owns a café and will have to decide whether business warrants the hiring of another *garçon*. This Harlequin teaches music while he composes his first opera. And poor Pierrot is a contractor who will never complete the building he was erecting, and will leave his family in want. Ah, my good people, if only the painter had been able to make you feel the reality of this scene, it would have torn your heart. Yes, and it might then have opened the eyes of Frenchmen to the folly of indiscriminate dueling out of mere pique or stubbornness which has corrupted our conception of true honor and true courage and caused us to appear ridiculous in the eyes of other nations."

Everyone waited for Dumas to resume. No one moved. But the silence which indicated respect for the author's words began to be stained with whispered voices, irritatingly low. Sharp ears, near enough to two men on the periphery, could pick up a give and take of such phrases as ". . . his own reputation . . . naturally has to defend himself . . . one should ask him . . . what was that name? Eugène de Mirecourt? . . ."

Embarrassment spread in concentric waves.

Dumas, towering above the group, pushed a firm step through the crowd toward the voices. "Somebody has a question to ask me?" There was utter silence. Dumas said, "I'm afraid I've been talking too much."

"Oh, no. Please continue."

So many voices joined in that Dumas, obviously warmed, shrugged and said, "There's not much more to be said. But we might ask ourselves such a question as this: Whence come these characters? From what milieu? From what kind of a masquerade ball? Obviously not from one of those *bals masqués* such as one finds in some bystreet where the walls are all grime badly concealed by a quick coat of whitewash, where a couple of tin quinquet lanterns hang from the ceiling and where we see on the walls such signs as this: *No smoking while dancing,* and WC with an arrow pointing. And naturally someone has thought it a good joke to turn the arrow the wrong way or write some remark underneath. In such places a quarrel would be quickly settled with fists or knives and no ceremony. Nor have we to do here with one of those aristocratic masquerades where the host issues a theme such as 'Le Petit Trianon' or 'The Gods of Mount Olympus,' and where therefore all costumes must accord to give the evening harmony and richness. Besides, in such a case, the coaches in the rear would be private equipages and the coachmen would wear livery. . . . Am I right?"

Everyone agreed, astounded that this small canvas should yield still further material for elaboration, and aware that this was not so much the talent of the painter Gérôme as the talent of the writer Dumas.

"We are reduced, therefore," Dumas continued, "to such a public ball as that of the Opéra, or some private ball of modest circumstances. Let us examine both possibilities. In favor of a public ball is the haste of the duel, carried out at an early hour of the morning, without change of costume. The contestants seem not to know each other very well and fear that if they delay their conflict they may never meet again. All this argues, I say, for the *bal de l'Opéra,* but as we shall see this deduction too has to be rejected. And I will tell you why although you may have already observed it yourself.

"Anyone who has ever attended these balls knows what they are like. A volcano in eruption, a typhoon off the coast of China, is peaceful indeed, when it comes to a comparison of fury and commotion. Five thousand gas jets multiplied by a thousand mirrors and reflected in the profusion of carved marble and bronze make the palace glitter. Three orchestras succeed each other as the musicians almost fall dead from the exertion of trying to make themselves heard above the thunderous crowds. And you must pardon me if I mention that the tone of licentiousness, the daring of the costume, is set by the habit of the management of using some fifteen hundred *filles publiques* to sell the tickets and introduce that note of shamelessness which makes these balls so popular.

"Now at what hour are we? The actual duel took but minutes. These affairs rarely take more. The ride to the Bois and all the rest of the details could not have consumed an hour. So we are dealing, then, with the condition of the ball at four or five o'clock in the morning. Have you seen it then? Yes, I am sure that some of us have. Any book or play that attempted to portray it would be struck down by the censorship. But all attempts to suppress the *bal de l'Opéra* have failed.

"At four o'clock in the morning the ball is in its agony—the agony of an idiot afflicted with *folie de grandeur.* By this time every lib-

erty that men and women dare permit themselves has been enjoyed again and again. Every coarseness has been played out to
satiety. Five thousand gas jets and five thousands dancers have
ruined God's fresh air to the point where it is a positive poison to
take it into one's lungs. Sweat has caused havoc with every skin:
one's powder has run and dried and run again until one's skin is
like the hide of a plucked chicken or a dead lizard. Mascara and
rouge have mingled on everyone's face into an Apache war paint.
There's not a costume that is not disarranged, if not both soiled and
torn. And I shall make no attempt to describe for you the condition of the ballroom itself, the floor where broken glasses, shredded
paper, the ends of cigars, the bones of chickens and chops sold at
the refreshment counters, the indescribable litter, as if wagonloads
of garbage had been upset here to make a barricade for a revolution against decency.

"And if you have seen the grand staircase when the dance is
over, you have never forgotten it. Those who are still on their feet
must step over the drunks that lie everywhere like corpses after a
battle. The ushers help by pushing the exhausted libertines to one
side so as to make a small passageway to the door. Yes, and at such
times to see waiting to each side the poor honest charwomen and
porters, with their brooms and buckets and mops, waiting and looking on, with sad, reproving eyes. . . . And the director of the Opéra,
tearing his hair at the desecration of an edifice that was built for
the arts, but who does not know how to stop these balls because
there have been riots whenever the attempt has been made. . . .

"So I have given you the truth of these balls, which were what
caused my colleague Victor Hugo, now so shamefully exiled from
a country which he honors by his genius, to write that wonderful
poem—you remember the lines: *'Hélas, que de jeunes filles, j'en ai
vu mourir,'* and *'Elle aimait trop le bal, c'est ce qui l'a tuée.'* Yes,
those balls, they do kill indeed. Ask any doctor about the pleurisy
of dances. To come out hot and perspired into the wintry air, one's
lungs already weakened by the vast amounts of carbon dioxide gen-
erated by the gas jets. Yes, how many young girls that has already
killed! You see, Madame, I may be Dumas the ignorant,* but I

---

* The reference is to the famous nineteenth-century chemist Dumas. To distinguish himself from this *Dumas the savant*, Alexandre Dumas sometimes
called himself *Dumas the ignorant.*

know something of physics too. One must know everything to be a writer of cheap fiction."

"Oh, Monsieur, don't say that. You don't write cheap fiction."

"Thank you, Madame. I only repeat what the critics tell me every day in the newspapers and the reason why they exclude me from their studies of French literature. . . . But to continue. So here we have this duel, at dawn, and these people who have not had time to change their costumes—in short, they have been at the ball through the night—and now look at them. They have not turned a hair in this Dantesque hell of a masquerade party. Their costumes are clean and fresh. Their make-up is perfect. Instead of being wan, overcome, dirty, drunk, feverish, as if issuing alive from a nightmare, they are as if they had just freshened their toilette for this occasion. . . . Is it not now abundantly clear, my friends, that Monsieur Gérôme has not only never been to a ball that would lead to such a mad duel, but he has never himself fought a duel, or even seen one fought?" *

"It is clear that you have fought duels, Monsieur," a lady ventured.

"Ah, Madame, that is an unfair change of subject. I beg you, *de grâce*, spare me."

The lady bit her lips and tried to efface herself in the crowd.

"We come thus to the final possibility. The duel is the result of a quarrel engendered at a modest *bal masqué* in the home of some good bourgeois who has invited some of his friends. But here again there are problems. Where did they get the dueling swords? At such short notice. Surely not from the host of the ball. He would have prevented such a tragic ending to an affair which he had undoubtedly dedicated to pure pleasure. At the Opéra one might imagine that the dueling swords could be secured from the property department. And even there one would be guessing. Indeed, those swords have already bothered me several times and I have only omitted the matter because there was so much else to criticize. If the seconds had time to go looking for a pair of dueling swords—that is to say, matched weapons in length, weight, flex-

---

* Gérôme was to fight a duel many years later, a duel with pistols that fractured his right forearm and for a while held out the possibility that he might never paint again.

ibility, sharpness and point of balance, which at four o'clock in the morning is not such an easy errand—then would not the principals have had time to change their costume, secure a coat against the cold, write a will, a few lines to one's wife, one's mother? . . . Because there are a lot of things to do before a duel!

"And then there are those mysterious feathers scattered there on the snow exactly where Pierrot's opponent would have been standing. We have assumed, because tradition would have it so, that Pierrot's opponent was Harlequin. But the feathers seem to say that it was the Mohican. But then the puzzle really overwhelms us, for the Mohican has on this cumbersome buffalo robe, which would surely have hampered him in dueling, whereas Harlequin is dressed as gracefully and as free as a trapeze artist. . . . I don't know if you recall the various sketches by Horace Vernet * in which he shows his studio and his home and with a fencing scene included. In his sketch of his atelier we see the master and his many pupils and assistants busy with canvases, while two students are dueling in the center, each holding his palette and brushes in one hand, his foil in the other. At first glance it appears ludicrous. But then you see that such a studio requires all sorts of properties and that armor of all kinds is hung on the walls. And then the mood of play where so many young men are at work must often show such eruptions of high spirits, so that the whole scene makes sense.

"But here, you see, it is all false," Dumas concluded. "Terribly false. And strange that such otherwise excellent critics as Edmond About and Théophile Gautier have found nothing but praise."

He stopped, and then, abruptly giving his arm to a pretty lady, he turned and left, while the crowd remained standing around the painting, silent, as if ashamed of themselves for not having had the wit to see in this little scene all the many points that Dumas had raised. For most of them were well aware that a cloud hung over Dumas, a cloud of fraudulence not only as scholar and writer but also as a man of courage and adventure, such as he pictured himself in his works, and here it was plain that the fraud had more brains than they had, and therefore possibly more brains than those who had discovered his fraudulence.

* In his day the most admired and affluent of painters, now well nigh forgotten.

Jules Verne looked after him thoughtfully—and perhaps with a little feeling of guilt.

Only Pierre Larousse hastened after Dumas and with a few steps overtook him. Dumas recognized the scholar and gave him a warm hand. "I listened to your talk just now," Larousse said, "and I derived the feeling that you know even more about this painting than you have told us."

"Not at all," Dumas said quickly.

"One might bet money," Larousse insisted, "that you had been present at that scene and therefore knew the truth of the matter. That you were either the Duke de Guise or the Mohican. Or possibly Harlequin himself."

"You would be risking your money."

"You mean you weren't there?"

"What makes you so sure that I was?" Dumas countered.

"The clarity with which you exposed the falsity of the scene. There were things you said that would never have occurred to me. Nor to most anyone. And yet I will not admit to being stupid."

"Monsieur Larousse," said Dumas, "what I did with Gérôme's painting I have had to do ten thousand times in my books in order to make a scene live. I could not possibly have been present at all the scenes of my plays and my books. And yet I had to make them live. One has for that a sixth sense: a sense of reality."

Larousse would have liked to continue the conversation and get it around to the question of how Dumas, who had once stood before the public as a great writer, now was accepted with more or less good humor as a kind of mountebank. It was difficult to phrase the matter without running the danger of insulting the man. But perhaps Dumas guessed what was in the encyclopedist's mind when he said a final word about Gérôme's painting: "An artist who has genius is forgiven his every fault, while an artist who has only talent is condemned for his every fault."

He made the phrase applicable to himself when he remarked rather ruefully, "I know, Monsieur, because I too once had genius, and now have nothing left but my talent."

Taken by itself, this scene as observed by Larousse and his friends was sufficiently memorable to be worth recording. But what made it absolutely unforgettable was still to come.

Some time later, on that same day, Larousse went to the offices of the management to make an offer on a painting which he wished to acquire. He saw Dumas leaving the desk of one of the commissioners. Dumas did not see him.

Larousse had a sudden flash of illumination.

He went to the commissioner to whom Dumas had been speaking and said casually, "So Monsieur Dumas is buying Gérôme's 'Duel after the Masquerade Ball.' "

"Ah, no, Monsieur. I had to inform him that the painting has already been acquired by the Duc d'Aumale." *

Then the commissioner gaped in surprise. "But how did you know? Monsieur Dumas asked me to keep his offer a secret."

"We'll both keep the matter secret," Larousse declared.

Nevertheless, some years later, after the fall of the Empire, when Dumas was already dead, Larousse did tell the story. You will find it in Volume D of his great dictionary. But you will find no answer to the mystery of why Dumas should wish to own a painting whose value he had utterly destroyed by merciless criticism.

It would be quite surprising if after the passage of all these years we should now be able to supply an answer.

CHAPTER TWO

How to Give a Horse a Ride

THERE WAS a veritable frenzy for dueling in Alexandre's blood. Dueling began no doubt with David and Goliath, but it did not really become a way of life, inescapable to anyone who wished to call himself a gentleman, until the modern era—reaching its apogee in the last two centuries. Then, from the dueling oaks of New Orleans, all the way across the world to Russia, men lashed at each other with bull whips, stabbed each other with poignards and bowie knives, hacked at each other with sabers, fenced with épées in an

* The painting is now in the Baltimore museum, a part of the Colonel Walters Collection.

exuberance of male energy that is a phenomon of history—a phenomenon that has just lately vanished from the scene.

Hamilton, Vice-President of the United States, died in a duel at Weehawken.

Pushkin the poet died at St. Petersburg.

The world over, the duel was once accepted as a fact of life.

And nowhere and at no time was the rage for proving oneself on the field of honor more in vogue than in France during the lifetime of Alexandre Dumas.

As a child of four he got hold of his father's matched dueling pistols and declared that he was going to fight a duel. Indeed, it can be said that Alexandre was conceived as the result of a duel, for it was through a duel that his mother and father met.

Thus our study of the mystery of the "Duel after the Masquerade Ball" must go back to that event.

It was one evening in June, a hundred and seventy years ago, as this is being written, that a detachment of the King's dragoons and a detachment of the Queen's dragoons happened to bivouac for the night on the outskirts of the same little town in France.

The King of France at that time was Louis XVI, who was half French, being the son of a French prince and a German princess, and the Queen of France at that time was Marie Antoinette, who was not French at all, being the daughter of the Empress of Austria.

The little town where these two detachments met was Villers-Cotterêts, located between Soissons and Château-Thierry on the classic invasion route to France, at this particular time nothing more than a cluster of white houses around a church, a number of fine country residences in the environs, and a royal palace for its main building. The reason for the King's residence was the near-by hunting preserve, a fifty-thousand-acre forest of ancient trees and dense underbrush, where the privileged had the right to hunt for boar and stag, and the poor had the right to gather up free all the dead wood lying on the ground.

On that June evening then, when these two detachments of dragoons happened to be quartered so close together, and the officers of both groups had gone to neighboring châteaux to be entertained for the evening, the rank and file of men flooded into the Hotel of the Royal Arms, the main drinking spot of the village.

It was in the courtyard of that inn that a dragoon of the King's regiment nonchalantly stopped a tall, swarthy dragoon of the Queen's regiment and said to him, "Want to know something, my friend?"

"Yes. What?"

"Then listen carefully."

"I'm listening."

"You know what our King does to your Queen every night?"

This tall, swarthy dragoon of the Queen's regiment at first looked puzzled as the group of King's dragoons roared with laughter. Then suddenly he snatched his saber out of its scabbard and shouted: "Now I'll tell you something. And this time you listen carefully. In this case you've got it wrong. I happen to know that it's our Queen who does it to your King every night! And this blade will prove it!"

Some further hot words were exchanged on the question of who did it to whom; then the matter was left to the sabers to decide. But so many men on each side clamored to be part of this fight that the matter had to be properly organized.

A big blackboard was rigged up in the courtyard, and every dragoon who wanted to defend the honor of his regiment either wrote down his name or else had it written down for him, and matches were drawn by lot under the supervision of a committee of seconds who decided that all duels would be stopped that threatened fatality.

Thus, before this historic night was over, in the courtyard of that inn, by the light of flares, over a hundred duels were held to decide the momentous question of whether the King did it to the Queen or the Queen did it to the King. The honor of the royal family was at stake and the blood of a hundred or more wounds was to testify, before the night was over, to the fierce devotion these young hotheads had for their particular side of the reigning family.

It was a frightening night of wild cries and clashing steel. In many neighboring cottages people, unable to imagine what was happening, stayed awake all night with loaded pistols.

Never had the Hotel of the Royal Arms enjoyed such a busy and prosperous evening. As soon as one wounded duelist ran bleeding

into the inn to be washed and bandaged, another took his place, and
the more wounded, the more the demand for food and wine. And
the more the men groaned with pain, the more they laughed over
the ridiculous beginning of this fracas, which neither side, however,
would give up, the honor of their colors being now so deeply involved.

Threading her way nervously between the crowded tables was
Marie-Louise Labouret, the daughter of the owner, just a slip of a
girl, slender and delicate as the first shoot of a tulip bulb in spring.
She was strangely attracted and repelled by all this fierce commotion, and annoyed that no one would explain to her what it was all
about.

Her persistent questions provoked constant fresh outbursts of
laughter among the men and repeated orders from her father and
mother to tend to her business or else be off to bed. All of which
only piqued her curiosity the more. Never had she been so conscious
of men's glances following her eagerly around the room where she
hurried with bandages and basins of water, or else with bottles of
wine and slices of roast, for it was as if the fighting had put a keener
edge on everyone's appetite.

Among the wounded whom she treated that night was the
swarthy dragoon who had first drawn his saber and who had fought
in four different duels before he was himself slashed on the forehead
and retired. He went into the inn and collapsed at a table, his head
slumped down on the wood where a lake of blood grew rapidly. He
seemed totally unconscious when Marie-Louise took off his helmet
to wash the wound and stanch the flow of blood.

She was struck then by his strange black and tightly curled hair.
She had never seen hair so black or so dense, and when she went to
fetch fresh water in her pan, she asked her father about it.

"Don't you know a colored man when you see one?" her father
asked her, annoyed at being interrupted in his work.

"A colored man?"

"*Mais oui!* An African. A black."

"But he isn't black," Marie-Louise insisted. "He's just very tan."

"Then he's a mulatto," her father said. "Mixed blood. His father
was a Negro. Or more likely it was his mother."

"Is he a cannibal?" Marie-Louise asked. "Surely he's no Christian."

"It's you who are no Christian, ninny," her father exclaimed. "Are you going to let him bleed to death there without a helping hand?"

Marie-Louise ran off to finish her job. But she was full of a kind of nervous curiosity that drove her to examine this huge man, as well as to keep as far away from him as possible, as if at any moment he might seize her in his long arms.

Finally he opened his eyes and said, "Thank you, my little one."

Marie-Louise jumped. "You speak French?" she asked.

The bronze man smiled. "What did you expect? That I should say tohubohu?"

He laughed and revealed teeth so white and so huge that it was like the yawning of an animal. "Are you afraid of me?" he asked. "Why? Is it because I'm black?"

Marie-Louise nodded. "Are you a cannibal?" she asked.

"Of course," he said. "But I like sugar best, because I was born in the Sugar Islands." And with that he grabbed her.

She screamed and tore herself loose, and his laughter followed her as she ran away.

For the rest of the evening, she kept herself at a safe distance from him. Nevertheless, she watched him when he left the inn later, a tall, lithe figure with a bandage across his forehead.

The following day, the King's dragoons having been ordered to ride out of town, the Queen's dragoons decided that they had been awarded the palm of victory and that the Queen's honor had been vindicated. They remained quartered in the little town, and almost every evening numbers of them gathered in the village inn.

The bronze dragoon was always among them, and Marie-Louise could feel his piercing glance following her as she helped with the service, and now and then she stole a look at him and saw him instantly catch her glance, his lips parting in a big smile while his white teeth remained clenched upon a cigar and his open lips expelled a big cloud of smoke.

At night, when she went to bed, she prayed to God for protection, for it seemed to her that in the darkness she could still see the gleam of those white teeth and the cloud of smoke pluming out.

Decidedly the man haunted her, and strange ideas began to fill her head. One evening she found herself asking her father whether white sheep ever gave birth to black lambs.

"What makes you ask that question?" her father asked.

"Nothing," she said. "It was just an idea that passed through my head."

Her father gave her a strange, wondering look. But as she went about her work at that moment, he said nothing.

As a matter of fact, he considered her future already settled. She would marry Blaise, the son of a farmer whose rich fields and crowded barnyard were one of the prize properties of the region. This farmer and Monsieur Labouret were having frequent conversations on the matter, and almost every detail of the engagement had been settled and remained only to be brought to the notary, Maître Menesson, for the contract to be formally drawn up.

Blaise was a heavy-set fellow who took pride in emphasizing his strength. He liked to clump into the inn of an evening in his heavy hobnail boots, a doubled-up bull whip in one hand, which he would crack against the leather of his calf. Then he would put a proprietary arm around Marie-Louise as if to announce to the company that this was his.

Blaise was not so stupid that he didn't notice the hidden courtship between the tall, dark dragoon and Marie-Louise. There began then a three-cornered duel of glances in which the whole inn became interested.

The young farmer evidently thought he'd get this matter over with fast by rousing the dragoon to a fight and whipping him thoroughly. And he took to passing up and down before the dragoon's table on one pretext or another, and each time he passed he'd pretend to stumble and accidentally would rock the dragoon's table so that the wine would slop out of his glass.

Then the farmer would put on a mock show of apology, and the dragoon would quietly assure the farmer that it was nothing.

"Marie-Louise!" Blaise would call, as if she were already his to order around. And both men would look on as she cleaned up the mess. The farmer would crack his whip and the dragoon would smoke. And smile.

Everyone awaited developments, which could not be long forthcoming. Surely a dragoon who had not been afraid to fight four saber duels would not shirk a fight with a farmer? Or was he frightened by that bull whip?

The local citizens who dropped into the inn almost every evening began to show money. Perhaps a few bets would get things moving. But the dragoons maintained that their man was still suffering from his wound, and, besides, it was obvious that though both men stood over six feet, the farmer was clearly the heavier, the more rugged.

It wasn't until the odds against the dragoon rose to four to one that dragoon money came into evidence. Blaise himself helped to provide some of the money. Monsieur Labouret was called upon to hold the bets and Maître Menesson, as notary, witnessed the amounts and entered them into his notebook.

Madame Labouret went about with a set face, annoyed with people for getting so excited about such brutish matters. "You'd think people would be too civilized nowadays for such pagan sports," she said. Besides, it would give Marie-Louise ideas. It would turn her head. There was nothing worse in a girl than giddiness caused by too much attention from men.

And still every evening, as if utterly unaware of what was brewing all about him, the dark dragoon took his seat in the inn and ordered his glass of wine, first stopping before the spit where the roasts were turning to light his cigar from a piece of burning charcoal. And every evening hobnails would shove the dragoon's table harder, until the dragoon would have to leap up to avoid the wine's soiling his uniform.

And again the parade of courtesies, and Blaise shouting, "Marie-Louise!"

The day when news spread that the detachment of Queen's dragoons was to leave the following morning the inn was crowded with bettors. The question that Maître Menesson had to handle was what happened if the dragoon left without fighting. The dragoons argued that the money should be handed back to each bettor. The villagers argued that the dragoon money was forfeit. A coward was the same as a loser.

This argument took on the proportions of a conclave. And when the decision was reached that the money was to be forfeited if there were no fight, the odds rose to six to one, and now the dragoon money really came into play.

The whole inn was watching when that evening the farmer passed the dragoon's table. This time he hit the table so hard that the glass bounced to the floor and broke.

"Lick it from the floor!" said Blaise and cracked his whip against his boot. "The floor in this inn is clean."

The dragoon rose quietly. "Come," he said, "let's us two have a little quiet drink at the counter."

The farmer hesitated, unable to make out the meaning of this reply. Meanwhile, the dragoon went up to the bar and Blaise followed.

The innkeeper and his stableboy had just moved a new tun of wine into position on the rack, preparatory to broaching it.

"Allow me to show you how one takes a swig from a cask," said the dragoon.

By this time the whole inn was coalescing toward the counter where the cask had just had its spigot pounded home.

The dragoon waited for his audience to collect and then he went behind the counter, seized hold of the cask and lifted it from the rack. "It will not be so easy for someone to upset this glass," he said.

"Open the spigot when I nod," he continued, speaking to the innkeeper. "And close it when I give another nod."

And then with a mighty jerk he lifted the cask and held it overhead, with the spigot directly over his mouth. He nodded and opened his maw. The innkeeper got up on a chair and turned the handle and the wine poured down. The soldier's throat worked convulsively to keep pace with this stream. Everybody's neck craned painfully to watch the performance. A nod from the dragoon and the innkeeper turned off the flow. The dragoon slowly lowered the barrel down to its place on the rack.

Then he turned to the farmer, who stood there as if stupefied. "Good wine. Excellent wine. I invite you to have a drink. My treat." To the innkeeper he said, "Take out the price of a glass of wine for Monsieur. Serve it to him in a glass." He emphasized the words "in a glass."

This obvious challenge could not be ignored by the farmer, not in front of this crowd. But it was clear that he was nervous as he said, "No glass, Monsieur Labouret. I'll have a swig too."

He laid his bull whip on the bar, went behind the counter and grabbed hold of the cask. He managed to lift it from its hollow on the rack, but to swing it up as the dragoon had done—that was beyond him. But by balancing it on the edge of the rack and getting under the cask, he managed to raise it into the air. His knees wobbled in the process, and he had to spread his legs to keep his balance. And then, too, he had not taken sufficient care of where the spigot should be in relation to his mouth when the cask would be overhead. It was far out of line. He had to push out his lower lip and keep his shoulders and neck hunched, and even then, when he gave the nod to the innkeeper he could hardly catch all the fluid. But even if he had, what with the exertion of holding the weight there, swallowing so rapidly was more than he could do. The wine gushed over his face, rushed into his nose and eyes, inundated his face and overflowed into his collar and over and under his clothes. He nodded quickly, but then, without giving the innkeeper an opportunity to turn off the wine, he let the cask swing down and barely managed to prevent it from smashing itself to bits on the rack. The innkeeper rushed to turn off the spigot.

"I pay for the drinks," said the dragoon. "Even the spilled ones."

The farmer was still wiping his face with his sleeve.

"Marie-Louise!" the dragoon cried. "Clean up the spilled wine!"

Marie-Louise rushed up with a towel, which she handed to the farmer, who brushed it aside angrily.

The dragoons smiled and the local citizens looked pained.

"Who cares to see a man give a horse a ride?" the dragoon announced to the company.

Give a horse a ride? Who had ever heard of such a thing? Did the man really mean that he would gallop off with a horse on his back? Everyone wanted to see this and was prepared to follow the dragoon to the stables.

The dragoon turned to the farmer. "Will Monsieur come too?"

The farmer was obviously unwilling, but could not see any way out.

"Don't forget your whip," said the dragoon, taking it from the bar and handing it to the farmer, who took it with a grumpy thank you.

Out in the stables the dragoon mounted his horse bareback, guided it with his knees to a position under a big beam, swung his arms around the wood and pulled himself up, holding his beast so firmly between his legs that he finally had the animal with its four hoofs clear of the ground. The horse snorted in fear to find itself hung up in mid-air, gripped as if with steel tongs by the dragoon's riding muscles.

When he had let his horse down and guided it back to its stall, it was clear that the dragoon had hopelessly outmatched his rival. The farmer had sunk back into the anonymity of the crowd.

One of the strangest duels in history had been fought and won— without bloodshed.

Everyone trooped back to the inn. Here the bronze giant declared himself willing to bet that in spite of his height and his muscle he had the smallest foot in the room. Indeed, so small that he could slip into the shoes of a girl. As he stripped off his boots there was no doubt in anyone's mind what girl's shoes he meant to slip into, and obviously no other girl would have dared pick up his challenge.

Marie-Louise, as if hypnotized, took off her slippers.

The dragoon wore no socks. And when his boots came off they revealed such trim brown feet, neat as the hoofs of a gazelle, that it was no surprise to see him glide them without effort into Marie-Louise's slippers.

It seemed as if by this act, as by some savage marriage ceremony, the dragoon had taken complete possession of Marie-Louise. And when he capped the evening by offering to prove that his calf muscle was bigger around than her waist, she offered him no resistance. She was in fact so utterly his already that she beamed with pride at the honor of having so remarkable a man courting her in so incredible a fashion.

While Monsieur Labouret and Maître Menesson were counting out the money to the dragoons who had so artfully underplayed their comrade's strength, Madame Labouret took the mulatto aside. She turned to her daughter and said peremptorily, "Marie-Louise. *Vas te coucher.* It's late."

Reluctantly, as if she could not bear to let the dragoon out of her sight, Marie-Louise obeyed.

"Apparently," the innkeeper's wife began, "Monsieur does not realize that we are honorable people."

"But absolutely," the dragoon assured her. "I never for a moment thought anything else."

"In the life of soldiers," Madame Labouret continued, "there are of course all kinds of girls. That's the way it is. But our daughter, Monsieur, is the apple of our eye. She is not a prize that is given to the winner of a popinjay archery contest at a fair."

"Naturally not, Madame," the dragoon agreed.

"I'm telling you this only to make it very very clear," she went on. "And also because I heard you call my daughter Marie-Louise, just plain Marie-Louise, a moment ago."

"I was only making fun of this fool—pardon me, your future son-in-law—because he always called her Marie-Louise when he would spill my glass of wine and order her to clean up."

"That is another matter," the innkeeper's wife said. "That man already has certain rights. He's one of the neighbors. I don't defend him, mind you. But when one is about to be engaged—when one has declared one's intentions, and they are honorable—excuses can be made for such conduct.

"Of course," said the dragoon.

"But you. Here today. Gone tomorrow. For all one knows, you may be a runaway slave from America."

"I am indeed from America," the dragoon declared. "But not a runaway slave. My name is Thomas-Alexandre. My father was the Marquis Davy de la Pailleterie. The manor house is in Normandy. In Bielleville."

Madame Labouret smiled quietly as if to say that it wasn't going to be easy to pull the wool over her eyes. "You mean to say there are black marquis in Normandy? I never heard of that."

"He is not black, Madame. He is white. Even his hair, now, is completely white. It is my mother who was black. She was a Negro woman who worked on my father's sugar plantation in San Domingo. When he grew old and tired of running the plantation, he sold off and came back to France, bringing me with him."

"So you are the future Marquis Davy de la . . . whatever you said?" she asked with the same fine smile of disbelief.

"The Marquis Davy de la Pailleterie. Yes."

"Yes. Of Bielleville in Normandy."

"That's right," said the dragoon. "Only . . ."

"Only what?"

"Only I must explain to you that my father and I have quarreled. That's why I enlisted in the Queen's dragoons."

"Now really! That stupid I am not, Monsieur," said Madame Labouret severely. "If your father were a marquis then you would be an officer in the dragoons and you would be quartered at one of the châteaux in this town. You would not be a simple private here in the Hotel of the Royal Arms."

The dragoon shrugged. "We quarreled, as I have said. He wanted to marry a white woman, while I still hoped—foolishly, I suppose—that he would someday marry my good mother. So I left him and took the name of Dumas. Marie-Cessette Dumas—that was the name of my mother—who meanwhile, however, has died. And I enlisted as plain Private Dumas."

"In short, to put it bluntly," Madame Labouret concluded, "you have no right to your father's name. There never was any kind of ceremony between him and your Negro mother?"

"Not so fast," said the dragoon, a little purple coming into his cheek. "I'm no bastard. My father acknowledged me as his son."

"Ah, you don't say?"

"Yes, I do. It's registered before a notary."

"My congratulations. But it is all none of my business. That is to say, unless Monsieur wishes me to make it *my* business. Do you understand what I mean?"

"Perfectly," said the dragoon. "And what if I should say, Yes, please make it your business?"

"Then I would have to say to you, Monsieur, come back here with a commission in the army, and Marie-Louise is yours."

"A commission in the army is not easy for a private," the dragoon said. "Particularly in peacetime, when officers have long lives."

The landlady shrugged. "That is your affair. After all, you do have connections. At least you say you have."

At this moment a dragoon came up and handed Thomas-Alexandre half a dozen gold coins. "Your share," he said.

The black dragoon gazed at the money in his hand. Then he said, "Madame. This money. If I do not come back with a commission—or if I die in war—add it to the dowry of your daughter."

"I will give you a receipt," said Madame Labouret, for whom there was a correct way of behavior for every occasion, no matter how strange it might seem to others.

"You noticed that I avoided a fight," said Thomas-Alexandre. "I mean with Blaise."

"Yes," she admitted.

"I might have spoiled his face in a real duel," the dragoon pointed out. "After all, your daughter may still have to marry him."

"Monsieur is very thoughtful," said Madame Labouret.

Only a few hours later, before sunup, the dragoons were mounted and in their dress uniform. Their horses were so currycombed that the flanks glistened like running water. Their boots were polished like mirrors, and the white bandoleers like a St. Andrew's cross over their chests had been freshly laundered. Swords for fighting on horseback, guns for fighting on foot, were clean and ready, and the traditional horsetail floated from their helmets.

From her little room under the roof of the inn, Marie-Louise could look out beyond the inn to the square in front of the old palace of Francis the First, where the dragoons were in formation. As the first glints of morning light were reflected on all this brilliance, Marie-Louise tried to distinguish which of the dragoons was the tallest in the saddle, but her eyes were misted, so she couldn't be sure.

The bugle sounded. Hoofs clattered against cobblestones. Leather harness squeaked. Pennons fluttered. And in a little while Villers-Cotterêts was as sleepy a little town as ever.

Marie-Louise wept.

How could a dragoon private ever become an officer? She thought she would never hear from her bronze champion again.

CHAPTER THREE

A Black Devil

THIS IS WHERE history took a hand. The month of the duels in the inn was June, traditional to love, but the year happened to be 1789, and in the following month, in July, there were riots of hunger among the poor of Paris, and the military was called out to suppress the mob.

The common people, in their fury at being met with bullets instead of bread, turned upon the Bastille, the prison fortress of Paris, as a symbol of the police power they hated. They captured it with their bare hands.

The French Revolution had begun, and with it an era of warfare opened up that was to provide many a common soldier with the opportunity to become an officer, and many an officer with the chance to put a crown on his head.

In August of that year, the very same King and Queen in whose honor dragoons had so recently been willing to have their heads split were imprisoned and were subsequently tried and put to death. And not a dragoon did anything about it.

Austria, Prussia, England, Spain, Holland had meanwhile formed a coalition to bring the French back to their senses. But this combined attack of all Europe was just what was needed to force France, where almost every household was split down the middle, to unite, stop its internal quarreling, and cement itself into a powerful military nation again.

Dragoon Dumas distinguished himself in battles everywhere. In the heat of combat he would be overcome with such a rage for fighting that his dark face would glow with a purple flush. Austrian prisoners first gave him the name of *der Schwarze Teufel*—the Black Devil. The name stuck and was translated into French, so that even among his own troops he was known as *le diable noir*. Newly formed regiments vied for his services. One made him a second lieutenant. Another snatched him away and made him a first lieutenant. The first seduced him back by still another promotion.* One day after particularly distinguishing himself he was dined by his general and rose from the table a major. A few months later he was dined again and left the table a lieutenant colonel.

It was as lieutenant colonel that the former private in the Queen's dragoons managed a leave of absence and rushed back to Villers-Cotterêts, to find himself welcomed everywhere as a returning hero. Indeed, it was not only in Villers-Cotterêts that he was known. His white stepmother from Normandy came down to be present at the

* It was St. Georges, also a mulatto and an outstanding athlete and swordsman, who first commissioned Dumas when he created the American Hussars, a regiment including many Negroes from the French colonies.

wedding between Colonel Alexandre Dumas and Marie-Louise Labouret. And the stepmother's name, signed with a great flourish to the marriage register—Marquise Davy de la Pailleterie—removed the last vestiges of doubt from Madame Labouret that she had made a fine match for her daughter.

A few days of visiting at some of the fine châteaux of the neighborhood, where the former dragoon was now welcome, and a few gay evenings at the inn, now rebaptized as the Hotel of the Sword (a safer name, according to Monsieur Labouret, since kings may come and kings may go, but the sword will very likely go on forever) and Lieutenant Colonel Dumas had to leave.

Marie-Louise wept, but history was on the march. When next she saw her husband he was a full colonel. And then a general. And he was still on his way up. He was becoming a popular figure in France. In a time of universal suspicion, of everyone's spying on everyone else, of endless investigations, of summary trials and mass executions, when judges with portable guillotines roamed the country smelling out internal enemies, General Dumas let it be known that he had little respect for this sort of patriotism.

One time his official duties took him to a town where several citizens had just been condemned to death for opposition to the government. The windows of Dumas' hotel fronted on the square where the public executions were scheduled to take place. It was noticeable to everyone that the General's windows remained tightly shuttered.

"You give a bad example," one of the judges said to him in a tone that did not disguise a threat. "The people will be forced to presume that your sympathies lie with the traitors."

"They will be right," said General Dumas. "I can understand a duel. I can understand a war. But don't ask me to have anything but contempt for an execution where a man with his hands tied is prodded up the steps toward a machine against which he is totally helpless."

General Dumas thus acquired still another nickname: Mister Humanity. And he cared so little about concealing his true feelings as to order one of the portable guillotines broken up one day and used for wood in his fireplace. He was immediately denounced before the Convention in Paris. "It was a cold day," said General

Dumas. Nothing further was done about the matter because the government now began to find him valuable for handling insurrections before they reached dangerous proportions. In this he showed himself far more skillful than General Hoche, who left a trail of bitterness behind him.

It was for this reason that when thirty thousand insurgents, tired of bloodshed and poverty, tired of the perpetual revolutionary oratory that gave them no bread, were massing for an attack on the Tuileries, the first name that occurred to the Convention was that of Mister Humanity.

Barras of the Convention sent a messenger to the Château des Fosses in the rue de Soissons of Villers-Cotterêts, where the General now lived in a style befitting his rank. The message said: "Come at once. Urgent!"

The General was out hunting, and Marie-Louise, who had seen her husband called back to the colors too often in the years of their marriage, sent the messenger off in the wrong direction.

It was not until late in the afternoon that messenger and general met. At once the General commanded a cabriolet for immediate departure to Paris.

"How is it that the messenger could not find me? You knew where I was hunting."

Marie-Louise, in tears, confessed that she had done it purposely. "Haven't you been through enough fighting? Can't we be together for a little while? Your daughter scarcely knows you as her father yet. You did not see her born. You did not hear her first words."

Thomas-Alexandre smiled and sighed. "Don't forget, if it hadn't been for fighting you would be married to a farmer with a bull whip."

The General drove at breakneck speed the fifty miles to Paris.

But when he arrived there it was already too late. The Convention, after waiting for him for hours, decided to put its protection into the hands of another general: General Bonaparte. And it was General Bonaparte who set up his cannons so as to give the people that famous "whiff of grapeshot" that ended the insurgent period of French history and set the stage for the Napoleonic era with its law and order and fitful war prosperity.

There were times, later, when General Dumas would say to his wife, not reproachfully, but sadly, "If not for your love, France might have had an Emperor Alexandre, mulatto from the island of Santo Domingo, instead of an Emperor Napoleon, Italian from the island of Corsica."

General Bonaparte put Dumas in charge of his cavalry, where he accomplished miracles.* The two men were soon on the most intimate terms, Dumas becoming one of that specially favored group that Napoleon admitted to the conferences he held while still in bed with Josephine. As for Josephine, she was at once fond of this fellow Creole from the Sugar Islands with whom she could chatter in her beloved patois. And Napoleon used to tweak Dumas' ear and say to him, "You'll go far with me."

It was not, however, until the Egyptian campaign that Dumas began to realize where the ambitions of Napoleon were sweeping the French republic. When he understood Napoleon's dreams of cracking the British empire and bursting through Asia Minor to swallow India, and perhaps encircle the globe, he had to ask himself, "Must French boys die in the sands of Egypt because of this man's grandiose plans?"

General Dumas was not one to hide his feelings. "I am at the service of France," he said to Napoleon, "and not at the service of any man's private ambitions."

"I could shoot you for insubordination!" Napoleon screamed at him.

General Dumas asked for a transfer home. It was granted at once. But no sooner had he taken ship to cross the British-infested Mediterranean than Napoleon suspected him of wanting to get to Paris and there promote himself for the role of commander in chief.

Whether Napoleon's own agents were back of Dumas' seizure in the harbor of Tarento and his imprisonment by the Bourbons of Naples is not clear. But one thing is certain: Napoleon made no effort to secure Dumas' release.

Dumas suffered horribly in prison. Repeated efforts were made to poison him just enough so that he would die of what might seem a natural disease. And when after two years he was finally set free

---

* Colonel W. R. Phipps, in his five-volume history *The Armies of the First French Republic,* says that even Dumas the novelist could not have done justice to the heroic exploits of his incredible father.

and returned to France, he found himself in the anomalous position of being neither in the army nor out of it, neither dead nor alive. He could collect neither pay nor pension. Napoleon had given strict orders: "I never want to see or hear that man's name!"

The result was that as far as the War Department was concerned, Dumas simply didn't exist. Even in the official paintings which had been ordered by the government to commemorate the victories of French arms, Dumas' face was painted out.

The man who eventually came back to Marie-Louise was still a giant in stature, but within he was gnawed by the stomach ulcers that were soon to kill him. Though for a while he continued to live in his old style, with servants and horses, he was actually without a penny. His one great longing was to have a son before he died, and Marie-Louise promised him one.

"It's going to be a black devil like you!" she would say gaily. She felt certain that it would be a boy because her previous child, a girl, had never kicked like this one.

Just as she was approaching confinement, she went to see the Whitsuntide fair, and especially the Punch and Judy show which she always loved. But this time that Faustian drama had a black devil puppet that carried on in such an uproarious fashion that it seemed to frighten even her unborn baby.

"It *is* going to be a black devil!" she moaned in fear.

And soon thereafter, when the child was born, the umbilical cord got itself wrapped around its neck, and the first glimpse the mother had of her offspring was of a dark-blue baby straining to gulp air.

"My God!" cried the mother. "A black devil!" She crossed herself and fainted.

But a moment later the baby managed its first cry, air flowed into its lungs, and it turned pink suddenly as if someone had lit a light within.

Alexandre Dumas had been born.

CHAPTER FOUR

The Omelet Masterpiece

As IN THE CASE of the great heroes of antiquity, signs and portents accompanied the appearance of the infant Dumas.

We have these legends from none other than Alexandre Dumas himself, a circumstance which, however, instead of adding weight to their authenticity, has in fact tended to discredit them in the eyes of captious critics. Even in his own day Dumas was strongly suspected of embroidering his life. For example, when a certain X began using the columns of the newspaper *Le Siècle* to attack Dumas in a series of stinging letters, there were those who immediately declared that X was Dumas himself, just making sure that a fair-sized controversy should rage around his name and keep it fresh in the public eye.

Dumas, of course, treated these aspersions with the silence that they merited. His own blistering replies to X, which soon began to appear in *Le Constitutionnel*, were surely proof enough that the quarrel was genuine. Nevertheless, the doubting Thomases continued to insist that the altercation was fraudulent. Yes, even after Dumas had boldly challenged his attacker to a duel.

As this dramatic story unfolded day after day in the Paris papers, it was followed breathlessly by millions all over France and indeed all over the world. And X's acceptance of the Dumas challenge was thus a major piece of news. And his stipulation that the duel could only take place if seconds could be found who would take the secret of his identity to their graves aroused many exciting speculations as to the noble identity of X.

Naturally, the diehards continued to resist. Nothing could possibly overcome their incredulousness, not even the appearance of Dumas on crutches, with his right leg bandaged up to the knee, nor the abrupt ceasing of the X letters in *Le Siècle*. "Wait," they said. "Soon the Y letters will begin. And then will come the turn of Z."

Needless to say, nothing of the kind happened.

In any case, to hear Dumas tell about the legends of his infancy at one of those fabulous kitchen parties of his, when his listeners would be reminded of nothing so much as the bravura-style performances of such piano virtuosos as Thalberg and Liszt, or even the incredible Willmer, who with his trills and staccatos kept his audience hanging on the edge of their seats—to hear Dumas, enormous frying pan in hand, as he would superintend his guests in the preparation of one of his Gargantuan and unpredictable omelets, that must have been a real treat.

He would order Paul Meurice, the playwright, to peel the potatoes, Théophile Gautier, the historian of the Romantic movement and author of *Mademoiselle de Maupin*, to bruise the parsley and chop the onions, and Fiorentino, the music critic, to prepare the mushrooms and blanch the almonds, and Delacroix, the painter, to stop his eternal sketching and get to work cracking the crabs and cutting up the *cervelat*.

For into Dumas' omelets went everything. There were people who claimed that they had found the manuscript of a rejected article in one of Dumas' omelets, which was an obvious lie, for Dumas always saved his rejected manuscripts, rewrote the title and the first paragraph, and got them accepted by the very same people who had formerly rejected them. No one ever claimed to have found a thousand-franc note in any of Dumas' omelets, which was far more likely with one so careless with his money, but that is because anyone who did would naturally keep the matter quiet and conceal the evidence in his pocket on the principle that it isn't polite for a guest to call his host's attention to a hair in his soup.

"I know a thousand ways to prepare an omelet," Dumas used to boast, claiming that the egg section was going to be the culminating chapter of his great cookbook.

Others insisted that the reason his omelets were always different was not because he knew a thousand recipes but because he didn't know any recipes at all.

It was on such a kitchen occasion that Dumas insisted that to become a great man one must have legends clustered about one's birth.

"Take our friend Delacroix here," said Dumas, "He has a legend. His father had his horoscope cast when he was born, and the stars said that little Eugène would have the most tormented life of any man but would become famous. And before the age of three Eugène had already been rescued from death by accidental hanging, rescued from death by fire, rescued from death by drowning, rescued from death by accidental poisoning, and rescued from death by suffocation—all of which convinced his distracted parents that he was indeed born to be famous and they gave him every opportunity to educate himself along any line he chose. Is not every word I've said true, Delacroix?"

"It's true," said Delacroix, annoyed. "But now I know, my dear Dumas, why when you come to my house you always bring paper and pencil."

"Just as when you come to my house," said Dumas, "you always bring a sketch pad."

"Yes," said Delacroix, "but to sketch a person is not to take anything from him."

"That's not what the Arabs think," Dumas retorted. "They believe that when you take down their likeness, you take from their spirit. And they are by that much lessened."

Delacroix loved and hated Dumas. It annoyed him to see Dumas a hundred times more famous than himself. Thousands of people who would never know Delacroix even dead already knew and admired Dumas alive.

Walking on the street with Dumas was a parade of "Bonjour, Monsieur Dumas!" and every woman's eyes turned upon the novelist, while as for himself, but half the weight of Dumas, he was as ignored as if he were Dumas' page boy trailing after his master with the royal umbrella.

No wonder Delacroix wrote in his diary with a kind of sneer: "Dumas' public is not mine." No wonder he was annoyed with Dumas' coming to see him and extracting from him all sorts of information that Delacroix had perhaps gathered painfully for one of his historical canvases. And before Delacroix had finished his historical painting, there was Dumas already in every newspaper with a serialized novel on the same historical period. It took Delacroix longer to paint a single scene than it took Dumas to write a whole novel.

And yet it was Dumas who was once in the box of the Prince Royal of the Orléans house when the latter decided to send Victor

Hugo a gold and diamond snuffbox, in return for a book of poetry
dedicated to the Duchess of Orléans by Hugo.

"How much is the snuffbox worth?" Dumas asked.

"I don't know," said the Prince. "Perhaps five thousand francs."

"For five thousand francs you can buy a painting by Delacroix
and give that to Hugo, making two artists happy instead of one."

The Prince agreed. "Find the right painting," he said to Dumas.

Dumas came rushing up to Delacroix's studio taking the steps
three at a time.

"I have good news for you, Eugène. I am come to buy one of
your paintings!"

"Ah, that's too bad," said Delacroix.

"Why too bad?"

"Because I cannot charge you, a fellow artist, more than a thousand francs a canvas. Go ahead. Take your pick."

"But it is not for me," said Dumas. "It is for Victor Hugo."

"Ah, so? Then it is even worse than I thought. For one cannot
charge a poet as much as a successful playwright. Victor Hugo can
have his choice of my works for five hundred francs."

"But you don't understand. It is the Prince Royal who is paying
for this canvas. He means it for a gift to Victor Hugo."

"The Prince Royal? What is he offering me for a canvas?"

"Five thousand francs!" Dumas cried.

"That's too bad," said Delacroix proudly. "I'd love to make a
sale, but I don't have at the moment a single canvas that I value
at less than ten thousand francs."

Thus the deal fell through.

He was a difficult man, Delacroix. He could not take life as a
lark, the way Dumas did.

Yes, he hated Dumas. And yet, there he was, in Dumas' kitchen
and somehow absorbed in Dumas' perpetual talk. Dumas was talking about himself, telling how as a newborn baby, naked, he was
laid before his father, and how he had suddenly begun to ease his
bladder. His father and everyone else who was present had stared
in amazement at this fountain arching high and falling way over
the boy's head.

"Never have I seen anyone cast his stream so far!" his father had
exclaimed. "He is destined to a glorious career!"

But then the stream had lost its first force and had come spattering down upon the baby's unmindful face, and then, petering out, had washed over his chest, then dribbled still a bit upon his belly with its umbilical bandage, to die finally exactly where it had originated.

"I'm afraid," his father had then said, "that he will just as easily cover himself with shame as with glory."

"Yes, legends," Dumas said. "Legends are what a man needs to make his way in the world. It is because of this legend of my first voiding that, from the beginning of my life, I always felt that I was born to go far in both fame and shame. Families without legends cannot develop greatness of character. Think of the legend of the Medici: that the founder of the family was graced with a supernatural male endowment which his successors later used as an insigne over their branch banks and which has since become in many countries of the world the sign of a pawnshop: three golden balls.

"That is what makes for greatness!

"Had my father gotten to Paris before Napoleon, when the Directory feared a royalist uprising," said Dumas, "and had he then become emperor, he might have founded the order of the Golden Fountain, as King Edward founded the Order of the Garter, which was obviously no garter but a sanitary belt which the Countess of Salisbury dropped, for no garter would have occasioned the smirks and the ribaldry that we are told of, and the king would not have tied the offending article around his calf saying, '*Honi soit qui mal y pense.*'"

"My dear Dumas," said Delacroix, "that is of course your trade: to spin out a nothing until it fills three hundred pages and is called a novel."

"What do you call a nothing?" Dumas demanded.

"Your first pee," said Delacroix sharply. "That is what I call a nothing. Even though you would found an order on it."

"With a necklace of yellow topazes, obviously," said Gautier.

"Let me tell you then how important a nothing can be," said Dumas. "When Victor Hugo was born he was not expected to live. He was misshapen. He was grotesque. His head was huge. Swollen. His neck was a thread. Doctors said he had little chance of surviving. Relatives shook their heads. Friends whispered that it would be better if he died. The least neglect would have sufficed. But his mother took more than just ordinary care of him. She lavished on him every possible affection. Why?

"Well, I'll tell you why. Because of a nothing.

"Because someone asked her, 'What makes a head heavy?'

"And she said, 'I don't know.'

"And this someone said, 'Doesn't your head ever feel heavy?'

"And she said, 'Yes. Sometimes.'

"'When is that?'

"'When I've been thinking too much.'

"'So it is thoughts that make a head heavy? Is that not so?'

"'Yes, but how can a baby have heavy thoughts?'

"'How else,' she was asked, 'does God bring new thought into the world, except through the heads of babies?'

"And so month after month passed and this mother did not give up. A year and still the child's head dropped. Fifteen months and it still could not raise its head. But this mother had decided that her Victor was a genius and that his brain would someday astound the world. And then one day the child was strong enough to begin to lift that noble head filled with weighty thoughts.

"That is why Victor Hugo wrote those lines:

> *'Je vous dirai peut-être, quelque jour,*
> *Quel lait pur, que de soins, que de voeux, que*
>   *d'amour,*
> *Prodigués pour ma vie, en naissant condamnée,*
> *M'ont fait deux fois le fils de ma mère obstinée.'*

"Yes, twice the son of his determined mother. I know every line of Hugo's by heart," said Dumas. "It is one case where I do not follow my motto, which as you know is *video nec invideo*—I see but I do not envy. For in this case I cannot prevent myself from envying Hugo's ability to versify."

"That's not your motto," said Delacroix.

"Why do you say that?" Dumas asked.

"Because I remember your giving me a different motto some time ago."

"Of course I did," Dumas cried. "Because I have every motto. I have Blanche de Castille's 'Death sooner than dirt.' And Rabelais'

'Do as you please; let happen what may.' And Monjouet's 'God is my yoke.' And Saint-Souplis' 'Live in order to die; Die in order to live.' And Longfellow's 'Excelsior.' I have them all. I love them all. A motto is a man's spiritual spine, as important as his physical spine. It reveals our inner secret. It forms a kind of promise to which we dedicate our lives.

"You will see, my friends. France will die because the habit of people's taking devices and mottoes is dying in France."

"You made the same gloomy prediction about cigars," said Fiorentino, lighting up his Havana.

"I did," said Dumas. "And I meant it. I predict that France, the most witty country of Europe, will in fifty years' time become as dull as Holland if the habit of cigar-smoking persists."

"There's a safe prediction," said Delacroix. "In fifty years' time none of us will be here to call you to account for your error."

"Or to praise me for my prophetic powers," Dumas retorted. "I am not afraid to make predictions. Just as you know the rules of perspective, my dear Eugène, and can draw a house that has not yet been constructed, so a historian like myself can draw the future. Alexis de Tocqueville does not hesitate to say that someday the United States and Russia will divide the world between them, although no one can see any such likelihood at this moment when Moscow and Washington are still paved with mud. But a hundred years from now, who knows? Nor do I hesitate to say that just as France is allied with Britain while Britain takes from her the empire of the world, so Britain will someday be allied with the United States while the United States takes from her the empire of the world. For nations always make the mistake of thinking political compatibility a good reason for alliance, whereas it is the worst of all reasons. And remember what Napoleon could say of China: There sleeps a giant; take care not to wake her. A historian is no good who can only read the past. Any fool can do that. The true test of a historian is to see into the future.

"And let me tell you this: I had in my childhood an affliction that revealed everything about my life. Nothing has happened to me since that was not predicted by and predicted on that affliction. Listen:

"Already at the age of six months I began to come out of the crawling stage of infancy and to get up on my feet. Only, instead of getting up on my feet, I got up on my toes. On the very tips of my toes.

"My mother took this for an abnormality, which it was, but my father took it for a curiosity that distinguished me from other children, which it also was.

"My father said, 'Why he's going to dance his way through life!' And he applauded my efforts. And no one can deny that I have had that urge.

"But my mother said, 'It's unnatural. We must do something about it.'

"My father consoled her, saying, 'Leave him be. Only too soon life will rock him back on his heels.'

"My poor father did not know how right he was, nor what event would do precisely that: rock me back on my heels.

"As months and even several years passed and I still didn't walk normally, but raced around like mad on the tips of my toes, my mother grew increasingly worried, my father increasingly delighted.

"My father showed me off as a ballet dancer, and people admired my astonishing skill.

"My mother, however, took me with her to the priest to ask, 'Is this Christian?'

"There was an old woman in our little town who every morning would go off to the Royal Forest to gather faggots, and, coming back in the evening with a huge bundle on her back, she would stop at our horse trough to dip her dry, gnarled hands into the water, push aside the green scum and bring a little sip of clear water to her toothless mouth. This woman would say to my mother, 'Well, have you tamed the youngster yet? He's like a colt that wants taming. Remember, if you don't break him in his youth, you will never break him.'

"My mother wanted me broken. But I guess I never have been properly broken. Never properly tamed.

"My father would not permit severe measures with me. He adored me and, like all fathers, expressed his adoration in indulgence, while mothers frequently express their adoration in discipline.

"We had neighbors who knew everything, just as neighbors know everything in all neighborhoods of this world. So there was a neighbor who said to my mother, 'It's the savage blood coming out in him.' She meant, of course, my African blood. And she advised my mother to put sabots on me.

"Whenever my father wasn't around my mother would force me to wear heavy wooden sabots. It would make her heart bleed with anguish to see me running around on the tips of my sabots, stumbling, falling on my face, but still getting up and racing off again at top speed, my nose and my face at the end of the day looking like a piece of beaten meat.

"She thought she was doing it for my good, because the neighbors warned her that if she didn't soon bring down my heels to the ground, my bones would never grow right, and I would run through life like an animal. Which is perhaps what I've done.

"She heard from the village smith to whom she went for a pair of iron shoes for me that a horse really walks on its toenail, which is the hoof, and she saw some connection between my style of walking—or rather running—and my father's love of horses. As well as my own rapidly developing love for them.

"My father's attitude was completely different. You must know that our little town of Villers-Cotterêts had so far produced one famous writer: Demoustier, already very old when I was brought into the world—indeed, my mother nursed him in his last illness— and who is still remembered for his wonderful rendering into French of Greek and Roman mythology. Because of Demoustier, there were people in our town to whom the classical myths were as real as Napoleon.

"One such man was our rich neighbor Monsieur Collard, who was reminded of Giovanni de Bologna's famous statue of the god Mercury whenever he saw me. You all know that statue where the god is seen poised on his toes, with a pair of little wings sprouting from each heel.

"One evening, at our home, this Monsieur Collard caught hold of me, though I fought like mad, for I didn't like to be fondled. I didn't like to have my mad dashes interrupted. 'Winged heels, that's what the little rascal has!' Monsieur Collard said. 'Like the god Mercury.'

"My father wanted to know what the wings of Mercury signified.

" 'Speed, of course,' Monsieur Collard replied. 'Flight! That's why Mercury is the god of thieves.'

"My mother cried out at this. Was her child to become a thief?

"Monsieur Collard explained to her that not all thieves are criminals. Spain stole the gold of the Indies. Prometheus stole fire from heaven. The bee steals nectar from the flowers in order to make honey.

"My father accepted this idea. But no one then present realized how often I was to be accused of stealing my thoughts from others, as my dear Eugène Delacroix has done here this very evening.

"In order to console my mother, Monsieur Collard went on to point out that flight did not only pertain to theft; we also speak of flights of imagination, and for that reason the winged god is also the god of eloquence.

"This alarmed my mother even more, for she remembered all the eloquent orators of the revolution who had perished, murdered or guillotined: Danton, Desmoulins, Hébert, Robespierre, Marat. She didn't want me to be eloquent. And perhaps I have been too fast a writer ever to achieve genuine eloquence.

" 'Then maybe he should be guided into commerce instead,' Monsieur Collard suggested. 'For Mercury is also the god of merchants.'

" 'Thief, orator, merchant? What kind of a combination is that?' my mother asked.

" 'Is that so strange?' Monsieur Collard replied. 'When you have a man with a gift for taking, and also with a gift for fluent speech, what have you if not a successful merchant?'

"There you have it, gentlemen," Dumas concluded. "Who does not know how often I have been accused of being a mere merchant of literature? Was ever a symbol more prophetic? Did I not once bet a thousand francs that I could write a novel in three days, and I wrote the *Chevalier de la Maison Rouge* with six hours to spare, being locked for the time of the bet in an empty room and slipping the pages under the door one by one as I wrote them.

"I must add that after all the attempts of my mother, with sabots and with specially made tightly laced leather shoes to keep my instep down, I still refused to walk except on my toes.

"Then there came a day when my father died. I was four years old. And suddenly my mother noticed that I was walking with my heels on the ground like everyone else.

"So much for prophecy," Dumas concluded amidst the silence of his friends. "Now for our omelet. Butter, butter, butter. My first and most important rule of cooking is this: You can't possibly use too much butter. Every man will agree with me. It is only women in the kitchen who are stingy with butter."

This was the moment when Delacroix seized Dumas' skillet and declared, "This time I am making the omelet!"

He could scarcely wield the enormous skillet, in which one could easily fry an omelet of three dozen eggs; nevertheless, he would not give it up.

"I'll show you an omelet that not one of you will be able to match!" Delacroix declared.

Dumas shrugged and let him have his way and started to crack eggs, separating whites from yolks.

"Tomatoes?" Delacroix asked.

"Here," said Dumas, handing him the crock of tomato purée.

"Chopped parsley? And green pepper?"

"Here."

"Saffron? And the *cervelat*?"

Everything was put within easy reach of him as he stood at the stove where the charcoal was glowing, thanks to the powerful bellows of Dumas' healthy lungs, unspoiled by cigar-smoking.

But what kind of a dish was this man Delacroix making? It seemed to have neither rhyme nor reason. Why did he pour in a little bit of yolk here, then a dab of white of egg there, then some yolk and tomato purée mixed. And here a bit of chopped parsley, and there some *cervelat*.

And the man worked at a furious pace that in itself was a puzzle. And the way he shook out precious saffron, not spreading it carefully, but here a little bit, and there a whole lot.

"It will be a mess!" cried Paul Meurice.

"He's ruining our omelet!" cried Gautier.

But the hair stood up on Dumas' neck, for he suddenly realized that this man Delacroix was not interested in the ingredients of his omelet for their taste, but for something quite different: their color! *Cervelat*, parsley, yolk, these were just so much brown, green and orange on his pallette.

And the frying pan was his canvas.

The man was painting. And suddenly the painting began to come into focus. Everyone leaned over the stove watching with amazement, as the empty places were filled in, as the forms took shape, and now one saw clearly the saffron and egg yolk desert landscape, with the tawny lion on its haunches defending itself against the rearing hoofs of a wild horse which was largely made of *cervelat*. Green parsley palm trees showed a near-by oasis. Over all a tomato-red sunset colored the sky.

As everyone crowded around, the omelet was finished.

"Incredible," murmured Gautier. "Never was more rebellious material forced to become art."

"Yes," said Dumas to Gautier, "you will have to add a new verse to your poem on art:

> '*Oui, l'oeuvre sort plus belle*
> *D'une forme au travail*
> *Rebelle,*
> *Vers, marbre, onyx, émail.*'"

"Instead of enamel, make that last word omelet," said Paul Meurice.

"Take it off the fire!" Dumas cried, for just then a thin acrid smoke began to rise from one side of the pan.

"You're burning a masterpiece!" Gautier yelled.

But Delacroix didn't move. And when the others tried to force the pan away, he resisted them. "It needs more brown to accentuate the scarp on that side."

"But you're ruining the omelet!" said Meurice. And they compelled him to remove it from the stove.

"It's altogether wonderful, Eugène!" said Dumas.

"It should hang in the next salon!" said Gautier. "Nothing in the Orientalist school was ever better."

Meurice, who had the handle of the skillet in his hands, let the huge omelet, well lubricated with butter, slip out onto a big platter. "Come on, *mes gars*," he said. "We shall now see what it feels like to eat the Sistine Madonna."

"I always knew that the painters of the Renaissance mixed their colors with egg," said Dumas, "but never before did a painter paint with egg."

"I will have the lion," Gautier announced.

"The horse of *cervelat* is for me," declared Dumas.

"Give me that sunset," said Meurice.

But Delacroix spread his arms above the omelet. "No one is going to touch this," he said truculently. "*C'est trop réussi.* It has turned out too good. I'm going to save it."

"But we're hungry!" cried Meurice. "Stand away, man!" And he started to push Delacroix aside.

Dumas and Gautier looked at each other. "It's a Delacroix," said Dumas, undecided. "It's worth thousands of francs."

Gautier sighed. "But in time of hunger . . . Don't forget the 'Raft of the Medusa' that Géricault painted, the shipwrecked sailors who turned cannibals from hunger. What would a tourist guide do if locked up in a museum for a week?"

"You're right," Dumas decided. "Away, my dear Eugène. There is no more powerful motive force in history than famine." And pushing aside the painter he began to serve huge portions of the enormous omelet.

Delacroix, in cold fury, glared at them.

"It's delicious!" everyone agreed.

"A double masterpiece!" said Dumas. "My dear Delacroix, permit me to salute you as the first artist to win the grand prize both in the salon and in the cuisine and that with the same exhibit."

"Why aren't you eating?" Meurice asked, chewing away.

"I'm not hungry," said Delacroix in a sullen voice.

"Ah, bah! *Mon cher!*" cried Dumas with a burst of feeling for his friend. "*Il ne faut pas nous en vouloir.*"

"And you?" he asked. "Suppose someone ate one of your manuscripts!"

"Don't be ridiculous," said Gautier. "Some of our stuff is absolutely indigestible. But your omelet is really good."

He let himself be persuaded to eat some of it. After all, he had achieved what he had set out to do: to shut up that eternal chatter of Dumas' and seize the center of attention for himself. "I feel like

Saturn devouring his children," he said. "But you're right. It's not
bad. Just a trifle overdone."

"You got that burned scarp," said Gautier.

"You see the lesson?" Dumas pointed out. "One must never try
to improve what is already nearly perfect. Which of us hasn't
found that out in his writing?"

Well, at any rate, that's the story. And when it got around Paris
it annoyed Delacroix, who denied every word of it. "Painting in a
frying pan!" he snorted. Nevertheless, he was often begged to repeat the trick. And a Parisian restaurant got itself a brief fame by
advertising an omelet *Salon de Peinture*, wherein the cook used egg
variously colored with spinach juice and tomato juice, thus achieving all the important colors except blue.

Others claimed the omelet story was a fact, but that the painter
involved was a much lesser artist, a man named Jadin whose excellent dog portraitures had won him commissions from dog lovers
all over Europe.

It was this artist Jadin who was announced repeatedly in the
papers as the man who would accompany Dumas on a trip through
Sicily, from which the author had already promised a serial of his
always delightful travel essays.

But at the last moment Jadin couldn't go.

Dumas went alone.

Nevertheless, when the feuilleton began to appear, there, day
after day, was Jadin and his bulldog Milord, off in Sicily with
Dumas. And the two men went sightseeing together, discussed history and geography, climbed Mount Aetna, and got themselves into
all manner of scrapes as a result of the escapades of the lusty bulldog Milord.

Thus it came about that while Jadin, in Paris, would be out
walking his bulldog Milord, that a friend would greet him and then
quickly apologize: "Sorry. I thought for a moment you were Jadin.
Good day, Monsieur."

"But I am Jadin."

"You don't say? But I was referring to the painter Jadin."

"But that's me, the painter Jadin!"

"No doubt. But I meant not a house painter, but the *artiste-peintre*
Jadin."

"*Sapristi alors!* I'm no house-painter. I'm the artist Jadin!"

"Just as you say, Monsieur. I'm sure you're an artist too. But I meant the one who is off with Dumas in Sicily, and whose articles I read every day in the feuilleton. Please excuse me, Monsieur."

Jadin boiled with indignation. He got so that he went around buttonholing people and saying: "I am the artist Jadin. There can't be any mistake about that, can there?"

People said: "Next thing you'll be saying that your bulldog is also called Milord."

"Absolutely!" screamed Jadin.

That, of course, was really carrying things too far. The police had to be notified. And the newspapers carried a word of caution to their readers with respect to an impostor who was calling himself Jadin and who also claimed to paint dogs. This pretender even sported a bulldog that answered to the name of Milord.

When Dumas finally returned to Paris, Jadin found that he himself had also returned. His friends greeted him again, and told him about the spurious Jadin who meanwhile had wisely made himself scarce.

Jadin held himself in check although he raged inside. Until he met Dumas on the street one day.

"You took four months out of my life!" Jadin exploded.

Dumas, lost, asked innocently: "What do you mean?"

"You pretended I was with you on your trip. People refused to believe that I was here."

"I couldn't help myself," Dumas said. "I had so anticipated this trip with you, that I felt all the time as if you were at my side. Besides I had to imagine someone with me, otherwise I would have been so lonely, so homesick, I would have run back to Paris without my promised travel impressions. Forgive me!"

Jadin, a good fellow at heart, forgave. Indeed he later really accompanied Dumas on one of his trips.

Defamers of Dumas are quick to point out that nostalgia probably had not nearly so much to do with Dumas' dragging of an imaginary Jadin through Sicily as did the old profit motive. Dumas, they argue, was paid by the line. Ergo, conversation back and forth, brought in several times as much money as the solitary reflections of a lonely wanderer.

Just figure out the returns on such a conversation as this:

"You don't say, Dumas?"

"On the contrary, my dear Jadin, I do say so, and emphatically."

"But my dear Dumas, can you prove it?"

"Of course I can."

"Then please do."

"With pleasure, my good Jadin."

"Very well, I'm all ears."

Obviously, being paid by the line, there was seven times as much money in a trip with Jadin as without him. So Jadin had to go along, willy-nilly.

Perhaps you think that this is not getting any nearer to the mystery of the "Duel after the Masquerade Ball." You would be wrong. To explain the mysterious connection of Alexandre Dumas with the "Duel after the Masquerade Ball," we must first understand our man.

We must understand a writer who could be in the process of writing the serial appearing daily in Émile de Girardin's *La Presse*, while at the same time he was accepting contracts for still undreamed-of serials to appear in daily installments in six other papers: *La Patrie, Le Constitutionnel, Le Siècle, Le Soleil, L'Esprit Public* and *Le Commerce*. So far Dumas had written nothing but the titles of these other serials.

And not only that, but scarcely were these serials announced and the subscribers of all these papers waiting for the promised treat, than Alexandre Dumas announced a grand trip to Madrid to attend the nuptials of the Duke of Montpensier to Isabella of Spain. He intended to see all Spain, and then go off to Algiers, and then . . .

The assistant editor of *La Presse* came storming into Dumas' study. "Ah! So you are here, after all."

"That would be difficult for me to deny," said Dumas.

"Good," said the editor, sitting down and wiping his sweat-covered face. "I was afraid you were really going to Spain."

"No, no."

"Well I'm glad to hear it."

"Not until tomorrow."

"What?! You are going off in the middle of *Joseph Balsamo?*"

"Your readers will wait."

"They won't!"

"They'll have to."

"But we have a contract."

"Ah, yes, that's true. I did sign something or other. What does our contract say?"

"It says that there are to be no interruptions, and you are to make no other commitments until the story is finished."

"Yes. I remember now."

"Well, I'm glad you see reason, my dear Dumas. Our circulation has gone up nearly three hundred per cent. Our readers are wild about *Balsamo*."

"You don't say. In that case I'm sure they will not mind waiting until I return."

"You mean you still insist on going?"

"Tomorrow, as announced."

"And our contract?"

"It says the book must be finished. And I am finishing it."

"When?"

"Right now! Look over my shoulder and read."

The editor looked and read what Dumas was writing: "Exhausted, Joseph Balsamo sank to the ground. He closed his eyes and expired."

The editor clasped his face in his hands. "He dies? He is really dead?"

"As you see," said Dumas calmly. And he wiped his pen and put it aside.

"You murdered him. Deliberately. It is monstrous!"

"Who is to prevent me?"

"What will our readers say?"

"That's the affair of your paper."

"But the plot is still up in the air. The story isn't rounded out."

"Perhaps. But that is the way death sometimes comes. In the midst of life, as the good book says. Man proposes and God disposes."

"This gave every promise of being a great novel. This can't be the end."

"Pardon me. I will prove to you that it is the end. Look." And Dumas, dipping his pen in ink, wrote with a flourish: *The End.*

The poor editor went out, tearing his hair.

And Dumas went off to Spain, while the owners of seven Parisian papers prepared subpoenas against his return.

It came to a big trial in Paris, where Dumas sustained with brilliance the right of an author to do as he pleased with the characters of his books.

"An author is like God with respect to his characters," Dumas declared in court. "He created them. No one can dictate what he shall do with them!"

The presiding judge said, "You compare yourself to God?"

"So far as my books are concerned, yes."

"Ten million Frenchmen are waiting for you to continue Joseph Balsamo's story," said the presiding judge. "Are you not a Frenchman?"

Dumas bowed his head. "I cannot resist the prayers of ten million Frenchmen," he said. "I shall revive Joseph Balsamo."

And what's more, he did revive him.

That's our man. That's the man we must know in order to understand his connection with Gérôme's painting.

CHAPTER FIVE

Duel with God

DUMAS HIMSELF has told us of his first duel.

He was four years old. His father had just been buried. And his mother came upon him as he was lugging two enormous pistols up the stairs. They were his father's fine pair of matched dueling pistols, so large and heavy that little Alexandre's clumsy and pudgy fingers could not cope with them, and he only managed to struggle them up, one after another, a step at a time.

There was such concentration, such determination in the youngster's actions, that for a moment his grief-stricken mother stood rooted, watching him.

Then she interfered. "What on earth are you up to? Here, give me those guns. You know you're forbidden to touch them!"

"Let me be!" the boy screamed in anger. "I'm going to Heaven!"

Madame Dumas was dumfounded. "To Heaven?" she gasped.

"Yes." And he pulled loose from her and went back to his tussle with the pistols.

His mother's skin began to tingle on the nape of her neck. "What's got into you?" she cried.

"I'm going to fight God," the boy said. "And I'm going to kill Him —for killing my father!"

His mother broke into tears. But then her grief passed over into fury. "Give me those pistols!" she shouted, and she tore them from his grasp. "There aren't going to be any guns in this house any more. I don't want any guns! Or wars! Or duels! I don't want any heroes. Do you understand me? You're going to be a musician when you grow up. You're going to study the violin. You'll handle a bow and a fiddle, that's what. Because I don't want any wars, any revolutions, any emperors. I don't want any history. Do you hear me? I just don't want any history at all from now on!"

As far as violin playing is concerned, Dumas did study it for years as a child. And in later days he used to say, "Yes, I'm a violin player. So was Raphael, don't forget."

But what I wanted to discuss was this story of Dumas' first duel. It's this sort of story Dumas tells about himself that makes critics smile. This incredible picture of a four-year-old still so naïve that he imagines he can reach God by going upstairs, and still so fanatically devoted to his father that he is determined to avenge his death, and so penetrated with the French code of honor that he doesn't mean to waylay God, but to fight Him a fair duel—well, it just makes us smile. That is, unless it sticks in our craw and makes us throw Dumas away entirely.

Dumas! You old-fashioned, overblown fraud, you with your cloak-and-dagger and your trap doors!

But you know what? I believe this little tale. It doesn't make me smile. I don't relegate it to the category of those family tales that arise wherever there is a doting mother and no witnesses to contradict her.

I just believe. Not that I think that Dumas would actually have shot God dead, for, as we know, he was never a man to bear a grudge, but that he was just that fearless.

Let's take, for example, Dumas' role in the revolution of 1830, when the Bourbon Charles X made the mistake of thinking that his prestige through the conquest of Algiers was so great that he could suppress the freedom of the French press. This king was so sure of himself that he issued the decree and went off hunting. And while he was gone the tables and chairs and pianos tumbled out of the windows of Paris and the barricades rose in the streets and the king's soldiers were met with boiling oil thrown from the roofs.

Dumas, then a young rising writer, ran to Lafayette, leader of the revolution, and said, "I'm at your orders. Command me!"

Lafayette said, "We need gunpowder desperately."

"I can get it for you!" Dumas cried. "I'm from Villers-Cotterêts, which is only a short distance from Soissons, where the royal powder magazines are. I know the place well. I played there as a child. Give me a company of men and I shall seize that supply and bring it back to Paris."

Lafayette said, "You have my order. But I have not a man to spare you for the expedition. You must do your own recruiting."

So what was the first thing that Dumas did?

He ran to Humann, the most exclusive tailor of Paris. Naturally, with Paris in such an uproar, Humann was tightly shuttered. Dumas rapped at the door. He pounded at the metal blinds until a head was poked out of the window upstairs. It was Humann himself.

"Open up!" Dumas cried. "I need a uniform. Quick. The revolution depends on it!"

Humann didn't care much for revolutions, but Dumas was a customer he could not offend, so he let Dumas into the dark store.

"What kind of a uniform do you want?" the tailor asked.

"Ah, that's the problem," said Dumas. "I don't know."

"Well in what branch are you? Cavalry? Diplomatic corps? What is it?"

"I really don't know," Dumas admitted.

"Bah," said Humann. "I don't know either. Do you know at least your rank?"

"No," said Dumas. "My commission is still oral."

"A fine revolution," said Humann in disgust. He opened up a volume of colored plates. "Well, here are all the uniforms. Pick which you want."

"But these are the uniforms of Charles X, whom we've just deposed!" Dumas cried. "Those are the uniforms of the enemy. What we want is something fresh. A new France is arising today. A new world is dawning."

He saw now that he must take charge of this matter. He ordered Humann to produce all his uniform cloths, and the tailor dragged out all the materials he had: serge, moleskin, velvet, whipcord, grosgrain, and in all colors—blues, reds, greens, as well as various shades of white and cream.

"Wonderful!" Dumas cried. "We shall do something completely original."

And the tailor began to catch the writer's fire, heaping before him all kinds of passementerie: gold and silver braids, fringes, frogs, piping. And all sorts of buttons, eyelets, sequins.

Well, in short, as a result of the meeting of two kindred spirits, the one with supplies and craftsmanship, the other with imagination and daring, there developed in that shop that afternoon a uniform which was like nothing else ever seen on earth. It expressed, so Dumas assures us, the élan, the victorious élan of youth toward liberty and a future without bounds.

And, late at night, thanks to the assiduous work of three assistants and the constant presence of Dumas himself, who didn't stir from the shop and kept taking fittings and having a stitch taken in here and a stitch let out there, when this uniform was finally finished, Dumas put it on, stuck pistols in his belt, girded on his sword, mounted a horse and was off to Soissons.

Alone. Of course alone. Not only because in Paris, at night, in the grip of a revolution, it would have been madness to start recruiting, but principally because he still had no uniforms for recruits. When you have only one uniform, you've got to make that one do.

Before dawn Dumas was rapping, pounding, kicking at the strong door to the commandant's house in Soissons.

"Open in the name of the people!" Dumas cried.

Now there are two versions as to what followed. Both agree that the door was opened and the fortress surrendered to Dumas with all its store of gunpowder. According to Dumas, it was the sight of his uniform that did the trick, as well as his commanding voice that obviously proclaimed his unswerving loyalty to the people's cause.

But according to another version, the wife of the commandant of the fortress was a former sugar planter's daughter, and in her youth she had witnessed many of the bloody uprisings of the slaves of Santo Domingo and, seeing Dumas' head of bushy hair through the peephole of the great door, she cried out in terror, "The blacks! It's another revolt of the blacks!" and she flung herself weeping upon her husband and begged him not to fight this thing, but to surrender at once.

And so Dumas, all by himself, forced the magazine at Soissons and hired drovers to bring to Paris the powder that won the revolution for the people.

This uniform of Dumas' became one of the big laughs of Paris. Everyone was nudging everyone else. "Have you seen Dumas' uniform? Have you ever seen anything like it?" They didn't actually laugh at him to his face, because the story was still circulating of how he had recently challenged Georges Pleubèque to a duel because Georges made a remark about a Quiroga cloak that Dumas was then wearing, and Dumas put his sword through Georges' right shoulder so that the man was never able to lift his elbow on that side again.

But everyone looked and smiled. There was no doubt about it. That uniform was utterly and fascinatingly unique. And since it was not adopted by the new army, it has remained unique to this day.

As for Dumas, he summed it up very simply: "If we're going to kill each other over the freedom to print what we please, what about the freedom to dress as we please?"

You see, the man was an utter popinjay.

Imagine wearing on one's massive paunch the sparkling orders of countries that never existed and sporting the colorful decorations of potentates who never reigned! Who would do such a thing but Dumas?

Why, a Prince of Scanderbeg once bestowed upon Dumas the highest order of the realm of Epirus and Albania: the Black Eagle with the four crosses, plus the oak-leaf clusters. All because Dumas responded so generously to the Prince's appeal for help in the cause of the Albanian movement of independence against the unspeakable Turk. One of Dumas' services was a flaming proclamation for national freedom addressed *To All Europe*. Another was opening an Albanian freedom loan by a first subscription of five thousand francs.

This loan was never redeemed because the Prince of Scanderbeg was just then taken up by the French police and sent to finish out the unexpired portion of an old sentence for pickpocketing at country fairs.

That didn't prevent Dumas from continuing to wear the decoration that the Prince had given him. Like his uniform, it was unique. A huge piece of glittering gold set with black diamonds. At least that it what Dumas thought until one day he had to dispose of it for some ready cash. That's when it turned out to be nothing but gold-plated brass. And the stones were nothing but artificial jet. So Dumas didn't sell it, and continued to wear it.

"But now that you know it's a fraud!" people said.

"It's beautiful," said Dumas. "And it seems I have the only one."

"But it isn't even gold."

"Yes. That's true. But I've thought of having it copied in real gold," Dumas said.

"But it would still be a fraud, my dear Dumas, since your Prince of Scanderbeg has turned out to be nothing but a common pickpocket."

"Oh, about that you can't tell," Dumas argued. "Who was Joan of Arc? Nothing but a peasant girl. Who was Bernadotte? Just an officer in Napoleon's army, until the King of Sweden made him his adopted son. And who was Napoleon? Ah, no, don't go disposing of people that way. Who knows the sublime future that may be in store for them."

No wonder people used to smile when they thought of Dumas.

And they still smile. Gustave Lanson, in his huge work on French literature, dismisses Dumas with half a sentence. Dumas just doesn't rate in official French literary history.

Why, only last year when Dumas' play *Kean, or Disorder and Genius* (based on the life of Edmund Kean, that drunken performer of whom Coleridge wrote that seeing him act was like reading Shakespeare to flashes of lightning) was revived in Paris and unexpectedly turned into the season's hit, an American newspaper reporting the matter said, "No one knows which one of Dumas' many theatrical hacks actually wrote the play. All that is known is that Dumas signed it."

Imagine! No one knows who wrote this play that a hundred and eighteen years after its opening can still be revived as a hit. The only thing that is certain is that Dumas didn't write it. Dumas only signed it.

You see the fraud that the man was? Some hack comes to him with a great play and says, "Please do me a favor, my dear Dumas."

"Certainly," says Dumas. "What is it, my good man. Speak out!"

"I can write a play, as you see, but unfortunately I am absolutely incapable of writing my signature. I've heard that you are very good at writing signatures. Will you then kindly sign this?"

And Dumas, ever obliging, says, "Nothing to it, my dear fellow."

Dumas himself thought all this fuss about who wrote his plays was just funny. "When a play of mine is hissed," he said, "no one doubts that I wrote it and that my talent is failing me. It is only when a play of mine is a success that everyone immediately wonders, Who do you think really wrote it for him this time?"

Dumas once went to Bourg, in Bresse, to do research for a novel that he intended to write and which appeared later as *The Companions of Jehu.* There he was told that the town's magistrate was the best local archaeologist and historian. He went to see him at once.

"Well, sir," said that magistrate with a smile of condescension on his face that was not far short from an open sneer, "so you are honoring our poor country with a visit in search of material for a novel."

"No, sir," said Dumas. "The material I have already located. In my head. I want only to consult certain documents and to visit the actual site."

"Ah, fine. But I didn't know that it was necessary to give oneself so much trouble in order to write a novel," the magistrate said with that affability that kind parents show to children and that kind historians show to novelists.

Dumas replied, "I find that the more exhaustive my research, the better my scenes."

"But there is so much to the history of Bourg," the magistrate said. "It will be fatiguing. Perhaps you should have sent someone else to do the work for you."

"How could I send someone else to do research for a matter which is still only in my head?" Dumas asked. "How would he know what to look for, what was significant and what was trivial? When I want to put my characters in an inn, or want to have them racing across country in a running fight, I must see the place myself, in order to know later how to fit my figures into the house or into the landscape."

"That is another matter. This then is a novel which you intend to do yourself!" said the magistrate as if a great light had dawned upon him.

"Alas, yes," said Dumas. "I am reduced to that. My valet used to do them for me, but he now pretends that he is also capable of signing them with his own name, so of course I had to dismiss him, since the signature is above everything else what I like to take care of personally."

But all this argument, all these clever retorts, could not stop our man from acquiring the reputation of a fraud. His own son—and this is a matter which we shall have to go into at length because this is the essential part of the solution of the mystery of the "Duel after the Masquerade Ball"—his own son said of his father, "The kindest man. Really. I've never known him to speak evil of anyone. Of course, I've never heard him speak of anyone but himself."

It was indeed his own son who coined one of the most famous lines of the century when he said of his father, "His vanity is such that he will ride on the outside of his carriage in order to make people believe that he is rich enough to afford a Negro groom."

As a matter of fact, Dumas did like to sport a Negro groom. When he was flush with money (whether freshly borrowed or freshly earned never made any difference to this man to whom money was once and for all money, just as a decoration was once and for all a decoration) Dumas always got himself a Negro groom. And why not? What set one off more in Paris than a Negro groom? This, more than anything else, dazzled. And to dazzle was always the object of the Parisian elite, whether aristocratic, revolutionary or Bohemian.

What could be more effective than a Negro groom dressed in puffy trousers of bright yellow silk, with a skimpy monkey jacket of red velvet elaborately befrogged with gold? What could be more correct than to stop your tilbury, or your spider, or your landau, or your berline, or whatever might be your most flashing and stylish carriage, stop it before Tortoni's, and have your Negro groom leap out and fetch you one of Tortoni's famous ice creams or sherbets, which you ate right in your own vehicle?

It was sheer Arabian Nights.

Most definitely it was not *peuple.* For with all the revolutionary zeal of France, no one wanted to be—or wanted to do—anything that smacked of "people." In the day when the penniless Nestor Roqueplan, by nothing but his determination to stand out from the masses, could live like a millionaire and be the style-setting dandy of Paris, that expression of his *"c'est peuple"* ("it's people") was withering. It surpassed for certain milieus the authority of a papal interdict. Why, when Nestor Roqueplan one day rejected a bottle of champagne proffered by the master of the cellar of the Golden House Restaurant with the expression *"c'est peuple,"* the whole champagne industry of France shivered and almost collapsed.

But to get back to Dumas' first duel. With God. One must imagine a little boy growing up in a household where there is not a penny in cash and yet where life is somehow still luxurious and where the mother runs off to Paris to cast herself at the feet of Napoleon in the Tuileries and beg for mercy.

And the father, left home with the child, entertains him by taking him along on his hunts. And by telling him stories of his military life. For example, how he captured the fortress of Mount Cenis in the icy fastnesses of the Alps, so as to break open a passage from France into Italy.

"Here, I'll show you. When I grab you from the rear, like this, you can't fight back, can you?" And the two would have a little scuffle to illustrate a point in military tactics. "But to take this fortress by the rear we had to scale a wall of ice, hundreds of feet high. Do you know how high that is?"

And the little boy listened wide-eyed, feeling the thrill of it without fully understanding.

"Put one tree on top of another. The tallest tree you've ever seen. And put another tree on top of that. And still another tree. And imagine all these trees made of slippery ice. And you had to climb that. —Do you know what I did?"

"You went to the smith," said Alexandre, who had heard the story before but for whom it was still as fresh and as magical as ever.

"Yes. I went to the smith down in the valley and I said, 'Make me three hundred pairs of frost nails that I can lace on the boots of my men.' You see, that was to give my men sharp talons, such as eagles have, so that their feet could dig right into the ice. And then I took these three hundred pairs of frost nails and I called all my men together and I said to them, 'I need three hundred men to volunteer for work tonight.' And all my men shouted at once. They all wanted to go along. But I said, 'The men I need must promise that if they feel themselves slipping they will keep their mouths shut and fall to their deaths without a cry.' You know why I asked my men that?"

The little boy nodded eagerly. "Because they mustn't wake up the men in the fortress."

"Precisely!" said his father. "And because it wouldn't have done any good to cry out. No one would have been able to save him. One slip and you were lost. You fell to your death. And if you cried out and the garrison was wakened, why then all of us would be killed."

And though he had heard the story enough times to know it by heart, still the little boy asked, "And did anyone fall?"

"Yes. Three men."

"And did they keep quiet?"

"They didn't utter a sound. All we heard was their bodies bounding from rock to rock as they plunged into the abyss. But not a cry. Not a moan. Not a murmur."

"And did you take the fortress?"

"We did indeed. The surprise was so complete that the enemy didn't even try to resist. They simply surrendered."

"And then what happened?"

"Well, now the road was open over the mountains and down into Italy. Into sunny Italy with its orange groves. And we went down there and we whipped the Austrian armies. . . ."

Such was the education of the young duelist.

And then his mother came home, her lips still white with rage. And she told of how she had cast herself at the feet of Napoleon; she told of how he had lifted her up and begged her not to cry and had asked her what he could do for her. But the moment he heard the name of Dumas, the Emperor turned away in anger and said,

"Haven't I given orders that this man's name must never be mentioned in my presence?"

Such was the conversation, such the atmosphere in which the child was nourished. Such was the drama on which his mind was gradually opened to consciousness and to growing intelligence.

And as if all this were not enough to stimulate the mind of the little duelist, his very education was designed as if to intoxicate him. He began it when at the age of four he was in a neighbor's house and disturbing everyone with his perpetual dancing around.

"I have something that will keep him quiet," the neighbor said, and she brought out one of the forty-four volumes of the great illustrated edition of Buffon's *Natural History*. As soon as the boy saw the big animal engravings, he remained for hours as if hypnotized. Walruses, giraffes, hummingbirds, snakes took hold of his mind.

One day, his sister, home for a visit from her school, said to him, "Why do you just look at the pictures? Can't you read?"

And she pointed out to him, in the text, the twenty-six letters of the alphabet.

Almost at once he caught on and could read. And he filled his mind with the sonorous sentences of Buffon, whose style was such that it was commonly said that he never sat down to work in the finely furnished study of his château without first donning his precious lace jabot and cuffs.

One day this neighbor watched little Alexandre as he was moving his finger along the line of print.

"You're reading?" she asked.

"Yes."

She couldn't believe it in one so young. "Show me," she insisted. "Read out loud."

And the child read, stumbling over some of the big words. But it was plain enough that he could and did read.

"Do you know what you're reading?" she asked.

"Of course," he said.

"Well, tell me," she asked.

"I'm reading French," he said. "My sister told me."

"Yes. But what does it mean?"

"I don't know what it means," he said.

"Then why do you read it?"

"Because I like to read."

He was reading for the sheer joy of accomplishment.

The neighbor took pity on the lad and to save him the trouble of going through the forty-four volumes of Buffon's prose she gave him a volume of Galland's translation of *The Arabian Nights,* the edition which first brought to Europe's attention those marvelous Oriental tales.

For the first time Alexandre realized that strings of words made pictures in one's mind. Now his imagination began to blossom. Soon he was reading *Robinson Crusoe.* And then the Bible. And Demoustier's Greek and Roman mythology.

It was for this Demoustier, who had been a neighbor, that Alexandre's mother used to cook a vegetable soup, which was the only thing the old man could digest. But as time went on she had had to make her soup finer and finer, and at last she had been reduced to feeding him nothing but hot water.

And then one day the old gentleman had said to her, "When your thick soup couldn't pass, you could make it finer, Madame. But when even water won't pass, then, my dear, it is clearly time for me to pass."

And now, to her great fright, Madame Dumas began to notice this same graduation from fine to finer soups, which she had to prepare for her husband, the General.

"Before I reach hot water and then cannot even pass that," he said to his wife, "I must make one more attempt with the Emperor. Rather than leave you without a penny I am willing to humiliate myself before him. And I will take along Alexandre to melt the man's heart."

And thus, at the age of four, Alexandre saw for the first time that city which is still the capital of dreams and visions: Paris.

Father and son stopped at the home of a little old man who had a very young wife. The young wife embraced the General in the very warmest way, but the old man didn't seem to mind. And then she caught the little toe-dancing Alexandre and hugged him too.

"Do you know?" she said. "I could have been your mother."

Alexandre struggled against the confinement of her embraces. "No, you couldn't," he said loyally. "I already have a mother."

"Of course you do," she said. "But tell me: does your father still drink his wine right out of a cask? Can he pick up a horse between his knees? And does he show his pretty feet and his beautiful calf to all the girls?"

"My father is terribly strong," said the boy stoutly and began to kick and cuff his way out of the arms of the woman. But then Alexandre stopped his struggle. "Did I hurt you?" he asked. "Why are you crying?"

"I'm just crying because it was I that wanted to be your mother," she said, and Alexandre found that very silly.

But he remembered it. And many years later it began to mean something. Because that is the way the human mind sometimes is: it remembers trifles as if knowing in advance that they will be understood later.

He remembered the little old man too. In fact he was fascinated by him because of his strange costume, which was like nothing the boy had ever seen before. He wore a taupe-colored coat, blue velvet breeches, candy-striped cotton stockings and red-heeled pumps with fancy buckles. But it was his hair that more than anything surprised Alexandre. It was dressed in a style which he later knew was called "pigeon wing" and which terminated in a plaited pigtail woven and tied with a black silk ribbon, so that it was almost rigid, and it did in fact point right up into the air because it stretched out over the man's stiff and richly embroidered coat collar.

"Why are you looking at me?" the old man asked, smiling. "Do you like the way I'm dressed? It's in honor of our king. Do you understand that? Louis XVIII, who will come back to the throne when Emperor Chameleon is gone. You don't know who Emperor Chameleon is, do you?"

His wife objected. "He's too young. Leave him be."

The General said, "You still dream of a return of the Bourbons?"

"And why not?" the old man asked. "Didn't the revolution ruin my career? Think of the marvels I used to do with hair. Why, I dressed the hair of Marie Antoinette herself. A frigate in full sail. What a wonder! What a delight to see! Oh, yes, powdered hair! The wigs of Louis XIV, the puffs of the Regency, the frizettes of Louis XV and the cushions of Marie Antoinette. What an art hairdressing

was. And now—destroyed, destroyed, destroyed! A great art annihilated! A great talent like mine doomed!"

His wife tried to console him and calm him, but he was a peppery
little man who danced around almost as much as did little Alexandre.

"Ah, but you don't know how wonderful it was in the old days.
Before Rousseau said, 'Back to Nature'! The idea! The ridiculous
idea! Why, let's all go naked then! No! Man's goal must be to get
as far away from Nature as possible. That's why we have artists!

"But I had my laugh out of it too. When, after cutting off all the
powdered heads, they then began to cut off their own unpowdered
ones. Oh, I tell you, when I saw that first *natural* unpowdered and
uncurled hair go under the guillotine, did I dance! I was right there
beside the guillotine, and I danced right into the blood with my
red-heeled shoes! And a man said to me, 'What are you laughing at?
Why, you look like an aristocrat yourself.' I laughed in his face. I
thought our business was coming back! And at first, with the Directory, it did seem as if I might soon be heating up my tongs, because Barras never did give up powder, and Citizen Moulins still
wore a queue. But then that Bonaparte had to stick his head in. And
can you imagine curling that man's hair? That flat short hair that
makes his head look as if he had just been rescued from drowning."

And this too Alexandre somehow remembered, though it made
little sense to him at the time.

Perhaps he remembered all this because the little old man advised
the General what to do about his son's habit of dancing on his tiptoes. "That's because you've neglected to pierce his ears," he said.
"There's nothing gives the body balance like a pair of gold earrings.
Why, any fool can feel that for himself. Just grab hold of the lobes
of your ears between thumb and forefinger. The moment you hold
them something happens—the eyes expand, the body feels as if it
had recovered its center, and the chest comes up. Oh, that Rousseau,
that fool with his Nature. What crimes he has to answer for! What
secrets we knew about life that will now die with us!"

And then he turned to his wife. "Come, give the lad some almond
water with honey, and then a sugarplum, or a glacéed chestnut, and
fetch your big gold chain and we'll go upstairs to the midwife and

she'll have holes in those little lobes before you can twinkle your
eyes."

The wife took three links off her gold chain. "One for the midwife, and one in each ear," she said, and the General agreed, and
they all marched upstairs, Alexandre dancing his way up; and a
little while later back they all came, Alexandre wearing two bright
tears, one in each eye, and two bright circlets of gold, one in each
ear, and sucking hard on the remnants of his sugarplum.

But there was no blood, because the midwife stabbed the holes
with a white-hot needle.

Why, of course such a scene would wake a little fellow up! In
precisely the same way that gardeners will sometimes hammer a
nail into a tree that refuses to bear, and suddenly, lo! the next season the tree is covered with fruit.

Or the way Benvenuto Cellini's father slapped him, saying,
"This is not a punishment. But just to make sure that you never
forget."

And because it was all so exciting Dumas remembered it all his
life. Remembered the great physician Corvisart who was Napoleon's personal doctor, and who was certain that he could effect a
reconciliation between the two men, but failed, even when he told
Napoleon that the General had only months to live. "I auscultated a
walking coffin," he said.

And Dumas remembered others who also tried to help his father:
Marshal Brune, who said to the little boy, "I'll never forget your
father riding his horse right into the Grand Mosque of Cairo. He
was whirling his saber around his head, cutting down the enemy
left and right. Everyone thought he was an apparition from hell."

And Marshal Murat, soon to be a king in Italy, who said to the
lad, "Your father was the greatest cavalryman France ever had in
her armies."

But no one was able to change Napoleon's mind. Not even Princess Pauline, Napoleon's sister, whom little Alexandre remembered
always as the most beautiful woman he had ever seen.

Yes, the little boy never forgot these people. Years later he would
go to visit the precise spot where, after Napoleon's fall, mobs tore
Marshal Brune to pieces. And he would visit the place where King
Murat was taken from his throne, tried, and executed before a firing

squad. And he would see after Pauline's death the marble statue that Canova had carved of her, and for which she was said to have posed naked, a statue of feminine beauty so lovely that all Europe came to worship there as if at a shrine, and the crush of visitors was such that the statue had to be surrounded by heavy bronze railings.

Yes, this is the world you must know to understand a child of four challenging God to a duel.

CHAPTER SIX

Out of Sheer Natural Abundance

THE MAN WAS ALIVE. Really alive.

Billions breathe. But how many are alive? To imitate the lives of others is to be no more alive than a ditto mark. To be alive one has to be oneself, and that takes courage. The courage to accept failure, to make enemies, to acknowledge that one has defects and can be wrong.

Dumas didn't come alive all at once. Only gradually did he realize that the large aggregations of men are just various conspiracies of successful browbeaters who insist on stamping you out with the same cooky cutter to which they have submitted. Precisely because they were suffocating for a breath of difference, so they were driven to insist that you suffocate with them.

But in his break with conformity Dumas fell into the opposite conformity: that of nonconformism. Thus, wanting to be a poet, and knowing that afflictions of the chest go well with tragic aspirations of the poetic muse, he walked the streets of Paris forcefully caving in his mighty lungs and coughing delicately into a handkerchief that he vainly hoped would soon be spotted with blood. When nothing of the sort happened, he despaired for a while of his literary talents.

Naturally he didn't despair long.

It was again pure nonconformism that led him to wear an excessively large Spanish Quiroga cloak. He didn't wear it so much because he liked it as because the *bourgeoisie* didn't.

When Byron died, Dumas dressed in mourning to go to the office where he worked as an envelope-addressing clerk, and all day muttered to himself fragments of poetry in Latin and German. Only foreign languages could have expressed at that moment the unutterably despairing mood that tore from him such phrases as "*Sic transit gloria mundi.*" The fact that few of the other clerks even knew the name Byron was but another proof of the dark destiny of the life of the poet, who must fling his priceless pearls to such inappreciative swine.

These were the days when artists would gather in dismal taverns to eat Italian spaghetti and macaroni (as when have they not?) and it was at one such place suddenly one evening that Dumas discovered he didn't like spaghetti. What was it but wet laundry ineffectually disguised under a spicy sauce? At the moment he didn't have the courage to come right out with it and take a definite anti-spaghetti stand. But from then on he began to realize that nonconformists are only a cleverly established branch organization of the conformists, the purpose of which is to trap the rebels, offering them an easy escape from general conformity into a different and smaller (that is to say, more exclusive) prison, where they can enjoy a pretentious illusion of freedom.

What a fuss it raised throughout the world of cuisine when Dumas later publicly abjured spaghetti!

What a storm blew through Italy! Newspapers there gave it columns of space. And all over Europe people split for and against spaghetti—that is to say, for and against Dumas.

Wherever Dumas wandered in Italy he was met with the reproof, "But, Signor Dumas, you can't have tasted *our* spaghetti!" Every restaurant owner begged him to come to dinner and enjoy the proof that at least one restaurateur in Italy knew how to prepare a really noble dish of spaghetti. When Bellini, Rossini, Donizetti came to Paris they seemed more anxious to convince Dumas that he was wrong about spaghetti than to open their new operas. After all, more was at stake in the matter of spaghetti than in the matter of opera, which a hundred Italians had already sufficiently demonstrated to the world that no one could write so well as an Italian.

"Would to God," Dumas cried to himself, "that I had cut off my tongue before ever uttering a word against spaghetti!" For previously he could eat spaghetti or leave it alone. But now a refusal to try a new spaghetti was an insult to a whole community, a whole nation. And still spaghetti remained what it had been before: a more or less tepid laundry, more or less rinsed of its suds, and more or less well masked under a thick sauce of unknown ingredients.

And each time, as truth demanded that he stick to his old estimate—"It's still spaghetti!"—all Italy reacted with fury and tightened her teeth on a dagger.

Though Dumas claimed that the riots against him in Naples, when he was director of the excavations at Pompeii, were provoked by King Victor Emmanuel of Sardinia, who was jealous of Garibaldi's popularity, one is inclined to suspect the additional hand of *agents provocateurs* detailed by the spaghetti manufacturers who were afraid that the diet of all Italy might change due to this vigorous anti-spaghetti personality in their midst.

Just because the rioters did not cry, "Down with the enemies of spaghetti!" should not obscure one historical fact: the riots occurred each time during the dinner hour, when Dumas sat down to table in the palace that Garibaldi had given him, sat down to a table groaning with every kind of food except *pasta*.

All this is mere tweedle-dee and tweedle-dum: a battle of grace notes. The theme of a man's life has something much more serious than these external adherences to conformity or to nonconformism. And here I don't just mean that even in the last days of his life, when Dumas was nearly seventy, Mathilde Shaw could burst in on him unannounced one day, and could find him half-undressed and surrounded by three naked girls, and what's more, so lacking in shame that he could say to Mathilde, "No, no. Don't run away, my child. We were just having a little fun, Adam and Eve style. But, of course, since nature so displeases you, we will all get dressed. Come now. Please be reasonable."

Of course Mathilde Shaw, respectable daughter of a respectable scientist,* and herself respectably wedded, could not take things that lightly. She ran home and spent the rest of the day calming her nerves.

No, I mean it rather the way Jesse Shepard did, who also saw Dumas in that same last year of his Paris life. Jesse Shepard had

---

* Charles Schoebel, noted orientalist, student of biblical linguistics

come out of Midwestern America, a handsome young giant who didn't know one note of music from another, and who nevertheless, with those huge hands of his able to span an octave and a half, improvised such enchanting music and accompanied himself with a voice equally untrained, but of such strangely haunting power, that the artistic circles of Europe stood in amazement. Crowned heads became his admirers. Countesses, one after another, fell madly in love with this man who had the beauty of a Wild West colt.

When Jesse Shepard, freshly come to Paris, wanted advice on how to get along, a friend took him to Dumas as one most likely to give him sound advice on this subject. Jesse saw a figure like a great Hindu bonze throned in magnificence and surrounded by worshipers of whom by far the largest number were young and pretty girls.

"I know very little about music," said Dumas.

"I know even less," said Shepard. "The first time I saw a piano, I just sat down and played. I don't know why. I don't know how. And I'm afraid to try to find out. Where's your piano? I'll show you."

"I have no piano," said Dumas. "As often as I've bought a piano I've had to get rid of it: it's a conversation stopper. In fact, it's the worst kind of conversation stopper, for the people who have something to say always shut up when someone starts to play, while the people who have nothing to say keep right on saying it and have to be shushed again and again."

"It's too bad you have no piano," said Shepard, "because I was hoping you'd advise me about making a career for myself."

"I'll advise you anyhow," said Dumas. "Take life in the same way you take your music. Accept it. Let it come to you as an improvisation. I remember Franz Liszt, how worried he was when he gave his first piano recitals in Paris. Then he found that people did not comment on his piano so much as on a big red cotton umbrella which he used to carry overhead when he walked in the sunshine along the boulevards. After that, instead of worrying about his piano, he gave his attention to his umbrella: he procured an even larger one, and of a more violent red. Thus he became a celebrity. He knew that people wanted not so much to listen to him as to talk about him. And he soon gave them plenty to talk about.

"Don't force. Let happen. Mankind is like an ocean: swim and you will soon be exhausted and you will certainly never reach shore. You can flounder around, you can be swamped, you can be drowned. But if instead you let yourself go to the currents of life, the waves will bear you up, they will carry you along, and maybe even toss you high up in the air. Remember this: Your life is yours. Don't accept any of the rules that other people have used and are themselves ready to throw away. But let life make her own rules especially for you. Then, when you are old, you will be able to say, I lived. And not, I might have lived."

One wonders if Shepard thought of that "I lived" when, years later (1927), he was old and penniless, in Los Angeles. His great novel *The Valley of Shadows*, which he had written under the name of Francis Grierson, lay forgotten. His improvisations, never recorded, were to become a vanished art. The case worker from the Los Angeles Assistance League was just knocking at his door as he expired. She had refused to believe that this old man had toured the world as a pianist and singer. She had refused to believe that he had been a well-known writer. She had refused to believe that he had just pawned his last piece of jewelry, a watch given to him by the King of England. It was her duty to investigate first. And meanwhile he died of hunger.

Yes, one wonders if he thought of Dumas in his last moments and was able to say, "I have lived." All we know for certain is that it was with Dumas in mind that he wrote, "Genius is not so much an infinite capacity for taking pains, as it is an infinite capacity for remaining young."

An infinite capacity for remaining young! Yes, Dumas had that. It goes along as a natural dividend to those who live their own lives, no matter what the cost.

Dumas once said with a smile, "I could have the biggest monument ever raised to a writer if I would only bother to pick up all the stones that are thrown at me."

And how many stones were thrown, particularly after Eugène de Mirecourt launched his slanders and Dumas failed to challenge him to a duel! Men who insist on improvising their lives, living according to their own rules, have their reward as well as their punishment.

Even John Bigelow, our American Civil War ambassador to Paris, threw a couple of stones in Dumas' direction.

Dumas let them lie. He was really too busy to bother with picking up pebbles. Life boiled and bubbled around him. He was perpetually in and out of a new love. He was forever having his old plays revived, or new ones staged, he was forever being translated and produced abroad, he was forever in the midst of a new serial, forever having to appear in court either because he was suing or because he was being sued, he was forever starting a new magazine or newspaper. . . .

And, incidentally, whenever he published a magazine he would pretty soon find himself writing the major part of the contents. And one day, during such a venture—whether it was the time he was publishing *The Month*, or the time he was editing his daily literary sheet *La Polichinelle*, or getting out his weekly *Monte Cristo*, or his tri-monthly *D'Artagnan*, or his daily *Musketeer*, or his *La France Nouvelle*, or *La Liberté*, or his *Theater Journal*—what difference, it was during one or another of these various ventures that one day he was about to go out to lunch and found his pockets empty.

He went into the adjoining office and asked his business manager for some money.

His previous periodicals having all ended up in financial debacles, Dumas had this time hired the toughest business manager he could find. This gentleman said to Dumas, "We are not a bank, Monsieur Dumas. We cannot lend money. Not even to you."

"Isn't there something coming to me?" Dumas asked meekly. "For my services or for my writing?"

"Not a cent. You are all paid up."

"Oh, so?" said Dumas. "Well, just a moment." He went back into his office and reappeared with a sheaf of papers. "I've just finished this story about my visit to the Prince of the Cossacks. You can pay me for this. It will print up in about eight hundred lines."

"Gladly," said the manager, and he opened his till and counted out the money.

Dumas looked at the sum in his hand. "Pardon me, there's some error here. This is not enough."

"On the contrary, your pardon," said the manager, obviously *froissé*, "that is exactly eight hundred francs."

"But that makes only a franc a line!"

"Quite right. That's what we pay—one franc a line."

"And that's what I've been getting?" Dumas asked, amazed.

"Exactly."

"All along?"

"All along."

Dumas exploded. "But I can get a franc and half a line, and even more, from any other paper in Paris!"

"No doubt, Monsieur. But our rates are one franc a line."

"But why?"

"For the very simple reason that that is all we can afford," the manager said.

"Ah?"

"Absolutely."

"Well, in that case," said Dumas, "you can give me back my article. I will walk down the street to *Le Drapeau*, and I will not only make myself an additional four hundred francs, but I will have myself a constitutional in the bargain. Both my pocket and my appetite stand to benefit."

"Just as you say," said the manager stiffly. "You are the editor and you have a right to accept and reject any article you please." He handed Dumas his story and took back the money, opening the till to replace it.

Dumas buttoned the collar of his shirt and adjusted his cravat (he always worked with his collar undone. "The blood must go to my head," he used to explain), and he got his hat and cane and was about to leave.

"There is something I must say to you, Monsieur," said the manager.

Dumas said, "Later, if you don't mind."

"No," said the manager. "Now! You understand that in taking that article to *Le Drapeau*, you are taking it to a competitor—?"

Dumas stopped. "Ah . . . I hadn't thought of that."

The manager continued, ". . . and that such an action is in the highest degree disloyal to the interests of your own paper?"

Dumas pondered this dilemma for a moment. Then he expostulated: "But why should I sell my work to myself, when I obviously can't afford to pay myself my standard price. It's humiliating to

think that others value me more highly than I do myself. But—
voilà—as you say, I'm just in no position to compete with them for
my own work."

"It's a matter of loyalty," the manager declared. "And as such I
must leave it to Monsieur's sense of honor."

"Bah!" cried Dumas. "Sense of honor, sense of honor! Can you
tell me what is dishonorable about selling an article where it will
bring the highest returns?"

"If that is how you see it, Monsieur," said the manager, "then I
have nothing further to say," and he slammed shut the till.

Dumas, furious, clapped his hat on his head, brandished his
cane, and went downstairs to the street, muttering angrily.

At the landing he heard the manager running after him, "Monsieur Dumas!"

"What now?"

"You realize that getting out a magazine these days, with such
high prices, is a costly affair, and debts press upon us all the time—
rent, paper, printing . . ."

"I realize it."

"I remind you only so that you will be sure to bring back some of
the money you make on that article. That is if you wish to continue
in business."

Dumas nodded. "I'll take care of it."

And in fact he did bring back the money. But in time he got tired
of writing for other papers in order to support a paper of his own,
in which, however, he could not afford to publish himself, particularly not after his own paper began to lose circulation because readers found that to get their Dumas they had to drop their subscription to Dumas' own paper and buy a different one; and then it
really took a lot of outside writing to support his dying magazine—
dying, as a matter of fact, because of lack of his own work, which
he had to dispose of elsewhere.

It was indeed a cruel dilemma, a vicious circle if ever there was
one, which for some unaccountable reason attacked all his periodicals.

But my point is: how could Ambassador John Bigelow say of a
man who thus compromised his sense of honor, because of the stern
mathematics of a given situation, that this man had no sense for the

ordinary rules of arithmetic? And, moreover, ascribe this lack of ability for figuring to Dumas' Negro ancestry?

Oh, these amazing geographers to whom only the continent of Africa was dark, but the course of the African blood stream everywhere completely mapped! A half century after Dumas' death Francis Gribble will still tell you precisely how this or that wayward or improvident action in Dumas was due, not to Dumas' determination to live out his own life, but due to that fraction of Negro blood in him. In his book on Dumas, which is one long essay in cold scorn, he has it all figured out. Not that he, Francis Gribble, is as good at figures as he is at mapping the blood stream. He will admit, for example, that Dumas was a colossus, since everyone who ever described him says so, but, nevertheless, says Francis Gribble, Dumas' height "was only five foot nine." How a man five foot nine could be a "colossus," Gribble doesn't explain, thus implying that like everything else about the man, his physical proportions too were a fraud, an exaggeration, and that he was no more the genuine man he appeared to be than he was the genuine writer, for of course Gribble is convinced that Dumas had his books written for him—the good ones at any rate. He considers the bad ones genuine and an additional proof of Dumas' lack of quality.

Gribble's inability to figure out that French feet (*pieds*) and French thumbs (*pouces*) are not the same size as English feet and English inches is of the same order that makes a channel fog isolate the continent, as the famous London newspaper headline is said to have put it. It happens that a French foot, for some arrogant and quite unjustifiable reason, is equal to thirteen English inches, and that Dumas was therefore six foot three.

John Bigelow too found his explanation for Dumas in the man's Negro blood. "It is the peculiar character of the African," Bigelow writes, reporting on his visit to Dumas, "that, for want of the reflective and logical faculties, he is incapable, except in rare instances, of measuring size, time or distance, or of thoroughly mastering the common rules of arithmetic. Dumas' blood was not sufficiently strained, or shall we say corrupted, to be an exception to this rule."

And he goes on: "He had no ability for reflection. The moment he began to reflect, he became confused and the train of his thought was irrevocably broken. He had run down like a clock."

Bigelow wrote this some months after Dumas died and as a result of an acquaintance which endured exactly one luncheon.

Dumas, at the time of this luncheon, was sixty years old. He had just come back from Italy, where he had gone with Garibaldi to help liberate Sicily and to overthrow the Bourbon Kingdom of Naples (an act that Dumas regarded as a belated revenge for the way that family had treated his father in their Neapolitan prisons), and he had stayed for a while in Naples as director of excavations for Pompeii, and at the same time he had published an Italian newspaper, the *Independente*, written some books in Italian, as well as in French, and then had returned to Paris with a new mistress, Fanny Gordoza, a singer whose beauty made up quite amply for her lack of voice.

John Bigelow, at the time, represented Lincoln's North in Paris and was trying desperately to keep Napoleon III from openly taking France in on the side of the Confederacy. Already the Emperor had laid his hands on Mexico through his puppet Maximilian of Austria, whom he had placed on the Aztec throne, and already he had in the process of construction a navy of the world's first ironclads, with which the South was to sweep the ships of the North from the Atlantic. A vast American empire was envisaged, based on Negro slavery, and extending from the Amazon to the Mississippi. Naturally, Granier de Cassagnac, the man whose name sounded like the chewing of pebbles, Dumas' personal enemy and France's greatest propagandist for Negro servitude, was behind the scheme.

Believing that a new atmosphere opposed to discrimination against the Negro was prevalent in the North, Dumas decided that the time had come for him to travel to America. And to discuss that project Dumas invited Bigelow to luncheon at his recently rented villa at Saint-Gratien.

Dumas' proposal was very simple: he would make a trip to America, see something of the Civil War battlefields, and write a book. "Nothing very much—four or five hundred pages at most," because speed was of the essence, and in a matter of a few weeks he hoped to bring out a volume that would stem and reverse the French tide for helping the slavocracy.

He wanted no money for his trip, but he did wish to be invited. "The proper auspices," said Dumas, "will open doors much more quickly."

John Bigelow half concealed a smile.

Dumas noted it. "I daresay you think a few weeks is not sufficient for both a trip and a book?"

"Alexis de Tocqueville," Bigelow replied circuitously, "took four years to write his great study of American democracy."

"But I am not studying American democracy," Dumas cried. "I accept it. I wish only to strike a blow for your cause!"

"Still, a few weeks—Americans may almost regard it as an insult. . . ."

"You don't understand," said Dumas. "I am not one of your slow writers whose mind moves like a glacier. I write out of sheer natural abundance."

This last remark—*I write out of sheer natural abundance*—is one that Bigelow remembered long afterward with fine scorn. And he mentally rejected Dumas' explanation that unless he wrote in a hurry he wrote badly.

"Don't you ever correct?"

"Never," said Dumas. "Though sometimes I tear up. Once when I was having a play rehearsed I suddenly stopped everything. The director wanted to know what was the matter. 'Call the fireman,' I said. 'What for?' 'Never mind. Call him.' And when they brought me the fireman I said to him, 'I saw your red hat in the back all during the first two acts. But in the third act you disappeared. Tell me why.' 'I remembered certain things I had to do,' said the fireman. 'Why didn't you remember them before?' I asked. 'I forgot. I was so interested in the play.' 'Enough!' I cried. 'Give me the third act!' And I tore the pages up. 'If that fireman forgot his duties during the first two acts and remembered them only during the third act, then there must be something wrong with it. I must write a third act that would keep this fireman from remembering his duties until the end of the play even if the house should be in flames.' And I sat down and wrote it."

But Bigelow was not impressed. He was himself to go down in history as a considerable writer and an editor, but somehow he was repelled by Dumas. He did not take at all to Dumas' theories of

animal magnetism by which one lets the forces of humanity stream
through one's organism, and life becomes the effortless activity
of a spark dancing in a conflagration.

Ah, thought Dumas, here is another one of those who believe the
De Mirecourt slanders and is convinced that I enslave ghost writers
to produce my books as American planters enslave Negroes to produce their cotton.*

"Perhaps you would care to see the manuscript of my latest
work?" Dumas asked. "I have just now finished it and it is ready
for the printer."

Bigelow smiled, thoroughly clear in his mind that Dumas was
showing him this manuscript only in order to persuade him of the
genuine nature of his works, a trick which had already been pointed
out to him. Nevertheless, he politely showed interest, and Dumas
had his secretary bring him the manuscript copy of his *San Felice*,
the first part of his enormous novel on Naples and on Admiral
Nelson's tragic love affair with Lady Hamilton. There was no doubt
that it was all written in a fine copperplate hand precisely such as
Dumas used when he left his address in Bigelow's office.

But Bigelow was still smilingly aloof.

Ho-ho! said Dumas to himself. The slander is here too. This man
has heard that I hire only secretaries who have first studied how to
imitate my handwriting to perfection, so that I can not only deceive
my contemporaries but also posterity as to who really writes my
books.

So Dumas gave up. There was simply nothing to be done with
these people who were certain that they had uncovered the truth
of Dumas' abundance.

Only a short time before, he had received a visit from a Swedish
journalist who wanted to know Dumas' real name.

"My name is Dumas," said Dumas.

The journalist insisted. "That's of course just the name of the
firm."

"What firm?"

"Why, the firm of five writers who issue all their novels and
plays under the name Dumas."

---

* The untranslatable pun here depends on the fact that in French the word
for ghost writer is *un nègre* (a Negro).

"Oh, I see," said Dumas. "Yes, of course. But my name too happens to be Dumas."

"What a coincidence!" said the journalist and marked it down.

"Yes, isn't it?" said Dumas.

Oh, yes, Dumas knew these wise ones who had taken their stand that no one human being could possibly write so much as Dumas. One man, for example, had counted thirty-six thousand historical personages in the works of Dumas, and obviously no single person could possibly have studied that many historical figures sufficiently well to know how they looked, how they dressed, and how they talked.

Dumas, despite his African origin, was overwhelmed when he saw this calculation. But then he sat down and did a little calculating of his own: he had written something under a hundred novels and less than a hundred plays. In no book or play of his had he ever introduced more than a handful of historical personages. There is a limit to the number of historical characters a reader will accept in a romance. Many of his books and plays contained no historical characters at all. And in many of his books and plays the same cast of historical personages appeared again and again.

Total historical characters in Dumas, alias Dumas, less than a thousand. A respectable figure, no doubt, but far from thirty-six thousand.

Perhaps a real discussion with Bigelow on Dumas' "writing out of sheer natural abundance" never got started because Dumas' mistress made her appearance then, and Dumas at once sensed a coolness in Bigelow that was even more marked than his disbelief in Dumas' ability as a writer.

In fact, Bigelow quickly took Dumas aside and whispered to him, "If you are really intending to visit America, you will of course come only with your wife. It would be fatal if you did otherwise, I assure you."

Dumas understood that to mean that there would be no official invitation or any auspices for a trip to America. Dumas pocketed his defeat and remarked pleasantly that, no doubt, after they had freed the black slaves, the Union would go on to fight to free white slaves from the tyranny of convention. "What anyhow is this inde-

pendence, this pursuit of pleasure, of which you Americans speak
in your great founding documents?"

Bigelow explained that while Americans did what they pleased
in their personal lives, they did not permit the same liberties to
those who lived public lives, whether by reason of their talents or
their positions.

"Would they rather I turned over a page?" Dumas asked.

Bigelow, who knew French quite well, nevertheless missed the
point of this question, thinking that Dumas was referring to turning over a new leaf, and the author had to explain that he was wondering what would happen if he went to America without his mistress, because of addiction to another form of love—namely, that
which caused the King of France, Henri III, to turn over the pages
of his court.

Bigelow smiled.

Dumas remarked that sodomy was the only crime that had never
been laid at his door. He then declared that he was certain that
America contained millions of women who were as attractive as
anything that France could show, and there was therefore no reason why he should bring his mistress along.

Upon which Bigelow really froze. He was now not merely convinced that Dumas had nothing to offer the Union, but that, on the
contrary, a visit from such an unconventional character was fraught
with grave dangers: an amatory scandal between Dumas and a
white American woman exploding at a crucial moment in the American press could do incalculable harm to the North, lending strength
to the Copperhead rumors that the Civil War was a war to surrender white womanhood to the lusts of the blacks.

And so they went in to luncheon, Bigelow generously waiving
prejudice and escorting the mistress of the house to the table. There
were half a dozen other guests, mostly concerned with Fanny Gordoza's musical ambition.

What a luncheon it was! Gargantuan! Befitting an African chief-
tain.

A huge ice-cold carp first. Jellied. Looking as if caught whole in
a block of ice. Served with a piquant sauce. ("First-rate," Bigelow
reports.)

Then a roasted leg of mutton. (Bigelow's judgment: "Delicious.")

Next veal and rice with tomato sauce. (Dumas' furious comment: "One can't trust a professional cook with the preparation of a proper tomato sauce. Tomato sauce requires the love and care that only the gifted amateur will devote to it." Bigelow: "But I've never tasted a better tomato sauce in my life." Dumas: "Then you haven't lived, Sir. You must come to see me sometime when it's cook's day off.")

Finally, the table was loaded with two huge platters, one piled high with fruit, mostly grapes, the other with cold crayfish. The table wines were removed and champagne was served. (Bigelow's comment: "He made enormous inroads on the crayfish, picking them up with both hands and eating them with audible noises of chewing and gulping. Sweat broke out on his brow. His breath came and went like a trip hammer. I never saw a person eat so much like an animal.")

When luncheon was over, Bigelow saw Dumas relax in an easy chair and was sure that he would drop off to sleep like an over-stuffed python. But after a few moments, when it seemed that the man was nodding, he was suddenly wide-awake and held every-one's ear with his fascinating conversation. "He talked rapidly, elo-quently," says Bigelow, "and there was a sweet smile on his face. Indeed, there was not a sordid or mercenary or selfish trait on his features. He had hatred for only one man: the Emperor Napoleon III, whom he called a conspirator, comparing him to jackals and foxes who eat in the darkness of the night."

One would think that this man with the sweet smile who had not a sordid or mercenary or selfish trait in his features would emerge as a less disreputable character from Bigelow's report. But no, Bigelow was actually happy when the luncheon was over and he could leave. He had, it seems, been warned that Dumas was always broke and that he would undoubtedly hit him up for a loan. Bige-low was later able to congratulate himself that nothing of the sort had happened. But in any case he had all along been firmly deter-mined to turn the man down cold.

What can one conclude from this amazing report where, against the evidence of his own eyes that saw the handwriting of the manuscript, against the evidence of his own eyes that saw not a selfish or mercenary or sordid trait in his features, Bigelow nevertheless was convinced that Dumas was a plagiarist and that he appropriated the writings of others? What can one conclude when, against the evidence of his own ears that heard Dumas' eloquence and the rapidity of his brilliant talk, Bigelow concluded that the man had no reflective or logical faculties? And when, against the evidence of the fact that the man treated him most hospitably, he nevertheless concluded that the man was out to steal money from him under the pretense of a loan?

The whole amazing exhibition of bias has to be read, chiefly in *Scribner's* magazine, 1871, to be appreciated and in order to understand how deeply the De Mirecourt slander had taken hold of the best people.

One is driven to conclude that but for a prejudice against the Negro, never would such slanders have prevailed against such evidence.

Take for example Dumas' too hearty appetite for crayfish. It had, of course, nothing to do with Dumas' African blood. It had to do with the fact that as a little boy, hungry as a lean she-wolf in a hard winter, Alexandre had copied the habit of other hungry boys— going hunting for crayfish that hide under the rocks of little streams. He had early learned to run barefoot through the icy brooks, turning over the rocks and quickly snatching at the agile crayfish that are so adept at disappearing before the hand can get to them.

And ever after in his life the very sight of this food, which his famished body had once so deeply craved, would excite him with a powerful appetite.

CHAPTER SEVEN

Iron Shoes for a Prince

THE TRUTH IS that his mother had utterly no understanding of the vast forces that were developing within the boy. She was indeed in the position of the goddess Juno who one day took pity on an abandoned baby that lay squawling in a ditch and, picking it up, gave it her breast, not knowing that this was the infant Hercules. Then the goddess, for all her mother love, saw herself under the brutal necessity of smashing at the infant's face with her fist whenever she wanted to loosen his voracious lips from her nipple.

Madame Dumas fed her son as best she could, but she never fed him enough. Her son was always hungry. Food was just not sufficiently abundant in the Dumas household. The General had died leaving no pension and little but debts. And Madame Dumas' parents soon followed, leaving an estate so encumbered that it was a source of expense rather than of income.

To add to her misfortunes, this was a period when Napoleon's secret police went ferreting about everywhere. And Madame Dumas' political situation was peculiarly bad because of the fact that while she was the widow of a Napoleonic general, that general was in disgrace with Napoleon. What side would take the risk of helping this woman? The adherents of Napoleon? No. They feared that Napoleon's anger against General Dumas would be carried over onto them. The Royalists then, since they hated Napoleon? But why should they help a Republican general who had fought alongside Napoleon? The result was that Madame Dumas was assisted only by her closest relatives, who did so in stealth.

You will find little in Dumas' *Memoirs* about his hungry youth. He glosses over it there. Look for it, however, in *Ange Pitou*, where his description of a hungry peasant lad in the care of a stingy stepmother is undoubtedly drawn from his own youth.

The truth of the dire poverty of the Dumas is shown by the fact that when this widow of a general and of a national hero was offered the chance to open a shop where she could sell the government monopolies of tobacco and salt, she seized it. Her shop was, of course, a mere hole in the wall, and the income from the sale of those two inconsequential items could have been no more than a pittance, distinguishing itself from poor-relief only in that she was forced to earn it herself.

Alexandre doesn't deny that for years he dressed in nothing but the cut-down and made-over uniforms of his father, and that he gaped with envy at every coxcomb that came from Paris in a suit of new clothes. No wonder, when at length he was rich enough to dress, he decked himself out like a peacock and would have liked to have been as pretentious as Beau Brummell, who kept a special artist employed in making nothing but the thumbs of his gloves, for he contended that it is by an ill-fitted thumb that even the best dressers often reveal the inadequacy of their costume.

And as for food, Dumas simply never got over his concern for it. When, overnight, as an unknown, he suddenly had a hit play in Paris and a ticket broker appeared on his doorstep the next morning and offered to advance him a goodly sum for all the tickets that accrue to the author of a play in production, what did Dumas do with this first chunk of money ever to land in his hands? Why, he ran out to a neighboring restaurant and arranged for a lump payment to have all his meals free there for a whole year.

Imagine! A whole year in which he need not worry about food! What bliss!

No man who has not repeatedly suffered the pangs of hunger would behave that way.

And what did that restaurant do? Naturally it went bankrupt before a month had passed.

What did Dumas do? He said, "I should have known better than to lay up treasures on earth where thieves break in and steal and moths and rust do corrupt."

But all his life he remained preoccupied with the question of food. His only real hobby was cooking. And the last book of his life—almost his testament, you might say—was his *Grand Dictionary of Cooking*, the result of a lifetime of recipe gathering.

His bird-sized mother, whose waist was not as large around as her husband's calf, could have no conception of the amount of food her youngster craved. She took her poverty as a sign from God that she had sinned the sin of pride, and that she had had no business to meddle with history. And she was firmly determined that her son should be a violinist and be as far removed as possible from the course of history.

But how could one keep history from Alexandre? Again and again invaders threatened France, and the frightened villagers buried their treasures and ran.

From a hide-out in a garret, young Alexandre saw a clash between French cuirassiers and German light cavalry. Wounded men bled to death before his eyes.

Peeping through dusty shutters, he saw Cossacks galloping down the road on the way to occupy Paris.

He saw the Royalists rejoice when the Bourbons came back to the throne of France, and he saw them become turncoats again when Napoleon escaped from Elba and made his hundred-day comeback.

Through the summer heat of 1815, along the hot and dusty road through Villers-Cotterêts, he saw the reconstituted Grande Armée marching. For three whole days they passed: foot soldiers, gaitered giants, with sunburned faces, plaited sidelocks and fierce mustaches. For three whole days they came, accompanied by the constant sound of drumming and interspersed with over a hundred regimental bands, so that the music of the last one faded into the distance only to have its melody taken up by another band appearing on the horizon. The standards of a hundred victories were held aloft, protected in leather casings.

Detachments of cavalry went flashing by, their gay colors revealing their different organizations: hussars, cuirassiers, dragoons, mamelukes. And between these went the lumbering supply wagons, the ammunition trains, the swearing cannoneers lashing at the beasts of their heavy caissons. And alongside went the sutlers with their ambulatory refreshment stands, from which the *vivandières* rushed with food and drink, in and out of the ranks of men.

What a sight it was, this three-day circus! Even those mothers who execrated the name of Napoleon as the murderer of Frenchmen were drawn into the growing crowd of admirers.

Napoleon himself had said that never in the world's history had there been such an army as his. "Even the old Romans did not march their men more than twenty-five miles a day. I march mine thirty-five. And my men think nothing of it. The Romans rested their troops for a day before they went into battle. My men march and fight the same day. And never was victory so certain!"

As the cries of *Vive l'Empereur!* grew in volume from the onlookers lining the road, Madame Dumas warned her son. "Don't you dare cheer that man. Don't you dare. You are orphaned because of him. You wear the rags you do because of him." And she forced him to go to the rear of the store and practice his violin.

But she couldn't keep him there. He escaped to mingle with the crowd along the road. In spite of himself his throat was thick with pride. In spite of himself his heart was gorged with emotion.

He ached to cry out *"Vive l'Empereur!"* But he bit down on his lip.

As the procession came to an end, a fast carriage rattled into the courtyard of the Boule d'Or, inn of the Golden Ball, where grooms changed the four horses with mad speed. A crush of people milled about. Alexandre pushed his way through. He could see into the interior, where a pale man sat deep in the cushions.

"Vive l'Empereur!" the crowd cried.

The pale man inclined his head in graceful acknowledgment.

Only Alexandre remained silent, staring.

The poet Heine had written a whole paragraph on the beauty and majesty of nothing but that man's hand. Heine declared that in the presence of Napoleon one could see a gold star shining in the sky in broad daylight. "His face," he said, "has a hue the like of which has to be sought in the marble busts of Greece and Rome. His features are more nobly proportioned than even the best that antiquity can show us. His expression is so imperial that it is like a commandment: 'Thou shalt have no other gods before me.'"

Alexandre's heart swelled within his chest. His mouth had to open. His throat had to speak. Carried away in spite of himself, he suddenly brayed, *"Vive l'Empereur!"* And tears burst from his eyes.

The pale head nodded and smiled upon the ragged boy.

Then came the rains of late June, and one day a mud-spattered carriage dashed at breakneck speed through the village, stopped abruptly at the inn and changed horses even faster than before. Going out, the Emperor's carriage had been last. This time it was first.

There was no crowd because rumors of a great defeat at Waterloo had already reached the village, and the turncoats were once more busy suiting their apparel to the new political weather.

And it was only by chance that Dumas happened to be around and to glimpse in the interior of the carriage the figure of Napoleon, his head more like a marble mask than ever, his body sunk deeper into the cushions.

All alone the boy cried, *"Vive l'Empereur!"* The grooms stared. The man in the carriage gave no sign that he had heard.

And afterward, for days, came the march of tired men. No bands played, no drums beat. Only scattered groups of men wandered by, many with bloody bandages, some pushing wheelbarrows in which were the severely wounded. All moved slowly toward Paris.

It was the funeral procession of an empire.

And filtering rapidly through these unresisting men came the hard-riding Poles. Then the Hanoverian light cavalry. And finally the solid marching British.

How was it that a man so hated enjoyed such an ascendancy over Frenchmen? Wasn't it because he decorated life? Transfigured it? Turned it from a chore into an adventure?

Which is precisely what Dumas would do later with his plays and books.

Fraudulent? Of course it was fraudulent. As fraudulent as Scanderbeg's Black Eagle of Epirus and Albania with its four crosses and its clusters of oak leaves. Napoleon, too, was to be sent back to prison to finish out an unexpired term for pickpocketing the thrones of Europe.

Fraudulent, yes. But, God, how it dazzled!

Madame Dumas thought of history only in the terms that the great preacher Bossuet taught in his sermons—namely, that it was God's way of punishing and rewarding us. She had no conception of history as a kind of intoxication, a pageant and a dance peculiar to only one creature on earth—namely, man.

She was determined to force her boy out of the current of history by making him a violinist, and to that purpose she scrimped and she saved, even out of their own food, that she might have three francs each week to pay Master Hiraux for Alexandre's daily lessons. That matter being taken care of, she was left with only one problem: how to get the boy to practice. Here, after trying every idea of her own, and every suggestion of friend and relative, she was reconciled at last to the necessity of beating her own flesh and blood.

After a couple of years of lessons, Master Hiraux came one day to Madame Dumas with tears in his eyes. "Believe me, Madame," he cried, "please believe me."

"Calm yourself, my dear Master Hiraux."

"I have tried and I have tried, good God, how I have tried. And no one knows better than you, Madame, how bitterly I need these three francs which you give me every week. But it is a crime. No, it is worse than a crime—it is a sin—to take from you what you need just as badly as I do. You will never make a violinist out of that boy."

"But, Master Hiraux," Madame cried, as with one little hand she caught Alexandre, who was about to run out of the door, "we mustn't give up so easily. I will punish him from now on twice as hard. You will see. He will be good. He must be good."

"Look, Madame. You see this bow that Alexandre uses? You see all these repairs? You see the gluing I have done? The tiny brass nails I have put in? The fine wire I have wrapped around? This is the fifth bow he is in the process of destroying. It is I who do all this repairing. It is I who do the replacing when the bow is too far gone. Why do I do all this, Madame? For the sake of those miserable three francs, and for nothing else!"

"How can he destroy so many bows?"

"Madame. Listen to me. On the way to his lesson, he stops to play with the boys. He takes out his bow. It is a gun. It is a spear. It is an arrow. It is a sword! He duels with it! He attacks, he parries, he ripostes! He does everything with it. That is, he does everything but play the violin with it. Please, Madame, do not tempt me any longer with your three francs. Let me die in peace with a clear conscience!"

And with that the poor man put on his hat and rushed out of the house.

Madame Dumas turned upon her son. "Stop it!" she cried. "Stop it at once!"

"Stop what, *Maman?* I'm not doing anything."

"You're looking like your father, that's what you're doing!"

"Like my father?"

"Yes. And at this particular moment, when I'm obliged to give you the beating of your life, it is cruel of you to look so much like your father."

"But I can't help how I look, *Maman.*"

"Then at least turn your head away and don't break my heart."

So Alexandre turned his head away, and his mother's ineffectual little hand came down on him as hard as she could manage it. "Duels! Swords! Guns!" she cried in exasperation as she rained blow after blow upon him.

Her energy was not great and was soon spent. *"Mais voyons,"* she said, utterly out of breath, "aren't you going to cry finally, so that I can stop? Have you no pity for me?"

"But, Mother," the boy protested, "you know very well that I can't cry unless I see you cry first."

Thus, as always, her beatings ended with the two weeping in each other's arms.

"Oh, what is to become of us?" Madame Dumas asked and hid her face in her hands. And then, in a habit that was becoming more and more frequent, she had recourse to prayer. She would force Alexandre to kneel at her side, and both would pray until illumination came to her.

Lumière was what she wanted, and Dumas would recall later how long it would sometimes take for that little light to come. But finally she got it.

"It's poor Master Hiraux whom we must pity," so the light informed her. "We have tried his patience. And we have cost him the three francs he needs so badly. Obviously there is only one thing to do. You must practice hard, my dear child, and go and beg his pardon and convince him that this time you have reformed."

Alexandre's face fell. "Oh, no, Mother!" he cried.

"And I say yes," said Madame Dumas. "I tell you it is God's will. It is God's answer to my prayer. So now you will practice, practice and practice, until you can return to Master Hiraux and positively astonish him."

How could she imagine that she would make a violinist out of Alexandre when every day he could pass the gunsmith's shop and look through the open doorway and see hanging on the wall the swords, the pistols, the guns that had belonged to his father, and which from time to time would diminish in number as they were sold off?

The owner, a man whose underlip hung like an open purse because a sword cut had severed the nerve there, and which perpetually dripped saliva, would take pity on the lad and invite him into the shop, show him how to hold an épée, show him how to fire a flintlock, teach him how to meet the recoil, how to hold a gun when climbing over a fence, so as not to discharge the gun into one's leg or groin (the way poor Philippe had done, dying, as a result, of lockjaw), how to keep powder dry even in wet weather, how to prevent a flash in the pan.

Alexandre would take these lessons with an expression of wonder and gratitude that was almost painful to behold. And to him, this gunsmith, with his lip perpetually glistening with a drop about to fall, was a man he ever afterward remembered with gratitude.

How could his mother imagine that she would make a violinist out of Alexandre when every day he had only to get up at dawn and run off into the forest of the old royal preserve and hide there all day long?

At night she might beat him and force him to cry, but she couldn't force him to play, for she begrudged the cost of the two candles that had to be put in the double brackets of the music stand, which was the reason, of course, he waited until dark to come home. Being out in all kinds of weather inured him to the cold, the rain and the snow. His health was ever after such that in all his life he scarcely knew what it was to be sick. But of course it also roused still further his formidable appetite and made his craving for food all the keener.

How could she make a violinist out of him when every day he could go into the forest and study better methods of setting snares for leverets, better ways of liming twigs above ponds where birds came to drink, so that the silly creatures would get themselves glued up and their necks could be twisted without trouble? How could she make a violinist out of him when he was deeply involved in learning how to set mirrors for larks and traps for squirrels?

He was growing every day sharper in ways of evading the forest guards. For example, he figured out that if he now and then showed the guards a trap he had himself secretly placed, he would give himself a reputation for honesty and of being on the guard's side, so that they would trust him instead of suspecting and spying on him.

There were other poachers in the huge forest, and sometimes he would come upon them. He made friends with them. But generally he hunted alone. It was safer. But it was from these poachers that he learned many of his tricks. For example, they taught him how to catch a jay and pluck its feathers while alive, thus wringing from the poor creature such cries that all the birds for a mile around would flock to the scene for the sport of pecking to death a jay that

was no longer able to defend itself. Nothing more was needed then
but the art of casting a net over the stupid and vindictive little birds.

Years later when he read Fenimore Cooper's *Leatherstocking
Tales*, he recognized himself. He was an Indian. He was a *coureur
de bois*.

Years later, too, when he wrote of his hunting exploits in Russia
and Africa and Switzerland, there were people who were quick to
point out that Dumas wasn't a hunter at all. He was never anything
but a poacher. He shot a rabbit that wasn't even running. He shot
a partridge on the ground instead of waiting until it was on the
wing as a real sportsman would.

Indeed, Dumas never really shot anything except with the
thought of eating it. And that, of course, isn't hunting at all. At that
rate even people who couldn't afford a fine horse, a good gun, a
pack of dogs, beaters and a fine-tailored hunting habit with a red
coat could call themselves hunters, and then the whole noble sport
would be degraded.

No, Dumas always had food in mind. Indeed, he would no
sooner have twelve little birds on a spit than he would set the thing
to roast and would pull a piece of bread from his pocket to catch
every drop of fat as it fell from the tiny carcasses, and his stomach
was so greedy that often he could not wait until the birds were
properly done before he was crunching into their tiny bones.

And nothing but the thought of his mother, dining at home on
yesterday's reheated *potage*, would intervene to spoil his total enjoyment.

One day he dared come home with a fresh-caught leveret. His
mother was occupied in front, in the store. Quickly he skinned the
animal and set it to roast.

When his mother came from the store, she smelled the meat at
once. "What is that?" she asked.

"Oh, a leveret," he said carelessly and blew on the charcoal.

"A leveret? And where did you get a leveret?"

"Found it."

"Found it? Where?"

"Just lying there."

"Dead?"

He nodded.

"Too bad," she said dryly. "Otherwise one might eat it."

"But why not, Mother? That's exactly what we're going to do."

"Not a rabbit that you found like that. Never. Goodness knows what it died of. A disease perhaps. Or from eating some poison. It must be thrown away."

"But, Mother, I know how it died."

"Oh?"

"Yes. I found it caught in a snare."

"If you found it in a snare, why didn't you run and tell the forest guards? They would have hidden near by and surprised the poacher when he came to get his catch."

"Yes, Mother, I should have done that. Only . . ."

"Only what? Wasn't it your duty to tell them?"

"Certainly, Mother. Only the poacher they would have caught— would have been me."

"You?"

"Yes, Mother, and now our rabbit is ready," he said, and indeed the odor spread by the fat, crusty meat was divine. But as he was about to take it from the spit, his mother stopped him.

"It needs a few more turns," she said, and, considering how many roasts she had made as daughter of an innkeeper, she was undoubtedly right. "When it is done you can carry it right over to the forest guards."

"But, Mother," cried Alexandre, "what can they possibly want with a dead rabbit? Except to eat it, as we can do by ourselves just as well as they can."

Poor Madame Dumas, trapped in these conflicting arguments, knelt in prayer with her son and asked God for light. "But," as Dumas later said, "I rather think it was not so much a light that struck her eyes, or her spirit, as it was an odor, an irresistible odor, that struck her nostrils. At any rate, after her prayers, and after my promise never to poach again, we sat down and ate."

The little larks and finches were less of a problem since they could not be considered as poached, there being no laws to protect songbirds at that time. But it took such a lot of them to make a proper meal, and this meant a lot of liming of twigs, a lot of mirrors for larks, and in particular a lot of plucked jays. "Plucking a jay is no doubt inhuman," Dumas confessed years later, "but, good Lord, it certainly saved me from many a beating from my dear, kind mother, who wanted so desperately to do the right thing for me, and those beatings hurt me chiefly because I knew then without a doubt that she was thoroughly displeased with me."

One time in the forest, as he was setting snares, he was suddenly surprised by a witch crashing in on him through the underbrush. He was ready to run at the sight of this frightening apparition, a wizened beldam in a black cloak with a mass of false hair protruding from a bonnet that was all awry, but he heard her say, "If we are both frightened of each other, little boy, then neither of us has any reason for fright." This struck Alexandre as a very sound observation, and instead of running he went up to her.

"I am lost," she said. "I left my carriage on the road for a stroll in the woods. I lost my sense of direction. Then I thought I heard ghosts, and I began to run."

"Ghosts?" the boy asked. "Real ghosts?"

"Naturally not," said the woman sharply. "There are no real ghosts."

"Then why were you afraid?"

"Because one doesn't have to believe in ghosts to be afraid of them," the woman said.

This again struck Alexandre as a sound observation, for he knew that though he too didn't believe in ghosts he was afraid to cross the churchyard alone at night.

As Alexandre led her through the forest, whose every path he knew by heart, toward the road, the old woman asked him his name. When he told her, she stopped and looked at him. "Then you are the son of the General."

"Yes, Madame."

"I know you through my daughter, who is Madame Collard, and who lives here in Villers-Cotterêts," she said. "But you do not know me, do you?"

"No, Madame."

She told him that her name was Madame de Genlis, and since that also meant nothing to him, she explained to him that she was famous for having laid down the rules of how a prince was to be educated.

This excited Alexandre. He wanted to know all about the education of a prince.

"You're not a prince," she said to him. "But you'd like to be, wouldn't you? And sometimes you like to imagine that you *are* a prince, don't you? You dream of it."

"Yes," he admitted.

"Well, it's not easy to be a prince. I made the princes in my care wear iron shoes all day long, so that every step they took would be exercise, and they wouldn't have to take time away from their other work in order to grow up strong. From the moment they woke up at five o'clock in the morning, they studied. I made them raise their own food in the garden and milk their own goats. And while they worked, they had instructors teaching them botany, mineralogy, astronomy in different languages. In the morning everything was in German. In the afternoon, with music study and painting, everything was in Italian. At mealtimes no language was permitted except English. Every evening, before they went to bed—they were not permitted a real bed, just a board of wood and a single light cover—we had magic-lantern slides to teach them the history and geography of the world."

"What's a magic-lantern slide?" Alexandre wanted to know.

Madame de Genlis laughed. "You have a lot to learn," she said.

By this time they had reached the road and her carriage, and Madame de Genlis got in. "It's not easy to be a prince, is it? But you're going to try, aren't you?"

"*Oui*, Madame," he said.

"Well, maybe you'll be a prince," she said and she patted the boy on his head.

Dumas never forgot this incident. For a long time his mind dwelt on the possibilities of being a prince. One day his mother told him of how she had made for him a pair of iron shoes when he was three years old, hoping that the weight would bring his heels down.

"I wore iron shoes?" he exclaimed.

"Certainly," she said. "But they did you no good, and besides they hurt you, so I discarded them."

"I really wore iron shoes . . ." he said, and his face with its shiny olive complexion glowed so that his mother asked him whether he was ill.

His mind was on fire with the thought that maybe he was a real prince, maybe he would someday live in a palace, and his mother would be a queen.

CHAPTER EIGHT

Six Hundred Glasses of Absinthe

WHAT ARE CHILDREN if not dreams? They are conceived amidst the dreams of their parents, and nursed by the dreams of their mothers, and then surrendered to their own dreams. And thus passing from dream to dream, they are gradually ushered into a world that is itself half a dream.

And half a nightmare.

But the point of this story of the encounter with the witch is that, years later, as a young man, Alexandre was to have a job as envelope-addressing clerk in the offices of the Duke of Orléans, who was precisely one of those princes educated by Madame de Genlis to wear iron shoes and to grow and grind his own grain and to sleep on a plank. And this Duke of Orléans was still later to become King of France at about the same time that Dumas was to rise to the height of his fame and to become known as the "uncrowned king of Paris."

Now as to the respective merits of these two kings, one with a throne of power and the other with a throne of popularity, there is this to be said: Everyone agrees that the Duke of Orléans, who became king under the name Louis Philippe, was so miserly that though he earned out of his private fortune every fifteen minutes what a moderately prosperous family would consider a year's income, he wrecked the French treasury with his demands for more money, even while in Lyons starving silk workers were rioting for bread.

Still, one day this crowned king complained to his minister Monsieur de Montalivet that being a king was often a pretty dull business, and Versailles was enough to bore one to death.

"It would be simple, Sire," said De Montalivet, "to change Versailles from a place where one dies of boredom to a place where one dies laughing."

"That's something I should like to know about," the King said.

"Alexandre Dumas," the minister explained, "has failed to report for his two weeks of National Guard Duty. Order him to report here and serve those two weeks in Versailles. You will see that Versailles will become the liveliest place in France."

"No doubt," said the King dryly. The idea of calling his former envelope-addressing clerk to rejuvenate Versailles did not appeal to him.

"Have you heard, Sire, how he keeps a Holy Water fount in the vestibule of his home at Saint-Germain, and how he has his publishers fill it with silver, and how he has a sign there saying, *A blessing for those in need.* And have you heard how a man came to him . . ."

"I am not interested, Monsieur de Montalivet," said the King in such a cold voice that the laughter and the words died suddenly in the minister's throat.

In the end, of course, both men lost their thrones. A revolution threw out Louis Philippe. And the slanders of Eugène de Mirecourt eventually undermined Dumas.

But I rather think that justice will in the end give the prize to the uncrowned prince, Dumas.

Madame Dumas, completely unaware of the future that awaited her son, having failed to make him a violinist, decided to make him a priest.

"A what?" the boy screamed.

"A priest."

"Oh, Mother, no!"

"No words, please. Make up your mind to it."

"Wear a skirt? And say prayers all day long? Never!"

"Enough. You've heard me. A splendid opportunity has just presented itself. Abbé Conseil, my cousin, has begged a place for you in the seminary at Soissons. You do not know how lucky you are. Your future is assured."

As Alexandre continued to plead and to protest, his mother informed him that another one of her cousins, Abbé Fortier, had promised to take him around with him for a few days to give him a taste for the priesthood.

This Abbé Fortier was a middle-aged man, rugged as an ancient oak. He enrolled the boy at once in the job of repairing the roof of his pre-Gothic church. And when Dumas flinched at scaling the steeple, with its crumbling stones, to set right the crucifix that had fallen to one side, the abbé tucked up his cassock and did it himself while Dumas gaped with surprise and admiration.

Called to minister to a dying woman in a remote and wild section of his parish, the priest took along his fishing rod and his gun, and on the return home he stopped at streams and forest glades to show the youth tricks that he had never even heard of. And then, finally, when Dumas saw the abbé enter into all the contests of the country fair and outdo all his competitors, even in the matter of who could eat the most hard-boiled eggs, consuming over a hundred of them to win the prize, Dumas felt that he had found his vocation: he too wanted to be a country priest. It was a rugged, demanding profession, of which any man could be proud.

When he returned to his mother she embraced him with joy. Finally all her problems were solved.

But suddenly everything changed: he refused to be a priest. And when his mother stormed at him, trying to understand what had caused this abrupt switch, he ran away to the forest and did not show up for three days. Not until his mother got Quiot-Biche, a notorious poacher of the town, to take a note to him, assuring him that she would no longer press him to be a priest, did he finally consent to come home again.

His mother burst into tears when she saw him. "I've promised not to ask you, but that's still no reason why you can't explain it to me."

Alexandre said nothing.

And yet the explanation was quite simple. Full of pride in his new vocation, Alexandre had gone around town telling everyone of his plans. Then he met the two Deviolaine girls, his rich and pretty second cousins, one twelve, the other fourteen, girls with whom, when he was invited now and then to the Deviolaines' home, he would play the craziest kind of bedroom games: ghosts, itching powder, frogs hidden under the sheets, and the like.

"Oh, Alexandre," cried Cécile, "we hear you are going to be a priest! How wonderful!"

"Yes," said Alexandre proudly. "I am entering the seminary in a few weeks."

"Perhaps someday you will be our priest," said Thérèse and she clapped her hands, and Alexandre preened himself.

"Certainly," he said.

"And you'll hear our confessions?" Cécile asked, her eyes twinkling mischievously. "And we'll have to tell you all the naughty things we have done?"

"You certainly will," he said.

"And we'll have to promise never to be naughty again," Thérèse inquired, "and say a hundred *mea culpas?*"

"Yes," said the future priest sternly.

"But after that, you know what we'll do?" Cécile asked.

"What?"

"We'll go right on being naughty again, so that we can come back to you and confess some more!"

With that the two girls put their pretty heads together and whispered and giggled.

"What are you giggling about?" Alexandre wanted to know.

"We're whispering naughtiness," said Cécile, "and we mustn't tell you about it until you're a priest."

That was all that actually happened. But it was like an electric shock to him. This is what sent him running into the woods to hide out for three days and dream about the magic of naughtiness that could bring to a girl's eyes a sparkle that was like an icicle in flames.

A different kind of poaching thus entered the life of Alexandre and exerted its fascination upon him until the end of his days. His mother, meanwhile, as a last resort, entered him into the local boys' Latin school run by Abbé Grégoire, who, with the heavy cane which he brought down smartly on his pupils' knuckles, tried in vain to instill some knowledge into Alexandre's mind.

But Alexandre's mind was on girls. Besides, he had little taste for arithmetic. Latin and Greek grammar he despised, though he loved to read the classical stories. Indeed, he was good in only one department: he wrote an amazingly good hand.

When Madame Dumas heard this about her son, she broke down and wept. "It is obvious that he is an idiot," she said, for she had never seen an important man whose handwriting could be easily deciphered.

One day Alexandre asked his mother point-blank, "Mother, can you dance?"

"I used to be able to," she said.

"Then teach me. You must teach me!"

It was a shock to his mother to realize that her son was growing up. She tried to give him a lesson in dancing, but the incongruity of their size and their family relationship upset her. "Let Abbé Grégoire teach you how to dance!" she said.

Alexandre approached the abbé on the subject and received such a verbal castigation on the evils of dancing that his ears burned.

He went about soliciting the help of his classmates. Didn't they want to learn to dance too?

Abbé Grégoire got wind of the movement among his pupils and met the danger head-on. "There will be no dancing in this school! No girls will ever enter here!"

But the whole school was suddenly caught up with a dancing fever. Perhaps because of the constant danger of war, the boys felt that they wanted to experience as much of life as possible before being snatched away to their death.

They approached Abbé Grégoire with the idea of pairing off among themselves and so learning to dance without girls.

"Sodom and Gomorrah!" cried the abbé. "There will be no dancing of boy with boy in this institution."

In the end, faculty and student body compromised by letting the boys dance holding chairs in their arms! Brezette, an ex-infantry corporal, was brought in as instructor and, coming as he did from Napoleon's army, than which there was never any more dance crazy, he taught all the latest and most complicated steps, *chassés-croisés*, traverses, *entrechats*, flic-flacs, and all the twinklings of the ankles and crossing and uncrossing of legs which were then in style. And also the new dances—the waltz and the polka—for these troops considered dances too as part of the loot which they brought home from every foreign country where they fought.

At his first real dance a girl of the village actually complimented

Dumas on his waltzing. As for him, all this energy which he expended in dancing seemed to return to him like the energy of strong drink, increasing his passion, winding him up for ever more spins and turns.

After he had whirled his partner until she screamed in ecstasy, she could not help exclaiming, "I've never danced with anyone who held me with such assurance!"

"That's because I've never danced before," he said, "and I had no idea that a girl would be so light in one's arms."

"You've never danced before?"

"Never," he said.

"That's impossible!" she declared. "You dance divinely! Surely you've had lessons."

"Yes," he said, "lessons, but not with a girl. With a chair. And from the first, when our class started to get instruction in dancing, it was taken for granted that the heaviest chair in the room, the teacher's own chair on the dais, was to be my partner. Everybody called that chair 'Dumas' girl.' And I guess it was from having to hold that big chair and dance with it in my arms that I was so surprised to find that a real girl is so light."

For this first dance of his, everything he had was borrowed—his clothes, his shoes and even his gloves. Indeed, he had totally forgotten about gloves, and only when he got his first partner did he realize that he would be the only male to extend a bare hand. He was horrified. In his desperation he approached a handsome dandy who was just pulling on his gloves.

"If you're not dancing," Alexandre begged, "let me have your gloves. Just for one dance."

"Certainly," said the dandy and, stripping off the glove he had already put on, he gave the pair to Alexandre.

"Thanks," said Dumas, and was about to return to his partner when he saw the dandy coolly pull out another pair of gloves and start putting them on.

"I always carry an extra pair or two," the young man said.

It was thus that Dumas met Adolphe de Leuven, son of the Count of Ribbing. This Swedish count, roused by America's battle for independence, had gone to the United States and enlisted in Washington's army. Returning home to Sweden, after the war, completely infected with the American spirit, he had soon joined a conspiracy against Gustave III, King of Sweden, who had declared with contempt that a single Swedish regiment would soon take care of any revolutionary rabble. Privy to the costume that the King was wearing at a masked ball, he had gone up to him and said, "There's a handsome disguise!"

This was the signal for a fellow conspirator, Anckarstroem, to fire. The King fell, mortally wounded.

They had supposed that in a masked ball they would escape detection easily, but they were all captured. Only Anckarstroem's guilt, however, could be fixed positively, because the gun was identified as his.

He was sentenced to be whipped with thorns for three days, then to have his murderous trigger hand hacked off, and finally to be decapitated. But at the same time that this sentence was passed upon him, he was told that his entire punishment would be remitted if he named his fellow conspirators. He refused. Whereupon sentence was carried out.

His decapitated body, exposed to public view, was found each morning crowned with laurel leaves. As a result of this expression of popular feeling for the American and the French revolutions, the authorities decided to get rid of the other arrested men by perpetual banishment.

Count Ribbing, arriving in revolutionary Paris, was hailed as the "handsome regicide" and feted like a potentate. Eventually he bought himself a château near Villers-Cotterêts, to which he would now and then retire from his duties as the editor of a Parisian newspaper.

It was the son of this man who was the dandy of the ball.

The two boys, despite their difference in present fortune, struck up an intimate friendship. Each had lusty republican forebears who had been in the thick of history. And each soon found another reason for intimacy.

"What are you going to become?" Adolphe once asked Alexandre.

Alexandre shrugged hopelessly. "I guess I'll be a notary's assistant, until maybe someday I can become a notary myself."

"I'm going to be a writer," said Adolphe. "A poet, and a dramatist."

Immediately Dumas was jealous. If this idea had ever occurred to him before he had never told it to anyone, but suddenly it seemed to him that he could be nothing else. "I'm going to be a writer too," he said.

"I want to write like Shakespeare," said Adolphe.*

"Shakespeare?" Dumas asked. "Who is Shakespeare?"

So Adolphe invited him to go to Soissons, where a company was touring in Ducis' translation of Shakespeare.

When Alexandre saw *Hamlet,* saw ghosts and murder and tragic love, saw insanity, poison, incest, revenge and dueling, all holding forth on the stage to the accompaniment of wild poetic imagery, he took such fire that he cried, "I too want to write like Shakespeare."

And then he leaped at once to action. "Let's write a play. Together."

They did. They wrote three one-act plays, which Adolphe then took with him to Paris. Alexandre lived on in a fever, waiting for every post to bring him money and fame. But one by one the plays were rejected by every producing company.

Thus several years passed, during which Madame Dumas became a feeble old woman, barely able to take care of her little salt and tobacco store. Alexandre worked in a near-by village with a notary and had little time for literature, and no money to go to Paris with, though once he managed to sneak off for a couple of days with his gun and literally shot his way to Paris, by poaching game all along the road and paying with the contents of his game bag for his meals and lodging.

It was as a result of the notoriety of this tale of successful poaching during an absence without leave that the notary dismissed Alexandre from his employ.

One evening, at the Boule d'Or inn, Alexandre tried to get someone to play billiards with him. He hoped to make a few sous. But no one would play against young Dumas for money: he was known to be too good.

Finally the innkeeper offered to play with him for drinks.

"But you know I don't drink!" Alexandre cried.

* He never did. But he is remembered for at least one bright little comedy, *The Postillion of Longjumeau,* and his fame is secure for having founded that great periodical the *Revue des deux Mondes.*

"Well, then we can't play," said the innkeeper.

But they played nevertheless and Alexandre won six hundred glasses of absinthe.

"What am I going to do with six hundred glasses of absinthe?" Alexandre wondered.

"You will drink them," said the innkeeper, laughing. "In time, perhaps, you will learn to like the stuff."

"Give me some money instead," Alexandre begged. "Half what it's worth."

The innkeeper shook his head.

"A quarter of what it's worth!"

Still the innkeeper refused. And the idle crowd in the inn watched this argument with amusement.

"Very well," said Alexandre. "Give me my absinthe."

The innkeeper took a bottle and poured a drink for Alexandre. He made a face as he brought it to his mouth but he tasted it anyhow and then spat with disgust.

Everybody roared.

"Faugh!" screamed Alexandre.

"Well, try another glass tomorrow. It takes a long time to develop a fondness for absinthe."

"I like it right now," said Dumas. "Give it to me."

"There's still some in your glass."

"That's just one glass. I won six hundred. I want six hundred glasses. And I want them right now."

The tables were reversed now, and the crowd was laughing with Alexandre instead of against him. The innkeeper tried to squirm out of this situation. Alexandre could have his drinks whenever he wanted. For himself and his friends. Or he would give Alexandre a dozen bottles.

But Alexandre kept shaking his head, just as the innkeeper had done before.

"Pour out six hundred glasses of absinthe," he insisted and, turning to the crowd, he asked, "Isn't it the rule of honor that gambling debts must be paid within twenty-four hours?"

And so in the end the innkeeper settled for ninety francs rather than make a fool of himself before his customers.

Ninety francs! Dumas had never seen so much money. Why, it

was a fortune! "I can go to Paris!" he cried. "I can become a great playwright! A Shakespeare!" And at once he counted out to the inn-keeper the price of a seat on the next evening's diligence.

But when he ran home to his mother and told her of his good fortune, she burst into tears. That her idiot son should try his for-tune in Paris was a hair-raising thought. She tried to reason with him. She wept. She knelt before him. She dragged him to the grave of his father and conjured him.

She took him to his old schoolteacher Abbé Grégoire, who re-minded Alexandre that far better students of his than Dumas had been content to settle down in Villers-Cotterêts and raise carrots and pigs.

She took him to their nearest rich relative, Monsieur Deviolaine, who had just been appointed Inspector General of the forests of the Dukes of Orléans. Monsieur Deviolaine, in his usual tempestuous manner, shouted, "I have nothing to say to the most notorious poacher in the whole province."

Instead he addressed Madame Dumas. "I am afraid your son has turned out to be a good-for-nothing, able to net larks and play billiards, but little else, and Villers-Cotterêts should be well pleased to get rid of him. However, if he is starving in Paris, tell him to come to my office and I will at least see that he gets a ticket to go back home."

Which one is the true story of Dumas' departure to Paris I don't know: whether because he, a teetotaler, won six hundred glasses of absinthe, or whether because he had lost his job and found that as a scamp he was completely played out all over Villers-Cotterêts and its environs and so could hope for nothing further there, this I can't answer. But my historical method is the same as that of Dumas: between two conflicting stories I always pick the most in-teresting.

In any case, one evening Alexandre and his mother went through the General's old correspondence to see what friends he might have had who could now be appealed to for help in getting established in Paris.

Here was a letter from the Duc de Bellune, who was now, under Louis XVIII, Minister of War. Here were letters from General Foy,

Marshal Jourdan, Sébastiani, Kellermann. Here was even one from Bernadotte, now King of Sweden.

They were all still alive.

Dumas noted down the names and determined to look them up in Paris.

Another visit to the General's grave, and the two, she tiny as a bird and in her perpetual widow's black, and he tall and as yet thin, poorly dressed and with his ungovernable hair wild on his head, walked in the growing darkness to the inn of the Boule d'Or.

One more kiss and one more promise to send for her just as soon as he could find an income, and the postilion sounded his horn, the driver cracked his whip, and the diligence clattered off into the darkness.

In the morning, by five o'clock, the coach would have made the sixty miles to Paris.

CHAPTER NINE

The Gold Is Gone

TALK ABOUT LUCK!

Just put yourself in Dumas' place. Imagine yourself like him: tall, young, strong, the son of a soldier who was a hero of France, and now, lo! in the full conviction of your talents and the certainty of your eventual success, you step off the coach at the depot of the Lightning Express Company in the rue du Bouloi, and Paris lies all around you.

Paris at dawn. Paris in the month of May.

Can you imagine yourself any luckier? Paris at twenty-one? Paris: the only city in the world, as Madame de Staël phrased it, where it is a joy to be alive even when you are unhappy?

Talk about luck! What else can you call it? Not that Dumas would have admitted it. To him, luck, as he said later, was nothing but the natural result of an energetic love affair between man and his existence. "Just as no woman can refuse her favors when a determined man really woos her," he said, "so life cannot help but give you her best when you court her *con brio*."

Well, in that case, never was there such a passionate courtship as
that of Dumas and life. Why, even when the man had made his mark,
luck continued to shower him with her gifts.

What author, for example, hasn't at one time or another wished
that some member of his family, or some very close friend of his,
would either commit a gory crime or be the victim of it? What relative's life would not be a cheap price to pay for a ready-made story
thus thrust into one's paws, along with a ready-made audience already clamoring for one's book?

But have you ever had such a piece of literary luck? No. Nor I
either.

But Dumas—yes.

The Dumas family had been intimate with the Collards of Villers-
Hélon before Alexandre was born, and young Alexandre knew the
Collard granddaughter Marie Cappelle from her birth. This girl
grew up and eventually married a fellow named Lafarge. Marie had
good reasons to regret that marriage. Lafarge, for all his courtship
manners, soon revealed himself as a country boor with perpetually
dirty fingernails, coarse, cruel and stupid, and with a fortune that
consisted only of some miserable ironworks supporting a mountain
of mortgages and debts. It thus seemed almost providential that the
man should develop a severe inflammation of the bowels and die
of it.

But after the burial, gossip raged like a forest fire and in time
compelled the authorities to exhume the body. And then there burst
upon Europe a scientific dispute that spread to all the famous chem-
ists of the period as to whether certain tests conducted on Lafarge's
intestines proved or disproved the opinion that he had died of a
dose of arsenic. Chemical analysis was still in its infancy, and, in
fact, a positive test for arsenic had been formulated so recently,
and the tests themselves so sloppily conducted, that there was room
for considerable scientific debate as to the validity of the conclu-
sions.

Nevertheless, Madame Lafarge was put on trial to determine
whether she had or had not baked arsenic into a cake she had made
for her husband. All Europe now split itself into passionate pro- and
anti-Lafargists. And so it was that at a time in history when some
fifty or more million people craved to know every detail about this

monster or this unfortunate beauty (according to which side you stood on), there was Alexandre Dumas, who not only knew her intimately but happened at the same time to be an already well-known author! And thus he acquired new glory.

How much literary luck is one writing man entitled to?

Of course, one will have to admit that this wasn't luck when seen from Marie Cappelle's angle: she was found guilty and went to prison for life, serving ten years before she was pardoned by Napoleon III only four months before she expired at the youthful age of thirty-six. Her tale is strangely pathetic, and her prison letters (full of gentle protests against her fate and convincing arguments demonstrating her innocence) have, since their publication, earned her the sad name of Saint Arsenic.

But for Dumas this was sheer luck.

And then, as if this man weren't already enough in the public eye, he had to become involved in the Dujarier affair, a grossly rigged duel in which Dujarier lost his life, and which led to a trial where Dumas figured as one of the principal witnesses and where his astute responses from the stand excited all France.

Luck even pursued this man after his death!

For example, in connection with the fraudulent duel that cost the life of Évariste Galois, Dumas' name will always have to be mentioned, because Dumas was the only person who bothered to note down the name of Galois' killer: Pécheaux d'Herbinville. Why should anyone have wanted to bother with this detail in what was after all an insignificant case? Who was this Galois but a young boy who had failed miserably in his entrance examinations for the polytechnical school, and was since then loafing around Paris taking part in radical meetings? Who cared about the death of this poor student who was not yet twenty-one years old? For it was only some fifty years after Galois died, and when Dumas himself was already dead, that a few pages that Galois had scribbled on the eve of his fatal duel became precious documents in the history of science, and showed that this young lad had possessed one of the great mathematical brains of all time.

Dumas could have had absolutely no inkling of this when he wrote about Galois.

Something of the same kind of posthumous luck working for Du-

mas occurs in the matter of Edgar Allen Poe. Dumas has left notes
about a meeting with Poe in Paris in 1836, relating how he found
rooms in Paris where Poe could work undisturbed through the night.
Scholars have always tended to reject this story as utterly fantastic,
but are forced to admit that for precisely this period in Poe's life
there happen to be absolutely no records with which to refute
Dumas!

Can this kind of luck—the luck of being able to keep one's name
fresh in the public mind even after one's death—can that really be
explained as the result of a love affair with life, no matter how energetic?

Doesn't it seem, rather, to require that famous hypothesis—the
hypothesis of God—that the astronomer Laplace told Napoleon the
Great he had had no occasion to call upon when he wrote his vast
treatise on the physics of the solar system?

Take, again, Dumas' luck in the matter of F. W. Reed.

This F. W. Reed was a poor boy in Whangarei, New Zealand,
than which nothing seems more remote from Paris. Moreover, he
labored in a drugstore at tasks that were beyond his strength and
that absorbed practically every minute of his waking hours from
dawn until his collapse from exhaustion late at night. Saturdays and
Sundays brought no surcease: indeed, additional duties were piled
upon him.

Then one day there fell into the life of this wretched child a tat-
tered paper-bound book: *Monte-Cristo.* He could barely steal
enough time from his work to read a paragraph a day, a couple of
pages a week. But the story gripped him at once and sustained him
wonderfully through his endless dull labors. Curiosity, excitement,
enthusiasm stole into a boy's life and transmuted its drabness into
adventure.

Who could this man be, this Alexandre Dumas, whose name was
on the title page of that book?

In little Whangarei, in those days, there was neither bookstore nor
library—Whangarei is as remote in New Zealand as New Zealand
is itself remote in the world—and all the boy could discover was
that Dumas was a Frenchman, that the *s* at the end of his name was
generally not pronounced, and that he was dead.

The boy grew up. His work remained as mountainous as ever.

But each week he managed to find a half hour or so that he could fill with Dumas. In time, from Auckland, then from London, and finally from Paris, he drew ever new books from the inexhaustible works of Dumas.

Slowly, with infinite patience, he used the minutes of his spare time to master French and thus enabled himself to read the many works of Dumas that have never been translated. And so, in the course of a lifetime of incessant travail, which only in his later years let up a bit, Reed made himself the world's authority on Dumas and owner of the largest collection of his works.

And today, when you hear again that old story of how Dumas copied out one day an article on snakes and sent it off as that day's installment for his serial, you may query F. W. Reed, who will tell you that he has found no evidence of any such installment and that the story is most likely another one of those exaggerations that the French people loved to tell about their favorite character. It belongs with the stories of how an autumn leaf once floated through the open window onto his desk and was promptly signed by Dumas and sent off to his printer as an original piece of work.

It belongs with the stories of Dumas' weird collection of medals, and how crowds would gather to stare at him when in full uniform he stood guard before the Tuileries. What a uniform that man wore: the gaudiest of the three authorized! Black cap with silver eagle and scarlet tuft, and with chin strap of solid silver links. White worsted epaulets. Festooned white shoulder knot with tags. Over his chest yellow cross belts. Dark blue coat, lined with scarlet silk and with scarlet piping and cuffs. Big silver buttons. Trousers, light blue with red seams. Black boots. Yellow gloves. Knapsack of deerskin with fur to the outside, and yellow straps to bind his blue, rolled-up greatcoat.

And all over the front of this uniform, his medals!

Paul Huet, the well-known landscape painter, passing him there one day, stopped and blinked. "And you call yourself a Republican?" he said. "Why a man could get a sunstroke just from walking past all this glitter."

Dumas exploded. "I'm a staunch Republican, and you know it!"

"For a Republican, you have a suspiciously large number of

royal friends," said Huet, running his finger underneath the overlapping medals.

"What about it?" Dumas asked truculently. "I like kings. It's the institution I am opposed to, not the man who happens to have been born a prince."

Huet grabbed Dumas and spun him around. "I thought so!" he cried. "The man has even got medals hung on his behind!"

To which Dumas answered simply and with a touch of sadness, "Those are from kings who have since lost their thrones."

Yes, it was an age of exaggeration, but also an age whose real accomplishments would be difficult to exaggerate. And perhaps the luck of Dumas in finding long after his death a shrine in the antipodes, in far off Whangarei in New Zealand, must be measured against his Herculean labors while he was alive.

Where are the publishers today who will race with gold across the seas to bid for an exiled writer's novel, as they did to the isle of Guernsey for Victor Hugo's *Les Miserables*, where a Belgian businessman carried off the manuscript after laying down 125,000 francs in gold as an earnest for more to come.

On the table lay the pile of sheets. Upside down.

Lacroix, about to set down his bags of gold, said, "May I have a little look?"

"No," said Victor Hugo flatly.

Lacroix paled. "But . . . but supposing it is all just blank paper?"

"You will still have the right to publish it with my name on the cover," said Victor Hugo. "That should insure a good sale."

"You are right," said Lacroix, and he put down his bags of gold.

Alas, that kind of gold is gone!

Where is there a writer who could do today what Dumas did in Russia in the middle of the last century? Meeting, deep in the Caucasus, a young and engaging fellow, Vasili, who wanted nothing so much as to be Dumas' valet, he said to him, "You're hired. Go to Paris and wait for me there."

Vasili jumped with joy until he remembered that he was due for his compulsory military service and never would the authorities grant him a passport. Furthermore, he had not a penny he could call his own.

Dumas asked for a sheet of paper, for pen and ink, and he sat down and wrote: "Greetings! Alexandre Dumas, of Paris and the world, respectfully requests all the nations of our globe to honor this passport and open the borders of their land to the bearer."

Then he added a P.S. asking all railroad and steamship companies to transport Vasili on account and send their bills to Dumas, Paris.

When Dumas came back from his trip, Vasili was waiting for him in his apartment with a passport that bore a dozen visas and, clipped to it, twenty or thirty bills from transportation companies and hotels, most of them marked *Paid*, and with an added note on this order: "A small return for the pleasure of reading *Twenty Years After*."

Yes, the gold is gone.

Dumas saw it when shortly before his death he visited the great Paris Exposition of 1867 and stopped in the Cours de la Reine, where the Palace of Industry was, and watched the huge walking beam going up and down over the great stationary steam engine, watched the great fly wheels spinning smoothly on ball bearings, watched the pistons working furiously.

After a long silence he turned to the beautiful Mazeppa, the American-Jewish actress Adah Isaacs Menken, who was his last mistress, and said, "You really think the human spirit can survive that?" He shook his head sadly. "It is a rigged duel. The machine is bound to win."

CHAPTER TEN

A Private Secretary for a Poor Lad

BUT TO RETURN to that first May day in Paris.

After getting off the coach, Dumas grabbed up what food was left in the basket his mother had packed for him, food at which he had nibbled all night between cat naps, and, checking the rest of his baggage with the clerk at the depot, he raced off, eating as he raced, crossing town and climbing the hill of Montmartre to the house of the Count of Ribbing.

The Count and his son Adolphe were having breakfast in the garden when Dumas burst in on them.

"I'm here!" he cried and spread his arms wide.

As Adolphe embraced him and the Count shook his hand, they asked in alarm, "Has something happened to your mother?"

"No, she's fine! But I've come to Paris to be a writer!"

"Hurrah!" cried Adolphe. "You've had something accepted!"

"No. Nothing yet."

"Then you have a job?"

"No. Not yet."

"Then you've come into an inheritance. Come, man, tell us the good news!"

"The good news is that I've decided to come here and write."

"But how are you going to live?"

"Why, by writing."

"Yes. Eventually, no doubt. But meanwhile?"

"Well, I'll get a job."

"How?"

"Easy."

"How easy?"

"Now, now, now," said the Count, "let's first ask our good friend if he's had his breakfast."

"I wish you hadn't asked me just exactly that question," said Dumas, looking eagerly at the good food.

"Why, how so?" the Count asked.

"Because if it comes to telling you whether I've had breakfast, I'll be forced to tell you the truth."

"Of course, my boy. I expect the truth from you. Always."

"In that case, yes, I've had my breakfast."

"Well, what's so difficult about saying it?"

"Because I'm afraid you will let it stand in the way of my having breakfast with you."

"Ah, so," said the Count, light dawning on him. "I accept the correction. I should have simply asked whether you cared to share ours."

"Delighted!" said Dumas and reached eagerly for the platter of eggs.

"Well, now, my boy," the Count said, "tell us how you are going to get a job so easily. This I would like to hear."

"Why, I went through my father's correspondence and picked

out all the names of his good friends who are still among us today: the Duke of Bellune, Marshal Jourdan, Marshal Sébastiani, General Verdier, General Foy, and so forth."

"And you have written to them?"

"No. I am going to see them personally."

"Ah," said the Count. "You are going to see them personally. And you have not even written them to expect you?"

"That's right," said Dumas, swallowing hard and reaching for another helping.

The Count cleared his throat. "That is to say, just as you are, you are going to knock at their door?"

"Yes," said Dumas. "Why not?"

"Why, nothing, my boy. Nothing."

The truth was that Dumas had as yet absolutely no notion of how ridiculous a figure he cut. He was so obviously fresh from the country, his coat was of such an antique cut and so violent and crude a color, and his hair had so clearly been trimmed by his mother that the effect was ludicrous, and the only reason one couldn't laugh was because his features expressed such bumptious and completely innocent eagerness that to laugh would have been like kicking a puppy that is wagging its tail and trying to lick your hand.

But though Dumas had no notion of anything's being wrong with himself, he could not fail to sense the lack of enthusiasm on Ribbing's part.

"Has it occured to you," the Count asked, "that perhaps you should have conducted your applications by mail first?"

"Why? What can they tell me by mail that they can't tell me to my face? And isn't it better if I am right there to take a job the moment they offer it?"

"Well, have you any idea of how many job-seekers importune such highly placed people every day?"

"I hadn't thought of it. In any case, they can't all be sons of their intimate friends."

"Well, have you any idea of how many would-be writers try to get jobs even on my little paper, every day?"

"No."

"Would it surprise you if I said dozens?"

"Dozens?"

"Well, dozens may be an exaggeration, but I assure you that not a day passes but that I have to tell some ambitious boy like yourself that I have no room for him."

Dumas' appetite failed him for a moment. He stopped eating and looked at the Count. "You are afraid that I'm going to fail?"

"Well, what difference? You will have had a vacation in Paris. And you will return to Villers-Cotterêts with fresh energy and new and saner resolutions."

Dumas said, "You think my coming here is doomed to failure."

"Well, let's call it a very risky venture."

"And you would have advised me against it?"

"What else could I do, as your friend?"

"So you, who assassinated the King of Sweden, would have advised me not to risk coming to Paris?" Dumas asked.

"My dear boy," said the Count, "it is precisely because I have done both that I can tell you that it is easier to kill a Swedish king than to make a killing in this city of Paris, where hundreds of eager young men pour in every week, each one determined to make his mark."

Dumas sat there for a moment, and the sweat began to form drops on his brow. It was the first time he had felt his whole life as a great big foggy question mark. Self-doubt paralyzed him. But after a moment he gathered himself together. In later years he was to say of self-doubt: "A person who doubts himself is like a man who would enlist in the ranks of his enemies and bear arms against himself. He makes his failure certain by himself being the first person to be convinced of it."

"Well, I must go," he said, swallowing another mouthful of tea and rising.

"Why are you rushing away?"

"I have so much to do. In the first place, I must buy a copy of the *Almanac of 25,000 Addresses*, so as to look up all the people I want to see."

"But an almanac costs five francs," said the Count. "Why spend so much money when I can let you look at our office copy?"

"Thanks, Count, but I have to hurry. I have so much to do. I still want to look for a room."

"There's no problem about a room. Paris is full of hotels."

"I mean a room for rent. I want to bring my furniture here, and my books."

"Yes, but of course you won't do that until you're settled. After all, you have to sign a year's lease. And you don't know yet whether you can stay."

"No," said Dumas, "I don't know whether I can stay." But after a pause he added, "All I know is that I'm going to stay."

He left as quickly as he could, anxious to be away from these good, kind people who had failed to give him a word of cheer just when he needed it most, these rich people who obviously liked him but just as obviously had weighed him and found him wanting.

As he ran down into the city, he made up his mind to succeed no matter at what cost to himself. His determination hardened within him until it was like a knot. And he drenched it in the tears of self-pity that he refused to let flow from his eyes. He steeped it in his own brine until he knew for certain that it could never come unraveled.

And it never did.

He bought his almanac and found the address of Marshal Jourdan in the Faubourg Saint-Germain. Jourdan, a former silk merchant, hearing of the rising of the American colonies against Britain, had joined a regiment of volunteers and fought under Washington. He had then returned to France and followed a military career through the French Revolution and the Napoleonic era, and had managed to weather every change of government and still come out on top.

A servant opened the door to Dumas and asked, "Whom shall I announce?"

Dumas was struck by the splendor of the furnishings and the startling silver-and-blue livery of the servant. Tongue-tied, he mumbled, "General Alexandre Dumas . . . I'm his—"

The servant had already left to report to his master.

Within seconds an old man ran out, threw his arms around Alexandre, but just as quickly withdrew them, crying out, "Impostor! How dare you?"

"I'm no impostor," said Dumas. "I'm Alexandre Dumas."

"Don't lie! You insolent dog! Alexandre Dumas was my bosom companion for years. I knew him as well as I know my right hand."

"I'm his son!" Dumas exclaimed. "My father is dead long ago."

"Get out!" cried the Marshal. "Alexandre never had a son. Get out before I throw you out!"

"Please believe me," Dumas begged. "I had no intention of passing myself off as my father . . ."

"Enough!" said the Marshal and walked back into his study, shutting the door.

Dumas shrugged and left. He quickly suppressed the poison of self-doubt that he felt rising again and looked up Marshal Sébastiani in his almanac. The Marshal lived in the Faubourg Saint-Honoré.

Once more, a sumptuous mansion. This time Dumas was admitted right into the Marshal's study.

"So you're the son of my good friend Alexandre," said Sébastiani, whose rise to fame was to some extent due to the fact that his family's cottage had been next door to that of the Napoleons on the island of Corsica. Now his study, bounded by four huge and lavishly decorated walls, contained four secretaries, to whom the Marshal dictated in turn, at four magnificently carved desks. As he passed from secretary to secretary, each would extend to the General a gold snuffbox, from which he would take a tiny pinch of the finest Spanish tobacco.

But when he heard that Dumas wanted a career in literature and not in the army, he lost his respect for the lad. "Here are four writers," he said, pointing to his four secretaries. "I couldn't write a word to save my neck, but I can have twenty writers any day I want them. The streets are full of writers. There is only one career for a real man and that is the career of arms."

Next was the Duke of Bellune, but this former Napoleonic general who had achieved a dukedom would not even see Dumas. He sent word through his servant that he would be glad to receive a letter from the boy.

After the Duke came General Verdier. This general, to Dumas' surprise, lived modestly in a top-floor apartment and painted pictures.

"I have been accused of conspiracy, my lad, and they have pensioned me off. Today you would be much better off if you had left your country in the revolution and fought against her in the armies of her enemies, for loyalty to your country's interests is not the way to rise. Remember this: Be loyal, not to your country, but to the party that happens to be in power, whichever it may be; that is the secret of success in this corrupt age."

Next, General Foy. The famous orator was busy in his study, writing his history of the Peninsular War, amidst books, maps, pamphlets, manuscripts, strewn over chairs, tables, desks and even the floor.

"So you're the son of General Dumas who commanded the Army of the Alps."

"Yes, General."

"I've been told that Bonaparte treated your father very unjustly and extended this injustice even to his widow."

"He left us in utter poverty."

"What can I do for you?"

"Anything. Because I'm at the end of my resources."

"Well, that shouldn't be difficult. I know a place where the only requirement will be that you know some mathematics."

Dumas swallowed. "It was my feeblest subject, General."

"Oh, I'm not speaking of higher mathematics. Just some algebra, conic sections . . ."

"I'm sorry, General," said Dumas, blushing. "But really . . ."

"Well, let's see. How about law? You've studied a bit of that, haven't you?"

"No, General."

"Well, Latin and Greek then."

"Well, Latin, General, but almost no Greek at all."

"How about modern languages: German, English . . ."

"Some Italian, but not much."

"Bookkeeping?"

"Please, General, let me confess at once, before I die of shame. I spent most of my time hunting, fishing, reading, dancing. I'm afraid I was a bad student. But that's because I had no direction. If you will tell me what you want me to learn I'll soon know it, because I'm not really as stupid as I may seem."

"Good. Well, let's see. . . . But by the way, have you something to live on in the meantime, while you study?"

"Not a thing, General," said Dumas and felt absolutely crushed.

"That makes it really difficult."

"Yes, General. But I assure you, whatever job it may be, it will be only a stopgap. You shall see, I will yet make something of myself. I will apply myself. I can. I will."

"Yes, I am sure of it. But at the moment there's nothing to be done. However, I'll look around. Here. Write down your name and address."

Dumas took paper and pen and started to write, saying, "I'll get my mail at the Count of Ribbing's . . ."

The General exclaimed, "We are saved, my lad!"

"How so?"

"Your hand! You write a beautiful hand."

Dumas felt utterly annihilated, being reminded sharply of his mother's judgment that a beautiful hand was nothing but a certificate of general incompetency. Foy, however, went on. "I happen to know that the offices of the Duke of Orléans need an address-writing clerk. You'll get twelve hundred francs a year, which isn't much."

"It's a fortune!" Dumas cried.

"Well, then it's as good as done. Come back tomorrow."

"I want to rent a room. Can I be sure—"

"Go ahead. This is a political matter. The Duke should be able to say that he has the son of a Republican general working for him."

So Dumas ran off, muttering to himself, "I must study, study, study. I must never stop studying." And all the while he went into innumerable houses and saw innumerable rooms, all of which were too expensive if nice and too mean if cheap. But finally he found one with a window on the court and with ugly yellow paper on the walls, but with an alcove that would accommodate his bed, leaving the rest of the room free to be his study.

The porter, who with a glance had recognized a fresh country bumpkin in this tall lad with his outlandishly long jacket hanging to his knees and his poorly trimmed hair aureoling wildly about his head, pressed his advantage.

"Ah, yes, an alcove. It isn't everywhere now that you'll find an alcove, Monsieur. *Les alcôves*, our fathers understood how to appreciate that. Nowadays, four walls, *voilà*, that's what they call a room." He sighed, as if indeed the world had fallen upon evil days since alcoves were no more.

And Dumas, though he had the sense to realize that his recognition of an alcove was no particular sign of any great artistic sense in himself, was nevertheless pleased.

He felt, however, that he had to be critical of the ugly yellow wallpaper.

"Oh, that's because Monsieur has no idea of how much that wallpaper costs a roll," the porter said.

And Dumas had to admit that he didn't.

"Well, that explains everything," said the porter.

Dumas, not sure whether that meant that the paper was extremely expensive or extremely cheap, was forced to let the matter drop or else expose himself.

The matter of the window, however, was more vital.

"I shall be working a great deal, early and late. And that window won't give much light."

"Oh, Monsieur mustn't let the matter of light bother him," said the porter. "Here we burn nothing but candle ends. They are of the finest wax. And cheap in spite of it."

"Candle ends?"

"Ah, you don't know about candle ends?"

"Of course. A candle end is the end of a candle. The part that is left in the holder when the candle begins to gutter."

"Ah, Monsieur, there's a lot more than that to a candle end."

"How so?"

"Well, Monsieur, let us imagine that you are rich—which for all I know you may be, for nowadays even dukes and princes prefer to travel incognito—and let us say you have fine guests coming to your home. Now, would you bother to light the little bits of candle left over from the previous evening? No, you would say, 'Blaise—' I'm imagining, you understand, that Blaise is your valet. . . ."

"Yes, of course," said Dumas. How good it felt to be taken for rich, successful, intelligent!

"Well, you would say, 'Blaise, fresh candles everywhere. I have important guests this evening.' And Blaise would say, '*Oui*, Monsieur, I shall attend to it at once.' But what will Blaise do with all the little candle ends? Why, he will put them in a box. And when the box is full, he will come to me. Why to me? Because he knows I do a modest business in candle ends. The whole neighborhood knows that, Monsieur. I don't wish to boast: it is a puny business. But it is all mine. And when I buy Blaise's box of candle ends, he has a bit of money to add to his wages, I have a bit more stock for my commerce, and there is no waste of a commodity which from year to year becomes more expensive and more precious: good wax. You have to admit, my friend, that all this works for the best of everyone concerned. The rich have their luxury, the poor have only the leavings, but both have their light, and there, Monsieur, lies the essential, for a candle, short or long, still gives as much light."

Dumas listened with appreciation. It was the beginning of his discovery that each person, in his own way, and on however humble a level, is a philosopher and worthy of being a character in a book.

And the porter concluded, saying, "Naturally, I give my own tenants every advantage of price when it comes to buying candle ends. And first choice of the best ends."

How could Dumas resist? And especially when the porter pointed to a piece of furniture which would be thrown in with the room.

"What do you say of that?"

"That" was obviously a tall writing desk. But then the porter proudly showed him that the side opened up and there was room not only for the receptacle which is ordinarily kept in a night table, but also for the user, though for Dumas it would be something of a tight squeeze.

"There is a *secrétaire* that can keep a secret," said the porter, playing up the expression *lieu secret*, which is French for privy, as indeed in English the word privy too has its nobler meaning in privy councilor and such expressions.

The porter did not lie when he said that this combination privy and writing desk was the latest style in Parisian furniture. "Nothing could be more decent," he explained. "If some evening you have guests, and if they saw something which was nothing but a *lieu secret*, it would strike the eye. And if a guest were to ask, 'What is that?' it would be most embarrassing. But this way you can always say, 'That's a writing desk.' And it is clear, from looking at it, that it is in fact a writing desk."

CHAPTER ELEVEN

Cherchez la Femme!

WHEN, IN LATER YEARS, the English would flock to Paris to see for themselves what they styled "the demoralization of the French theater," and an English critic (Percy Fitzgerald) would write: "From Dumas dates the inundation of the French theater with a bloody spate of slaughterings, incests, adulteries, violations, secret accouchements, represented with the crassest accuracy . . ." and that "Dumas started that rivalry in obscenity which in the end caused the sewer gates to be lifted bodily and a deluge of impurity to 'wash' away the last vestiges of decency from the stage . . ." one is forced to wonder how much of it may be blamed upon the Parisian furniture makers who launched the style of combination desk and night table where Dumas penned his earliest literary productions and, so to speak, formed his style.

Whether this should be set down as another piece of luck is debatable, but in the meantime this is perhaps as good a place as any to go into a little sketch of manners and morals of the period, with no intention, however, of browbeating the reader into believing that the manners and morals of any period can really be summed up, for there are no rules so consistently broken as those of manners and morals.

There is no doubt, for example, that around this period doctors launched a number of violent attacks on the Parisian habit of lolling in a warm bath. "Nothing," they declared, "is so much the cause of indigestion as frequent and prolonged hot-water baths." They even blamed various kinds of permanent invalidism on this pernicious custom.

But are we to assume anything from such medical warnings? Where do people actually obey doctors' orders? Certainly not in Paris. At this time almost every Parisian home of any affluence contained a popular style of tin bathtub with a heating device underneath consisting of a tube to hold the hot ashes which could be bought from the neighborhood baker, and a coquettish little chimney which rose from that tube to crook a little finger out of a hole in the windowpane. What a joy on a cold Sunday to immerse oneself into such a tub and steep there hour after hour. Balzac says he soaked himself daily for one hour in a hot tub.

The homes in this era were still miserably heated. Winter heat is a very recent invention, as a matter of fact. Goethe, at this time, expressed the wish that he might be hanged every winter and be taken down and revived every spring, for the cold months were nothing but an agony of chilblains, coughs and fluxions of the chest.

Stendhal tells us that to take off one's flannels in winter was certain death and that in an experiment being made in a hospital all patients so treated turned up their toes and died.

Balzac took to the habit of endless cups of hot coffee to keep himself warm. And no wonder Dumas infuriated people later when they saw him work in the depths of winter with nothing on but a thin white shirt, his arms and his neck bare, and only explaining cryptically, "I'm just naturally warm."

Is it possible that, in such an era, the pleasure of a hot bath really went out of style?

Of all the stories we read of this period, how much can we take as the truth and how much as just the winds of opinion and controversy forever blowing over the questions of manners, morals, customs and hygiene?

We are told, for example, that the year 1823, when Dumas came to Paris, was the year of the *Death of Socrates*, Lamartine having just published his book with that title. And that Herbault, who was to that era what Madame Éloffe was to Marie Antoinette and what Paquin was to Napoleon III and what Dior is to us today, would have nothing but shades of gray in his styles and long draping effects to remind us of the agony of drinking hemlock.

As for 1825, it was the year when the play *Jocko* made such a huge hit. Jocko was a female monkey in Brazil who fell in love with an exiled European, and he with her, out of disgust for humanity and its wealth-corrupted civilization. She was the sweetest little animal and so devoted that she quickly taught herself to sew and cook and to dance and sing so as to delight her master. Altogether she was the most charming little trick that ever hit the Paris stage,

so contemporaries insist. But one day, having tumbled into a gorge
filled with wild animals, she came out with a diamond. Then her
European lover gave her no peace, driving her again and again
down into the terrible gorge where the wild animals attacked her,
but from which she had to bring back the diamonds he craved. At
last she came back only to die.

Jocko's stage costume is still with us as the monkey jacket, scarlet
and gold-embroidered, and along with other similar garments it
was the rage of Paris—until the giraffe appeared.

Mohammed Ali, that Turkish brigand who became pasha of
Egypt and almost caused a war between France and England, presented this giraffe to the people of Paris. The public followed with
passion the tale of the travails of the poor beast, chained to the deck
of a ship as it crossed the Mediterranean amidst the fury of storms.
Five cows were brought along to provide milk for the delicate creature. For four weeks a specially built truck dragged the animal over
the roads from Toulon to Paris. And what a sensation when it was
finally installed in the Jardin des Plantes, where crowds of vast size
flocked to see the beast that stood on the first floor and ate its meal
on the second. Men's collars suddenly became an inch higher. Tall
girls were suddenly popular and admired. Hairdressers introduced
a coiffure *à la girafe*—ringlets of hair tight against the scalp to make
the head small on top of a long neck. Textile mills wove hundreds
of thousands of yards of giraffe cloth, spots of brown on a sand-
colored base.

I have not bothered to find out what the styles of other years
were, contenting myself with the old saying, *"Plus ça change, plus
c'est la même chose"*—The more it changes, the more it's the same
damned thing.

The battle of Waterloo, we are told, created a revolution in feminine psychology. In one day, the whole conception of woman developed over the revolutionary and the Napoleonic eras—that she
could die as bravely as man—was destroyed, and a new woman appeared who all at once dared not take a step without her smelling
salts, a mere scratch being enough to cause her to swoon. The
light, antique dresses, often of gauze, which were furthermore
dampened so as to cling to every curve of the body and thus imitate the *drap mouillé* effect seen on Greek statues, suddenly disap-

peared and the feminine body was once again corseted, and so tightly that it took two men and a bedpost to do the job. The feminine breasts, the nipples of which once stood out like knobs in the chill of damp gauze, were now well hidden, but the bosom itself expanded mightily under the pressure of the corseting and became twin pink blossoms delicately poised on a slender, stalklike waist.

The clergy, who necessarily take their occupation of saving souls much to heart, and who for some obscure reason sooner approve of the business of war in which men kill each other than they do the business of sex in which men and women merely roll in each other's arms without permanent damage to either and possibly some enjoyment, gave the new styles their unqualified endorsement and in fact their blessing: they saw the corset as an additional hurdle against unchastity.

But the new look in the matter of chastity was very real. And when the heir to the throne of France was stabbed and lay dying of massive loss of blood, and when his wife, the gay Duchess of Berry, was the only woman present to whom one could look for the means to make a quick ligature, the question of whether or not she might lift her skirt and fetch down her garter was a grave moment in history. Or so we are told. Considering the attacks against the institution of royalty, should not a prince die rather than a princess be convicted of open impudicity?

Dumas himself tells us that the success of his play *Antony* was due at least in part to the brilliant manner in which he solved the problem of how to commit a violent murder on a struggling woman without ruffling her clothes or exposing her feet to the titters of the gallery.

So refined did women become that they were shocked at the notion of using a single perfume and thus smelling like some recognizable flower, a rose or a carnation, which might give a man the strange notion that they were ready to be plucked. Fashion dictated the use of ten or twelve different perfumes which were calculated to confuse the male nostril and deprive him of any preconceptions whatsoever.

How, in the face of this, statistics continued to show one third of all children of Paris born illegitimate is beyond me.

All this new feminine refinement did not, of course, prevent a nurse from dressing in whatever old clothes she didn't mind staining, and it would take another forty or fifty years before she would don a clean white uniform, and then, of course, only over her indignant protest: "What? I should dress up like a bride just in order to give an old man an enema?" *

Such was the world into which Dumas engaged himself to make his fortune by writing.

As he was about to descend with the porter to sign a year's lease at ten francs a month, he noticed another door on the top landing.

"Don't worry," said the porter quickly. "Monsieur will have all the quiet he wants here. The only other tenant on this floor is a most respectable woman who, like me, has her little business. She does for laundries all those little repairs of buttons and little rips which laundries always promise their customers and always fail to carry out. She already has two assistants to help her."

A most respectable woman? *Peste!* That was too bad. Dumas imagined a dumpy woman of about fifty, with a mustache already darkening a stout upper lip. Yes, it would have been nice to have had the stimulation of a young and pretty neighbor. But, of course, one cannot ask for everything. One cannot hope to fall into the latest type of combination writing desk, plus cheap candle ends, and expect a ready-made mistress too.

No, that much luck no one has a right to expect.

And so he ran off to the depot in the rue du Bouloi to get his baggage and to make himself at home in his new abode, intending to pass the night on the floor. He was in a hurry to move in and be as settled as possible, because he wanted to go out and look at the town and see the theaters, which, of course, he wouldn't be able to enter since he was already so short of money. But just to feel the tingle of the air along the boulevards, see the crowds on the sidewalks or jamming themselves into the cafés, and look at the billboards outside the theaters!

---

* This, of course, does not apply to the various religious organizations and the municipal *crèches*, the *hospices*, for foundlings, incurable women, etc., many of which were conducted with exemplary cleanliness. Others, on the contrary, were notorious for carelessness, filth and a shocking death rate.

When he had put his baggage away in his still almost-empty room at Number One, Block of the Italians (across the street from the Opéra Comique), and was about to rush downstairs, he paused for a moment and looked at the door of that respectable woman.

Why not? he asked himself. He walked over to the other side of the landing and knocked. After a moment a clear voice came through the door. "Yes? Who is it?"

It was a voice that didn't sound at all like that of a woman with a mustache showing on her upper lip.

"I beg your pardon," said Dumas. "I'm your new neighbor. I've taken the room opposite. And I have as yet none of my things, which are being sent from the country. So, if I could have a glass of water. It would be a great kindness, which I hope to be able to repay."

"One moment, Monsieur."

Through the thick door he could hear faintly the sounds of a woman in slippers as she fetched a glass of water. Then the door opened, but only so far as the inside chain would permit, just sufficient for a hand to tender the glass.

But Dumas had seen enough: it was obviously the hand of a young person. Pale and smooth. Dimpled.

He took the glass. "*Merci*, Mademoiselle."

The voice corrected him coldly. "It is Madame. . . ."

"Your pardon," Dumas said quickly. "My name is Alexandre Dumas."

But the voice didn't answer. The door clicked shut.

"Many thanks for the water," said Dumas.

And through the door came the cool answer. "*Pas de quoi*, Monsieur."

There you are: which of us, as a young writer, hasn't wished for just such luck as Dumas had: a garret in Paris and on the same landing a young person with a clear voice and a shapely hand, with whom it would be a pleasure to develop an intrigue. And as forbidding as that word Madame might be, it was yet more attractive and promising than a Mademoiselle would have been, for it suggested a past that was correct and foreshadowed a future that might be even more interesting. In short, a widow. Young and yet not inexperienced.

She was, Dumas soon learned, Marie-Catherine Lebay, from

Rouen, poor, abandoned by her husband, and busily making a living for herself.

It is about time that we came to the woman in the case. For of course there was a woman involved in the "Duel after the Masked Ball." In fact, more than one. And was it not Alexandre Dumas himself who first summed up all criminological investigation in three terse words which have become famous: *Cherchez la femme!* Find the woman!? Words that he put into the mouth of his Monsieur Jackal, in what was probably the first detective story ever to be put on the stage.*

With that clear voice ringing in his ears, with that smooth white hand floating in his mind's eye, with the promise of all manner of delight ahead, Dumas fairly bounded down the steps.

By Jove! This called for a celebration! To hell with economy on his first night in Paris! He had an extra louis, a twenty-franc gold piece among the smaller coins in his pocket, and he took out this gold coin, spun it in the air, and said, "Heads I have dinner and theater tonight. Tails, the same!"

But as he came down to the street level, he met up with the porter, who in a tone of very gentle reproach, said, "Monsieur no doubt has many weighty matters on his mind."

"How so?"

"No matter," said the porter. "You will remember later."

"Remember what? What have I forgotten?"

"*Le denier à dieu,*" said the porter. "The farthing that belongs to God."

"Of course!" cried Dumas, and without hesitation he flipped his gold louis to the porter, crying, "Catch!"—which you can be sure the porter did.

The porter's wife, seeing the flash of gold, came running out and promised Monsieur Dumas that his room would be kept spotless for him—for a mere five francs a month.

"Agreed!" said Dumas, and walked on feeling wonderful.

* He was originally a character in Dumas' novel *Les Mohicans de Paris*, wearing green spectacles and constantly dipping into his snuffbox and forever saying, "*Cherchez la femme!*" Without a doubt the literary ancestor of all the great ferrets from Victor Hugo's Javert to Conan Doyle's Sherlock Holmes, and years before Hawkshaw of *The Ticket-of-Leave Man* (1863), usually given that credit.

But not absolutely wonderful, for something in him said, "What an insane idea to spend one's first Parisian evening in a gesture. What an insane idea to give two month's rent for a tip."

And yet it was grand. It was more than grand: it was superb.

It was the first of a whole train of gestures that Dumas loved and lived for.

Say what you will, say that it is nothing but cheap display, say that it is nothing but life lived for mere pyrotechnics—ah, but what else makes a man click, what else makes him give off a sudden burst of light, what else if not a gesture that spotlights him for a moment, picks him out of the obscure crowd, makes an individual of him, separates him from the nameless millions? What will you say of a man who has never indulged in a gesture? How will you sum up his life except that he left an estate of so and so many dollars, or a widow with so many children?

Would there have been a Dumas at all without the gesture? After all, what right had he to come to Paris and say, "I am going to be a writer"? Where is this talent you claim to have? Show me the evidence of it? How dare you aspire to be anything more than a *garçon de café*? Who is your mother anyhow but an old widow woman who goes from neighbor to neighbor and begs for last week's newspaper, which later she will carefully tear in squares and roll each square into a cone or horn, into each of which she will measure out a carefully weighed sou of salt or tobacco? What is it but the most piddling of businesses, carried out in pennies, with fractions of pennies as the net profit?

Yes, he should have come to Paris and taken a job in a café and run from sunrise until the gas was extinguished, from one table to another, with an "*Entendu*, Monsieur," and a "*Voilà*, Monsieur," to drag out his mattress at night from behind the screen where it lies along with warped billiard cues and broken checker sets and old watering cans, and sleep among the tables in the stale odor of spilled drinks and saliva-soaked cigars, no more and no less than ten thousand other garçons do each night in Paris.

What, after all, made him different? Nothing except the courage of bluff. Which is how every man starts if he starts at all.

For how can a man say that he will be this or do that, when he has never been anything or done anything before? Doesn't he have to start by saying I can build the pyramids, and I can beat the Philistines, and I can discover America, and I will fly?

The bluff, the gesture, is nothing but a man stretching himself and eventually, by dint of stretching, really filling out his new size, finally making his empty boast a reality.

It was bluff alone that saved Dumas' life against the Baron de B., who in seventeen duels had never failed to draw blood from his opponents, crippling one for life and putting two underground.

Once Dumas was standing behind the Baron in line to get his cloak and saw the Baron drop a copper coin into the attendant's saucer.

Dumas put down a hundred-franc bill as his tip.

"You have made a mistake, Monsieur Dumas," said the girl.

"I refuse," said Dumas out loud, "to accept the Baron de B. as a standard of what is right and what is a mistake."

The Baron responded with an immediate challenge to a duel. "Tomorrow morning at six o'clock in the Bois de Vincennes."

"I have the installments for three different serials to write in the morning," said Dumas, "and that will keep me busy until two o'clock in the afternoon, and at three I have a rehearsal at my Théâtre Historique, so between two and three is the only time I have free. Let's make it two-fifteen prompt, so I can be back in plenty of time."

Then he handed the cloakroom attendant a five-hundred franc bill. "Since I am so busy, will you do me a favor? Take the Baron's size and select a fine casket. Also place an order for a first-class funeral. Obviously, from the tip he gave, his death will be a genuine financial hardship to his heirs."

It was by pushing through with his bluff that Dumas turned the tables on the Baron, who for the first time in his life doubted his victory. "What a stupid thing," he said to himself, "if I should be killed over a matter of a few francs for a tip."

The following day he called on Dumas and the affair was settled with an apology and a handshake.

Above anything else, Dumas respected the fine gesture. He gave immortality to Morisel, who was nothing but an old wine sot dying of dropsy, because Morisel pulled off one of the supreme gestures of history.

"What is this I'm dying of?" Morisel asked Dumas.

Dumas said to him, "What? Hasn't your doctor told you?"

"Sure. He has said dropsy. But what is dropsy?"

"Dropsy—that's when your kidneys can no longer void the fluids of your body," Dumas explained.

"That too I know," said Morisel. "That is why they tapped me. And then when tapping would not drain me, they made me sweat. But still I know nothing. Imagine dying and being utterly ignorant of what is doing this to me. It's as if I had simply flunked out of life. It's a disgrace."

"What do you propose to do about it?" Dumas asked.

"Find me a surgeon who will open me up and show me exactly where the trouble lies and explain to me just exactly why. I must see it with my own two eyes. I must look my enemy straight in the face like a man."

Naturally no surgeon could be found who would do this for Morisel. "You couldn't stand an operation," they all said. "You'd be dead before we got well inside of you."

Then Morisel hit on this idea: let Dumas find him a corpse dead of dropsy.

To everyone's surprise Morisel remained alive while for a whole week the city morgue and the hospitals were searched for a man who had been killed by dropsy. As last they found one, and Morisel had Dumas buy it for the usual price of the day: six francs. Dumas also found a lecturer in surgery to do the autopsy: forty francs. The body was brought into Morisel's room and placed beside the moribund's bed. And the surgeon went to work and was able to demonstrate the situation in terms of the organs and tissues of the human body. It was an excellent *conférence*, in the best style of *l'école de médicine* of Paris: lucid, witty and at the same time profound.

"So that's it, eh?" Morisel said.

"That's it," said the physician and put aside his scalpel. "Now you know the whole story."

"It was the thought of dying in ignorance that was simply killing me," Morisel explained. "Now that I know exactly where I stand, I can expire in peace. You'll see. I'll give no more trouble. Thank you all."

Then he said to the doctor, "If you should want to repeat your lecture to your students, you may have my body."

The doctor, touched, shook his head. "One can get all the dropsy cases one wants in wine-drinking Paris."

Minutes later, Morisel was dead.

All Paris mentally doffed its hat to a man who could pull off a final gesture of such proportions. And Dumas was able to write a noble obituary for a man who otherwise would have passed on as just another name to be stricken from the registry of the living.

It was the same when an old actor named Perrinet came to him and begged him for a part. Dumas, who knew the man as the worst actor in the world, refused, but offered him twenty francs.

But this miserable actor was too proud to accept charity. "If you can't give me a part in your play, give me at least some little work, so that a man can keep his self-respect."

Dumas thought but couldn't dig up a single idea. After all, he had a dozen deadbeats always working for him as gardener, dog-keeper, fly-chaser, stagehand, walk-on—everything one can imagine.

"As a matter of fact," said Dumas suddenly, "there is a service you can do me. I'm in the midst of a story in which I must know the temperature of the Seine. See if you can't get hold of a thermometer and find out for me."

The man could and did. And Dumas gave him five francs. This was quite a fee to pay for so small a service, but Dumas figured he couldn't very well give him less.

Then to Dumas' surprise the man appeared again on the following day. "The temperature of the Seine has changed to fifty-seven degrees Fahrenheit today, Monsieur Dumas," he informed him.

Dumas handed him five francs and was on the point of saying, "Thank you, but I shan't be needing the temperature any more," when he realized that this would confront him once more with the problem of what to do with this man who refused charity and insisted on a job.

And so, every day, year after year, one might see an oldish, wispy man go to the middle of the Pont-Neuf, between the few shops that still stood on that ancient bridge, and carefully lower into the Seine a thermometer tied on a string. And afterward hurry off to find Dumas and convey to him this precious information.

All Paris saw it, and all Paris wondered how soon Dumas would grow tired of forking out five francs a day for the temperature of the Seine. But Dumas behaved with the utmost correctness. No matter where or when it might be that the former actor came to him with this information, Dumas would reach into his pocket and draw out the money.

"Sixty-two degrees, did you say?"

"Sixty-two and a half, Monsieur Dumas."

"Ah, you don't say so. Well, thank you infinitely, Monsieur Perrinet. Nothing is so important for a Parisian dramatist as to know the temperature of the Seine. There is an intimate connection between theatrical attendance and the condition of the atmosphere. You do me a great service."

And Dumas would turn to whoever was nearest him and say, "There's a man who never fails me. Never." You'd imagine he was saving Dumas' life and career each day. And once, when Dumas left town, he paid Perrinet, on his return, five francs for every temperature reading taken during his absence.

Naturally it could no longer be stopped. By this time it had become a gesture. And if Perrinet hadn't been taken one day to die at the Hôtel-Dieu, Lord only knows how long the gesture might have gone on.

For then it wasn't only Dumas who missed his faithful collaborator, all Paris missed a bit of mummery that had daily warmed one's heart and daily restored one's faith in human nature. And even strangers coming to Paris would ask their guide when they could see the man who took the Seine's temperature for Monsieur Dumas.

Dumas spoke a few words at the funeral ceremony. "Never," he said, looking around at the crowd that had followed the poor man to the grave, "never did you draw such a house while alive. Among all my collaborators you are the only one who never missed an appointment or failed to bring in your assigned share of the work. May the earth rest lightly on your bones."

Detractors of Dumas' claimed that the press of people at the funeral was nothing but a concourse of starvelings who thought that Dumas would now want someone else to take the temperature of the Seine for him, and each one hoped to be appointed to the sinecure left vacant by the death of Perrinet.

Dumas, however, with his sure theatrical instinct, realized that for Perrinet to have a successor would turn the whole business from gesture into a cheap publicity stunt, which some people had all along declared it was. These people insisted that this gesture was no different from the advertisements which Dumas kept inserting into the daily papers under the Personals. For example: "Will the gentleman who stared me out of countenance the other evening at the *Tour de Nesle* performance please be there tonight again? There will be a message for him. Signed, Heartsick."

Such little tidbits were said to pay off very well, some hundred or more Parisian gentlemen feeling themselves sufficiently deeply involved to purchase that many more tickets to Dumas' play for that evening.

CHAPTER TWELVE
Clique versus Claque

To RETURN NOW to the gesture of the flipped gold piece. Dumas went away feeling both elated by his gesture and downcast by the thought that he must now practice a double economy by skipping both dinner and theater. He had not yet learned how luck makes up to those who know how to execute a great gesture. He had scarcely walked the boulevards for ten minutes when he spied an old boyhood friend through the window of a café. It was the son of the music teacher who had tried so hard to make a violinist out of him.

Dumas rushed into the café. "Hiraux!"

"Dumas!"

And the two young men embraced each other.

"What in the world are you doing in Paris?" Dumas cried.

"Isn't it clear enough?" Hiraux retorted. "I own this café, and I'm here running it."

"This? Your café? Why, you lucky dog!"

"But you? What are you doing here?"

"I'm going to write."

"Write? What? Journalism? If so you've come to the right place. Half the journalists of Paris drop in here."

"No. I want to write plays."

"Ah, that's another story. Though most journalists try their hand at that too. But come, we must have a good talk about it all. Wait for me a moment; I'll go order a dinner for the two of us. Surely you'll dine with me?"

"With all my heart!" said Dumas.

"Well, sit down here while I take care of things. What paper do you want to read?"

"Any paper."

"You mean you don't have *your* paper yet?"

"I haven't had time to look into the matter. There are so many papers here."

"Of course, and you must get to know them. Every shade of political opinion has its paper here. This is the *Constitutionnel*, which is now the *Journal de Commerce*, because the *Constitutionnel* has been suppressed by the Censorship. And here's the *Drapeau Blanc*. And here the ultraroyalist *Foudre*, and here the *Réunion*, which has also had its censorship troubles and used to be the *Opinion*, and before that it was the *Pandore*, and before that the *Miroir*, and I don't know what before that. And here's the *Courier Français*, and here and here and here, other papers. You study them while I go order dinner."

Dumas leafed through the papers, trying to find his way into a tangled political argument over which every paper had a different story to tell and a different opinion to draw. He couldn't make head or tail of it, but he supposed that he would have to eventually since it appeared that everybody was making such a fuss about it. This too was something to learn.

After dinner Hiraux said to Dumas, "So you're going to write plays?"

"Yes."

"You'll make a fortune. That is if you write one as good as *Vampire*."

"*Vampire?*"

"You mean you don't know *Vampire?* Why, it's the sensation of Paris. No one has ever seen anything like it. Why are you sitting here talking to me when you ought to be going to the theater and learning your trade."

"Where is it playing?"

"At the Porte-Saint-Martin theater. Hurry. It's at the other end of town and there's such a line-up at the box office you'll never get in if you don't get there early."

Dumas ran more than walked, determined to be one of the earliest there. But though it was an hour before the performance was scheduled to start, he found all approaches to the theater blocked by a queue that wound itself around and around.

As he stood there chagrined at the thought that he might miss this great play he heard someone yell, "Hey! Hey you!"

Dumas turned around. "You mean me?"

"Yes, you, you with the frizzy locks and the coat down to your knees."

"What's wrong with me?" Dumas asked, bridling quickly at any aspersions to himself.

"Oh, nothing, my friend. Absolutely, totally, nothing at all. But it has given me the idea that perhaps I might be of service to you."

"In what way?"

"Do you want to see this show?"

"Yes, of course. That's why I'm here."

"I thought so. You see, right away I said to myself, There's a man who wants to see this show."

"Well, what about it?"

"Only that you will never see it if you go to the end of that line. At least five hundred people here tonight will never get into that building."

"You mean it's no use my waiting?"

"I mean I'll sell you my place." He held up two fingers. "Two francs!"

"Two francs?" Dumas exclaimed. "That's a lot of money."

"Well, you want to see this show, don't you?"

"Yes."

"Well, two francs does it."

"Where will I be sitting?" Dumas asked, for he was under the impression that the two francs the man was asking from him would entitle him to a seat inside, and not just to a position in the line-up.

"You have your choice of the whole theater," said the man in the line.

"I can sit wherever I like?" Dumas asked.

"Absolutely."

Convinced, and determined to see this sensational show that could draw such an avid crowd, Dumas paid the man two francs.

The man said, "Now, here. Stand close to me. Right up close."

"Why?" Dumas asked, puzzled.

"Because, you simpleton, if you don't the line will close up before you get a chance to slip in, and the place will be lost."

So Dumas stood close and, as the man pulled out, he pushed into his spot.

A moment later a tremor of life went through the line and it began to move. Soon Dumas stood before the box office. He wanted to move past and into the theater, but the way was barred by a man who said, "Ticket?"

"Ticket?" Dumas wondered. "No. I don't have a ticket."

"Stop holding up the line!" someone yelled in back of him.

The man behind the wicket said, "Well, aren't you buying a ticket?"

"Must I have a ticket to get in?" Dumas asked.

The people around laughed. "You think it's for free?"

"Move! Move!" the crowd yelled.

"But . . ." Dumas stuttered, "I already paid a man two francs. And he said—"

"Did he give you a ticket?"

"No!"

"Get going!" the impatient crowd shouted. "Come on! Make up your mind!"

"Give me the cheapest seat," said Dumas, feeling miserable at having already spent two francs.

"One franc for the pit," said the man behind the wicket, and Dumas paid, took his ticket and went in.

He looked around with curiosity at the theater, the huge proscenium with its fringed and embroidered curtain, the boxes to either side and the tiers of the orchestra and the gallery like gigantic shelves above. And everywhere oil lamps glittering and casting their rays of light.

Already he felt himself transported into a fabulous world of unreality.

Vampire, Vampire, he said to himself, wondering what the word meant.

And then he noticed that there were seats ahead in the pit from which one could get a closer view of the stage. Already some hundred people were sitting there, and Dumas wondered how they had gotten in, because his place in line had been about the fifteenth, and there didn't seem any way to explain how so many people could have gotten into the theater before him.

He moved up and sat among them.

"Who are you?" a man asked. "I've never seen you before."

"I'm new here," said Dumas.

"Duchard send you?" the man asked.

"Who's Duchard?"

"How did you get in?"

"I bought a ticket."

"Hey!" said the man to the others. "Here's someone who bought a ticket!"

Everyone looked at Dumas as if he were a freak.

"Is that a wig?" someone asked. "Or is that your real hair?"

"My real hair, of course," said Dumas indignantly.

"It's real!" the man screamed. "It's really real!" And everyone roared with laughter.

"What's funny?" Dumas cried, rising in his seat. "Anyone wants my address, I'll be glad to give it." He meant he was prepared for a duel. But no one took him seriously. And Dumas, standing amidst the sarcasm and the catcalls that surrounded him, grew purple with fury. Violence boiled within him.

But at that moment a tall man pushed his way toward Dumas.

"You're not a Roman," he said accusingly.

"A what?"

"Are you a Roman?" the man repeated.

"No," said Dumas. "I'm from Villers-Cotterêts."

This reply caused such a burst of guffaws that for a moment the people around him could only point at him and double up with laughter.

"I don't see anything funny," said Dumas, with a withering glare.

This only increased the laughter. "He doesn't see anything funny," people said to each other, gasping and slapping each other.

Dumas, white now with rage, let the back of his hand out against the nearest man, leaving four streaks from which the blood retreated only to return in a moment as four scarlet splotches.

"Ho-ho! A fighter!" the crowd shouted, their laughter suddenly stopping. They started to climb over the benches, piling in toward Dumas. But the tall man barred their way.

"You will please come out with me," he said politely to Dumas, but with an unmistakable ring of authority in his voice. "This thing has gone far enough."

"What have I done? I just came here to see a play."

"You have created a disturbance, Monsieur, and therefore you must leave. Now please don't drive me to the use of force, because I am inclined to believe that you will get the worst of it."

Dumas, mad as he was, could not but realize that he was outnumbered a hundred to one, so he followed the gentleman out of the pit and into the corridor and out past the ticket taker to the box office just ahead of the queue that was still filing past.

As the gentleman was about to leave him there, Dumas cried, "You mean I can't see the play?"

"Certainly. Exchange your ticket for any other seat in the house, but keep away from the pit."

"What ticket? I have no ticket."

"Your stub."

"What stub?"

"Why, the stub of your ticket, my friend."

"But I have no stub."

"In that case, Monsieur, you have no ticket. But you are at liberty to buy one at the office."

"What!" exclaimed Dumas. "I must buy still another ticket, after buying my way in twice already?"

"I'm sorry. But for an exchange of seats you will have to show either a ticket or a stub, and since I don't have any to give you, you will have to buy one. And let me give you this final piece of advice, Monsieur: never try to sit with the Romans again."

"What do you mean by that?"

"It's pretty clear, isn't it?"

"Romans? Romans? They're no more Romans than I am."

The gentleman stared at Dumas. "Are you really so green that you don't know what the claque is?"

"The claque?"

"Yes, the hired applauders."

"People are hired to applaud? What's the matter? Doesn't the public do its own applauding?"

"The hired applauders do it better," said the gentleman. "And they drown out the hissers."

And with that the gentleman left, shaking his head as if unable to comprehend such abysmal ignorance.

Dumas, furious, bought another ticket—this time for two francs fifty—in the orchestra stalls, though his mind kept adding the incredible total that this play had already cost him, and he decided that he was going to show the management what he thought of them and their play and their hired applauders by hissing the performance to its disgrace and failure.

He took his place, fuming, beside a gentleman who was calmly reading a book, and Dumas just sat there waiting for the curtain to rise so as to let loose his fury.

But the rise of the curtain startled him to the point of forgetting to hiss, for the stage was so dark that one could just see vaguely a scenery of rocks and stunted trees, and there was the sound of wind in dry leaves, and then a flash of lightning that revealed the interior of a grotto with tombstones and vaults, and after that a low growl of distant thunder threatening a storm.

Startled, then fascinated, Dumas forgot to hiss. Indeed, he was so enchanted that the only extraneous thing he noted was that his neighbor contined calmly to read his book, paying no attention to the performance. Meanwhile, on the stage, the storm gathered, and then a kind of unearthly light appeared in the grotto and one saw angels descending. The angels lifted up and set in place their great wings and then, in the most musical voices that Dumas had ever heard, they began to discuss the subject of vampires, wondering for what mysterious reason God permits such hellish monsters to inhabit the earth, to dwell in old graves and to leave their gloomy haunts at night and wander among the living, seeking a young and beautiful maiden on whom to wreak their horrible practices, sucking her blood until she gradually sickens and dies.

"Hush!" whispers one of the angels, and draws himself and his fellow celestials deep into the dark recesses of the cavern. "Here comes a vampire now." The monster, a tall and distinguished Scottish lord now appears, in a black cloak, the folds of which he manipulates like the wings of a giant bat. He moves the heavy cover from a tomb and lifts out a lovely girl clad in filmy white cerements. And as the angels in soft stage whispers inform the audience that the maiden is not really dead, but only in a deep trance due to a drug, the curtain falls on the prologue.

From the pit where the claque was there came a furious beating of calloused and highly experienced palms, along with the pounding of heels and the shouting of *bravo!* and *bravissimo!* And the audience, including Dumas, carried away by their enjoyment of the play, applauded enthusiastically. From all parts of the theater came cries of approval.

Only the gentleman beside Dumas let out a loud hiss.

This brought Dumas to his senses. He remembered that he too had intended to hiss. And at once he stopped applauding and joined his neighbor.

As if to drown them out, the vigor of the applause was doubled.

"*Chut!*" yelled the gentleman beside Dumas. And went into another hiss.

"*Chut!*" yelled Dumas. And he hissed again.

"Throw them out!" came the cry from the claque.

"Throw them out!" the cry was repeated in all parts of the house, and the fury of the hand-clapping swelled like a thunderstorm on a metal roof.

And the more the gentleman and Dumas tried to make their hisses heard, the more the audience drowned them out, until it seemed as if the applause would never stop, and Dumas grew worried lest he might have to pay a fourth time to get back into the theater.

But in the end it did die down, and the gentleman, red in the face from his exertions, turned to Dumas with an engaging crooked smile and said, "Ridiculous play, isn't it?"

"Ridiculous?" Dumas asked, genuinely shocked that this man could think for even a moment that this fascinating play was anything less than a masterpiece.

"Stupid. Silly. Vampires. Trances. Lot of rubbish, eh?"

"I found it wonderful," said Dumas with such a burst of sincerity that the gentleman was forced to believe him.

"Wonderful, eh?"

"The best thing I've seen since *Hamlet!*" Dumas declared, forgetting to add that *Hamlet* was about all he had ever seen on the stage.

"You don't say! Then why did you hiss?"

"Because that is my privilege," said Dumas stoutly. "Nobody is going to force me to applaud if I don't wish to. I defy them!"

"*Bravo*, young man. Freedom in the arts! I subscribe to that myself." And with that he returned to his book and went on reading to himself.

As for Dumas, he recalled now that his neighbor had been reading all through the prologue. Why, he hadn't given the play so much as a look. By what right, then, did he hiss? And what was he doing here in the theater at all, since all he cared to do was sit there and read his book?

Dumas' interest was provoked and he examined this strange man. He was tall and swarthy, and so slender that he seemed to have no real anatomy, just an armature of wires on which God had forgotten to sculpture a human being. And yet his face was very alive and friendly, and over his nose, which was pushed all to one side, there passed one twinkling smile after another as if the man were perpetually amusing himself with some private joke.

What book, Dumas wondered, could be so amusing and could hold this man's interest so strongly that he did not pay any attention to the spectacle on the stage? Bitten with curiosity, Dumas leaned around in his seat, twisting until he could read the imprint on the binding.

It said:

THE FRENCH PASTRY COOK
Containing recipes of all varieties
of French pastry
Together with Lenten dishes and
Sixty ways
to
Prepare eggs

"Forgive me for interrupting your reading," said Dumas politely, "but I see that you are as fond of eggs as I am."

The gentleman put a thin, transparent finger as a marker in his book and said, "On the contrary, Monsieur, there's nothing I despise more."

"But this book that you are reading, and which even made you miss the play . . ."

"Pooh! The play. But this book—that is something else. This book is one of the most valuable I have ever acquired."

"I should like to get one to give as a present to my uncle," said Dumas. "He is an abbé who once at a contest ate over a hundred eggs and would easily eat two hundred if he knew various ways of fixing them."

"My dear friend, this book is far too valuable and too rare to give as a present to an egg eater."

"Why, what's it for, then?"

"Why, to delight a bibliomaniac. I see you don't even know what a bibliomaniac is."

"No, Monsieur."

"Well, a bibliomaniac is a biped who can't afford shoes for himself or his children because he spends all his money on rare books. He himself is usually so poorly dressed that people sometimes give him pennies, thinking him a beggar. But actually there's no difficulty telling the two apart. Because a beggar washes himself at least now and then. A bibliomaniac hasn't time for such nonsense."

"I see."

"No, you don't see. You can't see, until you know that this pastry cookbook is an Elzevir, and that only eight copies are known to exist, and that this copy is the rarest of all because it has exceptionally wide margins. Now do you understand?"

"Yes, sir."

"Why do you say yes, sir, when actually you don't understand a thing. Who was Elzevir?"

"I don't know."

"There were any number of Elzevirs, cousins, nephews, sons and uncles, and they all published books in Amsterdam about two hundred years ago, and it's a study in itself just to separate one Elzevir from another."

"Yes, sir."

"Confound it, why do you say yes, sir, when you still know nothing?"

"Because now I've found out something, and I trust if I express myself politely perhaps you'll tell me more, and then I'll find out something else."

"Well, you're not so stupid at that, young man. What else do you want to know?"

"I want to know why you came to the theater if you are a bibliomaniac and didn't intend to watch the performance?"

"Why should I bother with these invisible spirits when I would much prefer to see the invisible snakes that exist in every glass of water, the invisible crocodiles that exist in every spoonful of vinegar, the invisible dolphins that play in every drop of milk?"

"What?" cried Dumas. "Crocodiles in milk and dolphins in vinegar?"

"Of course. Get yourself a solar microscope, latest model, and you can see it for yourself."

By this time the curtain had risen and the play went on and Dumas was entranced again as he shivered with fear when the vampire made secret assignations with the heroine for midnight in the cemetery, and when, amidst a volcanic eruption and a rain of fire, a further mysterious apparition displayed itself.

Dumas' neighbor calmly continued his reading until the end of the act.

"But you are missing a wonderful play," Dumas exclaimed when the curtain came down.

"Am I really?"

"You certainly are."

"I'd much prefer a play about things that really count: steam power, air balloons, piston guns, electricity, printing, gunpowder."

"Then you don't believe in vampires?"

"On the contrary, I not only believe in them, I have seen them with my own eyes."

"How so? Through a solar microscope?"

"No, face to face, in Illyria, which is the historic ground of vampires. I knew there a dead man who came every night to eat dinner with his son and his daughter-in-law, and then one evening he said, 'Now it is your turn to come and have dinner with me, beside my grave.' Then we all went to the cemetery and disinterred his body and found it pink as if in life. The heart was torn from him, swollen with fresh blood, and a flaming pitchpine torch was driven through the body. After that he never returned to trouble anyone again."

"You seem to know everything," said Dumas. "Then perhaps you can explain to me why there are people hired to applaud. I happened to sit among them and they threw me out."

"Ah, so it was you who created that disturbance down below?"

"Yes."

"Well, of course, the claque is an honored part of every theater."

"Honored? Don't you think it is ridiculous that the public should not be left to applaud or to hiss as they please?"

"My dear boy, you do not know the first thing about a claque, do you?"

"What is the first thing?"

"Why, that the claque was first established by Nero in Rome."

"Oh, is that why they are called Romans?"

"Precisely. And I'll tell you why the claque is a useful thing. Imagine some evening, when it is raining and a cold wind is blowing, that you come in to the theater. Imagine that you sit here wondering whether your feet are wet, whether you will be sneezing tomorrow, whether you wouldn't have done better to have stayed home. . . . The actors and actresses do their best, but it is a cold, damp house, and the cast cannot put its heart into its work, and the play fails not because it isn't a good play but simply because in wet tinder the best flint and steel can only fizzle out. Now do you see where the claque fits in? Do you see how they warm things up, start the ball rolling and create at first an artificial enthusiasm but which soon becomes the real thing as the audience quickly loses itself in the play, forgets the weather outside, and has a good time? You see how everyone is the better for the hired applauders? The actors and the actresses, the play itself, and of course the audience, which is an indispensable part of the theater."

"I see," said Dumas.

"No, you don't see anything yet. Because where the claque doesn't exist, there exists something worse."

"What is that?"

"The clique. Yes, it is either clique or claque in the theater, and personally I prefer the honest claque to the dishonest clique, for the clique can work against public opinion, and work to create an audience for poor taste, whereas the claque can never do anything but evoke public opinion. No claque would dare applaud a play that the public genuinely insists on hissing. Do you see?"

"Yes, I guess I begin to see," said Dumas.

"No, I am sure you don't. Because the claque too is part of the performance. A good joke on the stage is not merely good because you want to laugh but because someone starts the laugh going and the sound of this laughter is part of what makes you laugh, or laugh all the heartier. And especially if there is someone in the claque, as there always is or should be, someone who has a throat that is raw from brandy, and whose laughter sounds like an old carpet being ripped up from the floor. They call such members of the claque *rigolards* and they are paid particularly well, and the best of them are stout gentlemen who seem to be risking apoplexy by their laughter and who have the rare art of popping their buttons, which is something that always pulls down the house with gales of fresh laughter. Now perhaps you begin to understand."

"Yes, I think I do."

"But of course you don't. For you still know nothing about the women who are also members of every claque, and who play a wonderful role, especially the ones who sit scattered in the audience and at appropriate times know so well how to twist a handkerchief and catch their breath with a half-smothered gasp, and who can sniffle so gently that it is heart-rending and no woman can resist it. Do you see?"

"I am afraid to say yes," Dumas replied. "You will still deny that I see."

"Of course I will, for you still know nothing about the anti-claque."

"The anti-claque?"

"Why, most certainly. Don't you think that at a good play there should be at least one person who will hiss, so that others may shush him, and if he persists that there should be cries of 'Throw him out!' which excites everyone and makes for a play not only on the

stage but in the audience as well. The whole performance becomes
a kind of free-for-all in which there are no passive spectators, but
in which everyone participates noisily."

"Ah . . ." said Dumas.

"Ah what?"

"Ah, so it is you, the anti-clique. Now I understand why you do
not even look at the play, but just look up from your book now
and then and hiss."

"You just think you understand, my friend, but actually you still
understand nothing."

"What? Is there more?"

"There is always more to be learned, my friend. Always more."

"Well, I want to learn," said Dumas eagerly. "Because I want to
write plays myself."

"Oh, really? You aim to be a writer?"

"Yes. It is for that that I have just come to Paris."

But the conversation was interrupted again by another act. By
this time Dumas, in spite of the continued excitement of the play,
was more anxious to resume his conversation with his neighbor
than to learn about vampires. Nevertheless, the play continued to
hold him. After the curtain came down and the applause was over,
the gentleman with the crooked smile said, "So you wish to become
a writer?"

"Yes, sir."

"Have you already written something?"

"Nothing really good. No, sir."

"You are first finishing your studies, eh?"

"Well, not really. I mean, I don't know how one studies to be a
writer."

"Why, by first studying the best writers."

"I see."

"You've read Aeschylus, of course?"

"No."

"Sophocles?"

"No."

"Euripides, Seneca, Terence, Plautus, Aristophanes?"

"No, sir. None of them, I'm afraid."

"Well, what have you read?"

"I would rather hear from you what I should read," said Dumas, "than confess to you how little I have read."

"Well, then, let's proceed. After the classic playwrights, read the others: Shakespeare, Lope de Vega, Racine, Corneille, Molière, Voltaire, Beaumarchais, Schiller, Goethe. . . . Young man, what is the matter with you?"

"How do you mean, sir?" Dumas asked.

"Your lips are trembling so strangely."

"Oh, I am only repeating silently what you are saying. I want to be able to remember them all."

"Good. Above all read the three greatest works of modern times."

"Yes, sir. What are they?"

"In my opinion they are Goethe's *Wilhelm Meister*, Walter Scott's *Ivanhoe* and Irving Cooper's *Spy*."

Once more the play started, but this time Dumas scarcely paid attention, for he was busy trying to remember all the books and all the writers that he had to read.

And then the play was over and the audience filed out.

Out on the street Dumas didn't want to lose sight of his neighbor, but the latter obviously had not much interest in having the young man around him any longer.

"Good night, young man, and good luck to you," he said.

"Oh, Monsieur, I'm so grateful to you for everything you've told me. But frightened too, because with so much reading to do, I don't know if I shall ever again have time to write."

"You'll write, young man. You'll write when you're full, just as a pitcher overflows when too much has been poured into it. Fill yourself first, then you'll have time enough to pour."

"But there's so much to study: Aeschylus, Sophocles, Euripides, Aristophanes, Seneca, Terence, Plautus, Shakespeare, Lope de Vega, Racine, Corneille, Molière, Voltaire, Beaumarchais, Schiller, Goethe. . . ."

"Well, you've got a good memory at least. But of course you mustn't read only the playwrights, but also the great poets: Homer, Virgil, Dante, Tasso, Cervantes, Milton. . . ."

"Yes, sir."

"And then things are coming out all the time. For example, Latouche has just issued a volume of poems by André Chénier, of whom hitherto we knew almost nothing except that he perished thirty years ago under the guillotine, but who, from now on, will be known as one of the greatest poets of France. You must get that book and read it."

"Yes, sir."

"Well, good night."

"Just tell me one more thing, sir: are you really a member of the anti-claque? I can't believe it. And yet, without looking at the play, you hissed it. I keep asking myself, Why did you come at all?"

"Here, young man, I'll show you. See this?"

"Yes, sir."

"Well, what do you see?"

"The billboard."

"Yes, but what does it say?"

"It says: Marie Dorval and Philippe, starring in *Vampire* . . ."

"Yes, go on."

". . . a play by X."

"Ah. A play by X."

"Yes."

"Well, X—that's me. And can you imagine anything more wonderful than to sit in the audience and hiss one's own play and have people cry 'Throw him out!'? Well, it's an experience that I wish to you."

And the man walked across the street and got into a cab, leaving Dumas there gasping.

Yes, that was the luck of the man, for he was soon to know that this man whom he had met on his very first night in the theater of Paris was the leader of the new era in literature, the Romantic movement, Charles Nodier, soon to be appointed librarian of the Arsenal Collection of Paris, and there to have for his use sumptuous rooms where he would live and hold a weekly salon of literary figures, to which Dumas himself would eventually be invited.

What other writer coming to the capital city of his country would bump into the most important literary figure * of the day on his

---

* Nodier wrote many charming tales, still readable, and in addition some fantastic histories. His *Memoirs* are largely invention, his *History of the Secret Societies in Napoleon's Army* is largely fiction. His tale of his imprisonment under Napoleon and the frightful tortures to which he was subjected is utterly false.

first night? Such things happen only once in a thousand years.

Home, finally, late at night, in his barren little room, with only that lordly combination writing desk and night table, he laid himself down in his alcove, with his rolled-up coat for a pillow, and couldn't sleep.

And didn't want to sleep either.

He thought of General Foy asking him, "Do you know law? Do you know languages? Do you know mathematics?"

He thought of Hiraux in the café saying, "What? You don't know what paper you want to read?"

He thought of X in the theater saying, "Aeschylus, Euripides, Sophocles . . ."

Would he ever be able to talk like X, saying again and again, "No, you don't see, because . . ."

How filled one's mind must be with knowledge to be able to talk in learned essays. He must do that someday.

Tomorrow he would start to read and he wouldn't stop, he'd never stop, until he was so full that he would pour out like a pitcher. And then one day he would be in the theater while they were giving a play advertised as by X, and he, Dumas, in a box, would sit there and hiss, and the public would yell, "Throw him out!" And then the word would be whispered around: "Why, that's Dumas. He wrote the play. He's Monsieur X."

And everyone would laugh and applaud.

No, he couldn't sleep. He had to get up from the floor and walk up and down like a tiger in a cage.

He looked out of his window and saw the silent courtyard and the roofs and chimney pots. And in the silence, the silence of those dark, far-off days when cities at night were silent with a city-silence that is gone forever from the world, he listened to the soft whisper of the night wind. He felt that he had no need of sleep, that he would never sleep again. He was absolutely on fire.

Yes, he could feel himself burning, with a cold flame, and stretching out his hands before his eyes, they seemed to glow in the darkness, every finger haloed with a faint white mist.

He could feel an aureole of vague light spilling around his head. . . .

From that night on he felt himself a different person. An elect.

A favorite of fate. And the next day when he went to work he felt that his trancelike condition continued. The glow was always there with him. He knew it was, at the same time that he knew that no one could see it but himself.

When the office manager Monsieur de Broval ordered him to copy a letter, he obeyed, wrote swiftly, accurately, but all the while his mind was elsewhere, repeating the list of books he must read: Goethe's *Wilhelm Meister,* Scott's *Ivanhoe,* Cooper's *Spy.*

Monsieur de Broval looked at the copy and approved. "Excellent," he said. "Now fold it."

And Dumas started to fold it.

"What are you doing!" Monsieur de Broval cried. "Don't you know that envelopes for kings and princes must be folded in squares?"

"I'll remember that," Dumas promised, and he picked up a pair of shears so as to trim his page and be able to fold it square.

"Stop!" cried Monsieur de Broval. "Don't you know that a letter to a man of dignity should never show the marks of a scissor, that good paper must never be cut, only torn?"

"I'll remember that," Dumas promised, and proceeded to tear the heavy Montgolfier paper.

"Almost square envelopes are for letters addressed to ministers and ambassadors. Letters folded oblong are for chief assistants, inspectors, subheads of departments. Those below receive letters folded English style."

"I'll remember, I'll remember, I'll remember," Dumas promised.

And he did indeed remember. He became one of the best copyists in the office of the Duke of Orléans. His work was faultless and his writing clear as copperplate engraving. And yet all the while he was asleep. Or, rather, in a trance, working away with eyes and hands and some sort of automatic brain, so that all the while his real mind could go over the books he had read, could memorize a thousand scenes from plays, could remember ten thousand lines of poetry, keep in mind a hundred thousand details from history, science, art, until in his speech and his writing he never failed for an apt illustration.

Discussing one day the work of the Frenchman Ducis, who claimed to have "perfected" Shakespeare by eliminating the gross-ness in the same way that the Englishman Bowdler did, Dumas said, "In Rome, until Pope Gregory forbade it, there were doctors who had a sign on their door: 'Boys Perfected Here.' The sign meant that here a boy, with a twist of the wrist, could be made into a soprano for the Papal choir. Ducis and Bowdler have similarly 'perfected' Shakespeare."

So Dumas copied the Duke's correspondence and studied at the same time.

Next to him, at the same desk, worked a man named Lassagne, who had developed a fondness for the old chroniclers of French history—Joinville, Froissart, Monstrelet, Châtelain, Montluc, Saint-Simon.

Dumas added their books to the list of Nodier. He bought the newspapers and studied them, and went to see every show he could. His room bulged with reading material. He had twenty-four hours a day, and no need for sleep. The trance in which he copied letters, folding them into squares for princes, almost squares for ambassadors, oblongs for inspectors, English style for lesser officials, was in itself a kind of sleep whenever he wanted it to be so.

And as he went through the day, he felt the glow that wrapped itself around him, giving him poise, letting him march with sure steps forward into his life.

Daily he grew more certain of his power. He could feel it in his hands. And once when his fellow clerk Lassagne had to take his little daughter to the dentist and the little girl was howling with fear, Dumas passed his hands gently over her face. "The dentist won't hurt you a bit," he said to her.

And when she came back she said proudly, "It didn't hurt at all."

Some years later he was to run across the writings of Puységur and learn about Mesmer, and he would suddenly realize that everything they talked about he had discovered long ago in himself. The only thing he didn't know was that it had a name. It was called "magnetic" or "odylic," later "hypnotic" power.

Yes, talk about luck!

The man had everything.

CHAPTER THIRTEEN

"... A Prince of Wales Was Born to Me"

WHEN DID THIS MAN ever have time for love?

As a reader he was an abyss that engulfed whole libraries. As a writer he became a tidal wave that threatened continents.

"*Cacoethes scribendi!*" an American critic exclaimed in the *North American Review*, after Dumas had published his hundredth title. Dumas' art, so he implied, was actually nothing but a disease: the *writing itch!* Incurable!

"*Furia francese!*" screamed an Italian critic when not just one but half a dozen translators were busy at the same time turning Dumas into Italian, applying thus to Dumas the expression coined by Machiavelli to describe the maniacal impetuosity of the French soldiers at the battle of Fornovo.

But epithets never stopped Dumas. Like Mozart, from whose pen flowed a never-ending stream of concertos, arias, quartets, symphonies, operas, Dumas too claimed that his mind went on all the time whether he was asleep or awake, and that the business of producing a book with him was mostly a matter of copying down what already existed in pretty much of a finished state in his head.

Penniless in 1851, after years of unexampled profligacy, and threatened by a horde of creditors, Dumas escaped debtor's prison by going to Brussels.

"What do I owe?" he asked his money man Hirschler.

"Close to a million," said Hirschler in disgust.

"Pooh!" exclaimed Dumas. "What's a million words? I'll do it in less than a year."

"I didn't say a million words!" Hirschler burst out in fury. "I said a million. Do you understand? A million! And when I say a million I mean a million francs. Money. Not words!"

"And I still say what's the difference?" said Dumas, shrugging. "All right, so it's not a million words I must write, but three or four million. But it's still the same thing."

"No, it's not the same thing!" Hirschler declared. "Will you never learn that a hundred francs can be invested and will return two or three or four or five francs a year? For all eternity! And the capital will always be there? Forever! Can you do that with words? Can you invest a hundred words and get back four shiny new words every year in interest and still have your old hundred words just as good as new? No. In fact, your hundred words will be yours for only a few years and then they fall into the public domain. So much for words!" And he snapped his fingers.

"And a good thing for humanity," said Dumas, "that words are not property. How could the world ever pay the debt it owes to its poets if it had to pay interest every year for the use of the words of Moses, Homer, Virgil, Shakespeare and their heirs? It's hard enough to keep paying the landlords forever without expecting the people to pay their artists forever. Imagine paying again and again for the Ten Commandments and for Hamlet's Soliloquy? And yet who would not rather be homeless than without the shelter of such creations?"

Hirschler fumed at such unrealistic talk. But the question is: what is "real." Dumas thought people who were concerned about rents, interest, profit rates, were groping about in fog of confusion and fantasy. He felt like Balzac, who once interrupted a discussion on politics and politicians by saying, "Let's talk about serious matters. What did you think of my *Eugénie Grandet*? What about Felix de Vandenesse's proposal to Mademoiselle de Grandville?"

The characters in his books had to Balzac more reality than those in life. And was he so wrong? Is not Père Goriot a thousand times more alive today than Louis Philippe's minister of marine whose name you don't even know and, being told, will promptly forget?

All right. So one owed a million francs.

To work then!

Dumas rented himself a little palace on Waterloo Boulevard in Brussels and sat down in a garret room and wrote. Downstairs every evening, amidst the remnants of his Delacroix paintings and his Barye bronzes, and his enamel candelabras holding fifty wax tapers each, he gave balls and concerts, entertained now the exiled Victor Hugo and other political refugees, and now a troupe of dancing girls. . . .

And the volumes poured out of him. Novels, stories, plays. But in particular this was the period of his *Memoirs*.

These *Memoirs*, totaling well over a million words, scarcely take him beyond the opening successes of his career. And it is in them, on page 1062 (Volume III, page 54 of the English edition), that Dumas speaks of the birth of his son, which occurred in that yellow-papered garret in Paris, where he had discovered, on the other side of the landing, a soft voice and a dimpled hand. . . .

He writes in his *Memoirs*: ". . . a Prince of Wales was born to me. . . ."

That's all. Eight words. Not even the whole sentence.

Eight words for his first-born.

Where is reality? Where is the *furia francese*? Where the *cacoethes scribendi*?

Eight words. And not so much as one word about the mother either here or before or later. As much as to say: mother unknown.

What had happened suddenly to this cataract of words? Is this not the same man who will, at the age of sixty-eight, write to his publisher Lemerre (one of his army of publishers!): "After more than five hundred volumes—I stopped counting them a long time ago—I want to close my literary career with a book on cooking. . . ."

And what a monster of a cookbook he produced! Eleven hundred pages, with no less than eight pages devoted to the subject of mustard alone, exhausting it down to the detail of the necessity of preparing different mustards for men and for women.

To illustrate what a *haute cuisine* really is, Dumas will tell you about the duties of just one of the many personages involved in the maintenance of the *cuisine de luxe* at the court of Louis XVIII.

Monsieur Petit-Radel, for example, in addition to superintending the library of the Institute of France, selected peaches for the palace.

No jeweler could have brought to the appraisal of a diamond more care than Monsieur Petit-Radel lavished on a peach, rating it according to color and aroma first, then according to the savor and the creaminess of the juice, and finally according to the flavor and firmness of the flesh. For, to Monsieur Petit-Radel, the relishing of a peach was an experience involving the sum total of a sensitive man's ability to enjoy.

And this had to be so. Because at the table of Louis XVIII, a peach met some pretty heavy competition. For example, grilled chops. Have you any idea how grilled chops were prepared for the Bourbon palate? Three chops placed together and grilled as if one and then served as one. It was the guest at the King's table who himself separated the three chops and, discarding the two outer ones as mere husks, directed his attention only to the tender center chop into which all the rich juices of the outer chops had been driven by the heat of grilling, while itself at the same time escaping the rough touch of the flame.

With that kind of competition a peach had to rub its eyes open early in the morning. And no wonder that when Monsieur Petit-Radel brought his peaches to the King's table, his hands trembled, his eyes were filled with tears, as he waited for a word of praise to drop from the heavy Bourbon jaw.

That's the kind of cookbook it is: you almost want to eat the pages when you read it. Your lips drool, your mind is lost in a haze of exotic and exciting flavors and odors. Nothing, indeed, seems lacking to make this book the masterpiece of the romantic era of literature, nothing but a heavier charge of sex.

But everything else: geography, history, art, science—all appear, contemplated through the taste buds of man. Here is Louis XVI, fat and phlegmatic, more concerned with his belly than with his life, sitting through the debates of the revolutionary convention, his greasy hands tearing apart a roasted fowl, his gluttonous mouth chewing evenly, while polemics crackle around him and eventually force that monarchical head beneath the blade of the guillotine.

Here is Lucullus of Imperial Rome, budgeting his cook to the expenditure of a thousand dollars per guest per dinner, and his anger exploding when once he dines alone and discovers that his cook has spent less than the stipulated amount.

"But since you were eating alone," the cook excuses himself.

"Alone?" expostulates Lucullus. "But it is precisely when I'm what you call alone that the dinner must be extra choice. For it is then that Lucullus is the guest of Lucullus!"

Here are Talleyrand and Mr. Hahnemann the homeopath, and Louis XIV and almost anyone you can think of. For never did Dumas forget the lesson that Charles Nodier gave him in the theater, the lecture on the claque: read, read, read, fill yourself and then pour.

And he poured. He became a cataract of words. Wherever he went, out came the articles, the plays, the books.

Once, for example, during a hunt, Dumas, complaining of lassitude, shot one more partridge and then excused himself from his friends and went back to the inn and sat down in an easy chair before the fire.

There his friends found him still asleep when they returned from the hunt.

When he awoke they asked him, "Did you have a good sleep?"

"Just a cat nap really," Dumas said, yawning and stretching himself. "First wrote a one-act comedy." And he pulled the pages out of his pocket.

Were there any circumstances in which this man found it impossible to write? Why, he wrote travel books not only when he traveled, he wrote them even when he didn't travel. For example, he planned a trip to the Near East, but never got there. Do you imagine for one moment that the book about that trip was therefore not written? Then you don't know Alexandre Dumas!

The book appeared in Paris under the title *Fifteen Days to Mount Sinai*. London published it as *Traveling Sketches in Egypt and Mount Sinai* in a translation prepared by "a Biblical Student"; and New York saw it in a new translation under the title *Impressions of Travel in Egypt and Arabia Petraea*.

And it was a success! For years every tourist to the Near East wanted to repeat Dumas' exciting climb of the Pyramids and his amusing swim in the Nile. Even the Khedive of Egypt wrote to Dumas: "Egyptians themselves did not know the attraction of their own country until you visited us and opened our eyes."

Dumas never set foot in Egypt in all his life!

No, it's impossible to imagine a situation in which Dumas couldn't write.

In 1832, for example, he got involved in republican demonstrations against his former boss, the Duke of Orléans, who had meanwhile made himself King of France; and at the disastrous antiroyalist riots at the Cloister of Saint-Merri Dumas was almost killed.

Just how close an escape it was is shown by the report the newspapers carried the following morning: "Among the insurrectionists trapped at the Cloister was the recently successful playwright Alexandre Dumas. Along with the other prisoners he was tried by summary courtmartial and immediately executed by firing squad. Relatives may claim the bodies of the victims at the morgue this afternoon."

It was the day of his weekly dinner at the literary salon of Charles Nodier, of which he was by then a respected and beloved member. Dumas hastily penned Nodier a note: "Assure you my appetite unaffected by recent execution."

But that he didn't feel as cocky as his note is shown by the fact that he ran at once to Gosselin, one of his publishers. "I've got to get out of France! As soon as possible. And I'm broke. For four thousand francs I'll do you a book on Switzerland."

Gosselin said, "Your execution doesn't seem to have affected your need for money, but it has certainly damaged your brains. Books on Switzerland are a dime a dozen. Everybody and his aunt has done a book on Switzerland. The whole subject is passé. I'm convinced that people will soon give Switzerland back to her cows."

"There is certainly one book on Switzerland that no one has written so far," Dumas argued.

"What book is that?"

"A book about Dumas in Switzerland."

Dumas was right, but Gosselin couldn't see it. So it was not Gosselin, but another publisher, namely Dumont, who made his fortune out of what was to be for fifty years the most reprinted guidebook for Switzerland, a book in which the biggest piece of Swiss mountain scenery is undoubtedly Dumas himself.

Dumas toured Switzerland on foot, which is, of course, still the only way to tour a country. He learned to love the Swiss people and to hate the Swiss landlords. He conspued the beds of the inns in which for a man of his size the night was a long struggle between shoulders and toes as to which should have possession of the short sheet and the still shorter cover. He hated especially the four-franc *table d'hôte* dinners, where simple equity compelled him to eat a double portion of each food so that his meal should end up costing him only the two francs it was worth, although he was forced to admit that he was still four francs out of pocket, while his belly, stuffed with unsatisfactory food, was even worse off.

Tramping from Bex, he came to the Stagecoach Inn of the town of Martigny and there got less bed and less food than usual. This landlord he really hated!

But that's not how he wrote it up in his book. In his book the affair goes this way:

"Monsieur!" cries the genial innkeeper. "Welcome! You have arrived at a lucky moment!"

"How so?"

"Bear!" the innkeeper exclaimed, throwing wide his arms.

"Bear? Where?"

"In the kitchen! Where else? We are serving bearsteak today."

"Is that such a wonderful thing?"

"What? You don't know bearsteak? Bearsteak with butter sauce?"

"Never had it."

"Then, Monsieur, you are in for a treat. That is if Monsieur will dine *à la carte* instead of at the *table d'hôte*."

Dumas hesitated. Bears, for him, had always been cunning creatures, all roly-poly with fur, who, with a chain fastened to the nose, danced with charming clumsiness to the violin of a wandering musician.

Still, the idea of bearsteak with butter sauce was tempting and Dumas agreed to dine *à la carte*, as expensive as that would be.

A short while later the bearsteak appeared preceded by an odor that was divine and capable of overcoming all childhood scruples.

The innkeeper hovered over Dumas' table, while his guest cut up the tender meat.

Dumas paused with the first bite caught on his fork. "So this is really bear, Monsieur?"

"My word of honor!" said the innkeeper.

Dumas dipped the piece in the sauce and then popped it into his mouth.

"Hm! Why it's excellent!" he cried.

"What did I tell you, Monsieur?" said the innkeeper.

Dumas went to work on his steak, relishing each morsel with ohs! and ahs!

"Must have been quite a beast," said Dumas respectfully as he noted the size of the cut.

"Indeed, sir. Seven hundred and sixty pounds. A monster bear."

"You killed him yourself?"

"Ah, no, Monsieur. Not bear. That's for real hunters. Not for me."

"Put up a fight, did he?"

"You can imagine, Monsieur. Those beasts can rage! They are really dangerous."

"You don't say?"

"Would you care to know about this one?"

"Most certainly," said Dumas, continuing his advance into his steak.

"Well, this animal was stealing the pears from the orchard of a local farmer, a man named Mona. And this farmer asked one of his friends to stay up with him one night and ambush the animal. Which they did. But the size of the pear-eating monster upset them, and their two shots failed to kill it. Wounded, the enraged animal turned upon its attackers. The men used their guns as clubs. Then they ran. The owner of the orchard stumbled and fell. The other escaped, screaming desperately for help."

Dumas had regretfully reached the final segment of his meat, and cut it into halves to make two morsels of it and thus make it last longer. He picked up one in his fork and wiped it through the remaining butter sauce.

"What happened then?" he asked, putting the piece in his mouth.

"He came back with help and the brute was soon finished off."

"Yes. And then?"

"And then what, sir?"

"Why—the other hunter. The one who fell. The one protecting his pears."

"Oh. I'm afraid there wasn't much left of him."

Dumas was just wiping the last bit of butter sauce on the last piece of steak. "You mean . . . "

The innkeeper sighed. "A hungry bear, that's a mean customer. They'll devour anything. There wasn't enough left to make a burial."

Dumas suddenly felt no appetite for the final bite. He pushed it around for a moment on the plate and then laid his fork down.

"Monsieur is finished?"

"Yes, thank you," said Dumas. "I believe I've had enough."

"Wasn't I right? Nothing quite like bearsteak?"

"Absolutely," said Dumas.

"Since Monsieur enjoyed the steak, I'm sure he'll want to do his bit for the widow. The other hunters have turned over to her the total of the state bounty for each bear killed—namely, eighty francs —but we are also opening a subscription for her. If you would care to sign this paper and make some contribution, however slight . . ."

"I can do better than that," said Dumas, rising on unsteady legs. "I'll give her back her husband. . . !" And he ran hastily from the table.

From the moment this story appeared, first in the *Revue des Deux Mondes*, and then in book form, often reprinted and widely translated, the Stagecoach Inn of Martigny began to be besieged by tourists determined that they too must have the experience of eating a bearsteak.

"Bearsteak!" the innkeeper would moan.

"Yes, like the one you served to Alexandre Dumas."

"That Dumas! I'll have the law on him! Telling people that I served a bear that had eaten a human being!"

"Oh, but we don't insist on a bear that has fed on human flesh. Just bearsteak with butter sauce."

"But I tell you I have no bear! I never had bear! I never served Dumas any bear! And what's more I never will serve any bear in this inn!"

But still the tourists flocked to Martigny, and there were some heavily trafficked days when the innkeeper had to post himself in the yard of his inn and simply wave the people away. "No bear. No, no, no! Go on! Go on!" And he would tear his hair in his rage. "If ever that Dumas dares to show his face in Martigny again, I'll have him arrested. I'll sue him for every cent he has!"

Dumas finally had to admit that he had imagined the whole scene, simply to make something out of one of the dullest evenings he had ever spent in any inn of Switzerland, and one of the worst *tables d'hôte* he had ever sat down to. Just as Victor Hugo had to write his poem to the Hotel of Bedbugs, scratching it on the wall of an inn in Bray, because the little creatures had kept him up all night. And Carle Vernet, who was a *trompe-l'oeil* painter of great ability, painted a startlingly deceptive turd on the floor of an inn where he had passed a smelly night.

"What is a man of talent to do when he encounters human stupidity, filth and cheating?" Dumas asked. "Besides, a bear had indeed been killed in Martigny only the day before my arrival. And had mine host been a smart innkeeper he would have been only too delighted to have had the opportunity of offering his guests something exciting in the way of food. What right has a man to build a hotel, to set it down on the highway, luring in travelers, if he does not intend to offer them real hospitality? Besides, you know, if the man weren't so confoundedly limited, my little revenge on him could have been turned to his advantage. It was only up to him to have himself the most famous inn of Switzerland. All that was needed was for him to buy up the bear of the whole region, or even to have imported them from the swamps and forests of Poland, and people would have come to him from all over the world to eat his bearsteak with butter sauce. But no, instead of making himself a fortune he prefers to keep on running a miserable inn and have the satisfaction of calling me a liar."

No, no, Dumas didn't have to travel in order to write. And when he traveled, he didn't necessarily have to have adventures. Didn't he have his perpetually active mind as a substitute for reality wherever reality failed him? No, there was nothing that could stop that pen of his from racing on and being forever exciting, amusing, instructive and, if not always truthful, at any rate always truthlike.

Nothing, apparently, but the birth of his son.

What could possibly have happened in that garret on the Place des Italiens between that ardent giant and that woman with the soft voice and the dimpled hand?

The father said nothing except: ". . . a Prince of Wales was born to me. . . ." And the son, when grown and become famous as Alexandre Dumas *fils*, also said nothing. And when his mother passed away and was found to have left a diary which she had kept religiously all her life, the son made a little bonfire of it.

CHAPTER FOURTEEN

Birth—Adulterous

AND YET LIFE IS never completely destroyed. Even in the shifting sands of the Sahara desert, seen from an airplane, one can still spot geometric depressions arranged in quincunxes, where grew the trees of Carthaginian orchards two thousand years ago. For him who looks there is always a hint here and a hint there.

So serious a work, for example, as Professor Hippolyte Parigot's study of the dramas of Alexandre Dumas *père* contains flashes of material on the man's love life that will be found nowhere else.

We are in the middle of the nineteenth century, when, if ever, Paris confirmed her reputation as the sex capital of man. In that century of peace from Waterloo to World War I, victories, if any, had to be achieved in the boudoir for lack of any other field of battle.

All through the civilized world people stood aghast at the spectacle of pleasure-mad Paris. Nowhere else was the carnival season so dissolute. Nowhere else did the whole population seemingly go mad night after night, erupting from their homes at the stroke of twelve, dressed in fantastic costumes, or more often in a fantastic lack of costume, and, masked or unmasked, go singing and dancing through the streets, beating one another with blown-up pig bladders, shouting gay indecencies, and generally carrying on, until the morning sent them home in a state bordering on paroxysms.

It was an age of sexual scramble. Thirty thousand excess females in the city of Paris threw all previously accepted valuations of chastity, virginity, adultery, into question. And a flood of moneyed tourists, determined, no matter what the cost, to do in Paris what they couldn't do at home, contributed to the chaos. Nowhere else but in Paris could a magazine print a picture of a man drawing his pistol on another man while a woman throws herself before him clasping his knees, begging: "Have mercy on the father of your children."

In what other city would a dance orchestra dare introduce an anchor chain as one of its musical instruments, obvious though it be that nothing else in the world can make the precise startling and stimulating sound of an anchor chain? In what other city did composers of dance music vie with each other in setting off firecrackers or shooting off pistols? A form of orchestral competition that was to lead finally to Musard's discharging a mortar during his musical performances at the Opéra balls.

And then one evening Musard had the inspiration to hire a musician whose sole instrument was a chair. Yes, a chair that this gifted instrumentalist proceeded to raise high overhead and bring down with all his might again and again and again with insane deliberation until he had smashed it to splinters. Whereupon he grabbed up a fresh chair.

The crowd howled with delight. They stamped and kicked their legs into the air. They went into a delirium when Musard thus unveiled his "*contredanse* of the smashed chair." They mobbed the orchestra and carried off the conductor in triumph.

And then, when Alton-Shee, a peer of France, combined the frenzy of the *gallopade* and the madness of the *chahut* and achieved the indescribable cancan, pandemonium was reached: it was the deluge, the witches' sabbath, the feast of Belshazzar, the reign of Gog and Magog, when a couple of thousand screaming dancers launched themselves into the dissolute gymnastics of the cancan. Then the whole world pointed to Paris and cried, "Babylon! The whore of Babylon!" and entire populations waited with bated breath for a tongue of fire to come licking down from Heaven and consume this den of inquity.

The whole length of the Boulevard du Temple was given over nightly to amusement, to puppet theaters, to pantomime theaters, to intimate theaters, to circuses—all competing for the small silver of the average Parisian, while outside in the open air a horde of clowns, acrobats, tightrope artists, singers of popular songs, vendors of patent medicines, operators of popinjay trees and shooting galleries heightened the competition by appealing for the pennies of the poor.

Among the most popular of the sports of the period was that of the greased pole, the mast of Cockaigne, mythical land of plenty, which was supposedly reached only from the top of this slippery device.

What a sight, of an evening, amidst the feeble orange glow of whale-oil lamps and gas jets, to follow the contortions and maniacal struggles of a contestant, half naked, shiny with sweat and grease, as he would make his way up this lubricated pole to bring down the laurel wreath from the top, a laurel wreath that entitled him to the prize of a gold louis!

To watch the poor man squeezing his ribs and even calling upon his chin to help maintain the height he had managed to reach, and especially to follow his hysterical efforts to hold his position with only one arm, so that with the free hand he might reach into the sack of ashes which he carried tied to his middle, and with which he hoped to win for himself another boost upward—this spectacle held such a fascination for Parisians of this time that nowhere else did pickpockets do a better business than among the lovers of this sport. For them it was indeed the land of Cockaigne.

And the barker would shout his comments and encouragements, some of which came perilously close to wounding good taste, for it was altogether too easy to draw curious parallels: "Come on, young man! Only ten foot more to the laurel wreath. Don't disappoint us now. Is it encouragement you're waiting for? Very well, ladies and gentlemen, let's give the man the music. Let's add to the prize money. There's no melody like coins falling into the brass bowl. Let it sing!"

And from the crowd would come yells of advice and ribaldry. "Come on down, Gustave. I'll show you a different kind of climbing that's more fun and less work!"

And another would shout, "Use your head! Wipe the grease away with your hair!"

And still another, "There's a knothole to your right. No. Up a little higher. Crook your finger into that."

What a moment of drama it was when an exhausted climber could go no farther and all his multiplied efforts only made him lose height instead of gaining it. What a sight when a man, bringing into use not only his fingernails but even his cheek and his nose, still could not stop the downward slide that pushed the nasty tallow right up into his nostrils. How his muscles writhed in this futile combat against the steady pull of lubricated gravity!

And then the tragic heap a man made when, covered with a

mass of white grease and black ashes, he lay gasping at the foot of the pole. Never did a man look more defeated. Nothing was so symbolic of death putting an end to all of man's mounting ambitions and his overriding hopes than this final plunge earthward after all his expenditure of effort. Here was life perpetually slaying man's perpetual dreams of success.

But the barker wasted no time. "Who's next?" he would cry at once, shaking the bowl of contributed coins. "Our prize is getting bigger all the time! Up there is a louis of gold and down here this bowlful of money. Take one, take all! Come on, ladies and gentlemen! Prove to yourself that you have the strength and the courage to make a success of your life!"

And if no contestant appeared, he would change his tune a bit, taunting the people, declaring that the pole was easily climbed. "Come on, Jeannot! Show the public how easy it is to get to the top of the mast of Cockaigne!"

And without another word, Jeannot, his assistant, would smear his hands with ashes and leap up. His muscles under his tattooed skin would swell like boa constrictors as he climbed up as easily as a monkey.

"Ah, here we have a contestant. That is if this young lady will kindly release him. Mademoiselle, you should encourage your friend, not try to stop him. Young man, with your height you won't have far to climb."

The crowd cheered the tall, young, bushy-haired man as he quickly paid his franc and then pulled off his boots and socks. He then bared his torso and finally rolled up his trousers into two tight rings just beneath his groin. He was swarthy and powerfully built, and the girls went "Oooh!"

The attendant tied the sack of ashes around his middle.

And the barker cried, "Here's a man who is determined to reach the land of Cockaigne. Up there it lies, at the top of the greased pole, the land where the cocks lay golden eggs and the houses are built of sugar, where the streets are paved with blocks of cheese, the gutter runs nothing but wine, and the buttered geese fall roasted and ready to eat from the sky, with knife and fork already stuck in them."

"There he goes!"

"Look at that man climb!"

"Come on, ladies and gentlemen, let's hear the ring of your contributions."

"He's slowing down. He's slipping!"

"Ah, yes, ladies and gentlemen, it's easy enough when you start life. But as you go on, it becomes more and more difficult. That pole is thirty-five feet high. Calculate every foot of it to equal two years of life, and we see that our contestant is now fifteen feet up and therefore thirty years old. And now he's climbed five more feet and he's forty years old. And his strength is going fast!"

Indeed, the contestant had started to slip and was holding on now with an effort that involved every part of his body, even his eyelashes. Tallow got mixed into his dark, frizzy hair.

"You see how old he's getting," the barker shouted. "His hair has already turned gray."

For a while the young man flailed about like the previous contestant, trying every means of keeping his hold and exhausting himself in maneuvers. But finally he managed to bring ashes between the inside of his thighs and the pole and suddenly realized that by this trick he could hold on best and at the same time prepare for his thighs a new plaster of ashes further up.

"Ah, there's a man with talent!" the barker shouted.

But the plaster of ashes didn't always hold. Down below, previous climbers had worn off much of the grease, but here, up high, so few climbers had come that the grease lay thick on the wood and no amount of ashes would hold. And the climber began to slip. But what a struggle he put up! How he fought that tallow and the soap, until he brought his ribs against the wood with such desperate strength that he stopped sliding and held tight.

The crowd was silent. High up on the mast the climber was motionless, stuck there like a fly to a ceiling, his arms and his legs wrapped for dear life around the pole, and the only thing that moved was his torso, pumping air as visibly as a pair of bellows, and so loud that in the silence one could hear the wind whistling through the passages to his lungs.

No one dared move. No one dared say a word. The only other noise in the crowd was the soft sobbing of a woman who stared up with tears running down her cheeks.

Then suddenly the fly moved. It was almost as if he had gathered himself for a leap upward and had just been waiting for the tiredness to drain out of his muscles. His fingers just managed to crook around the wreath of laurel on top, and then his body started to slither down, slowly pushing a growing mound of foul grease, soap and ashes ahead of him.

"I won!" he cried.

"A victor!" The manager took the crown of laurel leaves and placed it on the mop of hair.

"Here's your gold louis. And here's the bowl of coins contributed by the generous public of Paris, always quick to salute and reward effort and ability."

The crowd applauded, and the young man said, "I don't know where to put the money. Catherine! Hold out your shawl and let Monsieur empty his bowl into it."

"What is your name, young man?"

"Alexandre Dumas."

"Ladies and gentlemen! I present to you a future hero of France: Alexandre Dumas, who will someday be richer than Lafitte and Rothschild."

With that he dismissed the winner and went back to business. His assistant gave the pole a new mopping of tallow and soap, and a new wreath of laurel leaves was placed on top. And the barker held up before the crowd another golden louis which was to be the prize for the next contestant. And Alexandre moved away with his pretty blonde companion.

"What a crazy, stupid, insane idea: to climb a greased pole!" she shouted at him.

"But I won! I won!"

"Good, so you won! And now what? You can't even put on your clothes, you're that filthy."

"I won! I showed them I could do it!"

"Just look at you! Smeared black and white, and smelling to high heaven of the foulest grease."

"What do I care? As long as you're beside me, and you smell like a garden of flowers, and you look like an angel."

"Don't touch me! Keep away from my dress with your greasy hands."

"I'm not going to touch you. I'm just making a gesture. A gesture of love."

"Well, make your gestures in the other direction. And don't walk so close. Imagine being seen with a man who looks as if he had just escaped from Charenton."

"You're not going to abandon me, are you?"

"No. Don't worry. I'll see you home."

"Then you love me. Now at last I have the proof."

"I don't love you at all. I just pity you."

"Then I must be satisfied to be pitied. It's still something. All I'm afraid of is indifference."

"I'd do as much for a dog."

"Good. Then I'll be your dog." And he fell on all fours and trotted behind her, barking.

"Stop it!" she cried. "Stop it!"

"Promise to wash me when we get home!"

"Wash you! You're mad!"

"But in your room you have a stove and a kettle and you can make hot water. I can't."

"Very well, I'll make you hot water. Only stop being a dog, for the love of Heaven!"

"You'll iron my trousers, when I've washed them?"

"Very well, I'll press your trousers."

"I knew you wouldn't abandon me completely. And what are you going to do with all that money?"

"What money?"

"The money you won. Because I certainly didn't climb that pole for myself."

"Do you think I need money that badly?"

"Then let me buy you a present."

"Better buy yourself another pair of trousers."

"Say what you please. But now at last I shall see the inside of your room."

"What makes you think that?"

"Why, to wash myself."

"Nothing of the sort. I shall heat the water and put it outside for you."

"You mean I got myself dirty all for nothing?"

"So it was just another trick? Like your scratching and miaouing the other night thinking I'd open up for a poor kitten."

"Why won't you let me into your room? I just want to see how you live. I just want to breathe the air you breathe. I promise to behave myself."

"Oh, sure. Like the last time we went dancing when you promised not to try to kiss me."

"But I wasn't trying to kiss you."

"Then what was it you were trying to do? Eat me?"

"I just wanted to have my face close to yours."

"You certainly did. So much so that I thought I was going to suffocate. I couldn't breathe. That's how you keep your promises. A person is a fool ever to believe a single word of yours."

"Oh, that's not fair. What do you know of the struggle I put up inside myself. Have you any notion of what it means to see you day in and day out and not—and not squeeze you to death in my arms? You don't have to see yourself. How lucky you are. You have no idea of the powerful impression you make upon a person. It's all very well for you to talk of promises . . . but it's I who has to keep them and see you at the same time. If I were blind, yes, and deaf too so I couldn't hear your voice . . . and had no arms . . ."

"How you talk. And two nights ago when you had tickets to the Théâtre Français, off you went with your fine friends, with no more thought of me . . ."

"But you would have been bored to death. A tragedy. A long, dull tragedy in verse by Baour-Lormian, whom everybody calls Balourd-Dormant, because you fall asleep during his plays . . ."

"You think I care with whom you go to the theater? I just wanted you to understand that I'm nobody's fool."

"So you think I'm trying to make a fool of you? Is that what you think?"

"No. Just that you exaggerate. And how you exaggerate!—Well, here we are, thank God. You go ahead. I don't want the porter to see us together in this condition."

"No. You go. After the porter opens for you, only pretend to close to door. Leave it open a crack and I'll dash through and close it myself without being seen."

"And I have your promise that you will wait in your room until I bring the hot water into the hall?"

"It would be so much easier if you would let me lift the kettle . . ."

And so it would go. On and on. Night after night. The struggle to keep him out of her room. And each night her defenses crumbling a bit, until at last, on one excuse or another, he had managed to enter.

And after that he was perpetually in or out. He had forgotten a book. His last candle end had been consumed. He had a splinter in his finger.

Or no excuse at all. Just entering and throwing himself on a chair and saying, "Pouf! Isn't it stifling!"

"Is that what you came to tell me? At this hour? When I'm just about to go to bed?"

"Well, yes, that's all. Except that you're ravishingly beautiful. I really must write a poem to you."

"Good. Go and do that. I'll sleep, while you write."

"Yes. And I will too. But you'll permit me to sit down for a second and rest?"

"You're sure it will be only a second?"

"However long it will be—it will seem but a second to me."

"Oh, I knew that once you were in my room there would be no driving you out," she would say.

"Why should you want to drive me out? Have I misbehaved myself? Am I so obnoxious to you?"

"I need some privacy. After all, I'm a woman. And I'm getting ready for bed."

"Please," he would say, "don't stand on ceremonies. Just tell me to turn my back or shut my eyes. I assure you I won't peek. My word of honor."

"Well, I'm telling you to get out. Whose room is it anyhow?"

"Oh, so it's come to that. Very well, if it's a matter of who pays the rent . . ."

"Must you always misunderstand me? I'm not really chasing you out, I'm just pleading. I'm just begging for a little consideration. Just a little."

And then when he'd finally leave and she would go to bed, she'd wake up at night to discover him sitting at her table reading by her candle.

"Oh! Where did you come from?"

"From my room. There's no air there. Your room is on the street and the air is so much fresher. I really didn't think you'd mind. Do you?"

"What time is it?"

"Three or four in the morning. I have no idea."

"And you haven't been to bed yet?"

"No. I have this volume I want to finish."

"Ah, well, you may be able to exist without sleep. But I need my sleep. I have work to do tomorrow. Please go back to your room."

"What difference if I'm here? You were sleeping for hours while I was reading. And it seemed to me I was your guardian angel. Go on, go back to sleep."

"But I can't fall asleep with you in my room."

"Very well, then let me read to you." And he'd come over to her bed and read. "Listen to this—it's Ronsard, Pierre de Ronsard: *'Quand vous serez bien vieille, au soir, à la chandelle . . .'*"

"Can't you sit on the chair?"

"Of course, if you insist."

"I don't see why you force me to insist. Isn't it natural that you should sit on a chair?"

"Why natural?"

"Why? Because this is my bed."

"Well, I'm not taking it from you."

"Yes, but—Oh, you drive me to such fury!"

"How so?"

"Because . . . because . . . well, to speak clearly, with my bed it's just the same as with my room. Bit by bit you're pushing yourself into it."

"Ah, you're crying. What is there to cry about? I've done nothing, surely."

"No, no, nothing at all," she'd sob.

And she'd continue to sob softly while he read on: "*'Regrettant mon amour et vostre fier desdain . . .'*"

And so it would go until finally it did not surprise her to wake one morning and find him curled up on her bed still in his clothes, but his cravat loosened and his boots off.

And the candle still burning.

Her frugal soul, deeply offended, reached out to snuff it out, unaware of how much she was exposing herself.

"You've put out one fire and kindled another," he said and caught her around.

"Stop it!" she cried. "Let me go!"

"Can't I even have my arms around you?"

"No, stop it!"

"But you've been in my arms often enough. When dancing, for example."

"Please! Surely there's a difference when we are out dancing . . ."

"What difference? A paltry few thicknesses of cloth? Is that such a difference? Don't you think when we dance that I can feel your heart beating through your dress? And smell the lovely smell of your perspiration."

"Oh! I say! Is that what you think of when you're dancing?"

"Why, what do you think of?"

"Really, you're impossible. You're low."

"What can I do? That's the way I am. Besides, it's you who bring such ideas to me. They never occur to me when you're not around."

"I'd like to be sure of that!"

"Would you really? Then I give you my word. My word of honor. Now despise me because my spirit is weak and you make my senses whirl. Despise me!"

"All I'm trying to do is ask you to behave yourself. I don't want to despise you. Why do you always jump to extremes?"

"All right. I'll behave. What must I do?"

"Keep your hands off me. That's the first thing."

"Very well. There. Are my hands off?"

"All right. Now go back into your room."

"Not before you promise to go out dancing with me this evening."

"Yes, yes. Only go."

And that's the way it went. After he had forced himself into her room and made himself at home there, he began to force himself into her bed and make himself at home there. And then there was only one more step: to force himself into her embraces and make himself at home in her body.

How often she resisted. And how often she called a halt and drew another line beyond which he was not to dare go.

And then finally there were no more lines that could be drawn.

She wept. She wept and was inconsolable. And he vowed her eternal affection and begged her pardon a thousand times.

"I didn't want another lover," she moaned.

"But surely you don't want somebody who doesn't love you?" he said.

"I've had lovers. I've had them. And it's only one heartbreak after another." She wept bitterly. "I wanted a husband. I wanted a husband."

"But you're married."

"Oh, stop that. You know I'm not."

"You call yourself Madame."

"Of course I do. How can I help myself? When I was living with a man I couldn't very well call myself Mademoiselle." She sobbed on.

"But when he left you—or you left him—why didn't you call yourself Mademoiselle again?"

"Suddenly call myself Mademoiselle? After telling everyone I was married? Are you crazy?"

"Well, what was I to believe when I first met you? And what am I to believe now? Shall I accept what you want others to believe, or only what you want me to believe?"

"Oh, that shows how little you really love me."

"You know that's not true. You know how much I love you."

"Then why? Why won't you marry me? Oh, you needn't answer. I know."

"What do you know?"

"Why should you marry me? What more have I got to give you? Haven't you everything? My rooms, my bed, my body. Why should you pay extra for what you have already."

"Don't be bitter, Catherine. It clouds the beauty of your eyes. We love each other. We have years of happiness ahead of us. I'll never leave you."

"I wish I could believe that. But I know better. I'm nothing but an address. Number 1, Place des Italiens. And all your love is the convenience of a girl living across the hall. A girl not too bad looking and dancing not too badly, and who will do until you move to another address . . . or there's someone who dances better or looks prettier."

"Oh, you're cruel!"

"I'm cruel! I like that. And yet you're wrong not to marry me. Yes you are, Alexandre. I would make you a good wife. Precisely because I'm not good enough for you."

"Don't say such things, Catherine. Who am I that I'm too good for you?"

"Oh, you have fine friends. And you have prospects. And I'll never be anything but a fool and a seamstress. But just because I'll never be anything else, you're wrong not to marry me. Because with me you'd always have someone who was satisfied just to trim your hair and boil your eggs and surround you with sympathy and with comfort and make no demands on you. . . ."

He knew she was right. But he knew too that this garret was not to be his world for very long. He was writing comedies like mad, one-act curtain raisers, and while they were all being turned down, someday one of them would be accepted, and then he would be a totally different person, moving in a totally different world.

"Marry me," she would say to him again and again. "Oh, I know you won't. But just listen to my reasons, so that years from now you can remember what I told you and say to yourself: Catherine was right. I should have married her. With me you will have someone who will never be a millstone around your neck. I can earn my own living and even if necessary a bit of living for you. It will be good, when you are running your chances out in the big world, to know that you have a cushion that you can always fall back on, a home you can always rely on, and a good soup always on the fire. And that no matter how high you rise and how jealous people may be of you, there will always be one friend who loves you for yourself alone."

"You're delightful," Dumas said, laughing. "Really delightful. First one can't get you to open up your door to let one in, and now one can't open the door the other way to let oneself out."

"Ah, so you're thinking of that already?"

"No! Of course not. I'm thinking of nothing of the kind. On the contrary. I'm happy as I am. Supremely happy. What I'm pointing out is that it is you who have changed. From the first moment I heard your voice through that door, I knew that I wanted you. And that's something you can't deny, can you?"

"No."

"No. You can't. But you—you've changed. And instead you accuse me of changing. I ask you, Is that right?"

"Very well, so I'm wrong. But still you don't understand how I feel. I want a husband, not a lover. Marry me, marry me. And you know what? You really want to know what?"

"What?"

"Don't you think I see you when you think I'm not looking? Don't you think I see you when your eyes go to other girls? But I don't care. Really I could take that too, if you would marry me. No woman could do more than that for a man. Some other woman will snare you, and she'll be jealous and make your life miserable. But I won't. I promise you. Just so I can know that you'll always come back to me. That I'll always have some of you at least some of the time."

And so she'd plead and they'd argue and finally he would drown all this talk in his kisses, and then while she slept off the drunkenness of love, he, as if love, on the contrary, were no more to him than a cup of coffee, would get up and turn to his books. And then, waking in the morning, often she'd find him exactly where she had seen him when she fell asleep. And at other times, curled up, half naked, on top of the covers, asleep in his kind of sleep, a greedy kind of rest, his nostrils taking in the air in great scoops, as if he could make up for his lost sleep by sleeping three times as fast as anyone else.

Then she would look at him in infinite tenderness. And she'd shake her head with the fear and the sorrow that surely she must soon lose this big, friendly, impetuous dog.

And she'd kiss him softly and whisper, "I'd like to let you sleep, lover, but my day begins so early. My helpers will soon be here."

But not a sign from him. Dead to the world.

She'd kiss him again, becoming more impatient. "Go. Go to your room, lover."

Silence. Except for the noise of his steady breathing.

Then she'd raise her voice. "Do you hear me? Get up!"

And she'd push him. At first gently. Then more rudely. And then, when that seemed to have no effect on him, she would tug and shove him. But nothing would rouse him and all her strength somehow seemed to ebb before his bulk.

And then as the minutes passed and her situation became ever more hazardous, she would reach the point of pounding him with her fists. "You devil, you! Wake up! Wake up and get out!"

But force made no more impression on him than kindness.

"Up! Up!"

He stirred finally beneath her blows. "Oh, it's you." And he would yawn and wrap his arms around her.

"No, no!" she would cry, struggling to escape. "It's daylight. It's too late for that."

But he was too powerful. She could not free herself from his strangling embrace.

"Imbecile!" she would mutter in her fury. "In a minute they'll be here!"

It was as if he were deaf. And perhaps even still asleep. For his eyes continued closed, and only his body forced itself upon her.

"My dress! Let me at least . . . Oh, you beast. Leave me be. Faugh! You disgust me!"

Neither her reasoning nor her anger mattered. It was as if one were to try to bar the way of a moving van rushing downhill on one of Paris's steep cobblestoned streets.

Then she stopped resisting and took the opposite course, trying to bring the matter to a quick conclusion. Which was precisely so it seemed to her, when, as if to increase her exasperation, he became deliberate. Her fire outdistanced his and, gasping for breath, she choked and cried and struggled, until at last it was over and, worn out, her body begging once again for sleep, she had still nevertheless to chase him from her room, adjust her rumpled clothes and get herself ready for the day's work.

And he? In a moment, dressed, his face bathed and his hair plastered down as well as it would go, he would step light and fresh into her workshop, where three women were now busily sewing, and he'd say cheerfully, *"Bonjour,* Mesdames. Did the heat bother you last night?" And he would smile and jest and leave for his office.

And each night it was the same. He smiling, forceful, ardent, mad. But somehow deep down always unruffled, always sure of himself, like the bottom of the ocean in a hurricane.

And she going from tears to cries of joy, from protestations to pleas.

"I have neither husband nor a lover," she would say.

"What? You dare say this to me? To me who worship every spot on your body!"

"Yes, but love, real love, that's something else."

"Ah, so you will teach me about love. I who have studied love in the Song of Solomon, in Ovid and in Shakespeare."

"Yes. Because all you know is passion. Not love."

"So? And what, pray, is the difference?"

"The difference . . ."

"Go on. Why do you stop?"

"I stop because you're not listening."

"I'm listening, I'm listening."

"Then take your hands away, will you?"

"Don't let my hands bother you. Speak. I tell you I'm listening."

"Yes, but how can I speak . . ."

"Oh, so now you admit that it's not because I'm not listening but because you are not speaking."

"Oh, God, you make life impossible. Why did you ever find your way into this house? My life was so peaceful. . . ."

"And will my going away make it peaceful again?"

"Yes, yes. Oh, no, Alexandre, no."

"Well, good. I'm not going. I'm not even thinking of it. No need for you to burst into tears."

"Oh, you make me so miserable. You destroy me. Sometimes I say to myself if only I had the courage I would kill myself. Or kill you."

"Promise me only one thing before you do."

"Yes. What is it you want besides my life?"

"To die in your arms."

"Ah, Alexandre, if only you understood."

"Understood what?"

"That I have so much love to give you. So much love. **That I** would really give you my life. But you don't understand that. You don't understand what it is to give. Only to take."

"You mean you have nothing from me?"

"Oh, yes. Dancing, laughter, everything but real love."

"And what is real love, my darling. Go ahead. Instruct me."

"Sacrifice."

"Sacrifice?"

"Yes. Sacrifice."

And thus it went on for months, until one night she said to him, "You know something?"

"What?"

"I'm making a baby."

"You're what?"

"I'm making a baby. Don't you understand French?"

He jumped to his feet. "Are you sure?"

"Of course I'm sure."

"You mean it will be my baby?" he cried. "My baby?"

"Do you imagine," she asked, "that I've been deceiving you? When I've scarcely had time to blow my nose, what with your arms around me every moment I can call my own."

"My baby!" Dumas said ecstatically.

"What do you propose to do?" she asked.

"A boy," he said, his face glowing. "A boy. It will be a boy."

"Either that," she said matter-of-factly, "or else a girl. One or the other."

"A boy," he kept repeating. "My boy."

"All right," she said. "So what?"

"So what? Is that how you look at it? How can you take it so lightly?" He scolded her.

"I take it lightly?" she screamed. "I? It is you! I'm asking you, What are you going to do about it?"

"It's going to be my son," he said. "Doesn't that mean anything to you?"

Furious, she shouted at him, "That's not the question. The question is, what does it mean to you?"

"Ah, you ask! You ask that of me—Alexandre Dumas, a father."

"Then we shall be married?"

"Ah! So it's just for that that you let yourself be caught?"

"How dare you say so! I trick you? Is that what you really think?"

"No, no, no. Forgive me. Look, I'm on my knees. I kiss your sweet body. Wait, I must run out and buy you a basket of fruit!"

And before she could stop him he was out of the room and rushing down the steps.

And then what happened was this: just at the time the baby was expected his own mother decided to give up her little business in salt and tobacco and move to Paris.

"I'm no longer young," she wrote to her son. "I get dizzy spells now and then. Doctor Rabail tells me that I shouldn't work at all any longer. If I sell this business and whatever else I own in this town, I will have two or three thousand francs—enough, I daresay, to keep us alive for three or four years, counting in your own earnings. And from then on, we must pray to God that you will either make a good marriage to some rich girl or that you will have a success in your career."

And thus, at the very time the midwife was coming to help Catherine Lebay bring a boy in the world a wagon was coming to take away Alexandre's furniture. He and his mother were going to live together at Number 53, Faubourg St. Denis.

"Isn't it terrible that things should happen just this way," he said to Catherine, "and that instead of being at your side in these difficult moments I must be running around, finding an apartment, superintending the moving, and doing a thousand things."

And she said nothing.

"You are angry with me?"

"Disappointed is the word," she said.

"I'll be back as soon as I can."

"No doubt," she said.

"You don't think for one moment that I'm abandoning you."

"No," she said curtly.

"Oh, come now," he said, "you really do, but just don't want to say so."

"Well, suppose I did think so."

"But it wouldn't be true!" he cried. "How could I be so loathsome!"

"Alexandre," she said, "somehow you always manage to do what you want even while denying it."

"But I will see you every day. Nothing will be changed."

"Yes, no doubt. But I'm sure of one thing."

"What?"

"I'm sure you haven't told your mother—about us. Not one word."

"Ah, but that's easily explained, my darling. My mother is getting on in years. And she's ill. One can't break news of this kind to her just like that. It might be a shock. She's counting on me to support her in her old age. She's figuring on my marrying into some rich family."

"Yes. Of course. But I was right, wasn't I? Your mother knows nothing. That's all I wanted to know."

"Darling, I must run now. But I'll be back this evening. Or certainly tomorrow morning."

"Why not this evening?"

"My mother again. It will be her first evening in Paris. I can't very well leave her. I've got tickets for the theater for her. I want her to make acquaintances quickly and thus create the best possible surroundings for her. Besides, that will leave us more free hereafter."

"I understand."

"Do you really?"

"Yes."

"Then give me a kiss!"

And thus a couple of days later, on the last day of July 1824, following the regulations of Article 55 of the Napoleonic Code, an officer of the "civil estate" climbed the steps to the top floor of Number 1, Place des Italiens, in Paris and verified the existence of a newborn child. Sex: male.

The mother, pale, languid, happy in the subdued, ethereal way of women who have just given birth, lay propped up, dressed in her blue lying-in gown, and watched the man as he unfolded a portable desk from crossed straps around his shoulders so that the writing surface protruded from his waist and he spread out on it his papers, his pen, his ink and drying sand.

He asked her the usual questions about her name, her family, her marital state.

She told him that her name was Catherine Lebay, that she had been born in Rouen, that she was unmarried.

The official marked it all down, in triplicate, and then he explained to Mademoiselle Lebay that the Napoleonic Code recognized only two kinds of births: legitimate and illegitimate, and that since she was unmarried this birth was not *legitimate* and therefore it must be *illegitimate*.

"Do you understand?" the official asked.

"Yes," said the pale lips quietly and turned to smile at the child lying in her arms. "Illegitimate. I understand."

"That means," the official went on, "that the father is unknown."

"Oh, no," said Catherine. "I know who the father is. He is—"

"Pardon me," the clerk said quickly, "but it is none of my business who you happen to *think* the father is. The father is still *unknown*."

"But I tell you, he *is* known. I know it and he knows it. And he will be here later and will himself acknowledge it."

The officer shook his head. "*Father unknown*," he wrote.

Catherine roused herself. "Why do you insist, when I tell you—"

"My dear lady," said the clerk, "don't you think I know my business? Before one can have a position such as this one must know the Civil Code by heart. And I can tell you that the *Code Napoléon* specifically, in Article 340, forbids the right of *recherche de la paternité*, the search for fatherhood. Do you understand?"

"But if the father himself . . ."

"Please. I see you still do not understand, or refuse to understand. According to the code, a woman has no right to name the father of her child."

"No right to name the father of her child?" Catherine Lebay exclaimed.

"That's right."

"How ridiculous! Every child has a father—and who should know better than the mother who the father is?"

"Undoubtedly. But that's not for the law. The law presumes that either the mother is married, in which case the father is the husband, whether actually so or not, or that the woman is unmarried, in which case there is no proof of who the father is, and if she chooses she may say the father is the King of Spain, and obviously the law cannot put down here on paper what can never be proved to be true or false. Now is that clear?"

"Well . . ."

"You see, this paper is a legal paper. And what I put down here would have to be accepted in every court of France. And if this paper were to say, here, that the father of your child is the Marquis de Carabas, then when the Marquis de Carabas dies, your son could go to court and collect his inheritance. Now perhaps you are beginning to see why I have to put down here 'father unknown.' "

"Yes . . ."

"Can you imagine what a state of affairs we would have in this country if every woman who has an illegitimate child had the right to declare who the father was? A fine confusion that would be! And what an opportunity for lies!"

"Yes," said Catherine meekly, "I guess it would be."

"Good. Well, now that we're over that, let's get on to the next point. Now follow me carefully. Illegitimate births are divided into three classes: simple, adulterous and incestuous. Simple is the name for those births where father and mother, both unmarried, are willing and free to marry and legitimize the whole situation. Now, is that the case here?"

Catherine closed her eyes. Lines of pain and bitterness appeared in her face for a moment, and then she shook her head. "No. It's not that simple."

"Good. Then we have only the two other possibilities: adulterous and incestuous. Now if you say incestuous, then this is the one case where the law makes an exception and permits you to name the father so that judicial proceedings may be had against him for violation of the criminal code against incest. But if you say no, then you must say the child is the result of adulterous . . ."

Catherine was tired. Her head was swimming.

"Yes," she said.

"Yes, what?"

"Adulterous," she whispered.

"I have only one more question," the clerk said. "What name will the child bear when he is christened. Christian names only, please."

"Alexandre," said Catherine softly, and she turned toward her nursling and planted a long kiss on his flushed scalp, which exuded an odor that was divine and of which she could never breathe enough. Tears dropped from her eyes and rolled down across the baby's pink head, on which the faintest fuzz of hair appeared.

The officer rose, folded up his little portable desk, and after having the nurse and the porter sign as witnesses, he handed Catherine a copy of the birth certificate, collected from her the cost of the stamp tax, and left.

And that's how little Alexandre Lebay came into the world, illegitimate offspring of an adulterous union between a mother unknown to the *Memoirs* and a father unknown to the civil records.

CHAPTER FIFTEEN

The Invincible Stomach

No MATTER how shamefully Dumas may have treated his little family, I must insist that he was fundamentally a kindhearted man. A very kindhearted man.

Take, for example, his behavior toward Bourriquet, a process server. During a period when Dumas was bedeviled with one lawsuit after another, and almost daily being served with another summons bringing him that much nearer to debtor's prison, there was no sight that he hated more than that of this knuckle-headed and barrel-chested individual who seemed to be constantly lurking outside Dumas' home waiting for an opportunity to force another paper into his hands.

And then one day someone came around with a collection sheet and asked Dumas to make some little donation toward the burial of an unfortunate man.

"Why, it's for Bourriquet! The process server," Dumas exclaimed, reading the name at the top of the sheet.

"Yes, it is. Died yesterday."

Dumas heaved a sigh. "Poor fellow," he said. "How could he die so suddenly? Why, I saw him only the other day looking so well!"

"Stood in the rain outside a brothel for hours waiting for a man whom he had to serve with a summons. Caught his death of cold."

"Why didn't he go inside?"

"In a brothel? While on official duty?"

"You're right," said Dumas. "Brave type. Died in the line of duty, like a soldier."

"Yes, indeed. I trust you will be generous, Monsieur Dumas."

"How much will it cost to bury him?"

"Third-class funeral: sixty francs."

"Here's a hundred and twenty," said Dumas. "Bury another process server with him."

That's the way he was: open, generous, free. So that his very hate had a way of transmuting itself into something rich and warm, almost an affection.

Not for nothing did Maxime du Camp, who, like Dumas, accompanied Garibaldi on his Sicilian expedition, dub him the "gentle giant."

But just as one would be foolish to go to Niagara Falls to rinse a teacup, where it would more likely be smashed than washed, so one shouldn't expect even a gentle giant to make the sort of home-loving husband and father that most women want.

Just picture to yourself one of Dumas' visits to his old garret. First there's the excitement of the reunion and the greetings and then the hundred little stories about the little boy's progress, potty-chair anecdotes, matter of teething or learning to walk or talk or read or count, depending on the stage he has reached. . . .

And then what?

Well, one can't be forever discussing infants. And infants have to be put to sleep fairly early. And thus, in the darkened room there would ensue such angrily whispered conversations as this:

"Stop it!"

And then again: "I said stop it! Don't you hear me?"

"Of course I hear you. But, after all . . ."

"*After all* is exactly what I mean. *After all* the trouble that I've been to, putting him to sleep, I don't intend to have him wakened."

"Just gently then. Very gently."

"Oh, sure, gently. How well I know your gentlies. One gently from you and look at me now."

So, in time, Dumas would get up and want to light a candle end and read.

"Don't you dare strike a light!"

"Well, what in the devil's name shall I do with myself?"

"Can't you lie in bed and sleep? What's the matter with you anyhow? Must you either be tearing into a woman or tearing into a book?"

"I've got to be doing something. I can't just twiddle my thumbs from now until dawn."

"Sleep is something to do. You can sleep for a change."

"Sleep is something? You don't mean that! On the contrary, sleep is nothing. Sleep is a hole in one's life. Sleep is the finger of death poking itself forward before his time. I refuse to sleep!"

"Of course you refuse to sleep. You can't sleep. Not after the meal you packed away."

"What do you mean by that?"

"I mean you gorge yourself, that's what. And naturally you can't sleep. Who could? With a bellyful of indigestion."

"Me, indigestion? Why, I don't even know the meaning of the word. I've got a constitution of iron. I digest anything and everything. I eat because I'm hungry and I work because I'm full of energy."

It's curious how often this indigestion theory crops up in order to explain the character of Dumas. Even Dumas *fils* raised it once when someone smilingly pointed out that his collected works were being issued in a dozen volumes or so, whereas no publisher had ever dared bring out a complete edition of his father's works, the nearest being the 292-volume set published by Calmann-Levy.*

Dumas *fils* fell back on the indigestion theory to explain his father's enormous output.

"If I haven't written as much as my father," he said, "perhaps it's because I sleep so well at night, while my father wouldn't even bother to go to bed due to the violent stomach cramps with which he was afflicted. I myself saw him up many times at night, working away busily with both hands, one hand writing as fast as it could, while the other was massaging his belly and coaxing from deep within him one lugubrious belch after another. And yet he insisted he was happy and that indeed there was no better way for him to forget his pains than by immersing himself in his work."

* It was still in print fifty years after Dumas' death, but is now no longer available.

Personally, I don't think that indigestion will explain the creative powers of Dumas in literature, no more than it will explain his strained relations with Catherine and his child.

That he did have stomach cramps now and then is true enough. Dr. Gruby, who might be called his doctor (though in all his life Dumas never really needed the services of a physician), once heard Dumas complain about his cramps.

"Do you think," Dumas asked, "that there might be something seriously wrong with me?"

"Let's look into this," Dr. Gruby suggested.

"In what way?"

"Follow this diet," said Dr. Gruby. "Three times a day have a meal of cold beef with an olive-oil dressing, a large cucumber salad and a big glass of milk. If you are hungry between meals take a cup of thick hot chocolate. Come and see me in a week."

Dumas followed the doctor's prescription to the letter.

As soon as he opened the door, a week later, at Dr. Gruby's office, the doctor said to him, "Go home. You're in fine shape. Forget doctors."

"No," moaned Dumas, "on the contrary, I've got the same pains I had before."

"Did you follow my diet?"

"Religiously."

"Then you're obviously as sound as a bell! The mere fact that you could come to this office on your own two legs after the diet I gave you, a diet purposely devised to put an ordinary man at death's door in three days, shows that you're as strong as an ox."

Dumas sighed, rubbed his aching belly, and went home to work.

He was indeed a tough man to kill. During the great cholera epidemic of 1832, when Dumas lived on rue Saint-Lazare and could see between fifty and a hundred funerals passing his window every day, he wrote his gayest comedy, *The Widow's Husband,* and consumed vast quantities of melons.

Liszt threw up his hands in horror. "You idiot! Melons are strictly forbidden!"

"I know," said Dumas, "but what can I do? I love melons, and never have they been so cheap and so good. —Here, let me open up one for you; you'll see for yourself."

"Not for me!" Liszt said.

His friends were convinced that they were seeing the last of Dumas, for during the epidemic fruit was the first thing that doctors looked upon with suspicion, and above all, melons.

Dr. Véron, a squeaky-voiced individual, rotund as an abbot, liked to think of himself not only as a doctor but as a financier, as well as a patron of the arts, and an artist too. He had some right to all these honors, since as manager of the Opéra he first produced Meyerbeer's *Robert le Diable*, and as owner of both a magazine and a newspaper he published Sainte-Beuve and such famous long-winded serials as *The Wandering Jew* and *The Mysteries of Paris* by Eugène Sue, and to cap it all himself wrote novels and memoirs. The doctor tells of a time when he went to dinner at Dumas'.

Véron had a cook named Sophie (said to have been his first mistress), who was so proud of her culinary achievements that she would sit in a corner of the dining room and accept compliments from the guests. She resented Dumas' fame as a cook, considering him an amateur and an upstart. And when accusations of plagiarism began to undermine Dumas' reputation, she voiced the opinion that just as his books were ghostwritten, so his dishes were probably ghostcooked.

Dumas was naturally deeply wounded. You might say what you pleased about his books, but about his cooking, that was another matter.

Véron tells of meeting Dumas on the street one day carrying an enormous shopping basket.

Dumas grabbed little Véron by the arm. "This time you don't escape me," he said. "You're coming to have dinner with me. Now, what shall I cook for you? Tell me, has Sophie ever made you a real bouillabaisse?"

"No," Véron admitted.

"Naturally not," said Dumas. "It's a dish that men make for men. I tell you that until you've tasted one of my bouillabaisses, you haven't begun to live."

So they went shopping together and Dr. Véron watched with rising incredulity as Dumas purchased oysters, mussels, prawns, lobsters, crabs, sea urchins, whelks, etc.

"All that goes into a bouillabaisse?" Dr. Véron asked, already regretting that he had let himself in for this dinner.

"You should take notes," said Dumas, "as I do when I find a new recipe. Then you can explain it to your Sophie. Tell her that one must cook all this in a good dry wine. Ah! Here is what I want: eels! And squid! Doctor, we're in luck today. The market has just what we want. Roe! Yes. Roe is wonderful in a bouillabaisse. And fish heads. We want lots and lots of fish heads."

"Fish heads?" Véron squeaked.

"My dear doctor," said Dumas, "without fish heads a bouillabaisse is little more than a mouth rinse. You wouldn't want it for brushing your teeth."

After the fish heads, Dumas went over to the vegetable counters. He bought knob celery, parsnips, onions, garlic, tomatoes, parsley, oregano, dill, laurel, saffron, pepper, and so forth.

"So much for the vegetables," said Dumas. "Now we need something for flavor."

"You mean," Véron exclaimed, "that so far you've bought nothing for flavor?"

"My dear Véron," said Dumas, "no doubt an ordinary cook—your Sophie, for example—would be satisfied, but the master cook reaches for the superlative; he wants to gild the lily and perfume the rose."

"To be sure," said Véron meekly.

So they purchased some dense, spicy Italian sausage, some Parmesan cheese as hard as rock, a little jar of the best and strongest Dijon mustard, and several bottles of vermouth.

"Have I forgotten anything?" Dumas wondered, standing there with his loaded basket and resting one huge arm around Véron's shoulders. "Think, doctor, think."

Véron, completely swamped, couldn't think of a thing.

But Dumas struck his forehead suddenly with the flat of his hand. "Mushrooms! What about mushrooms?"

"Right across the way," said Véron, "I see a mushroom vendor."

"A mushroom vendor?" Dumas cried. "Do you mean to tell me that your Sophie buys commercial mushrooms, grown in some abandoned mine or dank cellar? Shame on her."

Dumas signaled a cab. "To the *bois!*" he cried, jumping in and hauling Véron in after him. "We'll pick our own mushrooms."

"But picking your own mushrooms," said Véron, "that's risky. There are some similarities that only a trained botanist . . ."

"Ho-ho!" Dumas roared. "You say that to me, an old Leather-stocking who could live off the woods like an Indian."

"But there are toadstools so dangerous that they kill in three minutes," said Véron. "They contain an alkaloid that paralyzes the heart nerve." *

"Just you leave everything to me," said Dumas lightly. "None of your commercial mushrooms for me. Without taste! How can an abandoned mine take the place of God's woods?"

Once dismounted in the *bois*, Dumas pointed out an orange mushroom which, he said, was precisely the species indicated for a bouillabaisse. "That's the *girolle*," † he declared.

"This is the *girolle?*" Véron asked, picking one.

"For Heavens' sake, no!" Dumas cried. "That's the false *girolle*. It's deadly!" He snatched the mushroom from Véron's hand and threw it away.

"But it looks exactly like the one you picked," Véron pointed out.

"Of course it does. It's almost impossible to tell them apart, they look so much alike," Dumas said.

"But, good God!" Véron cried. "How do you know you are not going to commit a great blunder?"

"Never fear," said Dumas. "It's the eye," he went on, tapping his face just below that organ. "To a practiced eye there's a . . . well, I don't know how to describe it . . . a touch . . . a *je ne sais quoi* . . . that makes every difference in the world."

"A *je ne sais quoi!*" Véron shrieked.

"Calm yourself, my dear doctor," said Dumas, continuing to pick *girolles*. "*Tenez.* Here's a real *girolle* and here's a false one. Now look at them, side by side."

"They look exactly the same to me," said Véron, ready to burst into tears.

"Ah, yes, to you. But take a verse by Ronsard and a verse by

* Dr. Véron was the author of a popular book on toxicology.
† The *girolle* is known as the chanterelle in English.

Ponsard,* wouldn't a real poet recognize the difference at once?" Dumas tossed away the false *girolle*. "It's all in the gracefulness."

Véron sweated. "Ronsard, Ponsard!" he cried. "Poets! Gracefulness! Is that all you have to go on in a matter involving life and death?"

"That's all," said Dumas, "since color and shape are precisely the same, as you yourself noted."

"Only that the edible variety is more graceful?"

"Yes. Or the other way around," said Dumas, busily gathering.

Véron jumped. "What do you mean the other way around? Don't you yourself know which is the more graceful?"

"Oh, come now, doctor, you know better than to get into a battle over aesthetics. Some connoisseurs think the poisonous *girolle* is the more graceful; others hold that on the contrary it is the edible variety that exceeds the poisonous in the matter of gracefulness. Really now, shall we quarrel over this? Isn't it enough that there should be this subtle difference? Need we settle the question of which school of taste is right? As a scholar you know yourself that *de gustibus et coloribus non est disputandum*."

Véron was ready to die.

Of course the bouillabaisse had finally to be eaten and proved to be divine. But Véron tells, in his *Memoirs*, how he asked a servant if he could not find for him a little phial with a cork. When the article arrived, Véron delicately spooned a little of the soup into it, corked it securely, and put it into his pocket.

"Ah," said Dumas, looking up from his sixth serving, "Dr. Véron is taking a sample of our bouillabaisse to his Sophie."

"No," said Véron sharply, "that is not my intention. I just happen to have a patient with warts, whom so far I've been unable to help."

And a few days later he assured everyone that in Dumas' bouillabaisse he had discovered a new materia medica. "I have added it to my pharmacopial armamentarium," he declared. "Just a drop placed with great circumspection on the wart will cause it to slough off overnight. Beware, however, of any excess fluid as it will remove the skin too. Down to the bone. As to the effects of this

---

* Ronsard was a great poet of the seventeenth century, Ponsard a mediocre one of the nineteenth.

new medicament when repeatedly taken internally, for that I'm watching our friend Alexandre Dumas, and I will have a report to issue on the matter in due time." *

I take all this with a grain of salt. It is the jealousy of two impresarios both fighting to be the most talked-about character of mid-nineteenth-century Paris. But the truth is that Dumas had basically sound ideas on nutrition, as anyone can discover who will consult his huge cookbook. He believed, for example, very strongly in the eternal pot, *la marmite éternelle* and bemoaned the passing of this pot that remained forever on the back of the stove and was never washed or emptied, claiming that by this method of cooking, in which meat or fowl, vegetables and herbs, were kept simmering in a liquor that was never changed and constantly added to as it diminished, no nutritious principles were ever lost, and as a result health and hospitality were both reinforced.

The greatness of France, he categorically claimed, lay in the old eternal pot that produced a bold, healthy and virile race, alas now sadly in decline.

CHAPTER SIXTEEN
". . . and Palaces Where Kings Lay Dying"

THAT A MAN COULD LIVE so public a life as Dumas and still have his most intimate acquaintances dispute the question of whether he was a lifelong sufferer from indigestion or not demonstrates how difficult it is to pass a final judgment on people.

In the matter of his family one fact must be stressed: Catherine continued to raise her son to admire and respect his father. And the little lad grew up fully convinced that his father was the most marvelous father that ever was.

Trailing at the hand of his mother, holding back to watch some *saltimbanques* (sidewalk acrobats) doing their tumbles, little Alexandre would say, "Papa could do that."

And his mother would agree at once. "Yes, with a mattress under him," she would say, "there's no trick your father isn't up to."

* Véron died a few years before his guinea pig.

And if they passed a horse fallen to the cobblestones and saw the driver sweating to get the animal to its feet, Alexandre would boast, "Papa could get that horse up easily."

"More likely it's on account of your father that the poor beast fell," his mother would suggest.

And little Alexandre would agree proudly. "Yes, Papa could push any horse over. Papa is strong."

None of this childish worship, incidentally, went to the mother. And why should it?

Mother was quite different. Mother was forever washing her little boy, combing him, scolding him. Mother would say, "Stop scuffing your shoes! Do you imagine that I can buy you new shoes every second day?" Or else: "Blow your nose! What will people think when they see a boy of your age with a runny nose!" And she would pin a big square piece of sheeting to his blouse. "There. Now you'll remember. I hope!"

What a torture that rough piece of cloth was, screaming to everyone, "I'm a little boy who still hasn't sense enough to blow his nose when it runs."

Yes, that was Mama. Mama forever after him to sit up straight. "You want to know why you keep having those ugly coughs? Well, let me tell you. It's because you're always sitting all hunched up." And to teach him to hold himself properly she would sew to the inside of the collar of all his blouses a little button.

And whenever she looked up from her work and would see him sitting round-shouldered, she'd say, "Button, button!" And that was the signal for him to pull in his chin, push out his chest and bring his neck back to where he could feel the button.

"Ah! That's different. Now you're feeling the button. One can see it. Now keep feeling it."

How different life was when Papa came! His arms were full of bundles wrapped in newspaper, bundles which he would drop on the table in order to grab up his boy, run out with him onto the landing, and toss him high up in the air.

"Up we go! Up like a balloon!"

His mother would gasp and scream. Because there on the landing the stairwell yawned.

"Ho-ho! Silly Mama! Isn't she a silly to think that we're going to let our boy fall down those steps!"

"You can toss him in the room!"

"Not high enough. The ceiling is too low in the room."

"Must you toss him at all? Isn't he getting too old for that?" An angry spot of red would flare up on Mama's cheeks when she was aroused.

"As long as these arms can still toss," Dumas would say, "I'm going to toss him. That's what God made fathers for, with big muscles: to toss their children. He gave fathers big muscles and mothers big breasts. God knew what He was doing."

As for little Alexandre, he was never frightened by the yawning steps. He was never afraid of anything when his father was around. Only when he was with his mother, then, at night, he would often wake up out of his sleep and scream with fear.

After the tossing came the examination of all the packages that Papa had brought. Oh, the delight of opening Papa's packages! Always some new surprise! It was as if every time Papa came to visit them it was once again New Year's day, *jour d'étrennes*, day of gifts. There would be fruit and melons, and a cut of meat or fish, or even a whole fowl. And while mother went to put these away in crocks in the pantry, there would come the best part of all: the sweets, in little packages wrapped in striped or colored paper: sugared plums, or else *dragées* of almonds, or nougat, or—on rare occasions—delight of delights: rings of glacéed pineapple, about which father could tell stories of the distant tropics where pineapples grow, islands that rise up suddenly out of a warm blue sea like huge green gems.

What stories Papa could tell: of men in prison and of sailors in shipwrecks, and of the time he had gone boar hunting. And the boar could be heard grunting deep in a thicket. Grunting like this: *ugroink, ugr-groink*. Papa could imitate every kind of animal! And then of how fire was brought down from Heaven, and of the girl who was changed into a tree. . . .

Throughout the whole of his first six or seven years Papa's stories were just like a golden haze surrounding little Alexandre. And from year to year the golden haze was shot through with more and more streams of enchanting light, as if a fairy sun were rising out of banks of fog.

"Is this a time for sweets?" Mama would exclaim angrily, laying her hands on the striped paper packages. "Why, he didn't even finish his soup at lunch."

"You gave me too much soup!" Alexandre would cry. "No one could eat so much soup."

"I'll be judge of how much soup a little boy should eat," his mother would declare. (With Mama one could never say: "I don't like this or that." You had to finish what was on your plate.)

"Let him have at least one taste, Catherine," Dumas would beg. Little Alexandre was already breaking into a wail, but his father secretly nudged him and gave him a big wink, while Mama went on:

"Oh, well, if you're going to take charge of him from now on, I've nothing to say. Feed him all the sweets you like. But be prepared to hold yourself available if he gets sick. That's all I'm saying."

And while they were arguing, Papa would slip little Alexandre a piece of candy which he had hidden in his hand.

"Catherine, darling, please don't flare up. These visits to see the two of you are my moments of purest joy."

"Then you've nothing to do but make your joy permanent. All you have to do is tell your mother about us and we can all—"

"Please, sweetheart. Believe me, we will yet be a little family. But if you knew how sick my mother is. From day to day the steps become more of a problem to her. She can barely get to the street once a day. And meanwhile I work and work. All last night I did not shut my eyes. I was up with Schiller's *Vershwoering des Fiesko*. And tonight I must read Lessing's *Hamburgische Dramaturgie*. Now that I know enough German, I must read everything in the original."

"Well, of course, if you *must*, you *must*," Catherine would always say to such speeches. "Naturally, in that case you can't pay much attention to your family. Because there's no lord like the High Lord *Must*."

"Let's not squabble, darling," Dumas would plead. "Let's make this an evening of unalloyed joy, shall we?"

"Of course," said Catherine. "But why not make every day a day

of joy? Then you can not only feed him all the sweets you want
but you can watch over him the next day when he has the colic or
the fever."

But if the sweets roused Catherine, it was the toys Papa always
brought that really drove her mad.

"Another toy?" she would say. "Why, how did you guess that
that was just what this house needed most? Somebody with less
genius than you would have thought of the rent. Somebody without your ability would have looked at my shoes and wondered how
I was going to get through the winter with holes in them, or he
would have been bothered by the fact that charcoal has gone up
three sous. But not my poet. No. He knows that all we need is another toy. Of course, this is a special toy, isn't it? It's a surprise for
me? If I shake it money will fall out? You do think of everything,
don't you, Alexandre?"

And she'd shake the toy, but of course without so much as a
cent falling out.

"There's some trick to it, isn't there? Here, you show me how
it's done," and she'd push the toy toward Dumas. "I'll bet a fortune comes out. And we can move out of this garret, where the
child you adore doesn't have the chance to grow up strong and
healthy, as he would have, for example, in the sunny and roomy
apartment where your mother lives. —Oh, don't be frightened,
Alexandre. I would never dream of taking your little darling boy
in to see his dear grandmother. He'll get along without a grandmother. But sometimes we walk past and we just dream. We can
do that, can't we, Alexandre? You'll permit us to have dreams about
a grandmother, won't you?"

"I don't deserve that, Catherine," Dumas would say. "Really I
don't. Everything will come to us if only we're patient. Believe
me when I say that I want nothing so much as to see you two living
in a little cottage somewhere in the country. That would be nice,
wouldn't it?"

"Wonderful! Wonderful! And it would be nice too if we could
just pay the rent here. Perhaps you have a louis in your pocket?"

"Not a sou, Catherine. I'm broke. I spent my last few francs on
these gifts."

"Well, never mind, my dear Dumas. Never mind. I'll be happy

to sit on the floor and play with your toys until the bailiff comes
and throws us out."

And so the discussion would go on and on, with little Alexandre
waiting patiently for the storm to blow over and for Papa to show
him how to spin the new top, or how to make the little red monkey
climb up the coconut tree.

And Dumas would say to his son, "You must beg your mother to
love your Papa a little bit more. Papa feels so sad because Mama
doesn't love him."

And Mama would give a great gasp and close her eyes as if in
pain. "How can you do such a thing?" she'd whisper. "Deceiving
your own son."

But little Alexandre understood only that his mother had been
scolding his father and making him unhappy, just as she so often
scolded him and made him unhappy, and he would beg, "Please,
Mama, please be nice to Papa."

And Mama would turn away, clenching her teeth.

While Dumas would press his advantage. "Tell her I want a
kiss," he would whisper to the boy.

And Papa's little confidant would go up to Mama and say,
"Papa wants a kiss. Papa will be very unhappy until you give him
a kiss."

There was no way to end this miserable comedy except by giving in and allowing Dumas a kiss, which he, with his insatiable
carnal appetite, would greedily transform into a warm and promising embrace.

"Don't swallow me!" Catherine would gasp. "I've got to breathe."

Not that this would completely end the dispute. For Catherine
wanted to know just when she could count on some financial assistance and how much it would be. "I have to know exactly how much
I can spend on food, and exactly how much on clothing. Can't you
understand that?"

And she would go into her old litany of complaints about what
Dumas had done to her life. How, without him, her business would
have grown, and right now she might have ten or even twenty
girls working for her, and a couple of men with handcarts delivering
the finished work and bringing in fresh work. She might today be
a woman of substance. Instead, here she was: a nothing and a no-

body. The care of the child had prevented her from properly supervising her business. Her helpers had gone into business for themselves and stolen away her customers from right under her nose. Now all she had was her needle, and not much work for it either.

"And you? You're *so* helpful! You spend your money on toys."

"Please, Catherine, don't keep coming back to those toys. If only you knew how my thoughts go all week long to you and the boy, and of how I keep thinking, What can I bring that will delight the little youngster most? And then, if in my week of hard work I manage to find a moment I can spare and come running here to receive those wonderful shouts of joy—each one a jewel to my ears—when he unwraps my little presents . . . Really, now, Catherine, how can you have the heart to begrudge me that pleasure?"

"How well you put it, Alexandre," Catherine would say. "One would imagine that I spent all your money on gowns and furs and tickets for theater and ball."

"All my money," said Alexandre reproachfully. "What do you mean? The four francs and fifteen centimes that I earn a day? And with which I must pay rent and feed four people—myself, my mother and you and my son? And keep myself neat. For Monsieur de Broval inspects us again and again, and woe to the poor clerk whose linen isn't white and whose shoes aren't blacked. Nine hours a day I work at the office, and then I solicit copy work to take home for extra pay. Often I work all night copying music, invitations, documents. For pennies. Each time I buy a book I need, it is so many lunches that I must skip. I ask you, how can I resist making a holiday of my visits here?"

Much of all this was at first far beyond little Alexandre's understanding. But something of the tone in which it was carried on affected him like a sad song. It aroused in him a kind of undercurrent of dread, the great fear that his father would go away and never come back, and the feeling that if that happened it would be because his mother had chased Papa away. And thus there were those nights when, alone in the room with his mother, sleeping on a small mattress which was put on the floor at the foot of her bed, he'd wake up and scream, "Papa! Papa!"

And when his mother would rush to him and hold him in her arms and ask him what was the matter, he could only mutter in-

comprehensible words and burst into tears. It was against the background of this dreary life that his father's visits evoked from him
such loud yells of joy.

After the opening of the packages would come dinner. And here
Papa would take a hand himself, lecturing his mother on the right
way to do things. For example, how to season a salad. No, no,
Catherine. Heavens, no! The oil first. You see, let me give you the
science of it: everything—that is, every substance—has its own specific gravity, and the specific gravity of oil is lighter than that of
vinegar. If you use vinegar first, then the salad is drenched with it,
and when you add the oil, it just floats on top of the vinegar and
rolls down into the bottom of the bowl. It is wasted. But if you use
oil first, then the oil clings to your salad, and when the vinegar is
added, it sinks through the oil to the salad itself, and thus every
part of your salad will get the benefit of the seasoning. Do you
understand?"

What an appetite one always had for father's meals! Such delicious odors arose from its preparation and tempted one for an hour
before the food was ready. Yes, father brought festivity into the
home. Ordinarily one never ate anything except a vegetable soup
made with bones and thin meat scraps, or else one had bread and
cheese with watered wine. But with father dinner was an occasion.
He liked to serve courses instead of piling everything on the plate
at once, and he never insisted, as his mother did, that not one bit
of food was to be wasted, so that it seemed as if the taste of food
had no importance whatsoever. Father, on the other hand, wondered about each course, and sometimes, if a dish hadn't succeeded,
he would simply not eat it.

"What am I to do with all this?" Catherine would say when a
vol-au-vent or a timbale had failed, and Dumas would set the platter aside.

"What can you do with a failure?" Dumas would say. "Throw
it out, of course!"

"Throw it out!" Catherine would exclaim.

"Yes. Throw it out. What did I do with my five-act play on Ivanhoe? I realized it was no good and I threw it out."

"We'll eat this play," Catherine said with flat emphasis. "We'll
be glad to have an act or two for dinner for the next couple of days.

It may not be good enough for Monsieur the playwright, but our tastes are cruder."

And she would store it in the pantry, and little Alexandre knew he'd be eating it for the next few days, good or bad.

And with father too there was always dessert. Mother never served a dessert.

Also, father liked to talk while eating, which made everything last longer. And he was full of stories. Mostly funny ones, because Papa thought that with food one should laugh. Sometimes he was so funny that even mother would laugh, and little Alexandre would pretend to understand so he would have the right to laugh too.

"One must laugh while eating," Dumas claimed. "It helps digestion."

Really, it seemed at times as if father brought laughter into the house. And that when father left laughter went out along with him.

And just before little Alexandre's bedtime father would have still another story, one meant just for him. A story about a mother fish teaching her baby fish to swim without getting water up its nose, or else a story about a jinni in a bottle, or a story about grandfather, who was so strong he could lift a horse between his knees. Stories that were always suited to Alexandre's age and that would go circling around in his mind for days, becoming part of his daydreams and part of his nightmares and part too of his deliriums when he had a fever.

What a joy to be put to bed by Papa! And only one flaw in it, that one's heart almost froze with the thought that maybe when one awoke Papa would no longer be home.

Dumas would whisper to his son, "Why don't you tell Mama to let me sleep over tonight? Wouldn't you like that? Tell Mama you have a secret you want to whisper to her."

And then when Mama would come to kiss little Alexandre and to make him say his bit of a prayer, he would whisper to her, "Please let Papa stay overnight."

If there was anything that would infuriate Catherine it was this trick that he would play on her week after week. But what can one say in front of an innocent child?

"Don't worry," she'd say. "He'll sleep here all right. What else do you think he comes here for?"

"Wonderful! Wonderful!" Dumas would say to his son. "Your mother still loves your father a little bit. Of course I'll stay, and we'll have another good story in the morning. And maybe—you know what?—if you get up early, we'll both go for a little walk together, just you and I, before I have to go to the office. Now how would you like that?"

And yet, even with his mother's invitation and his father's promise, little Alexandre was often pursued deep into his sleep by his abiding fear that he would someday see the last of his Papa, that someday his mother would have scolded Papa once too often about that Miss German or that Miss English, for whom it seemed Papa sometimes stayed up all night.

Or perhaps mother would scold Papa just once too often for having bought his son another toy. Never, never did Mama think of buying him a toy. A hundred toy vendors might come along the street with the most wonderful toys in the world and his mother would just yank him along and say, "Just another silly and useless toy which your father will no doubt buy for you."

Still, there was something strange that the little boy observed for years without ever realizing just how strange it was, and that nevertheless made its impression on him: that though his mother didn't like his father, yet what a fuss she'd make on the days when one might be expecting a visit from him.

After she had cleaned him up, she'd warn him a thousand times to be *sage*, to behave, and she would refuse him sharply the permission to go downstairs and play with the little boy who lived in the rear of the courtyard.

"You're to play right here on the landing, you hear me? And don't you dare get yourself dirty. I've worked hard enough getting you clean."

And then he'd hear her filling the large tin basin in which she took her stand-up sponge bath, as he could very well remember from the times before the day she saw him looking at her, when she snapped, "What are you looking at? Tell me what you're looking at!" After which she always put him out in the hallway before she got herself undressed.

And then after her toilette, she would bring little Alexandre in and pass the brush through his curls once more, while the brush was still oily from the sweet-smelling brilliantine which she used on her own hair. And then she'd sit down at the table, her best dress on, with all the lace white and starched, and her good cashmere shawl around her shoulders, and the two of them would play lotto.

It was the only game she ever played. And these were the only occasions. The little boy would often grow tired of lotto, but his mother would not let him have the scissors to cut up paper. "You'll only be making dirt and I've just got through cleaning." Then he'd want something to eat, but that too she'd refuse. "No. You can't have anything to eat. Papa will be here and we'll all eat together."

The hours of waiting seemed endless. Often it would become too dark to see the numbers on the lotto, but they'd continue to sit in the gathering twilight, while outside one could hear the lamplighter going along the street, and across the way lights twinkled on in the windows. . . .

And finally one would have to resign oneself. Papa wasn't going to come this week.

"He might at least have sent a commissionaire with a message," Mama would say angrily.

No, there was no escaping it. The evening of waiting was over and Papa wasn't here. Mother would serve bread and cheese and milk, and neither of them would eat much.

Then the nice clothes would be taken off and folded up carefully, and they would go to bed.

And then sometimes, long after being put to bed, little Alexandre would be roused by peculiar noises. It was his mother making strange sounds in her throat, her teeth chattering, her breath coming and going audibly. And then a blowing of her nose.

Those were the nights when a great sadness would come over the little boy, the sadness of the silent night, the sadness of a lonesome walker ringing his heels down the empty street, the sadness of the distant cold sky with its sprinkling of stars, and then something even sadder, the thought of death, of not being allowed to move, not even permitted to open one's eyes, or to take a breath, and then having to submit to being shut up in a white box and put under the ground. And he would pull the covers over his face and cry softly to himself. And all the next day, even if the sun was shining, it would seem gray and long and dreary.

It was at such times that his mother would often say, "You'll drive me crazy with all your questions. Now leave me be. Go and play downstairs."

But, he wanted to know, Where is Papa?

"How should I know?"

"Is he with his mother?"

"No doubt."

"Does he have a mattress on the floor near her bed like I do?"

"That I'd like to see!"

"Could we really go and see?"

"No, we can't."

"But you said you'd like to see it."

"Yes, but we can't."

"Why not?"

"Because *his* mother doesn't like *your* mother, that's why."

"If we bought a lot of presents like Papa buys us, could we take them to her?"

"No, we couldn't."

"Why not? Wouldn't she even like us then?"

"Look child, once and for all, she doesn't like us and never will."

"But why not?"

"We're not good enough for her. Now do you understand? She wipes her feet with our kind."

"Doesn't she use a towel?"

"She's too good for towels."

"But I'll promise to be good too."

"Now you listen to me! I want you to go downstairs right now and leave mother to her work. Now go on and play."

"I don't feel like playing."

"What's the matter? Are you sick? Let me feel your head. You are warm. Well, then lie down. Lie down on my bed. And I'll make you a *tisane*."

And he would lie down on his mother's bed while she brewed him a herb tea, and all manner of strange ideas about his father would crisscross his mind and leave him faint.

He hated herb teas. And especially he hated having to drink them so hot that they almost burned his mouth.

And afterward he would lie dreaming, perspiring, imagining how wonderful it would be if suddenly there would be a knock at the door, as sometimes indeed it would happen, deep in the night when both of them were asleep, a pounding and a deep voice shouting, "Open up! Open up! It's me!"

Startled out of sleep, little Alexandre would burst into tears. And his mother would exclaim angrily, "Go away. This is no time to come visiting!"

"Visiting?" Papa would cry through the door. "Visiting? Is that what you call it when a father comes to see his family?"

"Family!" Catherine would sneer. "Please. Go away. I have to have my sleep. A customer is coming for a fitting tomorrow and I'm not half done with the basting. And the boy hasn't been feeling well either."

But the thought of his father going away without even being seen would bring renewed wails from little Alexandre and he would leap from his bed crying, "Papa! Papa! Don't go away!"

"That's right, my darling boy. Beg your mother for me! Beg her to let me in!"

"Oh, Mama. Please, Mama . . ."

"All right. Hush, hush. But you get back into bed. What do you mean out on the cold floor with your bare feet! Get back into bed at once!"

And then she'd get out of bed herself, obviously very annoyed, and remove her bed bonnet and freshen her face with a damp cloth, and loosen the tight braids of her hair, which she had done up for the night.

And then she'd put on the same pretty blue dressing robe that she had sewn for herself years ago, for her lying-in.

And she'd open the door.

Oh, what a world would come bounding into the room with Papa!

It was all the world of the Romantic Era that blew into that garret room with Papa. It was all the magic of that era of music and poetry, of art and invention, from the middle of the eighteenth century to the middle of the nineteenth, an era for which a thousand critics in a thousand books have sought in vain for the right definition.

Sought in vain because it was never so much a movement as a cry, part joy, part despair, part rebellion, wrung from the souls of millions.

It was never, anyhow, so much a theory of art as it was a state of intoxication with life.

It was man, the crippled god, born into a paradise forever just beyond his reach, assaulting the invincible gates of Heaven with the colors of his brush, the passions of his heart, the creations of his genius.

It was an era of defiance, an era of adventure, of heroism, of devotion unto death.

And also the era of melancholia, of unrequited love, of a secret and cruel disease, of a gypsy prediction of dire fate.

And stormy seas dashing themselves against rocky caverns, and nights in ancient forests, and moated castles stricken with a dark curse, and hovels of peasants embowered in roses and palaces where kings lay dying.

The whole world, and all history, everything strange and wonderful, everything beautiful and terrible, strode into that room with Papa—bringing mother a bouquet of hothouse flowers, and for little Alexandre a music box.

"Flowers!" said Catherine. "Hm. How did you ever guess that I wanted nothing so much as flowers?"

"Catherine, my sweet, my lovely keepsake . . ."

"I suppose you have just come from your latest flame to whom you've sworn some more of your undying love?"

"Please, darling. Please. To hear words more deadly than bullets come from lips as pretty as yours is too painful a paradox for me."

"What do you expect me to think when you come at three o'clock in the morning with useless presents in your hands? What except that your latest mistress has just shown you the door?"

"Just because I didn't visit you last week . . ."

"Nor the week before!"

"Well, Catherine, yes, since you insist, I must make a confession to you. I have another mistress."

"I knew it all along, my dear Alexandre," she sneered. "You and your fine words, your grand promises!"

"Catherine! Forgive me." Dumas kneeled before her. "Please. Listen to me. Let me tell you about my mistress. Awake or asleep, all I do is dream of her. Do you know that this room, or any room, no longer has four walls for me. Only three. There is always one wall missing and through that missing wall I see darkness and in that darkness—faintly—row upon row, the faces of human beings. An audience. And up there—the boxes. And on the red velvet cushions lining the boxes I see the bare white arms of countesses, and behind them the dark figures of dukes and barons. Catherine, I cannot even look at a candle but that it suddenly stretches out and becomes a whole row of footlights. The fireplace is no longer the fireplace. It is a prompter's box. Yes, and I can even hear the prompter whispering. Hush! Listen: 'Great Caesar fell. O! What a fall was there, my countrymen; then I, and you, and all of us fell down, whilst bloody treason flourished over us.' And then comes a noise that is like no other noise in the world. First low and then rising like a hailstorm, like giant hailstones beating against the roofs of a whole city: the noise that only human beings can make when they strike their palms together and stamp their feet to express their approval and admiration. A noise that grows in volume and is penetrated by a cry that takes your heart as in a vise, the cry of 'Author! Author!' Oh, Catherine, Catherine, this is my mistress! And year in and year out I labor so that someday she will clasp me in her arms!"

He lay sobbing on the floor, while little Alexandre, utterly lost, howled with fright.

CHAPTER SEVENTEEN

A New Religion: the Grotesque

THE THEATER, yes, that was his mistress.

Who had time for wife and child when Victor Hugo was crying, "Literature is our religion! The theater is our church!" And the young romantic writers were flocking to his standard to do battle against the entrenched classicists and especially against the state-supported theaters of Paris, the Théâtre Français and the Odéon, where nightly toga-clad actors went through the same old-fashioned classical dramas, reciting lofty thoughts in boring verses amidst an atmosphere of impeccable decorum—and to half-empty houses.

"I bring you a new religion!" Victor Hugo had written in the preface to his play *Cromwell*, with which he had hoped to beat down the doors of the state-subsidized theaters but had failed. "I bring you the grotesque—that is to say, the mixture of the sublime and the ridiculous which is characteristic of all human beings."

And his army of admirers shouted, "Down with literary despotism! Freedom for the artist!"

While the classicists and the academicians only bolted the doors tighter and warned that if the rules of "good taste" and the three unities of Aristotle and Boileau * were ever destroyed it would mean the revolution and an end to the purity and beauty of the French language. So Viennet, Arnault, Lemercier, Jouy, Andrieux continued to write their dull plays while the public groaned for something fresh.

All Paris joined in this battle. For the theater was the beating heart of that city. Rich and poor were equally passionate about the stage. Where else but in Paris could it happen that when a theater (the Porte-Saint-Martin) was built in the record time of twelve weeks, and the rich were afraid that the building would collapse, the management could announce a free evening with the best performers of France, and though word got around that the poor were being used simply to test the soundness of the construction, they yet crowded in at the risk of their lives, sat on each other's laps, filled the hall to the rafters, and proved that it would be amply safe for the rich?

Where else would rival singers such as Henrietta Sonntag and Maria Malibran split the Opéra every night into hostile camps, each trying to outdo the other in the noise they produced after every aria and the length of their applause. And pity the poor partisan of Malibran who happened to be seated amidst a solid phalanx of Sonntag admirers! And between the acts what arguments, what im-

* The famous three unities required a play to take place in twenty-four hours, in the same locality, and around a single main action.

precations, what fisticuffs, what challenges to duels! And after the performance still no letup, with each group trying to demonstrate to the other their greater devotion to their favorite diva, unhitching the horses of her carriage and drawing it through the streets with wild outcries.

The Latin Quarter of Paris began to swarm with fierce-eyed bearded men in sailor's hats of waxed leather, red satin vests and huge Spanish capes—men who looked more like pirates than writers or artists, men who swore lusty oaths, and in street brawls could be expected to account for themselves as experts in *savate*, able to knock a man out with a well-placed kick to the jaw. Men who expressed their enormous respect for women by making love to all of them irrespective of age or marital status.

These were the men who laid the foundation for what was to be called the Bohemian life—that is to say, the gypsy life of the genius in the garret, where marriage, career, regular hours of work are all easily spotted as nothing but sly traps set by the *bourgeoisie* to kill the true spirit of man.

These were the days when Gérard de Nerval, translator and poet, popularized midnight onion soup at Les Halles and drew a pet lobster after him on a string, declaring that a lobster was far superior to a dog as a pet, evoking the poetry and mystery of the sea, and never barking.

This was the day when Pétrus Borel raged through Paris, roaring his defiance of a civilization that was replacing cathedrals with factories and bringing the Paris police armed with skirts and trousers swarming to his house on the top of Rochechouart hill to stop a congregation of nudists.

It was for Pétrus Borel that Dumas devised lycanthropy ice cream made with red raspberries and to be eaten from the cranium of a human skull, that skull that every good romantic writer kept on his desk to remind him of Shakespeare's scene with Hamlet and the skull of poor Yorick.

Who had time then for wife and child?

All night long Dumas would study his Molière, his Goethe, his Corneille, his Calderón, determined to discover the secret by which the great writers cause the bones of their plots to become clothed with living flesh.

"I would lay each play before me as a surgeon lays a body on a marble slab. And I would dissect out each character, and dig out each scene, and slice into every line, and put each word under a microscope. I was like Harvey looking for evidences of the circulation of the blood. I was like Mascagni tracing the microscopic course of the body's lymphatics. I was Haller following up from the embryo the development of the human testicle. Yes, I was like an alchemist, spending each night in my laboratory, trying to find the secret of dramatic life, determined that someday I too would create my own homunculus in a bottle."

Often he would work until the wick of his lamp smoked and charred, because he did not have the money to buy more oil. Then he would extinguish the lamp to save the expensive wick and would recite by heart the plays he had studied, pacing up and down his room until dawn brought him enough light to resume his work.

These were the days when Dumas would wander about Paris as if caught in a wild dream, thinking, praying nothing else but "God, show me a plot! God, show me a magnificent plot! Please, God; and then like Archimedes who only wanted a fulcrum in order to move the globe with his finger, I shall take the theater of Paris by storm!"

It was in this state of mind that Dumas one day visited the Paris Salon and stopped short before a bas-relief done by a Mademoiselle de Faveau. It presented a startling scene: a man in the grip of two ruffians bent on assassinating him. They are awaiting final orders from a queenly woman at whose feet kneels a monk obviously pleading for the life of the victim. The power of the artist forces one to look to the queen and on her face one reads: No mercy!

What a scene for the theater! Dumas thought. Love and death both in the same scene!

"The Assassination of Monaldeschi"—such was the label on the bas-relief.

Dumas ran out of the salon, his mind on fire. Here was his plot! Here were his characters, here was his climactic scene!

But who the devil was Monaldeschi?

It was the day of the week when he would do his best to drop in on Catherine, but he never even gave the matter a thought. He ran instead to Soulié, rich owner of a nearby sawmill, who lived at his place of business and had a fine reference library. This Soulié was himself a devoted romanticist, a dramatist and a novelist not without talent.

Pretending to have nothing special on his mind except a friendly visit, and talking of this and that, Dumas took down a volume of Michaud's *Biographie Universelle* from the shelves. It was, of course, the right one of the M volumes for the name Monaldeschi.

He riffled the pages as if one page meant no more to him than another, but managed neverthless to stop on the page where Monaldeschi's name was to be found.

"Monaldeschi: *see under* Christina, Queen of Sweden," he read.

"*Peste!*" he swore to himself. Now he had to go through the same maneuver with a C volume.

Christina, Christina, Christina. There it was! A long article. But a glance or two sufficed to show him the dramatic possibilities of this willful and dissolute monarch, imperious, learned, coarse, who received her lovers naked on sheets of black velvet, the better to show off her fair skin. And who, abdicating her throne, traveled around Europe with her lover Monaldeschi, whom she later judged and condemned to death in a highhanded usurpation of the functions of the courts that aroused all Europe.

Dumas' brain whirled with the fire of creation: what an epic cross-purpose it was when Monaldeschi made love to the queen, concealing his true ambition, which was to get hold of the throne of Sweden, and the queen, thinking his love was for herself alone, decided to abdicate from that throne so that affairs of state would not come between her and the man she loved!

"What the devil are you looking up?" Soulié asked.

"Oh, just looking," Dumas said.

"I'll bet I know," Soulié said.

Dumas sweated. "What do you mean?"

"First the M volume. That was for Monaldeschi. Then the C volume. That was for Christina? Right?"

"How did you guess?"

"Guess? There wasn't any guessing. Everybody has been to the Salon, and every would-be dramatist in Paris has seen that bas-relief. Watch out: six months from now it will rain dramas about Christina."

"You too?" Dumas asked.

"Why not?"

"You too want to be ready with a drama for the Théâtre Français when Hugo breaks open the doors?"

"Who says it must be Hugo that is first through the breach?" Soulié asked.

The thought startled Dumas.

"Maybe it will be me," said Soulié.

"Or me!" Dumas shouted.

"Of course. It's a race," said Soulié.

Dumas rose to leave.

"Don't go," said Soulié. "We'll have dinner together."

"Thanks. But you said it's a race. And I'm starting."

Soulié laughed and tried to detain him, but Dumas left. When Soulié had said that in six months it would be raining dramas about Christina, Dumas had been ready to give the subject up, but now he realized that six months was precisely his advantage. He would write his in six weeks.

Already the subject was boiling within him. Already he could see his plot unfolding trap after trap, with every scene a surprise package, precisely like those that brought such cries of joy from his son.

Night after night he worked. Sundays made no interruption in his life. And five weeks later there lay on his table the play, copied out neatly. A romantic drama, but with two concessions to the Théâtre Français: it was in verse, and the characters were drawn from the aristocracy. But in every other aspect—in the violence of the plot, in the shifting of scenes, in the aging of the characters— it was a romantic play.

He didn't even know how one went about submitting a play to the Théâtre Français. The only person he knew there was an old prompter from whom he would sometimes get cheap tickets, a man with nostrils so huge after years of snuff taking that he could put a whole boxful in either nostril and with one sneeze extinguish every lamp in the house.

"I have a play," said Dumas. "How do I get it read by the theater?"

"Why, there's a playreading committee," said the prompter. "Just leave your play at the box office addressed to them."

"I see. And how long do they take to decide?"

"Oh, that depends. I don't think they are very far behind in their reading right now, so you should hear in about a year or two."

"A year or two!" Dumas screamed.

"Bah, an unknown playwright. Do you imagine they are going to rush yours ahead of better-known writers? Now, if you were a friend of Baron Taylor's, that would be something else again."

"If I were a friend of Baron Taylor's, what then?"

"Why you'd take it directly to him. He's the head of the theater administration."

"I'll make myself his friend!" Dumas declared.

He suddenly recalled that he had seen Baron Taylor's name linked with that of Charles Nodier as authors of a series of books on *Picturesque Voyages in France*, and Nodier was the man whom he had met on his first night in Paris, the man who had hissed the play he himself had written.

At once he ran to the Arsenal Library, where Nodier was librarian.

"Tell him I can't see him this month," said Nodier to his daughter Marie. She brought the message back to Dumas.

Dumas went away but he didn't wait a month. He didn't even wait a day. Three times in the same day he came back, and finally Nodier saw him.

"I want a note to Baron Taylor so he will read my play," Dumas said.

"I can't interfere with Baron Taylor's business," said Nodier.

"Remember the list of books you told me to read?" Dumas asked. "I've read them. Remember when you told me, Fill the pitcher and then pour? I'm pouring now. You can't stop me. Nobody can."

Dumas got his introduction to Baron Taylor and a day later had his appointment for seven o'clock in the morning, rue de Bondy, Number 42, fourth floor.

Dumas stayed up all night polishing his script. And at seven he entered an antechamber full of busts and books. Then a dining room full of paintings and books. Then a drawing room full of ancient weapons and books. And finally a bedroom full of manuscripts and books. And then a bathroom full of Baron Taylor in his bath and a gentleman who was reading a play to him from a manuscript.

What a dull play it was, and how long-winded! But obviously
very classical, obeying all the old rules. When finally it was over,
the bath water was icy, and Baron Taylor, shivering, escaped naked
to the bedroom and to his bed, where he lay with his teeth chattering.

Dumas' heart was in his shoes.

"All right," said Taylor, with the expression of a martyr, "for this
I am paid. So I am ready to listen to another play."

Trembling, Dumas drew from his pocket his manuscript. The
bulk of it made Taylor groan.

Dumas said, "Please, sir, let me read only one act. And if that act
has bored you, then I will read no more."

"Young man," said Taylor, "you are the first author ever to show
me even that much charity. Go on."

Dumas was so flustered that he could scarcely read. But when
the act was finished and he stopped and said, "Shall I continue?"
Baron Taylor said, "Of course. At last a work that is exciting and
full of meat!"

When Dumas had finished, Taylor leaped from his bed and
shouted for his servant. "Pierre! My clothes! Young man, be prepared to read this to the full committee. I am going to call a special
meeting for Thursday. It's time we had plays that were more than
wind!"

Thursday was the opening day of Dumas' career. For the first
time, in the green room of the Théâtre Français, he really met some
of the great people of his era. All the best-known actresses and
actors of the Paris stage were present, the ladies all in the latest
gay, flowery hats, and the men in tight trousers and in frock coats
that flared like little skirts.

And when the reading was interrupted repeatedly with applause
and with requests that he read again the monologue of Sentinelli
or the scene between Sentinelli and Monaldeschi, then it seemed
to Dumas that his heart must fly out of his ribs. And when it was
over and the play was accepted, with minor details to be concluded
later, he grabbed up his manuscript and ran home, so drunk with
his success that he looked everybody saucily in the face, thinking,
You, you, you—you haven't had a play accepted. And without
minding traffic he pushed his way across streets, shoving horses

aside and holding up cabs and being shouted at and stumbling in wet gutters, and finally he was home and he bounded into his mother's room crying, "By acclamation! Accepted by acclamation!"

How proudly he went to his office the next morning! It wouldn't be long, he thought, before all this letter copying was behind him.

An office boy brought him word that Monsieur de Broval, the chief, wanted to see him at once.

"Young man!" said Monsieur de Broval, glaring at Dumas, "who gave you permission to use the name of the Duke of Orléans in order to get your play accepted by the national theater of France?"

Dumas was nonplused. "But I did no such thing," he said.

He was shown the reports in the morning papers. "The Committee of the Théâtre Français announces that it has accepted for production a tragedy written by an employee of the Duke of Orléans."

"That must be me," Dumas admitted. "But I assure you I never said anything about the Duke of Orléans."

"And they accepted your play anyhow?"

"Yes. By acclamation."

Monsieur de Broval snorted. "You expect me to believe that the committee accepted your play when they have recently refused the work of such well-known and important playwrights as Viennet, Lemercier and Lebrun? Now deny, if you dare, that you pushed yourself in by making some crazy claim about the support of the Duke of Orléans. Deny it!"

"I must deny it," said Dumas. "Because I didn't. I was accepted because they liked my play. They loved it."

"You would do better to confess your error, my friend," Monsieur de Broval concluded. "For the truth is bound to come out. If your play is not produced, then it will be clear to everyone that the committee has found you out. And when they don't produce it, we will know how to deal with the schemer whose scheme did not work. I shall be sorry when that happens, sorry for your poor mother who has nothing to live on except the money you make here. But I shall not be sorry for you who have made such an arrogant and impermissible use of the Duke's name."

Dumas quaked for a second at the thought of being without a job, but of course there was really nothing to worry about. The play had been accepted. Everyone had been wild about it. Actors and actresses, even before he had finished the reading, had started to quarrel over the distribution of parts.

Nodier, hearing of Baron Taylor's enthusiasm for Dumas' work, invited the young man to his Sunday-evening dinners. And now the world of Dumas opened wider. He met such people as Lamartine and Alfred de Vigny, two of France's most applauded poets, and such artists as the painter Boulanger and the sculptor Barye. It was only the first of many such evenings that Dumas was to spend in the delightful Louis XV interior that the government provided for the librarian and his family, with Madame Nodier presiding at a fine dinner, with Nodier himself talking as a librarian should— that is to say, like an encyclopedist—with Marie Nodier afterward playing the piano, and then the rugs pushed aside, candles placed on the parquet floor so that the guests could dance between the flames and admire their fantastic shadows on the wall.

Only one thing disturbed Dumas and that was the presence of Victor Hugo, whose right to the opening shot in the romantic capture of the Théâtre Français Dumas could not help but feel that he was usurping.

But Victor Hugo could not have been more charming. "I would have hastened to congratulate you at once," he said, "except that I know only too well how many hurdles there are ahead of you. Acceptance by the committee means very little."

"How so? Why the actors and actresses are already quarreling about the roles they want."

"No doubt. But there are plays accepted by the Théâtre Français fifty and a hundred years ago that have still not seen the light of day."

"But Baron Taylor insists on immediate production."

"Of course. But what about Picard?"

"Picard? Who is Picard?"

"Haven't you ever heard of Picard?"

"I know a Picard who thirty, forty years ago wrote many plays that no one bothers to read now."

"He's not dead yet."

"What do you mean?"

"I mean that he no longer writes plays, but he still lives, a gimlet-eyed hunchback, who, committee or no committee, Baron Taylor or no Baron Taylor, still runs the Théâtre Français by virtue of the fact that he passes on the literary value of all plays. He nests in the Théâtre Français like some ancient spider and has the whole of it in his web. I'm surprised that he has not yet called for your script."

"Perhaps he has," Dumas exclaimed. "I received word this afternoon to bring a copy of my play to the theater tomorrow."

"Ah, you see. And woe unto you if Picard should find one limping verse, one rhyme that isn't rich, one misplaced caesura. He will make it his excuse for rejecting the whole play."

"But the committee . . ."

"He will fight the committee, he will go to the Academy and call upon them to stop this play for the sake of the preservation of the French language. He will run to the conservative newspapers and they will write editorials about the state's giving its money to a theater that is ruining France. And the management of the theater will take alarm at a possible cut in their budget, and the ministry will be worried and the whole government will be involved. Oh, you have no inkling yet of all that there is before you."

Dumas sighed. All his cathedral dreams were beginning to melt and run like a wax model in the heat of the sun.

Hugo said, "Would you be offended if I made a suggestion? Let me go over your script?"

"I would not be offended," Dumas cried. "I'd be delighted. But it must be done tonight. Tomorrow I must bring a copy to the theater."

Both Hugo and Alfred de Vigny spent the night with Dumas correcting the worst flaws of his poetry.

"You're not precisely the best poet in the world," Hugo observed.

"No," Dumas admitted.

"It needs more than a few hours to make good poetry out of poor poetry."

"I suppose so," said Dumas humbly.

"But there's no doubt you can write theater," Hugo added, with what sounded like a touch of envy.

"That's all I want to write," said Dumas.

But a few days later Picard called Dumas into his office.

"Are you rich?" he asked Dumas.

"Why, no, sir. I'm poor."

"Then whatever brought you into the hazardous profession of literature?"

"Why . . . my faith in my talent, I suppose."

"Talent? That's not enough."

"I have ambition. I apply myself without rest."

"Good. But still not enough to live on."

"I have a position that brings me in fifteen hundred francs a year."

"Well, hold on to it, young man."

"Yes, sir. I intend to do that, if I can. But why this advice?"

"Because here's your play. Remember this, young man: disorder is not liberty. Did you hear me?"

"Yes, sir."

"What did I say?"

"You said disorder is not liberty."

"Yes. And confusion is not genius. Are you listening?"

"Yes. Confusion is not genius."

"And instinct is not reason. And anarchy is not energy. And the ability to mutilate the French language is no proof of poetic ability. And the Théâtre Français has a higher purpose than merely to whip up the emotions of an audience. Good-by, sir."

Dumas, drenched with this catechism as if someone had capped him with a chamberpot, ran to Baron Taylor.

"I know, I know," said Taylor. "But we're all against Picard in this matter. And we're fighting back."

But a few days later a new force had entered the battle—the editor of the *Constitutionnel,* an extremely conservative paper.

"He too has something against my play?" Dumas asked Taylor.

"Nothing at all. But he does have a mistress. And this mistress has a friend, a classical writer by the name of Brault, whose doctor . . ."

"Whose doctor? How does a doctor come into this?"

"Listen and you'll see. This doctor is called upon to treat Brault, who is at death's door, and puts forward the opinion that nothing can save Brault except an unexpected joy."

"Ah!" said Dumas. "I understand. And Brault has written a play and the unexpected joy would be a production."

"Precisely. In fact Brault has written a *Christine* too. And you have no idea how dull his *Christine* is. But it is classically correct, and Picard is all for it. And the editor of the *Constitutionnel* has stepped in with an editorial on the functions of a state theater, and the Duke of Decazes and other important people are gathering for a campaign. . . . In short, my dear Dumas, we are surrounded."

"What are we going to do?"

"We must fight," said Baron Taylor. "We must answer influence with influence. What about your Duke of Orléans? If he could come out in support of your play . . ."

"Impossible!" said Dumas. "Already I'm accused of having used the name of the Duke to get my play accepted."

"It's our only hope," Baron Taylor said.

Dumas' interview with his chief, Monsieur de Broval, in which he pleaded for the support of the Duke, was extremely painful.

"Didn't you tell me," said the latter, "that you had not used the name of the Duke? And now you come to me and beg me to use my influence to get the Duke to back your play?"

"I repeat," said Dumas, "that my play was accepted by acclamation. But now Brault's friends are using their influence and one must fight influence with influence."

"How do I know," Monsieur de Broval asked, "that it isn't the other way around, and that Brault's play is not the better, and you, with influence, are seeking to push yourself ahead of him?"

"You can read the manuscripts," Dumas said. "See for yourself!"

"No," said Monsieur de Broval. "That will hardly be necessary. I think you'd better put your mind to your office work again."

A few days later the newspapers announced that in the Queen Christina competition, playwright Brault's script had won out over all others.

"I trust that's the end of this nonsense," said Monsieur de Broval severely. "It had better be."

Brault's play was produced, played to an empty house and died quickly. And Brault himself didn't live to see the opening.

And what was worse perhaps was that now indeed it did begin to rain plays about Christina. Soulié's play, for example, was being read at the Odéon. Dumas, disconsolate, tore up his script. But this was sheer theatrics, for he knew every line of his play by heart.

He thought it was the end of his dramatic career, but it wasn't.

It couldn't be. His mind raced on in spite of his misery. He dreamed
nothing else but plays.

Then, one evening, working late at the office, he ran out of letter
paper. He went around to the various desks of the other clerks
seeking stray sheets, and there, on one desk, lay a volume of Anquetil's big history of France.

Dumas casually opened it, and the first sentence his eyes lit upon
was this: "Here, Madame, in this hand, a dagger for your heart.
And here in my other hand a glass of poisoned wine for your throat.
Choose: which way would you prefer to die for your adultery?"

Dumas snatched the book toward him, devoured the page. Who
spoke those words? The Duke of Guise. And to whom? To his wife
Catherine of Cleves. And why? Because she was in love with Saint-
Mégrin. And who was Saint-Mégrin? One of the favorites of the
homosexual King of France, Henri III.

What a scene for the stage! A husband presents his wife with the
choice of poison or dagger.

Unfortunately Anquetil did not have much more. But surely
there were other writers with more information on this subject
matter.

Whom should he consult? Soulié again? No, not Soulié. Nodier,
then? No. Not Nodier either. Soulié was a rival. And at Nodier's too
many other writers gathered.

Who else was there?

Some weeks before, he had seen on the street a young woman,
small, thin, dark, intense, a bundle of nerves tied into a tight little
package. He had stared at her until she had turned to look at him
and he had then had a glimpse of eyes so smoldering with black fire
that they seemed ready to explode.

He had watched her enter an old private house in the rue de
Vaugirard, and he had remained there, observing the place until he
knew that she lived there. Her name was Mélanie Waldor, he discovered, and she was the wife of an infantry captain who was assigned to a provincial post. He found out further that she had a
small daughter, and that she did not get along too well with her
husband, so that she preferred to live with her father, Monsieur de
Villenave, whose home on the rue de Vaugirard he had seen her
enter.

This Monsieur de Villenave had devoted his life to the collection of old books, old autographs, old manuscripts. For fifty years he had done nothing else but devote himself and his money to this collection, until every grocer, every manager of a public comfort station—that is to say, whoever bought old paper, for whatever purpose—knew that Monsieur de Villenave paid well for old letters, old deeds and the like, provided they showed the signature of someone who had meant something in French history.*

Monsieur de Villenave, Dumas thought, that is the man who could lead me to the right books on Saint-Mégrin and his times. But how to get in to Monsieur de Villenave's home?

With an autograph, of course! Didn't he own all his father's correspondence with Napoleon?

Certainly Napoleonic autographs were worth something!

He ran home to his mother, asked for his father's papers, and pretty soon had found what he wanted.

The next step was simply to knock at Monsieur de Villenave's door. The fat cook opened up for him.

"Please inform Monsieur de Villenave that I have an autograph letter signed Buonaparte. Be sure to tell him that there is a *u* in the signature."

A few moments later he was ushered in and asked to go upstairs to the top floor, to Monsieur's study.

What a house Dumas entered. No better house could be imagined to contain his imprisoned beauty with the eyes of burning coal. A house practically without windows, for almost every window had been blocked up with shelves for books. A house that was a maze, for every room had been cut up with bookshelves built back to back from floor to ceiling, so that one room was indistinguishable from another, the whole place being nothing but a labyrinth of books— books everywhere, books jammed so close together that one could not have pushed a knife blade between them. And here and there

---

*The sale of old letters, records and so forth as wrapping paper (or for other uses) was a recognized business. It will be recalled that Madame de Hanska, that bird-brained Russian millionairess whom Balzac worshiped and who kept him dangling for so many years and finally married him when he was at death's door, immediately after the writer's burial sold all his manuscripts and correspondence to a neighboring grocer for wrapping mortadelli and marmelade.

a cul-de-sac of books, in which one ran into a blind alley and had to retreat before a solid wall of volumes.

As Dumas made his way up the stairs between these rows of books, and several times lost his way on landings where the next flight was hidden from him by more bookshelves, he thought he glimpsed down a long tunnel of books a form just disappearing around a corner.

It was she!

He stopped, his heart pounding. It was as if in a dark forest he had glimpsed a dryad, a woodland sprite.

When Dumas had reached the vast garret and found his way through a series of shelves to where he could make his presence known to the collector, he saw a gentle old man with his snow-white hair carefully done up in paper curlers, and he was greeted with a simple invitation to be seated for a moment until the master had concluded his conversation with another visitor.

Since every piece of furniture, and that included all chairs, was piled high with books, Dumas stood and waited until Monsieur de Villenave had finished.

It was obviously his contractor or architect to whom the old man was talking and who was saying, "No, Monsieur, I will not build you another story on top of this house. I don't care about your life, because you are not a human being, just a catalogue of books, but I have too much respect and love for your family. Don't you realize that there isn't a wall of this house that hasn't cracked and that I haven't had to repair and to brace? Don't you realize that the foundation is unsafe in spite of all the shoring I have done?"

"But, my dear friend, I have more books coming in, and, as you see, books are piling up on the floor. I need more space."

"Stop buying books."

"What shall I do with my life? Do you want me to die? Why, if I live another fifty years I will still not be tired of collecting."

"Then build another house."

"That is too expensive. It would waste the money that I need for buying books."

"Monsieur de Villenave, your problem is beyond that of an earthly architect. I leave you in the hands of God, Who alone can take on such architectural assignments."

With that the visitor left and Villenave turned eagerly to Dumas. "So, young man, is it true you have a Buonaparte signature, with the *u*?"

"Yes, sir. It is a letter that was sent to my father, General Dumas."

"Ah, let me see. Why it's dated Frimaire! This is wonderful. You understand, do you, how important this is? It will help determine exactly when the ambition to rule France came to General Bonaparte, for it was then that he began to eliminate the *u* from his name, which smacked of Italian origin and which he was afraid might render him unfit to rule this country. Yes, this I must have. How much do you want?"

"Oh, I wouldn't think of selling it," said Dumas.

"I understand, young man. It is a precious autograph. I too never sell anything."

"Would you accept it as a gift?" Dumas asked.

"What? You give this to me?"

"Please. I have other mementos of my father's. Besides, I realize that in your hands this document will be well taken care of and appreciated and will have meaning in connection with the rest of your Napoleonic collection."

"Yes, it will. But, young man, since you too have a deep respect for these things, why don't you come to my Monday evenings, when we discuss books and manuscripts and the like?"

"I would be only too happy to," said Dumas, "but . . ."

"But what?"

"I was about to ask another favor from you, and now I no longer have the right, since I am already in your debt for permission to come to your lectures and discussions."

"Ah, no," said Monsieur de Villenave. "Please tell me how I can be of service."

"I want information on Saint-Mégrin of the time of Henri III. I have read only Anquetil. I want anything else . . ."

"You must read the *Mémoires de L'Estoile*," said Monsieur de Villenave at once.

"Ah, the *Mémoires de L'Estoile*."

"Yes. And the *Confessions of Sancy*."

"Sancy."

"And let's see. Yes. *The Island of Hermaphrodites*. And then . . ."

"But I have none of these books!" Dumas cried. "Where shall I find them?"

"I have them. And knowing you too have the proper attitude toward such valuable material, I shall not be afraid to lend them to you."

After loading his arms with books, Monsieur de Villenave dismissed him with the repeated invitation to appear at his Monday evenings. "I will tell my daughter, Madame Waldor, to admit you."

CHAPTER EIGHTEEN

Thunder in Your Fist

DUMAS did not fail to appear at Monsieur de Villenave's house promptly at eight on the following Monday evening. But he paid little attention to the lecture, which dealt with the horrors of the troubled days of the Revolution in Nantes when Carrier loaded his victims in boats and had the sea cocks opened in what he would call "Sentences to downward exile." Instead, Dumas was watching for a moment when he could slip a beautifully handwritten poem to the dark and lovely spirit of the bookshelves.

How had Dumas guessed that Mélanie Waldor was interested in poetry?

The answer is simple: in those days of the Romantic era it was presumed—just like that—that no woman of feeling was without a taste for poetry.

And that he was right was shown the following week when he not only found a way of slipping her another poem, but she found a chance to slip him one in return.

At the next lecture he had the temerity to add an inscription to his poem, an inscription reading: "In the woman one loves lies all a man's genius."

She too added an inscription to her next poem: "Life is a prison through the bars of which only our words can slip."

From inscriptions and poems they passed to letters. At first letters about literature, and then letters about themselves.

Soon a letter a week was not enough to contain all the thoughts and emotions that boiled up in them. They wrote each other between lectures. They wrote each other every day. And then twice a day. And even three, four and five times a day. Something that would be quite unthinkable today but was easy in the Paris of that slow horse-and-buggy period when the mailman called at the house seven times a day.

They deluged each other with mail. He tempestuous, crying out his love and his pain, calling upon all the gods and all the philosophies for illustrations and arguments to explain the depth of his passion, overwhelming her with adulation, minutely describing the effect upon him of every detail of her person, lingering on the astronomical importance to him of a single word that chanced to drop from her lips, the earthquake she had caused in him by a single flutter of her dark eyelashes which seemed to him to express somehow a sliver of doubt, a grain of negation, and which would not permit him to rest or to work until she had assured him to the contrary, and without which assurance his brain must meditate on a crime that would rock through the corridors of history forever.

And she rather less violent, but no less minute, in her descriptions of her feelings, begging him at first to spare her, frankly confessing herself inadequate to give him the ecstasy he had a right to expect, and first begging for mercy because her body was full of bruises, and later complaining because two trysts a day showed a diminution of his love, which had once demanded three and four.

Their letters burn with ten thousand million kisses. They are full of wild declamations. Reproaches, scorn, self-pity, tears. All of which was considered quite proper to the romantics of that day, who did not pretend to an integration and a collectedness which they didn't have, only to run to psychoanalysts as we do today so as to have someone to whom to confess one's insanities. They knew then that the grotesque is the truth of human beings. They accepted it and made no attempt to deny or conceal it. They showed their wounds, and if they were not healed, at least they were comforted.

But for all the excitement of this love affair, not for a moment did Dumas forget that his real mistress was the theater. He was all the while writing his new play, *Henri III and His Court*. In prose this time, so that no one could refuse him for any fault in his poetry.

And now too he decided not to seek acceptance by acclamation but to work through what Brault had shown him was more powerful than acclamation—namely, influence and intrigue. He had Mélanie invite actresses, writers, producers, critics, and whatever important people she could reach for evenings of reading at her home, and thus he made his play a bone of contention between classicists and romanticists even before it was ever submitted. Through the Paris papers, which printed columns of tidbits, echoes, snappers, squibs, Dumas, keeping himself hid, managed to set rumors afloat that his play about Henri III was intended as a sly slap at the whole institution of royalty. This was playing with fire in a day when so popular a poet as Béranger could be fined and sent to prison for writing a poem against the King. But it worked wonders in making his play the subject of intense discussion.

Even before he had submitted his play to the committee of the Théâtre Français, delegations of conservatives were rushing to the palace to demand that *Henri III* be denied the right of production because the author, by making his principal character a king who happened to be a sexual pervert, was inferentially implying as much of all kings and was thus preparing the ground for another bloody revolution in France.

At the same time Dumas managed to stir up the republicans to march upon the Tuileries in the interest of historical research, to insist that truth must not be sacrificed on the altar of politics, and that any attempt to gloss over the fact of sexual perversion in Henri III would be considered an affront to every serious scholar in the world.

Ah, this was living at last! To be talked about everywhere. To be able to pick up any newspaper and see one's name in print. What difference if the article was unfavorable? It was still in reference to oneself.

Dumas really got to know himself at this period. He could intrigue with the best of them hereafter. And never again would he permit himself to be ignored.

"Oh, yes, I'm a windbag," he would later admit. "But, filled with the gas of vanity, what a glorious balloon I make, and how I go sailing!"

At his office, where he was visited now twenty times a day by friends, by actresses, by critics, his superiors soon had enough of him.

Monsieur de Broval called him into his office one morning and showed him a slip of paper. It read: "Suspend all further salary to Alexandre Dumas, who apparently has his hands full with his literary pursuits."

The note was signed: *Louis Philippe, Duke of Orléans.*

There was nothing that one could really object to in that note. It wasn't true, since Dumas was fulfilling his work just as before, but it should have been true. It would have been true of any other man than Dumas, who somehow almost managed the trick of being in two places at one and the same time.

"So I must either deny that I'm occupied with literature, and thus petition to go back on salary, or confirm that I am occupied with literature and leave. Is that it?"

"Exactly," said Monsieur de Broval.

"Then I must leave," said Dumas.

"You still have ten days until the end of the month. You may stay here until then and collect your final salary," said Monsieur de Broval.

"Thanks," said Dumas. "But after such a note I cannot stay here one minute longer. Please consider me suspended as of twenty days ago."

"But you are sacrificing two thirds of a month's salary!"

"Please ask the Duke to contribute the sum to the poor," said Dumas grandly, and walked out.

His mother, upon hearing the news, took to her bed, declaring that if she must starve to death, she would prefer to do so lying down.

As for Dumas, true to his new attitude, he did not grieve; he only wondered what advantage to draw from this event. And the answer was simple: to spread the rumor that he had not been fired because he was not doing his work, but to imply that he had been fired for deep and dark political reasons.

This rumor had two facts to make it believable. In the first place, the clerks in the office of the Duke of Orléans knew perfectly well that Dumas had always done his work. If the Duke had nevertheless fired him, the reason must then lie elsewhere. And where could that elsewhere be but in the play that Dumas had written? A play that betrayed the Duke of Orléans' secret desire.

After all, in Dumas' play there were Henri III and the Duke of Guise, cousins. And the Duke of Guise was scheming to get the throne from Henri III.

And in the day of Dumas there were Charles X on the throne of France and the Duke of Orléans, cousins again. Could it be that the parallel went further and was meant to suggest that the Duke of Orléans was scheming to get the throne from Charles X? And could that be the reason the Duke had fired his clerk? For letting that deadly secret out of the bag by means of this play?

As Dumas set this rumor flying, and it gathered power at every whispered retelling, so did the fame of Dumas' drama grow. Now there was not an actor or actress in all France who would not have given his right arm to have a role in such a notorious play. And no theater, not even the Théâtre Français, that would have dared turn it down.

Nothing could stop the play now but the royal censor.

These rumors about the Duke of Orléans grew to such proportions that the Duke finally felt compelled to go to his cousin, Charles X, and explain to him that there was absolutely nothing to them.

"I fired Dumas because he spent all his time on literature instead of tending to his envelopes. Your Majesty has no more faithful, contented and humble subject than myself. I swear to you!"

"In that case," said the King, "I have no excuse to forbid the play."

And to the next delegation who came to plead with him to have this anti-royalty play forbidden, the King said, "When it comes to the kingdom of the drama, I'm a subject like anyone else, and my authority is limited to a good seat and the right to hiss or to applaud."

No doubt if Charles X could have looked a year and a half into the future he might have taken a different stand, since he was then to run for his life, and his cousin, "his faithful, contented and humble subject" the Duke of Orléans, was to take over his throne.

Ah, well, when a duke fires you, and a king talks about you, you are a made man, no matter what the reasons. And the more his mother moaned about their poverty, the more Dumas proudly retorted, "I'm famous!"

"Your father was famous, and where did that get him, or us?" his mother groaned.

The next day, with the utmost aplomb, Dumas rang the bell of France's biggest banker, Lafitte.

"So you're the young man everyone is discussing," Lafitte said.

"If I weren't," said Dumas, "I would be seeing your secretary instead of you. And maybe only the secretary of your secretary."

"Quite right." Lafitte laughed. "Now what is the object of your visit?"

"I want a loan," said Dumas. "Three thousand francs."

"Certainly," said Lafitte. "What collateral have you?"

"This," said Dumas, and he pulled from his pocket the manuscript of his play.

"A manuscript?"

"Yes. The manuscript of my play: *Henri III and His Court.*"

"But you're joking, my friend. A manuscript is not collateral. Not in a serious bank."

"Do you mean it is worthless?"

"Well, it may be worth a great deal in artistic terms, and it may earn you a lot of money if it should prove successful. But from a business standpoint it is worth exactly nothing. You do not even have a prior success on which to base any predictions."

"And yet," Dumas pointed out, "a thousand people would gladly give not only three thousand francs but their eyeteeth as well to have their names on this script, which, unproduced, is already more famous than many a play that has been produced."

"No doubt. But that still makes it of no value as collateral."

"No value? This thing that is making me the talk of Paris?"

"Ah, yes, the talk of Paris. But, my dear boy, you know how long a Parisian rage lasts. One week. One night even, and the next morning no one remembers you."

"Not me, Monsieur. I shall always be talked about. I have climbed the mast of Cockaigne, and I mean to stay on top. Jean Jacques Rousseau got dressed up as an Armenian to be sure of being the talk of Paris. He threw away his watch, abandoned his children, broke his sword, took off his wig, did everything but let the public forget him. I would do the same. I would go naked with a snake coiled around my waist before I would surrender what I have struggled for so long: the privilege of not being ignored, which is to me the most precious right in the world, the only thing that makes me feel really alive."

Lafitte looked at the man before him and said, "I almost believe you."

"Almost? Look, Monsieur, I have still another manuscript in my pocket. Do you know what this is? This is a parody. You know that in Paris every successful play is parodied for laughs. Well, I have taken no chances that I might be parodied by somebody without talent. So I have written my own parody. *King Dagobert and His Court*. You see, I have turned my own drama into ridicule."

Lafitte looked at Dumas for a moment and then he drew from his pocket his heavy purse and counted out three thousand francs.

"There you are," he said quietly. "You owe me three thousand francs."

"Thanks," said Dumas. "Thanks from the bottom of my heart. Now what must I sign?"

"Nothing," said Lafitte with a smile. "This transaction is so irregular I would prefer to have nothing in writing and just make it a matter of your word of honor."

"But I would prefer something to sign," said Dumas. "With a copy for you and one for me."

"What?" Lafitte exclaimed angrily. "I'm willing to trust you, who don't have a penny, but you are not willing to trust me, who have millions?"

"It is not a question of trust," said Dumas, "but, with a piece of paper, I would have gone to the newspapers and shown them that Lafitte, a banker who never loses, has gambled an important sum of money on my play. That would be news. And more talk about my play. And also talk about you. And more certainty of success all around."

"Young man," said Lafitte, "if ever you're tired of writing plays, there's a job waiting for you in my firm. Together there's no limit to the fortune we could make!"

Dumas ran to the bedside of his mother and put the money into her thin hands. "There's two years' pay. Are you still worried?"

"How did you get this money?" she cried. "Alexandre! I want the truth from you."

But Dumas was already out of the room. He was needed at rehearsals.

On the day of the première, on the Saturday of February 11, 1829, Dumas, oppressed with fears, determined on his boldest step. He went to the palace of the Duke of Orléans and quietly announced himself as if an audience with a prince were an everyday affair with him.

The servants were impressed by his manner and instead of refusing him point-blank carried the message to their master.

The Duke received his former clerk with a smile.

"Sire," Dumas said, "I have come to invite you to the première of my play this evening. There is nobody whose presence would help more to make the play a success than your appearance, nailing the lie to all the stories that have circulated."

The Duke shook his head. "Impossible, my good Dumas. But I wish you every success."

"Because this means so much to me," Dumas said, "may I ask you why you refuse?"

"Because this evening I am having a flock of princes and ambassadors to dinner."

"Sire, forgive me if I insist. For nearly six years now I have squeezed two hours into every hour, split every minute and even broken every second into fragments so as to reach the goal where now I almost stand. I am like a man who has been fighting a lone duel without seconds year after year, and now, with my life at stake, my enemy's sword at my throat, I ask you, be my second this evening and at least encourage me to fight on."

The Prince was moved by this fervent appeal. He no longer smiled. "I'd like to. Indeed I would. But, as you see, I can't."

"If you'd like to, you can!" Dumas cried. "You have only to bring all your guests with you to the theater."

"But you're all sold out. Where would we sit?"

"In the whole first circle. I've reserved it for you!"

"But we dine at eight, and your curtain rises at seven," the Duke countered.

"I'll hold the curtain. And if you'll advance your dinner, it will still be possible."

"Very well, then. We'll be there."

"The play will wait for you," Dumas said and bowed himself out.

He ran to the theater, but a messenger was already there waiting for him to tell him that his mother had suffered a stroke. He ran home.

He pushed his way through a crowd of neighbors and found his mother in bed, still unconscious, breathing noisily. Someone had already summoned a doctor, who diagnosed a hemiplegia. The best that could be hoped for was a long invalidism before death.

Fighting tears and self-reproach, Dumas hurried back to the theater. Already the queue had formed, knots of people obstructed traffic, and vendors of sweets, sidewalk singers, acrobats added to the crush.

Soon the doors opened and the house began to fill with the combatants, two groups whom Gautier was already calling the dry-as-dusts and the flamboyants, and whom one could distinguish by their dress. The sober ones were the conservatives, the classicists who were not only fighting for their position of dominance in the world of art, but also for what they felt was the necessity of preserving the reign of order and reason, good taste and good sense, against the danger of the mob's becoming the arbiter and elevating to the rank of art whatever it happened to like.

Arrayed against them were the colorfully clad young artists, determined to gain recognition and the right to express themselves in new and exciting ways.

Victor Hugo was in a box with Alfred de Vigny. Dumas rushed to greet them. "This should be your night of triumph," he apologized to Hugo. "You made the breach, but I rushed through."

Hugo smiled graciously. "There's thunder in your fists, Alexandre. We are here to enjoy your victory."

Dumas saw the De Leuvens and pushed through a throng of people to welcome them. The old regicide smilingly foretold the fall of a dynasty in the world of art tonight. "A new king will ascend the throne," he said.

Dumas saw Soulié assigning husky workmen to seats. "I've brought you a claque beyond compare. My workers. They have hands with skin as tough as the bottom of your heel. I've instructed them to watch for my signals."

"But I've got the claque with me," said Dumas. "I've paid them."

"No claque is ever paid," said Soulié. "Not if the other side has paid them more."

Nodier came in. "I promise not to hiss tonight," he said.

"I'm still waiting for the day when I can afford to hiss my own play," Dumas said.

The theater was filling up. There were Sainte-Beuve and Malibran. And Barye the sculptor. And Lamartine. And both Boulangers.

But suddenly all artists were eclipsed by the entry of the Duke of Orléans and his dinner guests. Now the audience took on éclat: furs and jewels shone in the boxes of the circle. Behind the women in their lavish evening gowns sparkled row upon row of decorations on the breasts of the powerful men of the kingdom.

In a box sat his sister Aimée-Alexandrine, whom Dumas had scarcely seen in all these years. In another box was his new mistress, Mélanie Waldor. The house was packed except for two seats in the gallery.

And Dumas refused to let the curtain go up until those two seats were filled.

A stagehand came up to him. "There's a woman asking for you."

"A woman? But I'm . . . Is she alone?"

"She's got a boy with her."

"Well, she should have tickets for those two seats. I sent them to her."

"She has the tickets. But she still insists on seeing you."

Dumas ran to the stage door. He embraced his son.

"But you have your seats," he exclaimed. "Why don't you go there? I'm holding up everything for you!"

Catherine lowered her voice. "The boy's hungry. He had nothing to eat today. No money."

Dumas choked. "Get up to your seats," he said. "I'll have something to eat sent up to you."

And he rushed to give the order for the curtain.

The three knocks were given. The house darkened, and the curtain rose on the first scene: the laboratory of the alchemist Ruggieri. The scenic artists of the Théâtre Français had outdone themselves. The medieval room with its fantastic Renaissance décor, the clutter of chemical paraphernalia and the telescope pointing through a window giving one a glimpse of the roofs of old Paris, was breath-taking. The costumes of the actors were studied works of art, colorful and bejeweled.

And when the scene shifted to the Royal Palace, every luxury of the time was displayed. As well as all the degradation of a dissipated court where homosexuality reigned.

Act after act, classicists and romanticists battled it out with shouts and hisses, with stamping of feet and clapping of hands. Scene after scene had to be delayed or replayed because the noise of the audience drowned out the voices from the stage.

The play that should have been run through in two hours took five.

But in the end, the neutral public, drawn to Dumas' play because they loved it for its startling beauty and strong drama, began to take such violent sides in favor of the romanticists that the classicists no longer dared hold up the scenes with their whistling.

From the scene in which the Duke of Guise bruises the arm of the Duchess and wrings a heart-rending cry from her as the black and blue marks of his fingers become visible, the play became a rising triumph, a constant ovation, until at last the curtain fell after the Duchess's lover, Saint-Mégrin, was strangled with her handkerchief. "That should make death sweet to him. It bears the arms of his beloved Duchess of Guise," said the Duke in the play.

Pandemonium and through it the cry "Author! Author!" until Firmin, the leading actor, drew Dumas to the stage and presented him to the public, and then it was seen that in the first circle a man stood up: the Duke of Orléans himself. The whole theater rose. Even the classicists did not dare remain seated before this howling mob of admirers. "Down with Lemercier! Down with Viennet!" the romantics shouted. "Freedom! Freedom!"

Through an army of well-wishers who almost tore his limbs off, Dumas drove himself a path and escaped to run home to his paralyzed mother.

On the floor, under the door, some notes of congratulations had already been pushed, among them one from his former chief, Monsieur de Broval. "I could not go to sleep without congratulating you on your amazing and amply deserved triumph!"

The next day the newspapers, practically all conservative, leaped into the fight. The *Corsaire* cried: "Monstrosity!" It declared that the author was undoubtedly paid out of secret Jesuit funds to destroy France. The *Gazette de France* spoke with horror of a situation in which "conspiracy against throne and altar dares to show itself right out in the open." And the *Constitutionnel* foamed about "sacrilege" and described a "devil's saraband of would-be artists" attempting to tear down the bust of Racine, the great classic playwright of France.

But they could not deprive Dumas of his night of triumph. They could not stop the run on the box office for tickets.

And it was only the beginning of triumphant first nights for Dumas. He was to have them with his tragedies, and with his melodramas, and with his highly plotted and sprightly comedies. He was to have plays that would run eight solid hours without interruption, and plays that would go on in installments three nights in succession, and plays in which the actors would take over the whole theater, running along the aisles, storming through the audience, fighting in the boxes. For thirty years he was to startle the Parisian public again and again, sometimes in smash hits and sometimes in equally smashing failures, but never would he leave the public indifferent.

In this city of twenty thousand millionaires and twenty thousand prostitutes, where the rumble of revolutionary talk was like a background of thunder, and the chief of police let it be known that of every three men who stopped to discuss politics over an apéritif on the boulevards at least one would write him a report before the morning—in this city you were either a firecracker or a fizzle. There was nothing in between but boredom.

One evening as Dumas was coming out of the Odéon theater, a woman called to him from her carriage. She drew him inside and embraced him. "Please write a play for me," she begged. "I love the way you can handle a woman in your plays."

She was Marie Dorval, an actress famous for her ability to keep an audience in tears for one heart-rending act after another. She was also the poet Alfred de Vigny's sweetheart, and she would often have occasion to say to Dumas, in the succeeding years, "Darling, please don't. You know how terribly susceptible I am to men." Once she added, "You must spare me and even help me, because Alfred really thinks of me as an angel with white wings. Why, when I had a pimple on my shoulder he swore it was wings sprouting. Please, darling."

Dumas wrote for her what was perhaps his greatest stage success: *Antony*.

What an opening that was, with the susceptible Marie Dorval in the role of Adèle, who commits adultery out of an irresistible passion for the man she loves, while in the audience sat Mélanie Waldor, who in real life had been just that woman, and who now was watching her own love affair unrolling on the stage in a dramatization by her former lover.

And that lover, meanwhile, sat in his box beside his latest flame, a provincial actress, Bell Krebsamer, a beauty with blue-black hair and violet eyes and a body that already betrayed a fullness that was to be a girl, Marie Alexandre Dumas.

Looking up, Dumas could see his earlier flame, the blond Catherine Lebay, with her young boy, and looking down on the stage he could see a future flame, Virginie Bourbier, a developing actress.

And in the audience one of the noisiest applauders was a young woman dressed as a young man: George Sand, who was to make her fame soon as a novelist and almost, but not quite, become the mistress of Dumas.*

Antony was a howling success. The audience went wild and mobbed the author when the curtain fell, literally tearing the clothes from his body, perhaps because the play dared to say that sometimes there may be more love and beauty and virtue in an adultery than in a marriage that had long gone sour, and that was something that Paris, and the whole world, was aching to hear.

Anyhow, for one reason or another, not long after this, one fine

---

* Since she made novels out of her love affairs, her editor, Buloz, once proposed that she take Dumas to bed for her next subject. Ah, happy days of long ago, when novels were what moving pictures were to be, and writers could be stars!

day in spring, Dumas drove his latest tilbury or briska, a light-blue gig drawn by a spirited bay, drove it at breakneck speed up to Number One, Place des Italiens, and reined in his horse so that the beast reared back on its haunches. Dumas bounded out, tied up his animal, and ran up the five flights of stairs, crying, "Catherine! Catherine! Will you tell me what everyone is doing indoors on a beautiful day like this? Come on, no more loafing. Let's get out for a spin and have dinner somewhere."

Catherine, who was ironing, brushed her hair from her sweat-stained face.

"Well, look who's here," she said, while Dumas whirled his son around until the boy screamed with joy. "Formerly we didn't see Monsieur because he was too busy *trying* to get rich, and now we don't see him because he's too busy *being* rich. Just look at that white leather outfit! Why, it's soft as butter. That must have cost a pretty penny."

"Stop it, Catherine. You're wasting time. We want to get out into the country somewhere."

"Then get out in the hall and let me dress."

"Ah, such pretensions! We know you, don't we, Alexandre? He's your son, and I'm your old husband."

"Out!" said Catherine.

So Dumas took his son out into the hall while Catherine fixed herself up. And afterward she dressed her boy, and all the while Dumas fretted, saying, "Good time is being wasted. Come on. Let's go."

"*We* only waited six months since your last visit," said Catherine. "So now *you* can wait six minutes."

But at last off they went in Dumas' fast tilbury, with proud little Alexandre being allowed to hold the reins. Through the city and across a bridge, and into the outskirts, and everywhere people nodding to Dumas, rushing to his carriage to stop him for a handshake and a bit of talk, and everywhere on the sidewalk people gaping and saying, "That's Dumas. That's Dumas."

And Dumas saying to everyone, "This is my little boy. What do you think of my little fellow? Isn't he the image of his father?"

And then out into the country. To Passy, where behind walls stood one pretty little cottage after another.

"Ah," said Dumas suddenly. "I have a friend who lives here. Let's drop in. Now, where is it? Here. This must be the house. Stop the horse, Alexandre."

The carriage stopped, Dumas leaped out and tied the reins, and then offered his hand to help Catherine down.

He pulled the knob that rang a bell deep inside.

There was no answer.

"Hm. Could it be that no one is home? How irritating."

He rang again. Still no answer. He pushed the gate. It was merely on the latch, unlocked.

He entered a tiny garden. Directly in front was the door to the kitchen.

"*Holà! Holà!*" Dumas cried.

Silence.

"Come," said Dumas to Catherine and the boy. "Let's go around the garden to the front."

Dumas peered through the glass. "No one home. How ridiculous! And leaving the key in the door, too. How careless."

He opened the door. "Want to see the place?"

"No," said Catherine. "You can't do that. One can't just enter people's houses when they are out."

"Ah, nonsense. We're good friends. We'll wait for him inside."

And he pushed them in. "Hm!" he said. "Smell that! Dinner must be in the oven. They will be home any moment. And we'll have a feast. Wait, Alexandre, let's see if we can find something to amuse you. They have a child of their own here. I think that's his room."

And he opened the door and there indeed was a child's room full of toys.

"What a beautiful room!" Catherine exclaimed. "Don't touch anything, Alexandre. You might break something."

"Come, come," said Dumas, "so what if he breaks a toy or two? I'll pay for it. Go ahead and play, Alexandre. And sit down, Catherine. We may have an hour or so to wait."

"I don't like this," said Catherine. "I don't like it at all. I don't feel comfortable being here."

"Oh, they'll understand. They're human too. Hm. Hm. Do you think that roast could be burning? They must have banked the fire, but . . . I'll have a look."

He went into the kitchen and examined the stove where the charcoal glowed through the slits.

"That roast should come out," said Dumas, and he opened the oven door.

"What a fine joint! Lucky I was here to pull it out. It might soon be overdone. A tomato sauce is what should go with this, don't you think?"

"What business is it of ours?"

"I wonder if he has tomatoes already stewing in butter?" Dumas uncovered one pot after another. "No! But how foolish! This roast calls for nothing else. Let's see if he has any tomatoes." And Dumas went around uncovering crocks and looking in bins.

"Sure he has. Lots of them. Wonderful!" He turned to Catherine. "Now you know what I'm going to do? I'm going to fix up the tomatoes. Here, tie this apron around me, Catherine."

By the time the sauce was done, the owners still hadn't shown up.

"For Sunday dinner, they're certainly going to be late. And I'm hungry. Hungry as a bear after hibernation. Really, I can't keep my fingers off that roast. If I were to cut a piece from the underside who would know?"

"I won't permit it!" Catherine cried. "Enough of this. Let's get out!"

"But I'm hungry," Dumas insisted. "Come on, set the table. We'll eat. There's plenty here for everyone."

And over Catherine's opposition, he made her help him set the table and then he sliced the roast and they all sat down.

"You're not eating, Catherine," Dumas observed between great mouthfuls. "Isn't it good?"

"Wonderful," she said. "But I don't like this. I'm jumpy."

Dumas looked at his watch. "Good God!" he exclaimed. "I'm late. I have a rehearsal at the theater set for sharp on the hour."

He tore off his apron and ran out to his carriage. Catherine grabbed up her boy and ran out after him. But, encumbered as she was when she reached the street, Dumas was already whipping his horse into action.

"Alexandre!" she yelled frantically.

Already a hundred feet away, he pulled in his horse. "The place is yours!" he yelled back. "I bought it for you. You'll find some money under the mantelpiece clock!"

And he gave his horse the reins and was off in a cloud of dust.

CHAPTER NINETEEN

A Plundered Man

THE "Duel after the Masked Ball"?

No. I haven't forgotten it. How could I? But what can I do, swamped as I am in this vast material? Here, take for example these four closely printed volumes: Dumas' story of his trip to Russia. Four volumes that will have to be gone through even though they contain only a crumb or two of the information we happen to be searching for.

(And what mad volumes they are! What tales of Russian grandeur and horror! And when he comes to discuss the purpose of his Russian trip, which was to witness that amazing stroke of the pen by which Czar Alexander would free twenty-three million serfs from the degradation of slavery [at a time when the United States was still legally enforcing the condition of slavery on millions of blacks, which was something that Dumas could not very well forget], for the description of this, the greatest single act of manumission in the history of mankind, Dumas does not hesitate to dig back for a hundred and fifty pages into Roman and medieval history to give us a résumé of the whole problem of human liberty and human slavery!

(And when he tells his tales of Russian horror—the men sprayed with water so as to become prisoners in blocks of ice in the terrible Siberian winter, and others condemned to suffer confinement in egg-shaped stone cells where it is impossible to sit, stand or lie down, and every articulation of the human body is thus subjected to stresses that soon induce inflammation and pain beyond man's ability to bear—how wonderfully he tells those horror stories. The bailiff, for example, who wanted to go gambling but didn't have any money, but easily collected it: simply by announcing that he

had found a dead baby obviously drowned by its mother and de-
creeing an immediate mammary inspection of all the muzhik
women within his jurisdiction in order to discover what woman
had milk in her breasts and no baby to suckle, and since infanticide
must be common where poverty so largely exists, it was easy to
wring a ten-ruble bribe from all the women who wanted to avoid
inspection, and go off to one's friends with a well-filled purse. . . .
No, never before, and perhaps never since, have Russian horror
stories been so well told, though it is a field in which a lot of pens
have exercised themselves, and Dumas even asks himself whether
the stories are really true, recalling that similar horror stories circulated about the Bastille in Paris, and yet, when that prison was captured by the people in the French revolution, it was found to be
just an ordinary prison, the cells just ordinary cells, and more than
three quarters of them empty, and no instruments of torture whatsoever. And so, when Czar Alexander moans that people will go on
repeating these fantastic lies about the Russians, Dumas remarks,
"So long as you have closed doors people will imagine horrors behind them. Denial will do no good. Opening the doors will.")

How can one be short with this man who spreads himself out
everywhere like an inundation?

His style of writing is contagious. It is light and frothy and yet
has body. It is like Seltzer water, and indeed it came into existence
at about the same time that carbonated water became popular.
And unconsciously I find myself imitating his style. So that just as
you will have to bear with Dumas when in his cookbook, under the
subject of turkey, for example, he tells you not only all sorts of
recipes for cooking this fowl, but also the story of how Boileau, the
great French satirist, as a boy, playing about in the barnyard, fell
down and got his clothes so disarranged that a turkey, spying
what it thought a succulent worm, so mutilated the poor child that
he never quite became a man, and all his life thereafter hated the
Jesuits who had brought this bird to Europe from their missionary
voyages (for which reason the bird is called turkey in English and
dinde—really *d'Inde*—that is to say, from India—in French—though
it actually comes from America), I say, when a man sandwiches all
that in his cookbook, along with recipes for cooking panther (caution: panther liver is poisonous), and peacock done in sour cream,

and filets of kangaroo (and here a heart-rending digression on how
the kangaroo is subject to cataract of the eyes, frequently becoming
totally blind), I say, just as you've got to bear with Dumas in his
endless excursions, so you'll now have to bear with me in mine.

I ask you, How can you possibly force this man to sit for a
miniature?

With Dumas, there's just no such thing as a good story for which
he couldn't find the right spot. Faced with a good story it's a writer's
business to create the right spot! And he attacks Voltaire, who in
his *History of Russia* says, "This will be the public life of the Czar,
the life that has been of use to man; not his private life, of which
all manner of amusing anecdotes are told which will be omitted
here."

Imagine omitting amusing anecdotes!

And what is the result? When it comes to telling about the death
of Peter the Great's son, Alexis, Voltaire is stuck and breaks off,
deciding to write something else for the moment.

"Naturally!" cries Dumas. "Because this business of a public life
and completely separate private life is a myth. There can be no
such two completely independent categories to life. Czar Peter's
private life was also his public life. He had to kill his own son to
save the Russia that he was trying to create. And the story of that
crime is fascinating."

Voltaire also says, "Write nothing that posterity will find unworthy!"

"Nonsense!" Dumas retorts. "How can we possibly know what
posterity is going to find unworthy? Who are we to say how posterity shall look at the world? Let us rather write whatever we may
find that's worthy of being recorded, and let posterity pick what it
likes of our works and throw away the rest."

(Dumas didn't like Voltaire. In his voyage to Switzerland, being
shown the chapel that Voltaire erected to God, with the Latin inscription *Deo erexit Voltaire*, Dumas remarked, "So the little gnome
was finally reconciled to the deity, eh? Wonder who took the first
step.")

No doubt Dumas, like most of us, would have liked to have left
posterity an exaggerated picture of his own worth. But he couldn't.
He was driven strongly by the life forces within him.

When, for example, a certain Countess de B. committed suicide in Paris, leaving a note that blamed her unhappiness on the beastliness of men, Dumas was immediately brought into the picture but readily cleared himself when the facts became known.

One woman said to Dumas, "You're lucky you weren't actually involved."

"Why, I didn't have so much as a nodding acquaintance with her," Dumas protested.

"I know. But this should be a lesson to you. You and your beastliness are tending to exactly the same kind of tragedy. Mend your ways or else watch out!"

To which Dumas retorted, "What's one woman who commits suicide because of man's beastliness compared to the number of women who would commit suicide if deprived of it?"

In his later years, as we have already mentioned, a rough estimate on Dumas' lifesaving activities put the figure at well over five hundred.

And the reward for such a labor of love?

"I'm a plundered man," he once complained to Delacroix while taking a walk with him. "I've earned upward of a quarter of a million francs a year for thirty years or more, and today I have next to nothing."

(This was the walk that Delacroix mentions in his *Journal*, when Dumas, as "plundered" as he was, nevertheless took Delacroix up to see his latest mistress, for whom he had just furnished a cozy little apartment, and the girl managed to get Delacroix aside and moan to him that as genuinely as she was attracted to Dumas she did not think she could take it very much longer, that the pace of life he was forcing upon her was wrecking her physically, and she was afraid she would end up with a galloping consumption.)

Is it necessary to think evil of Dumas because Catherine Lebay, once having spent the little money she had found under the clock on the mantelpiece, had some difficulty extracting further sums from Dumas?

Just to locate Dumas, to say nothing of thereupon getting money from him, was already something of a task. He was forever moving from one apartment to another.

"I really don't live anywhere," he once said. "I'm like a bird. I alight here or there, perch for a moment and am gone with the wind."

As for money, he was always generous. And this means that he was chronically short. How can one be expected to have money and be generous at the same time? It is mathematically impossible. And yet, to satisfy his critics he should have been able to do both!

Paris was full of people who were forever saying, "Watch out for that Dumas. He's an expert walleteer!" (The French use the expression *boursiller*.) What is meant is that in a restaurant or in a coach with friends, it was always Dumas who would somehow manage to say first, "Devil take it! I've left my wallet at home. Say, old man, you wouldn't have a tenner to spare me, would you?"

For Dumas repeatedly to get the drop on his friends naturally started some malicious tales, for hell hath no fury like an expert walleteer who has been outwalleted by a rank amateur (which I take Dumas to have been).

In short, when Catherine would come to Paris and go to the rue de l'Université, it would be only to discover that Dumas had meanwhile moved to the rue Saint-Lazare, and from there to the Square d'Orléans, and so on.

And finally when she had found where he lived, he was somehow never in. And if she said to the janitor that she'd wait, he'd shrug and tell her that he hadn't seen Monsieur Dumas for days.

So it would be a chase all over Paris. From the Porte-Saint-Martin theater to the Vaudeville, to the Odéon, to the Ambigu, everywhere asking porters, watchmen, even charwomen. "Have you seen Monsieur Dumas? Is Monsieur Dumas here?"

And the worst of it was that one wasn't the only person looking for Dumas. It was all right that actors and editors and commissionaires were looking for him, but oh, the humiliation of running across a couple of women who were doing the same and—who knows?—perhaps for the very same reason!

But the money was needed; the boy had been sick. It had been necessary to have a doctor. And so one pocketed one's humiliation and went from the Café Anglais to the Café de Paris to the Café Riche.

And everywhere the same lack of exact knowledge, and the same disputes as to whether Dumas was even in Paris at all. "But surely he's gone to England for the Derby!" "I tell you I saw him this morning on the Boulevard." "Impossible, I happen to know for certain that he's in Trouville writing a play." "The fact is you're all wrong. He's gone to Venice to repeat Byron's exploit of driving a pair of horses across St. Mark's Place. And afterward he'll go to Naples to see Vesuvius in eruption. He spoke to me about his impending trip only the other day."

And then, if you finally found him, what good? A horde of actors, starveling poets, loose women had got ahead of you. And he would show you his empty pockets and instead of money would offer you a medieval illuminated book of hours, or an Egyptian tear flask, or a piece of rag which he would tell you was a precious bit of quipu from Peru. "Those people wrote, not with pen on paper, but by tying knots in string. Imagine a form of writing that the blind could read too! If only we had that!"

And of course promises. He had an important sum coming in next week and would send out five hundred francs by special messenger. (But instead of five hundred he'd actually send only a hundred. "Dear Catherine," he'd write. "Temporarily out of funds. Will make it up soon. In the meanwhile please sign the papers the bearer has. They are in connection with the house I gave you.")

Someone once pointed out to Dumas the big gold letters over a certain entrance. "Can you read that?"

"Of course. It says BANQUE."

"Good. You will find such signs all over Paris. All over the civilized world. That's the place to deposit your money the moment you receive it. Not in your pocket, where everybody's hand can reach in and grab it."

"That's well enough for those who have money," said Dumas, "but when do I have money? No sooner do I touch a sum than I'm surrounded. I already owe every cent I'll get and more. I'm never out of debt. I work mainly for the usurers. I'm paddling furiously just to keep from drowning."

This was true. In order to have cash on hand, he was perpetually borrowing, and with the borrowing came payments of interest, and compound interest following that, and then brokerage fees and discount fees and chattel mortgages and finally writs of seizure and long-drawn-out suits and endless lawyers' fees, and the constant threat of debtor's prison—in short, the whole witches' brew of small finance.

You see, he knew only one way to make money: to write something that would amuse. While other professions meanwhile had invented a thousand ways to take his money away from him. And in ways that were not always equally amusing.

The story of the faded little man who came to Dumas once with a handsome gold watch and begged him to take the piece as collateral for a loan of one hundred francs is an illustration of what a deadly maelstrom these financial transactions could become.

"My good man," Dumas said to him, "with a fine watch like that you don't have to come to me for a hundred francs. Anyone will gladly lend you a hundred francs on that, and even much more."

"Yes," said the man, "but this watch is the only memento I have of my dear father, and I would not like to lose it. And you know what happens when you fail to meet your date for payment. You are sold out before you can say boo!"

"You needn't tell me," Dumas sighed. "But for all that, I'm broke. Haven't got a penny."

"Ah, Monsieur Dumas," the little man begged, "surely there must be some way that you can help me out. If I pawn it, the interest alone will prevent me from sleeping at night."

"Oh, if it's just a matter of the interest, then have no fears. Let me take the responsibility for the interest on your loan. And I promise you that you shan't lose your precious watch. How does that suit you?"

"You are indeed a good man, Monsieur Dumas, and I go now in complete assurance to arrange a loan for a hundred francs on my watch."

"Good, good," said Dumas, and returned to his work, only to interrupt himself almost immediately and call after the man with the watch. "Wait a moment. Why take only a hundred francs for your watch? Since I make myself responsible for everything, get all the money you can, and bring me back the difference. I could use a little cash myself."

So the man pawned his watch for three hundred francs. Fifty francs were deducted at once for the usual fees connected with this sort of transaction, and two hundred and fifty francs were given in cash, of which the owner of the watch retained a hundred and brought a hundred and fifty to Dumas.

"Thanks, my dear friend," said Dumas, pocketing the money. "And now don't forget to come back at the expiration of the loan and I will give you enough to cover both principal and interest."

So a few months later the faded little man reappeared.

"Yes, my good friend," said Dumas, utterly blank.

"But, Monsieur, surely you remember me," the man whined.

"No, frankly. I don't."

"But my watch . . . !"

"Oh, your watch. Yes, of course, your watch," said Dumas, striking his forehead. "Let's see now. How much do we owe on that?"

"With interest we must return four hundred francs."

"Whee! Four hundred francs. You don't say so. That's bad news. Right now I couldn't be flatter."

"Ah, Monsieur Dumas, after all your promises."

"*Nil desperandum*, my friend. Let's see now. Your watch isn't lost yet. All we need to do is take care of the interest, isn't that right? And the loan can be renewed."

"That would take a hundred and fifty francs," said the man.

"Devil take it!" Dumas exclaimed. "And right now I'm without a cent. And you—you are completely broke too?"

"Monsieur, my entire fortune amounts to exactly a hundred and fifty francs."

"But that's precisely the sum we're looking for! Lend them to me, and I'll make out a promissory note to you, and then you can go to the broker and make sure that your watch is safe."

"But, Monsieur Dumas, if you take my hundred and fifty francs what will I live on? I will have nothing left to do but throw myself in the river."

"Live on? What do you need to live on? My table is always set, and there must be room here somewhere for a bed to be put up for you. Move in with me until we settle this thing."

So from being in debt to a usurer, Dumas went on to be in debt to the owner of the watch, and, moreover, responsible for his keep. And though in time he managed to redeem the watch for the man, he somehow could never manage to pay off his debt to him, so that for years the little faded man went on living at Dumas' expense, while Dumas' debt to him grew and grew.

What shall I say except that one day when Dumas concluded an arrangement with Michel Lévy for a sum running into half a million francs for all future books that he might write, the faded man appeared, took his share in fifty crisp bills of one thousand francs each and went off finally to buy himself a tobacco farm in the Périgord section of France.

And he still had that precious heirloom, his father's gold watch.

CHAPTER TWENTY

Love for Love

SUCH WERE DUMAS' financial transactions.

Can one wonder then that Catherine Lebay finally resigned herself to seeking customers for her needlework, emulating Dumas in being busy day and night so as to earn her own living.

At this particular period, little Alexandre was a quiet lad, gentle, dreamy-eyed, suppressed. Catherine's heart would tighten when she would see him so thin, apathetic and round-shouldered.

"Why do you sit in the house all day long?" she would ask. "Get out into the fresh air."

"*Oui, Maman,*" he would say obediently.

"Put on your scarf because the wind is nippy. And be active. Play. Run around."

"*Oui, Maman.*"

"And remember your posture. Feel the button."

"*Oui, Maman.*"

And through the window, looking up from her sewing, she would see him, with his scarf tied carefully around his neck, running around as she had ordered him to. The sight would make her break into tears. It was so clear that he missed his father and that the joy had gone out of his life.

One day she went out to buy some warm material to line her big fringed shawl and make it serve for the winter, when she saw a boy lashing a big top with a whip, making it spin and hum.

Instead of buying her lining she went into a shop and bought a similar toy for little Alexandre.

"Is it from Papa?" the boy cried out with wide-open eyes when she brought it home.

For a moment she didn't know how to answer. A kind of bitterness obstructed speech. Then she said simply, "No. It's from me."

"And—I can play with it?" he asked incredulously.

"I guess I can give you a present too if I happen to want to," she said gruffly.

"*Oui, Maman,*" he said.

Then afterward, looking up from her work and seeing him through the window as he lashed the top furiously, a strange thought came to her: that she had never really thought of this child as hers, but always as Dumas', and that in a way she had always been angry with him for being the child of his father.

"But that's not his fault!" she exclaimed to herself suddenly. "If it's anyone's fault, it's mine!" And then she took a fierce resolve: "He's going to be my child!" And her heart was flooded with a new joy of motherhood that she realized she had never experienced before. "My child! My Alexandre! Mine!"

From then on life changed for both of them. Theirs was no longer a house in which mother ordered a child to be neat, or to eat all his food, or to dress warmly. But a house in which mother explained to her child the sort of dress she was making, took him along when she was shopping, told him little bits of her own childhood, and let him lug her heavy reticule to show how grown up he was.

"I'm strong like Papa," he said.

For a moment the old urge to a sharp retort was in her, but then she replied calmly, "Yes, I'm sure you will be someday." And then she added, "I'm strong too, you know. You've never seen me sick, have you? What? You don't believe that I'm strong? Then you try and catch me." And she ran off down the lane. And after a moment he ran after her.

It was a new experience for both of them, and for a moment there was awkwardness. But increasingly now she took time out from her work to play with the child, and the child responded in the strangest manner. He began to do something he never had done before: he would fling his arms around her in pure joy.

Laughter began to resound through the little house in Passy. And Catherine found herself wishing that Dumas might never show up again. She didn't want him. She didn't need him. Life was better without him. They were both happy this way. And happy all the time, instead of just now and then when Dumas might take it into his head to visit them.

They were good companions now, and when it would happen that Catherine was so busy with her work that she could not find all the time she wanted to play with him and would have to refuse to go out in the garden and play, she would have the rare pleasure of hearing him beg her, "Please, *Maman*, please. . . . Play with me! Just for a few minutes!"

And when she still had to refuse and had to explain to him how she had to work so as to make money for them to eat, then she had the delight of hearing words such as this: "Pretty soon you won't have to work any more. I'll be grown up and I'll work for you. And we'll be rich."

She would feel herself flooded with love and happiness such as she hadn't felt for years.

"What will you be when you grow up?"

"I'll be like Papa."

"You'll write plays too?"

"Of course."

"Ah, too bad, because then you'll always be away and I'll never see you."

"No, I won't go away. I'll never leave you. We'll go together to the theater every night."

In this new atmosphere of love in which they were both drawn by their sense of having been abandoned to each other, they began to find endless ways of being gay. They played that old French game of holding each others' chin and saying, "*Par la barbe je te tiens*"—that is, "By the beard I hold you, and the first one who laughs . . ." It was a forfeit game, and the forfeits had to be redeemed later by imitating a duck or drinking a glass of milk without pausing for breath. At the end of the game he would say, "My sides ache from laughing."

And then there were games of hide-and-seek, and singing games, and guessing games. The house grew noisy and the laughter went on all day long.

The evenings were perhaps best of all, because to save expensive oil, they played in the dark, and games became mysterious mutual pursuits that were never clearly defined, games that were punctuated with shrieks of terror and laughter, half puss-in-the-corner, half hide-and-seek, sending sweet-sour shivers down one's back. And how cozy then to be tucked into bed and kissed and to fall asleep immediately, tired and happy.

And between games, when she would go at her work, she would more and more often say, "Now you must work too." She taught him how to tell time, and how to do simple sums. And she would say, "We're going to get more and more serious. If you want to be a writer like your father, you've got to study. Do you want to? An ignorant boy can't write a play. Your father studied hard."

"I too want to study," he'd say staunchly.

And one Sunday she spoke about it to the curé at the parish church, and the latter gave her a few books for the instruction of the very young.

She spread them out before Alexandre the next day. "Look at what all we have to study. Latin. Grammar. Spelling. Catechism. Euclid. I don't know them myself. But we'll do them together. And what I don't learn you'll teach me. And what you don't learn I'll teach you. And when we both don't understand we'll go to the curé and he'll explain it to us."

That way learning was fun. There were times when Catherine would have to say, "We laugh too much. I never hear any laughter when I pass the school. Maybe we're doing something wrong. I think maybe we have to be serious."

But in spite of themselves they had to laugh. Everything seemed so droll.

And yet, when the curé examined them one afternoon, he was amazed at their progress. "At this rate," he said, "the boy will be ready for *l'enseignement secondaire* long before the usual age of twelve."

"Then we'll have to go slower," said Catherine.

"Oh, no, *Maman!*" Alexandre cried. "Not slower. Faster!"

"You mean you want to leave me and go to a school, where no one ever laughs?" Catherine asked.

"Oh, no. I never want to leave you. But I want to study fast anyhow."

And thus, in this new atmosphere, the time passed swiftly, and one day Catherine had to say, "You know what? In a whole year you haven't been sick once? And not once have I had to say feel the button."

One afternoon there was a knock at the door and two men entered.

Catherine was not very surprised. Usually after the receipt of a little money from Dumas there would be a couple of men at the door with a note that they were to pick up this or that object: first the clock and the candelabra on the mantelpiece, then a painting, and then the living-room rug or a bust that stood on a pedestal in the corner.

She realized that he was gradually selling her out. But as long as she had a roof over her head and a pot to cook in, she didn't mind.

But this time she was in for a surprise. The men had an inventory and began checking off everything in the house. Catherine demanded an explanation.

"We're putting everything on sale next month," one of the men said.

"What do you mean?" she cried.

"House and contents," said the man.

"House and contents? But this is my house. These are my things."

"Yours? Are you then Madame Lebay?"

"Of course I am."

"Well, then you surely have no reason to be surprised that we're selling you out next month. For a whole year you've paid nothing on your mortgage, and we've petitioned for a writ to take possession."

"Mortgage? Writ?" Catherine cried. "What do you mean? This house and everything in it is mine."

"No doubt, Madame, but when you fail one quarter after another to make your payments on the mortgage, you lose your house. Surely you know that."

Catherine was beside herself. "Mortgage? I know nothing about any mortgage!"

"Up to the hilt, Madame. Two hundred and fourteen francs due every three months. And not a single payment has been made."

"Please, give me time. I'll pay. You'll see."

When the men had gone, promising to return in a few days, Catherine dressed Alexandre quickly and ran with him to the omnibus stop. All the way to the city she was oppressed with the sense of calamity impending, and she could scarcely talk to the child, to whom a trip by omnibus was still a wonderful experience.

At Dumas' apartment she was told that he was not expected in that evening. As to where he would be, no one could say.

And as he talked to her, the servant looked from the boy to Catherine and back again, and it was only too obvious what he was thinking.

Furious, Catherine turned away. "We'll be back," she said, and walked off, dragging little Alexandre with her.

"Is that where Papa lives?" Alexandre wanted to know.

"Yes," said Catherine curtly. She suddenly felt all her old antipathy to the child rising up in her again, in spite of herself.

"It's beautiful there," the child said. "Someday can we look inside?" he asked.

"No, never," said Catherine brutally.

"Why not?"

"Because I say so!" Catherine shouted, realizing that she was not making sense, but being too angry to care. Imagine! The old fraud! Giving her a house and then mortgaging it without telling her. She remembered the several messengers who had called at the house and asked her to sign some papers. Yes, that was it! She herself had stupidly permitted him to mortgage her house!

As she went from café to theater asking for Monsieur Dumas and everywhere saw glances going to the boy, her fury grew. For herself she didn't care, so she told herself, but when she thought of the boy growing up under this cloud of other people's suspicions and scorn, she felt herself knotting up inside.

She found herself suddenly on the street where Madame Dumas

lived, not far from the Luxembourg Gardens. All her anger against
Dumas welled up to a resolution. She would go to see the old
woman. Why shouldn't the grandmother know of her grandchild?
Why shouldn't she know how he neglected his son and let strangers
come and sell the roof from over his poor head?

The concierge directed her to the third floor. Through the door
one could already smell medicine. And when a typical slatternly
garde-malade opened up, the heavy odor, carried by warm stagnant air, struck them an overpowering blow.

"I want to see Madame Dumas," said Catherine.

The woman took in the situation with the same glance from child
to woman that everyone had given Catherine and the boy that
afternoon. "Madame is too sick to see anyone," said the nurse.

But Catherine pushed her aside and entered, holding Alexandre
tightly.

She hastened down the hall to a small room with curtains so
drawn that the place was steeped in gloom lit by darts of blinding
light that slipped past the edges of the drapes.

In an easy chair, propped up with cushions, and beside a little
table loaded with a crushing array of medicine bottles, was a wisp
of a woman, with one sleeve pinned across her chest, from which
dangled crooked and withered fingers, like wilted celery spilling
over the top of a paper wrapper. Her sallow head, in which the eyes
were two dark holes, was drawn askew by shrunken neck muscles.

"Madame Dumas . . ." Catherine began, but the old lady was
staring at the child.

"You're my Alexandre's boy!" she cried. "You must be! Oh, my
child! My wonderful child! Tell me your name."

"Alexandre," the boy muttered, frightened by this contorted figure.

The old woman began to breathe heavily, her frame shook, and
she reached trembling fingers toward the table for her smelling salts.
As she calmed down, Catherine said, "Where is Monsieur Dumas?
I must find him at once."

"Come here, my child. Stand before me. I want to see you. Give
me your hand."

"Madame," Catherine said. "I must find Monsieur Dumas
quickly."

The old lady turned her head with pain. "Why? What do you want from him?"

"I'm losing my house. There's a mortgage payment I must meet. That's why we must locate Monsieur Dumas at once."

"Money," said the old lady. "A house. Is that what you want? Is that all anybody wants nowadays? I understand everything now. You're just another one of those women who keep taking advantage of my son's good nature. But you'll get nothing here. Nothing at all! Get out. Get out!"

Catherine reached to take Alexandre's hand. But the old woman held on to the boy.

"You'll not take my grandson!" she cried.

For a moment it seemed as if there would be a tug of war over the boy, in which the nurse would help on the old lady's side. But it failed to materialize when the old woman was suddenly taken with a seizure of shakes and the nurse was at once so busy among the medicine bottles seeking the one indicated for such attacks that Catherine was able to grab Alexandre and flee with him.

The little boy was himself filled with dry sobs of fear, and it took minutes to calm him down.

"Was that my grandmother?" he asked.

"Don't ask questions," Catherine said flatly.

They were walking along the street when suddenly the boy pointed down a side street. "Look! Papa! There's Papa!"

Catherine, following the direction he was pointing, saw a man beside a carriage, a man so tall and crowned with such a forest of hair that it could not have been anyone else but Dumas.

"Run!" she cried. "Hold him!"

"Papa!" Alexandre screamed and raced down the street.

The moment he did so, Catherine regretted her haste in sending him off to his father. For she saw a nurse in provincial costume carrying a little baby and being helped out of the carriage by Dumas, who then gave his arm to a dark-haired beauty.

But Dumas himself was not in the least put out at the unexpected appearance of Catherine and Alexandre. He introduced his two families as if it were the most natural thing in the world for a man to do. And indeed as if nothing could have been more apropos and luckier than this encounter. He was all smiles.

The beautiful Jewish actress, Bell Krebsamer, seemed pleased to meet some other members of Dumas' family.

"Alexandre talks about you all the time," she said and stroked the boy's blond curls. "Do you want to see my baby?" She turned away the soft cashmere lace from the baby, and the nurse presented a dark little thing as thick-lipped as the father.

The comparison between this baby who would certainly never grow up to be a beauty and her own handsome boy provided Catherine with a fleeting moment of pride.

"Come, everybody! Inside," said Dumas.

"Is this where Madame lives?" Catherine asked.

"No. This is my notary," said Dumas. "I'm registering myself as father of the little girl."

"What do you mean?"

"So she'll have the right to my name," Dumas explained. "And to my fortune, if ever I leave one," he added with a laugh.

Catherine pulled Dumas aside and whispered at him angrily. "You never did as much for your son, who deserves it far more!"

"Why should I?" Dumas asked. "Who would ever dare deny my son his name! Look at him. If ever a man had himself reproduced in miniature, this is it! But a girl, that's different. She needs protection."

"So you refuse!" Catherine cried, her cheeks in flame.

"Calm yourself, my dear Catherine. Of course I don't refuse. Come in. We'll have papers signed for everyone."

But as they were going in, Catherine still had another matter to settle. "What about my house? The payments aren't being made on the mortgage, and they're selling everything."

"I'll take care of it," Dumas said. "Don't let it worry you."

From long experience Catherine knew that when Dumas said of anything, "Don't let it worry you," that was precisely the time for worry. But it was not until the notary handed her the pen to sign the papers that she seriously wondered if she was doing right.

In the back of the room she could hear Dumas telling his son that someday soon he would take him to Humann the tailor and have him outfitted with a special British hunting suit, tweed and leather, and then they would also visit Revette, who made child-sized guns for the children of the Prince Royal. And after that they would go hunting.

It seemed to Catherine now that no good could come of this. Every time she had signed anything for Dumas it had resulted in a loss. Men had come to take away her clock and her rug and even her house. What would they take now?

"I'm afraid," she muttered.

"But what is there to be afraid of?" the notary asked. "Is it not all to the advantage of the child that he should have the legal right to his father's name, even though he can never have—unless Monsieur Dumas marries you—the honor of full legitimacy?"

"Yes," said Catherine meekly. And she signed.

And then Dumas signed too—with a flourish of his beautiful handwriting.

Then he caught up his son and held him high in the air. "Ladies and gentlemen," he announced, "I present to you Alexandre Dumas, future Count Davy de la Pailleterie! Never forget, my son, that you are descended from the Knights of the Holy Ghost founded by King Henri the Third, and that you are the grandson of Napoleon's bravest general, and the son of France's best dramatist! You have a great lineage to live up to."

When he put the little lad down, Alexandre's face was seen to be radiant, transfigured with pride.

"Now, what is the motto of our family?" Dumas asked.

"Love for love," said the boy.

"Then, quick, give me a kiss," said Dumas, and boy and father hugged each other.

But Catherine was right in her forebodings. A few months later two men knocked at the door and this time they did not come for a painting from the house, nor for the house itself. They wanted nothing less than her son. His father had picked out a boarding school for him.

Catherine, white, trembling, said to them, "Wait here. I'll find him." Then she ran out into the garden where Alexandre was playing. "Hide!" she whispered wildly. "Run and hide. Come back only when it's dark! Go quick!"

"Why?" he asked.

"Don't stand there!" she flung at him. "Go! There are men here who will take you to your grandmother! Do you want to go and live with her?"

That made an impression on the boy. He dashed down the garden, climbed up a tree that branched over a neighbor's wall.

"I can't find him," Catherine lied.

The men waited a while and then left.

Then Catherine rushed to Paris. She didn't know whom to consult, except the old notary who had drawn up the papers.

"He wants to take my son from me," she cried to him.

"Of course," said the notary. "Isn't that to your son's best interest?"

"No! He's no man to have a child. He will stuff him with pastry one day and forget to feed him the next!"

"There's nothing you can do, Madame. He has the law."

"I should have denied that he was the father. I should have lied."

"That would not have helped. You have no rights, don't you see? Any man, a totally unknown stranger, for example, could have declared himself the father of your child and could have taken him away from you. The only person who could have stopped a stranger from doing that would have been another man who would have disputed the stranger's right to your child. But you yourself could have said nothing one way or the other."

"When he was born I was not allowed to say who his father was . . ."

"That's right."

". . . and then afterward I have no right to say who his father isn't."

"That's right."

"And there's nothing I can do to save my child?"

"Nothing! He's not really your child. Not in the eyes of the law."

As if torn inside with a deep wound, she rushed back to her little home. She found Alexandre still hiding in the garden, hungry and cold.

"Is grandmother gone?" he asked.

"No," she lied. "And she has policemen after you. We must watch for them every moment of the day and night."

"What can we do?"

"You'll hide. You'll stay always in my room. You'll sleep under my bed. I'll put a mattress there."

In her frenzy she saw herself running away at night with the child. And she began to pack things wildly, realizing all the while that her plan was insane, that she had no money, no means, and only a basket in which to carry anything.

And in the midst of her hysterical preparations there was a knock at the door. Alexandre ran to hide under his mother's bed, and his heart beat furiously as he heard heavy steps tramping about and saw a flickering candlelight moving near and then away.

But the candlelight came back again and again to spill under the bed, and finally there was the light itself, right in his eyes.

He screamed. And he heard his mother scream. And a man's arm grabbed hold of him and pulled him out.

His mother's arms laced themselves around him, tore at him. "My Alexandre!" she sobbed, and he could feel her wet face upon his.

He was tugged at, jerked at, as if he were a package; then he felt himself pulled free, then someone running with him out into the cold night air; and a moment later he was dropped on the bottom of a carriage, a heavy horse blanket was thrown over him, and he was being jounced up and down as the horses were whipped away.

Behind him he could still hear the screams of his mother.

Neighbors were tending to her with cold-water compresses and smelling salts when Dumas entered. Catherine begged them to stay and shouted at Dumas, "Go away! Go away!" But Dumas shooed them out and closed the door.

"Look, Catherine, let's be reasonable!"

"I don't want to be reasonable! I want my child!"

"But you have your child! Every Sunday he is free to see you. I am only putting him in a school."

"I have nothing now. Nothing," she moaned. "You took my business, you took my body, you took my child. Now what do you want? My life?"

"Catherine, darling, you are upset. But when you've rested you'll see things more clearly. Surely you want the child to have a good education, don't you? Tell me: don't you? Of course you do. And

I'm going to settle a good pension on you, enough to keep you in comfort."

"No!" she shouted. "No! You can't pay me for what you've taken. You can't! I don't want anything from you!"

"Now, Catherine, please, please listen to me. Come to the notary's tomorrow morning and we shall settle everything for your future welfare."

"Go away. Just go away," Catherine begged and, covering her face with her hands, she wept inconsolably.

Dumas sighed and went to call in a neighbor to watch over her, and then he left.

Just exactly what happened at the notary's, or whether Catherine even went, is unknown. But soon after this the house in Passy was sold to cover the mortgage, and Catherine was back in a garret, once more living alone and earning her livelihood as a seamstress.

It was as if a storm named Dumas had come into her life, picked her up bodily, tossed her about for a while, and then had blown itself out, leaving her stranded almost exactly where it had found her.

As for Dumas, whose intentions, as I say, were of the best, he could and did congratulate himself for having started his son off properly toward a sound education.

CHAPTER TWENTY-ONE

Duelist?

THE MAN was really a clown.

All France laughed when Dumas told the story of how for once in his life he had known fright. He was traveling in Livonia, where he had come to know and love a thick mushroom soup and, arriving one night late at an inn, he had sat down in the common room and asked the landlady for a bowl of hot mushroom soup. Only he had forgotten the word for mushroom. But having made clear his desire for soup, he took paper and pencil from his pocket and drew a mushroom.

It was only when he saw the landlady's eyes bulging in horror, only when he saw her show the piece of paper to the peasants gathered in the room for their evening drink and saw them stare open-mouthed at him, it was only then that he realized that with his lack of ability in drawing he might have sketched a mushroom that looked like something he had absolutely no desire to have in his soup or in any other dish.*

Sweat broke out on Dumas' brow when he noticed the whole room emptying with the landlady. He expected at any moment that these rough peasants would be returning with pitchforks to rid the world of this stranger with the foul appetite. Or even worse, to set before him some unholy dish. He thought of escaping but felt himself glued to his seat with terror.

Until the landlady and the peasants returned with an umbrella, and Dumas out of sheer relief was ready to carry out his side of the bargain and consume this object, whalebone ribs and all.

Yes, all France laughed, and it is no doubt a great achievement to become a nation's clown, but what about the bastard son of this clown?

Even deep in his old age Dumas *fils* could not refer to his school years without suffering such pain as to force him to close the subject at once. His longest reference amounts to a single paragraph in a letter to Cuvillier-Fleury, tutor to the princes of the House of Orléans, in which he says:

"The teasing was continuous. The insults never stopped. Not a day passed that I was not involved in one or more fights. And I was always beaten. Never for a single moment was my body free of painful bruises. I despaired. I stopped growing. I was weak, sickly, utterly without interest for either games or studies. And yet I would not give in. Nor could I say a word of this to my parents. On my mother it would have had the effect of a reproach. To my father it would have seemed a sign of weakness. I had to suffer in silence and take what consolation I might from the conviction that things could not continue this way for very long without my dying."

To understand this and other brief references that Dumas *fils* has left us of these painful years, let's take a look at the school itself.

---

* This resemblance has resulted in a family of mushrooms with a scientific name from the Greek φαλλός.

Picture to yourself a bleak square of barracklike buildings, two-storied, stuccoed, once white but now leprous with age, surrounding a courtyard of uneven cobblestones. In the center an iron pump, ringed with puddles of stagnant, muddy water. It might have been a prison. It happened to be a boys' school.

The director, Prosper-Parfait Goubaux, considered himself something of a journalist, since he wrote now and then for the newspapers under the name of Pierre Aubry. He was also something of a playwright, since, under the name of Dinaux, he had had a hand in that most successful of all nineteenth-century melodramas *Thirty Years, or The Life of a Gambler.* He had also brought to Dumas *père* the germ for a play which the latter developed into *Richard Darlington.*

That with all this he still ran a school must be set down to his credit. Unless we choose to go into the question of how he ran it. We know, for example, that now and then, when he or one of his theatrical friends would open a play, the whole school of a hundred boys would be taken to the house to function as a claque, the director himself giving them the signals. This was a real lark. And for the moment the world of Paris had the impression of a gay school flourishing under the enlightened guidance of an artist.

Such was no doubt Dumas *père's* own impression and his reason for charging Goubaux with the upbringing of his son.

But such excursions were rare. Much more typical of the school would be such a picture as you would derive from watching the twice-weekly compulsory foot washings. Then, no matter how freezing the weather, a couple of the bigger boys would man the pump, and all the rest of the students, herded by the older lads acting as monitors, would be forced to take off shoes and stockings and raise their trousers above their knees and file past the leather hose from which spurted an icy stream of water.

The boys were made to soap their feet well and return for a rinsing.

Hygienically this was no doubt sound enough. But consider the effect of this cataract of water on the spirits of the bolder lads, the urge to shove, the battle to get possession of the hose, the gradual covering of the cobblestones with a soapy slime and the expansion of separate little pools of water until the courtyard was a veritable lake. And then the final melee as spirits reached their climax, and a free-for-all ensued from which one was lucky to escape with no more than a good drenching.

Meals were similarly Spartan.

Of the three feedings a day, only one was served at table. The other two were taken standing up, milk and bread being served in the morning and bread and hard cheese in the evening. Quantities were perhaps large enough, but only the noon meal was warm, consisting of a dish of thick vegetable soup, a slice of meat, and a piece of cake or fruit. Watered wine was served only to the older boys.

That morning hunk of bread was generally treasured to munch on whenever one was hungry during the day. But perhaps precisely because it was such a treasure, it was also something to be snatched, something to battle over. It served as a ball in impromptu tennis games and as a missile for snowball fights when there was no snow. Thus there were times when these precious crusts of bread would fly through the air thick as arrows at Agincourt.

In one way or another Alexandre lost his share almost every day. If nothing else, two boys would snatch it and keep tossing it to each other, high over Alexandre's head, who meanwhile rushed in vain from one boy to the other, always meeting a bland expression and two mocking empty hands that said, "Why come to me for your bread? I haven't got it. Look! He's got it over there."

It was a sport impervious to pleas or to indifference.

Tears were worst of all, for they only added to the general amusement. "Ah, poor boy, we've made him cry. Here. Take back your bread." But woe if you reached for it: the treacherous hand would suddenly fling it to the other boy. And woe if you didn't reach for it, for then the thief was entitled to say: "Well, he doesn't want it." And it would probably be immediately broken into pieces and gobbled up by a half-dozen famished lads.

Often the bread would end by falling into the mud around the pump. To attempt to pick it up was to have your fingers stepped on by someone who would say, "Oh, excuse me, I didn't know you were buttering your bread." And to wait for someone else to pick it up for you was to have him say, "Oh, look. It's dirty. Wait. I'll clean it for you," and then spit on it and rub it with his sleeve. And then, in addition, pretend to insist on your accepting it: "Here. It's clean now. I washed it for you."

In his fury little Alexandre would launch himself at one or the other of his tormentors, until he couldn't fight any more and wanted only to lie gasping on the cobblestones.

The ringleader in this sport was a lad named André. Others had their occasional fun out of molesting Alexandre, but only André made it his life's vocation.

It was André who, on Alexandre's first day at school, bent his quill pen into a spring and flipped a gob of ink that landed right on the back of Dumas' neck. The ink stained the lad's collar and splashed up over his ear.

Alexandre, not knowing what had struck him, reached his hand around, felt a strange wetness there and in drawing his fingers forward, smeared the ink not only over his whole hand, but over his cheek too.

André roared. What fun! And feeling himself secure because of his size, he had no hesitation in claiming the merit for this well-aimed shot.

Alexandre realized at once that he had no chance of beating this hulking fellow, who was at least twice his weight. But he didn't hesitate for a moment: he attacked nevertheless.

Why?

Courage?

Perhaps. But something more than that: necessity. Stark necessity. He had to uphold the good name of Dumas. Or else perish.

What else did he have to cling to? He had to prove not only that the name of Dumas was one to be proudly borne, but that he had a right to bear it. That he was a true sprig of the valiant Dumas.

And meanwhile the name of Dumas was in constant dispute.

For example, a caricature circulated in Paris showing Dumas, his features purposely distorted to make him seem more ape than man. This ape, equipped with an enormous pair of shears, was slashing at volumes marked Schiller, Shakespeare, Goethe, Lope de Vega and Victor Hugo, cutting out whole sections which he was piling up to make another volume, one marked Alexandre Dumas.

Some of the boys brought this cartoon to school. André even

pinned one on little Alexandre's back, without the latter's being aware of it until the gales of laughter following him everywhere called it to his attention. The boy's suffering over this cartoon is not to be described. The implications of the cartoon were so plain, the insulting nature of it so brutal, that wherever it appeared it was enough to send him into a frenzy of fighting.

And at night he couldn't sleep from pondering some impossible and telling revenge by which he and his father would turn the tables on their maligners.

Dumas, all the while, his ego puffed up by the never-ending theatrical successes which made his name known, in translated versions, on every stage of the civilized globe, took the caricature with a hearty laugh and never stopped working.

As to his son's ordeal, he had not the faintest inkling of it. No doubt he was aware that in every home of Paris the question of Dumas was being debated, quarreled over and laughed over, and that was precisely what he wanted; but that from these homes boys would return to school after every free day to bring back some new tale with which to tease his son, that was something to which Dumas apparently never gave a thought.

It was not only the question of whether he was the real author of his plays that was debated, but the question of his sex life, his financial affairs, and most of all, no doubt, his life of honor—that is to say, his duels.

About these the most fantastic stories circulated and were widely believed.

"Want to know how to get a great reputation as a redoubtable duelist without risking your skin? Well, this is how Dumas does it. All it takes is an actor who can play his part in a little scene. There's nothing difficult about that. First of all, in Paris actors come ten francs a dozen and, secondly, what actor would refuse Dumas a favor, considering that Dumas puts on six shows or more a year, and actors are always looking for good parts. So he has no trouble on that score. Now, actor and Dumas go to some fine restaurant or other well-frequented place where Dumas is always sure of a crowd of listeners. Dumas plays his usual self, and at that game there is no one like him. Meanwhile, the actor sits apart, dressed like some member of the Jockey Club of Paris, a dandy *tiré à quatres* *épingles,** but after a while he starts to listen to what Dumas is saying, takes offense, breaks in to argue with Dumas, to contradict him, to insult him, and finally to decry him!

"The crowd grows ever larger. The argument ever more explosive. One can see the blood mount in Dumas' swarthy face. Apoplexy seems to threaten as he takes insult after insult, and again and again tries to pass the matter off in a humble and conciliatory fashion. Then just at the right moment when the crowd is beginning to conclude that Dumas is a coward who will swallow any insult, suddenly, with his right hand, he tears at the kid glove on his left hand (which he has carefully failed to remove for precisely this bit of action), tears it so violently that he rips through the stitching and has nothing but ragged pieces to whip across the dandy's face, where they leave pink welts.

" 'My seconds will call upon you!' Dumas shouts, and stalks off, breathing like a volcano in eruption.

"Bystanders, certain that they have seen one of the most dramatic moments of high life among the fast set of Paris, race off to tell their friends of the incident that fate was kind enough to put before their very eyes.

"Soon all Paris is talking about another Dumas duel. And after a while news leaks out that it was fought early one morning in the Bois de Vincennes, or else in the Bois de Boulogne, and a day later one sees Dumas walking around with his arm in a big sling, or with a black patch on his forehead covering one eye.

"And maintaining a silence that is intended to speak volumes.

"Of course, only the gullibles are impressed, but is there any city in the globe that counts more gullibles than Paris? Those who have witnessed the scene before, and to whom it is now as familiar as the bearded lady in the circus, simply smile and walk on. But it's precisely the gullibles that Dumas aims to impress. It is they who rush to his plays, they who eagerly snatch up his books.

"However, when, instead of a dressed-up actor, it is a real live journalist like Granier de Cassagnac, or a genuine bibliographer like Quérard, or a social satirist like Eugène de Mirecourt, who publicly piles one insult on another against Dumas, and nothing happens, then it's sad. Very sad. Because the great battler, for those in

* Right out of a bandbox.

the know, has turned out to be nothing but a clown with a blown-up pig's bladder."

Fitzgerald, obviously one of those in the know, in his two-volume study of Dumas, insists categorically that Dumas' duels were all fakes (Volume II, page 62).

One of these make-believe duels, Fitzgerald tells us, in order to be made still more believable, was carried to a "real" bit of fighting where the seconds were also being deceived, and Dumas, to impress them the more, raged about, exhibiting a wonderful martial ardor, whipping his sword through the air and exclaiming, "Come, defend yourself. Ha! A victory over you would be but a paltry thing!" until eventually his "opponent" had more than he could stomach and gave Dumas a little "prod" in the arm.

Dumas, aghast, seeing a bit of red staining his sleeve, dropped his weapon. "What's that for?" he asked, going pale.

And Fitzgerald comments: "It was not in the programme."

Then Fitzgerald goes on to tell of another prearranged duel, in which it was agreed that the bullets were to be fired into the ground, but unfortunately the bullet from Dumas' pseudo-opponent ricocheted and buried itself in Dumas' calf, taking along pieces of his leather boot and his tweed trousers, which later had to be dug out and caused the author to go about on crutches for a little while, much to the amusement of those in the know and to the further amazement of the gullibles.

Now, as for myself, much as I dislike being a gullible, and little as I can know at this late date, when more than a century has passed since these matters stirred the air for a brief moment and then disappeared, still I cannot help remarking that it does seem strange in these two "duels" with actors, both no doubt carefully rehearsed (for it cannot be imagined that so experienced a showman as Dumas would go into an exhibition of this sort without being sure of his performance), and both duels furthermore conducted with actors who were looking to please Dumas for the sake of their careers, that yet both should somehow result in Dumas' being wounded.

Does that sound plausible?

Fitzgerald, however, certain that he has proved his point, now goes on to ridicule two other duels of which we happen to know the protagonists, neither of whom were actors, both being writers. And here it seems that the writers did a better job of faking their duels than the actors did, since both these duels were bloodless.

One has already been referred to. It was the duel with Jules Janin, well-known novelist and critic.

Janin had gone to the opening of Dumas' *Les Demoiselles de Saint-Cyr,** and there he had laughed himself sick, and after the performance had come to Dumas' box to thank him personally for a wonderful time.

"When I can sit for three hours and forget the gout that is stabbing my toes, then I know that I have seen a great comedy," Janin said.

But the next day Dumas found in the paper the most devastating attack that he had ever sustained in any review. And the article was signed J. Janin.

Dumas sent back a fulminating reply.

Janin's defense was quite simple: anyone can sit in the theater and enjoy a play. But criticism is another matter. Here you are no longer part of the playwright's audience, but have an audience of your own to take care of, and there's nothing the newspaper reader likes so much as a perfectly savage review, which it was Janin's job to serve up to him.

As already described, each of the duelists declared himself unwilling to fight with his own favorite weapon for fear of killing the other, whereupon, carried away by admiration for each other, by common impulse they embraced, weeping.

The second bloodless duel was one that was reported as far as the United States, for it was fought between Dumas and Frédéric Gaillardet over the authorship of *La Tour de Nesle*, a terrific success not only in Paris, but especially in the United States enjoyed a vogue that swept the country, Brander Matthews stating that it was in the repertory of half the theaters across the continent.

When this hit was first put on in Paris, it was billed as written by XXX, with everyone aware that XXX meant Dumas. Whereupon a totally unknown young man named Gaillardet appeared and declared that he was XXX and demanded that his name be billed.

---

* This was Queen Victoria's favorite play. A special gala performance was put on for her when she visited Paris in 1855.

The producer refused, declaring that Gaillardet's script had been only the starting point for a completely fresh play.

Gaillardet went to court and produced documents and contracts and won his case, but only insofar as his name was concerned: Dumas was able to prove such extensive rewriting that he retained the major share of the royalties.

Dumas, in fact, claimed that he had never even seen the original Gaillardet script, having been shown an already extensively reworked script done by someone else. The producer, Harel, sided with Dumas, stating that he had bought the Gaillardet play knowing that it was entirely unfit for the stage but convinced that it contained a good idea. But to satisfy the ruling of the court he changed the billing on the play to read: "XXX and Gaillardet."

Gaillardet sued again and won again, and the billing on the play was reversed to read "Gaillardet and XXX."

Six suits were won by Gaillardet, and all Paris began to side with him, until he made the mistake of writing another play, *Struensee*, which failed dismally, and then still another one, *Crime for Love*, which failed even worse. After that people were strongly divided.

Gaillardet's battles with Dumas continued in court and newspapers until it came to a duel.

Dumas proposed swords, declaring that even a bad shot such as Gaillardet was said to be might by chance kill. As for himself, he only wanted to let a little blood out of Gaillardet and then as far as he was concerned honor would be satisfied.

Gaillardet insisted on pistols, saying that he had never held a sword in his hand.

When the principals and seconds appeared at Saint-Mandé early one morning, just off the Bois de Vincennes, Gaillardet was seen to be dressed in deep black from head to toes. It is well known that solid black makes a difficult target to shoot at, the eye finding no point where it can fix itself. Dumas, on the other hand, had taken no such precaution. He had on a light shirt and tan trousers.

Gaillardet's advantage was clear.

Then suddenly Dumas noticed, so he tells us in his *Memoirs*, that Gaillardet had failed to remove a little plug of white cotton from one ear.

"I shall aim at that and split his head open," Dumas declared to one of his seconds. "Watch me!"

Ah, if only he had! Yes, if only he had, it might have been most tragic for Gaillardet, but the vexed question of Dumas' duels would have been settled. Who would have dared raise again the story of faked duels, after a body had been carried from the field of honor? Who would have dared raise again the question of whether Dumas was the author of his own works or not?

Just one life, and all problems would have been solved. And Dumas says that he had meant to settle things once and for all. He was strongly tempted. And to prove it, he had taken his seconds around to a pistol-shooting gallery the night before. He had had the boy load ten guns and had picked them up one after another and split a clay pipe every time—shooting almost as fast as one can count.

Bixio, the scientist, had been present and had said, "I've still to see a man die of a fatal gunshot. I understand that when mortally struck a man spins around once and only then falls to the ground."

"You'll verify it tomorrow," Dumas had promised him.

He himself had been prepared to die in this duel, having made his will in favor of his son and daughter, and having stayed up all night to write thirty-six letters, one of which was to be sent to his mother every month from a different Italian city, thus giving the bedridden woman still plenty of time to die without ever knowing that her son had predeceased her.

But, instead, what happened was this: as the signal for firing was given and Dumas was slowly bringing his pistol down from overhead to take aim, Gaillardet, nervous, fired immediately. Dumas' finger was on the trigger, his aim was on that cotton plug, but he hesitated, waiting to see if he still felt whole or not. In a fraction of a moment he realized that Gaillardet's bullet had not even touched him. He still had a bead on that bit of white in Gaillardet's ear but he found himself unable to pull the trigger on a completely undefended head. He deflected his weapon and let the shot go far to the side.

Another bloodless duel was over. Obviously another fake.

And so in school more teasing for Alexandre, and thereafter a greater effort than ever to prove by the expenditure of his own reckless courage that the duel had not been faked and that his father was still the bravest of men.

Bixio had to wait until the revolution of 1848 when, being struck in the street fighting, he spun around and was heard to mutter, "So it's true."

Dumas' attitude toward killing was that only passion could excuse it. Cold-blooded murder, and capital punishment, he hated. And since his anger tended to evaporate quickly, he could not bring himself to take a life. His *Thousand and One Phantoms*, besides being a classic collection of shiver tales, is also a powerful argument against the use of the guillotine and against capital punishment in general.

Like his father, he was Mister Humanity.

But the result of deflecting his bullet from that cotton plug was that sixty years later the Gaillardet matter was still live enough to be an issue, and Dumas *fils* had still again to rise to his father's defense when a statue to Dumas *père* was unveiled in Paris and showed on the base a partial list of his father's works, including the much disputed *Tour de Nesle*. The children of Gaillardet wrote an angly letter to the press of Paris, insisting on the immediate removal of this work from the inscription, declaring that they could produce court records to prove that the play was written by their father

Dumas *fils* saved the day for his father's reputation by the following note to the papers:

It cannot be doubted that my father had a hand in the writing of the *Tour de Nesle*, since the courts did not deprive him of the major share of the royalties. I am therefore willing to enter into a compromise arrangement with the heirs of Monsieur Frédéric Gaillardet: if they will not object to the play's remaining on my father's statue, I will engage myself not to object if the name of the play also appears on a monument to their father, whenever it may be erected.

This was, of course, a safe arrangement and a sly dig as well, since it was hardly likely that anyone would ever raise a statue to Gaillardet, though he has the merit of having come to New York, purchased the dying *Courrier Français des États-Unis*, which had

been founded by Joseph Bonaparte, and changing it from a Bona-
partist sheet to an organ for all French people, from Canada to
New Orleans, no matter what their party affiliation. This newspaper,
which some years ago celebrated its hundredth birthday, is still
being published.

But while Alexandre was thus taking the brunt of his father's
extravagant career, Dumas went right on embroiling himself in
other dubious duels—for example, one resulting from the affair of
the Duchess of Berry.

This Duchess, it may be recalled, was the charming and young
wife of the heir to the French throne until that prince fell at the
hands of an assassin, whereupon the Duchess would have still been
the mother of the new heir to the throne if the revolution of 1830
hadn't thrown her, along with a lot of other Bourbons, out of France
altogether.

The Duchess ran off to England, but from there she launched a
one-woman invasion of France, thinking to rouse the country to her
side and force the new government to acknowledge her son as still
the heir.

She was captured and locked up in a castle.

And now comes the piquant part of this exceedingly French tale:
two doctors were summoned in the utmost secrecy to examine the
Duchess, and they came to the conclusion that she was in a condition that in the case of widows always leads people to resort to
their fingers—and in this case the mathematics could hardly be
to the Duchess's credit.

Since in France, as in most civilized countries, nothing gets
around so fast as a secret, and since everybody has fingers on which
to figure, the whole country was thus split, with one half crying that
this story was a filthy lie against a lovely and tragically widowed
princess, and the other half declaring itself as certain of the diag-
nosis as if they had had a finger in it.

Duels began to explode on all sides, and so fierce was the popular feeling concerning the Duchess's condition that the contagion
spread everywhere, and no sooner was one duel fought than the
seconds immediately challenged each other, thus creating two new
duels for every one that was settled. So involved did these cross
challenges become that the duelists had to line up their appoint-

ments, and the newspapers began to publish lists and schedules, as today they might do in some sports tournament.

Naturally a man like Dumas, whose father and mother had met as a result of a similar epidemic of duels over another insult to royalty, immediately sent in his name to be put down on the list of those who thought the princess was *enceinte*, and would fight any challenger for it. But already the police had begun to interfere, dueling being naturally forbidden by law, and as all those whose names were listed for duels found themselves watched night and day, Dumas never got a chance to match his blade, and the whole affair gradually calmed down.

Anyhow, when the Duchess gave birth to a fine baby, the correctness of the medical prognosis no longer seemed an issue worth dying for.

But once again people pointed out that Dumas the duelist had increased his reputation for dueling with little expense to his personal safety. Some even claimed that he had sent in his name when he was already aware that most of the duels would never be fought.

CHAPTER TWENTY-TWO

Annexation versus Stealing

AT SCHOOL, meanwhile, every new gossip about Dumas continued to bring new misery to Alexandre. For example, when the cartoon of Dumas' plagiarisms came out, André conceived the idea of attaching the same slander to Alexandre. He drew a smaller version, with Alexandre as a small monkey pasting up his own compositions and exercise papers out of pieces cut from the work of his schoolmates.

He labeled the monkey Jocko.

Alexandre, who had never given anyone the least cause to imagine that he copied his papers from those of his fellow students, was amazed that this unjust accusation should gain credence, and that throughout the school he should be called Jocko.

The mere mention of this word was soon enough to send him into a frenzy of fighting. He would look around, guess at the possible utterer of it, and fling himself at the boy, no matter what difference there might be in size.

He found the writing of his compositions, the drawing up of mathematical exercises, ever more onerous. He felt himself already suspected of copying, even before he had set anything down. And in classroom, he kept his head ducked in lest anyone taunt him for trying to peep at his neighbor's work.

Added to this there were whispers. Things not openly said, but intimated. Things he didn't understand, except in a vague way. Insults that he realized were terrible but that made no real sense, reminding him of snatches of nightmare, fleeting, obscure, horrible, and yet somehow taunting, compelling. A hundred times a day they would come to his mind, and then disappear before his reasoning faculties could grasp them.

All he could understand was that he had done something terrible, something that no decent person ever did. He felt permanently separated, exiled, from everyone else.

No wonder the boy looked forward all week to Sunday, when he could flee this school and go home to his mother or his father.

But Sunday was a day so thick with its own problems, problems that in their way were even more of a torture than those of the weekdays, that no sooner was Sunday at hand than already he wished it were over.

Sunday, after a very early Mass, preparations were made by most of the boys to go home. Some few lads came from distant parts and remained in school all day, but by far the greater number were from Paris or near by, and their parents would begin to call for them right after Mass. They would come in hired cabs, in ordinary carriages, in fancy coaches with coachman and footman both in livery, and with coats of arms emblazoned on the glossy woodwork.

And all the while Alexandre knew that down the street, hiding in an angle where the wall was built out to include a tree, his mother stood, wrapped in a brown shawl, waiting for him. And the question the little boy had to solve every week now confronted him again: until what hour could he still expect Papa to show up? Or, rather, how long should one keep one's mother waiting there while one continued to hope for Papa and his shining tilbury? For, obviously, only if father didn't show up would one go off with mother.

And as the minutes passed and his father still didn't appear, Alexandre's heart sank both with longing for his father and with anguish over his mother, whose presence he sensed at all times, waiting for him to resign himself to having to spend the day with her. . . .

And that was so wrong, so cruel. Because it was not at all the way Alexandre felt. He loved his mother. And he loved his father. And it was sheer brutality to force him every week to undergo this test of his affections! Not that he could possibly have formulated it that way. He could only suffer it, not explain it.

Nor did the torture stop when the situation was resolved and all hope given up of seeing his father for that day, whereupon he would take his bundle of dirty clothes and go find his mother in the angle of the wall.

What he wanted then with all his heart was to have her throw her arms around him and love him, love him hard, love him both for herself and also for the father who was absent. And sometimes she would do just that. But more often, irritated by her long wait, she would fling something of this sort at him: "Too bad your father didn't come, isn't it?"

And if he didn't answer she would insist. "Well, isn't it?"

What could he say? What could he really say? The word *yes* would be the truth, but an insult. And the *no* would be an outright lie. So he would try to embrace his mother and wheedle her out of it, feeling all the while that the honesty had gone out of the situation. But he would do it nevertheless, for children live in the passageways left between the emotional walls raised by the adults, zigzagging here and there, darting for an escape wherever they find a loophole, behaving like animals in a maze that is full of delights and dangers and traps.

"So you want me to believe that you love me?" his mother would mock.

"But, *Maman,* I do. I really do. Oh, *Maman,* if you only knew . . ."

"Well, that's fine. But it would be a lot easier to believe you if you didn't look so glum about it."

"Glum? Do I look glum?"

"See that dead tree that has fallen down there? It looks ten times as gay as you do."

"But, *Maman,* really . . ."

"I can just imagine what a different expression you'd wear if your father had shown up. Oh, don't think I haven't watched you driving off with him. I know exactly how you look. As if the gates of paradise had opened up. I've never seen you looking that way for me. Never!"

How could he explain to her (when he was, as a matter of fact, himself still struggling in the quicksand of all these painful experiences) that it was not that he wasn't fond of his mother, but that precisely the infrequency of his father's visits made it all the more important that he shouldn't miss a single one by failing to wait as long as possible?

And then there was a fact that couldn't be denied: it was so much easier to be gay with his father! But this was the mystifying element in the situation, something which of course he never analyzed at that time, but which he felt just the same: that with his mother he wanted to be gay but couldn't. While with his father, he just naturally felt gay, but somehow always with a sense that he shouldn't.

Just to see Papa's bright tilbury come bounding up, its wheel spokes glittering, and every piece of silver on the harness flashing in the sun, and father sitting there with a big smile on his ruddy face, and beside him a beautiful lady whose skirts overflowed, so that when she made room for you, you were pressed on one side by her satin and on the other side by Papa's soft corduroy, and you breathed lilies of the valley here and eau de cologne there. . . .

And father immediately handing you the reins and in a second you had turned the horse around and with a flick of the whip you had the horse dashing down the street—and too late you realized that you had passed by the angle where mother was hiding without so much as a glance at her.

And father already talking of something exciting. . . .

Alas, it was too late then to change one's expression of joy, and yet one did change one's expression, not outwardly, but within: for merely at the thought of that quiet figure in a brown shawl, deep in the angle of the wall, one would be stricken with such a pang in one's chest that one felt as if someone had stepped into one's lungs with a hard heel.

And all day long, despite the joy of being with father, there would be moments when it was as if a brown shawl passed before one's eyes, and outside one's laughter might continue, but inside it would die.

And thus, whether it was his mother who took him to her little room, or his father who took him to his latest apartment in the rue Bleue or Chaussée d'Antin, there was always an undercurrent of tragedy to his Sundays, so that in spite of his six days of misery, there were times when he awoke to Sunday with a sense of dread and found himself wishing that it were Monday already. Then, instead of having to suffer at the hands of the parents whom he loved, he would only have to suffer at the hands of his schoolmates whom he hated.

And then, as if that weren't enough, there was still the matter of his dirty laundry. Obviously there was no sense in bringing a bundle of dirty clothes to his father. He never knew when he would see his father again. So it was not until his father was ruled out for that Sunday that he would go and fetch his dirty clothes and bring them to his mother.

But of course his mother noticed that when his father took him away, Alexandre dispensed with the matter of his laundry, and thus it was as if that bundle was her allotted share. This was what she was entitled to. Dumas got the joy. She got the work.

And yet if Alexandre would forget to bring her his clothes, she would remind him of it. And she would even say, "If you go off with your father you can still give me your laundry, you know. At least I'll have something to remind me of you."

But this was sheer bitterness. And the boy realized it. The whole business of the dirty clothes was upsetting and irritating—not only bringing the bundle with him when he went to meet his mother, but also her insistence on carrying it ("I'm used to carrying bundles of clothes") and her continuing concern with the problem when they were finally home. She would have him undress and would wash and clean and mend and press everything he had on.

And keep shaking her head. "How could you possibly get an ink stain on the back of your blouse?"

Or: "I never saw so many torn-off buttons. What do you children do anyhow? And of course you didn't save the buttons, did you? No, naturally not. Well, I'll have to see what I've got in my button box."

In the matter of undressing, it was his bruises that bothered him especially. He would take off his clothes piecemeal and stand in such a way as to make his worst ones inconspicuous. Because his bruises always set her off. "That's not just a bruise. That's a real contusion. You should have leeches on that."

"It's all right, *Maman*. It doesn't hurt."

"You can't tell me that that doesn't hurt. It must. How did you get it anyhow?"

"Playing."

"Playing? Playing what? What kind of game can you possibly play that would give you a bruise there? Explain that to me."

"Oh, games of all kinds. How can I remember how I got that one?"

"Can't remember how you got that one! Why, it's a wonder no bones were broken."

And the questioning would go on and on until it was maddening. And then she'd finally subside, muttering, "Imagine taking children away from their mothers and putting them in a school. Who could ever have invented such a cruel thing?"

Then her lips would tremble and her eyes would close and tears would be pressed out from beneath the lashes, and she'd say suddenly, very harshly, "Here! Thread this needle. I can't see any more. My eyes are getting old," and she'd turn away to grope for her handkerchief.

Oh, yes, this would have been the moment to put his arms around his mother and kiss her, and afterward, back in his dormitory, when the assistant had gone off with his lantern and plunged the big room and all its cubicles into darkness, this moment would come back to him and he'd regret not having done it and promise himself that next Sunday he would behave differently to his mother. But somehow, at the same time, he knew that everything would be the same, and he would always be left with nothing but his regrets and his tears.

Years later, looking back on it, he would wonder what else was to be expected from a day that began with his mother saying, "So you have to spend Sunday with your mother instead of your father. Well, too bad, because I'm dull. *On s'embête avec moi.* I don't know how to make things gay like your father does. All I know is how to wash and to sew. Really, I don't blame anyone for not liking my company. I don't like it myself."

For years he did not know why every Sunday with his mother would end in a headache. Even when on nice days they would go out to Saint-Cloud or to the Jardin des Plantes, a Sunday with his mother would always end up with a headache which would destroy his appetite when finally they sat down to eat their evening meal in her room.

It was the one meal in the week he might have eaten in peace, but somehow he had no desire to eat. He felt flushed, dizzy, and he longed to be back in school.

His mother, perceiving it, would say, "Can't wait to be back with your ruffians, eh?"

"No," he would say. "That's not it."

"Of course I don't blame you for not eating my cooking, after the wonderful meals your father serves."

"It's just that I have a headache," he would tell her.

She'd feel his head and verify that it was warm. "You're not going to be sick, are you?"

"No," he'd insist. "I'll be all right."

Sometimes he made an effort to speak to her about his studies. There were moments that were not without interest. For example, in natural history the boys were going to repeat Franklin's experiment with a kite in a thunderstorm to prove that lightning was the same as the spark that one could get from a Leyden jar. But then he would see his mother's glance go to her night stand, where she still kept the thin volumes that the curé had given her, those books on elementary grammar, spelling, natural history and arithmetic, which they had once studied together during that short year when they had been so happy with each other.

And thus, the day, begun in glumness, would close in gloom, and they would walk together to the school, where she, conscious of her workingwoman's clothes, would kiss her son good-by a good block or two from the school, and he would somehow be glad to be back.

With his father life was so completely different that it was as if one had gone to live in another world.

No one understood so well the art of making life sparkle as his father. Sunday might be anything: a hunting party, for example. Or a visit to one of his friends. Dinner might be in some crowded café where everybody knew Dumas and Dumas knew everyone, and the conversation and the laughter crackled on all sides.

"Ha-ha-ha! Did you understand that, my boy? Well, you can't yet. But you will someday. It's because these days they are starting new periodicals for everything: for artists and architects and bookbinders and just lately one for nursing mothers, and Monsieur Heine has just announced a magazine for fetuses. And he is assigning subjects for articles to all the famous writers and scenes for illustrations to all our best painters! Ha-ha-ha!—Come. You must meet Herr Heine. Thiers, our minister, has just declared that this German writes the best French in Paris."

And thus little Alexandre would later remember meeting all the great people of the era.

Or it might be an evening at the theater, in father's box, with visiting back and forth of all the notables, everybody distinguished for something, and father constantly whispering to him, "That's Taglioni, the great dancer. And that's her rival, Fanny Elssler. Those are the two Johannot brothers, both wonderful illustrators. That's Buloz, the editor of the *Revue des Deux Mondes*. And that's Dr. Véron, of the *Constitutionnel*." And everywhere opera glasses were aimed here, there, everyone looking, recognizing each other, shouting to each other, exclaiming over this and that.

There were evenings when Alexandre would suddenly find himself in costume. He was a stork, in white, with a giant yellow beak that he could make go *clack-clack* by pulling a hidden string. Father was made up as a greased pole.

"I'm the mast of Cockaigne. Come on, my little stork. Up you go!"

And off they went to a masked ball at Amaury Duval's.

Or it might be an evening at Liszt's, with the pianist playing madly, for he was determined to have an execution unequaled anywhere in the musical world, but stopping anyhow to order all the children to gather around and providing them with horns and drums

and triangles and leading them in an impromptu performance of
Haydn's toy symphony.

How wonderful to be in these salons, with their mirrors and their
polished woods and their soft carpets and crystal chandeliers, and
the walls hung with stretched silk, so that everything glistened,
even the people, and the men, Musset, Vigny, Soulié, making a fuss
over him, and the women putting their sweet-smelling, powdered
arms around him.

How rare those days were! In between what months of desola-
tion!

For in spite of all this constantly rising popularity of Dumas'
throughout the civilized world, or perhaps because of it, the attacks on him never let up.

There were people in Paris who felt that they had the key to this
underground war. They insisted that all these ugly stories originated from a single source. "There's someone sets these rumors
afloat," his friends said. "Somebody who wishes to harm you."

"Who could possibly wish to harm me?" Dumas would ask, "when
there's no one I hate."

"Of course you remember that caricature of you as an ape with
a pair of scissors, cutting up the classics to make yourself a play?"

"Yes, sure I remember it."

"Have you any idea who perpetrated it?"

Dumas shrugged. "Never thought of it."

"Well, it was Granier de Cassagnac."

"Granier de Cassagnac? What can he have against me?"

"Nothing. But then he didn't think it up for himself, but to please
someone else. Have you any idea for whom?"

"How should I know?" Dumas asked.

"Yes, but if you wanted to know you could, by just studying it."

"I haven't even a copy."

"No, but if you remember it at all you ought to be able to find
the clue in your mind."

"A clue in the caricature itself?" Dumas asked.

"Yes. Can you recall whose works were pictured in it?"

Dumas thought for a moment and he exploded. "But, no! That's
impossible!"

"So you do remember something strange about it?"

"Call it strange, if you like, that among all those dead classics—Schiller, Shakespeare and so forth—from whom I'm supposed to be cutting my play, there's only one live person, a Frenchman, who will certainly one day belong among the classics, but who surely is out of place there as yet."

"So you've finally noticed it. Victor Hugo, young, alive, hardly to be ranked yet with those others."

"And you want me to believe that this is proof that he ordered this caricature made?"

"How else did he suddenly become a classic? Who else but himself would already put him among the classics?"

"But Victor Hugo and I, we love and respect each other."

"Speak for yourself. That is no doubt the way you feel about Victor Hugo, but are you sure he feels that way about you?"

"How else?"

"Remember that he opened the battle against the classicists, but it was you who stole the show away. You beat him by a full year."

"But don't you know that he stayed up through a whole night to smooth out my verses before I submitted my *Christine*?"

"Yes. But that was before you had made a success. You were a nobody then. He could be generous. Now you are somebody. He can only be jealous."

"Nonsense!"

"And your plays run months, where his run weeks. And sometimes not even weeks."

"He's still a giant compared to me."

"A giant in genius, no doubt. But not in popularity. And Victor Hugo wants everything. He wants to be the greatest in every field: novels, plays, poems, history—he even wants to be the ruler of France."

"Why shouldn't he be?" Dumas asked. "He would be the best France ever had."

"Did you notice that this caricature appeared just as Victor Hugo was producing his *Marie Tudor*?"

"What about it?"

"Wasn't there talk about *Marie Tudor*'s being very much—in fact too much—modeled after your *Christine*?"

"There will always be people who will talk that sort of thing."

"Well, Victor Hugo is now preparing to open his *Lucretia Borgia*, which is rumored to resemble your *Tour de Nesle*. Let's see if once again he tries to turn the question of plagiarism toward you, so as to keep it away from himself."

A few months after that the answer came: a long, three-part article in the newspaper *Les Débats*. Signed *Granier de Cassagnac*.

This time it was no mere caricature. This time it was a detailed accusation. A full bill of particulars. Here, for example, was a whole column from Schiller's *Don Carlos*. And parallel to it another column with a scene from Dumas' *Henri III*.

There couldn't be much doubt about this scene: it was practically word for word a copy.

Schiller's Don Carlos says: "A letter for me? And for whom is this key?"

Dumas' Saint-Mégrin has it: "This letter and this key for me?"

Schiller says: "Be silent as the grave. I know sufficient now."

Dumas alters it to: "Silence. I know all."

Schiller's page boy says: "With her own hand."

Dumas' page boy says: "She herself."

Schiller says: "It is not delirium."

Dumas changes it to: " 'Tis not a dream."

And so it goes. On and on. And more: this piece of Dumas is from Schiller's *Egmont*, and that piece from Lope de Vega's *Love and Honor*. Christina's abdication speech in Dumas is the king's speech in Victor Hugo's *Hernani*. Only reversed. The scene of the challenge in Dumas' *Térésa* is the same as in Schiller's *Brigands*. And Dumas' *Don Juan of Marana* is Mozart's *Don Giovanni*, plus a lot of Goethe, plus some other sources.

"How does Dumas work?" Cassagnac asks. "Very simple: he pillages. He loots. He doesn't need a pen. A pair of shears suffices. He simply lays out his ground plan, dividing the work into so many compartments. To fill in these compartments he rummages through all the literature he can lay his hand on for a scene that will fit. Sometimes the scene must be cut a little, sometimes it must be stretched. Sometimes it needs a piece snipped off here, sometimes a piece tacked on there. And so without the pains of composition, he composes one play after another, scarcely ever resorting to pen and ink."

Dumas was incensed. "Why, this is monstrous!" he cried. "Why, by this method any man who has written twenty or thirty plays can be shown to have stolen any number of scenes, because no writer is unique. And there is no facet of human behavior that has not figured somewhere before in the vast body of literature, and what can two people say when one of them brings a key and a letter to the other? It's bound to be pretty much the same. Had I written my play first, they would have had to say that Schiller had taken his scene from me!"

So Dumas went around as before, as if nothing had happened, and there were people who felt compelled to take him aside to explain to him that his honor was at stake and he must do something about it.

"My honor?" Dumas asked. "How so?"

"Why, these scenes that are so close, almost word for word. . . . That's so, isn't it?"

"No doubt," said Dumas. "But if that scene was good in Schiller's play, why isn't it good in mine? Answer me that! And indeed perhaps better, since mine is the better play."

Who else but Dumas would have dared to brazen out these flagrant thefts?

"Who speaks of stealing?" he once asked, in company, glaring around at everyone. "Does one speak of Alexander the Great stealing Greece? Or India? Does one speak of Rome stealing Egypt? When I take, I don't steal: I conquer! I annex!"

This *conquer* and *annex* became part of the slang of Paris. For months no one ever used the word stealing, only the word conquer. Before a judge, a pickpocket would admit only that he had "annexed" a man's gold watch.

And along the boulevards people were saying, "The man is through. He must either challenge Cassagnac to a duel or never show his face in Paris again."

"Challenge Cassagnac to a duel? Are you mad? Dumas wouldn't dare."

"Why do you say that?"

"I thought by this time everyone knew that Cassagnac is a man to be afraid of. Haven't you heard of the duel he fought with an

Englishman a year ago? Cassagnac had the choice of weapons and elected for each man to carry two pistols, one in each hand, and no changing of hands permitted. The point is that Cassagnac is an equally good shot with both hands. At fifteen paces he can hit the head of a pin."

"Yes, but at fifteen paces any man is a pretty big target."

"Sure, but Cassagnac insisted at starting fifty paces apart, each contestant free to walk forward as far as he pleased and to fire at will."

"What happened?"

"The Englishman fired first and wounded Cassagnac in the groin. But with this bullet in his belly, Cassagnac kept walking forward until he was within fifteen paces of the Englishman. Then, just as the latter was about to fire his second shot, Cassagnac fired and destroyed the Englishman's weapon right in his hand. The Englishman was now weaponless and Cassagnac still had a bullet. He walked up to his opponent, put his gun to his forehead and while the Englishman stood his ground unflinching, Cassagnac fired and dropped him dead to the ground."

"Good lord!"

Many people were certain that Dumas would go storming into the office of *Les Débats* and, ripping off his glove with such violence as to tear the stitches, would throw the rags of kidskin into Granier's face, crying, "My seconds will arrange the details!"

Such a duel, people said, would be sheer murder!

But as all Paris waited, some shivering for Dumas, others smilingly insisting that nothing would come of it, that's precisely what happened: nothing came of it.

Then the story went around that Dumas had discovered that Granier de Cassagnac was just a puppet for Victor Hugo. Victor Hugo was a powerful influence on the newspaper *Les Débats*. Not a line went into that paper without Victor Hugo's knowledge and consent. Granier de Cassagnac himself owed his job on the paper to the recommendation of Victor Hugo.

Now the rumor was that the reason Dumas wasn't fighting Cassagnac was that he scorned the underling and would soon have to do with the chief of the conspiracy.

Everybody waited for this one. What a duel that would be for history! The two greatest names of modern French literature facing each other in mortal combat!

But once more time passed, and nothing happened.

Those in the know—and there are always people who will claim that—declared that Dumas had been to see Hugo and had said to him, "Never would I have done a thing like this to you, Victor. Never would I have permitted an attack on you in a paper on which I had as much influence as I understand you have on *Les Débats*."

Hugo replied, "My dear Dumas, you've no idea how terrible that article was before I toned it down."

"What?" Dumas cried. "You only toned it down? Why didn't you destroy it?"

"I as much as did. I ordered it set aside."

"But you should have torn it up."

"An oversight. Believe me."

"Victor," Dumas said, "people are saying that you are jealous of me. That isn't so, of course."

"Why, yes, it is. Of course I am jealous of your popularity."

"You are? Then is it true also that in your *Lucretia Borgia* you have imitated my *Tour de Nesle?*"

"I did my best, my dear Alexandre."

"Then everything they say is true?" Dumas cried, overcome.

"Yes. But one thing they do not say, I am sure."

"What is that?"

"They do not say that you are jealous of me," said Victor Hugo.

"Why should they? I'm not jealous of you," said Dumas.

"No. But you should be," said Hugo.

"Why?"

"Because, as far as I'm concerned, I have already written poems that I am sure are immortal, for me to be jealous of your popularity is pardonable. But for you, Dumas, you having not yet written anything that is immortal, not to be jealous of me, that is unpardonable. A person who has your talent does not have to steal scenes. That is only because you want five successes a year instead of two. If I had thought only of myself, I would have torn up Cassagnac's article and let you continue to kiss the heel of the public and run after the clink of money forever. But I think of France and what a talent is being lost in you because you are able to write a successful play in a week or a month, and therefore won't give yourself the time to write a great play in a year."

Dumas was silent. "You're right," he said, deeply chastened. "Everything is too easy for me."

"Beware of borrowing and collaborating, and all the devices by which literature becomes business," Victor Hugo said. "For today there is a profit in it, but for tomorrow there is nothing but regret."

"You have given me a very needed lesson,'" said Dumas humbly. "Instead of straining to be better, I am satisfied to be good."

Yes, thus, so people said, any notion of a duel between Victor Hugo and Dumas came to an end.

CHAPTER TWENTY-THREE

The Whole World for Ten Sous

IN ALL THIS there was naturally very little to satisfy Alexandre at his school.

And whenever he would be with his father, he'd try to get him away from company for a moment to whisper to him, "When are you going to fight him?"

"Fight whom, my boy?"

"Why, Cassagnac. Or Victor Hugo. When? Tell me."

"Victor Hugo? I'd never fight him. Why, he's my best friend."

"Well, Cassagnac then," Alexandre said, trying not to show how deeply this affected him.

"Oh, as for him, I'll take care of him, don't you worry."

"Really?" Alexandre cried.

"When your father tells you something, you can go out and borrow money on it. It's that sure."

"You'll kill him, of course."

"Kill whom? Oh, you mean Cassagnac? Oh, I trust not. You wouldn't want me to go around killing people, would you?"

Alexandre's face fell. "But he'd want to kill you."

"Just let him try," said Dumas.

That sounded better. And Alexandre went on: "Will you hurt him?"

"Why, you little rascal you. You're aching for a fight, I swear!"

"You can beat him, can't you?"

"Of course I can. You wait. He'll be sorry he ever started with me."

How wonderful to take that back to the boys at school, and when they were teasing him worst to be able to shout to them, "My father is going to make Cassagnac sorry he ever started anything. You'll see. My father isn't going to kill him, because he doesn't like to go around killing people. But he's going to hurt him. He'll make him sorry!"

At first the boys tended to be impressed, but as week after week passed and there was still no story of a duel, their teasing only increased. Tears of indignation would spurt to Alexandre's eyes as he threw himself into fight after fight.

And all the while he was gnawed by doubt, as if by a cancer. Not that he ever really lost faith in his father. How could he? What then would he have had left to live on?

He worried, too, lest there be any truth in what some of the boys brought back from conversations heard at home, about Cassagnac's having shot an Englishman in a duel. Killed him, just like that. Could such a terrible thing happen to his father?

One Sunday he was able to ask, "Papa, how good a shot are you with your left hand?"

Dumas shook his head. "Very poor," he said. "Very poor."

This was bad news for Alexandre. "They say that Cassagnac can shoot equally well with his left and right. Is that true?"

"So I've heard."

"And you're not afraid?" Alexandre asked.

"Me? Afraid? When have you ever seen me afraid?"

"You wouldn't let him kill you, would you?"

"Never fear. When it comes to trouble, I know how to take care of myself." And Dumas embraced his son, overwhelmed by this evidence of his son's fear for his safety.

Alexandre, meanwhile, took this for assurance that the duel was about to be scheduled. He trembled and at the same time was filled with pride.

But again the weeks passed.

Then one Sunday, being once more with his father, he whispered, "Are you really going to fight Cassagnac?"

"Don't worry about it any more, my boy. Your father is in no danger, God be thanked. There, let me kiss you for showing such concern."

Alexandre felt himself trapped. He struggled to hold back his tears. "But you said—you said you'd make him feel sorry."

"I said it. And I did it."

"Oh, really? When? What happened?"

"Why, when my *Angèle* opened at the Porte-Saint-Martin."

"Yes? What did you do to him?"

"I sent him tickets."

"You sent him tickets?!"

"Yes, for a box. For the opening night. Naturally I didn't let him know that I had sent them. I had someone else write the invitation and make some illegible signature. The note said: 'Dear Cassagnac: You'll join us of course in our box this coming Tuesday to hiss Dumas' play *Angèle*. They say it's worse than his *Son of the Émigré*.' —You remember, of course, how they hissed my *Son of the Émigré*, and everyone said, 'Poor Dumas, he's through, he's lost his touch.' Oh, my dear boy, you've no idea yet how many pallbearers there are just waiting around for the chance to carry you out—all the failures, the envious, the deceived, the bitter, the lazy who stand by and only wait for the industrious to fail so that their own laziness may be excused and even justified—well, someday you'll know."

"Did he go to the play?"

"Of course. My suggestion that he come to hiss was irresistible. There he was opening night with his fiancée and her mother or his mother and some friends. All ready to hiss. But we had a grand success, and I must say he behaved admirably. He scowled at first, but then the play caught hold of him and he applauded with everyone else. What an ovation! I will bet you right now that this play will run as long as my *Antony*. Already it is being performed in Madrid and in Brussels. It will go all over the world."

"And what did you do to Cassagnac?"

"Well, when the public shouted for me, that's when I gave it to him."

"Gave him what?" Alexandre cried.

"A great big pair of shears. Just like those he gave to me in that caricature they say he was responsible for. Did you ever see it?"

"Yes," said Alexandre.

"It was so big, that pair of shears, that three ushers had to carry it to his box. And several ushers carried big editions of the works of Schiller, Goethe, Shakespeare, Lope de Vega. The whole of Ladvocat's *Théâtre Étranger.* Along with a note, this time in my handwriting, saying, 'Dear Cassagnac: Since you know so well how I write my successes, I can't see what prevents you from writing similar successful plays, except that you don't happen to own a pair of scissors, nor the necessary books from which to cut out all the scenes you need. Here you are, then, fully equipped for a great theatrical career. And now I challenge you to do what you say I do. You will discover that the snipping out of scenes here and there to make a play is virtually impossible. Anyhow, I challenge you to do it. And since it was I who sent you the tickets for the box you occupied tonight, I shall await with impatience your return invitation for a box in the theater when you present your own play done entirely with scissors—without pen and ink.' —How do you like that, my boy?"

Alexandre didn't know yet if he liked it or not. "I thought you would fight him a duel," he said.

"Why, of course! Didn't I challenge him to a duel? And with the weapon he himself suggested in his caricature—a pair of scissors! Now we both have our weapons. And let's see if he can make a play that way! I know he can't. No one can!"

"Yes, I see," said Alexandre, beginning to understand the cleverness of Dumas' riposte.

"The duel is on!" Dumas cried. "But, of course, he'll never even try to match me. He can't. It takes a playwright to write a play, whether he plagiarizes scenes or not. Do you see? Now what would it have proved if I had shot a bullet into his heart? Nothing except that I can shoot better than he can. But a challenge to write a play,

that is the real duel! I fired my first shot with my *Angèle*. It was a
hit! Now it's his turn! Let's see if he can hit the target too!"

"Oh, yes!" Alexandre cried. "Now I understand!" And suddenly
he could see the whole scene before him—the crowded house, the
applauding audience, the man in the box forced to accept the
presents that turned against him the ridicule he had tried to cast
upon Dumas. Yes. This was a real duel. A duel over plays.

"And you know how I signed my note?" Dumas went on. "I
signed: Alexandre Davy-Dumas de la Pailleterie!"

"What did he do?" the boy asked, breathless.

"Nothing. Just went pale as he read the note. Then crumpled it
up and walked out of the theater. Leaving the presents behind."

"He left the presents?"

"Yes. You see, that means that he refuses my challenge. He is
dishonored."

"Good!" said Alexandre.

"You see, here was my problem: I had to find a way to revenge
myself without killing him. You understand?"

"Yes."

"Because I could have killed him, you know that."

"Oh," said Alexandre, openmouthed with admiration, "I know
you could."

"And there would have been no escape for it. Because I'm a dead
shot. You've seen me often enough. When I have a bead on a rabbit,
it's time to heat the frying pan. But Cassagnac is a good man with
the pistol too. Or so they tell me. So you see my dilemma."

"Yes, Papa," Alexandre said.

"You understand the word dilemma?"

"Yes, Papa."

"From the Greek meaning 'two premises.'"

"Yes, Papa."

"I would have had to shoot him dead at once to save my own
skin! In a duel with a bad shot, I might have taken a chance and
wasted my bullet. But not in a duel with a marksman. Precisely
because he is so expert with the pistol, it was necessary to find a
way out without going to the field of honor. And just as when I'm
writing a play, and have a problem to solve, and must think out

my characters and my scenes in order to lead to my climax, so here too I had the same thing. Only this was in real life. For earnest. I had to plan it all. I wrote *Angèle* for no other reason. I needed a new smashing success."

"Why, it's like a story," said Alexandre, inspired. "You built a trap for him."

"Exactly. He made me a monkey with a pair of shears, and I made a monkey out of him with a pair of shears. Neat, eh?"

"Oh, I wish I could have been there!"

"I wanted you to. But there were so many details, last minute changes, all the cast at odds. In the theater one must be as much a general as on the field of battle. You understand."

"Yes, Papa."

"I suppose you want to write for the theater too someday?"

"Oh, yes!"

"Well, study hard. Read a lot. You will. I know you will, my boy."

Truly it was a glorious revenge, and never did the boy admire his father so wholeheartedly. But to convey that to the boys at school, that was another matter.

"Dilemma!" they exclaimed scornfully. "Dilemma! Ha-ha!"

"It's from the Greek," said Alexandre manfully. "My father would have had to kill him!"

"If your father was so sure of killing him, then why didn't he challenge him?"

"He didn't want to. He would have regretted it all his life."

"You mean Cassagnac would have nailed him dead, that's what!"

"He would not!" Alexandre shouted. "My father would have killed him with the first shot. He would have had to."

"Your father wouldn't have had time to. Cassagnac can aim and fire faster than any man alive."

"I tell you my father—"

"Go on! Your father. He isn't even your father!"

With that Alexandre threw himself at one of his tormentors and wouldn't let up until his limbs were so exhausted that he was near paralysis.

One evening, months later, the two Dumas, father and son, were at the home of Countess Dash, that birdlike woman who was one

of the earliest of female journalists to twitter about fashions and
social doings in the style that is now so commonplace, and to whom
Dumas had dedicated his *Angèle*. She showed the boy a collection
of dolls which she had, dolls made many years ago by seamstresses
who, working in expensive materials, materials woven with gold
and silver thread and sewn with pearls and with gold sequins, could
not afford to make full-sized samples, but used *mannequins*, who
in those days really were manikins—that is to say, puppets—to show
their creations to the ladies of the court.

And suddenly she looked at the boy. She brushed her hand
through his hair and picked up his chin with one finger.

"Smile," she said.

He smiled.

"Stand up."

He stood up.

"Stand up straight. Square your shoulders."

He pushed back his shoulders and stuck out his chest.

"How old are you?" she asked.

"I'm twelve," he said. "That is, I'll be twelve soon."

"You're a nice boy," she said and she embraced him and gave
him a little peck on his forehead.

Then she went over to Dumas *père* and whispered to him, "Do
something for that boy."

"What do you mean?"

"Look at him. He's twelve and he looks like seven. Do something
for him, you hear me? That's an unhappy boy. A profoundly unhappy boy."

"What are you telling me?" Dumas exclaimed.

"All I say is do something for him, or you won't have him for
very long."

Dumas considered his son. He was in truth undersized. "Come
over here, Alexandre," he said. "How do you feel?"

"Fine, Papa."

"Hm. You know what? Yes, I think you need a change in your
life. Something new. Something exciting. You know, I have always
been of the opinion that it is not great men who make great plans,
but that it is great plans that make great men. Mine has been to
explore, describe, study the entire Mediterranean basin, the sea it-

self and the lands that drain their water into it: Egypt, Palestine, Asia Minor, the Caucasus, Russia, the Balkans, Turkey, Greece, Austria, Italy, France, Spain, Algiers, Morocco and Libya. That is the scene of ancient history. That is the seat of classical learning. Art, science, civilization, the whole modern world was manufactured in that basin. The world as we know it was born there, and when I have finished someday all the books that I intend to write about that inland sea, the world will have finally sat for its own portrait, and I will have been the artist."

Alexandre listened, fascinated. It was like years ago when his father would tell him stories before putting him to bed.

"Do you know why we say longitude for the breadth of the world and latitude for the height? Why this reversal? Because the Mediterranean was our first geography, and it is broad from north to south and long from east to west. That's how deeply the Mediterranean life still lives in man. Do you understand?"

Alexandre nodded, although he didn't really. But he was caught by his father's enthusiasm.

"Now this is my project. Already I have done Southern France. And parts of Italy. Now I must return to do Calabria and Sicily. I must climb Mount Etna. Also Vesuvius and Stromboli. I must see Venice and Constantinople. Much of this we must do on foot. Did you hear me, my boy?"

"Yes, Papa."

"Did you hear me use the pronoun *we?*"

"Yes, Papa."

"I said *we* because you are going with me. Do you want to?"

"Oh, yes, Papa! Oh, yes, yes!"

"Good. Now, as I say, I do much of my traveling on foot. There is no other way to see a country and its people and learn its ways and its stories. So, from tomorrow on I want you to study in your geography books everything you can find on the Mediterranean and on Italy. And every morning and evening I want you to take off all your clothes, rub yourself briskly with cold water, and then do a hundred knee bends, until you are thoroughly warm again. Will you do that?"

"Yes, Papa," said Alexandre, his eyes glowing.

"You won't forget?"

"No. I promise you!"

"Good! In a couple of weeks we leave. Work hard until then. Be healthy and fit to accompany me. I shall make you my assistant, my secretary and my comrade."

Later that evening Countess Dash said to Dumas, "You've saved that boy's life."

Alexandre went to work seriously on his father's plan. Much as he hated that leather hose during the semiweekly foot washings, he got up every morning before the other children and, taking off his clothes, stood before it and rubbed himself all over with water. In the chill dawn, even a hundred knee bends were scarcely enough to bring warmth back to his frozen body.

"I'm getting ready for a big trip," Alexandre said. "Papa is taking me to see the whole world, and I've got to be strong and healthy."

"The whole world?" the boys asked, and the project was so huge that for the moment they stopped teasing, because it is difficult to make fun of someone whom you envy.

"Yes, the whole Mediterranean world, which is where our civilization was born. We're leaving in a week or two."

Yes, it was an impressive thing to be able to say. Even André was disconcerted for a bit.

Then came Sunday, a drizzly day that threatened worse. Alexandre was so certain that his father would appear that he ran down to the street to his mother's corner.

"Hurry," she said. "It's cold. And there's no reason to keep me waiting this morning."

"But I'm still expecting Papa," he told her excitedly. "Papa is taking me on a trip. I'm going to be his assistant, and then later his secretary." He deliberately held back the third word his Papa had used—comrade—because it had fastened itself already too close to his heart.

His mother pulled her shawl around her. Then she said, "Did he tell you that?"

"Yes. Last Sunday. At the Countess Dash's. He said we'd leave in a couple of weeks and be gone a long, long time."

"Oh."

"So I'm sure he'll be here today. We'll have lots to talk about. And things to buy for the trip."

"Oh."

"So perhaps you better not even wait. Not in this rain."

His mother uncovered a small basket. "You see what I made: a lunch for us. Chicken. Your favorite. I thought we'd go to Saint-Cloud."

"Oh, too bad."

"Yes, with this rain we'll have it at home. Let's go."

"But I told you, Papa . . ."

"He won't come," she cut him off sharply.

"Oh, he'll surely . . ."

"I tell you he won't come. He left four days ago."

He couldn't grasp it all at once. "I . . ." he began. "Papa said . . . the whole classical world . . . our civilization." It was too great a betrayal, too great a disaster, to be expressed in words.

"Your father says a lot of things," she declared. "Now you know."

"He probably just went away for a few days. He'll be back. He said *we*. . . ."

"He's gone," she said flatly. "So come, let's not stand in the rain like fools. Where are your dirty clothes? How often must I remind you to bring me your dirty clothes?"

"I'll get them," he said. But he didn't move.

"Do you think I'm lying?" she asked. "Like once I lied about your grandmother wanting to take you?"

He shook his head.

"Then go for your clothes," she said.

He still didn't move. He couldn't. The sobs began to tear through his body. His mother threw her shawl over him and drew him toward her, holding his racked body against her warmth, while the rain increased.

When he had exhausted his tears, she said, "Shall we go to your father's apartment to make sure?"

He nodded, and they walked off through the downpour.

His father's furnished apartment was already occupied by another tenant, and the concierge knew nothing of any message.

As a matter of fact, Dumas had simply picked up and gone, completely forgetting the promise he had made to his son. Gone off with Jadin, the painter, and Jadin's bulldog Milord. They encountered earthquakes, climbed volcanoes, went through storms and waterspouts, came up against bandits. As a man suspected of revolutionary principles, Dumas had to sneak into Naples under the name of Guichard. At Rome he had a friendly interview with the Pope. But the next day the police threw him out of the city, declaring that his plays aroused the dangerous spirit of democracy. Six volumes of travel impressions, a couple of plays, his first novels and some short stories were all he could manage to squeeze out of this trip, which in later years he would often speak of as the happiest days of his life.

Of his son's they were the most dismal.

Monday morning Alexandre was more pleased than not that his throat was sore and his head so dizzy that when he tried to stand up from bed he fell over on the floor. He had to be taken to the infirmary, and there was no need to explain to anyone why his father had gone off without him. He wasn't well enough to go on such a trip.

It was during this period that Alexandre began to understand better the whispers that floated around him, piling up ahead of him, parting before him, and closing in again behind him, surrounding him like a ghostly prison, isolating him, exiling him.

He was sick for months.

He would be well for a few days and then down again. For weeks on end he never left the little infirmary.

At long intervals there would be a letter from his father. No more than a brief note: "Are you following my articles in *La Presse?*" And once a long letter on the books he must study. "You must read Shakespeare and Goethe in the original. Homer and Tacitus too. Not even the Bible has been well translated. Indeed, the real genius of a language is untranslatable. Shall we ever be able to know Confucius and Lao-tse unless we learn to read Chinese? I doubt it."

On Sundays, his mother, as inconspicuous as a charwoman, would cross the court to the infirmary, bringing Alexandre a pot of soup, still warm, having been carried all the way under her shawl.

Everyone took her for no more than what she looked: a servant.

She would feed Alexandre first and then sit by his bedside and knit. Never, while anyone might have been present, would she kiss him or even touch him.

The hours would pass, and neither of them would speak much.

No sooner was he well again than he emerged once more into the atmosphere of whispers.

Alexandre knew already that he was a bastard. In French history, when the name of Dunois, the Bastard of Orléans, or some other bastard of nobility would be mentioned, as could not fail to happen (for example, in the story of Joan of Arc), at once all eyes would be turned upon Alexandre, who would have liked to be able to slip through the floor.

But this referred only to his father: that his father had had a son from a woman to whom he hadn't been married. Never had he thought of it from his mother's side.

Until one day he heard André saying, "Half a franc. That's all it costs. I never pay any more than that."

And then André turned to him. "Tell us, Alexandre. Where does your mother live?"

A sudden rage came over the boy. He ran at André kicking and scratching and had to be pummeled almost into unconsciousness before he would desist.

He grew so sensitive about this matter that he had but to hear coarse whispers followed by a burst of laughter for him to fly into a rage.

But the greatest hurt came from a feeling that gradually invaded him and that he could not shake off—that perhaps his mother had really been that kind of woman. And that perhaps she still was. And that perhaps boys around him, in this very school, had been to her and had found her cheap and good, as sometimes he would gather from snatches of whispers that happened to reach his ears. This thought came near to driving him mad. Worn out by his never-ending struggle against shame and ignorance, and hating himself for the images that would leap to his mind, he found sickness almost a blessing, and the only drawback to life in the infirmary was the visits of his mother, whom he could now scarcely look in the face because of the ugly thoughts that would awake in him. One day he discovered himself wishing that he might never see her again, a thought for which he immediately reproached himself, and yet a thought that returned to him again and again and cut through him like a knife.

Their meetings now became more taciturn than ever. He was almost afraid to open his mouth lest he reveal some of the horrors that stirred within him.

The most damnable part of all this was that as the boys became bolder in their attacks on him, Alexandre found himself curiously excited. While he would rage at an obscene drawing that he had found slipped into one of his books, and that depicted a moment of debauchery with his mother, whose name the boys had somehow discovered and which they printed underneath the woman's figure, and while he would fling himself headlong at whomever he suspected of having perpetrated this filth, still the image itself would continue to burn in lines of fire in his mind, and to his complete horror he would realize that he was looking forward to the next piece of filth.

Sometimes a few boys would surround him and make him a proposal that would affront him to such a degree that he did not know whom to attack first and would look wildly from boy to boy and finally fall to the floor in a paroxysm of frustration.

One Sunday, in order to avoid seeing his mother, he ran off early, wandering all day long through the streets, keeping clear of the busy ones where he was afraid that someone might recognize him. All manner of crazy ideas of never returning occupied his thoughts. But in the evening, tired out and hungry, he turned back toward the school. Going through a dark lane, he moved aside to make room for a woman who was coming from the other direction.

But instead of accepting the space, she too moved, confronting him.

She smiled and said, "You don't have to be afraid of me."

"I'm not afraid, Madame," he said, shaken.

"Good. Then come with me. For ten sous, I'll make you happy."

"I'm late," he gasped. "I have to get back to school."

"That's just an excuse," she exclaimed, and threw her arms around him. He fought free and raced off, hearing her laughter behind him and never pausing until he was utterly exhausted.

Thereafter, for days he remained haunted with the idea that that was how *he* had happened: his mother meeting his father in a dark lane and saying to him, "I'll make you happy for ten sous."

But along with that abysmal thought there existed another

strange feeling that was perhaps even more disconcerting: a regret that he had not taken advantage of the woman's offer. He had happened to have ten sous in his pocket at the time, and that was all the woman had asked for making him happy. Had he gone with her he would have known everything.

Tormented by this desire, he promised himself that the following Sunday at about the same time he would find himself in the same lane, and this time he was determined to have the courage that had failed him before.

"Well! So we meet again."

"*Oui*, Madame," Alexandre said, his knees trembling so that he felt they must give way.

"Well, what about it? Have you ten sous?"

"Yes."

"Show me. You young scalawags are full of tricks."

He dug the money out of his pocket.

"Ah, that's it." She took the money and said, "Come along." And put her arm about his waist.

That was when his courage left him. His body was like jelly. He felt that he must either run away or sink to the ground.

He ran. And behind him he could hear mocking laughter and too late remembered his ten sous.

CHAPTER TWENTY-FOUR

Marriage à la Mode

MONTHS WENT BY. But young Alexandre's torment from outside as well as inside causes never abated. One Sunday after Mass, he remained in the chapel and talked to the young priest of the school. During the interview he burst into tears.

The priest, a gentle man, saw in this distracted youngster a soul seeking peace, perhaps a future servant of God, and he began to lead him toward the comforts of religion.

They would meet frequently, and together would read some passage from the Bible, one of the psalms, one of the parables of

Jesus, or his Sermon on the Mount, and then they would talk over
the problem of modeling one's life upon Scripture.

The priest knew well the stories of all the saints, and he would
tell them to the boy, emphasizing the battles against the spirit of
evil that all saints had had to endure, and the strength they had thus
acquired to face martyrdom and achieve holiness.

Alexandre found it difficult to turn the other cheek. He tried
desperately not to let himself be drawn into fights, but as the teasing was always there he did not succeed.

But at night, instead of dreaming of revenge, he would pray God
to forgive his tormentors, passing all the insults of the day in review and trying to put himself into a frame of mind that could say:
I hold nothing against them. Vengeance belongs to the Lord.

Sundays he would spend in prayer on the stone floor of the
chapel until he had exhausted himself, after which he would go
quietly to meet his mother.

Daily he grew thinner, more hollow-chested. He found ways of
achieving complete privacy, even in this beehive, and he had made
himself a knotted rope with which he would flagellate himself. He
would continue until he could find a stain of fresh red on the rope.

At night sometimes he would take a handful of nails to bed and
strew them around his body so that sleep would become impossible
and he would be forced to endure a vigil.

There were moments when he would think of himself as another
Christ. He was certain that he would die soon, and then he saw
miracles manifesting themselves on his grave. He would be another Saint Alexandre, and the evil boys of the school would make
pilgrimages to his tomb and to the shrine erected over it, and there
they would become aware of their sinfulness and pray to him in
Heaven to intercede to God for forgiveness.

All day long his lips murmured prayers. Often he raised his eyes
to Heaven, expecting that at any moment the firmament would declare the glory of God and the clouds would burst asunder to reveal
some vast apotheosis. Every night he expected the last judgment
and saw the graves of the world spewing forth the dead.

And then, one day, to this emaciated and tense boy, this recluse,
this desert anchorite, yet living so close to the heart of Paris, there
came a note from his father:

MY DEAREST BOY:

This afternoon, in the Chapel of the Chamber of Peers, I am being
married. Sunday afternoon you will come to my apartment and greet
your new mother, who already loves you dearly.

What was there in this letter to make Alexandre feel that God had
answered his prayers and that the miracle had happened? How
could he possibly have deluded himself into thinking that his father
was now about to marry his mother, and that his greatest wish was
about to come true and he would have a father and mother like
other boys, and no one would dare insult him again? Perhaps it was
the words "your new mother, who already loves you dearly" that
misled him and made him jump to the conclusion that now he was
to have a home, instead of two homes, neither of which had been
a real home.

Naturally he couldn't wait until Sunday. He put on his best
clothes and ran out of the school, his heart singing with joy.

The story of Dumas' marriage swept through Paris like wildfire.
No one believed it, of course. That Dumas should marry was a con-
tradiction in terms. It was a joke. "That man just can't stand people's
talking about anyone but himself, so he has to keep inventing some
new mystification every day."

But others declared themselves *au courant*, and even named the
girl: Ida Ferrier.

Of course, this made the story even more incredible, for Ida
Ferrier was a cute little blonde—that is to say, she had been cute
and little when Dumas first met her and starred her in some of his
plays. But at once she began to take on weight and people said that,
instead of letting her success go to her head, she had let it go the
other way.

She grew indeed so monstrously fat that Gautier once pro-
pounded the following riddle: "What is the best-kept secret in
Paris?"

The answer was: "Ida Ferrier's skeleton."

With all that, she had the morals of an alley cat. People declared that for every horn that Dumas would put on Ida's head,
she would put two on his. The whole thing was somehow a coarse
joke.

Chateaubriand, who witnessed this marriage, commented afterward that when Ida Ferrier bent over to sign the register, he leaped aside, fearful lest one of the huge things he suddenly saw peep out from her décolleté should break loose and avalanche down upon him.

Alfred de Musset claimed to have the correct information as to why Dumas was marrying her. Dumas had gone with her to a ball given by the Duke of Orléans (son of his former boss, who had since become King of France) and had presented Mademoiselle Ida Ferrier to the Duke.

The Duke had pointedly greeted her as Madame Dumas.

Dumas, smiling, had corrected the Prince, but the latter had insisted and finally had drawn Dumas aside to say to him, "My dear Dumas, she *must* be your wife."

"But, Your Highness . . ."

"Enough. I am not in the habit of being introduced to whores in my own home," said the Prince sharply.

Dumas cleared his throat. "Naturally not, Your Highness, and my objection was not intended as disrespect, but merely to point out to Your Highness that the ceremony has not yet been celebrated."

"In that case, I must ask your pardon," said the Prince, "for having used an ugly word. Let me be the first to congratulate you on your approaching wedding."

That clinched it, and Dumas, who had just been in the process of ridding himself of Ida, found himself now attached to her as never before.

But this is not the story that others told. According to them it was Ida's hope to marry, not Dumas, but an elderly admirer of hers who was a multimillionaire. But this ancient sport had other flames whom he preferred to her. He promised, however, to see her safely married. To someone else.

This wealthy old roué was Monsieur Dumange, of whom a multitude of stories are told. He amassed a fortune from the ordure business of Paris, employing a host of latrine cleaners and selling his product all over the farming area around the city. He had, so encyclopedist Larousse informs us, a wonderfully beautiful daughter, who, of course, had a flock of suitors. But the old man knew that they were after his money and he was determined to have only a son-in-law who would not be ashamed to take over his business.

It was his custom to take each suitor to his warehouses. Those who could not bear the odor were immediately disqualified. Even those who penetrated these fetid cellars were still not eligible. He would lift the cover from a well-filled vat and say, "Get in."

"What? Get in? Get into that?"

"Yes. In with you. Dive in!"

And even when a suitor was found who was willing to get in bodily, that still didn't satisfy Monsieur Dumange. He had to duck his head in too.

The man who finally got that far became Monsieur Dumange's son-in-law and heir.

But as far as Ida was concerned, he got her married off by going around town and asking all the usurers what bachelor had a lot of notes outstanding. And who should turn out to be the most prominent bachelor with a lot of loose debts around? None other but Ida Ferrier's flame Dumas, who would, of course, never marry anyone.

Monsieur Dumange, however, bought up all Dumas' obligations, waited until many of them were overdue, and then went to the author.

"I know there are people who say that you sign things you haven't written, but I presume you will recognize these papers as genuinely yours?"

What could Dumas say? "Yes, those are my signatures. But I must tell you that at the moment I am absolutely flat."

"You realize that I can send you to prison with them?" Monsieur Dumange asked.

"Good Lord!" Dumas cried. "Surely you aren't serious. . . ."

"Do you know why I took the trouble to buy up two hundred thousand francs of your debts for forty thousand francs of my good money?"

"No."

"Because I promised to marry Mademoiselle Ida Ferrier."

"Ah, so? Then, congratulations, my friend. And it is really sweet of her to ask you to do this for me, who mean nothing to her now."

"She did not ask me to do this."

"Then I don't understand."

"It's nevertheless very simple. I promised to marry Mademoiselle Ida Ferrier. She insisted on it, before she would open her arms to me. Yes, I promised to marry her, but I didn't say to whom."

"Oh?"

"Yes. And now you see that I intend to marry her to you."

"Either that or prison?" Dumas asked.

"These papers for two hundred thousand francs will be the dowry she will bring to you. The moment you produce a certificate of your marriage to Mademoiselle Ida Ferrier, you shall have these papers to burn, if you like."

What could Dumas do?

But whatever the story, Dumas married Ida Ferrier in the Chapel of the Peers.

And just as the witnesses, Chateaubriand, Nodier, Roger de Beauvoir and Villemain, were lined up at the register, young Alexandre burst in, looked around and said, "Where's mother?"

"Here," said Dumas. "Here, my son, is your new mother."

Alexandre was horrified. "That fat thing!" he cried. "You are marrying that fat thing? I thought you were marrying my mother."

And he ran out sobbing.

Naturally Ida Ferrier said, "Don't you ever let me catch him around my house."

The story goes, furthermore, that Monsieur Dumange deceived Dumas. He didn't give him the notes as dowry. He gave them instead to Madame Dumas, and she held them like a whip over Dumas, forcing him to endure the marriage for five years, after which she retired to live in Florence on sixty thousand francs a year, which Dumas sent her until her death.

As for Alexandre, he returned to his school, now more alone than ever. And yet the succeeding five years were not as bad as the first five years of school had been. Many of the boys had got too old for that kind of teasing. And Alexandre kept ever more strictly to himself. He abandoned most of his religious devotions and took instead to gardening.

Behind the school was a big plot of weedy ground, once intended to be the school's garden, where the children would grow their own food. But this idyllic dream of the pedagogues did not succeed. The land became the scene of pitched battles, with gardening tools as weapons and stones for bullets, and food had to be bought as usual from the grocers. Alone Alexandre gardened, growing flowers.

Though he had fewer fights, his stand for his father never faltered. Even many years later he could not forgive those who had cast any aspersions on his father's good name. For example, walking one day on the boulevard, he was accosted by someone who greeted him as if he were a long-lost brother. "Why, it's Dumas! As I live and breathe!"

It was André, now a grown man—in fact, already mostly gray.

Alexandre stared at him coldly.

"Why, you devil, you!" André cried, pleased as punch. "I've often thought of you, and with pride too. Our little Jocko has become a success. I always knew you had it in you! Come, let's have an apéritif, and you'll tell me all about it."

"Get out of my sight!" said Alexandre.

"You're joking. I'm André! Don't you recognize me?"

"I said, Get out of my sight!"

"Why, what's the matter with you? Say, you don't mean that you took those little tricks at school seriously? Ho-ho! Just because we called you Jocko? Didn't you realize that it was all in fun?"

"Do you want me to murder you in cold blood?" said Dumas *fils.* "Do you?"

"Oh, come now. Just because we had a few scraps." But, seeing that Alexandre was starting to pull the blade out of his sword cane, he went off shaking his head and afterward told people that Dumas *fils* had lost his mind. "That man should be locked up. For the public good. Imagine! He's still mad over some little tricks we used to play on him at school. Why, that's all of thirty-five years ago!"

CHAPTER TWENTY-FIVE

"I Want to Be a Legend"

WHAT A MOMENT it was for visitors from abroad, and even for Parisians, to whom the sight was already familiar, when they had the good fortune to catch a glimpse of the two Dumas, father and son, canes in hand, striding along the boulevards—two giants, each well over six feet, erect (showing the victorious bearing that seems to have disappeared from the world since people have taken to cultivating athletics instead of posture), each man topped by his own magnificent brush of woolly hair and, crowning that (veritable Pelion piled upon Ossa), the stylish *haut de forme*, the tall opera hat, either black or fawn colored. People just had to stop and gaze. With admiration and with envy. For there is nothing that human beings take such innocent delight in as pure swagger: *crânerie*, which is the image of God displaying itself to its best advantage.

It was royalty. It was dynastic.

And Dumas would buttonhole his friends and say to them proudly, "Well, what do you think? About us. My son and me. We make a fine pair, eh? And both of us exactly the same age."

"Both of you exactly the same age?" would be the incredulous exclamation.

"That's right. Both of us exactly twenty years of age. His first. My second."

This witticism about their ages, Dumas thus picturing himself and his son as two young sports out for a good time together, must, in the interest of historical veracity, be contrasted with another witticism that was undoubtedly being whispered about. You will find it recorded by that recorder of scandalous whispers Count Horace de Viel-Castel, whose six volumes of *Memoirs* for very obvious reasons did not see the light of day until 1883, twenty years after the Count died.

Viel-Castel writes: "Dumas uses his son to break in his new shoes and break off his old mistresses."

The first part of this witticism must be denied at once, and categorically. Dumas already had such small feet that the strictest elegance could not have insisted that he wear any more tight-fitting shoes than he normally did. Besides, he was never without a valet, and Parisian valets have always considered it one of their duties to have a slightly larger foot than their masters and thus be able to take on the task of "breaking in."

They accepted this task as gracefully as they picked up soiled gloves, it being the custom of the master upon coming home to strip off his gloves and toss them on the floor with studied carelessness.

As to the second part of this witticism—namely, that Dumas used his son to break off his old mistresses—here too a denial must be registered.

Actually, few men have solved the vexatious problem of what to do with an old mistress, and particularly with that variety known in France as *la femme collante*, the close-fitting, skin-tight, hard-to-remove kind, so brilliantly and with so many interesting variations as Dumas. He had, to be sure, a great many opportunities for exercising his inventive faculties in this particular field. To give only one example, as reported by De Villemessant, the journalist who founded *Le Figaro*, one of France's most successful newspapers: one day Villemessant asked Dumas why every time he visited him he saw a cart outside and men either loading or unloading furniture.

"Are you in business?" Villemessant wanted to know.

Dumas explained. "It can be nothing new to you, my dear fellow, that I am constantly being harassed by bailiffs who are forever on the point of attaching my worldly goods and selling me out. This is by no means an enviable situation; however, I have not only learned to live with it, but even to derive therefrom a certain benefit. Thus I will often deliberately allow matters to go from bad to worse until the bailiff is ready to put the seals on my door. Meanwhile, I will tell my mistress that if she hurries I can perhaps convince the bailiff that the furniture in her room is her own, and that she has thus a right to take it with her when she leaves me. At once she will manage to find a cart and some men and they will empty her room even to the pictures on the wall and the rug on the floor. That over, I adjust my debts somehow and refurnish the room."

"Only to begin all over again with some other woman?" Villemessant asked.

Dumas shrugged. "What can I do?" he asked. "I am once and for all so constituted that to me a home is not a home unless there is a woman about."

"Which in turn explains why the bailiffs are forever after you," Villemessant said.

I wish that with these two denials the Viel-Castel witticism might be considered sufficiently refuted. But when a man takes pride in the fact that he and his son are of the same age, and that same age is not the age of the father, but that of the son, the question of father, son and mistresses takes on an anomalous aspect that seems to require a little further exploration.

Viel-Castel does not have the reputation of being a liar. A senile *voyeur*, yes, with a strong penchant for recording pornography, yes, but not a deliberate liar. Viel-Castel did not invent his tales about the Countess Dash's giving herself to whatever man happened to take her home from a dance. He simply recorded them. They were the gossip of the day. Just as when he asks Delacroix, "Did you ever sleep with George Sand," and Delacroix answers, "Why do you ask? Hasn't everybody?" he is being merely the conscientious reporter in noting it down.

Though it may sometimes be wondered in what circles he picked up all those filthy little stories—for example, the one about Rachel, the great tragedienne, Dr. Véron's mistress, tearing her hair out at night in bed and screaming to him, "Then go and get your brother!" (this brother being a gawky, unlicked giant who still ran the little family stationery shop), since clearly neither participant would have told it, and it could only have come either from the brother or from some eavesdropping servant who had no right to be believed and recorded. It may therefore be asked whether certain other factors didn't play a role in his choice of stories—for example, the fact that he was a rabid reactionary.

Rabid? What am I saying? This man prayed night and day for bloodshed. He was no rabid reactionary. He was a sanguinary one.

An iron broom is what he wanted, one that would sweep across the entire surface of France, raking out all the *canaille*. And by *canaille* he meant in the first place Victor Hugo, and then George Sand, and Eugène Sue, etc.

Dumas? Yes, Dumas, of course.

Viel-Castel wanted heads to rain into the basket, until the whole romantic movement had been extirpated and along with it all those socialistic and communistic and Saint-Simonian ideas, all those Proudhonist notions of leveling of incomes, mutualism and every other sort of utopian scheme which he considered so many diabolical tricks to steal other people's money and property.

Curiously, he himself—but only in his youth—had been something of a romanticist. He had written verses and novels, all of which had fallen flat.

In addition, Viel-Castel was for a dynastic France. As a child he had been brought up at La Malmaison along with various Bonaparte children, and he considered all France as rightfully belonging, if not to the legitimate Bourbons, then at any rate to the Bonapartes.

To cap it all, Viel-Castel hated Negroes—that is to say, free ones.

Thus, when it comes to talking about Dumas the Negro, Dumas the Republican, Dumas the son of a general dismissed in disgrace by Napoleon, Dumas the romanticist and Dumas the successful writer, what can a Viel-Castel do but pour out his hate, a Viel-Castel who was a comparative failure at literature, a Viel-Castel who was an antiromanticist, a proslavery man, and an archreactionary?

And so again and again these two men would dine together at the evenings of Princess Mathilde Bonaparte, and afterward Viel-Castel would go home to write in his diary all the scandalous gossip he could pick up about that "vain, lascivious, cowardly Negro Dumas."

While Dumas would go home and write more books like *The Three Musketeers, The Count of Monte Cristo, Twenty Years After, The Black Tulip,* and so forth and so on, and become more and more famous. And never once mention Viel-Castel, either in his own *Memoirs* or anywhere else, so far as I know.

Don't imagine that Viel-Castel was not aware of the enormous difference between the roles they played in each other's minds, and that he didn't often say to himself, "That toad! I know he never gives me a second's thought, whereas I, I have to keep thinking of him again and again. But wait, just wait, my friend. I'll get even with you yet. When I'm dead these *Memoirs* of mine will be published and then people will know exactly what one of your contemporaries thought of you!"

With what relish then, with what secret, slobbering satisfaction, Viel-Castel would put down, for example, the tale of how Dumas had finally been able to get rid of his wife Ida Ferrier and thus fetch his son home from school.

Telling Ida one evening that he had been invited to go to the Tuileries, Dumas left, but did not go to the palace. Instead he went to see a woman named Valerie des Brosses.

This Valerie was scheduled to play some small role in one of his plays, and she had approached him during rehearsals and had said to him in the saddest, sweetest tones imaginable, "Oh, Monsieur Dumas, my part is so small."

This *double-entendre* was not lost on Dumas. He had, as a matter of fact, often complained that future literary historians would belabor him for his lack of dramatic restraint and proportion, when it was not for want of literary ability but from absence of moral fiber that he had expanded many a role that should have been tightened or even cut out altogether.

Furthermore, this Valerie des Brosses, whose husband was a wealthy manufacturer of barometers and thermometers, had no need to be seeking parts on the stage and was only drawn to do it because of the opportunities it afforded for a dissolute life.

"I have a wonderful inspiration on how to develop my role," Valerie told him. "Perhaps you could come to a little supper at my home and let me explain to you my ideas? Unfortunately my husband is off to Almaden in Spain to buy mercury, so we shall not have the pleasure of his company."

No need to say any more. Dumas could already tell without the use of any Des Brosses instruments that the weather was going to be fair, and the temperature cozy.

At that time Dumas lived on the rue de Rivoli, in a beautiful apartment on the first floor. In addition, he had a small apartment on the fourth floor where he could work late into the night. That evening, then, pretending that he was off to the Tuileries, he left Ida and went on foot to Madame des Brosses'.

Valerie had had her servants prepare a delicate little supper of roast squab and then had dismissed them for the day. Then she made her toilette as a Javanese, wrapped only in a cashmere shawl, her arms and feet bare. On her wrists and ankles she wore heavy silver manacles between which stretched silver chains, as if she were a prisoner. A prisoner to chastity.

The obvious comedy that was indicated by this costume was played out to the full: squab was eaten in primitive style, with bare fingers, from the wooden platters laid upon the Turkish rug, and then as the curtain came down, the silver chains were torn asunder by passions that thus visibly demonstrated how irresistible they were.

About midnight, having written a dozen more lines for Madame des Brosses' role, Dumas started back for home. He still had all his installments to write for the next day's papers, along with an article or two, so he was anxious to get to his writing table. But as he was on his way home, the skies suddenly opened up and rain fell by the barrel. The weather turned quite chilly. At that hour it was impossible to hope for a cab, and Dumas struggled through the downpour, arriving at his home dripping wet. His fourth-floor apartment turned out not only to be icy cold but without a single stick of firewood around; moreover, he couldn't find any dry clothes to change into. Annoyed, he went downstairs to his other apartment to fetch himself some wood, or at least a change of clothes.

To his surprise he found a nice fire crackling in Ida's bedroom. Ida herself was already in bed and angrily resented his intrusion, declaring that she wanted to sleep, but the scene was so inviting that Dumas drew a table up to the fire and said that he would work there.

Ida huffed and puffed, but Dumas went right on throwing a couple more logs into the fire and laying out paper and ink.

"Is that how little you care for my sleep?" she asked.

"What about me?" he retorted. "I'm wet to the bone."

He stripped himself down to his skin and, taking a candle from the table, went to the wardrobe to find himself some dry clothes.

To his amazement there stood a man just as naked as himself.

"Why, Roger de Beauvoir!" Dumas exclaimed, the blood mount- ting to his swarthy face.

"Good evening, Alexandre," said Roger meekly. "I was just trying to slip into my clothes."

"*Coquin!*" Dumas screamed, grabbing the boulevardier around the middle and lifting him from the ground as if he were nothing but a sack of potatoes.

Ida screamed, "Don't hurt him. Alexandre! For God's sake, you don't know your own strength!"

"You!" Dumas went on, apostrophizing his prey. "A witness at my wedding, and now bringing trouble to my household, dishonor- ing the roof that has so often given you hospitality. . . !"

As for Roger, he whimpered with pain but said nothing.

"Open the window!" Dumas shouted to Ida.

Ida leaped from her bed, drawing a filmy nightgown around her. "Alexandre! Please!"

"You!" he snorted at Ida. "Pretending I was disturbing your sleep. Open up, I say! Or I'll strangle him in mid-air!"

Frightened by this fury, Ida pulled back the heavy curtains and opened up a window. Wind and rain raged into the room. Dumas flung Roger's clothes out into the street. "Now you follow your clothes!" and he was about to fling Roger after them when he sud- denly stopped. "Why, this weather isn't fit for a dog!" he said. He pushed Roger into an easy chair. "Stay here, then. Ah, *sapristi alors.* And me with three installments to be completed before morn- ing. Out of my way, everyone. I have work to do. Ida, you get back to your sleep! As for you, Roger, you false friend, I'll take care of you later!"

And, naked as he was, he sat down by the fire and started to work. His fury had raised a sweat on his brow, so that for the moment he disdained any clothes.

Ida, having fought the window shut, stood there, not knowing what to do. Finally, chilled, she went back to the warmth of her bed.

And meanwhile Dumas wrote, line after line, without pause ex- cept to dip his pen, never going back to cross a t or dot an i, never stopping to think, never going back to scratch out a word, but moving on and on and accompanying his writing, as usual, with all sorts of strange ejaculations, bursts of laughter, muttered imprecations, broken cries.

Ida, subdued by the warmth of her bed and after casting a helpless glance at the poor naked Roger, who sat shivering in the easy chair, fell into a sort of languorous doze and woke, not knowing how many quarters of an hour later, to see the same scene continuing. Dumas still muttering and laughing as he wrote, and poor Roger now so chilled that his teeth could be heard chattering all the way across the room.

"Alexandre," Ida begged. "Alexandre. Don't you hear me?"

"Yes, my sweet," he said, still deep in his thoughts, his pen never stopping.

"The fire has gone out. Put some more wood on."

"Certainly," he said. But when he went to the wood box, it was empty. "*Peste!*" he said. "There is no more wood. And now it is decidedly getting cold." He went back to the wardrobe, found the dry clothes he had been looking for before, and drew on an old pair of trousers and an old jacket.

And he went back to work.

After a while Ida said, "Have you no pity? Look at Monsieur de Beauvoir, catching his death of a cold."

Dumas looked up from his writing. "*Tiens? C'est vrai.* Your teeth are chattering, Roger. You must really be suffering from the cold."

"A-a li-ttt-tle," said Roger, his trembling chin interfering with his speech.

"Well, then, for God's sake, jump into bed. Get warm!"

Roger stared pop-eyed at Dumas. "Into bed?"

"Where else?"

"Ah, but . . ."

"But what? Don't tell me that you are shocked. Do you expect me to believe that you weren't in that bed before you heard me entering my apartment? Come, come, now Roger, none of that false modesty. Not with me."

"Now just a moment, Alexandre," said Ida sharply. "This is my bed. And I think I have something to say. . . ."

"Ho-ho! So it's you who are going to play the prude! No, no, I'll never cast you for that role. Not any more. Why, it seems I'm the only honest one here and will own up to being less than a saint. Well, you can both do as you please, but, as for me, I'm going to bed. I must be up early to finish my work."

With that he threw off his clothes, snuffed out the candles, and put himself under the covers.

Off in the dark Roger's teeth could be heard crepitating.

Dumas nudged Ida. "Ida. I say, Ida, do you hear me?"

"Yes, yes, I hear you."

"This Roger, you know, he's a gentleman. You understand what I mean? The kind who will never get into a lady's bed without a clear invitation. There are some men that way, Ida. They are polite and always ask a lady's permission. No savage like me. So why don't you say something kind to him? You know he may really catch his death of cold."

"If only *you* would," Ida snapped.

"That's hardly likely," said Alexandre. "Meanwhile, we're all missing our sleep. So, come on, be nice to Roger. You know, I'm sure he's secretly very fond of you and only too bashful to show it."

"Get into bed!" Ida ordered Roger. "Let's not give him any further opportunities for the exercise of his wit."

Roger whispered, "Thanks, Ida," and groped his way to the bed, and since Dumas made no room for him on his side, he had to slip in next to Ida.

"Now that's what I call being sensible, Roger," said Dumas. "Good night all." And a moment later the great bellows of his chest were breathing like a storm in a forest.

But at the crack of dawn, he was awake. He sat up in bed and by the slivers of light that shot through the slits of the draperies, he silently observed the sleeping pair beside him. Then he leaned across Ida and shook Roger awake. "Sh . . . sh. Not a sound. We must not wake her up. Roger, my friend. I am ashamed of myself. My fit of jealousy—it was unworthy of me. I insist on buying you a completely new outfit to replace the one I threw out of the window."

"No," said Roger, "you owe me nothing. I behaved like a wretch. How shall I ever earn your friendship again?"

"Roger, in ancient Roman days, when two friends had had a misunderstanding and had said ugly things to each other, when the

storm was over, they met in some open place and publicly reconciled themselves. We must do the same."

"You are very generous, Alexandre."

"Nonsense. Here, reach me your hand. Across Ida. We would not
possibly find a more public place to stage our reconciliation."

"I like that!" said Ida, who was already quite awake.

"And now. Enough of this lazing in bed. My clothes are dry. I
leave you, my friends, to go to my apartment upstairs. I have work
to do. As for you, Roger, to show you that my heart is in the right
place, I relinquish Ida to you. I give her to you. She's yours."

Ida gave vent to an "Oh!" of dark fury, while Roger said, "You
are generous to a fault, Alexandre. But, really, I cannot accept such
a sacrifice."

"Why not? Surely not account of your wife, your Léocadie? Because I know you have definitely split with her."

"No. It is not that. It is . . . that I know how much Ida means to
you. . . ."

"You're right, Roger. But I would never be able to forgive myself
for last night unless I made it up to you in some striking way. Take
Ida. Take her!"

"Really, Dumas, you overwhelm me. I cannot accept. . . ."

"Come, come, Roger. Please, I insist."

"No, Alexandre, I beg of you. . . ."

"Get out!" Ida screamed. "Get out! Both of you. I don't want
either one of you! I'm packing. I'm going to Italy!"

And she did. She went to Florence and lived out the rest of her
life there.

Such is Viel-Castel's story.

With Ida finally out of the way, Dumas could realize his old
desire: to bring his son home to live with him.

But before we go into that we must continue to consult Viel-
Castel in order to understand how mightily Dumas had grown in
the past few years and how his ambition craved even greater success, so that we may understand the new problem Alexandre had
to face with respect to his father.

If once again we follow Viel-Castel, it is because, as much as we
may dislike him, he does not seem to have been an inventor of un-
truths. He had plenty of opportunity to hear whatever stories were

going around. He was one of the curators of the Louvre museum, and his connections gave him a front seat in the theater of his times.

It may not be textually true, for example, that Dumas, being asked to acknowledge himself as the father of a certain child, said, "I would recognize that child anywhere as mine. But the mother . . . I just can't place her." But it does sound like the Dumas we know. Something of the sort either happened or could have happened.

And so, too, another story of the time when Dumas wanted to recognize another child of his and give her his last name, but the mother refused, saying, "You've succeeded in making the name of Dumas common as dirt. I won't have it for my child."

Oh, no, Viel-Castel made no pretense of liking Dumas. Or, indeed, of liking anybody. But he did make it his business to find out two things about everyone: in the first place, how much income he or she disposed of (and just how fraudulently it may have been acquired) and, secondly, who slept with whom (and how), two facts of enormous importance which ordinary historians make it a point to omit from their books—no doubt in order to palm themselves off as serious-minded students who have risen above such trivialities—but as a result of which the past never seems to make much sense to us of the present wherein these two problems of sex and money somehow always loom so confoundedly large.

Yes, he had a front seat at the theater of his times—but he himself never mounted the stage, and maybe that is what hurt. He was one of those unnumbered multitudes to whom life is like something glimpsed in the display window of a shop. Never will they have enough courage to go into the store and buy some life—or even discover that many samples of life can be had free—and so they must remain forever with their noses pressed to the glass and compensate by scorning, mocking, decrying.

No wonder Viel-Castel says somewhere in his *Memoirs*, "Even my closest friends do not know how often and how much I weep. I am the saddest of men in this the saddest of all centuries."

And here was this Dumas who thought—the shallow fool—that the nineteenth century was one of the wonders of the world! Who went everywhere and everywhere enjoyed himself hugely, and wrote and spoke about it in such a way that everyone suddenly wanted to go there too and be as happy as he had been.

And Princess Mathilde, after listening to Dumas for hours at her dinner table, would exclaim, "That Dumas, he's a circus!"

And Viel-Castel would burn. It disturbed him that a Bonaparte princess should fall under the influence of a Dumas who could not but tarnish a reputation already somewhat compromised, for the Princess, though married to the wealthy Russian platinum king Demidov, was actually living with the Count de Nieuwerkerke, a mediocre sculptor. And night after night, Viel-Castel would grind his teeth to see a comedy played out before everyone, which must have struck the servants as most odd, with the Count dressing in his rooms, putting on his coat and hat, and taking his cane too, and then going downstairs by the back way and appearing at the front entrance as if he were just a visitor. And the butler, who had watched this deception for years, would call out the Count's name without a smile, and the Princess would welcome this man with whom she slept every night as if she hadn't seen him for months.

And then, the evening over, the Count would bow and kiss the Princess's hand, and polite hopes would be exchanged that they might see each other again very soon, and then the Count would be handed his hat and coat and cane, and would leave (not to go to his wife, who lived in the country, but just to skip around through the garden and go up the back stairs to his rooms).

Yes, that iron broom would have to get him too someday, but meanwhile Viel-Castel took out his fury on Dumas. "Listened to that man talk for four solid hours, no less," he writes, "never once deviating from his favorite subject: himself. Nothing but one self-aggrandizing impertinence after another."

What Viel-Castel called impertinence was Dumas' growing habit of speaking of himself in the most flattering terms, as if he were quite the most outstanding personality of the century.

It could not be denied that when, in the short space of about six months, Dumas had given to the world two such successful novels as *The Three Musketeers* and *The Count of Monte Cristo*, his reputation, already considerable, had ballooned to fabulous proportions. But that scarcely entitled the man to go around calling himself "the uncrowned King of Paris."

"My dear Count," Dumas would say, "it is not I who have insisted on this title, but the public who has spontaneously offered it to me, because it is so delighted with my books.

"My books, you know, have swept around the globe like a tidal wave," Dumas continued. "In the remotest villages the people would gather at the post inn to meet the mail coach and snatch up their copies of *Le Siècle*, containing the latest installment of my *Three Musketeers*. Woe to the postman who had forgotten to bring his papers. In Bescançon a driver who had merely failed to bring a sufficient number of copies was so manhandled that he had to take to his bed.

"Only the writers of the gospel have been translated as often as I have. Why, I can now be read in Mandarin Chinese.

"Do you realize that in Spain, for example, no fewer than six different translations have appeared of my *Monte Cristo*? Do you know why? Because although my rights are not protected in Spain, and no one has bothered to send me so much as a penny from there, each publisher's own rights are protected, and no one publisher may infringe on the translation of another, so each one must make his own separate rendering. And thus you can see the strange sight of one publisher taking another to law over a supposed infringement of his Dumas translation, and the law will actually ponder this case, which is exactly the same as if the police would give chase to the thieves who have stolen my watch and my billfold, but not in order to recover those articles for me, their rightful owner, but simply to see to it that the robbers do not cheat each other over the division of the loot.

"With my books selling the world over, it should not surprise anyone that there should be remote regions where the children know of only one living Frenchman, Alexandre Dumas, and should the question arise as to who is the King of France, this is the name that comes to their innocent lips.

"And thus at the post office of Paris, when they receive letters addressed to the King of Paris or to the uncrowned King of France, they know already that the letters are meant for me.

"Go ask any ten visitors from abroad who is the Frenchman they would most like to meet, and eight out of ten will tell you 'Dumas!' This I know for a fact, since a poor man came to me once begging for help, and I told him I would make him rich. 'How so?' he wanted to know. 'I will tell you, and you only, where I intend to be each evening. In what restaurant I shall dine, or where I shall go to the theater. You will have a monopoly of knowing where Dumas is.' He thought at first that I was laughing at him, making fun of him: what was the value of a monopoly on Dumas' daily schedule? But when he discovered that tourist guides were anxious to buy this daily information from him for the sake of pleasing their clients, he knew that he was in business. And I am assured that he has at present a nest egg which I myself might envy, so anxious are people to get a glimpse of me in flesh and blood.

"Thus you see I do occupy a throne. And it will not be easy to dislodge me. For it is the people who have crowned me, and since I need no army to keep that crown on my head, my position is unbeatable.

"Ever since I worked as envelope-writing clerk for Louis Philippe, before he became King of France, and ever since, one day, he took the trouble to write a note saying, 'Suspend all further salary to Alexandre Dumas, who is too much occupied with literary pursuits'—as though because I worked late into the night to write plays, my salary, which amounted to a pinhead fraction of his total income, had now become a drain on his treasury—ever since then I have considered myself his rival, determined to come out ahead of him in the race for historical importance.

"And as he mounted the throne and looted the public funds to the point of causing bread riots in Lyons and elsewhere, as he became the king of misers, so I have perforce become the king of spendthrifts.

"And one day I had the satisfaction of hearing the story of how the King, reading his newspaper at Versailles, threw away the sheet in disgust, saying, 'Why there's more in this paper about Dumas than about me.' Then I knew that I was winning. Just as he knew that he was losing.

"Not that people don't keep trying to minimize me. When my *Three Musketeers* was running in *Le Siècle*, the editors of that paper began taking bows for the enormous increase in the paper's circulation figures, although they should have known better, since even Prime Minister Guizot, whom they were roasting daily in their paper, subscribed to *Le Siècle*, but with the written proviso 'Please cancel subscription the moment the Dumas serial is concluded.'

"But it was only when my *Monte Cristo* began to come out in the columns of the *Journal des Débats*, and suddenly the circulation figures of *Le Siècle* dropped into a mine shaft while those of the *Débats* soared up into the clouds, that editors began to understand what was taking place, and they started to queue up outside my study and haven't stopped since.

"My price per line soon reached and then surpassed that of Balzac, who up until then had been the highest paid *feuilleton* writer of Paris. Balzac ran to his editor, Émile de Girardin. 'You mean that savage is to get more money than I do?' he shouted.

"Girardin tried to explain to him that it wasn't because I insisted on more money, but simply that editors were outbidding each other for my services and were themselves driving up my price.

"But Balzac wanted no explanations. 'From now on,' he declared, 'I demand three quarters of a franc a line!'

"'What? Even more than Dumas?' Girardin exclaimed. 'Out of the question, my dear fellow.'

"'Enough!' Balzac cried. 'I will not be put on the same footing with that Negro!' And he tore out of the office."

The Princess laughed and leaned forward for more, but Viel-Castel drew back, shocked to the depths of his being. "The crassness of it," so he recorded in his diary. "You'd think the man would at least pass over his African blood in silence, instead of openly joking about it."

But Dumas went right on. "Poor Balzac. He still had to endure the humiliation of having his novel *Les Paysans* stopped while only half completed in the columns of *La Presse*, and my *Reine Margot* substituted.

"Yes, I am so much the King of France," Dumas went on, "that, like him, I enjoy immunity from arrest. Did you know that a policeman who recently joined the Paris force, being required to take the oath to enforce the law without fear or favor, asked and obtained the right to one exception: Alexandre Dumas. 'That is one man I would never be able to arrest,' he said. 'He may do what he pleases so far as I am concerned. Besides, to lay hands on him would be to risk being mobbed.'

"But it was not until Dr. Véron got up at a meeting of doctors called to hear the latest reports on the American use of anesthetics in dentistry and surgery that I knew I really had become a king. He said, 'For my part, the problem of pain has already been solved and by a Frenchman. I simply give my patient a copy of Dumas' latest romance, I wait until the reader is well immersed, and then I operate freely, and never hear a murmur.' "

This was really too much for Viel-Castel. Unwilling to attack Dumas directly, he turned instead to the Princess. "I trust Your Highness finds this sort of conversation amusing."

Dumas said at once, "Her Highness will, I am sure, forgive an old Republican for his outspokenness."

Viel-Castel threw up his hands. "Now suddenly the King of Paris becomes a Republican. Which are you, anyway?"

"Both, of course," said Dumas calmly.

"Oh, of course," Viel-Castel mocked.

"Is is possible today for an honest man to belong completely to any one party?" Dumas asked. "I took part in the movement to force Louis Philippe off his throne. But when, as one of its first acts, the republic that followed decreed the pulling down of the bronze equestrian statue of Louis Philippe, I decided to protest.

"Friends warned me not to. They begged me not to stand up for Louis Philippe. 'You will be marked down as a Royalist,' they said. 'You will get into trouble with the new government.'

"One man said to me, 'Don't you ever want to have a government in power that favors you?'

"I said, 'I'll never have a government that likes me, because I insist on speaking my mind, and while there are many governments in this world that tolerate free speech, there is no government in the world that likes it.'

"So I wrote my well-known letter to the papers. I said, 'A republic that pulls down the statue of a king demonstrates that it is afraid of the mere image of a king. Such a republic is obviously timid, weak and given to inconsequentialities. It will not last long.'

"Was I right? It scarcely lasted two years. And I can say the same of the present government. It will not last. For it has exiled Victor Hugo and a hundred others of whom it is afraid."

"Suppose you tell us what kind of a government you would really approve," the Princess said.

"Gladly. I will tell it to you from an incident in my life. Years ago Louis Philippe gave a great ball at the Tuileries. It was announced that no one would be invited who was not an aristocrat. The newspapers wrote sensational articles about the lavishness of this spectacle, which the reporters were privileged to watch from the balcony where the musicians were seated.

"I decided that this ball must be answered. I had at that time a large four-room apartment. But on the same floor was another apartment with four much larger rooms. I rented them for a couple of weeks, opened a connection between the two apartments, and invited my friends to an artists' ball.

"Everyone understood that a challenge had been flung to the King, and that the aristocracy of talent was going to pit itself against the aristocracy of birth.

"All the artists offered me their services. Ciceri painted the ceilings for me. Delacroix did a number of murals from the plays of Victor Hugo. The Boulanger brothers and the Johannot brothers did murals from my plays and from those of Vigny.

"The sculptors Barye and Nanteuil modeled plaster ornaments that outdid anything to be seen in the Tuileries.

"The rest of us, myself in the lead, organized a huge hunt in the forest of Villers-Cotterêts, and we came back with such quantities of deer and other game that we got the best chefs in Paris to exchange with us and secured in return two buck roasted whole, a fifty-pound sturgeon jellied whole, and a huge veal and turkey roll. A vast quantity of other food was ordered to be delivered on the night of the ball. Bordeaux, Burgundy and champagne by the hundreds and hundreds of bottles were set to warm or to cool or put on ice, according to the rule for wines.

"The Paris theaters emptied their wardrobes to lend our friends the most magnificent costumes.

"Seven hundred guests showed up. Only four hundred had been invited. But three hundred more came, and I didn't mind. 'Your talent is your ticket of admission,' I declared, and whoever had distinguished himself in any field that demanded talent and application was welcomed.

"Under the blaze of hundreds of candles and with two orchestras playing, there was displayed such a pageantry of color as was never seen since the Field of the Cloth of Gold. We had astrologers and Chinese warriors, and Turkish slave girls, and executioners and Madame du Barrys. Delacroix came dressed as Dante. Lafayette appeared as a Venetian Doge. Alfred de Musset was got up as a weather-cock. Rossini came as Figaro. Barye as a Bengal tiger. Jadin as an undertaker.

"At nine o'clock in the morning guests were still dancing, and all went out onto the sunlit streets for the final galop.

"The Tuileries were never able to match that ball. Never were so many celebrities gathered together, never such a display of talent and beauty and wit.

"That is my answer, Your Highness: that talent should reign, rather than birth; that personal achievement should count, rather than inherited money. That would be my conception of the perfect government. And if ever there should be such a government in the world, it would be like a sunrise in the history of man."

"And of this government," Viel-Castel said, smiling, "I suppose you would want to be king."

"Not at all," said Dumas. "My ambition goes beyond that."

"What?" Viel-Castel exclaimed. "King is not enough? You want to be the emperor, I suppose."

"Higher than that," said Dumas.

"Dictator, pope, what can you possibly want to be?" Viel-Castel exclaimed.

Dumas continued to shake his head. "Greater than that. Greater still. Is it possible, my dear Count, that you have no conception of what the greatest estate is that mortal can aspire to?"

"No, I cannot follow you in your power-mad ambition."

Dumas smiled. "Neverthless it is very simple: I want to become a legend."

"A legend?!"

"Yes. Isn't that the highest that man can reach? Do you know of anything greater? When history perishes, what survives? Are not kings and conquerors forgotten from eras whose legends are still alive? Ah, my good Viel-Castel, aim for that—to make yourself into a legend—and the world will forever keep your memory green.

Palaces will fall into ruins, and cities will lie covered with dust, but never can you destroy or bury a legend. Let all my books be burned like Alexandria's library, but if I shall have meanwhile succeeded in becoming a legend, nothing will ever erase me."

"Bravo!" said Princess Mathilde.

CHAPTER TWENTY-SIX

The Font of Money

WELL, NOW WE ARE finally getting at the heart of the Viel-Castel witticism about mistresses and shoes. When you have a father who is aiming to become a legend and a son whose sole idea over many years has been to merit the great name of Dumas and to prove that it is a name worth bearing, then you have a truly strange and powerful father-and-son combination.

Let's see what happened.

When Ida's departure enabled Dumas at last to take his son into his home, he found a boy who had meanwhile grown into a tall, blond and handsome young man. Years of gardening had developed him physically, but the unending conflict with his fellow students had made him taciturn, indrawn.

His old tendency to stoop had reasserted itself.

"Is that how you stand?" Dumas asked his son.

Alexandre remembered his mother's old injunction: "Feel for the button," and he brought his neck back hard.

Dumas shook his head. "No. You can't force it. Either the spirit wants to stand straight, or it doesn't. Now listen to me. Are you listening?"

"Yes, Papa," said Alexandre.

"Remember this: animals are a part of geography. Man is a part of astronomy. Animals have shapes and forms. Only man has posture. When a real human being walks, his spirit is aware of the fact that with every step he takes his foot strikes against our great globe, which is one of the heavenly bodies of this vast universe. And you especially should realize that the entire surface of this globe you are treading rings with the name of Alexandre Dumas, a name that only two people, you and I, are privileged to bear!"

And then Dumas said, "*Now* let me see you walk—astronomically!"

And Alexandre walked. With tears in his eyes.

This was not the same as feeling for a button. This was reaching for the unattainable. It was more difficult. More exhausting. But it was also more inspiring. What was a button compared to the stars? This bastard had suddenly to learn how to be crown prince to a legend!

Though there was nothing that Alexandre desired more deeply than to live with his father, he felt it his duty to inform him that he was far behind in his studies. He had several years to go yet before he could take his baccalaureate.

"But I thought you wanted to be a writer," his father said.

"Yes, I do. I do."

"Then why are you worried about degrees? You don't suppose that a degree will get you a play accepted, do you?"

"No, but . . ."

"Surely you don't imagine that with a diploma in your pocket you will no longer have to study?"

"No, Papa."

"A writer, my boy, never stops studying. Only professors can afford to do that. There are no degrees for us. Only performance counts. Come, you shall see that writing is not easy. I intend to start you off at once, as my assistant."

He showed Alexandre into a room next to his own study. The shelves were heaped with books, many of them huge old tomes. On a small table stood piles of paper and a supply of pens and ink.

Dumas took one of the big volumes from the shelf. "Villehardouin," he said. "In the Paulin-Paris edition, published not so long ago. And this is Louis Cousin's *History of Constantinople*. Written a hundred and fifty years ago, but still excellent. Sit down, son."

When Alexandre had seated himself, Dumas, walking up and down the room, said, "As you may know, I have a far greater demand for my work than I myself can supply. So, like my fellow writer Scribe, whose librettos are wanted by every composer, I like to have a little preliminary work done by an assistant. Just as

Rubens would have one of his pupils paint in the feet of his goddesses, another pupil the drapery, a third the sky and the clouds, while he reserved for himself the important work of the conception, the composition, the faces and so forth—just so, in my case, I like to have something already half formed which I can recast, rewrite, expand, supplying all that distinguishes a rich piece of writing from a poor one.

"Now, some time ago I promised the *Revue de Paris* a novel based on the sack of Constantinople. You already know something, I presume, about that catastrophic historical event?"

"You mean the fall of Constantinople to the Turks?"

"No, no. That came two centuries later. I'm speaking of the time when the Crusaders from France, on their way to conquer the Holy Land from the Mohammedan, joined instead with the city of Venice in an expedition against the city of Byzantium or Constantinople, which, far from being pagan, was a stronghold of Christianity.

"Constantinople at that time was still the heir to all that was classical. It was a city that had never been conquered by Goth or Vandal. The Dark Ages had never descended there. All that remained of the art and the wealth of the Roman Empire had taken refuge there, defended by walls that were eight hundred years old and had been added to so often that at the time we are speaking of they stood over two hundred feet thick—massive masonry, topped by a forest of turrets and flanked by a multitude of redoubts and casements. It had been attacked and besieged many times, but never had it fallen. It had, moreover, not only its walls but it had the sea and the mountains to make it impregnable whether assaulted by arms or by starvation.

"It was this city that the Crusaders looted. Among the prizes were one thousand colossal bronze statues that had once stood in Rome. The Venetians when they captured the city melted them down and struck them into coins.

"The story must begin with Isaac the Angel, who was on the throne of Byzantium just shortly before the siege. His brother Alexis coveted that throne and, by sticking hot needles into Isaac the Angel's eyes and blinding him, was able to wrest the crown for himself.

"Blind Isaac the Angel had a son, whose name was also Alexis. This Alexis had been shut up in a prison, but he managed to escape and in time reached Venice and there laid before the Doge of Venice, Dandalo, a man of eighty years of age, who was also blind, a scheme for leading the next Crusade, not against the Mohammedan, but against Constantinople. Venice would supply the ships, France would supply the Crusaders, Alexis would supply the secret of how to conquer the city in spite of its walls.

"Pope Innocent III was furious at this scheme. He did not want to show the Mohammedan world the spectacle of Christian fighting Christian. But he could not stop the Venetians, who were anxious to destroy Constantinople, their commercial rival for the Mediterranean trade. He could not stop the Crusaders, who wanted the chance of looting this rich city. He could not stop Alexis, who was bent on revenging his father.

"So the deed was done. The loot was enormous. Blind Isaac the Angel cursed his son Alexis for betraying his country to the enemy merely to secure a throne which was now valueless anyhow.

"That's the story, my boy. In brief. And here are your authorities. Villehardouin, who himself took part in this enterprise. Here is the Greek historian Nicetas. Here is Gunther. Here is Gibbon, who studied every possible source. And here are a lot of other books you may find useful: books on the Crusades in general, books on Constantinople, books on manners, morals, costumes, art of warfare, and so forth.

"Best of all there is my good friend Delacroix' excellent painting 'Entry of the Crusaders into Constantinople.' It tells you everything on one canvas. All the characters are there. Isaac the Angel, Alexis, Baldwin and so forth. And a magnificent view of the whole city is shown. I cannot recommend anything better than a thorough study of that painting. It will save you a trip to Constantinople.

"Well, what do you think? Doesn't it excite you? Isn't it the best material in the world for a big, colorful novel? French swords battering Byzantium?"

"Yes, Papa," said Alexandre, concealing his panic as best he could.

"Then to work, my son!" Dumas cried. "We shall have another and finer *Monte Cristo*! *Au travail!*"

And with that he left, going into the adjacent room, where he had his study, and where he fell to work at once, as Alexandre could tell from the screams, the whistles, the laughter and the groans that reached his ears.

As for Alexandre, he was left absolutely flabbergasted by this rapid transition from school to this study, where he was as if locked up and told to produce a novel better than *Monte Cristo*.

He had no idea how or where to start.

After a moment he picked up a volume from a series on the history of the Byzantine Empire. He opened at random and began to read. The more he read the less he understood. It was all about a subject called *monothelitism*, which apparently was a diabolical ideology threatening the church, the people, the throne, everything.

He opened another volume. But it was the same story. Everywhere he met words that were completely unfamiliar to him, references to arms, to dress, to coinage, to religion.

Ah! Here on this shelf were books that would explain such words to him. Here was *Costumes and Furniture of Old France* by Count Horace de Viel-Castel, curator of the Louvre museum. And here was another set of huge volumes on *Arts and Costumes* by Bibliophile Jacob (Paul Lacroix). So now he must work his way through all these books systematically? Nothing appealed to Alexandre less than this sort of close, methodical study. He had avoided it all through his school years. And now every few pages he had to stop and collect himself. He felt that his mind was a mere blur of facts, with nothing clear and certain. And when he contemplated all the other volumes still untouched, he quailed. Desperately he repeated to himself that he must succeed, that he must have his father as proud of him as he was proud of his father. But the going remained rough.

After some hours his father came into the room. "My François— who will be your valet too—tells me that your wardrobe is in a deplorable state. Come. Let's go on a shopping tour. I've already ordered the tilbury harnessed."

Passing through Dumas' study, the father stopped before a holy water font, a handsome marble and bronze affair that must have done duty once in a rich church.

"We'd better take along some holy water, to bless our shopping," said Dumas.

As Alexandre approached, he saw to his surprise that the basin was filled, not with water, but with coins, largely of silver, but with a rich sprinkling of gold, and an even richer sprinkling of paper bank notes, many of them of a thousand-franc value.

Here and there, dispersed through the money, were pieces of jewelry, mostly chains, watches and fobs. Beneath all this, like some sort of murky sediment that had sunk to the bottom, lay a heavy foundation of scorned copper coins.

"Holy water?" Alexandre asked, impressed by the sight of this treasure.

"Unholy, if you prefer," said Dumas. "But I will bet you that if any communicant were to answer honestly, he would confess that he would rather dip his finger in this basin than in the one that stands in every church."

"Is this the way you keep your money?" Alexandre asked.

"Why not?"

"I mean, out in the open?"

"Do you imagine it might spoil? No fear. Money never rots from age, not in this house."

"Suppose someone should steal it?"

"I assure you I would not lose a moment's sleep over it. Or miss the next installment of my *feuilleton*. I'm only annoyed that not one of these watches which have been forced on me as collateral for loans keeps time."

"You should have a man of confidence to run your business affairs," said Alexandre sagely. "You'd more than save his salary."

"No doubt," said Dumas. "But you know what people would say? They'd say, 'Dumas is no longer Dumas.' And that would cost me more than any possible theft. Now, enough talk. Fill your pockets."

Dumas grabbed a couple of handfuls of money and stuffed it in his purse. Then he turned to Alexandre. "Take," he said.

Somehow Alexandre couldn't bring himself to dip his hand into this mass of money. It intimidated him. He had not yet completely sloughed off his role of bastard.

"Go on," Dumas encouraged. "Put your hand in. It feels good. And, besides, yours has more of a right here than many a hand that's dipped into it. Remember, I have only one rule in regard to this holy water. You may take what you need, whenever you like, except when there is less than two hundred francs in the basin, in which case you will not touch more than half."

'Whenever there's less than two hundred?" Alexandre exclaimed. "When could that be? There must be much more than fifty thousand in there now."

"That is no assurance that there will not be less than two hundred there tomorrow," said Dumas. "So go ahead and fill your pockets while it's there."

And as Alexandre still hesitated, Dumas added, "After all, we're going to be working more and more closely together. And I shall therefore soon be owing you money, which is more normally my situation anyhow."

"But, Papa, there's nothing I need money for."

"What?" Dumas almost screamed. "Nothing you need money for? How can you possibly say that?"

"But it's true, Papa. And even more since this very minute you've been saying that you intend to take me out and buy me a wardrobe. What can I ask for when I've got my rooms, when I have servants to wait on me, when the kitchen is ready to give me any food I may desire? And I have books and a study in the bargain. What would I want with money?"

"Look here, my boy," said Dumas seriously. "When one is the son of Alexandre Dumas, one has certain obligations. One must be seen constantly in the best restaurants. One must deny oneself nothing in the way of clothes or amusements. One's mistresses must be stared at and envied. One's scrapes should interest the authorities and give newspaper editors something to shake their heads over. In short, of the two categories of people that make up this world—namely, those who gossip and those who are gossiped about —one must definitely belong to the class of select individuals who live out the stories that others will later amuse themselves by repeating. Such are the duties of a son of Alexandre Dumas. Now see that you do not disgrace me by passing unobserved in a crowd."

"Yes, Papa," said Alexandre, trying not to show his dismay. The word "mistresses," not just in the singular, but in the plural, had particularly disturbed him.

"Good," said Dumas.

"Yes, Papa."

Gingerly Alexandre's hand went to the money and took some of the coins. But then, feeling his father's eyes upon him, he took one of the thousand-franc notes and a couple of the hundred-franc bills and stuffed them all in his pocket.

Dumas embraced his son and kissed him on both cheeks. "Come. Now let's shop."

They went first to Staub's for some gaudy waistcoats of brocade, of plaid and of chamois. Then to Darnet's for shirts of the finest cambric and batiste. After that to Walker for the latest in stocks. And to Collman for shoes. To Humann and Renard for suits and for cloaks. They chose black for formal wear, blue for fashion, gray for everyday use, tweed for sport, white linen for summer boating, and a couple of novelty weaves, pepper-and-salt, herringbone, hound's tooth and the like for casual wear, and finally a soft velvet suit for cold days. Cloaks, of course, to match.

Then to Pinaud's for cosmetics—cold cream, hartshorn, patchouli and the like. To Verdier's for canes, in particular a fine ebony stick topped with a distinguished-looking lapis-lazuli grip, for evening wear.

And last of all, to Breguet's for a gold chain, several fobs, a gold toothpick and a handsome timepiece.

Alexandre had to gasp again and again at the prices of the articles his father bought.

"It's nothing, my boy," said Dumas. "It costs money to make a splash. Did you notice my new tilbury? I had to order it two years in advance from Binder. And I paid him a fortune."

"It's beautiful," said Alexandre.

"Not only that," said Dumas. "Did you count the springs?"

"No."

"Then you didn't do what every Parisian does. A few years ago four springs were enough. But today if you have only four springs, you'd do better to ride around in a Roman chariot, which had none, for in a Roman chariot you'd still attract attention, whereas with four springs today, you only date yourself. And to be dated is the worst thing one can do."

When they had returned home and Alexandre had worked another couple of hours, he asked his father if he might have the tilbury for a while.

"Certainly," his father said. "Go, my boy. Amuse yourself."

Alexandre drove to the outskirts. As he crossed busy streets it seemed to him that he could feel people's looks going toward him. He sat bolt upright, thinking of his father, and of the solar system, but just the same he was disturbed, and he flicked the horse with the whip so as to get through town as fast as possible.

The building before which he eventually stopped was a neglected structure at the end of an impasse. Broken panes had been stuffed with rags. Some of the window openings had been bricked in, protection against cold being more important than light. The hallway, open to any comer, was crowded with snot-nosed children and mangy dogs. In the rear, across a courtyard where a couple of pigs grubbed, was a low building even dingier. A flight of rickety steps led to the upper floor.

Alexandre went down a hall and knocked at a door.

From inside came the sound of shuffled slippers and a voice asked, "Who is it?"

"It's me, *Maman!*" Alexandre cried. "Open up!"

A gray-haired woman opened up and screamed. Alexandre took his mother in his arms.

"Why, *Maman,*" he cried. "What frightened you?"

"Come in," she said. "For a moment I was carried back so far that I was dizzy. This is exactly the way your father would burst in on me—unexpectedly—and dressed just like you are—in the height of fashion. And of course immediately announcing that everything was changed, that life was going to be completely different from now on. . . ."

"Well, so it is!" Alexandre declared. "This time it really is. Look!" And he pulled from his pocket the money he had taken from the baptismal font and strewed it across the table—gold, silver and bank notes.

"Where did you get that?" she asked.

"I've left school, *Maman.* I'm living with father from now on. And I've got all the money I want."

"Congratulations," she said dryly.

"He keeps his money, thousands and thousands of francs, in a

baptismal font. Calls it his holy water. And he insists I should dip
my hand in and take as much as I want."

"What will you have?" she asked. "Tea? Or chocolate?"

He followed her to the little stove, where she blew on the embers
and added pieces of charcoal. "Is that all you say? Doesn't it mean
anything to you that at last you can move out of this slum and stop
working? Why, I've brought enough for you to live on for a year or
more. In comfort, if not in style."

"And after that year? What then?"

"There will be more," he said.

"Perhaps. Or maybe less. Or nothing. No, thanks. I too have all
the money I want. Dr. Delarue lets me take from the kitchen whatever is left over. I come and go there as I please, and as long as his
drawers are filled with clean linen, every button in place and every
rip sewed up so that it is almost invisible, he doesn't care what hours
I work. It's as if I were an independent person. Why should I
change that?"

"But surely you could find a more attractive place to live. It's
something I've always wanted for you."

"Did you earn this money?"

"Not really," he said. "But I will be earning it. I'm working for
father. Preparing his next novel."

"But you didn't earn it, did you? Not yet?"

"No."

She shook her head. "His money never brought me anything but
heartache. Your money would be quite different. Your money I
would have a right to, because I'm your mother. We're related. But
his money? What right have I to it? We're nothing to each other.
It's ten years or more since he's laid eyes on me. And with my gray
hair coming in, he probably wouldn't know me today even if he
should bump into me on the street. We're total strangers."

Alexandre didn't know what to say. His heart pained him as it
had so often in the many years since he had experienced the
estrangement and bitterness between his parents.

His mother served him his chocolate. "Move your chair this way,"
she said. "There's a bad spot there." She pointed out to him on the
floorboards a spot where the wood was powdering away. One could
already see through to the floor below. "I should get a piece of tin

from the *quincaillier*," she said, "and nail it over that spot. But then I live alone here and as long as I know where it is, even in the dark, it doesn't matter."

He drank his chocolate in silence. And as usual, when with his mother, in spite of his love a desire rose in him to get away as fast as possible.

"Don't forget his money," Catherine said to him, indicating the bills and coins still spread upon the table.

A little sheepishly he gathered in his wealth. "I'll have my own money to bring to you soon," he said. "Very soon."

"I can wait," his mother said quietly. "This place isn't so bad. There would even have been enough room for you to move in with me—when you had finished school," she added. "It was a dream I permitted myself. You would have been alone most of the day, with no one to bother you while you wrote. And I would have cooked for you and taken care of your clothes. And the money from your work would soon pay for a better life."

He had no answer for that. It only stung his eyes. He just kissed her, promised to return shortly, and left.

CHAPTER TWENTY-SEVEN

New Shoes and Old Mistresses

BACK HOME in his study Alexandre fell to work upon the sack of Constantinople with all the more determination. The struggle was prolonged and bitter. It was weeks before he began to feel himself oriented amidst this vast material. It seemed to him that he should know all about the Crusades so that his characters might be able to talk Crusades with the familiarity of people who were at home with them. He had to know the history and the government of Venice, and the prominent families of that city who strove against each other for political power. He had to know the schism between Roman Catholic and Greek Orthodox. And above all he had to know Constantinople.

He was grateful that his father never questioned him as to how his work was advancing. For he was now coming to the worst of the problem of writing a historical novel: the use of history within the plot of the book. And here the trouble was that for lack of the research one couldn't write the story, while at the same time for lack of the story one did not know how to value the bits of interesting material that one uncovered. One became glutted. A way had to be found to merge the two aspects so that they could advance together.

Time and again he tackled the problem of an outline. But the result gave him little satisfaction. It either seemed more history than novel, or else, if he stressed the novel part, the whole thing threatened to become unbelievable.

He decided boldly to write some of it to discover how the finished product would sound. At first things seemed to move along fine. But more and more his characters began to behave independently. Obstreperously they insisted on living their own lives, making havoc of his outline. Suddenly he found himself without a story.

Again and again he wrote new outlines. But again and again his characters lined up against him, like enemy soldiers determined to die before succumbing to his plot. And when, furious, he forced them nevertheless to do his bidding, the result was so hollow, so wooden, that it was unreadable. Joints creaked, plaster split, the scenery tore like paper. The whole thing collapsed upon him like a badly made stage setting.

In the first case his characters had killed his plot. In the second the plot had killed his characters.

In his irritation he would again and again crumple up masses of pages, throw them on the floor, and kick them aside with his foot.

Then, manfully, he would start fresh.

But when he had done the next version he would ask himself, In what way is it any better? Is it not, as a matter of fact, far worse?

More crumpled sheets on the floor, and another version in the making. And a couple of days later, when that one was done, it would join the rest of the crumpled sheets. Until suddenly it occurred to him that perhaps that first version hadn't been so bad at that. All at once he remembered it as alive with color and excitement.

Frantically he searched through the crumpled sheets on the

floor to find his first version. It was a puzzle to get the sheets correctly together again.

So this was his best work?

Yes, it was good. But this part he had done better elsewhere. And this part still better in some other version.

He set to work to uncrumple every crumpled sheet and search out the best from each version. Good. Now all he need do was fit all these pieces together.

But it didn't work. The seams bulged and gaped. From version to version his transitions swayed like rope bridges across the chasms of the Himalayas. And once more he found himself crumpling up one essay after another.

In the midst of this patchwork he found his mind giving way. He could no longer keep track of what he had included and what he had left out. He began to despair of ever getting his opening finished. And yet, after the opening there was still the whole book to be written.

At last there came a day when he felt himself floundering around so helplessly amidst a vast accumulation of crumpled sheets, a long succession of discarded outlines, masses of notes, that he could see no way out. He was lost. Finished.

And yet he had to succeed. He not only had to prove that he was the son of his father, he had to prove himself to his mother too. He had promised to bring her his own money, and when he thought of her in that room saying, "Watch out. There's a bad spot on the floor," he would be spurred on to yet another effort.

"Having any trouble?" Dumas asked one evening, coming into his son's study.

Alexandre shrugged. "It's my first attempt at writing. I mean, serious writing."

Dumas nodded. He looked around, saw all the crumpled sheets, and in particular noticed those that had been crumpled and then uncrumpled. He recognized the familiar literary battleground of his early struggles: the paper corpses, mangled and discarded, strewn upon the floor; the anguished cries of mutilated paragraphs; and the general, armed with quill and ink, still marshaling his decimated cohorts for another futile assault.

At length Dumas said, "The art of writing can never be taught. It can only be learned."

"In that case," said Alexandre, "I'll learn it."

"Take the evening off. You've worked hard enough."

"Where shall we go?" Alexandre asked.

"I'm staying home," said Dumas. "I have work I must finish. But you, why don't you go out?"

"I have no place to go," said Alexandre.

Dumas said nothing for a moment; then he asked, "In that case I'm sure you would not mind running an errand for me, would you?"

"Certainly not," said Alexandre.

"Good. I've made a few changes in the role of one of my actresses, and I would like her to have the corrections tonight so she will be well prepared for the rehearsal tomorrow. Could you do that for me?"

"At once."

Dumas went back into his study and returned in a moment with an envelope. "The changes are inside. And here is the name and address: Madame des Brosses on the rue Taitbout. Take the tilbury if you like. In any case, I won't use it tonight. If I should go out, I'll walk."

It was near the middle of the night before Alexandre returned. He thought everyone would be asleep, but there was a crack of light coming from his father's study, and as he passed in the corridor his father called out to him, "That you, Alexandre?"

"Yes, Papa," said Alexandre.

Dumas came to the door. "Well? You took good care of my errand?"

Alexandre said, "Yes," and hung his head.

"Going to sleep? Or to work?"

"I'll go to work," said Alexandre.

"Good," said his father. "Sometimes the night is the most rewarding."

As Alexandre started toward his study, Dumas held him back and looked at him with a smile. "It must cost her a pretty penny to keep having those silver chains repaired."

Alexandre, startled, stared at his father. "How did you . . . ?" he began and stopped short.

His father laughed and took his son in his arms. "You will see. In a few months all Paris will know about those chains, and the man who has never broken them will feel that he has been left out of something important."

He laughed and clapped his boy on the shoulder.

Alexandre laughed too. But he did not laugh like his father. There was something in him that did not permit him to roar lustily, much as he wanted to.

"Obviously she likes to think that to possess her a man would climb mountains and break down walls, go through fire and water. But her jeweler, what must he think when, day after day, she brings him silver chains to be repaired?"

"She takes them to a different jeweler each time," Alexandre suggested.

"Of course she does!" Dumas said. "Why didn't I think of that."

Alexandre liked that compliment. And, stimulated, he threw out another thought. "No doubt a day will come in her life when no man will care to break that chain. What a terrible day that will be for her."

"Why, you're a writer," Dumas cried. "That's a story you must write."

And with that somehow Alexandre could release his laughter. And both men laughed together: two men who had shared an adventure and now shared a memory.

Well, that's how it started. Viel-Castel's criticism, I mean.

Alexandre, discovering that it was easier to live up to his father's sexual expectations of him than to his literary expectations, abandoned Constantinople and took to the gay life.

And if at first he tended to follow in his father's footsteps, that was only natural since with his father's mistresses the ice was, so to speak, already broken, and entree was facilitated by a natural curiosity on both sides.

You see that I have not hesitated to go down deep into mud and slime to fish out another fragment of the explanation I owe the reader with regard to the "Duel after the Masquerade Ball." And since obviously anything human has at least one foot in the mud, my explanation would have failed to explain had I not pointed it out.

Naturally, Alexandre was not content to remain permanently in this particular relation to his father. Viel-Castel tells us of a moment when the young man protested against being saddled permanently with his father's new shoes and old mistresses. Whereupon Dumas is said to have replied, "Don't you see it is an honor I am doing you by giving you my new shoes and my cast-off mistresses?"

"No, Papa, frankly I can't see it."

"What? Am I not proving in this way that you have both my small foot and my big v. . . .? * You should be proud and happy!"

Thus fortunately endowed, Alexandre soon went out to try his own wings. Viel-Castel tells us how ". . . young Dumas, Alfred de Musset and a third young man of the unbuttoned literary set were once in conversation with Princess K . . . , Madame de N . . . † and Madame Z . . . , three fabulously wealthy Russian ladies who had come to Paris to do that which they would never have dared do at home in Moscow. The subject of prostitution came up, and the question arose as to whether prostitutes were to be considered as tragic figures, or whether they enjoyed their profession, and perhaps even got the best out of life."

Viel-Castel continues: "Young Dumas, that badly bleached product of three adulterous Negro generations, cried out at once, 'Why don't we find out for ourselves?'

" 'How so?' he was asked.

" 'With three pretty women here,' he said. 'we have enough to start up our own brothel. What's to prevent us, if we really wish to know?'

"The idea was so attractive that everyone immediately caught fire, particularly the Russian ladies, who thereafter devoted half of the week to their necessary Parisian social life, and for the other half became inmates of their own house of prostitution.

"With the volumes of the Marquis de Sade's *Justine and Juliette*

* This word *v* . . . . is as Viel-Castel gives it. No doubt it has an English equivalent, but I cannot find it in my dictionary.

† Madame de N . . . has been identified as Madame de Nesselrode.

as their textbook, with three eager instructors and three even more eager pupils, the entire range of lupanarian activity was thoroughly explored and the ladies proved themselves apt and rapid learners, even going out into the streets, like the Roman Empress Messalina, to pick up in the cabarets further material for study and for practice."

Viel-Castel doesn't tell us what conclusion the ladies came to—I mean as to the life of a prostitute—whether tragedy or joy. Instead he launches into a sociohistorical study blaming all this debauchery on the Marquis de Sade, the writer who spent so many years of his life in prison, both under the old regime and under Napoleon, and whose name has given us the words *sadism* and *sadistic*.

"One cannot exaggerate," says Viel-Castel, "the nefarious influence that this man and his ignoble novel have had on the entire body of French literature of the nineteenth century. No author since De Sade has dared write a novel into which he did not fling a morsel of obscenity. Victor Hugo does it in his *Notre Dame de Paris*, Jules Janin does it in his *Dead Donkey*, Théophile Gautier in his *Mademoiselle de Maupin*, Dumas in every one of his plays, George Sand, Eugène Sue, Alfred de Musset, all, all are close relatives of De Sade, all have been infected by his debauchery." But Viel-Castel doesn't go into the question of who debauched De Sade.

And no doubt about it: Alexandre had discovered that to be his father's true son at the desk was not so easy as being his true son in a lady's bed, and thus he neglected the sack of Constantinople to the point where his father eventually gave the *Revue de Paris* some other work instead.

Those were the days when the Dumas baptismal font was always full of holy water. When Paris was full of pretty women. And the two Dumas were, as the father said, both of them twenty years young.

As for his mother, Alexandre avoided her.

CHAPTER TWENTY-EIGHT

The Dueling Code

NO. HE COULDN'T possibly have been any happier.

Feeling himself at last completely accepted by his father, and backed by all the money of that fabulous baptismal font, it wasn't very long before Alexandre had taken the lead in the wild *jeunesse dorée* (golden youth) set of Paris. To that period of his life belong those insane cross-country horse races, real medieval treasure hunts, with clue leading to clue and if correctly followed guiding one finally to the prize: a naked maiden chained in an abandoned tower. And there were gladiatorial combats, and revived tourneys of knighthood, executed in authentic suits of armor, and hashish parties right out of the times of the Crusades. And forfeit games requiring one to bring an eighty-year-old woman from the aristocracy to a costume ball, failure being punished with a compulsory leap into the Seine while on horseback.

And such mad affairs were mere moments in a perpetual routine of fencing matches, hunting parties, all-night sessions at baccarat and lansquenet, and the usual round of theater, opera, balls and so forth.

This was the "famished lion" era of European morals, when it seemed that nothing could ever satisfy man's appetite for perpetual intrigue, romance and adventure; and families trembled lest even the walls of convents, supplemented by chaperons and the constant preaching of hell-fire and damnation, should prove insufficient to protect the virginity of their daughters. Émile de Girardin used to say, "Sure, the times are corrupt. But one can fight corruption without denying that the periods of depravity coincide somehow with the eras when the greatest artists flourish. Study history and tell me what upright Sparta ever produced that can be compared to wicked Athens. Whether you like it or not, flowers grow best in manure."

This was the time when General Galliffet (at that time still a colonel and not yet infamous as the man who butchered the Paris Commune with thirty thousand summary street executions) was said to have met his lieutenants one morning and declared, "Gentlemen, my wife deceived the lot of you last night. She slept with me."

It was he who started the understandably rather short-lived Parisian vogue of not only drinking a toast to his latest love, but reinforcing it by crunching the champagne glass between his teeth and swallowing the whole mess. His comment to those who wished to imitate him was "You can't make it the first toast of the evening: you're not drunk enough. And you can't make it the last toast because you'll start worrying about those razor-sharp splinters going through your gut. You've just got to keep drinking until you pass out. When you wake up you discover to your surprise that it's not as bad as you thought."

It was that kind of an era. An era when the Count de Châteauvillard invented a new game of billiards: played from horseback. Games of mounted billiards were the rage of Paris—for three weeks.

And Alexandre was in the thick of it all. He seriously threatened to surpass his father, especially since he added to the parentally practiced vices three that Dumas had always shunned—namely, hard drinking, heavy smoking and gambling for high stakes—besides giving his dissipations practically his entire time, instead of sparing them only an occasional few hours as his father did.

Victor Hugo, who had long had a fondness for Alexandre, seeing this development going on year after year, finally had the opportunity one evening of taking the handsome lad aside and reading him a rather serious lecture on the difference between virtue and vice.

"Vice rewards us with immediate delight," he said, "while virtue must be patiently practiced for many years before we obtain any joy from it. But in the end there is no comparison between the results: the practice of vice results in boredom, while the practice of virtue results in bliss. You know, Alexandre, I wouldn't want you to discover this fact too late in your life."

The young man, embarrassed for Hugo's sake, since the whole thing struck him a little like a scolding from some spinster, thanked the older man profusely. He admired Hugo, but as a poet, not as a mentor.

As for Hugo, he realized that he had wasted his wisdom, so he gave the boy a friendly pat and said, "Assure me of only one thing: that you are really and truly happy."

"Deliriously so," said Alexandre.

Hugo smiled. "Good. In that case, go, my son, and sin some more."

Which Alexandre promptly did.

But as for catching up to and eclipsing his father, that wasn't so easy.

In the Dujarier case, for example, it seemed for a while that Alexandre was close to the center of this celebrated affair, for he had actually been present at that extravagant evening of drinking and gambling when the mysterious dispute had started. It was in an upstairs private room of the Frères Provençaux, at that time perhaps the most expensive restaurant in the world, where a group of *bons vivants*, including Roger de Beauvoir, the Count de St. Aignan, Dujarier and several others, had been entertaining some of the loveliest and most accessible (but expensive) ladies of the town. Everybody had been having a wonderful time and everybody had got quite drunk, and then just when the party was breaking up a certain Beauvallon, whose sister was married to Granier de Cassagnac, had suddenly declared that such an insult as Dujarier had offered him that evening could be wiped out by nothing but blood.

Dujarier, a slight, bald-headed man who had never so much as held a weapon in his hand, protested that he could not recall having insulted anyone. True, the conversation had been at times pretty free, but it had all been in good fun.

"Are you calling me a liar?" Beauvallon shouted.

"No," said Dujarier, "but you are mistaken if you see any occasion for a dispute."

"That means only one thing," Beauvallon screamed. "That you are too cowardly to fight!"

This insult was more than Dujarier could take. "My seconds will call on you in the morning," he declared.

"But you don't even know how to fire a pistol!" Alexandre cried. And, turning to Beauvallon, he said, "This is my fight," and, ripping off a glove, he flung it into Beauvallon's face.

Stung, Beauvallon stood there, face flushed, breathing heavily; then he said, "One duel at a time!" and walked off.

If Alexandre knew how the quarrel had started, his father had already predicted the result: misfortune was bound to come to Dujarier. Dumas had said that weeks before the quarrel, and for this strange reason:

Dujarier's mistress was Lola Montez, the ravishingly beautiful Irish dancer of fandangos who gave herself out to be the daughter of the well-known bullfighter Montez. She had been briefly Dumas' mistress and had stalked about his home in velvet trousers, cracking her bull whip and shooting off her pistol, two weapons without which she never walked abroad.

Dumas had got rid of her as quickly as he could. "She has the evil eye," he told friends. "She draws misfortune to her neighborhood just as surely as a magnet draws iron filings."

And when Dujarier had taken up with her, Dumas had said, "She'll bring tragedy to him. Watch and see." *

It hadn't been necessary to wait long.

Dujarier was editor of the newspaper *La Presse*, and so clever at his work that he had pushed *La Presse* forward to one of the highest circulations of Paris, beating out *Le Globe*, which was then edited by Granier de Cassagnac. As *Le Globe* got into difficulties, Granier de Cassagnac had to borrow money, and Dujarier was secretly buying up Cassagnac's obligations, preparing to sink *Le Globe* completely.

Granier de Cassagnac knew that his career hung by a thread.

Two days after the quarrel at the Frères Provençaux, Dujarier was dead from a shot in the face. Beauvallon, who had done the killing, fled to Spain along with one of his seconds.

Balzac and Dumas, who had both had novels published in Dujarier's paper, were pallbearers at the funeral. And Dumas clamored for immediate police investigation, saying, "This was no duel. It was an incident in the battle for circulation between *La*

---

* Dumas' prediction about Lola Montez was to be remembered again when she became the mistress of the King of Bavaria and shortly cost that monarch his throne. And again when she died young and miserable in New York and was buried by charity in Greenwood cemetery, Brooklyn.

Presse and *Le Globe*. Beauvallon, Cassagnac's brother-in-law, was nothing more than a hired assassin. I know this Cassagnac, this Marat of slanderers."

The police did investigate. Beauvallon and Ecquevillez, his second, were extradited back to France, and the whole affair came to a head in one of the great trials in the annals of French justice, held at the Assizes of Rouen.

Dumas drove up there in state, squeezing his son and three or four beautiful actresses into his carriage.

With his usual ability to combine the serious with the comic he made himself the sensation of Rouen. The courtroom was packed on the day he testified.

He began by disclaiming the title of Marquis Davy de la Pailleterie. "I do not wish to be known even as *Monsieur* Dumas, but simply as Dumas, *tout court.*"

"What is your profession?" the presiding judge asked.

"This being Rouen," said Dumas, "the city that gave France the great playwright Corneille, I do not dare describe myself as a dramatic author."

"There are degrees in everything," said the judge charitably.

"Put me down simply as a writer who knows something of duels," Dumas decided.

"You have fought duels, then?" he was asked.

"*Monsieur le président*," said Dumas. "I happen to know that the legal code of December 15, 1837, declares that dueling is only another form of assault with a deadly weapon and that both parties to a duel must be punished accordingly. Do you insist that I incriminate myself? I cannot afford to go to prison. I am too busy keeping up with my serials."

The judge explained: "I only wish to assure myself and my colleagues that you have the qualifications for testifying here as an expert on dueling."

But Dumas continued to insist. "I admit nothing except that I have had so many years of experience in the matter of dueling that by this time I know the French Dueling Code by heart."

"The French Dueling Code? What is that?"

"What, sir," Dumas exclaimed in surprise, "you do not know of the great dueling code that was drawn up by the Count de Châteauvillard? And which was eventually adopted by a committee composed of representative members of the nobility of France and by another committee chosen from among the most talented members of the literary circles of our country?"

"I have never heard of it," said the judge.

"Then permit me to have a copy sent to you," said Dumas.

"What bearing has this code on the case we are considering?"

"Why, this, sir," Dumas explained. "The aim of the state law is to wipe out dueling. On the contrary, the aim of the Dueling Code is to perpetuate the old and honorable tradition of dueling by surrounding it with such regulations as to enable a man to defend his reputation at all times, weapon in hand. In the eyes of the law no difference is made between one duel and another. But according to the code, if the affair was properly conducted, then no matter what the outcome, whether bloodless or resulting in injury or death, the affair is a credit to all concerned."

"Is that your opinion on the case we are considering?"

"No, it is not. On the contrary, so flagrant were the violations of the Dueling Code that I can look upon this as nothing but a brutal assault, a premeditated murder. Though disguised as an affair of honor, it was in fact no more than a cleverly laid ambush."

"Can you point to specific infractions of your dueling code?"

"I can indeed. In the first place, the matter of the time of the duel. The duel was set for ten o'clock in the morning in the Bois de Boulogne. The weather was cold. It was snowing. Dujarier arrived promptly. But Beauvallon did not show up. He kept Dujarier waiting for an hour and a half. And he arrived only when Dujarier had just decided that all the requirements of honor had been satisfied, and he might leave without disgrace. In my opinion, the fact that Beauvallon showed up just in the nick of time before the duel would have gone to Dujarier by default indicates that Beauvallon was actually never far from the scene. He could very well have been waiting in a carriage hidden among the trees near by, himself able to see while remaining invisible. Thus he could keep himself warm while his opponent was getting chilled. He could keep his fingers flexible, while watching his opponent becoming more and more numb and fidgety. Such tricks, *Monsieur le président*, have been foreseen in the code. Dujarier need not have waited at all. His seconds should not have permitted the duel when Beauvallon finally showed up, warm and fresh, while Dujarier was already chilled and in addition mentally and morally exhausted."

"Can you point to other infractions?"

"Certainly. It is the business of the seconds to do everything possible to reach an arrangement without armed encounter. The code recognizes dueling only as the last resort of a vital clash between two persons. And, indeed, even at the final moment it is still the duty of the seconds to seek a reconciliation. In this case all efforts to reach an agreement were frustrated by Ecquevillez, one of the seconds. This man did not so much act as one of the seconds as he acted the part of one of the conspirators."

"Go on, please."

"The moment the fatal shot was fired, while everyone was gathered around poor Dujarier, this Ecquevillez quickly picked up the pistols and disappeared with them. This shows that he was afraid that the weapons might be examined for evidence. It is known now that the weapons belonged to Granier de Cassagnac. The Dueling Code, however, specifically insists that a duel shall be fought with weapons completely unknown to both combatants. Since Beauvallon is the brother-in-law of Cassagnac, it seems unlikely that these weapons were altogether unknown to him. Indeed, one of Dujarier's seconds has already testified here that when he touched the pistols before the duel his fingers came away smudged with black. The weapons had obviously been recently used and very likely heavily practiced upon. Thus Beauvallon, in my opinion, came to the field with a weapon with which he was thoroughly familiar, while into poor Dujarier's stiff fingers was pressed a gun that he knew nothing about."

(It was at this point that Granier de Cassagnac, who was himself in the audience, made an angry outcry.

"Do you wish to testify?" the presiding judge asked him.

"I am not involved in this trial," said Granier de Cassagnac.

"Then please leave," said the judge.

Attendants ushered Granier de Cassagnac out of the room.)

"Anything else?" the presiding judge asked Dumas.

"Yes. It was agreed that both men were to exchange one shot upon a given signal. Dujarier fired upon that signal and, seeing that he had missed, threw away his gun and waited for Beauvallon to fire his pistol. The latter took such a long careful aim that one of the seconds yelled a coarse word at him. Even that did not disturb him. When he fired, he smashed Dujarier right in the face with his bullet. Obviously he knew how to aim this gun. But more than that."

"Yes, go on."

"I mean that his seconds had clearly not given Dujarier all the instructions he was entitled to. For instance, he should not have thrown away his gun. He had the right to keep that gun and hold it up before his face and thus shield with metal at least that much of his body from injury. Thus with criminal conspiracy on one side and ignorance of the rules on the other, Dujarier was permitted to go to his death."

"I cannot understand, Monsieur Dumas," the judge said, "why, in the face of this tragedy, you still defend dueling. Would it not have been simpler and would not Dujarier have been alive today if he had refused to fight and gone to the police for protection?"

"Oh, no," Dumas cried. "That would have been a great mistake."

"How so? On the contrary, it would have saved his life."

"Of what use," Dumas asked, "to save the life of a man when his honor cannot be saved at the same time?"

"Was there then no way of saving his honor without going through with this fantastic duel?"

"None, *Monsieur le président*. Not in our circles of politics, journalism, literature and art, where honor is a sacred word."

"Why is that? Explain yourself."

"Because that is the way it is in our land. Because Dujarier was both challenged and insulted. As a man of importance in Paris, as editor of a great newspaper, he could not refuse that challenge or, refusing it, he could not fail to answer the insult with a counter challenge. Honor dictated it."

"Yes, but suppose he had ignored all that. He would at least be alive."

"Alive, yes," said Dumas gravely. "But no longer a Frenchman. He would be one of the living dead. Every salon in Paris would have been closed to him forever. His best friends would have passed him by on the street without a sign of recognition. You could not

have sold a single copy of his paper *La Presse*, except to people
who would have bought it to throw it into the gutter. What good
is a newspaper edited by a man without honor?"

"In that case, what is to prevent any clever editor from being
eliminated either by being killed or being dishonored?"

"Nothing but his determination to sell his life dearly," Dumas
declared fiercely. "Every man of honor who is exposed to the hot
competition of talents and ambitions in our capital has only to
spend a couple of hours a week in a fencing academy and on a
pistol range to be respected and feared. Hired assassins never pick
a quarrel with a man who can handle a deadly weapon. That kind
of canaille wants first of all to be sure of saving its own skin. Thus,
by all men being prepared, we are guaranteed that if a quarrel
should arise it will be a genuine one, based on a real collision of
politics and personalities, and not based on some vague pretext."

"And so, in spite of this tragedy, you continue to justify dueling?"
the judge asked.

"Yes. Under the Dueling Code, which should be recognized by
the law."

"And you still feel that this antiquated mode of personal combat has a place in our modern world?"

"More than ever," said Dumas firmly. "Because today, alas,
France is no longer the richest or the strongest country in the world,
as once she was. Of Du Bellay's great line, *France, mère des arts,
des armes et des loix,** only the arts are left, in which we can still
hold our own at the center of the world's civilization. And that requires us to take our arts, our culture, with deadly seriousness. We
must be willing to stake our lives on our ideas and on our ideals.
Only if we do so shall we continue to be the greatest people in the
world, the one to whom the world will always look when it seeks
the true meaning of the words courage and honor, beauty and
truth."

Saying this, Dumas looked around the courtroom as if he himself
were challenging anyone to dare hold him or his France cheaply.

The audience, including some of the greatest literary figures of
France, was swept away with patriotic admiration, and as Dumas
excused himself from the stand, he received an ovation. Flaubert

* "France, mother of the arts, of weapons and of laws."

rose to shake his hand as he passed down the aisle. Taking his seat beside his son, Dumas whispered to him, "Your turn now. See that you make a like impression."

Alexandre did take the stand. Of course, he couldn't equal his father by going into the philosophy of dueling and relating it to the position of France in the world, but when he told of how he had tried to draw upon himself Beauvallon's fury, so as to protect the unexperienced Dujarier, there was a murmur of approval throughout the audience for his chivalry and heroism.*

The repute of the two Dumas was never so high.

CHAPTER TWENTY-NINE

Down with the Stars!

OF COURSE IT WAS not to be expected that Alexandre would soon outshine his father. That man came nearer than ever to being a legendary figure during this period.

Montficaud, a contemporary, speaks of him as "the express train of literature" and describes him as a steam locomotive, tearing across all the countrysides of the world, roaring through all the tunnels of history and coming to a screaming stop in all the capital cities of the globe, bringing mankind the booty of two milleniums of human activity.

And a cartoon of the period, adopting much the same simile, shows him as the dark-skinned, frizzy-haired engineer of such a train, bringing his express into a station and turning to look out of the window of his cab and survey the horde of passengers milling about his coaches, each coupé of which is a volume of his works.

The face of the engineer looms forward to a life-size portrait, in a style which the cartoonists of the time favored. His forehead seems like a banner. Above, his hair, just beginning to gray, is like storm clouds cut by flashes of lightning. The cranium is massive,

---

* The law never was able to touch Granier de Cassagnac. But Beauvallon and Ecquevillez eventually went to prison, condemned to eight and ten years respectively. The disorganization during the revolution of 1848 enabled them to escape after serving only a few months.

the temples enormous. Babylonian is the way someone once described them, and indeed it is as if looking along them one could glimpse the perspective of an ancient colonnade.

His eyelids, fringed with long black eyelashes, seem to indicate the sweep of his thought. The bulging eyeballs add to the face something of royal arrogance, while the dusky pupil, like a smoldering coal, reminds one of the dominance of a lion tamer.

Humility? Reticence? Not a sign of them. The gaping nostrils are like double doors flung open to the world, welcoming everything, indiscriminately, accepting with appetite whatever life has to offer, without bias and without aversion.

A ragged line of powerful teeth, bloated lips, a few scraggly bristles, all so many mementos of a hotter climate, a fiercer sun. (And the voice that issued from the mouth was likened, by those who had heard it, to copper striking copper, the sound of something left over from a pagan religion.)

The chin is fat and mobile, as if a meal too rich were forever dripping from the corners of his lips. But, within, one senses a jawbone, robust, active, hinged to a muscular neck, stubborn, gorged, but at the same time peaceful, like that of a grazing ox.

Such is the engineer who turns in this cartoon to watch his train spilling out its passengers, passengers that are all little tiny replicas of himself: Dumas men and Dumas women, Dumas children and Dumas elders, Dumas saints and Dumas tyrants. All eager, all strong, all determined to know and to relish. All colorful and crackling with desires, all instinct with the insatiability of modern man, struggling, fighting, leaping, loving, wiping the gravy dish with a sopping piece of bread, as if they had all taken vows to outdo one another in cramming into their one allotted life span every conceivable experience and convinced that by the omission of even a single sensation, by so much must life be accounted a failure.

And all this the engineer of the express watches, nodding his head, smiling, approving, encouraging.

Never was a writer more prolific and more popular than Dumas at this period. Books fairly tumbled from his pen in one continuous stream. Novels such as *The Queen's Necklace, Memoirs of a Physi-*

cian, The Forty-Five Guardsmen, Twenty Years After, each one a crashing success.

Nor was this all. This was the time when Dumas dazzled Paris with his own personal theater, built to his own specifications, the Théâtre Historique, which he opened with the play *Queen Margot.* People spent forty-eight hours in the queue to make sure of having tickets for the opening night. The curtain rose at half-past six and did not come down for the last time until three o'clock in the morning, after eight and a half hours of solid melodrama, played to torrents of applause.

And even that was not a record for Dumas. He put on his *Monte Cristo* in three nightly installments because it was too long to be shown in any other way.

Théophile de Gautier thus described this amazing playgoing experience: "A curious change comes over one. One ceases to be a spectator and becomes an inhabitant. One no longer lives on this or that street, at this or that house number, but one lives in this or that box or seat in the orchestra or loge. On the first night, you still behave as generally in the theater: the person sitting next to you is and remains a complete stranger. But when you see the same face the following night you start becoming friends. By the third night the stage can barely be heard above the buzz of conversation as all these new-found friends exchange ideas and reminiscences. And one hears such conversations as this: 'Have you been to see Madame X lately?'

" 'Why, no. To tell you the truth I don't even know her new address.'

" 'Oh, she hasn't moved. She's still in Box 18.'

" 'Then I must certainly go and pay her my respects.'

" 'Do so, old fellow. She receives as usual every night between the third and the fifth act.' "

Nor does this sum up all Dumas was doing. He wrote, in addition, two books of history on the reigns of Louis XIV and Louis XV. And edited at different times three political magazines of staunchly democratic and republican outlook, and in the turbulent years between the revolution of 1848 and the coup d'état of Napoleon III, he presented himself several times as candidate for deputy in various districts.

"Ships sail the ocean," he orated to the people during one of his lightning campaigns, "ships whose sole and entire cargo consists of books by Dumas. Yes, I am a laborer just as you are, my friends. You build houses or plow the fields, while this right hand of mine holds a pen and puts in fourteen hours of work a day, and thus keeps six hundred and ninety compositors and pressmen constantly at work. To say nothing of hundreds of binders, packers, shippers and salesmen. And of course I cannot even begin to count the numbers of people who have a livelihood in other countries through my books and plays, which are translated and produced everywhere. (Cries of Bravo!)

"In Paris alone, my plays employ hundreds of actors, scene decorators, costumers, set-builders, musicians, supernumeraries, firemen, hairdressers, ushers, lamp-oil merchants, to say nothing of the members of the claque. (Scattered bursts of applause.)

"I do not have the figures for the people employed in our provinces, but I can say this: Counting only Paris, I make steady work for one thousand six hundred and ninety-two people at an average rate of three francs a day, and I've been doing it for upward of twenty years. Children have been born and grown up to manhood and womanhood whose whole living has come from this brain and this right hand. Figuring but four members in a family for every working person, there are nearly seven thousand people making a living from my industry. Seven thousand people—that's a city in itself! (Long applause.)

"The worker!" Dumas cried. "The future belongs to him!" (Furious cries of approval.) "Priests, kings, aristocrats, bankers, all have had their day. But now it is our turn. The world belongs to us, the workers, the creators!" (Noisy demonstration and loud cries of *Vive Dumas!*)

He lost, and not because of Paul de Kock's * ridiculous posters soliciting votes for himself, claiming that the number of women who wrote to him asking him for a lock of his hair kept four hundred hairdressers at work making him new wigs since he was totally bald, etc., etc.

The fact is that Dumas was genuinely surprised and chagrined

* Paul de Kock was the author of numerous novels and plays now rather forgotten.

at losing. "I drew the biggest crowds of any candidate," he said ruefully.

"Ah, Monsieur Dumas," a constituent explained to him, "we would all have gladly voted for you. But we thought of those seven thousand people, that whole city. You remember?"

"Yes, well what about that city?"

"Think of all those people being out of work and hungry because you were now making speeches in the Chamber instead of writing more books. A whole city devastated."

Yes, the man was at his top performance during those years when he was lodged so magnificently just outside of Paris, first at the Villa Medicis in Saint-Germain, and then in his own mansion at Marly-le-Roi, years during which the *Registre Annuaire* recorded his income as 800,000 francs a year, which, at a time when a man was expected to support a family on three francs a day, was a truly baronial revenue.

But baronial, too, were his expenses.

This was the era when Dumas took delight in giving a Roman picnic to as many as six hundred people at once on the grounds of his home, suiting dishes and costumes and service to the Roman theme, and when neighbors for miles around would climb their roofs to watch the fireworks being discharged as the finale of the festivities.

Dumas himself often had to miss these grand picnics because of the press of his commitments, remaining in his room and writing busily while his guests were entertained.

But he never missed the fireworks.

Following a star rocket as it traveled up into the sky and watching it explode and release its rain of gold and blue meteors, he would sometimes be so stirred that he would scream *"Enfoncées les étoiles!"* Down with the stars!

And he would shake his fist at the Milky Way and shout, "The earth too shines! Yes it does!" And then it was as if he were seized with a fury to tear down the great canvas of heaven and repaint it with some more dramatic tableau, one in which the earth (with Dumas aboard, of course) would move to some more prominent place in the universe and surround itself with rings like Saturn and a whole chorus of comets.

This was his old unfinished duel with God (which had once caused him to lug pistols up the steps when he was four years old), still working and churning within him.

Just about this time, too, Foucault was scientific editor of the Parisian *Journal des Débats*, and he would now and then inflame Dumas with descriptions of what he and Fizeau in friendly competition were doing to devise machines that would measure the exact speed of light, which was so great that it could circle the earth's equator seven times in a single second.

This was something to make even "the express train of literature" burn with envy. At least momentarily. And his ancient desire to dance on his toes, to cast his water over his head, to lift himself up by his bootstraps—in short, to become legendary, to be transported to the stars like the heroes of the Greek myths and become one of the constellations—would yeast up mightily in him.

Thus his income and his expenditures held a kind of running battle to see which could outdo the other: production or profligacy. With the result that as successful and as rich as he was during this period, never was he so harassed by debts and financial obligations.

This was the time when his son, pointing to his father's untied shoelaces, got this answer: "Thanks, my boy. But you've just cost me forty francs, for I figure the tying of each shoelace to run me easily twenty francs of my writing time, which I can ill afford to waste."

This was the time when a man brought him the skin of a boa constrictor.

Dumas threw up his hands. "Ah, no, no! For once I am going to say no. I already am the proud owner of a whale skeleton, which is still in the crates in which I bought it, and I also have the mummy of an Egyptian cat, as well as a stuffed aurochs. So, no, I don't want to buy your snake skin."

"What?" the man exclaimed. "You would refuse to buy the skin of a boa shot by your own dear father?"

"My father, the general, shot this snake?" Dumas asked. "Are you sure?"

"Positive," said the man. "Here. You can still see the bullet hole."

This, of course, threw the whole matter into a completely different light, for, as Dumas later explained, though it could not be demonstrated that this bullet hole had actually been caused by his father, yet it was a well-known fact that his father had used a gun in hunting, and thus it now seemed up to Dumas to prove that his father hadn't shot this snake.

"And this I was in no position to do," Dumas pointed out.

In short, he bought the snake skin, but not so much for the skin itself as for that piece that was missing—namely, the hole, the hole that his father might conceivably have made. And never was a hole so expensive, since on the strength of it the man deemed himself Dumas' best friend, turned up for dinner, stayed the night, and for three years practically lived with Dumas.

Dumas had a kind of natural shyness when it came to asking people what they were doing in his house.

Once, at dinner, he whispered to the man sitting next to him, "Introduce me, please, to some of these people."

The man shrugged. "I'm a stranger here myself," he said, pouring himself another glass of champagne.

The incident with Rusconi illustrates the nature of the household over which Dumas reigned. (I'm afraid the word "reigned" is not the *mot juste* to describe Dumas' function in his own home.) But at the monthly line-up of his servants to receive their pay, Dumas noticed an elfish, gray-haired man who was a complete stranger to him.

When it came his turn, Dumas looked at him wonderingly. "You're . . . working for me?"

"Ah, Monsieur Dumas," said the little man, obviously hurt, "have you so soon forgotten? I'm Rusconi."

"To be sure, to be sure," said Dumas quickly, covering up his forgetfulness. "And now, how much was it?"

"A hundred and twenty francs a month, Monsieur," said Rusconi.

In the succeeding months and years no one could fail to observe this gnomish little man scurrying busily about the house. But just what he was so busy about no one could fathom.

"You should know," someone said to Dumas. "After all, you evidently hired him."

"I suppose I must have," Dumas said. "But for the life of me I can't remember what for."

"Well, what does he do?"

Dumas shrugged. "Several times I've stopped him as he was hurrying by and I've asked him to do me some slight favor. On such occasions he always turns to me with tears in his eyes and says, 'Ah, Monsieur Dumas, if only I had more than two hands I would gladly put them all at your disposal.' Or else he will say, 'If I could manage to be in two places at once . . .' In the face of such devotion how can one quibble?" Dumas would ask.

"Well, you can fire him any time," Dumas was told by one of his friends.

"Fire him?" Dumas recoiled. "You mean without any reason? Of course if I could find out what he does I could easily find fault with his work and discharge him. But as long as I don't even know what he does I must presume that he does it well."

Eventually it was taken for granted that Rusconi's job was to rusconize. And thus the matter went on for many years. At any rate, one finds mention of the fellow still rusconizing around years later.

The few people who were ever able to a engage this hard-working man in a conversation never heard him say more than this: "I used to be chief of police of the island of Elba; thus these two old eyes have had the privilege of looking upon the two greatest men of our century: Napoleon and Dumas."

Then he would hurriedly excuse himself because of pressing duties.

CHAPTER THIRTY

A Bagatelle

No ONE WOULD take more delight than Alexandre in these tales of profligacy about his father, and he repeated them on every possible occasion to his young friends. And if he began to discover that as a result of these extravagances, the baptismal font was more and more often emptied of everything down to its copper dregs and its shoddy gold-plated trinkets, he did not mind, for he had only to wait a day or two to find it full again and to fill his pockets before it drained away.

Still, there came a day when he had gambled heavily and had left the green table owing two thousand francs, and, it being a matter of honor to pay one's gambling obligations within twenty-four hours, he queried his father about the empty font.

"What's to stop you from doing what I do when I'm pressed for funds?" Dumas asked.

"What do you mean?"

"Why, borrow, of course."

"Borrow? From whom?"

"Why, *parbleu*, from the people who make it their business to lend. Where else? I can give you the names of every usurer in Paris. I know them all. Intimately."

"But I've never borrowed before in my life," Alexandre protested.

"Well, there's a first time for everything," said Dumas.

So Alexandre went to a moneylender and readily got two thousand francs upon signing a note to return three thousand in six months.

"Was that so difficult?" his father asked.

"Easiest thing in the world," Alexandre had to admit.

"Well, there you are, my boy. Personally, I've never been able to understand this vulgar prejudice which considers a man who lends ten thousand more fortunate than a man who borrows ten thousand. Do they not both have ten thousand? What's the difference whether borrowed or lent, so long as one has it?"

Nevertheless, it was about this time that Dumas *père* decided that it was necessary to simplify his style of living. The crowds at his place gave him no elbow room. The race for more and more production threatened to give him no free time whatsoever.

Walking one afternoon on the outskirts of Saint-Germain, he climbed Mont Ferrand and stopped on the brow of the hill to breathe and admire the sweep of scenery that overlooked the whole Seine valley.

"Ah," he said, "what does a man want from life but to view one little corner of God's magnificence, to eat a crust of bread and drink a cup of tea. And, of course, paper on which to write."

He took his son out to this spot one day and said, "What do you think? To have a little hut here and be alone, and work in peace. Away from all the crowds? Don't you agree?"

"A beautiful thought," said Alexandre.

"This very day," Dumas decided, "I shall arrange to purchase a bit of a lot here."

In the near-by village of Port-Marly, he found a local builder. "I'm really ashamed to disturb you for so small an item," he apologized. "All I want is a shack. Just protection from wind and rain. Nothing but a roof over my head, a door to get in and out, and a window for light. And no more room than is necessary for my little table and a chair. Do you think you want to bother with it?"

The builder declared himself willing.

"How long will it take?" Dumas asked.

"Four, five days," said the builder.

"And how much?"

"Three hundred francs."

"A bagatelle," said Dumas.

And thus, on succeeding afternoons, Dumas, after his many hours of work, would put on his light linen suit, pick up his Panama and, cane in hand, would wander off from the mob at his villa in Saint-Germain, go to Marly and climb Mont Ferrand.

"While you're about it," he would tell the builder, "you'll put in a little bit of a kitchen. Just an alcove where I can make myself some tea or an omelet. That will be no trouble, will it?"

"Another day or two," the builder said. "But it will add something to the cost."

"Naturally," Dumas agreed. "How much?"

"Maybe a hundred and fifty francs."

"A bagatelle," said Dumas.

Only his most intimate friends were privileged to accompany Dumas on these walks to his secret retreat. His trusted co-worker Maquet, also Bibliophile Jacob, whom he frequently consulted in matters requiring deep historical research, or his best actor Mélingue, and so forth.

On each of these trips Dumas had some little improvement to suggest to the builder. For example: "While you're about it, I think you should add just one small room to the side. For a cot. In case my son or a friend is here late. One can't just show a man to the door at two in the morning, can one?"

"That will be another couple of hundred francs, Monsieur Dumas," the builder would say after a bit of rough figuring.

"A bagatelle," Dumas would answer.

The next day it would be another friend and another request to the builder. "You understand I need a lot of books in the course of my work. I have thousands of historical works that are indispensable to me. We must have enough room for shelves."

"We can lengthen the sides of the main room, which will give you . . ."

"Exactly."

"Another week of work and another five hundred francs . . ."

"A bagatelle."

One day he said to the contractor, "You know . . . a little room . . . rather tastefully done . . . after all, who knows? my life may still hold many joys. You understand?"

He was really a jewel of a contractor, this builder. He understood perfectly. "A bit of a boudoir?"

"Exactly!" Dumas cried.

And then on another occasion, a day or two later, he told the contractor about his extensive collection of paintings and bric-a-brac, bronzes and ivory fans and the like. "It's good to surround oneself with such *objets d'art*," he said. "It stimulates the muse. It rouses the sluggish imagination. It colors one's prose. . . . You understand?"

"Of course," said the contractor. "I think that what you need, Monsieur Dumas, is not a shack but a house."

"A house?" Dumas exclaimed with surprise. "What do you mean by a house?"

"I mean . . . well, something substantial, with upstairs and downstairs. . . ."

"A brilliant idea!" Dumas said. "And my workroom will be upstairs, where no one will disturb me."

"But for a thing of that size, Monsieur Dumas," the contractor said, "I would feel better if I had architectural plans."

This is how the architect Plante came into the picture.

Plante first designed a house to cost twelve thousand francs, and than a bigger one to cost fifteen thousand and then he threw caution to the winds and designed one to cost sixty thousand francs. With that he figured he had reached the maximum.

But meanwhile Dumas had widened his holdings from the plot to hold a cabin to a half acre to hold a house, and then to an acre to hold a mansion, and finally to six acres to hold a palace. And the costs rose from sixty to a hundred and then to a hundred and fifty thousand. And that was not nearly the end.

The land itself was not solid enough to support such a structure.

"We must dig down to bedrock," said Plante.

"Then we'll have cellars!" Dumas exclaimed. "Secret passageways, trapdoors, mysterious corridors and tunnels."

"That will mean arches," said Plante, "which will increase the cost again."

"How much?"

"Fifty thousand more."

"A bagatelle," said Dumas.

At bedrock a spring was uncovered. The contractor cursed this new obstacle. But Dumas leaped with joy.

"Pipe it!" Dumas cried. "We'll have waterworks, fountains, a moat and drawbridge, swans and goldfish. We could even have a lake with an island! There could be a little kiosk on that island where I could be really alone and work undisturbed."

The estate was now conceived of as entirely walled, with four floors, stables, kennels, a conservatory, a zoo, an aviary and so forth. The place was to be decorated inside and out with friezes, sculptures, carved stone and woodwork. Everywhere hardwoods, marble and bronze.

And great crowds of people came every week end from Paris, picnicked on the ground and watched Monsieur Dumas' palace going up.

The contractor put up a sign that read:

PRIVATE PROPERTY
NOT OPEN TO THE PUBLIC

But the crowds still continued to flood the place.

When the contractor tried to stop them, indicating the sign prominently posted, they each and every one protested that they did not

consider themselves as the "public." They were friends of Dumas'.
They had voted for him. Or they had shaken his hand at such and
such a time, and he had personally invited them to drop in any time.

And if Dumas himself was appealed to, what could he say except
that yes, yes, he remembered the occasion quite well.

And then there were the women with babies—well, it was best
just to let a woman with a baby alone to wander around, and not to
risk a scene. Who knows who she might be?

Thus, what was meant to be built in a week took nearly three
years. Which isn't surprising when you consider the iron grillwork
balconies done by master forgers, the façade with sculptured marble panels, the number of towers and turrets, each topped with some
gay gonfalon bearing a device such as "*Au vent la flamme! Au
Seigneur l'âme,*" meaning "My colors to the wind, my soul to the
Lord." And the rooms that were built by authentic Moorish wood-
carvers to resemble the Alhambra of Spain, and other rooms that
were Chinese or Persian or Louis Quatorze, or Renaissance or
Gothic. And the landscaping, the fruit trees, the stocking of the water
basins with fish, and the greenhouse to supply a constant floral
display. . . .

Why, for nothing but the vintage wines with which to stock his
huge wine cellars, this man who never touched wine spent I don't
know how much!

And when you add to all this the fact that during this same period
Dumas was building and launching his Théâtre Historique and
equipping it with the most advanced stage machinery in the world—
well, it can be no surprise that a permanent condition of drought
settled on the famous baptismal font.

Even the copper dregs and the pinchbeck watchcases were consumed.

As a result, young Alexandre was driven to gambling for ever
higher stakes in order to meet his expenses, which was fine when
luck was with him, when in fact he could be more extravagant than
ever, but not so good when luck ran against him, when he would
be forced to hide out from bailiffs who were after him with all sorts
of writs.

"We're quite a pair now," Dumas would exclaim, embracing his
son fondly. The two would now frequently have moments of deep

manly affection when they would compare notes on the art of out-
witting process servers and escaping the jaws of debtor's prison.
(An art, incidentally, that Baudelaire was later to carry to such a
high degree of proficiency, spending nearly his whole life eluding
these twin evils.)

All the while, Alexandre never really stopped his luxurious style
of living, keeping two saddle horses and one harness horse, giving
his mistresses expensive presents and always, just like his father,
ready to subscribe ten or fifty louis for a new hospital or a new mission for the savages of Africa.

And if he had to disappear occasionally, when the chase was hot-
test, there would always eventually be a new round of note signing
for higher sums and stiffer interest charges, which would set him
afloat again to resume his old life.

CHAPTER THIRTY-ONE

The Incomprehensible Red and White Camellias

ONE AFTERNOON he was hurrying along the Place de la Bourse, having a long-coveted appointment with a woman who had done over
her bedroom, making walls and ceilings a solid expanse of mirrors,
and he was thinking of nothing else but the various pleasures that
were soon to be experienced when an elegant blue coupé pulled to
a sudden halt beside him, and an astonishingly lovely girl, with
black hair and ivory complexion, skipped nimbly to the ground,
passed in front of him and disappeared into a shop.

All that remained with the young man on the sidewalk from this
brief vision was the memory of something ethereally beautiful,
something young and slender, draped in a gold-embroidered cashmere shawl.

And a vivid impression of such girlish, flowerlike innocence that
he walked on with the word innocence singing in his blood: innocence, innocence, like some kind of intoxication, and suddenly he
couldn't bring himself to go to that assignation, and instead went
into a store and bought flowers and fruit and took a cab to his
mother's.

It had been many months since he had seen her.

"Flowers?" she said dryly. "Don't you see I've always got nasturtiums and geraniums growing in my window? And what do you suppose I want with pineapples and hothouse grapes? If I want a piece of fruit, I can easily buy myself an apple from a pushcart."

He sat down, saying little.

As usual, she warned him about the bad spot on the floor and then asked him whether he would have tea or chocolate.

"Chocolate," he said.

"You always did love chocolate," she said. "You used to make me boil it until it had a thick skin on top, and that you loved especially."

It was while drinking this hot chocolate that reminded him so much of his childhood that tears began to come to his eyes, and he got up and went to the door.

His mother tried to stop him, but he tore himself loose. "I'll be coming every week from now on," he said, and hurried away as fast as possible.

He didn't keep his promise. He went back to his usual life, with the same crowd of rich young idlers who whored and gambled their lives away, but there can be no doubt that this was out of mere habit, and that within himself he felt an ever-increasing sense of loneliness, an ever more irresistible thirst for innocence and purity, such as had emanated from that lovely vision in the cashmere shawl.

The strangest part of this peculiar conversion to innocence was this: that if Alexandre had waited until the girl had left the shop and then had entered it and made inquiries about her, he would have discovered at once that she was Marie Duplessis, one of the more notorious prostitutes of Paris, long a favorite of the millionaire members of the Paris Jockey Club, who passed her back and forth among themselves, and seven of whom had at one time got together to set her up in the most luxurious style of living.

In fact, he could not, considering the small size of Paris at the time, have remained very long in ignorance of who she was. And yet he continued to be convinced of the girl's innocence to such a degree that when, less than a year later, he began to notice his unknown angel of purity quite regularly occupying a ground-floor box at the theater, and he could see that for twenty-five days of the month she invariably carried a bouquet of white camellias, while during the other five days the bouquet was made up of red camellias, thus boldly flaunting her shameless profession to the entire audience, Alexandre could nevertheless write of this strange custom of hers as if it were completely incomprehensible to him.

Indeed, he went so far as to insist that no one else understood the meaning of it either. He actually wrote later: "No one ever knew the reason for this change of color, which I mention though I cannot explain it. It was noticed by her friends and by the habitués of the theater which she generally frequented. She was never seen with any other flower but camellias. At her florist's, Madame Barjon's, she had come to be called the 'Lady of the Camellias,' and the name had taken gradual hold until she was finally known by no other."

If he did not understand the reason for the red and white camellias, he must nevertheless have understood the nature of her work; and yet even on this he was to comment that she was a "virgin whom some slight mischance had cast for the role of prostitute, and who therefore by the same slight chance might someday be turned back again into the purest of virgins."

His original impression was thus only confirmed. "Only to see her," he wrote, "was to realize that she was still in the virginity of vice," whatever that may be.

And he was to argue that "her profession, far from disqualifying her for true love, had in fact made the acquisition of her love all the more desirable and precious, since the marriage vows of a real virgin might be due largely to curiosity and to carnal itch, while the love of a prostitute could never be anything but the most unselfish and spiritual of devotions."

To be sure, along with her air of innocence, Marie Duplessis had other things to recommend her. Imagine perfectly arched eyebrows and eyelashes, both like black velvet, and as if printed on the smooth ivory of her face, in which scarlet lips made the only splash of color.

"It was a face to put geometry to shame," Théophile Gautier wrote of her.

The effect was like the work of some master jeweler. And when she smiled, it was as if a piece of fine jewelry could also sing. One saw teeth that were almost transparent in their glossy whiteness and a fine tongue as pink and as clean as that of a snake.

Women envied her corsetless figure with its narrow hips. Men could not take their eyes away from the lovely expansion of her bosom. Her wrists and ankles, mere bone and tendon, had about them the precision of a race horse.

To these natural endowments she added a delicate and costly elegance. Beneath her invariable cashmere shawls with their lovely embroidery one caught a glimpse of some rare silver-shot fabric, some precious brocade or jacquard silk. For jewelry she preferred a plain gold chain, though sometimes she would stud her hair with pearls, diamonds or emeralds to set off its blue-black sheen.

She stood out as unique despite the competition of beauties from all over the world who flocked to Paris and who caused Mrs. Trollope to exclaim, "Surely these are not terrestrial creatures!"

But they were very much terrestrial, as the Bey of Morocco discovered. "They only seem to be disembodied angels. One must see them dripping with sweat after a frenzied *varsovienne* and then afterward wolfing a beefsteak done rare to know otherwise."

One evening when Alexandre was in the theater with his father and with Eugène Déjazet, son of the actress, his father said, "Well, what do you think of her?"

"Who?" Alexandre asked, lowering his glasses quickly and obviously quite flustered.

His father laughed. "Why, Marie Duplessis, of course," he said. "Haven't you been staring at her all evening?"

Alexandre's embarrassment was very plain to see.

"You're in love with her," Dumas said.

"I've never even met her," Alexandre retorted.

"Well, there's nothing easier—that is, providing one has the cash to spare. See that blowzy woman in the orchestra? The overdressed one whose face looks as if it had been torn from a chunk of raw meat? You can hear her coarse voice all the way over here. She's the moneyman in the company. She arranges the price—which is high. And she delivers the goods, which, as you can see, are first-rate."

It hurt Alexandre to hear his father talking about his angel of innocence in such fashion. And he tried to cut the conversation short by saying, "I don't like commercial affairs, and besides I haven't the money."

But his father went right on. "Money? Do birds pay for their food? Poets and artists must always be admitted free. The world of beauty belongs to them by birthright. You must make yourself her *amant de coeur*, the man she loves for love."

And he urged the two young men to go to her box.

"But I tell you we don't even known her," Alexandre protested.

"When one's name is Alexandre Dumas," Dumas said, "that is in itself a letter of introduction."

Noticing that his son was still blushing, he went on. "Surely you have nothing to be embarrassed about. You're no schoolboy. And I assure you she's no duchess. She's a kept woman. Indeed, she's as much an article for hire as a public cab. But wait. Someone has just taken our public cab. You see that man who has just entered her box and who keeps himself well in the background as if he didn't wish to be seen? That's the Count de Stackelberg, who once helped Metternich form the Holy Alliance. That's a long time ago. He's eighty years old now and I doubt if he's capable of much alliance forming today, holy or unholy. I'm sure he must demonstrate his love for Marie more in his jealousy than in his passion. Nevertheless, he considers Marie his mistress and he spends a fortune on her, so that her other lovers have to be carefully squeezed in when he's not around. And that's the job of that blowzy woman, Clemence Prat, her procuress."

Thus it was that later that evening Alexandre found himself in a sumptuously decorated apartment that was almost like a hothouse, so luxuriously grew the trellised camellias and other flowering plants from lacquered boxes set around the walls. The rooms were large, the furniture massive and expensive, the walls crowded with paintings, and everywhere precious candelabra, vases and figurines of bronze, porcelain or enamel. The drawing room was large enough to accommodate a billiard table and a piano in addition to sofas, easy chairs, tables and bookcases.

There were other men present. And Marie, amidst this crush of luxury, sat at the rosewood Pleyel piano playing very badly and singing a song that was not merely risqué but actually dirty.

To watch those perfect lips in that angelic face frame themselves around a word that swine would have avoided in the gutter was pain so bitter Alexandre thought he could not endure it.

And then to hear her subsequent rollicking peals of laughter.

Was it possible that she enjoyed this kind of life?

He went up to her and implored her in a whisper not to use such words.

"My, how proper we are!" she said, laughing.

"It's not because of me," he said. "I mind it only because of you."

"Oh, come now," she said, smiling. "Don't be a baby. Can't you see that I'm long past such things? And what about yourself?"

And, as if to spite him, she launched into such repulsively coarse talk that Alexandre was forced to turn away. But she, along with the rest of the company, laughed hilariously. Alexandre stole glances at her now and then and each time suffered a pang to see her drinking like a drayman, shouting like a fishwife and laughing uproariously as one filthy observation followed another. Toward the end of the evening her color grew unnaturally high, and her laughter was often broken by fits of coughing, when suddenly her face would be crossed with pain, and she would press her handkerchief convulsively against her lips. Finally the handkerchief came away stained with blood. She ran into her dressing room.

"Don't disturb yourselves," said the procuress. "She's just spitting a little blood. It often happens when she's been laughing too much. You'll see. She'll be back in a moment."

But Alexandre, troubled, could not check himself. He followed her. The dressing room was empty, but beyond through the open door, was her boudoir, and he went into that little room that was decorated as if it were a candy box, with the walls hung with yellow silk and the furniture all of rosewood, the dressing tables covered with a hundred articles of ivory, gold or enameled silver, the whole arsenal of a coquette: brushes of every kind, scissors and files, and jars and boxes of every conceivable cosmetic, and bottles of every kind of perfume.

But the only thing that Alexandre saw was a taboret on which sat a basin of water stained with streaks of bright blood.

And Marie, leaning against the mantelpiece, exhausted from a fit of coughing.

"You're ill," he exclaimed.

Touched by his evident sympathy, she gave him her hand, and as he bent over to kiss it, she could feel the wetness of his tears.

"What a child you are," she said, laughing.

"If only I were a relation of yours," he said.

"Why? What would you do?"

"It would give me the right to make you live a different life. Prevent you from doing harm to yourself."

"Oh, I've got to amuse myself," she said. "I can't sleep. So this is how I live. Besides, girls like me—one more, one less, what does it matter? You can be sure someone is already waiting to take my place."

"If you knew how much I love you," Alexandre said, "you would not say things that hurt me."

"This must be stopped at once," said Marie. "I cannot have you, or anyone, in love with me."

"But you can't prevent it."

"I must prevent it."

"Why?"

"Are you rich?"

"I'm not exactly poor," Alexandre countered.

"Have you the means to spend a hundred thousand francs a year on me?"

"A hundred thousand francs a year?" Alexandre exclaimed.

"That's what I spend. I like luxury—as you can see. What share of that can you assume?"

Alexandre shook his head slowly. "Very little."

"Then, please, let's be friends. Let's talk. Let's laugh. Let's amuse ourselves. But let's say nothing more of love."

"But surely," said Alexandre, "the Count—he can't possibly represent love in your life."

"No. But he's gentle. He's affectionate. And he's wealthy. I respect him. That's just about all."

"Then I don't understand . . ."

"It's very simple. If I should let you be my lover, how soon before you'd be jealous? How soon before you'd cause difficulties that would jeopardize my hundred thousand francs a year? I will not have you creating trouble for me."

Like a drowning man pleading for help, Alexandre poured out to her all that she had meant to him since the first time he had glimpsed her, how he had treasured her image in his heart, how it had changed his whole outlook upon life, and how much it meant to him now to be finally in the same room with her alone, talking to her.

"Please don't send me away," he begged.

"I really ought to," she said. "And maybe I'll regret not doing it."

Seeing that he had made some impression upon her in spite of her hard words, Alexandre put an arm around her and for the first time felt her slenderness and the lightness and flexibility of a body that was almost as if cut from paper.

And when she did not resist his arm, he drew her close.

"So you really love me?" she asked, and for the first time he noticed that there was not the slightest trace of raillery in her voice.

"I swear it desperately."

"Do you love me enough to be different from other men, who insist on knowing everything about their mistresses, past, present and future?"

Alexandre said he loved her enough to be exactly what she wanted him to be.

"In that case, we shall see," she said.

"When?" he asked.

"Later on."

"Why later on?"

"Because," said Marie. And, releasing herself from his arms, she went to her night table and selected from a bouquet of red camellias a single flower and pinned it to his buttonhole. "It is not always possible to carry out an agreement on the very day the contract is written."

"You are dismissing me?"

"Yes. Until this flower changes color."

"When will that be?"

"Tomorrow night between eleven and twelve. Are you satisfied? And now, not a word to anyone."

She kissed him, and before he left she said, "Does it seem strange that I should agree so rapidly?" She took his hand and placed it beneath her breast, where he could feel her heart, which was palpitating frantically. "I haven't long to live, so I must live quickly."

"Don't say that, please," he begged.

"Oh," she said, laughing, "don't be put out. Of one thing we can both be sure: as little as I have to live, it will be longer than you will want to love."

And, giving him no chance to answer, she started a gay song and went back into the living room.

Thus their association began, an association that was a succession of stormy quarrels, final and irrevocable partings—and tearful reconciliations.

"So this is the love without jealousy that you promised me?" she would sometimes ask. He had no answer, except that within himself he would have a similar—but silent—recrimination: "Is this really the innocence that I was hoping to find?"

And yet, how wonderful were those reconciliations, what moments of tenderness and of passion when they would lock the apartment and live as if they were alone on an island in the tropic seas.

And then how proud he was to go driving with her in an open barouche, or appear with her in her box at the theater, feeling himself envied by every man in the audience, by the whole golden youth set, and by all the aging *bons vivants*, and by every writer and artist. He could feel the whole theater turning their glasses toward Marie and then toward him: Roger de Beauvoir, Gautier, Dr. Véron, Lord Seymour, Fernand de Monguyon, Pierre de Castellane, etc.

In any company she was always the most strikingly dressed woman and at the same time the most tastefully. Everything about her was always selected with exquisite care. She might be too sick for anything else, ordered to bed by the fashionable Dr. Koreff on a diet of asses' milk, but she was still not so sick that she couldn't receive her modiste, her jeweler, her hairdresser. And no sooner on her feet again than she was once more running in and out of shops, the first to discover a new note in fabrics, a new color, a new cut in style.

And never twice in the same outfit.

In the brief moment when they could love each other with unalloyed devotion, they had wonderful evenings at her home, in restaurants or at dances—and for one short month in the country, a stolen vacation which she had obtained from the Count de Stackelberg by lying to him that Dr. Koreff had ordered it for her, a lie which lay in Alexandre like a rotten worm during that whole month of joy.

But such drawbacks to pure happiness were not to be compared to the anguish of those days and those nights when he found himself excluded. When, through the infamous Clemence Prat, her procuress, she would send him a note saying that she was too ill to receive him, and he would realize at once that something was afoot.

Then he would go out at night to the street beneath her apartment and spy out who visited her: what carriage stood outside, whether the phaeton of the Count de Stackelberg, the demi-daumont of the Count de Perrégaux or the coupé of Dr. Koreff. Or some unknown's carriage. Sometimes her apartment would be dark, and the street empty. But he would take his stand nevertheless, hidden in a doorway on the opposite side, and wait through the cold or the rain until he saw some sign of life, either the glow of a light in her bedroom or else the arrival of a carriage that would stop before her door. If he then saw her coming out with a strange man, he had to use every resource of his will power to prevent himself from assaulting them bodily.

And then, later, after a day, or maybe a week, when he was readmitted, what battles would be fought between them. She might talk or cry or wheedle herself out of the Count de Stackelberg, since she insisted on the right to continue her extravagant way of living, which only that man's millions could provide for her. And she might even talk herself out of the Count de Perrégaux, since he had formerly been her lover and might still be only her friend. But these unknown men!

There would come painful moments of mutism which neither could break, both being choked with unexpressed and even inexpressible feelings. And other moments when he would rage and she would laugh at him. And still other times when she would be cruelly cold, pick up a book, and say, "Let me know when you're finished, and I'll be glad to show you to the door, if you no longer remember where it is."

And there were occasions when she would be tearfully contrite and confess to having piled up debts that the Count de Stackelberg had refused to pay, and gradually she would reveal a tale of a bit of prostitution that was nothing more nor less than a business transaction with a visiting German nobleman, or a gross bourgeois from the provinces who wished to know what Parisian high life was like, people whom Clemence Prat was always finding and proposing to her.

Then he would ask questions, each one of which was a double-pointed dagger that stabbed him just as much as it did her. "Did you love him—this boor?"

"Of course not!"

"Oh, you didn't love him? But you were willing . . ."

"I had to have money, I tell you!"

"How much money did it take to get you to behave that way?"

"A lot. Believe me."

"Would you have done it for less?"

"What do you think I am?"

"Do you have a scale of payment for each different caress?"

"How dare you!"

"And that being the case, how much do you imagine I owe you by this time? Have you kept figures on it?"

Until she would scream at him in a fury that would sometimes bring blood into her mouth.

"You won't rest," she would cry, "until you see me poor again. Oh, if you only knew how I despise poverty!"

"You despise poverty?" he would sneer. "And you buy enough dresses in a month to clothe five hundred families for a year!"

"I need five hundred dresses!" she would yell back. "It would take a thousand dresses to drown out of me the taste of poverty!"

"I've been poor too," he once retorted.

"Poor?" She laughed. "You poor?"

"Yes. Poor. And hungry. Without food in the house. And everything sold. And my father off on some trip. And my mother ready to go begging on the street for bread."

"Oh, you don't know the first thing about poverty," she retorted. "Nor about hunger either. You never watched a man eating soup from a bowl and had to stand there rooted, wishing you had the privilege of licking the dregs of soup that you could see he had left sticking to his mustache. That's the kind of hunger I had! I was ten years old and had never worn anything but rags—rags that even the ragman didn't want. I had never had a comb through my hair. I had never had a bath! I had never had a pair of shoes! My father, my sister and I slept in a sheep-shearing shed."

No, he couldn't match that kind of poverty.

She told him how the man with the bowl of soup one day beckoned her into his hut and placed hot soup before her. She started ladling it down as fast as possible. But suddenly he jerked the bowl away from her. "Later," he said. And he pointed to a bed of straw in the corner.

"I didn't know what he wanted, but there wasn't anything—no, not anything—I wouldn't have given for that bowl of soup. I didn't hesitate for a moment. And afterward I ran home and told my older sister how easy it was to get a bowl of soup. She slapped me and spit in my face. But I didn't care. I had food, and that was what I wanted.

"I was eleven when I got to Paris. I was still barefoot, still in rags, still in need of a bath. I didn't know how to read or write. I knew nothing. Nothing except that men would sometimes give you money or food. A butcher, whose wife had just died, gave me my first real dress. Out of his wife's wardrobe. It was a cheap piece of cotton, but to me it looked as if woven with diamonds. It was far too big for me.

"I began to understand that I was attractive. I began to realize that once I had a dress there were men who would give me a coat, or shoes. And then when once I was dressed there were men who would give me jewelry. I began to realize that there was always a still richer man. That there was always something better, something more luxurious, something more extravagant.

"And I wanted everything. I taught myself to read and to write and to dress and to live. And when I finally had my own apartment, I wrote to my sister and told her to come to Paris. She had someone read the letter to her and she dictated her answer: If ever she saw me she would spit in my face, just as she had done years before.

"I'm twenty-two years old. I have a couple of years to live, maybe even only a couple of months. And I don't ever intend to live a single second of it in poverty again."

These details of her career as a prostitute were unadulterated torture to Alexandre. But hearing her speak of the little life that was left to her would cause him to forgive everything.

"After all," she would ask, "did I ever make a secret of my way of life? Did I ever try to pretend to anything except what I am? I have nothing else to exchange for what the world gives me except this body of mine."

"But since you say you love me," he would sometimes argue, "how can you see me suffer?"

"And you?" she would argue back. "Are you determined to make me suffer? Can't we tolerate each other and just be happy?"

Once he dared to revenge himself by having an outside adventure. Then she clawed back at him with fury.

"Ah, so *you* can," he said, "but *I can't*. Is that it?"

And she answered firmly, "Yes. That's it."

"And what makes it right for you—and wrong for me?"

"Because I'm a whore," she flung at him. "I do it for money. When it comes to love I can give you all you want. But when it comes to money, you can't give me all I need! That's the difference!"

Thus, instead of diminishing, their quarrels grew ever more violent, their periods of estrangement longer, their reconciliations shorter. He began to find more and more fault with her continued prostitution, he began to add objections to her language, to her irregularity in eating and sleeping and to every other aspect of her life, and especially to her generous consumption of champagne.

"Won't you let me have a little happiness during my last few months on earth?" she would plead.

"Those last few months of yours," he had the cruelty to say, "have stretched out pretty long, haven't they?"

And yet, somehow, whatever good days they had were so heavenly that he could only compare it to having a love affair with a flower. Never had there been anyone who could be so beautiful, so tender, so adorable.

It was during such a period of bliss that he one day met his father on the street. Dumas rushed up to his son and clapped him heartily around the shoulders. "Well, we're off!"

"Off to where?" Alexandre asked. "To the Frères Provençaux for lunch?"

Dumas roared. He began to pull wads of money from his pockets and sheafs of railway bonds. "Does this look like lunch money to you?" And right there on the street he went into a fandango. "Spain!" he cried. "Granada! Seville! Bullfights and oranges and señoritas on balconies!"

And as Alexandre still didn't seem to understand, Dumas demanded, "Well, are you with us?"

"Who's us?" Alexandre asked, fencing.

"Why, Maquet, Boulanger, you and I and my valet. I've just signed seven new contracts for serials. And I'm selling my last railway bonds. I'm on my way right now for a big letter of credit from the Rothschilds. You know I like to travel in style! Besides, we're planning for a six-month voyage. Maybe longer."

And as his son still didn't seem to rise to the occasion, Dumas shook him. "What's the matter with you? You don't seem too pleased. What is it? A woman?"

Alexandre nodded.

"Come on, boy," his father said, "you're not seriously thinking of giving up Spain for a woman. There are millions of women in the world. But there's only one Spain."

Alexandre was torn between love for Marie and love for his father. His whole being cried out to go to Spain with his beloved Papa. All the tears shed years ago, when his father had gone off to Italy leaving him behind, now demanded their satisfaction.

"When are you leaving?" he asked.

"Right away!" Dumas cried. "We take the train tomorrow for Orléans, which is as far as the railway goes. Then a coach which I've already arranged to buy. Hurry, make your farewells and get your clothes packed."

CHAPTER THIRTY-TWO

"As Little Time As I Have to Live, It Will Be Longer Than You Will Want to Love"

No SPEECH had ever cost Alexandre such effort as the short sentence: "I'm going away," which he had to tell to Marie.

He waited to tell her for what he thought might be the best moment, which of course never came, so that it was dawn when he finally had to break the news.

She rose up in bed. "Oh, no. You're not leaving me now!" she cried wildly.

And when he assured her that he was, and in fact that very day, she clenched her arms around him, twined her wiry fingers together and declared that he would never obtain his release except by cutting them off with a knife.

With tears she conjured him to have pity on her. "Don't let me die alone," she pleaded. And when he persisted, she promised him that she was now prepared to give up everything, that she would change her life completely, that she would live, if he insisted, in a hut and wear nothing but a hair shirt: all she wanted was for him to stay with her.

"It won't be for long," she said, weeping. "I'll do anything you say."

This was what he had always craved: a new life together. This was finally the life of innocence he had been seeking. He mingled his tears with her and assured her that together, in some remote countryside, he would help her recover her health and defeat death.

Although he swore that he was leaving her only to say good-by to his father and explain to him why he was not going to be one of the expedition, she did not fully trust him. He had to swear a dozen times by everything that was holy that he would be back within a couple of hours before she would let him out of the room.

When he found his father amidst a welter of trunks and suitcases and a retinue of servants, he said to him, "I'm not going, Papa."

"Are you crazy? Why not?"

Alexandre sighed. "It's awkward for me at the moment. I'm in love. Desperately in love."

"Ah, well," said Dumas, "don't distress yourself. For any other but you, I would not delay my trip. But since it's you, we'll wait. Will a couple of days finish your affair?"

"I'm afraid it's more serious than that."

"*Sapristi!*" cried Dumas. "You chose a poor moment for love. Who is it this time?"

"Oh, somebody," said Alexandre. "I cannot tell you right now." It would have been quite impossible for Alexandre to have explained to his father that he was still involved with the same Marie Duplessis from whom he had broken a dozen times. He had never dared tell anyone what this relationship really meant to him.

Besides, how could he have justified denying himself a trip to Spain for the sake of a prostitute? How could he have explained the strange illusion of innocence that continued to radiate from her and to bewitch him all over again after each betrayal?

"My boy," said Dumas grandly, "when I am in Spain I shall be representing in my person all that is best in the glory and culture of France. You have no conception of how highly I am regarded abroad. It is no exaggeration to say that I am worshiped. The red carpet will be rolled out for me everywhere. I shall be welcomed like a visiting potentate. Imagine yourself at my side. Imagine my pride in you. And your joy. No. I will not permit you to miss the greatest experience of your life for the sake of a woman, even were she a princess."

In pain Alexandre cried, "Then let's go at once."

"That's exactly what we're going to do," said Dumas. "We haven't a moment to lose. *En route! En route*, everyone!"

And a couple of hours later they were rolling toward Spain.

What a trip it was! Dumas did not lie when he said he was worshiped abroad. The moment they reached the frontier, one sensed all Spain bowing to the great writer.

When a customs officer had opened Dumas' baggage and was starting to examine it, his superior came running out of his office, his face flaming like a beet.

He elbowed his way through the crowd and, reaching the inspector, yelled, "What! You dare subject the baggage of Alessandro Dumas to an ordinary inspection?" The purple of anger fairly leaped from his face as he shoved the impious inspector aside with a gesture that was almost a blow.

"Alessandro Dumas?" the inspector gasped, retreating.

"Yes. *Los Tres Mosqueteros!*" his superior shouted and then, bowing, he begged Dumas to forgive Spain for such an affront right at the start of his trip. "Pass, pass, Messieurs!" he said, stamping the baggage right and left with a flourish.

Trip? No. Call it a procession. Call it a national holiday. A fete stretching from one end of the country to the other. With the *Giralda*, the chief newspaper of Seville, able to express its feelings only by printing itself in gold letters on the day Dumas entered that city. And at court festivals in Madrid, grandees accepting neglect as their proper share as all flocked about this tall, stout man with the smiling moon face.

And then the book Dumas made of it upon his return! Another volume in his series studying the Mediterranean world. Already famous for his sprightly travel books, this time Dumas surpassed himself, proving once again that the most fascinating bit of scenery in any country was that walking attraction, Alexandre Dumas.

In this unending carnival Alexandre had soon recovered his boyish spirits. He felt himself surrounded by admiring glances, and indeed he was at that time something to stop a woman's heart: a copy of the great Dumas, but done by an artist who knew how to refine and improve—slender where his father was stocky, tan where his father was swarthy, blond where he was dark, and with hair more curly than frizzy, but with the same eyes of icy blue.

It wasn't long before the party began to miss Alexandre for a night, and then for as long as a week, and several times he rejoined the caravan on the road, his horse in a lather after a wild ride that was probably an escape.

And so the travelers wandered from city to city in Spain, everywhere overwhelmed with bullfights and balls, and even experiencing a brush with bandits, and then going on to Gibraltar to be entertained by the British governor. And afterward crossing over to Africa and lingering on there, Dumas practically commandeering a French war vessel for his private use, and as a result receiving a twenty-one-gun salute when the ship came to anchor at Tunis. This was but one of many episodes that was later to be investigated and reinvestigated by the French authorities to discover who had permitted this cavalier use of a government vessel for a private party, particularly when Dumas took to presenting himself as the rescuer of some French prisoners who had been captured during the wars with Abd-el-Kader.

All this misuse of the French navy was estimated as having cost the government eleven thousand francs. And there was a demand that Dumas be forced to pay. Whereupon Dumas presented the French admiralty with a counter estimate. A bill against the French navy for a hundred and nineteen thousand francs.

The astounded ministry gasped. "What's this for?" they asked.

"Will you deny that I am at least as important to France as Walter Scott was to England?"

"What do you mean?"

"Are you saying," Dumas thundered, "that I have not, like Walter Scott, inspired our people to know and love their country's glorious past?"

"We cannot deny that, Monsieur Dumas."

"Well, the English navy took Walter Scott to Italy at a cost of a hundred and thirty thousand francs. The French navy spent only eleven thousand francs on my trip. As long as this matter has come up for an airing, I would like to state my claims: France owes me a hundred and nineteen thousand francs. Here is my bill. And I propose to sue. France must not neglect her artists!"

That closed the investigation and shut up the investigators.

But what about Marie Duplessis during this long absence?

If she suffered, no one knew it at first. She dressed more strikingly than ever, laughed louder, drank more champagne.

But her head ached, she couldn't sleep, and coughs tore through her chest like saw blades. Her life became more dissolute than ever. And more expensive. And the Count de Stackelberg was called upon to advance her ever larger sums. At the same time she treated him to a series of caprices and infidelities, as if to revenge herself for the fact that her attachment to his money had cost her the one great love of her life. Until the Count at last had had enough of her and broke with her.

Then her lavish style of living made necessary a rapid succession of other lovers, until she had exhausted herself and brought on an attack that confined her to her bed for weeks.

Dr. Chomel advised her to live on bread and vegetable soups. Dr. Davaine recommended a diet of grilled meats. Dr. Koreff advised quinine enemas and spice fumigations. One specialist suggested the baths at Ems. Another referred her to the water at Baden. A third said Spa. A fourth Wiesbaden.

Whatever they told her, she did. She ran from remedy to remedy and from watering place to watering place. And wherever she went, her illness went with her.

"These are my stations of the cross," she said, and wept. But then she called her hairdresser, her modiste, and, attired in a new and lovely creation of fine India muslin and draping about herself another embroidered cashmere shawl, she went out smiling, carrying her bouquet of camellias.

For life was now more expensive than ever, what with doctors and hotels at the finest bathing resorts.

Liszt, who had recently run away from Lola Montez, became her lover. He was as handsome as a prince out of the Arabian Nights, which, coupled with his talent, should have been enough to make her forget Alexandre.

Liszt swore that he would take her to Venice and to Constantinople, and that just the sight of the marble palaces along the Grand Canal, just the sight of the minarets on the Golden Horn, would cure her by stimulating her zest for life.

In his old age Liszt was to remember this promise and to regret that he never fulfilled it. But at the time he was in demand everywhere for concerts and recitals, and he left Marie again and again, and finally was heard of no more.

Then she took up once more again with the Count of Perrégaux.* Their love flared up violently. Or so it seemed, for she went with him to England and there was married to him. But when they returned, she had no sooner painted his coat of arms on her coupé than already they were separated. She dropped her brief use of the title Countess, became Marie Duplessis again, and once more was seen in the theater with her bouquet of camellias.

* He was the grandson of Napoleon's banker.

Someone called her "the phantom in furs." For, thinner than ever and inclined to shiver, she discarded her cashmere shawls and took to wearing warm chinchillas tailored by Révillon. In her pale face her eyes glowed larger with a new astonishment, as if she saw for the first time that no matter how one may run from poverty and wretchedness, there is nowhere any happiness, only disenchantment and melancholia.

She was scarcely twenty-three years old and she did not want to die. That last winter she bought herself a prayer stool, beautifully carved and upholstered, and spent long hours on her knees begging for life. Her eyes grew misty and red from weeping. And afterward, looking at herself in the mirror, she would wonder if life without beauty was worth having.

Then she would take to a new flurry of shopping, going to Tahans, where one bought boxes that were works of art and miniature pieces of furniture done in tropical woods with inlays of ivory and tortoise shell. Or to Mottet's, whose parasols were each a creation. Or to Mayer, whose gloves were known from Moscow to Rio de Janeiro.

But nothing could hide from her the fact that her days were numbered.

Koreff had said to her that consumption of the lungs was totally unknown to stableboys and that he could only draw the inference that the emanations of wet hay and manure must have in them a natural preventive.

So she had a stable installed beneath her bedroom, quartered cows and horses there and had holes bored through the floor. At night she would remove the corks and let the fumes fill her bedroom. Nothing helped. Neither the stable manure that grows flowers nor the social manure that grows artists.

And meanwhile merchants were asking for payment on her bills. From her deathbed she wrote her creditors sweetly worded notes on perfumed paper, inviting them to come to her bedside and discuss the matter.

Then she would sit up in a cashmere robe with blue silk lining and stave them off with some piece of jewelry, some painting, or just the promise that when she died everything would be sold in settlement.

It isn't true, as Dumas *père* was to write later in his newspaper *The Musketeer*, that the merchants took the pink brocade curtains from her bed and ripped up the very carpet from her bedroom floor. And therefore there was no reason for him to say, "How wonderful the law that forbids creditors from seizing one's bed, otherwise she would have died on the bare floor."

No. She died in luxury. Leaving whatever might be left from the auction of her goods to the sister who had spit in her face.

It was this auction of the effects of Madame la Comtesse de Perrégaux that was about to be held when Alexandre returned. The announcement of the four-day sale said that the apartment was open for inspection. Thus he was able to wander again through the sumptuous rooms, see again the costly furniture he had known so well, and be reminded anew of the girl who had put his hand under her breast so he could feel her palpitating heart and had said, "If I give myself to you so quickly, it is because I have so little time to live."

And when he had objected, she had laughed. "Don't be put out. Of one thing we can both be sure: as little time as I have to live, it will be longer than you will want to love."

At the auction, Alexandre watched with pain and distaste the crowds of eager buyers vying for her furs and her shawls, for her mahogany and rosewood furniture, for her piano and billiard table, for draperies and carpets and spreads, for the fifty pounds of silverware, "much of it adorned with enamel," as the catalogue described it, and for her jewelry "enriched with fine diamonds, pearls and other precious stones," for her horses, her saddles and harnesses and her coupé upholstered in blue satin—and even her petticoats and the basin which he had once seen filled with water and blood streaks.

Janin, Gautier, the Goncourt brothers, other newspapermen were there, busily picking up every bit of gossip to put into the articles they would write for their papers.

Charles Dickens, who attended the sale, thought ill of all this excitement and sympathy over the death of a young prostitute. "I rather imagine she died young of boredom and overindulgence," he wrote. Stories were told him of society women outbidding each other for a pair of Marie's Cinderella-sized shoes, and of Eugène

Sue's strange determination to own her *Book of Prayers* at no matter what cost.

Alexandre, in tears, kept in the background.

On a rainy Mardi Gras, with all Paris preparing to go mad for the celebration of the closing day of the carnival season, Alexandre went with the Count de Perrégaux to witness the disinterment of the body. The Count wanted her removed from the common grave where she had the right to lie for only five years and reburied in a costlier grave, "purchased in perpetuity." And in such cases the law required two witnesses to identify the body.

Under a black sky with a cold, steady rain falling, the coffin was opened. There she lay on a bed of fine white lace, with camellias and a crucifix pressed against her bosom under her crossed hands.

The Count de Perrégaux told Alexandre of her last days. How Liszt had been far away in Hungary, while he himself, out of town, had heard nothing of her sickness until the end was close. It was the Count de Stackelberg who had come to visit her and had wept that he should still be alive at eighty while she, scarcely more than twenty, was dying.

She was going fast when the Count de Perrégaux finally arrived. "She cried a great deal," he said.

The coffin, after identification, was reburied in its new plot and surmounted by a big marble block topped by a funerary urn. The tablet did not give her married name, the Countess of Perrégaux. It bore her maiden name, her real one—Alphonsine Plessis—and the dates showed that she had reached the age of twenty-three years and nineteen days when she died.

That strange innocence that Alexandre had found in her continued to spread its magic even after her death.

She became a saint.

An unconsecrated saint.

For more than a hundred years now that marble block on Saint-Charles Avenue of the Montmartre Cemetery has rarely been without its blanket of her favorite flower: camellias, both red and white, the offering of countless girls who hope through her intercession to find what she never found: happiness in sex. And many of whom, to help matters along, leave their visiting cards along with their bouquets.

What with the calendar of properly consecrated saints being so full of virgins, it is understandable that there should be a need for a shrine where one might bow one's head and mumble frivolous prayers.

CHAPTER THIRTY-THREE

The Two Writers

THERE'S NO ASPECT of Dumas *père's* life and character about which we are more in the dark than his superstitions.

He himself angrily repudiated the charge. "Me superstitious? Why, there's not a superstitious drop of blood in my entire body!"

Which is what makes his behavior, on specific occasions, all the more puzzling. Take, for example, the time he went on a tour of his estate with his head gardener Michael, and at one point made the following comment: "You know, Michael, we seem to be quite plentifully supplied with members of the canine race."

"And why not?" Michael demanded angrily. "Is there a dog in France that doesn't dream of retiring to this spot someday and living off your table scraps? Ever since you've forbidden me to use the whip on them, there's nothing I can do to get rid of these strays. As for trying to feed one without feeding the rest, why that only fills the garden with a pack of snarling wolves tearing each other to pieces."

"Ah, yes," Dumas admitted, "we have here a pretty problem."

"We certainly do," said Michael. "Has Monsieur any conception of how many dogs this property can now boast of?"

"No, Michael, I have no idea."

"Well, Monsieur Dumas, let me tell it to you. We now have thirteen dogs. And not one of them, outside of your own Scotch pointer Pritchard, worth the bullet it would take to kill him."

"That's bad, Michael," said Dumas seriously. "Very bad."

"Yes, sir. I never saw such a lot of useless mongrels before."

"I'm not referring to their pedigree, Michael," said Dumas, "which is something that I would no more hold against a dog than against a human being. But I am worried about their number. Thirteen dogs sitting down to dinner together is sure to bring misfortune to one of them before the year is up. You know that."

"Well, you just give me back my whip," said Michael, "and I gaurantee you that you'll be down to your original dog Pritchard in less than an hour."

"That's a bit harsh, Michael. In a way, you know, these dogs do me an honor: where else in France is there an estate where thirteen dogs can be fed from table scraps?"

"Monsieur is too modest," said Michael. "From your table scraps I could do much more than feed thirteen dogs. I could open up a first-class canteen for the French army."

"It's that number thirteen that worries me," Dumas went on. "If something should happen to one of those dogs I would have to hold myself personally accountable."

"If that's all," said Michael, "then I can soon help you. Even without a whip I can find some way to get rid of one of them. That will leave only twelve."

"That's fine," said Dumas. "Get rid of one." Then he reconsidered. "But isn't that precisely what the number thirteen predicts? Misfortune to one of the number? No, let's not allow ourselves to become the instrument of a superstition. I tell you what, Michael. Why don't you let in another stray, which will bring the figure up to fourteen? Then everything is saved."

Michael sighed and gave up. "Since those are Monsieur's wishes," he said submissively. "But permit me to remark that I'm very much surprised to find so educated a person as Monsieur so superstitious."

"Superstitious?" Dumas snorted. "But I'm nothing of the kind!"

And take the occasion when, during an after-dinner conversation, Jadin the painter flung the same accusation at Dumas. "You know, you're the most superstitious person I've ever met."

"Go away!" Dumas exclaimed. "I'm far too intelligent. Why, only the other day when a group of us was discussing the question of what was the wittiest line in all classical literature, I voted for that famous sentence that Cicero attributes to Cato the Elder: 'Two fortunetellers cannot look at each other without laughing.' A line so clever that it is claimed that for a time it wiped out the lucrative trade of the soothsayers of ancient Rome."

"You can't fool me with that kind of professorial talk," said Jadin.

"Only half an hour ago, when we were seated at table, you suddenly stopped eating and went pale just because I happened to lay one fork crosswise over another."

"But, *parbleu!*" Dumas cried. "That's no joke. One doesn't play around with things like that! Crossed forks! There's nothing more unlucky!"

"So you admit it!" Jadin shouted.

"Admit what?"

"You've got to admit it," Fiorentino * broke in. "You and I, Dumas, patronize Adam the shirtmaker, and Adam was telling me only the other day how you canceled an order for shirts because you found him working on them on a Friday. You actually screamed at him, he tells me."

"Of course I screamed at him," Dumas said heatedly. "Imagine a shirtmaker not knowing that to sew a shirt on a Friday is to sew not a shirt but a shroud."

"Everybody knows it," said Jadin, "but everybody isn't such a fool as to believe it."

"Are you calling me a fool?" Dumas cried. "Do you imagine for one moment that I believe it?"

"Then why do you behave as if you do?" everyone asked. "Explain yourself."

"A man wants to have his mind at ease," Dumas said. "Just because I'm too intelligent to believe in this nonsense doesn't mean that it can't be disturbing. After all, I'm both a scholar and a poet. And it's as Pascal says, '*Le coeur a ses raisons que la raison ne connait pas.*'" (The mind cannot always fathom the reasoning of one's heart.)

Though this would seem to be a very simple matter to understand, somehow it was always easier, for the intellectuals especially, to misunderstand Dumas.

There was, for example, the time when he was writing the *Vicomte de Bragelonne* as a serial for *Le Siècle* (containing the adventures of the Four Musketeers, now grown old), when one

* Using a pen name, Fiorentino was music critic for two different Parisian papers and carried on a bitter feud with himself for many years. This duplicity was not revealed until both these contrary critics heaped praise on the same soprano. Such a thing had never happened before. She turned out to be Fiorentino's mistress.

day his son came upon him seated before his little writing table
with his mouth hanging open and great tears coursing down his
cheeks.

"Papa!" Alexandre cried. "You"re ill!"

"No, my boy," said Dumas, throwing his arms around his son and
sobbing violently. "But I've had to kill him. Just now."

"Kill whom?"

"Porthos. My great big lovely noble Porthos, my wonderful
Musketeer whom I myself created as the best of all the gentlemen
of France next to D'Artagnan, Porthos with whom I've been living
on such intimate terms day after day for six years or more. I've had
to kill him. And what for? Why, to make story interest. To make
exciting reading for my millions of devoted readers. Slaughter him.
Yes, slaughter him in the gladiatorial arena of the *feuilleton*. Sport
for the public. Ah, shame on me. Shame. To have killed my own
child."

And when, two days later, France opened its paper, they found
the installment of their favorite serial missing and instead a note
saying, "Monsieur Alexandre Dumas, overcome by the death of
Porthos as told in yesterday's installment, has retired for a week of
mourning to his birthplace, the town of Villers-Cotterêts."

Of course not absolutely everyone in France took this seriously.
Certainly in England, where his installments were being pirated
as fast as they could be sailed across the Channel, it was immediately pointed out that this period of mourning coincided suspiciously with the opening of the hunting season, and indeed it wasn't
long before the news came from Villers-Cotterêts that Dumas was
boasting of having killed three fat buck on opening day. Which invited from one English critic the thought that Dumas had killed
Porthos in order to have an excuse for a holiday.

But, of course, in England just then Dumas was being attacked
for what was called his "philosophy of Aladdinism"—that is to say,
the substitution of daydreaming for work in the attainment of one's
goal in life—and an English industrialist was saying openly that he
could readily spot every reader of Dumas among his operatives
by the poor quality of their output.

But it is particularly in connection with the famous Eugène de
Mirecourt affair that the question of whether Dumas was supersti-

tious or not has enormous importance. This affair started one evening at a meeting of the *Societé des Gens de Lettres*, the Association
of Men of Letters, the French equivalent of our Authors' League, an
organization to which both Dumas *père* and Dumas *fils* belonged.

It must be explained first that by this time Alexandre had already
become something of a writer. This had come about as follows:

He was hiding one day from the bailiffs when through the window he noticed a process server entering the estate. He ran to his
father and pointed out the man.

"Don't worry," said his father. "We'll get him. Watch!"

And as the bailiff crossed a little wooden bridge spanning a pond,
Dumas pulled a lever and the planks of the bridge separated and
dropped the man into the water.

"Now he's where he belongs, with the other cold-blooded animals," said Dumas, and laughed heartily.

Alexandre's laugh sounded rather sour. "It's all right for you to
laugh," he said. "You have a paying profession that keeps pouring
money into your coffers no matter how fast you keep spending it.
But I, I have no income, nothing but increasing debts and no
prospect of ever having anything else."

"*Ventre saint-gris!*" Dumas exploded. "What's the matter with
you? Have you no fingers to hold a pen?"

"Fingers, yes," said Alexandre. "But talent, no."

"Talent, talent!" Dumas cried. "Who has talent? Not I!" He
pounded his table top. "It's this plank that has all the talent. And
it's only by leaning against this piece of wood for fifteen hours a
day that I'm able to rub off some of the talent into my writing. Why
don't you try the same?"

"Didn't I?" Alexandre asked. "On that Byzantine novel? What a
miserable botch I made of it."

"Does that one failure mean you're through with the ambition
to write?"

Alexandre shrugged. "I write a few verses now and then."

"Verses," said Dumas, making a little grimace. "My compliments.
That's hardly the means of a livelihood today. Still, who knows?
You've got to start somewhere. So let's have a look at those verses
of yours."

"Why do you want to look at them?" Alexandre asked.

"Why, to see if they can be published," said Dumas. "A book with your name on it is what you need."

"But these verses weren't written to be published," Alexandre said. "They're . . . well, they're personal, private . . ."

"None of that, my boy," said Dumas. "An artist has no private life. What are we, after all, but merchants of our dreams? Even a prostitute sells nothing so intimate as that!"

So, some days later Alexandre showed his father a number of lovelorn lyrics he had written, vague fugitive pieces, many of them concerning an unnamed and unfortunate beauty who could not have been anyone else but Marie Duplessis.

"Why, they're wonderful, my boy," said Dumas. "Magnificent! Here. Let me embrace you. I predict that, like Byron, you will go to sleep unknown and wake up famous."

"You really think they should be published?" Alexandre asked, troubled.

"Why, publishers will leap at this opportunity!" Dumas declared. "You let me handle everything."

But the publishers didn't even nibble, much less leap. Dumas' own publisher at the time, Cadot, turned the poems down cold. "I don't intend to ruin the good name of Dumas," he said. "It's my stock in trade."

Dumas was furious, and to prove the publishers wrong he himself made the investment of printing his son's poetry.

Sins of Youth the little volume was called, and one critic immediately wrote: "Undoubtedly the main sin the author had in mind was the sin of publishing this rubbish."

Fourteen copies were sold—fourteen copies, which in time Alexandre succeeded in buying back and destroying so that today even the great Bibliothèque Nationale of France does not possess the book.

"Now!" Dumas cried. "Right away another one!"

"Another book?" Alexandre asked. "After this total failure?"

"Yes," Dumas ordered. "And without delay! And after the next failure another book. And so on. Without end. For with books it is the same as with artillery. Never trust to winning the battle with a single bull's-eye hit, but follow the practice of Napoleon: just keep firing in the direction of the target without any letup. Wars are rarely won by sharpshooters; it's the volleys that count."

"But what shall I write? You know already that I cannot write historical novels like you."

"Never mind what you write," said his father. "Only write! For just as appetite comes while eating, so literature comes while writing."

So Alexandre wrote his novels *Life at Twenty* and *The Adventures of Four Women and a Parrot* and *Césarine*, thin-blooded romances with too much suet and too little muscle, books that Dumas pressured his friends on various newspapers to publish as serials, overruling their objections, saying, "After all, it will bear the name of Dumas," and they saying, "No one will be fooled," but in the end giving in, which caused a critic to write: "Watch out for those four little letters *f-i-l-s*. The genuine article is still signed Dumas, all by itself."

Which made Alexandre feel ashamed of himself, for he knew his own lack of talent.

And then, one night, as he was sitting at his desk leaning on that plank of wood that has all our talent and feeling that kind of misery, that dark sense of incompetence that writers know so well, he found his thoughts going back to that saddest and guiltiest of all his days when he had just come back from Spain and had seen the announcement of the auction of Marie Duplessis' possessions and realized that he had had his part in killing her.

And then, before he knew it, he was crying.

And then suddenly he found himself both crying and writing.

For the first time he was writing as he had always known his father to write, overwhelmed by his own material. And somehow ashamed of it. So he took a room at a near-by inn where he could be sure of being alone and feel free to give way completely to his emotions.

The story he wrote was the story of the *Lady of the Camellias* as we know it. He could never have written it exactly as it had happened. That would have cost him too much. What he wrote was the story as it should have happened. Gone is that father who does a fandango on the streets and says to his son, "Come to Spain." And

gone, above all, is that unfaithful lover, himself, who went off to
Spain and left his love to die alone.

He made it instead the simplest story in the world, so simple as
to seem like the dream of a little boy. Only three characters: father,
son and the beautiful, wayward girl. And the father interfering to
save the son from this forbidden love. It might almost be a modern
version of Adam and Eve in the Garden of Eden. It might almost
be a modern *Oedipus Rex*. And, pervading this simple story, such
a sense of early childish innocence that white and red camellias
have a meaning too mysterious to fathom.

It was a complete rehabilitation of everyone: his father is no
longer the unpredictable Bohemian with a string of mistresses, but
a real and legal father, a solid bourgeois who carefully saves his
money and who interferes between boy and girl only because he
wants his son to live an equally honorable and correct life. And the
son is no longer either a bastard child or a young man striving to
outdo his father in dissolute living, but a well-brought-up youth
ready to enter the serious profession of law who is having his short
fling at life before he settles down. And as for Marie, it is not
caprice or love of luxury that leads her to betray the boy, but a
secret agreement wrung from her by the father, by which, in return for one more night of love, she promises the father to make
the son hate her forever by going back to her old immoral life.

And then the deathbed scene which clears up all misunderstand-
ings—but, alas, too late—leading to the moral that true love en-
nobles even the most degraded woman, which is thus not merely a
rehabilitation of Marie Duplessis, but of another fallen woman, also
close to the heart of Alexandre, Catherine Lebay, his mother.

Had not dreadful things been said about his mother's immoral
life? Had she not nevertheless radiated innocence? And had not he
as an innocent child lived with her and loved her—until his father
had come between them, saying, not, Come to Spain! but, Go to
school! and causing him, as a result, years of anguish? Thus in one
sad little tale two of the errors of his life were as if erased and his
deepest wishes endowed with a certain amount of truth.

Critics received the book more favorably than anything Alexandre had written so far, and it seemed for a moment that it might

be headed for success. But sales dropped off suddenly and the
book died.

"This material was not meant for a novel," was Dumas' explanation. "It should have been a play."

Though Alexandre had given Marie Duplessis the name of Mar-
guerite Gautier in his book, his father easily recognized her.

"You've made me cry," he said. "It's so sad and beautiful. And
yet she was one of the very fortunate women of this world: it is not
granted to everyone to have been loved by two writers."

"Two writers?" Alexandre exclaimed. "Who was the other?"

"What? Do you still refuse to think of yourself as a writer?" his
father replied.

Alexandre said nothing. He was for the moment too shocked and
confused.

This was the evening that the Societé des Gens de Lettres was
scheduled to meet. So father and son went to Paris by train.

By the time they reached the city, it had begun to drizzle, and
every cab had been snatched up. Dumas yelled, "Cab! Cab! *Holà!*
Whistle, my boy! Whistle loud! There's one! No. It's taken. Whistle
again. There, he sees us. He's turning around to come to our side.
No, the devil! He's picking up that lady! Here! We'll take this
wagon."

"But, Papa," said Alexandre, "that's the mail pickup wagon."

"What's the difference. . . . You'll give us a lift, won't you, my
friend?"

"But, Monsieur, this is no cab for hire. This is the mail."

"You mean you don't recognize me?" Dumas exclaimed, with one
foot already on the riser.

"Who doesn't know our Monsieur Dumas?" the driver retorted.

"And this is my son," said Dumas.

"An honor, Messieurs. But the law . . ."

"You mean you would refuse a ride to a colleague?"

"What do you mean a colleague?"

"Why a man of letters—like yourself."

The driver laughed. *"Monsieur, on ne peut rien vous refuser.
Montez donc."*

Naturally Dumas wrote him out a pass for the theater, invited him to bring his wife and children out to his Monte Cristo estate of a Sunday and see his little zoo, and in general arranged matters so as to lead eventually to an expenditure that a dozen cabs would not have entailed.

Father and son were, of course, late for the meeting. As they entered, a tall man with a soft lock of dark hair falling over his forehead stopped reading from a paper. Thirty or more authors, seated around a huge oval table, stared at the two Dumas.

"Sh . . ." Dumas whispered hoarsely to his son. "You sit down here. I just want to go over and shake hands with my dear Maquet." All eyes followed him as he tiptoed around, and the speaker waited until Dumas should shake hands with Maquet. But on the way Dumas saw Pommier and stopped to ask him, in a whisper that could be heard around the room, "How is Madame Pommier recovering since her miscarriage?"

The aged Viennet, last remaining practitioner of the ancient art of writing letters in verse, rapped on the table and said in his wonderful voice: * "Can we have quiet, please?"

"A thousand pardons," said Dumas. Then, mischievously poking one man in the ribs while winking at another, he dropped into the nearest empty seat and began to clear his throat noisily. That concluded, he yawned and sank back into the upholstered chair, contentedly crossing his hands over his belly and obviously prepared to have himself a little cat nap, or, as the French say, a little dog.

The speaker, ready to resume half a dozen times and each time forced to wait for Dumas to come to order, finally began. "Is this some inconsequential personage whom I accuse of dragging literature into the marketplace and there prostituting her? I would not waste your time at this meeting if it were. I will not name any names, but lest you fail to recognize the man, picture to yourself a drum major with the muscled limbs of a Hercules. Add to that a squashed nose. Item: a pair of bulging lips. Item: a wild bush of hair. There you have his portrait."

Alexandre, listening with amazement, turned his eyes toward his father, but the latter was lying back in blissful peace.

* He had snatched the papers from Lafayette's hands when the latter was reading the proclamation of Louis Philippe as King of France and had demonstrated how such a document should be read.

The speaker went on: "Shall I be more explicit? Shall I describe him as half marquis, half savage? Shall I tell you that as marquis he is the intimate of kings? But as savage he importunes them for ribbons and medals, which to him are like so many colored beads. Shall I describe his behavior in a restaurant, ordering the most exotic dishes? That's the marquis. But if the dishes are not prompt in appearance, his hunger may cause him to invade the kitchen, gobble up whatever he sees, raw meat or half-cooked potatoes, afterward dropping off to sleep in a corner on the floor. That's the savage. . . . Mistresses? Any number of them. That's the right of a marquis. But the ladies know enough to take a smelling bottle to bed with them to cover up a doubtful perfume. That's the—"

A tremendous blow from a suddenly aroused Dumas struck the huge table so that it shivered.

"What's this?" he thundered.

The whole gathering, excepting the dignified Viennet, was on its feet at once. Young Alexandre, in a quick rush at the speaker, was stopped by three or four members. The room suddenly resembled a battlefield frozen into a tableau.

Viennet rapped again and again, calling upon everyone to sit down. "Calm! Calm!" he kept repeating.

Dumas stood there, breathing like a harpooned whale, drops of sweat popping from his brow. And bunched around him a kind of living wall of authors bent on preventing a physical encounter.

Viennet spoke out forcefully. "I will hold myself accountable for permitting this incident. And I will ask the speaker to be seated."

The speaker, brushing away the lock from his forehead, said, "My subject is still the necessity of this body to take cognizance of the growing wholesale manufacture of literature and take steps to prevent it."

Dumas blew out his breath and glared around the room. "If that's the subject," he declared haughtily, "it has nothing to do with me. Continue! I'm going back to sleep."

The speaker, once more brushing away the falling lock of hair, went back to his paper. "This body, representing the highest traditions of the profession of letters in France, must ask itself how it is that some writers can turn out fifty and sixty books a year, while other writers require a year to do a single volume. Is it possible that there are factory methods for producing books? That a dozen impecunious writers can be hired by an entrepreneur, some set to work ranging through German, English, Italian literature in order to steal plots and ideas, while others are busy going through books of travel and of history, mercilessly pilfering them of their best passages, and others meanwhile adapting to the new stories stolen scenes of love or of battle or of chase, while still others whip in the dialogue, to make the mixture light and frothy to suit the modern taste? And with all this patchwork confectionery, finally pasted together and copied out, the owner of the workshop has nothing to do but sign his name with a flourish on the final product, which is then pushed into the market, where it crowds out the honestly written homemade novel."

Suddenly Dumas smacked his forehead, then shot to his feet again and, pointing an angry finger across the table at the speaker, he shouted, "Jacquot! Now I remember you. Jacquot!"

"My name is Eugène de Mirecourt," said the speaker, prudently pulling back a step.

"And I say you're Jacquot! Twice you came to me with romances you had written wanting to sell them to me, assuring me that all they needed was my touch. But I turned them down."

"That was my trap to expose your literary-brokerage business!" Mirecourt yelled.

Once more the whole room was in commotion, and young Alexandre again had to be bodily restrained.

"Trap indeed," said Dumas, laughing. "What kind of a trap did you expect me to fall into when you brought me such miserable stories?"

"You asked me to try you again, didn't you?" Mirecourt cried. "Promising to buy if I brought something better."

"And why not?" Dumas asked, again glaring around the room. "Aren't stories bought and sold every day in this country? What's wrong with that?"

"There's nothing wrong," said Viennet, "provided you do not afterward sign them as your own."

"Well, who then should sign them?" Dumas roared at the president. "Jacquot here? Who cannot write a publishable story on his own?"

"But it is inconceivable," said Viennet, "that one should sign a story that one has not written in its entirety."

"What?" cried Dumas. "Would you then refuse Shakespeare the right to sign his plays? Just because he took his plots from others? Factory! Workshop! Poppycock! Here, this right arm of mine, that's my factory."

"Is that arm able to write sixty volumes in one year?" Mirecourt shouted. "Why, the fastest secretary cannot *copy* that much, to say nothing of *composing* that much *original* writing. Deny here that Maquet did your *Three Musketeers*! Indeed, your whole D'Artagnan series. Deny that Théaulon did your *Keen*! Deny that Fiorentino and Maquet did your *Monte Cristo*! Deny that Paul Meurice did your *Ascanio*, and that De Leuven did your *Lorenzino*. Come on. Deny it. Maquet is present. Deny it before this body!"

Maquet, sitting at the far end, looked very uncomfortable as all eyes turned toward him. For a moment he was torn with the desire to appear before this assemblage as the author of the D'Artagnan series and the *Count of Monte Cristo*, but then he shrugged and said, "My association with Monsieur Dumas is entirely honorable and needs no discussion here."

"That's right," Dumas rumbled. "This is a lot of humbug, gentlemen. What? Are we to be put on the witness stand because someone brings trumped-up charges against us? Surely serious charges such as these must be better founded before the accused is forced into the defensive. I won't deny I've bought stories. And I'm not going to say that Maquet and I haven't worked closely together. Very closely indeed. In fact, in the press of my work I've had to turn to many, many others for help."

"Help? Association?" Mirecourt shrilled. "Euphemisms! Shall I give you an example? Here," he shouted, holding up a volume, "is a book called *Jacob Ortis*. And by whom is this work? Here, on the title page is the author's name. It is Alexandre Dumas. Read it! 'By Alexandre Dumas,' that's what it says. But is it really by Alexandre Dumas? It is not. It was written in Italian by Ugo Foscola. This is nothing but a translation. Well, is this translation at least by Dumas? No, it is not! It was done by one of Dumas' assistants, Fiorentino. And even that's not entirely true. Because all Fiorentino did was take a translation made years ago by Gosselin and alter a word here and there. Now, gentlemen, I ask you, Can any-one saddle a more ingeniously complicated bit of imposition on the unsuspecting public?" He tossed the book on the table. "There you have one small example of literary merchandising!"

Viennet rapped. "I will call for a vote of adjournment. We shall meet next time to appoint a committee to investigate . . ."

Mirecourt jumped up on a chair and screamed at the top of his lungs, "Delays! A trick to bury this! But we young writers who have been waiting for years to get ourselves published and always everywhere finding that nothing is wanted except by Dumas, Dumas, Dumas, we are determined now finally to break up this monopoly that has blocked all doors to us. And we have the proofs here! Page after page stolen outright. Book after book turned out by factory methods. Plagiarism and theft and deception! This will be published! I am giving you notice!"

"Vote for adjournment!" came the cry from various parts of the room from members anxious to have this rowdy and embarrassing scene done with.

"A lot of falderal!" Dumas snorted. "First show us the *Monte Cristos* and the *Three Musketeers* that have remained unpublished because I blocked the door. First submit those unpublished literary masterpieces here, to this body. Gentlemen, this is nothing but the old trick of incompetence determined to rise by tearing down the competent! Granier de Cassagnac and others have tried it before!"

And though Mirecourt cried out frantically, "A committee is the kiss of death!" and "I will not permit these facts to be buried in committee," the meeting was adjourned.

While the two Dumas were being ushered out of one door, Mirecourt was being escorted out the back way.

Alexandre said to his father, "I, too, have seen that man before. He exercises regularly at Fabien's fencing academy."

At the door Mirecourt succeeded in giving his conductors the slip and ran madly toward Dumas, but a number of authors managed to throw themselves between as a living barricade.

Mirecourt screamed, "Tell me, you! What does it take to get you to fight?"

Dumas smiled. "I don't fight any Jacquots-come-latelies."

"Not even when they insult you by calling you a coward?"

"I've been called coward by better men than you," said Dumas evenly.

"So it's true what people say—that all your duels are just play-acting. Put-up jobs to give you cheap glory and your books cheap publicity!"

"If that's what people say," said Dumas, "then what good is that kind of publicity?"

"What? Is there no insult so deadly that it will make you fight?"

Dumas' face went hot. He suddenly spread his huge arms and pushed everyone aside. "Sure there's an insult that will make me fight."

"Then do me the kindness to reveal it to me. I beg you."

Dumas glared at him, and then relaxed and smiled. "Why, all you have to do is intimate that I resemble you in even the slightest way. That will be insult enough for me."

Mirecourt was stopped for a moment, while smiles broke out here and there on the faces of the spectators. But then Mirecourt accepted the suggestion. An ugly smile distorted his lips. "Very well. If that is what it takes to make you fight. Yes, *you* resemble *me*."

"That," said Dumas, "is more than I can stomach. You may expect my seconds."

"They can find me and my seconds at the office of *La Silhouette*," said Mirecourt. "Opposite the Odéon."

CHAPTER THIRTY-FOUR

"This Time I Want a Corpse!"

WORD OF THIS explosive meeting at the Society of Men of Letters had already reached the literary ghetto of Paris, spreading rapidly from café to café, and by the time the two Dumas were on the street Dumas' friends were coming on the run, one after the other. Fiorentino, Mallefille, Lacroix, Brunswick, De Leuven, Bourgeois, Meurice, and so forth, all of them at various times collaborators with Dumas or originators of some unsuccessful story or play which they had transferred to Dumas for a price for him to turn into a success.

Dumas, surrounded by his little court, felt in fine fettle standing bareheaded in the continuing drizzle, the water drops sparkling like jewels in his frizzy hair.

"Ha!" he was saying. "I wrote of King Charles IX looking out of the window at the great Huguenot massacre and being so excited that he yelled, 'Bring me a Huguenot! I too must have someone to kill!' But only now do I really understand how he felt. Bring me someone to kill!"

"Papa!" cried Alexandre. "Let me be one of your seconds!"

"Always before in my duels," Dumas said, "I've studied carefully how to avoid loss of life. Both mine and my opponent's. After all, I'm the son of Mr. Humanity. I don't like killing. But this time no mere show of blood will satisfy me. This time I want a corpse!"

"Please, Papa!" Alexandre begged. "Let me be one of your seconds. Please. Please."

Dumas roared with laughter. "Look at the boy! Look how excited he is! Embrace me! Of course you may be."

"Who will be the other second?" Alexandre asked.

"Oh, we have time, we have time," said Dumas. "I have the choice of the finest friends in the world." He gestured to the men around him. And then, suddenly pulling himself up straight, he barked, "Members of my literary workshop! Attention! What kind of sloppy factory have we got here? Line up there! Let's show some discipline. Dress ranks! That's better. And now, parade rest! Men, you're invited out to my castle of Monte Cristo tonight. We're going to cook ourselves the meal of our lifetime! Come on, Alexandre. Quick, two or three cabs! We'll have no trains tonight. We'll ride out in state!"

And on the way out, he was in especially fine spirits. "A duel!" he said. "Danger! That's when I show my real mettle. When did I ever write better than when seven editors at once sued me for serials I had promised them? The court order was: Write those serials or go to prison. So I called upon you to help me. And you did! Why, that year I alone published twice as much as the whole forty immortals of the French Academy. Twice as much as the whole lot of them put together!"

"Ha!" he snorted. "*Jacob Ortis*. Not written by Alexandre Dumas! Who then wrote it? Ugo Foscola? Well, of course he did. Which of us in literary work doesn't know that it was written in Italian by Ugo Foscola? Imposition? What nonsense! Why, I found this masterpiece lying in the gutter. An orphan. Twice translated into French and still ignored by the public. So what did I do? I did what any noble-hearted man would do. I adopted this literary waif. I gave it my name. I gave it some of my light touch. And lo! Hundreds of thousands of people were suddenly enjoying a book that previously no one would read. Literary merchandising! What rot! Why, it's a service to literature that I did.

"Didn't I do the same with the *Iliad* and the *Odyssey*? Sure I took a few liberties with Homer. But Homer himself would thank me for making him once more popular and readable. Imagine people reading Homer again as a serial with their daily paper!

"Ah, no! You can't do that! Out of their towers swarmed the scholars, crying, Blasphemy! Heresy! Lese majesty! And they frightened the poor editors until the serialization of Homer was stopped, and the scholars wrapped him up again like a mummy and took him back into the tower. But the people! The people! What do they get out of all this scholarly protection of the classics? Nothing! And do you remember? All the dry-as-dusts saying, Next thing—you know what?—that terrible Dumas will be selling the Bible for a serial. And why not? Do you know of any better story than that of Moses rescuing the Jews from Pharaoh? Do you know a better story than the passion of Our Lord? Of course I shall make it into a serial someday! And it will be one of my best, too!"

"Hurrah!" cried Brunswick. "The Gospels according to Saint Alexandre Dumas!"

And when they were all gathered in the baronial kitchen, with fire crackling both in the stove and in the giant fireplace, Dumas cried, "All right, men! No more cooking for the brain now. Let's cook for the belly! I propose roasted squab, along with a pilau of rice done with almonds, and egg yolks and mushrooms and tomatoes. And a big salad of endive, rings of hard-boiled whites of egg, red caviar. Accepted?"

"Motion passed!" said Lacroix.

"All right, Fiorentino, you tend to the eggs. Hard boil four dozen. And then slice, pick out the yellow for the rice, leave the rings for the salad. . . . You, Brunswick, crack almonds. Here are bitter almonds and here sweet. Mix about one bitter to ten sweet. . . . Alexandre! I charge you with the mushrooms. Peel and sauté in butter! . . . De Leuven, you know my cellar as well as anyone. Take Maquet and fetch up the wines. I never drink, so I leave the choice to you."

"Have you noticed what attention I give to color?" Dumas asked, as he started preparing to spit the squabs. "We eat with our eyes too. I have white, yellow, green, brown, red. The whole spectrum. Also notice that I have something hard and something chewy, as well as something soft and something crisp. And something bland and something spicy. Something light and something filling. Something cooked and something raw!"

"It's the same mixture you use in your novels," said Bourgeois.

"Why, of course," said Dumas. "What else is civilization but the art of cooking! Comb your history books and see if any civilization has ever arisen except where two or more styles of cooking have clashed and mingled. The crossroads of man's appetite are also the crossroads of man's culture! Rome. Athens. Jerusalem. Why, did you know that King Solomon had twelve high chefs? Each chef cooked for one month and for the other eleven went traveling to bring back to Jerusalem new foods and new ways of preparing them."

Working with the long spit and the squabs gave Dumas the feeling of already holding a rapier in his hand.

"Come on," said Dumas to Mallefille,* a wiry individual who was likened by his contemporaries to an eagle pressed flat. "While our squabs are getting done to a turn, grab a spit and let me show you the thrust with which I mean to disembowel this Mirecourt and wrap his intestines around his neck."

Mallefille took another spit, and the two men gave the customary fencers' salute and started to feel out each other's style. Alexandre immediately withdrew his sautéed mushrooms from the fire and ran up to watch, for he was terribly anxious that this duel be brilliant. His father must not be merely invincible, but strikingly so.

---

* Mallefille supplied the background material for *George*, Dumas' novel about Mauritius Island plantation life.

And Mirecourt must not just die, but die ingloriously, crushed, slaughtered, so that with one fell blow, so to speak, all the terrible moments at school when Alexandre had been laughed at and beaten would be wiped out. This was to be the moment of his great vindication! This was to be the moment when he would prove the truth of the expression "*que la vengeance est douce au coeur du vindicateur!*"

But this was also precisely what made the performance of Dumas so heart-rending. Alexandre stood there feeling an icy dagger pushing itself deeper and deeper into his vitals. Was this corpulent man, wavering on his feet and thrusting around so inelegantly with his spit, as if he were stirring up a fire with a poker, was that his father? This *ferrailleur*, as fencers say contemptuously, this ironmonger, who all the while that Mallefille was repeatedly lunging through to strike him in the breast yet was cockily saying, "Beware now, Mallefille, don't press me too hard, or you will force me to use the famous flanconade of Girard,* which I know better than Girard himself!"

And all the time Mallefille was backing him to the wall and poking him in his fat belly any time he wished. Until Dumas laughingly begged off, saying, "It's not fair. Mallefille, your ugly face inspires me with love instead of hate. I would have to fight you blindfolded in order to beat you. To show my prowess I need someone who looks like Mirecourt."

"Papa!" Alexandre cried at last in a voice that was almost a groan. "You're so terribly out of practice!"

"Nonsense, lad! I have what is known as a natural technique. Inborn. I never need practice. And this hand never loses its cunning."

"But your stance is all wrong. And your footwork. And your grip . . ."

"Ah, so? Indeed? And I daresay you will teach me?"

"Why, Papa, you know I exercise three times a week with Fabien! That's where Mirecourt goes."

"Fabien!" said Dumas with fine scorn. "Do you imagine for a moment that this Fabien could hold up a candle to an old-timer like Grisier, who taught me? We had the real thing then, my boy. Never

---

* To Girard, the author of *Traité des Armes,* 1711, was ascribed this sensational thrust into the flank.

will there be a fencer like St. George, my father's friend and also a mulatto, the greatest sportsman the world ever produced. Fencing today is a lost art, just like the making of stained-glass windows!"

"But, Papa," said Alexandre, almost in tears, "your life depends on your knowing at least the fundamentals of protecting yourself."

"Look who will teach me fundamentals. Why, boy, I fought my first duel when you were still in swaddling clothes."

"Please, Papa, listen," Alexandre cried out in despair. "In a few words I can explain to you Fabien's method. After all, it's Fabien's methods that Mirecourt will be using against you!"

"Now look, my lad, but really . . ."

"Here, just for a moment, Papa. Stand like this." Alexandre turned his father around, raised his arm, pushed his elbow in toward his body. "See. You must form a triangle. A big triangle. The point of the triangle is the point of your sword. That point must protect your hilt. The sword guard in turn protects your arm. And the arm, held so, protects this whole side of your body, which again in turn protects the left, or heart side. Thus a single point of steel, Papa, functions as a shield—in fact, as a steel armor for the whole body, and from behind this steel protection, you make your lunges and your ripostes. Try it, Papa. Try it!"

"Bah!" said Dumas. "Away with your parlor fencing, where you have masks on your face and buttons on your foils, and the floor underneath is smooth as glass. That's why the best fencers in the academies go out on the grass in a real duel and lose their lives! Here! Watch me! Float! Dance! Be loose and light! Remember that you can easily pierce wood, but try and stab through a curtain that's blowing in the wind."

Alexandre's heart wept tears of blood to see his father prancing awkwardly, like a circus bear. "He's going to his death," he thought, "and I don't know how to stop it!"

"Watch my rapier! Watch my wrist!" Dumas went on. "Nimble, alive! And the arm fluttering in and out! *De l'audace, de l'audace. Toujours de l'audace!* That's what wins. Not the defensive triangle!"

Then, contemptuously, he threw away the spit, crying, "*À table*, everyone. The squabs are done. Brunswick, bring the whole marmite of rice. We're friends here. No need to serve in china. All this transfer from pot to dish often kills the flavor."

Alexandre had difficulty restraining his tears. His big Papa going so lightheartedly to his death.

"Papa," he pleaded. "As your second, permit me to arrange it so that you fight four weeks from now. And meanwhile you can put yourself in practice again."

Dumas put on arm around his son. "Your concern touches me, my boy. Touches me deeply."

"Please, Papa, don't disregard my advice. At least let me do one thing: since you are the insulted one, and it's your choice of weapons, let me choose pistols."

"Pistols? Is that really your advice?"

"Yes, because pistols, one shot each . . ."

"But you're mad!"

"No, Papa."

"Well, you must be. Don't you see that I, with my bulk, am three times the target that this spare Jacquot is? Don't you see that by giving him three times the advantage of hitting me that I have of hitting him, it is as much as if I gave my opponent three shots to my one?"

"Yes, but, Papa, I know this man. He can fence. But he can't shoot."

"Oh, come now, you're not serious. Even if he is a bad shot, don't you know that a misaimed bullet in the hands of a bad shooter can sometimes kill, while no bad swordsman ever won by luck?"

Alexandre made one more effort. "Papa, please believe me. I assure you . . ."

"He assures me," Dumas said, laughing. "But, my dear lad, don't you think that I know how to fight a duel? A thousand thunders, boy. I can't serve a dinner and have you hovering about my elbow all the time. Either help or get out of the way."

Alexandre crushed his hands in frustration and pain. He had never had such a sense of impending tragedy. While the others ate with relish, he barely nibbled at his food.

Roger de Beauvoir, sitting next to him, leaned toward him. "Don't worry about your father," he whispered. "No cat ever had a better developed faculty of always landing on his four feet than your father."

Dumas said, "Right now, my boy, if you would suggest to me a good epigram for this duel, I would be more grateful to you than for any instruction you can give me in how to hold my sword."

"Epigram?" Alexandre asked in amazement.

"Of course," said Dumas. "The best duels are always those that are accompanied by a striking epigram. Without an epigram a duel is just a duel. With an epigram it becomes a work of art. The perfect duel is one in which blood is mingled with wit."

"Sainte-Beuve's epigram was the best," said Paul Meurice.*

Everyone laughed except Alexandre, who had never heard of the Sainte-Beuve epigram. Dumas, spitting out a few squab bones to clear his mouth, explained: "The reference is to a duel on a very rainy day, when Sainte-Beuve came to the field of honor with a big umbrella held over his head. Being requested to remove the umbrella before the fight, he stubbornly refused. 'Honor,' he said, 'demands that I take my chances against a bullet, but it cannot force me to take any chances with a cold in the head.'"

"I've seen that umbrella," said Brunswick. "It has a hole in it to which Sainte-Beuve still points with pride. But it could just as well have been made by poking a finger through the cloth."

"For my part," said Paul Lacroix, "I think that Sainte-Beuve took his cue for that epigram from a duel that Benjamin Constant fought with Fortin des Issarts. Constant was too sick to stand that day. 'Is there anything in the rules,' he asked, 'that forbids me to die while comfortably seated?' So both contestants were placed in armchairs, thirty paces apart, and exchanged three bullets each. Afterward Constant was able to say, 'We would have done better to bring along an upholsterer instead of a doctor.' Now that's what I call a duel! One can talk about it afterward."

"That's so," said Maquet to Alexandre. "In our profession it is more important to get a good story out of a duel than blood. So don't postpone this thing until your father learns how to fence, but only long enough for him to provide himself with a good epigram. I assure you, it counts more in the end."

* He was the brother of the most noted goldsmith and jeweler of Paris, and perhaps for that reason Dumas' collaborator on the novel *Ascanio*, whose hero is the famous Florentine goldsmith Benvenuto Cellini. Independently he wrote other works—for example, the play *Fanfan la Tulipe*, of which there was recently a French motion picture. He became a close friend of Victor Hugo's and his literary executor.

"The best was still Cyrano's," said Dumas. "Meeting on the field of honor, neither of the opponents could remember what the quarrel was about. 'What difference?' said Cyrano. 'Since we're here, let's fight. We can always have our quarrel later.' "

All this hilarity caused Alexandre great distress. Unable to restrain himself, he burst out, "This is cruel!"

"Oh, now," said Roger, "really you underestimate your father, Alexandre."

"I would rather underestimate," he said, "than overestimate. And I tell you that my father is as unprepared as Dujarier was!"

Dumas smiled. "Please. Let's not get lugubrious. After all, I've fought many a duel. And as a matter of fact, it doesn't become you, my lad, to speak so cocksurely on a matter in which you've had less experience than any of us. All of us here have fought duels. I know you have, Roger, and you, Mallefille. And you and you. Yes, all of us. The one exception is you, my boy."

Alexandre suddenly felt himself reduced to a timid and callow youngster. And he would have left the room except for the threat of tragedy which he felt he must somehow avert.

"As for myself," Dumas went on, "I guess I've fought about as often as all of you put together."

"Just how many duels have you fought?" Roger de Beauvoir asked.

"Oh, I don't know. Let's see. There was my duel with X. You remember Baron X.—Now, wait. I might as well take this thing in order. My first duel was with a fellow who made fun of my Quiroga cloak. Stuck him through the shoulder. Then, when I was traveling in Germany with Gérard de Nerval, there was the duel at Ems. Pistols. No injury. Then the duel that grew out of my affair with Mademoiselle Bourbier. And then the duel with Maurice Alhoy of the *Figaro*, when I got a bullet in my calf."

As he spoke he ticked them off on the fingers of his hands. "Next was the duel in Italy with Fuselli. Bloodless. Then here, the duel with Gaillardet. Then the one with Adolphe Dumas . . ."

"Adolphe Dumas?" Alexandre asked somberly. "Who was he?"

"Dramatist," said Dumas. "Wrote *School for Families*. I had to warn him once too often not to use the name Dumas. 'Your name is Adolphe Dumas,' I said to him repeatedly, 'and I demand that you

never again call yourself plain Dumas.' 'I've got a right to call myself Dumas as much as I please,' he said, 'and no one can stop me,
because my name *is* Dumas.' 'No,' I said. 'All over the world when
anyone hears the name Dumas, it is of me that they think. Therefore it is tantamount to forgery for you to call yourself Dumas.
You must always specify Adolphe.' 'No,' said he, 'you must specify
Alexandre.' Well, he kept insisting, and so I had to force him to a
duel. The terms were that we would fire at each other until one or
the other consented to change his mind. After four shots, none of
which touched anyone, but of which he heard all my bullets whistling past his ears, he realized that if my patience wore out I could
shoot him through his brain. And so he relinquished the name of
Dumas to me."

"Any more?"

"Oh, I mustn't forget the duel I had in La Vendée, when I was
there on a special mission given to me by General Lafayette during
the 1830 revolution. And then the duel already mentioned, with X.
And then the duel—the time I was shot through the flesh of the
thigh. Also the duel in Marseilles when I was pierced through the
arm—here, you can see the scar. And then the duel which came
about as a result of my being one of the seconds for Saint-Auban.
We got into a dispute and the seconds challenged each other, and
immediately following the duel of the principals, we seconds each
exchanged a shot. And then ... then, let me see ... well, I guess that's
all."

He went over them again in his mind, ticking them off once more
on his hands. Suddenly he cried out in a choked voice, "God! God
save me!" He gasped and leaned back in his chair, his face, under
the lamplight, so pale that his skin had the hue of old parchment.

"Papa!" Alexandre cried.

"Give him water, quick!" said De Leuven.

Alexandre held a glass to his father's lips.

Dumas pushed it away. "I'm all right," he said, breathing out
heavily. Then he rose slowly to his feet. "Gentlemen—" he paused,
while the table, in complete silence, waited for him to speak—"may
I announce my last duel! My thirteenth. Can there be any doubt
that it means my death?"

He sank back into his chair.

Everyone began to talk at once, some taking it as a joke and others seriously, some trying to reassure him, others seeking to cajole him.

Dumas raised his hands for silence. "Please. Nothing you can say will change my destiny. A showman like myself instantly recognizes when the game is played out. *Finita la commedia!*"

"But, Papa," Alexandre pleaded, "you can't let a vulgar superstition defeat you."

Dumas gently motioned his son aside. "Forgive me for having disturbed your dinner, my friends. Let's continue as if nothing had happened. Bourgeois, pass the fruit bowl around. You can have cake with tea or coffee, as you wish."

Fiorentino said, "Are you sure you counted correctly?"

"You all saw me count twice," said Dumas. "Twelve duels I have fought so far."

"But I didn't hear you mention your duel with Janin."

Dumas smiled. "We each refused to fight with our favorite weapon. With the result that instead of fighting we embraced. That was a reconciliation, not a duel." Then he turned to the rest. "Let's not have any sorrow here. I've had a good life. The best, in fact. I've been poor and I've been rich, and thus I have had the blessings of both conditions. Born of a slave people, I've dined with kings. I would be a miserable wretch if after all these bounties I did not know how to make a proud exit."

He turned to his son. "My boy, you were insisting I should fight with pistols?"

"Especially now," Alexandre pleaded, "with this mood of yours making good swordsmanship impossible."

"Very well. It shall be your way. It was anyhow always fated that I should be dispatched by pistol shot."

"How do you mean, always fated?" Alexandre protested.

"I mean since Pushkin," said Dumas.

"Pushkin?" Alexandre asked, completely puzzled.

"Surely you know Pushkin," said Dumas impatiently. "The great Russian author."

"Yes, of course," said Alexandre.

"Did he not die in a pistol duel?"

"Yes, but what has that got to do with you?"

"Was not his name Alexandre, like mine?"

"Yes, but still . . ."

"Was he not part Negro, like myself?"

"Was he? I didn't know that."

"Yes, he was. And, moreover, boasting of a parent who was a general in the Russian army, as your grandfather was a general in the French army."

"I wasn't aware of that either."

"Yes, a general under Czar Peter, called the Great, as my father was a general under Emperor Napoleon, called the Great. Wherever you turn there are parallels. Did not both of us draw our inspiration from Shakespeare and Byron? Did we not both give our pens to the service of freedom and democracy? Did we not both of us go back into the history of our countries to inspire our readers with patriotism and love of liberty? He wrote of Eugene Onegin. I wrote of Henri III. He wrote his *Boris Godunov*, I wrote my play on Napoleon. He wrote his *Revolt of Pugachev*. I wrote my *Gaul and France*. But I have yet to mention the most tragic parallel of all."

"What, Papa?" Alexandre asked in anguish.

"Tell me, my boy, who was Anthes?"

"Anthes? I know no Anthes."

"No. Nor will anyone know this Mirecourt. But Anthes the nobody killed the genius Pushkin. And Mirecourt the nobody killed the genius Dumas. It is clear that Pushkin and I were born under the same terrible star!"

He leaned back once more in his chair and sighed heavily. "Forgive me, my friends. And please leave me. Tonight, for the first time in my life, I feel strangely tired."

"Shall I help you to bed, Papa?"

"No, my boy. Thanks. I shall be very well here. Do me only this one kindness: replace me tonight as the host. See that everyone has a comfortable place to sleep. Good night all." He lay back and closed his eyes.

Alexandre picked up a lamp in order to light the guests to their rooms. But first he bent over and kissed his father gently on the forehead. Dumas did not stir.

Alexandre's tears flowed unimpeded as he lit the way down the corridor from the kitchen and up the great staircase with its carved bannister, along the walls heavily paneled, where paintings in deep rich frames crowded each other for space, and where every corner held a pedestal with a marble or bronze statue.

Dumas' friends did their best to console Alexandre, and before they retired to their rooms, they assured him that there was no need to be worried.

"Your father," said De Leuven, "is not one to throw away his life —he enjoys it too much."

"He's too good a general," said Maquet, "not to make sure of a road for a quick retreat if necessary."

"In my opinion," said Brunswick, "Dumas is simply starring himself in a little play—of which we've seen only Act One. Before we give way to despair, let's wait for the curtain to rise on Act Two."

The men smiled and Meurice said, "Your father never could resist a dramatic situation, Alexandre."

And Lacroix added, "You'll see, there will be a nick-of-time rescue, in which Dumas, at the risk of his life, saves the life of Dumas. No need to worry."

Everybody laughed, and De Leuven clapped Alexandre warmly on the shoulder. "Of course not. Dumas is not a person, my boy. Dumas is a role. And your father must always be playing it to the hilt, frightening everyone but himself."

"Ask yourself this," said Mallefille, "do you suppose he quailed before his thirteenth mistress? Did he hesitate to write his thirteenth play? Or his thirteenth book?"

"Besides, those thirteen duels don't sit too well with me," said Fiorentino. "How is it I never heard of any German or Italian duels before?"

"Alexandre," said Meurice with a smile, "your father is so used to writing romances and plays that he keeps on writing them even when he has no pen in hand! But you can be sure of this: he has the outline of his plot in his head." This brought a general burst of laughter, during which Alexandre excused himself as decently as he could. Inside he boiled with indignation that these so-called friends and collaborators should express the very same insults that his father's enemies did: that his father's duels were invented, that he was a braggart and a sham.

How could they go to bed so calmly, after having seen his father hopelessly outclassed by Mallefille, after having seen him pale as a sheet, when he had suddenly discovered by counting that he was facing his thirteenth duel?

Acting? Was that acting?

And even if it was acting, wherein did that change the fact that no matter what course events might take, the outcome could only be tragic? For Alexandre to call for a duel with pistols was now out of the question. Not after his father had drawn the fatal parallel between Pushkin and himself. If in such a pistol duel his father lost his life, Alexandre would have to shoulder the blame of having sent his father to his death. So it must be swords! But with swords too the result must be disastrous since his father could obviously not hold his own against Mirecourt.

What then? What way out was there?

No duel at all?

But that would be disgrace. His father would be dishonored. His books would be flung into the gutter. All his previous duels would come under suspicion.

Suddenly Alexandre had the solution: he, as Dumas' son, had the right to take upon himself his father's quarrel. "Yes," he said. "You've been my father all these years; now it's my turn to be father to you. I'll fight your battles!"

This decision taken, he felt himself flooded with a great tenderness for his big Papa, whom he had seen dancing so awkwardly with the spit in hand, his big belly shaking. And sleep being impossible, he felt moved to write a poem to his father. We still have that dawn-written poem so full of respect and devotion for his father, because years later in *Le Figaro* of January 26, 1872, De Villemessant published it, and there we can read of that night and how Alexandre felt about the snide opinions that were expressed of his father. "Let others say what they will. Little I care!" he writes. And he bids his father, *"Travaille obstinément! Moi je veille à ta porte."* Meaning: "Work on obstinately. I stand guard at your door."

Then too he wrote a letter to his mother, to be sent to her only in case of his death, a letter begging her to forgive him for having neglected her.

And now he was prepared for the worst. He folded and pocketed his writing, then went down to the kitchen to see if his father was sleeping well.

To his surprise his father was not in the kitchen. But through the kitchen window he could see out in the garden a light in the kiosk where his father often worked. Alexandre ran out quickly into the garden and across the little bridge to the kiosk. Before he had opened the door and mounted the steps, he could already hear the choked cries, the groans that always accompanied his father's creative efforts.

Alexandre burst in. "Papa," he scolded (from the height of his new authority), "this is no time for you to be working. You should be in bed."

"In bed?" Dumas laughed. "With four serials waiting for installments? You know how I feel: to waste time is to commit suicide a little bit."

Yes, there he was, just as always, at his deal table, the window wide open, his shirt sleeves rolled up, his collar unbuttoned, his mop of frizzy hair wild as ever. And above him the circular ceiling he loved—painted blue, with the constellations done in gold.

"You were worried about me?" his father asked, touched.

"I couldn't sleep," said Alexandre.

"Nor could I," said Dumas, "but it was not from worrying about myself, but from worrying about my public. I kept thinking of that good man of letters who gave us a lift in his wagon. And I thought of all the other millions of people who have come to depend on me for their daily installment of something that will continue to make life worth the struggle, something that will raise their flagging spirits, instruct and amuse them at the same time. I thought of all the poor people chained for their lives to some thankless task, to whom I bring the only bit of sky they know. I thought of the sick and the afflicted, to whom each day I bring a fragment of forgetfulness. And I said to myself, Die tomorrow if you must, but meanwhile go on working. For mankind."

"Oh, but you mustn't fight tomorrow!" Alexandre cried.

"You're right, my boy. It is a grossly unfair duel, in which that wretch has the opportunity to kill a man, and I can only crush a worm. But if I refused, the world would misunderstand. They would tear me to pieces. Even your reputation would be sullied."

"I will fight him, Papa!" Alexandre cried. "Let this be my duel. My first!"

"Out of the question! The sentiment does you honor, but it would be the height of folly."

"Please, Papa . . ."

"Not another word," said Dumas. "Let me write as long as blood still flows through my veins. Take Maquet to be my other second, and go and make all arrangements."

With that he embraced his son and gently pushed him out of the room.

CHAPTER THIRTY-FIVE

"If He Can Fight for His Father, Why Can't I Fight for Mine?"

ALEXANDRE DID NOT GO to Maquet. He could already hear the latter saying, "So. Now we have Act Two." No, this was something he had to do alone. He went to his room, changed his clothes and rushed off to take the first early-morning train to the city.

Mirecourt had been true to his threat. As early as it was, already sandwich men with placards were marching along the boulevards advertising the sensational exposé in *La Silhouette*: "The Romance Factory: Alexandre Dumas and Company."

Alexandre went to find the offices of *La Silhouette* opposite the Odéon theater. He dashed in, and before anyone could oppose him, he was swinging his cane around, brushing papers and inkwells from the desks, smashing lamps and overturning chairs.

The clerks leaped out of the way of this madman, and Mirecourt, entering from an inner office, hid behind a door, holding it by the knob like a shield.

"A hundred francs if you grab him," Mirecourt shouted.

One clerk threw a carafe of water at Alexandre, and as he ducked it so that it went crashing to pieces against the wall, another clerk jumped him. Then they were swarming all about him, and in a moment two of them had his arms firmly pinioned against his back.

It was then that Mirecourt came out and faced him.

"I'm here to pick a quarrel with you!" Alexandre yelled hysterically.

Mirecourt smiled and shook his head. "My quarrel is with your father. That duel is going to be part of the exposé I'm writing. I wouldn't miss it for a gold mine."

"I'll force you to fight me!"

"In other words, the great Dumas won't fight and has sent his son instead. Is that it?"

"No! You lie! It's I who won't let him fight!"

"You'll have to let him fight. Or be disgraced!"

"No!" Alexandre cried again, and with fury he gathered saliva in his mouth and spat it at Mirecourt. Then he screamed, "There! Now you'll fight me!"

"Yes, I will," said Mirecourt. "And with the same weapon—spit at two paces." And he suited his actions to his words. "Now you've had your duel! Throw him out!" he said, wiping his face.

"I won't quit!" Alexandre shouted. "I'll find some way to make you fight!"

"One moment," said Mirecourt to the two clerks.

He stood looking at Alexandre thoughtfully. "There is one way you could get me to fight," he said. "The right insult would do it."

"Tell it to me!"

Mirecourt smiled. "All you've got to do is say that I have Negro blood in me. That is something I shall have to consider as the deadliest insult in the world!"

As if bitten by a snake, Alexandre tensed in the arms of the clerks. How diabolically clever this man was to think up this way of getting even for the insult that Dumas had proffered him the night before.

But there was no way out. "You have Negro blood in you," Alexandre muttered.

"That insult you must answer with your life!" Mirecourt shouted.

"I'm prepared. Where shall our seconds meet?"

"Send them here any time you like." He motioned to the clerks, and they roughly ushered Alexandre out of the door and into the street.

Alexandre immediately went to some former friends of his, two companions of his golden-youth days, and begged them to be his seconds. And an hour later the duel had been set for the following morning at eight, at Saint-Mandé. The weapon: swords.

Alexandre did not return home. He thought for a moment of going to his mother, but that too he rejected. He was in too great an inner turmoil. His mind raged with the desire to kill. He must extinguish this viper and stamp his heels into his dying coils. This duel must repay him for every insult he had swallowed in his life, for every defeat he had pocketed.

He sat, most of the day, in a little café drinking nothing but water and trying to calm himself.

A terrible thought had begun to gnaw at his brain: what if his father had truly never intended to fight Mirecourt? What if the scene he had played on the thirteenth-duel theme had truly been no more than Act One? And the scene in the kiosk nothing but Act Two?

He tried to reject such ideas as unworthy of himself. But in the late afternoon, as these thoughts still battered at the walls of his mind, he fled up the hill to the Montmartre cemetery. Kneeling at the grave of Marie Duplessis, he thought of her sad fate and finally found in tears a certain measure of peace.

He spent the night at a little inn unable to close his eyes and in fact only loosening his clothes and getting what rest he could in an easy chair.

In the morning he and his seconds were the first on the field. A few minutes later Mirecourt and his escort drove up.

For the sake of form a brief attempt was made at a reconciliation; then the conditions of the duel were set and the selection of swords was made from among several matched pairs.

Meanwhile, issuing evidently from the interior of the fiacre in which Mirecourt had arrived, could be heard the cries of a little boy: "Papa, Papa!"

"Pay no attention," said one of the seconds to Alexandre, "that's an old trick to soften up an opponent and disturb his fighting. Just forget he has a child. He had no right to bring him. So forget it absolutely. Do you hear me?"

"I'll forget it," said Alexandre. But his heart sank. He realized that the cry of that child had deeply affected him and drawn from him some of the desire to kill which up to this moment had animated him.

"Papa! Papa!" There it was again. Infuriating and at the same time paralyzing. Inundating him with memories of his own childhood. Of his own Papa.

Now the two contestants were brought to a little clearing in the woods, given their positions and told to wait for the signal to commence.

But just then the little boy, about eight or nine years old, came running toward his father. Pointing to Alexandre, he said, "He's fighting for his father! Why can't I fight for mine?" And suddenly wresting the rapier from his father's hand (who surrendered it far too willingly), he turned and began to thrust at Alexandre.

Alexandre's seconds tried to interfere, but they were blocked at once by Mirecourt's seconds, both men evidently chosen for their size and their ability to handle precisely this situation.

Mirecourt himself would in any case have made it three to two, had it been necessary. But as it was he had nothing to do but stand by, brushing the lock from his forehead and looking on with laughter.

As for Alexandre, he didn't even use his sword at first. The idea of using that deadly weapon against a mere lad of eight years didn't occur to him right away. He only leaped aside as the boy lunged at him again and again.

As for the lad, he was far from being a match for Alexandre, but he had obviously had some training, and his rapier was not any the less sharp, and he went at Alexandre like an angry wasp, clearly capable not only of inflicting a severe wound but even of killing.

It was this real and present danger that finally made Alexandre stop his leaps and bring his sword into play. But purely defensively.

After all, what attack can one use against a little boy? Not that Alexandre's brain wasn't awakening to the horrible possibility, the incredible disgrace of being wounded by this ragamuffin. He, the son of the great Dumas! Never would he live it down, neither in the public's eye nor in his own!

And worse still—horror of horrors—if the rascal should kill him! Why, he would rot with shame in his grave to have been done to death by such a diminutive snotnose!

And it was as if the lad was thoroughly aware of all his advantages, for he went after Alexandre with a recklessness that could only have been based upon his realization of being protected by his age.

And so Alexandre continued to fend and parry and retreat, and pray to God that he shouldn't slip or stumble, for he knew the lad would have that needle-pointed rapier through his throat or his heart before he could blink his eyes.

Indeed, as the minutes passed and the sweat poured from him, he realized more and more the masterful trap that Mirecourt had set for him, and he felt that he must at all odds escape from it before something catastrophic happened.

Suddenly he let his rapier fly out of his hand toward the boy, forcing the lad to duck, and, taking advantage of this moment, he fled through the woods to the road where his cab was. He leaped to the box, crying, "Off!"

The driver gave the horse a sharp crack of the whip and away they went, and just in time, for the boy was almost upon them and made a futile attempt to stab the horse. Clinging shamefaced to that coachman's box and hearing behind him the jeers of Mirecourt and the victorious yelps of the little boy, Alexandre felt the total magnitude of his blunder. Was not this precisely the kind of duel that his father had described as the greatest—namely, the kind you can afterward talk about because wit has been mingled with blood?

Only it was not Alexandre who had worked this trick, but Mirecourt, leaving the name of Dumas forever humbled.

He could picture Mirecourt hastening back to Paris and going from café to café, exhibiting proudly his little son who had made the big Alexandre Dumas tuck his tail between his legs and run for his life. He could picture the little boy enthusiastically describing how he had snatched the blade from his father's hand, crying, "If he can fight for his father, why can't I fight for mine?"

It would be only a matter of hours before all Paris would be laughing, and only a matter of days before the whole world joined in. And the epigram "If he can fight for his father, why can't I fight for mine?" was so perfect that it was unanswerable and blocked every possibility of getting even.

It was an absolute checkmate.

"Hah!" cried Dumas when his son brought him the fatal intelligence. "You have robbed me of a sensational revenge, my boy. A feat that would have crowded Mirecourt into a mouse hole for the rest of his life!"

"I'm sorry," said Alexandre, feeling miserable. "But it was because I was afraid of your life in a fight with Mirecourt. All I could see was how bad your swordsmanship was. And that you yourself expected a pistol shot to kill you in your thirteenth duel."

"Then it's all to your credit, my boy," said Dumas, "that you rose to my defense. But did you imagine for one moment that I, a Davy de la Pailleterie, ever seriously intended to cross swords with that canaille?"

"But you had to fight him, father," Alexandre exclaimed, flabbergasted. "You yourself challenged him to a duel. And how could I know you didn't intend to fight him when already you were calling it your fatal thirteenth duel?"

"Ah, thirteenth, thirteenth," said Dumas with impatient ferocity. "To an intelligent man no superstition is a final condemnation. It's but a goad to force him to discover a way around. What did my namesake Alexandre the Great do when he confronted the Gordian knot? Whoever wanted to conquer Asia had first to undo this knot. That was the tradition, and Alexandre couldn't undo the knot. And yet he was determined to have Asia. So he took out his sword and hacked through the knot, thus demonstrating both to himself and to the world that Asia was not to be conqured by some political sleight of hand, but by the sword! And the same way with me. My problem was how to defeat my enemy and yet not fight my thirteenth duel, which I knew must be unlucky for me. And my mind, which never yet has failed me, soon brought me the solution: model yourself upon the famous Count de Saint-Foix, it said. Like him, throw down your sword on the dueling grounds and boldly proclaim, 'I will not fight this man!'"

"But, Papa," said Alexandre, "you couldn't have done that. It would have been a disgrace!"

"Hah!" said Dumas. "Disgrace! Was it disgrace for Saint-Foix when he did it? Didn't his seconds plead with him to fight? Didn't they say, 'You will be called a coward forever'? But was he moved?

No, he was not. He said, 'Why should I fight this man who sat down next to me in the theater and whose odor was so upsetting that I had to tell him frankly, "You stink!" Where's the sense of a duel over that? If he kills me, will he stink any the less? And if I kill him, will he not stink all the more? No. No. A thousand times no! He cannot have a duel with me just to avoid taking a bath!'

"That, my boy," Dumas concluded, "was the triumphant scene with its perfect epigram that I was going to play out on the dueling grounds, both to conquer my enemy and overcome my fate, casting down my sword and refusing Mirecourt the satisfaction of evading the laws of libel by covering up his crime with a duel! What do you say now, my boy? Would that not have been brilliant? As brilliant as my defeat of Granier de Cassagnac with a pair of shears!"

Alexandre didn't know what to say. Too many thoughts were suddenly in frightful collision in his brain. All he could grasp at the moment was that he had blundered doubly—not only in engaging himself in a duel in which he had cut such a ridiculous figure, but also in being denied the consolation of feeling that he had done it for his father's sake.

"Is it too late?" was all he could think of asking, hoping somehow that one could still achieve a revenge against Mirecourt. "Shall I act as one of your seconds?"

"No," said Dumas, throwing up his hands. "A duel is now out of the question."

"But why, Papa?"

"Because I'm too angry. I tremble lest confronting that wretch I should lose control over myself and perpetrate some frightful mischief."

"Wouldn't that only be what the man deserves?" Alexandre cried. "Do you suppose that if I had stumbled in my fight with that little rat that he would have hesitated to plunge his sword into my throat?"

"Yes," said Dumas, "you are probably right. Maybe something frightful is what I must give the world. Perhaps it is for lack of it that there are people who actually accuse me of having fought fraudulent duels."

"It is!" said Alexandre. "At school I suffered from nothing so much as the teasing that went on about your duels. I used to hope that you would kill someone in a duel so that there would finally be proof that no one could doubt."

"You wanted your father to kill?" Dumas asked.

"Yes, I did. I prayed for it."

"That means that you yourself doubted me. Yes. You did!"

"No, Papa," said Alexandre. "Not really. And yet, it would have been so good to have had something that would convince everyone that you were not a fraud."

"Huh! Convince everyone. Who will ever do that? Not Christ Himself could do that. Go try to find yourself a genius to write your masterpieces. Go try! Spend a lifetime at it! And yet there are people who believe that that is what I have done fifty times or more."

"Yes, Papa."

Dumas paced his study angrily. Then he said, "You know, of course, my boy, that I must take care not to act in a rage, when I might do something which I would later have to regret?"

"Yes, Papa."

"It would sour the rest of my life and perhaps wreck my talent. But maybe someday I will have to give these wretches what they want! A corpse! Fling it into their faces!"

"Do it for my sake!" Alexandre begged impulsively, all the suppressed longings of his dreadful schooldays bursting through.

"Don't worry," said Dumas. "Someday it must happen that I shall not be able to master my fury. Someday, to protect the good name of Dumas, I shall have to give the world the corpse that it wants. Yes. I can promise it to you!"

And suddenly his mood changed. "Enough talk. To work!"

And he sat down and began to write, while Alexandre went out filled with elation at the thought that someday his father would not be able to master his fury.

But as far as Mirecourt was concerned, Dumas did not let his fury get out of hand. He had the man routinely charged with the crime of libel, and at the end of a trial Mirecourt saw himself sentenced to fifteen days in prison and to a fine of three hundred franc.

So it would seem that Dumas had won.

But it was Mirecourt who exulted. "Victory! The great duelist has been exposed. I forced Dumas to reach, not for his sword, but for the police, and thus reveal his true character to the world!" As for his sentence to prison, Mirecourt considered it a cheap price to pay for the right to occupy the center of attention in Paris. Moreover, the success of his exposé of Dumas caused him to look around for new worlds to conquer. For the next quarter of a century he made himself a lucrative business of undressing all the prominent men and women of France and indeed of Europe. "Contempory History," he called his series of pamphlets that ran eventually into the hundreds. Until one of his hireling writers one day exposed him for precisely the practice he had accused Dumas of: commercial literature. He retired to a monastery, where he died.

CHAPTER THIRTY-SIX

The Secret That Must Be Kept Inviolate

IT WAS PERHAPS Alexandre who was the chief victim of the Mirecourt affair. From this time on he began to feel so uncomfortable in the presence of his father, so full of unuttered and unutterable questions and reproaches, that he invented a good pretext and moved back to Paris. Meanwhile everything had foundered around him. The last vestiges of his golden-youth era were gone for good. He rented a cheap room and buckled down to earning his living as a writer.

He suffered. His sensitivity was out of all proportion. Even children obstructing the sidewalk with their wooden sword play would cause him a momentary feeling that it was all staged expressly as an insult against him. He knew it wasn't so, but he cringed nevertheless. He had to avoid even his closest friends. Their most innocent expressions seemed to him charged with mockery, and their most commonplace observations to be full of concealed scorn.

Day and night he sat in his room and wrote. Or tried to write. And again and again he had to do over a page because tears of anger and self-pity had made words illegible.

As for Dumas, he sailed on as if absolutely nothing had happened.

"Oh, I'm finished," Dumas often admitted. "I know that. No self-respecting critic will have anything to do with me. Which leaves me in the sad predicament of having to write exclusively for the reading public.

"Posterity, or at least so I'm told by those who apparently know posterity intimately, has already crossed out my name. Which, you see, forces me to count only on my contemporaries, who, however, pay cash for my books, a habit which posterity has yet to acquire.

"As for my plays, Paris refuses to see anything in them except an evening's amusement, which is disgraceful and crassly lucrative. And as for my serials, no newspaper will print them now, except for strictly business reasons—that is to say, to increase circulation, a vice to which journalism is generally addicted.

"Worst of all, my lifelong ambition to be elected to the forty immortals of the French Academy is absolutely done for. I'm as excluded as if my name were Molière, or Descartes, or Pascal, or Rousseau, or Beaumarchais, or Diderot, or Stendhal, or Balzac. . . .

"Never will my name be seen among such immortals as Féletz, Jay, Pongerville and the rest.

"Ah, to think that I shall never be entitled to wear this uniform. Look at all that silver-thread embroidery. And the hat! Oh, what a magnificent plume! Ambassadorial, isn't it?"

"What," he was asked, "you own the uniform of an organization to which you can never hope to belong?"

"Where's the harm?" Dumas asked. "I was at the funeral of Casimir Delavigne and went over in my mind who could possibly take his seat, and, being then still in the unexposed stage of my fraudulence, it seemed to me that in all France no one deserved it so much as myself. So right after the speeches at the grave I ran straight from the cemetery to my tailor and had him make me this uniform. Beautiful, isn't it? But getting a little worn."

"You mean you actually wear it? And so often that it shows signs of use?"

"Yes, on rainy days," said Dumas, "when my mood is somber and I go to the kitchen to fry myself up some *pets de none,** I like to pretend that I too am an immortal. It cheers me up!"

You see, still the incurable clown!

* Untranslatable as such, but signifying apple fritters.

And of course the women still came and went, taking away such gifts as a queen might envy and leaving Dumas with new debts to add to his old ones.

His continued popularity with the fair sex was thus explained by Dumas: "Thank God, I've only been exposed as a writer and a duelist. By now everyone has heard about my collaborators, but somehow the women still labor under their old impression that when it comes to love I dispense with assistants and that the signature of Dumas is absolutely genuine."

No, it was not Dumas who suffered from the Mirecourt fiasco. It was Alexandre.

It was really a bad time for young writers who still had their mark to make.

Indeed, it was a bad time for almost everyone. It was that mid-century period, when, as Victor Hugo described it in his notebooks, the despair of the rich equaled, if indeed it did not surpass, the despair of the poor. The rich showed their frantic efforts to over-come their despair by organizing endless balls. The poor showed despair by equally frantic efforts to erect barricades. On one night, that of February 24, 1848, for example, the police counted 1,574 fresh barricades, raised by militant workers in a futile effort to keep the authorities from swooping down on their little political clubs.

The world thus had the spectacle of two objects occupying the same space: a rich nation and a poor nation, like husband and wife who must live with each other and can't and dream only of either murdering or else enslaving each other.

France, which so often had found a rebirth of its glory and en-thusiasm in bleeding itself, was about to try the old remedy again. And it was to a song written by Dumas for one of his plays, *Mourir pour la Patrie* (To Die for the Fatherland), that the crowds of im-patient people finally surged upon the royal palace and sacked it.

The King, already stricken with the fatal illness that was soon to carry him off, ran away with the Queen, first stuffing his pockets with whatever bank notes he could find and filling two big sacks with gold coin, securities and jewelry. As the couple drove off to England, the King said to the Queen, "I've never seen you look so old."

In Paris the police had to take over empty warehouses for space to lay out the bodies of the dead. And for days mothers and wives came here searching for their loved ones.

Then Louis Napoleon, later Emperor Napoleon III, became President of France.

And one day Victor Hugo noted: "Poor Europe. Consider what the most important brains of this continent are busy with at the present moment. Louis Napoleon is playing hot cockles with Miss Howard, the pretty English girl. And the Pope is busy writing a book on the Immaculate Conception. Obviously all our problems will soon be solved."

Dumas' brain was also busy. He was publishing a political magazine. He was running for office. He was speaking everywhere. And he was fighting. Or at any rate, going about armed with enough weapons to equip a brigade. For all that, he never stopped his serials or his succession of new plays. And in addition he continued to manage his theater, the Théâtre Historique, where he had scheduled an early performance of his son's dramatization of *The Lady of the Camellias.*

But these were bad days for the theater too.

On evenings when rifle fire could be heard crackling here or there in the distance, people did not go out much.

One evening, for example, a single spectator showed up. Dumas went to the apron and announced that, due to conditions that were only too obvious, there would be no show. If the gentleman would kindly go to the box office, he would get his money returned.

"But there must be a performance, Monsieur Dumas," said the sole customer.

"But since we tell you that we are canceling—"

"Yes, I know," said the gentleman, "but I happen to be a lawyer, and as such may I point out to you that this ticket stub that I hold is in the nature of a sales contract. I have done my share by paying out my money. Now you must do your share. Otherwise I shall sue."

A suit? No, this theater couldn't stand another one. The management owed everyone money. Even the charwomen had to be content with a fraction of their pay.

So the play went on.

And was the lone spectator pleased? He was not. No matter how the actors tried, they could not wring from this man a single sign of approval. On the contrary, he hooted the performance.

Finally Dumas went outside and found a policeman.

"We have a spectator who is whistling," Dumas said.

"Ah, my dear Monsieur Dumas," said the policeman, "that is not forbidden. Unless it is really serious."

"It is so serious," said Dumas, "that not another spectator in the house can hear what is being said on the stage."

"That's another matter," said the policeman, "I shall have to run him in."

Thus the lawyer went to the guardhouse, and the actors got a chance to go home early. But at this rate it wasn't long before the theater had to close its doors and the property had to be surrendered to the creditors. The company scattered to find whatever employment it could. Anything to put food in one's mouth in these difficult days.

Dumas, who took a personal loss of over half a million francs, which he had invested in the theater, nevertheless was as cheerful as ever.

"You take it very lightly," said Alexandre, admiring his father in spite of himself.

"Oh, I know that it deserves serious consideration," said Dumas, "but I just don't have the time to give to it."

It was again Alexandre who suffered most: that failure canceled the scheduled performance of his *Lady of the Camellias*. Now he had to go and peddle his play, like any other playwright.

One day as he was returning from an unsuccessful reading and, in his growing melancholia, anxious only to be unobserved, he passed a bookstore whose whole window was given over to a display of the works of Dumas. Alexandre couldn't help but stop and stare at his father's vast output. And that big question, that question that he had so often forced aside as unworthy, now compelled itself to his attention: how could any one man have produced these yards and yards of books? His mind rang again with the shrill voice of Mirecourt, saying, "In one year you wrote more than the most industrious secretary could manage to copy, let alone create!"

Could one argue with that? Could one really? Didn't that seem to clinch it? Didn't that prove fraud without a doubt?

This sort of thinking was extremely painful, for in destroying his father Alexandre felt that he was destroying himself, and yet somehow he couldn't stop. Of course he knew that his father purchased some help in his writing. He knew that he bought books that had failed to come off and somehow managed to rewrite them into successes. He knew too that he relied a great deal on old chronicles and on memoirs.

But, even so, to publish in one year more than the hand of man could set down on paper in that one year, let alone create out of his imagination, how was this possible?

Alexandre thought of his own Byzantine novel and all the work he had done on that—and in vain. How could so much be written so fast? And yet his father certainly showed no sense of guilt. In the most unashamed way he boasted that in one particular year "I published more than all the forty immortals of the Academy put together."

A host of anecdotes that circulated in Paris had managed to dig themselves into Alexandre's brain even though he had always instantly rejected them as spurious. For example, the story of a man who had said to Dumas, "I found a terrible blunder in your novel *God Disposes*."

"Ho-ho!" cried Dumas. "I'm glad you called that to my attention. Xavier de Montépin did that one for me. I shall have to box his ears properly."

"I'm amazed you let such an error pass your scrutiny," said the man.

"Scrutiny? Do you think I have time to read all I publish?" Dumas asked, roaring at his own wit.

As Alexandre stood thus lost in his distasteful thoughts, a dwarfish, chubby-cheeked young man, with olive complexion and kinky hair, ran up to him and sought to embrace him. When Alexandre resisted, he began to make such gestures as deaf and dumb people make, displaying big toothy smiles of love, while repeatedly first pointing to Alexandre, then digging a thumb backward into himself and finally gesturing to the display of books.

Alexandre made the mistake of pretending to be unable to understand what was, after all, crystal clear—namely, that this dwarfish creature was claiming kinship with him on the grounds that he too was the son of the great and prolific writer Dumas. Thus, instead of releasing himself quickly from an embarrassing situation, Alexandre gave the dwarf the opportunity of extending his gestures and capering around Alexandre in such a way that escape finally became impossible.

People began to stop to watch this dumb show. And Alexandre could sense their amazed and amused expressions as they caught on to the tragi-comedy unfolding before their eyes. It was now more difficult than ever to call a halt, since the implication would be that a handsome offspring of Dumas was refusing to a less favored offspring the acknowledgment of an obvious kinship.

And Alexandre, sweating at thus being exposed before the world, not only as the son of a father who carelessly authored bastard books, but also as the son of a man who just as carelessly authored bastard children, indeed children so numerous that they did not even know each other (as his books were so numerous that he did not even read them), Alexandre had the feeling of being trapped in a kind of parody of the Mirecourt duel. In the end he grabbed the dwarf's hand, shook it warmly and then suddenly bolted through the spectators, with a horrible *déjà vu* sense of repeating his dash for the cab in that ridiculous duel.

Thereafter he did his best to stay off the streets of Paris, quailing in advance at the thought of whom he might meet next. He had, of course, often heard about his father's supposed hundreds of children scattered all over the map. But against all such rumors he had hitherto been able to shut his mind. These other bastards were mere shadows, insubstantial and distant, compared to himself and to his half-sister Marie-Alexandrine, who were the only ones who had been legitimized.

Actually, what proof did he have that this deaf and dumb man was not an imposter? Perhaps some half-wit whose only solace was to imagine himself the son of Dumas? And yet, from this moment on, Alexandre had the skin-crawling feeling of being surrounded by unknown brothers and sisters, and sometimes, seeing ahead of himself a blind man or a cripple, or a nodding hydrocephalic, and catching a glimpse of dark complexion or frizzy hair, he would cross the street to avoid an encounter.

The question of his bastardy, which he imagined he had long

ago put behind him, now once more obsessed him, and for that reason he could not but suppose that it was also obsessing others.

A new gruffness designed to forestall any contemplated slights on his parentage began to intrude in his manner. He became cold, sharp, belligerent. And this put a strain especially on his female friends so that he was soon down to a single companion of the opposite sex. And even this friendship soon broke, when Alexandre began to irritate her with questions designed to discover, without asking her outright, if she had ever had an affair with his father.

After an angry interview that ended in tears, Alexandre decided he had had enough of people. They were nothing but fiends in disguise. From now on he wanted solitude.

Not that he was alone in his solitude. His father's image still pursued him, looming in every direction like a Colossus of Rhodes.

His life became an endless, harsh inner dialogue between himself and his father. Day and night, wherever he might be, he found himself wrestling with this brazen giant who laughed at him, mocked him, overwhelmed him with crushing arguments.

"Get out of my life!" Alexandre would find himself screaming inside of himself. "Isn't it enough that you separated me from my mother, that you took me from school before I was finished, that you are leaving me now saddled with debts?"

"Ha-ha! So I ruined your life, did I, my boy? What about those all-night games of cards and dice? When did you ever see me doing that?"

"It was because you started out by debauching me!" Alexandre cried.

"Ah, yes," said his father. "No doubt about that. You would never have craved debauchery without me, would you?" And he laughed as if he knew Alexandre's darkest secret: the obscene drawings of his mother made by his schoolmates, drawings which had fascinated him in spite of himself.

"You abandoned my mother!" Alexandre shouted in retort.

"Look who's lecturing me on abandoning his mother!" the giant laughed.

And Alexandre would be forced to recall with hot shame his own endless abandonments of his mother, Sunday after Sunday keeping her waiting in that angle of the wall, while he dawdled, knowing very well that he was breaking her heart, but nevertheless unwilling to give up all hope for his father's appearance.

"It's because you blinded me with your glitter!" Alexandre cried out in self-defense. "Yes! You dazzled me! How could I know how false you were! That nothing was true about you! Nothing! Not your name, and not your books! Not your love and not your duels!"

At such moments he felt that it was lucky for him that his father was not there, or he would have attacked him physically. His hands itched to grapple with him. Even to the tomb of Marie, his father's image pursued him. He could not help but remember that it was his father who had first urged Marie on him as his mistress. And when he had objected that she might be expensive, his father had insisted, saying, "The world of beauty is free to artists and poets." That had not meant anything in particular to him then, but later, when his father had read his book and had wept, saying, "Still, she was fortunate in having been loved by two writers," and had generously allowed that his son might be the other writer, he had begun to see that even here his father had preceded him.

Was there nothing in the world that that man had not sullied! And this was the great Republican who was now going around prating of liberty and democracy and other high ideals, as if he knew how human beings should be governed, he who had certainly never been able to govern his own impulses.

What a *fanfaron*!

As for himself, Alexandre cared nothing about finding a better government. The political ferment of the times left him indifferent. Surely if man were prepared in his heart for a better government he would have found it long ago in all the thousands of changes of government that history has produced at the cost of so much blood.

Thus torn by hate for his father and remorse over his behavior toward his mother, Alexandre took one day the road to her apartment.

It had been so long since he had knocked there that he hesitated in embarrassment. But his mother greeted him as usual. "Well, well, a stranger," she said, in her dry, mocking voice.

That stopped him, and he stood on the threshold while tears came to his eyes. "*Maman*," he explained, "I want to stay here and live with you."

She took him in her arms. "Is that something to cry about?" she asked. "Did you imagine I'd say no?"

Though his mother never asked him what had brought him, and though she did her best to make him comfortable in her poor quarters, Alexandre was not happy. It was another complaint that he voiced against the giant: "You made me despise poverty and now you have left me without a cent!"

He tried to concentrate on his work, but the neighborhood swarmed with noisy children. Animals brought smells and flies. And he found himself constantly comparing the luxury of his father's life with the penury of his mother's.

Once he spoke to her about Monte Cristo, his father's estate. "Have you ever seen it?" he asked.

"I've heard about it," she said.

"But have you ever seen it?" he asked again.

"No! No!" she said sharply. "Why should I?"

"There's room enough there for a dozen families like us," he said.

"Then what are you doing here?" she asked. "You're free to go."

He said nothing further. But his mood grew ever more somber while his inner fury flared up higher.

His condition was not helped by his continued lack of success with his play. He had humbled himself and gone to the actress Rachel to beg that proud woman to let him read his play to her, thinking that with her in the lead production would be automatic, and censorship difficulties would be erased.

She consented and set aside an evening for him. But when he arrived at her house at the specified time he did not find her at home. He was told that she had gone out to play lotto. He felt certain that he had been handed this slap only because his name was Dumas. He was being included in her disapproval of his father, which was notorious.

At one theater his play was handed back with the comment that it too closely resembled *Manon Lescaut*. At another theater he was told that his play was too much like Murger's *La Vie de Bohème*. Alexandre sensed two rather unsubtle accusations of plagiarism and was convinced that he owed them entirely to the reputation of his father.

At still another theater he was told that he could pick up his manuscript at the concierge's lodge. There he discovered that the concierge had been using it to protect her tablecloth from hot pots, with the result that the outer leaves were scorched and that splashes of grease had penetrated through the whole script.

When Alexandre, heartsick at the necessity of recopying his play, ventured to protest the careless handling, the concierge flew at him. "Pooh! A little grease. So take another play!" And she shoved plays at him by the dozen. "We have so many plays here that we use them for anything we like. Go on, you're lucky you had only grease on yours!"

Alexandre realized that in the campaign against Dumas, since his father still enjoyed a popularity that nothing seemed able to shake, people somehow found it easier—and safer—to vent their feelings against his son. Hadn't his schoolmates done exactly that years ago? He was still and forever Jocko the monkey.

At such times Alexandre's rage would threaten to burst out in some kind of violence. His hands ached to grab, to crush, to snap or choke. And for lack of anything else, he would pick up a stick of wood and destroy it.

God help him, he sometimes thought, should he at such a peak of inner rage happen suddenly upon his father. Extreme violence must result. He had many years of suffering to pay back.

One gray day in December, when a thin powder of snow went stinging around the corners of the streets, Alexandre was walking along, immersed as usual in his battle with his father and breaking a twig in his hands in order to dissipate his rage, when suddenly he was aware of his father's two-wheeled, open-air britska, a smart new wickerwork trap, bearing down on him.

Dumas, hatless and coatless, standing up like a Roman, was driving his bay directly at him, horse and driver breathing great plumes of fog into the cold air, both man and beast superbly defiant of the winter, while the little Negro servant Alexis huddled shivering under the heavy woolen horse blanket.

Dumas brought his horse to a rearing stop. "Hop in, my boy," he cried. "Where have you been keeping yourself during these terrible days?"

It was, as a matter of fact, just a week or so after the *coup d'état*, when Napoleon seized power in France and had his soldiery create riots in the city and shoot down innocent people to give the world the impression of a strong man's taking hold of things in order to suppress a dangerous conspiracy threatening chaos in the very heart of Europe.

Alexandre found himself surreptitiously brushing away the bits of twig from his hands and meekly, quickly, getting into the basket, where Alexis moved aside to make room for him.

"You look pale," said Dumas. "You haven't been ill, have you?"

"No, Papa."

"Good. Then, listen: I have important news for you." He lowered his voice. "I'm fleeing to Brussels! Tomorrow! Early in the morning."

"What?" Alexandre exclaimed. "Are you on the proscribed list?"

"Before I explain, will you promise to keep what I am about to tell you as an absolute and inviolate secret? Promise?"

"Certainly, Papa."

"Well, then, the terrible truth is that I'm fleeing, not from the police, but from my creditors, who have already stripped my house of all its furnishings and who are about to sell me out completely—this very horse and this carryall too. Everything, everything must go under the hammer and be knocked down to the highest bidder. Everything, that is, except my books and a very few pieces of my art collection. And even that sacrifice will not satisfy my creditors! They want more."

He put his hand on his son's shoulder. "I trust now that my frightful secret is safe with you."

"What frightful secret?" Alexandre asked.

"*Parbleu*, my boy!" Dumas shouted. "Have you, or have you not, been listening to me?"

"Why, yes, Papa, but I still don't see what the frightful secret is."

"Why, what's the matter with you? Have you no imagination? Don't you see what effect will be created in the newspapers of the world when it is reported that the great Victor Hugo is being hunted down by Napoleon's soldiers armed with guns and instructions to kill on sight, while the great Alexandre Dumas is being hunted down by bailiffs armed with nothing more dangerous than overdue promissory notes and with instructions not to kill him but just to search his pockets for concealed cash? What! Would you have your father appear before the eyes of the world as any less heroic than Victor Hugo? Is it my fault that after all my anti-Napoleonic tirades Napoleon still insists on thinking of me as his friend? Ha! Coming so soon after the Mirecourt affair, this bad publicity would be hard to take. Well, are you clear now?"

"Yes, Papa."

"Good boy. Then you'll be coming out tonight to a last celebration at Monte Cristo? The keys must be surrendered by me at dawn. So I'm inviting all my friends—such as still remain faithful to me— and you may bring any friends you like, too, and we shall eat up whatever food is still around, drink up whatever wines still remain in the cellar and shoot off whatever fireworks are still in my storehouse."

"Yes, Papa."

"Remember, costumes and masks are required. You understand why? Who knows but that even Victor Hugo or Schoelcher * may come. And you can realize that with rewards of twenty-five thousand francs offered for the heads of the people on the list, my house will be swarming with would-be informers and secret police. So tell me what you'll be wearing. I want to be able to recognize you."

"Why . . . I don't know yet, Papa."

"Well, you'll always be able to recognize me. I'll be wearing my usual Musketeer costume. So just come up and make yourself known to me."

"Yes, Papa."

"Good. Kiss me, my son, and see you tonight. There. Now be off with you, my lad, I've got a million things to do. Oh, by the way, before I forget, you don't happen to have a couple of hundred francs on you?"

"No, Papa."

"Well, fifty, then?"

"Not even five, Papa."

"Ah, well. Too bad. I must somehow manage to secure an orchestra for tonight. But, no matter. I'll manage. See you later."

And he snapped his whip and was off, leaving Alexandre on the sidewalk raging against himself.

* Victor Schoelcher was France's great antislavery man.

Dazzled again, that's what had happened! Why, there the man had been—right in his hands, so to speak. And perpetrating still another one of his frauds. Pretending to be politically important! Pretending to be under sentence of death!

And what had he, Alexandre, done? Nothing! Just exactly nothing. Hadn't said so much as a word. Not a word. Not so much as an inflection of his voice just to let the man know that he wasn't taken in any longer. And now he'd be off to Brussels. And out of reach!

So furious was Alexandre with himself that he could not help but talk about it to his mother. "What kind of a simpering coward am I, anyway?" he cried. "There he was calmly figuring out still another way of deceiving people. And asking me to keep his secret. His inviolate secret! The hero! Ha! Always, always, he must be the great hero. No matter how many lies it takes.

"And what was a I doing? I was saying *Yes, Papa,* and *Of course, Papa* and *Certainly, Papa* all over the place.

"Just think! I had him there red-handed. Good God, what better chance did I want than finally to be able to cry out, You cheat! You! You cheat! Always cheating someone. Your public. Your bankers. Your women. My mother! Me!

"But no. I'm too much like him for that. I'm too much of a coward! Break twigs. Yes, that I can do. But confront him? Confront him with the truth? No. For that I'm as afraid as he is when it comes to a real duel.

"Now that he's lost his money what have I got from him? Nothing but his cowardice. That's my inheritance. Cowardice and frizzy hair. And debts I'll never be able to pay!"

In his blind anger, Alexandre didn't notice his mother's hand until it had landed flat, hard and stinging on his cheek.

"Stop it!" she yelled.

Frozen with amazement, he stared at her.

"Yes," she shouted at him. "I'm telling you to stop. You can't talk about your father that way. Not in front of me!"

For a moment they just faced each other, panting like animals. "You?" Alexandre cried out at last. "You're defending him? Didn't he destroy your life just as he's destroyed mine? What have you got out of all his fame and his money except this pigsty?"

"I'll tell you what I've got! The memory of a great man who

once loved me. That's what I've got. And I'm not going to let you spoil that for me."

"Great man!" He sneered. "Great skirt-chaser! Great dazzler! Great nothing!"

"I forbid you to say such things!" she screamed.

"I've heard you say as much yourself," he retorted.

"That's my business. But I won't allow others to say it. Not in my presence. And especially not you. If I've got nothing but this pigsty it's not because of him—but because of *you*. Show me *your* great books! Show me *your* great plays! Why, when he was as old as you he was known all over—from one end of the world to the other! Who knows you? Who? Answer me!"

She stopped, her voice choked off by her anger and by her tears.

The very sound of her sobs twisted his heart as if it had been caught in a machine. He reached out a hand to console her. But she pushed him away. "Let me be!"

He got up and ran out. Because suddenly he knew exactly what he wanted to do. He wasn't going to be dazzled any longer.

CHAPTER THIRTY-SEVEN

Duel after the Masquerade Ball

ALEXANDRE HAD BEEN to Babin's establishment many times. There wasn't a larger costume place in Paris, and the proprietor knew him well and would surely trust him for a couple of suits.

"What I need this time is something that will even disguise my voice," Alexandre said to him, doing his best to appear calm, although his head felt as if on fire.

"Oh, any mask that covers the mouth will muffle the voice enough to alter its effect," said Babin. "You'd be surprised how little it takes to make a voice unrecognizable. Take, for example, this domino—the kind we call a wolf's beard, with lace that falls over the chin. . . ."

"But I must be doubly sure," said Alexandre. "Absolutely sure."

"Then perhaps you want a costume like this," said Babin, taking a Man in the Iron Mask outfit off the rack. "This is specially designed to defy anyone to guess who you are. Inside this helmet is a metal mouthpiece that you grip between your teeth, and that mouthpiece is like a reed. There isn't a chance of your voice giving you away."

"Yes," Alexandre repeated thoughtfully, ". . . defy anyone to guess who you are. That's precisely what I want. Is that helmet heavy?"

"Heavy? Just cloth pasted over stiff paper and painted to look like iron. The stockinet hood that goes over the back of the head holds it on securely."

"And you have my size?"

"In carnival season I wouldn't be sure, but right now we have everything."

"And a sword to go with it? A dueling blade?"

"A sword? No, the Man in the Iron Mask was a prisoner. He didn't wear a sword."

"But that's what I want. A real dueling weapon."

"Oh, we have plenty of real swords, when it comes to that. But you understand that you can't carry a weapon when your face is masked. That's against police regulations."

"I understand that," said Alexandre impatiently. "And now I want still another costume. A Pierrot outfit. For a friend. Who is even a little bigger than I am."

In the standard biographies of Dumas, of which A. Craig Bell's recent study (London, 1950) ranks as the best, this final night at Monte Cristo is sometimes referred to as the night of the prunes because Dumas, when he emptied his larder for his guests, found mostly prunes and, serving them, remarked, "Enjoy them, my friends, for you are eating the last of one million francs!"

To Alexandre, when he entered, dressed as Pierrot, the whole spectacle of that last evening was revolting, emphasizing again the kind of useless and ugly orgy that had dissipated the wealth he might have expected to inherit from his father. The drawing room, the billiard room and the dining room of the first floor—rooms that he remembered so well as warm and friendly places, glowing like baroque jewels—were now stripped to their walls and lit only from the fireplaces and from some few candles guttering in bottles placed here and there on window sills or mantelpiece. And in this half-light, a mass of champagne-drunk guests cavorted and shouted, beating each other with inflated pig bladders, while a remnant of Dumas' zoo, brought indoors against the cold, huddled frightened in the corners: monkeys and dogs and macaws and Dumas' famous pet vulture Jugurtha, which had cost him fifty thousand francs to bring back from his African trip.

Three incompetent gypsy musicians screeched away on their instruments, while a Madame de Pompadour in the arms of a gorilla and an Egyptian cat goddess in the arms of a decapitated aristocrat, his guillotined head in the crook of one arm, danced around with some seventy other equally fantastic disguises.

On the naked walls where once had hung the paintings of Boulanger and Delacroix, a drunken artist had just finished scrawling in chalk reproductions of some of the more obscene murals of Pompey.

Dumas, in his Musketeer costume, an old tablecloth passed around his belly and tied in the back, was just bringing in some big pots of steaming food, assisted by a Praying Mantis and a gentleman with a bloody ax buried in his false skull. Alexandre raised his domino and made himself known to his father.

"Welcome, my boy!" Dumas cried as he and his helpers, for lack of a table, placed their pots on the floors. "Be the first to sample our cooking."

"Beware!" groaned the Praying Mantis. "It's the great gunpowder plot all over again! Your father has cooked for us nothing but beans and prunes. We're all to be blown up tonight!"

"He is determined that we shall give him a twenty-one-gun salute for his departure from Monte Cristo," said the man with the ax in his head.

"Beans and prunes is all I found in the pantry," Dumas protested. "So that's what we're having. Why not make the best of the occasion and reorganize the society of the *franc-petteurs*! * Come, Alexandre, you and I shall be the charter members and perform a duet."

* A mythical eighteenth-century society, supposedly organized to bring about an utterly natural and shameless mode of living, as the name well indicates.

The crowds of guests, and the animals too, attracted by the odor of food, swarmed about the pots and enabled Alexandre to escape. Slipping unobserved out of a side door, he ran through the dark cold garden to a tool shed behind the empty monkey house. Here he had already hidden the rest of his disguise as well as his street clothes. Despite the almost total darkness, he managed to divest himself quickly of his Pierrot costume. Underneath he already wore the major part of his prisoner's garb. All he had to do was pull the iron mask over his talcum-powdered Pierrot face and then belt on his sword.

When Alexandre returned to the house, the meal was already well under way. For lack of dishes and cutlery, guests were eating from champagne glasses with their fingers. They weren't long in discovering the fun of flipping prune pits at each other. The air was soon full of flying missiles, and in no time the floor was so slippery with them that the guests were tumbling over each other in Babylonian sportiveness.

Suddenly Dumas roared, "I'm forgetting the fireworks! Alexis, go around and put out all the candles. We want as much darkness as possible. And bring us the two bull's-eye lanterns from the kitchen." Dumas flung open the doors and ran down the stone staircase to the grass below, where boxes of rockets and Roman candles lay covered with a sailcloth. Near by was the stand from which they were to be fired.

Dumas was followed by many of the guests, but the cutting wind, whipping up the fine, powdery snow, drove most of them back toward the house, where they collected on the terrace or inside at windows. Only some half dozen or so remained below with Dumas, including the Praying Mantis and the man with the ax in his skull.

And also a stranger in an iron mask.

Now! said Alexandre to himself. But for a moment he was too overcome by his own daring, too shaken by the step he proposed to take, to make the attempt.

Alexis came up with the bull's-eye lanterns, and Dumas, opening one of them, began by lighting up a Roman candle and leaping with childish glee as the colored balls shot out into the dark sky, red and green and orange lights succeeding each other.

It must be now. Now! Alexandre said to himself. Now or never. But the thought of challenging his father, the thought of forcing him to a choice here, before all these witnesses, before all the people at the windows, a choice between fighting and dying, or not fighting and being disgraced, that thought whipped his blood to a froth.

And it was not until the Roman candle sputtered to a finish that Alexandre approached Dumas and, reaching beneath the tablecloth apron, half pulled his father's sword from its scabbard.

Dumas turned to the Iron Mask with a wondering smile.

Gripping his mouthpiece between his teeth, Alexandre said, "I just wanted to see if your blade was made of wood."

"Of wood?" Dumas asked.

"Just whether it was a toy or the real thing."

"Well, now you know," said Dumas, still smiling.

"Yes," said the Iron Mask. "The sword is real. But so is your apron. The only question that remains is what about the man who wears them both? Sword or apron. Which are you really?"

Dumas' smile froze. He handed a rocket which he had just picked up to the Praying Mantis. "*Who* are you?" he asked the Iron Mask.

"You wouldn't know," said Alexandre.

"I might," said Dumas. "You wouldn't be wearing a mask that disguises your voice if you didn't think I might recognize it."

Alexandre trembled. "You should know who the Iron Mask is," he said. "You wrote a book about him, didn't you? You made me the secret twin brother of Louis XIV. Which was an idea that you stole from Voltaire. Wasn't it?"

The Praying Mantis had just fired off the rocket, which, sailing up into the dark sky, let out a spray of red and white stars that exploded like musketry as they fell.

From the house and the stone terrace came an "Ah!" of admiration.

"Yes," said Dumas quietly, his eyes attracted to the display rather than to the Iron Mask, "I did adopt Voltaire's theory for my novel. It was an orphan idea worthy of better—"

"Always adopting orphans," said the Iron Mask. "You adopt

quite a few of them, don't you? You adopted your *Paul Jones* from Fenimore Cooper's orphan book *The Pilot*. You adopted—"

Dumas reacted violently. "*Mille bombes!*" he thundered. "I trust you are joking. But I call it a very poor sense of humor."

"If that's the way you wish to look at it," said the Iron Mask, "that's fine. I'll go right on insulting you, and you can go right on criticizing my sense of humor."

"Now I know who you are!" Dumas exclaimed. "One of Napoleon's *mouchards*, sent here to provoke a riot!"

"But obviously unable to provoke it," the Iron Mask retorted.

Dumas pushed back his apron and tore at the hilt of his sword. But he did not bare his weapon. He paused, changing his mind, and let the blade slide back. "You're right. And I'm not going to let myself be provoked. Not this evening, when I have eighty guests to entertain."

"Now you are criticizing my timing," the Iron Mask said. "Are you aware that that makes your third excuse not to draw your sword? What will your fourth excuse be?"

Dumas clenched his fists. "You are really determined to enrage me," he said.

"And you," said the Iron Mask, "are just as determined to swallow any insult."

Another rocket had sailed into the sky. Watching it, Dumas said, "In the face of such beauty, it will be difficult to rouse my anger."

"In fact it will be impossible," said the Iron Mask. "How many have tried before me and failed—Granier de Cassagnac, Mirecourt . . ."

"O-ho!" said Dumas. "So that's the quarter from which the wind blows! Ah, if only I didn't have to take the train so early tomorrow morning, you'd have exactly what you're looking for, my friend."

"The trains run on schedule! Excuse number four!" cried the Iron Mask triumphantly. He was feeling wonderful now. Exhilarated. Gone forever was the burden of groveling before his father as before a demigod. He was free!

"I've kept you too long from your firecrackers," he said to his father. "You'll forgive me, I hope."

"Certainly," said Dumas with a smile. "And now that you know there will be no fight, you may retire and relieve yourself of that coat of mail."

"What?" Alexandre exclaimed. "You accuse me of wearing a coat of mail?"

"It gives one courage," said Dumas, "to provoke a duel when bare skin must fight steel."

"Excuse number five!" Alexandre cried, incensed by his father's suspicion. "I'll be glad to furnish proof to your seconds that my skin is as unprotected as yours!"

"Then take off your mask!" Dumas cried.

Alexandre leaped back a step and drew his sword. "You take it off! That is, if you can and dare!"

The Praying Mantis and the others stopped their activity and stood around watching. As the last rocket faded, the darkness was accentuated.

The veins on Dumas' forehead had swollen like puff adders. "Beware," he said in a hoarse voice. "Don't go too far. I *can* be provoked."

The Iron Mask laughed. "That will be news to a lot of people all around the world."

Dumas stood there, panting, rubbing his hands together nervously. More and more people were coming out on the terrace above to follow this altercation. Others were watching from indoors.

Dumas relaxed. He blew out air. "This is all so ridiculous. We aren't even equipped to fight a duel."

"Why? Don't we both have swords?"

"Yes, but the Dueling Code forbids a duel with weapons with which we may be familiar."

"So now it's the fault of the Dueling Code," Alexandre said, laughing. "You can find excuses for not fighting faster than I can count them. Very well, then let us fight with unfamiliar weapons. I'll give you my sword, you give me yours. How is that?"

"But why are you so determined to fight me? What have I done to you? Who are you, anyhow? Who sent you?"

"Who sent me? I sent myself. To prove to myself—and to all these guests of yours—that you are a fraud. That your books are not your books, and your—"

"Enough!" Dumas roared.

"Does that mean you will fight?" Alexandre asked, mockingly.

"Yes!" Dumas yelled. "At the first peep of light! At dawn!"

"At dawn?" the Iron Mask ridiculed. "As well say never."

Dumas jumped. "Then now!" he bellowed. "In ten minutes."

"Excuse number six!" the Iron Mask scorned. "Ten minutes. Time enough for you to disappear from a house that everyone knows is no longer yours, and to which you need never return!"

"No, no," cried Dumas almost as if pleading. "Just time enough to arrange a few matters—and find my son."

"Your son?" Alexandre asked, stopped for a moment. Then he laughed scornfully. "Is your son to do your fighting for you once again?"

"By God!" said Dumas. "You do know how to drive a man to a frenzy. And I'm already nervous enough, facing my thirteenth duel."

"Now it's nerves! Excuse number seven!"

"No!" said Dumas. "No excuse. Just to make one last plea—because thus duel must end in someone's death."

"What?" the Iron Mask demanded. "Still another attempt to evade a duel?" But for a fraction of a second he wondered if perhaps he had not gone too far. If it came to a real duel—what then?

"I promised my son a corpse," Dumas said solemnly. "A corpse to prove once and for all—to him, and to everyone—that my duels are real enough. That corpse must be you."

"What makes you so sure?" Alexandre asked, sneering, but with a tiny sharp edge of fear slicing into him.

"Or me, then," Dumas said. "But in any case, a corpse. Mine will do as well as yours to prove myself to the world." He paused, breathing hard, and then, leaning forward to the Iron Mask, he yelled, "So prepare! This will be *à outrance*! Do you hear? *À outrance!*" *

"If that's what you want," said the Iron Mask, simulating a calmness he was far from possessing.

"Yes," said Dumas. "I am the insulted one. And it's my right to choose. A duel to death."

"Where do we fight then?" Alexandre asked.

* A duel *à outrance* is not finished until one participant is dead.

"Right here," said Dumas. "Any objections?"

"None," said Alexandre. "Except that it's dark."

"Then we'll fight like the bravos in the dark streets of Naples," said Dumas. "Each man will hold a lantern in one hand, a sword in the other. Where are your seconds?"

"I have none and want none," said Alexandre, to whom the duel had now taken on a fantastic aspect that he had never dreamed of.

Dumas addressed the Praying Mantis and the man with the ax in his skull. "Just make sure that he wears no coat of mail."

He turned to some of the others around. "Where's my son?"

"How was he dressed?" someone asked.

"Pierrot," said Dumas. "With a domino ending in lace."

"There's a Pierrot!" someone cried.

"Alexandre!" Dumas yelled. But the Pierrot gave no sign of being called and indeed in a moment proved to be someone else.

"Alexandre! Alexandre!" Dumas shouted. And then he turned to the crowd. "Please, everybody. Try to find my son."

A man in a toga, with harp in one hand and laurel leaves on his brow, came up to Dumas. "Look, don't be a fool. You're not going through with this."

"Hirschler!" said Dumas gratefully. "I was looking for you. Have you seen my son?"

"No. But listen to me—"

"Please. I have no time. You realize that I must make a will."

Hirschler laughed. "You? A will? What for? You have nothing to leave but debts."

"Yes, while I'm alive. But you know that it is only life that stands in the way of my being rich. Once dead and unable any longer to waste my money, I shall be a millionaire. My books and my plays will go on earning a fortune in royalties and if I am not here to spend anything there will soon be wealth in plenty for my son and daughter. This is what I want you to take care of."

"Take care of an oral will?" Hirschler asked scornfully. "How do you expect me to do that?"

"How can I write a will without writing materials?" Dumas flung back.

"Here. I have chalk," said the pornographic artist.

"Chalk will do," said Dumas, accepting a piece. "Here on the terrace wall I will write my testament. Alexis! Hold up one of the lamps."

"Don't be idiotic," said Hirschler. "Who ever heard of a will in chalk on a stone wall?"

"Why not?" Dumas asked. "It will be a holographic will, than which nothing is more valid. Don't forget that I was once a law clerk."

And Dumas began to write his last will and testament on the wall of the terrace while his guests crowded around to watch.

Alexandre too stared at this performance through the bars of his mask, while his hand held the weapon with which he might put that will into effect. For a moment he was stricken with horror of himself, but then he suddenly remembered another incident just before a duel: Mirecourt's son crying "Papa, Papa!" from inside the carriage. Just a trick, he thought. Another delay. Or still another scene out of his father's "thirteenth duel."

Fraud! That's all it was. An elaborate theatrical performance.

But one had to admit that the man was a master at this kind of dramatics: the sure *coup de théâtre* with the final wrench of the heart. Really, he held his audience in the hollow of his hand.

When Dumas had finished, he signed himself with a flourish: Alexandre Dumas, Marquis Davy de la Pailleterie. Then, as if impatiently brushing an unworthy tear from his eye, he said, "I need two witnesses. Who is present who has nothing to fear from the police and doesn't mind being known by his own name?"

Two masks approached and Dumas, breaking his chalk in half, gave them each a piece. "Sign," he said. Then, turning around: "And my son? Has anyone seen him?"

"We've looked everywhere," the gorilla reported.

"Gone off with a girl," someone suggested, and a nervous titter ran through the crowd.

"He'll be back soon, in that case," said Dumas. "We can wait a few more minutes."

"You wanted ten minutes," the Iron Mask said. "It is long past that already. Are you hoping to chill me to the bone? Is this excuse number eight?"

Dumas cupped his hands to his mouth so as to carry his voice. "Alexandre!" he cried in a voice so full of longing and sorrow that

the Iron Mask wished he could stop his ears. "Alexandre!" he
shouted again in the most heart-rending tone of a bereaved father.

But there was no answer. In the silence that followed all one
could hear was the screeching of the three gypsy musicians, still
playing on in the now completely emptied rooms.

Dumas groaned. "This is something I have long promised my son:
a kill. Well, no matter. He will have to content himself with seeing
the corpse as a *fait accompli*. Alexis! The lanterns!"

The Iron Mask was offered his choice of lanterns and shown how
to operate the blinker with a push of his thumb. The seconds then
measured the two men's swords and found them to be about as close
as could be expected from two unmatched weapons. Then, in order
to satisfy the Dueling Code, the weapons were switched.

Now the seconds put the two men into position, with swords at
salute, and cautioned them to wait for the signal.

Perhaps only then did Alexandre realize with a sharp pang that
he was finally and irrevocably committed to what had, until the last
moment, seemed impossible: he was actually facing his father with
naked, cold steel.

He could kill him! He had the opportunity. And the right. And
he might even be confronted with the necessity.

Yes, he could kill his father.

But, no. As much as Alexandre had wanted that in his angry
dreams, he knew at this moment that he couldn't bring himself to
do it. Not when he saw this clumsy bear before him, his apron still
tied around his middle, brushing away the Praying Mantis, who
wished to remove it.

Poor clown, Alexandre thought, forced to pay now for all his
years of boasting. Trapped. I'll have to manage somehow to wound
him just enough to leave him lying in disgrace on the ground, while
I run away, Alexandre thought.

But in a few seconds he was to become aware that this scheme
was not going to be so easy to execute. In the first place, as clumsy
as Dumas might be with his weapon and with his footwork, he apparently had had considerable experience with the Neapolitan
style, for he managed his blinker light with such fiendish cleverness
that Alexandre found himself alternately in darkness and then again

dazzled into a state of blindness by a sudden flash of light swinging right into his eyes.

In addition, he had to put up with his father's voice crying either "Ha-ha!" or "Ho-ho!" and constantly interjecting phrases of unasked advice, such as "Look lively there!" or unwanted sympathy, such as "Too bad. Better luck next time." And if the man was not talking, then he was laughing or else letting out squeals of pain as though he had been stuck to the heart and was about to expire.

All this clowning, this dancing and prancing about, kept throwing Alexandre off so that it was no wonder he couldn't find his usual dexterity. In addition, there was of course the undeniable fact that though his father's swordplay was ridiculously awkward, it nevertheless had a disconcerting unexpectedness about it that made it most effective, due entirely, of course, to its complete lack of style, though his father had once labeled it the "curtain blowing in the breeze" style, which was obvious nonsense.

Alexandre had begun the duel with the idea that it would be a simple matter to prick his father lightly, more than once if necessary, until the man had enough reason to quit. Indeed, he rather imagined that his father would be looking in the fight for just such a way out. Another and final excuse. And now to discover that it was he, Alexandre, who was himself put on the defensive—that was most irritating. And worse than that, to find himself, time and again, obliged to strain every fiber of his being in order to extract himself from a dangerous situation, soon changed his irritation into apprehension. The first cold prick of a long sliver of icy fear began to dig into Alexandre's heart. Had he started something he would be unable to finish?

It was then that the will to live bounded up mightily in him. He decided on a sly waiting game. Just to hold his own until, with all this furious bounding about, his father had worn himself out. Then he'd take care of him.

But things didn't go that way. Dumas, too, it seemed had decided on a change of tactics. Instead of going directly at Alexandre, he suddenly went after his lantern and with one quick whip of his blade he had smashed the glass and extinguished the candle. Suddenly Alexandre was without his precious light. And the sole source of illumination was under the control of his father.

By swinging his light far to the right or to the left of himself, Dumas could keep his opponent dizzily looking for him and thrusting here and there, blindly protecting himself against an assailant who might surge up from any quarter.

This is when the tears of self-pity and anger began to run down inside Alexandre's mask, and when cold drops of sweat trickled down from his armpits underneath his clothes. I must kill him, he thought. I must. I must. God forgive me. But now it is kill or be killed.

And as if stripping himself down for better action, Alexandre tossed away the wreckage of his lamp.

"You fool!" Dumas roared at him. "The broken lantern was still a weapon, with glass splinters that could shred a man. And you threw it away! Ha-ha-ha!—Here, let me show you what one can do with a lantern!"

And, attacking Alexandre *corps à corps*, he smashed his lantern right into the Iron Mask. For a moment Alexandre thought he had been permanently blinded as the burning candle came right at his eyes. Broken glass fell around him. His head reverberated.

"Aie!" he screamed, and leaped back to safety. With his eyes full of lightning flashes, he could make nothing out in the pitch darkness that now enveloped him. He lashed about himself blindly, guiding himself by what he thought was the sound of his father's step. At any moment he expected to feel a cold sword penetrating his body.

"Rockets!" Dumas yelled. "Give me light for the kill."

There he made his fatal mistake, Alexandre said to himself with a fierce explosion of joy. The moment I can see him I will let nothing stop me. I will run him through! And as the first rocket burst and made everything below suddenly startlingly clear, Alexandre saw an opening for his blade and quick as a flash he had lunged for it.

But it had been a trick. Dumas had purposely exposed himself and invited the thrust in order to turn aside and let the blade slip between his body and his left arm and, locking it there instantaneously, he had leaned his heavy body around on the blade with such sudden weight that the hilt twisting in Alexandre's grasp forced his fingers apart and left his hand tingling and aching down to its fingernails.

His sword went whipping off and fell on a patch of snow, where

Dumas leaped to straddle it and stood there hunched, his butcher's apron stretched between his heavy thighs, his rapier ready to thrust.

Alexandre, weaponless, panting, knew that to reach for his sword was to die.

And Dumas, gasping, also stood there, the sweat pouring from him, preparing for the next move, which he obviously intended as the final one.

From the stone terrace, as from an amphitheater, came cries: "Thumbs down! Kill the spy!"

While one lone female voice said, "Run for your life!"

Dumas interrupted his heavy breathing to say, "Unmask. And I will spare you!"

Alexandre shook his head. "No," he said hoarsely. "No." Rather death, he decided, than be revealed as the would-be murderer of his father and, worse still, as a son who had so doubted his father as to presume to teach him swordsmanship only to suffer a quick and ignominious defeat. No, he preferred to die sooner than face such shame.

Suddenly Dumas bent down and snatched up the fallen sword with his left hand.

"Here!" he said, offering it, but as Alexandre made no move to take it, he tossed it high up in the air, crying out, "Catch!" but then only waiting for Alexandre to reach his hands for it, when, bent double, he rushed upon him and bowled him over.

In an instant he had his sword's point tight against the Iron Mask's throat.

"Not a move!" he warned.

Then he snorted. "Hah! You're lucky that I have so little hate in me. Keep your mask on, if you like. My rage is spent. But never forget to whom you owe your life. Whoever you are, and wherever you may be, remember this: every time you see the sun rise, every time you take a breath of air, every time you drink a drop of water, every time you kiss a woman, it is Dumas you can thank for that pleasure. And even when you are in pain, remember me, for the ability to suffer, that is still life, and still more than nothing at all, and it is from me that you have that gift! And now, go! Here. Take your life, and take your own sword and go."

Alexandre didn't wait to be asked a second time. The moment he no longer felt that sword's point threatening his throat, he rose to his feet and, accepting his weapon from his father's hand, he headed as fast as he could for the nearest clump of trees.

Behind him he could hear cheers and jeers, whistling and hand-clapping, while a rocket burst overhead and splashed colored light all around.

Alexandre's body was still twitching from the violence of the strain he had been put to, his eyes were still scorching from the bitter tears he had shed, and in his chaotic thoughts and emotions he could make no sense of this noisy demonstration. But already he understood that as long as his own connection with the Iron Mask remained unsuspected, he might set aside his personal humiliation and enjoy to the full the satisfaction of knowing that his father was no mere bombast when it came to dueling, and that he had proved it before a large enough audience to make sure that the news would soon spread to all Paris.

He had lost, yes, but he had also won, and now again he could be proud of his Papa.

And it was with this thought beginning to spread a kind of warm glow in him that he quickly circled around to the shed behind the monkey house, hustled himself as fast as possible out of his prisoner's disguise and into his street clothes, drawing his Pierrot costume over the whole thing, and then with his winter cape around his shoulders and his domino over his face he returned to mingle with the guests.

It was only then that the meaning of the hissing and the applause was made clear to him.

A Grand Turk was laughingly pocketing some money. "Easiest fifty francs I ever made," he said. "The moment I clapped eyes on that ancient business of trying to provoke Dumas to a duel, and the moment I saw him playing his same old slow-to-anger role, I knew we were back at the old Dumas repertory theater. And right away I said to Lepage here, 'Fifty francs, old sport, that not a drop of blood gets shed.' And he was fool enough to fall for it. Ho-ho-ho!"

And Lepage was saying ruefully, "Well, it looked so damnably real at first."

Everywhere Alexandre went in the crowd he could overbear similar talk. A Crocodile was saying, "The moment I saw him writing his will on that stone wall, I was on to him. That was pure theatrics."

A Madame de Pompadour was saying, "It's really a scene from one of his old plays, isn't it? I'm sure I've seen it or read it before."

And another was asking, "Who do you suppose was hiding behind that iron mask? Mélingue? Bocage? Fechter? Lemaître?"

To which a Polichinelle said scornfully, "Don't be foolish. Those famous actors? Do you imagine they would lend themselves to such a farce? And play an ignoble part for the greater glory of Dumas? No, Dumas had to hire some deadbeat actor who couldn't have got any other role to save his neck. Besides, you could tell: did you ever hear such awkward lines? That Iron Mask mangled his part, if you ask me."

Alexandre boiled with indignation.

A Guillotined Aristocrat with his head in his arms and his voice coming from between his built-up shoulders, said, "I refused to make up my mind until I saw them fighting by the light of rockets. That gave the whole thing away. Dumas was always too much of a showman. And of course when he let the man go without forcing him to take off his mask, and with that obviously well-rehearsed curtain speech about giving his opponent sunshine and women, then there was no longer any room for doubt."

A Savage in beads and woolen blankets reported, "You know, I went to congratulate him on his victory, thinking he'd laugh in my face. But he took me very seriously. I guess he thinks he's fooled us all completely."

"Good old Dumas," a Harlequin said, laughing. "Of course he was bound to try to regain his reputation after that unfortunate Mirecourt affair, so you can't really blame him."

"Yes, good old Dumas," the Savage said. "We'll certainly miss his wonderful parties."

Alexandre felt like bursting out before these cruel and stupid fools and bellowing at them that none other than himself had been in that Iron Mask, and that as one of the participants he could vouch for it that never had there been a more real, a more terrible, kill-or-be-killed duel. But wouldn't that be proving the precise opposite? Who would believe in this father-and-son duel? Especially between such a father and such a son, who had been so long hand in glove to the point even of sharing each other's mistresses!

No. Such a revelation would only confirm people's convictions that the duel had been a hoax. And that was the most harrowing thought of all: that while for himself he had proved his father's courage and ability, for others he had only succeeded in reinforcing the story of the hoaxes and adding another one to his father's discredit.

It was this realization that made it so embarrassing for Alexandre to face his father. But he could not very well leave without saying good-by to him and having a word with him about the duel.

When he went down from the terrace to the lawn below, Dumas, his tablecloth apron still tied around his middle, had just nailed up a pinwheel and set it off.

"My boy!" he cried, embracing Alexandre at once.

"Papa!" said Alexandre.

"Then you've forgiven me!" said Dumas.

Alexandre was stopped. What did his father mean by that? "Forgiven you for what, Papa?" he asked.

"Ah, I forget. I'm still so excited. You do not even know that just now I fought a duel?"

"But of course I know," said Alexandre. "I watched it all from a garret window. Unfortunately I was in no condition to show myself when you called."

His father burst into laughter. "I might have known you were up to something of the sort. Who was she?"

Alexandre shook his head discreetly.

"But you were able to see everything?"

"Everything," said Alexandre.

"Hah! And what do you say now to my style? Was I not in good form? Don't you think now that I could have beaten that Mirecourt?"

"I'm sure of it, Papa."

"Hm. Why, I could have worsted the world-famous Angelo himself."

"Yes," said Alexandre seriously. "I think you might have."

"And you do not doubt, do you, that I was in a position to give you the corpse I so often promised you?"

"I don't doubt it for a moment, Papa."

"And you forgive me for having failed you again?"

Alexandre swallowed and for a moment he couldn't talk. "There's nothing to forgive, Father."

"Ah, but you don't realize that here everybody took it for a joke." Dumas said. "And the fact is that never did I have such an opportunity to prove myself once and for all. Just think, here was a man whose life I could have ended without ever having to look on his dying face, and thus I would never have had to carry any image in my mind to bring me subsequent regrets and to interrupt my work. Besides, I am fleeing to Brussels in a matter of hours. Who knows whether I shall ever return. You see? This was my chance. My one big chance. And I wanted so much to do it for you."

"Yes, Papa," said Alexandre, preventing the tears from coming into his voice. "I understand. But it doesn't matter, I assure you. Those who truly love you, Papa, they don't need convincing. And those who don't love you—not even a corpse would convince them."

"You're right," Dumas said. "But that is not why I spared the fellow's life. It was selfishness. Egoism. Because I have never been able to resist making a gesture. A big gesture. Imagine holding a man's life in your hands and being able to give it to him. How many people have had that experience?"

"Yes, Papa."

"Do you remember, my boy, how enviously I wrote of the Duke of Buckingham when, at the spot where Queen Anne revealed her love for him, he dropped a precious jewel. 'I want someone to find it here,' he said, 'and to be as happy on this spot as you have made me.' Ah, Alexandre my boy, if only one could mark the big moments of one's life by dropping jewels. But to how few of us that is granted. Who can be a Duke of Richelieu and make his entry into Vienna with four hundred horsemen, and each mount shod with silver shoes, and every shoe so badly nailed to the hoof that all along the route of the parade the animals keep casting their shoes, and the whole population of Vienna is out on the streets scrambling for horseshoes that are worth a fortune! Hah! To build pyramids and astonish man forever. Or write one's name on a continent like Amerigo Vespucci . . ."

Overcome with his impotent desire for grandeur, Dumas fell into the arms of his son and wept.

And Alexandre wept under his domino. "Papa," he said, "Papa . . ."

"Come with me to Brussels," Dumas begged. "We'll start life all over again. Here there is nothing but ruins. Let Hirschler bother with it."

"I must stay in Paris, Papa," Alexandre excused himself. "I must."

"At least you will drive me to the station?"

"Of course, Papa."

"Good. Then I can leave the britska in your care, to turn over to Hirschler. Alexis! Alexis, where are you? Just one moment, my boy, and I shall change my clothes and be with you."

No, Alexandre did not want to be with his father any longer than he could help it. Already a dreadful doubt was corroding his mind, the possibility that his father had known all along who was under the Iron Mask and had only begged his son's forgiveness so insistently in order to conceal that he knew. And thus explain away his real reason for not killing his defeated opponent.

CHAPTER THIRTY-EIGHT

Visit to a Dead Man

PERHAPS IF AT THE END of their long night ride to Paris, Dumas had not expressed the desire to see his friend Heine, Alexandre might have been able to rid himself of this nagging suspicion that was to haunt him henceforth to the end of his days. For that visit was as if specially chosen to underline the thought that his father had used the duel only to drive home a lesson to his son, the lesson that no matter what one may suffer in life, life was still man's greatest good. Yes, good to the last and bitterest dregs.

"I must see Heine before I leave Paris," Dumas exclaimed, "and we still have enough time before my train leaves."

"At this early hour?" Alexandre asked. "Why, it's still dark."

"Oh, never fear, Heine will be awake," Dumas said. "He and I are two of a kind: we never sleep. I, because of too much health. He, because of too little."

And Heine was indeed awake. In a room thick with the odor of unhealthy flesh and powerful drugs, lying in a bed over which hung ten ropes by which he could pull himself into various positions, there the great humorist suffered.

His pretty wife, with a parrot on her shoulder, pushed two chairs forward.

"Ah, look who comes to see me!" Heine cried, holding up a paralyzed eyelid and then dropping it to reach out blindly and shake hands with Dumas. "Mister Scheherezade. Mister Scheherezade himself."

Then, opening his eye again, he looked at Alexandre and said, "Are you going to be as great a storyteller as your father? Ah, you don't know what it means to the sleepless to have your father's books. See? Here is a whole row of them, within my reach."

"It's so long since you've been to see me," he scolded Dumas. "Ask Mathilde how often I've threatened to look you up myself."

"His threats!" Mathilde scorned. "Why, there stand his crutches. In the corner. He hasn't been able to use them for two years. I shall break them up for firewood one of these days."

"Get out!" Heine shouted at her.

"You needn't say it twice," said Mathilde. "It isn't often that I get a chance to leave you with company, while I escape from this drugstore where the odor is enough to make you vomit." And she flounced out, her parrot squawking as she slammed the door behind her.

"Oh, she still loves me," Heine said, his thin face lighting up with puckish amusement. "I know. She wouldn't have left so readily if my visitors had been two pretty girls. Naturally, she cheats on me. But then, that's my fault. I can no longer beat her, so she does what she pleases."

"I see you are still writing," said Dumas, indicating the heap of papers on the bed.

"My memoirs," Heine said. "My millionaire relatives will give anything to prevent their publication. They have promised Mathilde a pension, and if they do not keep their promise, after I am dead, Mathilde can always threaten them with their publication."

He laughed. "You know I once told Mathilde that I wanted her to be rich when I died. Her answer was 'I deserve it, after all the years I have cared for you.' 'It's not out of gratitude,' I explained to her, 'but because I want to feel sure that you'll be married again when I'm out of the way.' 'Why, naturally I'll be married,' she said proudly. 'I'm still young and pretty.' 'No doubt,' I agreed, 'but money will help make it certain.' That made her suspicious. 'Why are you so anxious that I should be married?' she asked. 'I want someone to mourn me,' I told her. 'Bah!' she mocked. 'And you think that if I'm married again, I'll ever have occasion to mourn you? On the contrary, I'll forget you completely!' 'It isn't to you that I look for mourning,' I explained to her. 'It's to your husband. He will often have occasion to say to himself, That poor Heine. I wish he were still alive. Because if he were, I wouldn't be married to his widow. You see, my dear Mathilde, that's why I want you to be rich when I die!'" Heine laughed until pain forced him to moderate his emotion.

Dumas laughed heartily and Alexandre was compelled to join in, although he felt like anything but laughter.

"Is there no possible cure for you?" he asked. "What does your doctor say?"

That brought on more laughter. "My doctor says pus!" he exclaimed. "Dr. Gruby believes in nothing so much as pus. Laudable pus, he calls it. Really, if he were a poet, he would write a sonnet to pus. Pus, he claims, takes away all disease. Pus is the body purging itself. And when I don't produce enough pus for him, he helps me along by giving me setons. Do you know what a seton is? It is a medicated bristle that is stuck under the flesh. It causes inflammation and then copious pus. I have a half a dozen of them on me right now. Oh, they produce pus all right, and pain especially, but as to carrying away my disease, of that I'm afraid they are incapable."

"Perhaps you should change physicians," Alexandre suggested.

Heine smiled gently. "Changing physicians is like changing religions. Either it has no meaning at all, in which case it is a sign of frivolity, or else it has a meaning, and then it is a sign of despair. In my lifetime I've been through every brand of medicine and every variety of religion. But for me at least there were never but two conditions: when I was well I was always a pagan at heart, no matter what religion I happened to profess. And now that I'm sick, I'm nothing but an old Jew, no matter whose God I happen to pray to."

"My friend," said Dumas, "I can see one thing. Your wit is still sharp, and you still laugh as much as ever."

"Does it cost anything to laugh?" Heine asked. "You see this knife that Mathilde uses to cut open the pages of my books? Do you see this bottle of opium powder that Mathilde sprinkles on my sores so that now and then I can sleep for a few minutes? Either one, knife or opium, could give me death any time I wanted it. But life is still too exciting.

"Karl Marx writes to me and tries to make a communist out of me. I flirt with him. I don't like communism. But when I think that someday that philosophy may become such a force as to crush those German aristocrats who have hounded me all my life, why I love communism, and I love Karl Marx.

"It doesn't even require such powerful thoughts to make me happy. I can look out of the window and see a dog lifting its leg against a tree. That's enough of the beauties of nature to fill me with joy.

"It's true that a sneeze practically explodes me. And a cough is like an iron rake pulled through my lungs and throat. And when my feet get twisted, I have to ask someone to straighten them for me, put the toes up and the heel down. It's true that there's barely enough blood left in me to keep my lips alive, and that someday I shall have to apologize to the worms for having nothing but bones to serve them. But as long as I'm alive I must consider myself lucky."

"Lucky," Alexandre breathed. He was pale. And the heavy odor of the sickroom, with its windows tightly shut against the cold, was beginning to affect him.

"Why, of course I'm lucky," said Heine, twinkling through his one good eye. "Whom else do you know so fortunate as to be able to speak authoritatively on the subject of life after death? How many are there who have been granted the gift of certainty on this important question? And now behold me! I can be positive of surviving death, since I have already done so. Yes, look at me: a living demonstration of immortality: Elijah on a mattress instead of in a golden chariot."

Never would Alexandre be able to forget this early-morning visit to Heine. For it underlined his suspicion that his father must have known from the start who was behind the Iron Mask and had deliberately, with the sure hand that only such a master plot weaver as himself could command, chosen not to turn the duel into an ugly embarrassment for his son by unmasking him, but instead had used the situation to teach him the most glorious lesson of all: to love life under all circumstances. The lesson that love of oneself and of one's life is the basic love, without which one can neither love God nor obey God's commandment to honor one's father and mother.

No, never would Alexandre forget this night and its lesson. And as long as Dumas lived, which was some twenty more years, never would Alexandre fail to demonstrate his filial love, respect and admiration when in the presence of the man who had twice given him life. To be sure, he took care thereafter to find himself in the presence of his father as rarely as possible.

Which is quite understandable. He wasn't precisely proud of his behavior.

Thou Knowest

WELL, THERE YOU HAVE IT: our long-promised explanation of Gérôme's painting, "Duel after the Masquerade Ball."

To be sure, that canvas presents a somewhat different scene from
the one we have just described. But that is readily explained. In the
first place, Gérôme wasn't even in France at the time of the Dumas
duel: he was off to the Orient to study its hot, rich colors, the one
indispensable trip for painters of this period. In the second place,
when, upon his return, Gérôme heard some talk of the Dumas affair, all he wanted of it for his painting was that striking central
idea: a duel in masquerade costume, and for the rest he wanted to
remove his scene as far as possible from any connection with what
he, along with almost everyone else, took to be just another Dumas
publicity hoax.

And in this project Gérôme succeeded so well that when his little
painting was exhibited at the Salon of 1853, even his contemporaries
wondered as to the identity of the participants. No one dared mention Dumas. Obviously not. This painting was too real. Here one
might see one of the principals actually expiring on the snowy
ground. Here was none of your prearranged, bloodless pretend
duels. This was genuine!

Conceive now, if you please, the scorn of Dumas as the very same
people who prided themselves on being too smart to be taken in by
his duels rushed to heap their praises on this little canvas for what
they termed its "unpitying realism"!

No wonder he could not restrain himself from standing before the
painting like a museum guide and giving an impromptu lecture exposing all its faults. And no wonder, too, that he made an offer
to buy the picture. He wanted this wretched thing to hang on his
own wall, so that if ever a discussion arose about his duels he could
lead his critics to it.

"What do you think of this duel?" he could hear himself challenging them.

And of course they would mouth the usual platitudes of the critics of the day: its brutal actuality, its stark air of having been experienced in person, as if sketched on the scene. And Dumas would nod and agree wtih them, and then he would quietly wonder about the overcoats.

"Overcoats?" his listeners would say. "What do you mean overcoats?"

"Well, yes," Dumas would say. "After all, it's winter. Realistic people aren't likely to forget to pick up their overcoats from the cloakroom just because a duel is going to be fought. Not in this iron cold. Oh, yes, the principals perhaps, because they are too excited. But wouldn't the seconds remember? And remind the principals for their own good? Of course, that depends somewhat on the kind of ball it was. What do you think? Was it a private ball? Or public?"

"I can't see what difference that makes."

"Oh, it's not important. Just a question of where they managed to pick up those swords. A writer of romances has to think of such minor things. A realistic painter can dispense with such questions."

Oh, he'd nail them! Nail them fast in a dozen unanswerable questions that would prove how little genuine concern the artist had shown for reality in his painting, and in general how deceptive that word reality can be.

It would have been the sort of revenge that Dumas liked. The same sort that he had practiced on Granier de Cassagnac, presenting him with a huge pair of shears and a library of plays and challenging him to write a play with scissors. But when he made his offer to buy the painting, he found that the Duc d'Aumale had already acquired it. Which didn't really disconcert him very much. After all, his scorn, his anger, had already evaporated.

Yes, it would have been wonderful to have known this man personally. In the flesh. In his towering mass of warm flesh, never tired and never cold, six foot three in his stockinged feet. Laughing at all his enemies and his increasing host of detractors, shrugging off all their sharp darts of ridicule and saying, "What do you expect of me? I'm once and for all simply incapable of hate. Rage? Yes, I can be enraged. Because rage is brief. But hate? No, I can't hate. Hate endures."

Yes, it would have been wonderful to have known him in the flesh. Failing that, I have had the pleasure of knowing him in spirit.

I have lived with this spirit of his, stayed up nights with it, taken long walks with it. Eaten with it. And gone to bed with it.

And now, when the time comes to write finis to this book, it is almost as if I were called to the funeral of a close friend.

Ah! he so loved life! He would have wanted to live and enjoy life forever. And for a time it seemed almost that he had discovered the magic of perpetual youth. It was the dying off of his friends, one by one, that shook his confidence in his own robust sturdiness. Shook it again and again until at last it was destroyed.

It was the Johannot brothers dying so young and so talented. It was Gérard de Nerval found hanging one wintry morning from a lamppost. It was his former star and mistress Marie Dorval dying in poverty and writing him a last frantic appeal from her deathbed. "Dumas, my dear Dumas, for that love that we once bore each other, please don't let me be thrown into the paupers' trench."

And he, being as usual out of funds, sold his lovely Grand Order of Nizam, the one that the Sultan of Turkey himself had hung around his neck, and bought her a plot.

And Balzac, swollen with dropsy, lying in stench and agony, while his wife entertained her lover in an adjoining room, and the doctor shaking his head and saying, "Behold the victim of fifty thousand cups of black coffee. Ten thousand nights of work, during which he kept himself awake with pot after pot of a tarlike brew."

Dumas and Victor Hugo were among the pallbearers of the body.

Oh, how many he had carried to their graves! In how many processions he had walked, and in how many black draped churches he had stood. In Notre Dame itself, steeped in black, when his good friend the son of King Louis Philippe had been thrown to his death from a horse.

How proud he had used to be, in former times, that so many people called him their friend, so that when he walked the streets or went into a café, it was everywhere: "Ah, Monsieur Dumas! Bonjour, Monsieur Dumas!" And Dumas here and Dumas there.

But in the end what did it add up to? Why, simply that the more people you knew the more funerals you eventually had to go to.

Indeed, there came a time when Paris, that city he so loved, became a nightmare to him. Romanticism had died when Baron Hauss·

mann had ripped open the medieval city to build great modern
avenues through it. And the modern people living there no longer
had any respect for him. His ways were already antique. Swash-
buckling. Cloak-and-dagger stuff. Trap doors. A joke!

Then a walk through Paris became a walk through a cemetery:
every corner, every restaurant, almost every house, would remind
him of someone who had passed on. Delphine Gay, Vigny, Murger,
Musset. The number was endless.

The army of the living became ever smaller, and the army of the
dead ever larger, until he felt choked. And he wanted to cry out,
"Take care! We are outnumbered! *Sauve qui peut!*"

But he battled on. He devoured life. His love affairs, his cooking,
became ever more extravagant, as if a champion appetite was
enough to make an impregnable bastion. He wrote massively, as if
he intended to use his books someday as a barricade. He threw himself into one adventure after another, as if sheer excitement would
frighten away the reaper.

He traveled back and forth through France. He went to England.
He went to Russia. He joined Garibaldi in the war against the Bourbons of Italy, buying a ship with his own money, stocking it with
weapons of war, recruiting soldiers, hiring tailors to sew them red
shirts. He even published an Italian daily newspaper. And showered
Garibaldi with the advice of a man who has read deeply of the
knavishness and trickery of princes and of peoples.

It is true that amidst his growing despair there still flowed the
strong current of his life, like a stream of water rushing through
a desert. For example, his little warship boasted a female admiral,
which ordinary warships don't. And this pretty admiral gave birth
to another one of Dumas' children, Micaella, a girl, for whom Garibaldi stood godfather.

But he never stopped writing, and some authorities state that Dumas' dispatches from the Garibaldian war front entitled him to be
called the world's first war correspondent. Others consider the
whole business just another piece of clownishness. Larousse, the
encyclopedist, had this comment to make on Dumas' dispatches:
"Wasn't there once a man named Garibaldi who had something
to do with this war against the Kingdom of the Two Sicilies? Or did
General Dumas cashier him?"

Yes, it was all very exciting. Very alive. But no matter how fast you juggle the balls, no matter how you dazzle yourself and everyone else with the speed of your living, the days still pass by, the months pile up solid, the years move forward ponderously, and then break off suddenly like huge icebergs dropping from a polar glacier.

And yet, for Dumas, funerals were eventually to provide him with one consolation: he could be sure of seeing his son, now a dramatist more famous than his father.

The two men, tall, bareheaded, solemn-faced, stood there while the speeches droned on. Then, afterward, they embraced stiffly.

"You are well, Papa?"

"In perfect health, my boy. And you?"

"Fine, Papa."

They stood there, as if there were words that still wanted to be said. But neither spoke. A secret wedged them apart. It was as if one or the other, or both, were too embarrassed to break the silence.

Then at last, awkwardly, almost like strangers, they would shake hands and part. And Dumas, afterward, would say to a friend, "I see him only at funerals nowadays. I suppose the next time will be the occasion of my own funeral."

And yet they continued to love each other. When the *Lady of the Camellias* had been finally brought to production, Dumas had rushed from Brussels to be at the opening performance. No one had applauded so frantically as he.

What a triumph! And when the cry of "Author! Author!" had resounded through the hall, Dumas *père* had risen big and proud in his box.

"What," people had wondered, "is he going to claim that he had a hand in this too?"

"Yes," Dumas had said in a loud voice. "I demand a share of the credit. Because I am the real author—I authored the author! And who knows but that someday I shall be remembered in history only because I was the father of the playwright Alexandre Dumas."

The house had broken into wild applause, and Alexandre, who admittedly had sweated for a second or two, joined in.

Afterward Dumas *père* said to Dumas *fils*, "Well, let's celebrate.

That's what I always did after a successful opening. Do you remember the gay times?"

"Of course, Papa," said Alexandre. "But for this evening you'll have to excuse me. I have a rendezvous."

"I might have known you would," Dumas said, smiling, and clapped his son on the shoulder heartily. "After all, you're still mine, root and branch."

"No. It's not what you think. It's Mama, who has already gone home to prepare a little supper for me."

Dumas said nothing for a moment. Then he smiled. "Of course. You're right, my boy. Convey my respects to your good mother. How is she, by the way?"

"Why not come with me and see for yourself?"

Dumas shook his head. But Alexandre begged him so insistently that at last Dumas agreed. It turned out to be an awkward evening at 22 rue Pigalle, in the neat little apartment to which Alexandre had moved his mother.

Catherine, seeing two men and not immediately realizing who the second one was, exclaimed, "Why didn't you tell me you would bring a guest?" But when she recognized Dumas, she screamed, and then, for the rest of the evening she was so distraught that it was painful.

She complained that she should have been warned. She declared that she would have planned a completely different meal. She would not have taken off her good dress. She was sorry about her coiffure.

Her hands kept fluttering to her gray hair. Her weak eyes glistened with tears that she had to restrain by force.

"My jam," she said. "Do you like it as much as ever?"

Jam? Jam? Oh, yes. Dumas remembered suddenly that once he had praised a bottle of jam she had passed on to him through Alexandre. And since then she had never failed to set aside a jar for him every year when she made preserves.

He couldn't very well explain to Catherine that he was being remembered constantly by his former mistresses with jams and cookies and knitted socks and whatnot. "Always something very domestic," he would point out to his friends. "All of them trying to make me see what I have missed by not marrying them."

"Recognize that little table?" Catherine asked.

"This little table? No. Can't say I do."

"You mean to say you don't remember the table on which you wrote your *Christina*? Don't you recall how you used to keep me up all night with your writing?"

"Yes, yes, of course," he said. "Of course. . . . And you've kept it all these years?"

"Why, certainly," she said. "Why, I even have some of the quills you used." And she brought out, wrapped in old tissue paper grown yellow with age, half a dozen goose quills.

"And look at this," she said, fetching out a bulky package. Inside were green rags. "Remember the jacket you wore the night of the triumph of your *Antony*? And how the crowd tore it to pieces in their admiration of you? I rescued these bits."

"You saved these things?" he said, overcome.

"Yes," she said. "That's the way I am. I never throw anything out. If you had married me, you would be a millionaire today."

"No doubt," he said and he nodded pensively.

It was a difficult meal that followed, with Dumas talking rapidly about this and that, as if he had to fill every crevice of time with a funny story lest the past suddenly surge up again.

Afterward Alexandre said, "I'm sorry. But I thought we would be happy together. *En famille.* I thought she would remind you of your youth."

"She did," said Dumas. "She did remind me of my youth. But— well, you see, she was unable to remind me of hers."

Such was only one of the walls between father and son. Indeed, their very careers brought them into a sort of silent warfare. In order to get the censors to pass *The Lady of the Camellias*, Alexandre had argued that while it was true that the play showed a prostitute enjoying a lavish income and moving in the highest circles of France, yet that was only for the sake of driving home the moral that the wages of sin are death. The actual play, he maintained, was merely incidental to this greater truth which it was designed to illustrate and support.

And after this first smashing success, Alexandre had the intelligence to realize that he had hit on a profitable vein of ore: namely, to draw from the depraved lives of Paris society still further moral lessons for the theatergoer, thus satisfying at one stroke both the censors and the public, both the puritan and the prurient. No actual figures were ever produced as to which group frequented his plays most assiduously, but the lump sum was enormous. Enough, indeed, to make him the acknowledged foremost dramatist of the third quarter of the nineteenth century. His influence on succeeding dramatists and in the formation of the whole Ibsen school of playwriting is part of the history of literature.

Some say that it was only to measure up to this role of modern Savonarola which had been thrust on him that he began to live an exemplary life, marrying a woman of the Russian nobility, investing his profits cannily, having children. Others simply say that with advancing age he settled down, as so many of us do, and they say further that even this settling down was not too painfully abrupt, and they point to the fact that throughout his life he carried on some rather delicate (or indelicate) correspondence with various actresses; and they even go so far as to prove with dates that he did not actually marry his wife until she had born him his first child.

The truth is, of course, that, deep within, Alexandre had always yearned for innocence as for a drink of pure water. And in the end he had found peace in being a sober, quiet, hard-working father of a family.

But because gossip never quite dies down, and because his plays did betray an intimate knowledge of the worst elements of society, Alexandre thought to reinforce the moral side of his plays by adding to them long sermonizing prefaces, which, of course, appeared only in the printed versions.

In one of these prefaces he wrote: "A man who deliberately (and it cannot be otherwise than deliberate) fathers a child without having previously considered and assured its moral and social well-being is a malefactor to be classed somewhere between thieves and murderers."

People pointed out this passage to each other and asked, "Does he mean his own father?"

And they read eagerly the passages where Alexandre advocates society's returning to an old tribal severity in which fornication is classed, not among the pleasant incidents of life, but among the crimes. He demanded that all extramarital intercourse be punished by five years in prison (plus half a man's income if a child should result) and even ten years if the mother had been a virgin.

The spectacle of this bastard son advocating such strict morals while his father meanwhile carried on a life as outrageous as ever had Paris chuckling again and again over the years. And it is not to be wondered that various rumors circulated, according to which the younger Dumas had actually wanted to murder his misbehaving father for thus making a fool out of him. There was a strange story, for example, that one evening the son had drawn a knife on his father. And that later he had excused himself, claiming a breakdown due to overwork.

The case of Adah Isaacs Menken brought the two men into the sharpest opposition.

Adah was the New Orleans Confederate beauty who had made herself the sensation of two continents by introducing nudity to the stage, appearing in *Mazeppa* and in *The Pirates of the Savannah*, two otherwise silly plays, both of which, however, required an actress to be dressed in pink silk skintights and to be lashed to the back of a wild horse.

Wherever she had appeared she had been able to interest not only the mob but men of culture and talent: Mark Twain in San Francisco, Walt Whitman in New York, Swinburne in London.

And Dumas in Paris.

By that time Dumas was sixty-six years old and more corpulent than ever. But he and Adah became as inseparable as love birds. They were seen everywhere together. They had themselves photographed together and their pictures were displayed in the photographer's window and some more enterprising rival photographers snipped their heads from the real photos and made new negatives by pasting the heads on figures taken from the most obscene pictures. These pornographic monstrosities became for a while the rage of the town.

Paul Verlaine wrote a doggerel verse about it.

And Villemessant noted in his *Memoirs*: "Out pops the Negro, and Dumas the white slave must work all the harder as the black master flings his money to the winds."

There was indeed something to excite people's sense of scatological humor in this girl of the Confederacy consorting with a colored man, in this wisp of femininity in the arms of a giant, in this young girl loved by an old man.

And when Victor Koning (who was later to make and lose a fortune in the theater) wrote a vicious lampoon in *La Vogue Parisienne* and Dumas, boiling over, challenged him to a duel *à outrance*, then the affair really came to a head.

All the old stories about Dumas' duels circulated again, and bets were taken that there would be no fight, or that whatever fight took place would be rigged and no blood would be shed. "Publicity!" everyone cried. "It's all publicity."

Dumas shouted back, "This time there will be a corpse on the ground. Either mine or his. That will settle it."

Once again, Alexandre felt that he had to take a hand. He ran to Koning. "Are you seriously thinking of accepting a life-and-death challenge from a man old enough to be your grandfather?"

Koning declared himself quite willing to play the coward and to publish an apology. The duel was accordingly canceled.

Dumas was furious with Alexandre. "While all Paris is taking bets that I won't fight, you have to go and prove that my enemies are right!"

Alexandre stood his ground. "I couldn't permit you to fight, Papa. Not at your age."

"Age! Age!" Dumas ranted. "What better way to end one's life than on the field of honor?" Will you never have done with spoiling my duels?"

Alexandre stared at his father. "What do you mean by that?" he asked.

But Dumas either avoided or ignored the question. "Hah!" he snorted. "I never felt more vigorous in my whole life!" And, pretending to hold a foil in his hand, he lunged and riposted about him furiously, until the great mass of his body shook with his heaving breath. "My last chance to prove myself has gone!" he moaned.

Oh, he was still active enough. It was not he but poor Adah who died a few months later, suddenly forgotten and alone, and was buried in the Jewish section of Montparnasse cemetery, where she still lies, with the enigmatic inscription which she herself asked to be put on her tombstone: *Thou Knowest.*

MORE EPILOGUE

A Penny to Your Memory

AND THUS DUMAS struggled on.

While the Cassagnacs, bribed with millions from the bloated financiers of the Empire, screamed for war against Prussia, a war that was soon to throw France to her knees, Dumas went out to the battlefield of Langensalza where the blind King of Hanover had stood with his little army against the might of Prussia and had been so brutally bowled over, and he came back to write a book, *The Prussian Terror*, warning France of her danger.

But Dumas was no longer of any consequence in France. Whether as clown or prophet, he was quite passé.

Gone were the days when customers punched each other in bookstores to reach for copies of his latest novel before it was sold out. Gone were the days when editors queued up before his study door.

Nothing was left for him but the dregs of a literary career. His books no longer sold. His plays no longer played. Out of charity a few editors still paid him small sums for bits of writing, for souvenirs, chats, squibs. And in the outlying halls he could still gather some sort of an audience for a lecture—for example, on his friend Delacroix, who had died not so long before.

As bills accumulated and money became scarce, he would not even turn down an offer to write a paragraph of publicity for a milliner.

"I'll pay you well for it," Madame Mabille assured him. "Fifty francs. But of course only when I see it in the newspapers," she added, as Dumas was already stretching out his hand for the money.

"Oh, they'll print it," he insisted. But the milliner clicked her purse shut and would not budge.

So Dumas wrote the pathetic little tale of a poor prostitute who had decided on suicide because she had no food and was even too weak to leave her tiny garret room. But before killing herself, she made one last attempt to move the heart of the kind people of Paris, writing her appeal on a bit of paper and tying it to the leg of her pet canary. Then, opening the little bird's cage, she gave it freedom.

"The poor bird," Dumas wrote, "fluttered into Madame Mabille's millinery shop. But it was too late. The young girl was already dead of starvation. The curious may still see the bird by visiting Madame Mabille's establishment, rue des Bons Enfants, and may verify the truth by the little bit of string still dangling from the bird's leg."

This little tale was picked up by all the Paris press, and hundreds of people crowded into Madame Mabille's place. After all, there's nothing moves the Parisian public to tears so much as the death of a young sinful girl.

Delighted with the results, Madame Mabille came running to Monsieur Dumas. "Here is your money," she said.

"But this is only forty-two francs," Dumas said.

"Precisely," said Madame Mabille.

"You promised me fifty," Dumas reminded her.

"Yes, but when I promised you that amount, I did not expect that I would have to run out quickly and buy a canary. That cost me eight francs."

"But you are not going to make me pay for the canary!" Dumas exclaimed.

"Isn't it because of your story that I was put to that expense?" Madame Mabille asked.

"Yes, of course," Dumas admitted.

"Then it's only right that you should pay," Madame Mabille concluded.

Since Dumas knew that no one had ever gotten the better of a Paris shopkeeper, he made no further effort to collect the eight francs.

When he was not working on such puffs and other trivialities, Dumas labored on his giant encyclopedic cookbook.

And meanwhile his living conditions deteriorated. His two servants robbed him and neglected to clean his apartment. Dumas himself, often penniless, did not bother to buy clothes or replace those that were worn out or had got stolen.

"But you must have clothes!" Mathilde Shaw said to him one day.

"Why?" he asked. "I've sold my last medal, you know."

He had never needed clothes for warmth, just to hang his decorations on, *ergo*, now that he had no decorations . . .

Occasionally his daughter Marie Alexandrine, who had finally split with her husband and was now earning her own living as a writer of theosophical articles, would come in and drive the servants briefly to work. She would tidy up the place, do her best to straighten out the author's finances, and show him her latest Buddhistic writings.

One day she burst into her father's study saying, "Today, Papa, you may lighten your karma of a thousand of your blackest sins." *

"How so, my daughter?"

"By doing your son a great favor."

"In what way?"

"By fulfilling his greatest wish."

"But what may that be? I don't understand."

"You mean you do not know what your son has been hoping for all his life?"

"No. I can't imagine. He seems to me to have everything he wants. Fame. Money. Family."

"Yes, but his father and mother were never married, and that is what he has always wanted more than anything else: to be the real son of properly wedded parents."

"The deuce you say!" Dumas exclaimed in surprise. "You're joking".

"No, I'm not. And if we hurry, you may still do him that great favor. His mother is dying. She will not last the day. They have just sent for the priest. Come quick."

Dumas remained pensive for a moment. He wiped his eyes with the back of his hand and said, "If you say so, then let's go."

When the carriage dropped them off at 22 rue Pigalle, passersby, hearing the boy ringing his bell, were taking off their hats in honor of the body of Our Lord, which the priest was bringing to the dying woman.

Upstairs the doctor cautioned the priest to hurry. "Do not be misled by her appearance. She has only moments to live."

---

* We have this incident, hitherto ignored by every biographer of Dumas, from Emily Crawford, Paris correspondent of the London *Daily News,* who knew Dumas well in his old age.

Alexandre was kneeling at his mother's bedside, his face buried in the spread to choke his sobs.

When Dumas entered, Catherine saw him at once. In her gray, fallen face, her eyes lost their exhausted look and glowed briefly.

"Alexandre," she gasped.

The priest raced through the ceremony of extreme unction and went on to the marriage ceremony.

When Catherine realized that she was going to be married, she gathered all her strength to say, "Alexandre, Alexandre, you will make this the happiest day of my life."

Dumas faltered. His legs trembled and he sat down on the side of the bed.

Alexandre sobbed out loud.

"For this shall a man leave his father and mother and cleave to his wife and they shall be one flesh . . ." The priest spoke rapidly. Then he said, "Join hands."

Dumas picked up Catherine's limp hand, white, with heavy blue veins.

"Repeat after me," said the priest. "I, Alexandre Dumas take thee Catherine Lebay . . ."

As the ceremony continued, her fingers slowly cramped themselves around Dumas' hand. But she no longer had the strength to repeat the priest's words after him. It was Dumas alone who uttered the lines "To have and to hold, from this day forward, for better for worse, for richer for poorer, in sickness and in health, till death do us part. . . ."

Then, at the bidding of the priest, Dumas slipped the ring on Catherine's thumb, then on her second finger, then her third and finally on her fourth, while the priest intoned, "In the name of the father, the son, the Holy Ghost, Amen."

When Dumas, tears streaming from his face, bent over to kiss his bride, she was already dead. He groaned out loud, abruptly embraced his son, and left.

His daughter caught up with him on the stairs. "Are you angry that I got you into this?" she asked.

He shrugged, unable to speak.

"You've no idea how happy you've made Alexandre."

"Good," he said. "But I'm tired. I can't remember when I've been so tired."

The next morning, for the first time in nearly half a century, when he sat down to his deal table and took up his pen, he didn't write.

Day after day he sat there, pen poised, quiet. And not writing.

He sat half awake and half asleep, dozing quietly, thinking of nothing in particular.

On the great billiard table his mail accumulated, unopened and unanswered.

Before him lay his deckle-edged paper, made especially for him by a Lyons admirer who happened to be in the paper business—blue for romances, yellow for articles, green for plays, so that he would not get his manuscripts mixed up.

His eyes were as perfect as ever. His hand was just as steady.

It wasn't that he couldn't write any more. It was only that he no longer felt any urge. After fifty years the machine had suddenly stopped.

He still possessed a few of those *objets d'art* that, so he used to claim, stimulated him to creation: Moorish carvings, Bohemian glassware, Russian icons, just a fragment of the once vast booty of outlandishly shaped and garishly colored objects that he had dragged home from his endless travels, the small fragment still left over after a hundred despoiling creditors and a thousand greedy women had garnered their share.

On the wall hung the single Delacroix he still owned. And also the framed "world's largest visiting card" that Delacroix had once sketched and left at his door when he hadn't found Dumas in.

And there too hung the two letters from Abraham Lincoln. The first thanking him for $100 contributed to the Fund for the Widows of Abolitionists, but remarking that an additional $125 had been realized by selling the Dumas signature from the bottom of his letter. Lincoln's second letter thanked Dumas for the receipt of a hundred signatures which he was sure would sell quickly at a hundred dollars apiece.

But all these mementos that had usually filled him with the zest to work no longer had any effect on him.

He felt himself just another object among a lot of objects. And he remained thus—quiet, content in a strange, lethargic way.

The servants came to him for orders and for money and he simply stared at them, seeing no need to answer them. One after the other, they paid themselves off with some piece of furniture which they took out to sell and disappeared.

The days passed and Dumas dozed on. He remembered how when he had been a little child he had used to run on his tiptoes. And then finally he had come down on his heels. Yes, but only outside: inside, in his mind, in his passions, he had raced on as before. Raced on for over sixty years.

Until now. Now at last he was at rest.

The weeks passed and he did nothing. Occasionally visitors dropped in. Then Dumas would rouse himself temporarily and even get dressed and go out. And for an hour or two he would seem to be his old lively self.

But the moment he found himself alone, he relaxed. And returned to his pleasant somnolence.

One day his son made an unexpected visit.

"Bonjour, Papa," said Alexandre.

"Bonjour, *mon fils*," said Dumas.

"How are you, Papa?"

"As you see, my boy," said Dumas. "As usual, hard at work. I have half a dozen stories and articles that I've promised to turn out." And he dipped his pen into the dry inkwell.

Alexandre saw the piles of unopened mail, the newspapers and magazines unread. With his finger he traced a track through the heavy dust that had accumulated on the mounds of blank deckle-edged paper.

"Why don't you come out and spend the summer with us at the beach?" said Alexandre. He had a little cottage at Puys, a lovely spot that George Sand had recommended.

Dumas shrugged. "Thanks. Really, I'm very comfortable here."

But he didn't resist when his son put a cape around him and led him away.

He liked to sit on the beach, in the warm sun. He heard his grandchildren screaming around him, and he smiled and dozed as if fifty years of missed sleep had now turned in their bill and were insisting on immediate payment.

Since he took no interest in the war, it was decided to say nothing to him about it. And Alexandre, seeing that the Prussian armies were headed for Paris, decided it might be safer to remain for the rest of the year at Puys.

When the cold autumn days came, Dumas began to spend less and less time up. Finally one day the maid put his clothes away. And Dumas realized that he would never wear them again.

When she emptied his pockets, she found a gold Napoleon and some change. Alexandre handed the coins to his father. Dumas laughed. "Look, my boy, that's precisely the sum with which I landed in Paris, fifty years ago. Imagine: a half century of high living and it hasn't cost me a cent. I'm still as rich as when I started out. Now let anyone accuse me of extravagance!"

The doctor came to see him, but only to confirm what was quite apparent: his body was no longer voiding its waters properly and the tissues were becoming flooded. It would be necessary, from time to time, to resort to artificial means.

Dumas understood the sentence of death and did not seem to mind.

Only now and then, when alone, he would sometimes cry softly. He would think back to the moment of his birth when he had cast his water over his head and his father had been so proud of him and had prophesied that he would go far. And now, here he was, and could no longer do at all that which he had once performed so superbly well.

One day his son found him in tears.

"You're in pain, Papa!" he cried out, alarmed.

Dumas shook his head.

"The children are too noisy?" Alexandre asked.

"No, son. I'm fine. But I've been thinking of the time Victor Hugo advised me not to write so fast, nor so much. 'You have money now, and reputation. Now write for the ages. Mature something that will live forever.' How I wish now that I had taken his advice to heart."

"But, Papa, you *have* written things for the ages."

"No," said Dumas. "I wanted to make myself into a legendary character. But I've failed—all around. Long ago, in my play *Antony*, I wrote: 'Oblivion is the shroud in which the dead are buried for the second time.' That line was meant for me."

Alexandre, tortured, said with simulated cheer, "But for that line alone, Papa, you should be remembered."

Dumas shook his head slowly. "No, my boy. The famous writers, the ones who really carve their names in history, they write the serious, the difficult, the incomprehensible. My works are too easy. A child can read them. And you know it's the dinner you can't digest that you remember long after you've eaten it. My stuff was always too digestible. It tasted too good. It went down too easily. Oh, I often thought of changing—but when I got to writing I could never put my mind to anything else but the problem of how to keep the reader interested, keep him excited, startled. I wanted to have him laughing or crying, amused or frightened. And never did I try to appear more intelligent than the reader. On the contrary, I strove to make the difficult as simple as possible, I wanted to share everything I knew with the reader, in the most pleasant manner possible. For this I will be forgotten."

"But, Papa, who will ever be able to forget your *Three Musketeers*, your *Monte Cristo*, your *Twenty Years After*?"

Dumas smiled incredulously. "You honestly think they are good?"

"Why, Papa, they're classics."

Dumas shook his head. "No. I don't believe it." He sighed. "I wish now that I had read them. I often promised myself that I would. But when did I have the time?"

"What?" Alexandre exclaimed, all the old ghosts rising in him again. "You never read them?"

"How could I?" Dumas asked. "I had to choose between reading and writing. I did not have time for both. So I decided to do the writing and leave the reading to the public."

"Well, you have time to read now," said Alexandre.

"But have you my books here?" Dumas asked.

"Can you imagine a French home without your books?" Alexandre said. "Without at least your *Monte Cristo* and your *Three Musketeers*? And if not, they can be purchased in every village."

He left and came back with an armload of Dumas volumes.

His father smiled sadly. "I shall scarcely have time to finish all that."

Nevertheless, he began to read. "You know, it's quite good," he said to his son once.

But in the midst of *Monte Cristo,* he became tearful. "I shall never know how it all comes out," he moaned.

Alexandre choked back his tears. "Papa," he said, "Papa . . ."

"Yes, son." The old man's eyes were closed and his voice far away.

"Forgive me, Papa. Forgive me!"

"What for, my boy?" his father asked. Those were his last words, spoken just as it seemed finally possible for father and son to have an explanation.

He had sunk into a somnolence from which he never again roused himself. Soon an attack of apoplexy in the midst of this sleep sent his daughter on the run for the priest. And while in the distance the Prussian artillery could be heard battering at Dieppe, Dumas received the last sacrament, only the fluttering of his eyelids betraying that he was aware of what was going on.

Thus he passed away. It was the fifth of December, 1870.

On the eighth, a raw morning, when the Germans finally invested Dieppe, Dumas' body was taken to the neighboring village of Neuville for temporary burial. The family, a few neighbors and a German patrol were at the ceremony. After the war it was expected that the body could be brought to its final resting place at Villers-Cotterêts.

Alexandre, in a voice broken again and again by sobs, spoke the last words. "It is not right, Papa, that I, your son, should stand here and say those final words that custom dictates should come from someone other than a relative. But we are surrounded here by an implacable enemy, and your friends cannot even know that you have passed away.

"You came to this world in the age of the great appetite. The age of man the devourer. A poem or two, the *Iliad,* the *Odyssey,* were enough to satisfy the Greeks for centuries. But today a new epic must be forthcoming every day.

"Such an age requires heroic workers. And nature has provided such workers. African sunshine, American grandeur, were needed to make your ancestors. Your father was a soldier who could strangle a horse between his knees and crush a helmet between his teeth. Rome would have made a consul of him. But our age produces too many heroes. Just as it produces too many Homers.

"Indeed, our country is so crowded with Homers that it could never even find room for you in her Academy.

"Son of a soldier, you flung yourself into literature as your father flung himself into battle.

"For nearly fifty years you fought, casting plays, comedies, trage-dies, novels, books of travel and history into the insatiable maw of the public.

"France, Europe, America, fed on your work. Secretaries raced to keep up with you. Producers, publishers, translators, plagiarists, like looters after a battle, battened on the field of your energy.

"Like Vulcan at his forge, you labored. And in the heat you some-times tossed bad metal into your fire. But you did not linger over your error. You went on. Around your hearth gathered a multitude of writers whose genius could only flower where your heat was.

"The envious, passing by, spoke of plagiarism, they spoke of lit-erary industrialism, but you never stopped your work.

"I used to see you sometimes in your workshop, Papa. There were moments when you were tired, and when you would let your hammer lie for a moment on the anvil, and, with your chest bared, your sleeves rolled back, you would come to the door for a minute or two to breathe the freshness of the night, to look for a moment at the stars, and wipe the sweat from your forehead. But only for a moment, and then you were back at work.

"And when, avid for something new, you would rush off to Africa or to the Caucasus, it was your whole workshop that you loaded on your shoulders, and, as you climbed Mount Etna, as you camped among the Tartars, you never for a moment interrupted your gigantic labors.

"And the mob, loving energy, loved you for your feats of labor and courage.

"But just when you were at your best, another mood seized the crowd. What once had seemed magnificent suddenly seemed clownish. People whispered evil stories about you. But you didn't mind. You laughed. And even when people began saying, 'It's the son who really has the talent,' you didn't mind either. On the con-trary, you took me around the shoulders and said, 'Yes, you're my best work. Someday I shall be known only as your father.'

"I might have become conceited, as certainly I must confess that

I was sinfully envious, but you taught me a lesson. You taught me much more than how to write: you taught me to love life.

"When I think of how, years ago, all the world knew you and, today, in the midst of gunfire, no one even knows that you have crossed the last milestone and gone to your long home without any of the honors that are due you, I cry—but I know that someday all those who have ever had their lives lightened for a moment by the reading of one of your books will contribute a penny to your memory, and then we shall cast a monument for you out of solid gold."

It was from a German paper found on the body of a German soldier that Victor Hugo, weeks later, learned of the death of Dumas.

"He was as kindly as a summer shower," he said. "His black clouds, his rumble of thunder, his flashes of lightning, deceived no one. Everyone knew that he was as gentle and as generous as a summer rain on the parched earth."

A Final Word Indeed

❧ A FINAL WORD ❧

What shall we call this book anyhow? Novel? Biography? Is there any truth to it whatsoever? And if so, how much?

The answer is that it is exceedingly true. For it is a work of fiction not only solidly based on research, but going beyond research.

To illustrate, take one of the very minor episodes concerning Dumas' love for medals. The painter Paul Huet did actually, according to the records, come upon Dumas standing guard duty in a uniform so dazzling with medals that Huet felt impelled to spin the man around to see if perhaps he did not have some extra medals hung on his backside.

And there our recorded story stops.

But this is outrageous! A landscape painter such as Paul Huet may consider that a good story, but not a writer. It just isn't funny enough. One feels hung up in mid-air. One wants to know if Dumas really did have medals pinned to his rear end. And if so, how did he explain it? Dumas was of course quite capable of hanging medals on the seat of his pants, but he would certainly never let himself be caught without an appropriate explanation. Very likely some simple, convincing and at the same time touching remark such as I lend him—namely that the medals on his backside came from kings who had since lost their thrones.

Now the anecdote is complete.

Was it wrong of me to have corrected this little story? With a man like Dumas, of whom so many delightful stories have come down to us, surely it is a harmless assumption that many more stories, and perhaps better ones, would have survived had his friends been more diligent in collecting and recording them. No doubt it cannot be given to every man to have his Boswell, but are we to hold that against Dumas when it is obviously not his fault but the fault of his friends?

Occasionally Dumas himself cannot be trusted to do his own anecdotes, even when acting as his own Boswell. As for example in the bearsteak story. There he omits so obvious a curtain line that I have felt compelled to supply it: I refer to the line in which he tells the innkeeper that he will do for the widow of the man eaten by the bear more than merely give her some money; he will give her back her husband.

Was it wrong for me to have corrected Dumas' oversight in this matter? And if so, may I know, please, whom I am wronging?

Dare we show ourselves less generous toward Dumas than Dumas

496

showed himself toward his historical characters in his own books? Surely
not. And thus if at times throughout my book I have done a little touching up of the tales of Dumas' cookery, his uniforms, his remarks about
women or about writing, and so forth, consider it as nothing more than
writers have been doing since the dawn of literature, gradually boosting
some anecdotes from India into the tales of Boccaccio and from there
into Shakespeare's plays, and, who knows, some day perhaps beyond that.

All this, so far, has concerned itself only with the passementerie of
my book.

More serious are my inventions of conversations that never took place.
For example the conversations between Dumas and Véron, between
Dumas and his business manager, between Dumas and Viel-Castel,
Dumas and William Wells Brown, etc. But note that in each instance
these are conversations that should have taken place! Take the case of
William Wells Brown, that free Negro from America who tried so hard
to have a conversation with Dumas. And then there he was one evening
in the same theater with Dumas. He in the orchestra, Dumas in a box.

What did Brown do?

He did nothing.

But how criminal of this colored man from America to have come
thirty hundred miles, and then to have failed to take just thirty more
steps to talk to the most famous colored man in the world. And apparently all because of mere pique: because Dumas had failed to answer his
letters! It's obvious that Brown had jumped to the conclusion that
Dumas was ashamed of his Negro blood. What Brown probably didn't
know was that Dumas was constantly being subjected to practical jokes
about his Negro ancestry. For example, when Barnum's circus came to
Paris some wag hired the entire Negro troupe to burst in on Dumas at his
apartment, crying, "Cousin, we are here!" and dumping their baggage on
the floor, prepared for a long stay. Naturally Dumas had become wary.

Thus it was left me to supply a conversation that should have taken
place but didn't. Lies? Well, yes. But the question is not whether I lied,
but whether the conversation, had it taken place, would not have been
pretty much as I give it. Fact is that my conversation goes beyond a real
conversation, since actual recorded conversations, even between men of
genius, often fail to touch upon essential points, due to accident, lack of
time, embarrassment, tiredness, who knows what. While imaginary conversations are able to go at once to the point.

Dumas' contemporaries are unanimous in calling him a brilliant con-
versationalist. Shall we fly in the face of these authorities simply because
we fail to find certain conversations recorded, and others recorded but
lacking somewhat in brilliance?

You see, the more one studies the Dumas material, the more one is
forced to the conclusion that research alone will never do justice to the
man. Personally, in my reading of Dumas biographies, I always seemed to

hear deep subterranean groans, as if Dumas were there in the cellar, struggling against the shackles of research.

And yet it was not without some trepidation that I dared follow the lead of Goethe and combine truth and invention, *Dichtung und Wahrheit*, for the sake of a closer approach to reality. After some groping around I found my way to a novel that would rely on research without being bound by it. And I hit at last on a novel written in the form of research, as other novels have been written in the form of letters, or extracts from diaries, and so forth.

For this I had some justification in Dumas' own statement to the historian Michelet: "Admit, my dear Michelet, that historians are better the more their works read like novels, while novels are better the more they read like history."

And for my motto I adopted the Italian expression *Se non è vero, è ben trovato;* roughly: *If it isn't the exact truth, it's at least a valid lie.* My goal, you see, being a book in which the lie would be indistinguishable from the truth.

This proved indeed the only solution of the problem of writing Dumas' life. For note that if one were to stick to research and nothing but research, then it would be impossible to write five full pages about Dumas' duels, and much of that would be mere speculation. Such episodes as the saliva duel at two paces, the dinner discussion of duels and epigrams, the story of the thirteenth duel—all that has for its actual historical support only this one small incident: Dumas fils, smarting from the insults flung at his father by De Mirecourt, had his seconds go to the journalist's apartment to arrange for a duel. But the door was opened by De Mirecourt himself, carrying in his arms his two-year-old boy and saying, "If Dumas sends his son to fight for him, then here, I offer you my son, who will fight for me."

That ended that. And no encounter ever took place.

Obviously this is not much of a scene properly to illustrate the immense devotion and love that, in those early days, young Dumas had for his papa. And this climax, a mere line of dialogue, is neither sufficiently startling nor sufficiently bitter to give the reader a sense of the tragic rebuff that it must have occasioned Alexandre. The affair cries for more light and shadow. The metal of truth wants bumping up here to a higher and sharper relief.

Nor was any great amount of invention required to achieve this. Only that De Mirecourt should delay his pronouncement regarding his son fighting for him until the appearance of the principals on the dueling grounds. Then only one thing more was needed to produce the grotesque performance that convulsed Paris: the age of De Mirecourt's son had to be raised from two to eight. And the little scamp had somehow to be supplied with a real sword.

However small, these are no doubt serious deviations from the truth, especially when they are allowed to expand into the scenes they evoke. But the question is: in what direction do they deviate? Is it in the direction of more truth? Or less truth?

Perhaps this question lets itself be examined best in connection with the scene in which Delacroix makes a masterpiece of an omelet in a frying pan. Here we have not one iota of truth on which to base ourselves. Nothing but research. And from that research we know first of all that such cooking sprees were a feature of Dumas' life, and, in the second place, that Delacroix was often present. Now, if you will look into Delacroix' diary, you will discover that Dumas plays an important role in Delacroix' private emotional life, because the painter both envied him for his enormous popularity and scorned him for his cheapness.

To have limited myself to the truth as it is given to us in the records would have prevented me from bringing these two great personalities to grips in my book, and their strange friendship and antagonism would have had to remain something in the shadows, unlived, without benefit of climax, a matter of a few words scattered here and there in Delacroix' private journal.

Ask yourself which brings these men more to life—the strict truth, or the invention based on that truth?

This same question of whether the lie tends in the direction of more truth or less truth comes up particularly strongly in the romance between Dumas and his first Parisian mistress, Catherine Lebay, where the absence of information is nothing less than shameful. Only eight words and a few sentences to cover everything: the romance, Catherine's pregnancy, the birth and registration of the child, the various events of a boy's schooling and growing up to manhood.

Who will say that those eight words from Dumas' Memoirs, those few sentences from a letter by Dumas fils, are closer to the truth than the expansion that I have given them out of my imagination?

One would of course have no excuse for adding a word to the existing records if human beings were not so obstinately determined to conceal the truth about themselves. Even writers, who do not shrink from exposing the characters of their stories to the public gaze in their most intimate moments, insist on preserving for themselves large areas of mystery. Why this happens to be so is not for discussion at this point, but its prevalence is such that today there exists a whole branch of medicine that bases itself on the theory that the only truly honest and trustworthy fiber left in man has taken refuge in his dreams, where it is almost beyond his will power to destroy it.

Thus, in order to restore to Dumas' life the truths that belong to it, one is called upon to supply material that is not to be found in any research however thorough.

And something more.

For there is often a vast amount of documentary material that by its sheer quantity tends to distort a man's life especially where other facets of his life have left little or no record.

An outstanding example is the question of Dumas' plagiarisms. Here one can easily be snowed under. Nothing is more certain than that Dumas was haled into court again and again on charges of literary fraud and was repeatedly forced to pay damages and make good in other ways. And in addition to the attacks on him during his lifetime, only recently there have been renewed investigations, for example, of his books on Spain, where a student was able to demonstrate with parallel columns how ideas, sentences, even whole paragraphs had been copied from previous travel books.

And then there is Quérard. In my novel I have had the nerve to dismiss Quérard out of hand. Can that be justified on any grounds?

Quérard was that indefatigable book salesman turned bibliographer who in the first half of the nineteenth century, in the course of amassing his huge lists of French books, ran across so many cases of deceit, so many instances of fraudulence and plagiarism, that he eventually devoted a separate five-volume work to this subject all by itself.

Seemingly nothing could escape the microscopic eye of this dry, mousy man with the sour and furtive air. And Dumas—yes, our good friend Dumas—rates the biggest entry of all in Quérard's *Supercheries littéraires devoilées*, his *Literary Frauds Unveiled*. Quérard sets aside for Dumas not less than 150 closely printed columns! So enormous is this listing of Dumas plagiarisms and Dumas deceits that Quérard felt it necessary to furnish this colossal article with its own private index so that the reader might find his way around in it.

Quérard is no cheap scandalmongering journalist such as Eugène de Mirecourt. He's no ambitious political charlatan like Granier de Cassagnac, a man determined to make a big name for himself no matter over whose dead body. You cannot brush aside his work as you can the short sketch by Loménie, who pictures our hero sitting at his desk turning over with his left hand the printed pages of a published work as fast as his right hand can copy out another original Dumas story, handwritten and ready now for the printer.

No, Quérard is one of France's great bibliographers, whose works are in every major research library of the world.

So when it comes to the facts about Dumas' literary frauds, there you have them. Written out in detail by a famous scholar who lived in Dumas' day and whom Dumas never dared sue. There are the facts. But for me they don't count. They don't add up. I wipe out all those 150 columns, just like that. And for this reason: from Quérard you will learn that one of the ghost writers most frequently deprived of his rightful author's credit by Dumas was his old boyhood friend Adolphe de Leuven (son of the Swedish regicide), whose plays Dumas put on the stage time and time again under his own name, eventually including them in his twenty volumes of collected plays with no acknowledgment to their true author.

But what Quérard couldn't possibly know was this: that when Adolphe de Leuven would die at the ripe age of over ninety, surviving both Quérard and Dumas by many years, he would leave his considerable estate, including a house and grounds . . . well, to whom do you suppose? Why, to the son of the very man who, according to Quérard, had so vilely misused and defrauded him.

Yes, he made Dumas fils his heir!

Now ask yourself what truth about Dumas there really is in all the 150 columns of Quérard? Facts, yes. Plenty of facts. But truth? Obviously not a shred of it.

Oh, to be sure, one wants and needs facts. All the facts one can get. And compilations of facts are very valuable. But at the same time one must never forget that all the facts about any person will never add up to the living man or woman. That is why the living Dumas somehow never leaps out of the pages of his biographers in the same way as Dumas' own creations leap out of his pages. Which is no reflection on Dumas' biographers, for he has had several excellent ones.

It is rather because when an author has absorbed all the available facts on the subject he is going to write about, he is still nothing but a supersaturated solution. And everyone knows that nothing can crystallize out of such a solution unless some foreign matter manages to get into it. For a snowflake to grow, more is required than the existence of water vapor and freezing temperatures in the upper atmosphere. Each and every snowflake requires a grain of dust or some other impurity around which to develop.

This foreign matter, this impurity—call it a lie, call it imagination, or truth beyond research—call it whatever you prefer, but without it all the research in the world will never produce anything. It must always remain sterile.

Now to come to the heart of my book: the father-son duel during the masquerade party. We will have to admit at once that there is absolutely nothing in the records even remotely suggesting such a father-son combat. And yet, once one has accepted the theme of dueling as eminently befitting a tale on Dumas (and I don't see how this could be avoided), then the eventual father-son explosion is in the cards.

In the records all we have is this one isolated fact—a fact, however, that like the fact of Adolphe de Leuven's will speaks volumes: one day Dumas fils found himself, knife in hand, about to enter a room where his father lay asleep. Dumas fils afterward pleaded illness and exhaustion as the cause of a temporary aberration of his mind.

But was this really no more than a temporary aberration of the mind? Was it not more likely a bit of that really honest and trustworthy fiber of man revealing itself in this walking nightmare?

We know that between these two men there existed not only a deep bond of affection but also certain hidden feelings, such that for years on end they never saw each other except at funerals.

How intolerable, then, to an author who wishes to portray the real Dumas that this powerful mixture of emotions existing between father and son should have found expression in nothing more overt than this little knife incident, a lapse so slight that it isn't worth more than a sentence or two in any Dumas biography.

Here are two men in whose novels and plays there are uncounted duels. Two men therefore whose imaginations ran riot in gunplay and swordplay. Is it fair that history should forever deny such men the one big encounter of their lives?

We know from any number of witnesses that Dumas really lived his stories to the hilt, played them out so intensely that he would sit up all night at his little deal table, busily moving his pen and all the while keeping up a constant shouting, groaning, weeping, laughing. At such moments he was not merely Dumas; he was also Ange Pitou storming the Bastille, he was the Queen Mother slinking through the corridors of the Louvre, he was the Iron Mask staring through the barred window of his prison, he was Cagliostro scheming up the affair of the diamond necklace, he was the future Count of Monte Cristo letting himself be buried alive in order to escape from the dungeons of the Château d'If.

Surely a man deserves as much as he gives. How can the hero of your book be the real Dumas if you yourself will not feel like shouting, groaning, weeping, laughing while you write about him? That this father-son rivalry should have eventually dissipated itself in other ways than one grand piece of swordplay is just one of those accidents of life whereby many a potentially heroic man never finds the opportunity of demonstrating his real size.

Thus the crucial importance for me of Dumas' criticism of Jean-Léon Gérôme's painting "Le duel à la sortie du bal masqué." This criticism is not out of my imagination. True, he did not make it before a crowd at the Salon, but he did write and publish it, and you will find an excerpt from it in Larousse's Grand Dictionnaire Universel du XIXème siècle, in the D volume under the title of the painting.

All other art critics of Paris—Saint-Victor, Gautier, Pesquindoux, Delescluze—had nothing but paeans of praise for Gérôme's canvas. Only one critic, Dumas, took it upon himself to lecture Gérôme on what is reality in a duel and what is not reality. Could one ask for better proof of the fact that Dumas was eaten with scorn and envy, to see this painter get away with so obvious a fake duel, while he could not make the sophisticates of his day believe in his real ones?

Here is part of what he says: "The conception of the scene in Gérôme's painting is dramatic. But not so the result. And the failure stems from this one factor: the artist did not concern himself sufficiently with the problem of the real and the false.

"In brief: it is absolutely unbelievable that anyone could leave a masquerade party to go out into the snow to fight a duel and not in some way mar his fancy dress costume. And no matter how you may imagine this quarrel to have arisen, no matter how anxious the principals may have been to effect an immediate and bloody settlement, even to the point of denying themselves time to go home and change clothes, still the scene remains incredible because merely to leave the hall the combatants would have to pass the cloakroom and they could not have failed, in midwinter, to redeem their overcoats. And even had their headlong thirst for the clash of steel prevented them from stopping for a moment at the cloakroom, they still would have found time to divest themselves at least of wigs and ribands, tear off some of the hampering cloth, if only to feel freer to kill.

"But here we see nothing of the sort. The artist is determined that his Pierrot and his Harlequin shall appear on the field of honor as flawlessly attired as if they were about to go into their dance on the stage of the Paris Opéra. Now do not accuse me of being a stickler for inconsequential details. I say this is basic to the declared purpose of the artist. And I say furthermore that precisely the effect he hopes to achieve is nullified by the complete absence of anything that might call to mind the life of our day and the usual dress of our times.

"In fine, standing before this painting I do not feel myself the spectator at a tragedy, but rather in the theatre at the final tableau of a pantomime. Oh, a well-staged pantomime to be sure. Pierrot handles his role with talented mendacity. No one could possibly play dead any deader. I applaud enthusiastically. Really I am thrilled—but you don't catch me shuddering. For I can see with my two eyes that this Pierrot has only been stabbed with a trick sword. And that the stain of blood on his white doublet was done by himself with a sponge previously soaked in red paint. Not for a moment do I doubt that when the curtain has dropped for the final time, our Pierrot will leap to his feet, rush to his dressing room for a quick change and then home and to bed. Bravo Pierrot!"

Is not this the sarcastic cry of a man who had to suffer under the suspicion of faking his duels? And just as Adolphe de Leuven's testament opened my eyes to all the gossip and even the facts about Dumas' literary frauds, so this bit of art criticism opened my eyes on the subject of Dumas' supposedly staged duels.

And rightly, or wrongly, around this impurity my snowflake grew.

Whether I have done a good job of growing my snowflake, that is another matter. Time will tell whether the lie I have constructed is just an ordinary lie, or whether it is one of those special lies that are truer than the truth. Because there are such lies. For instance, the ostrich who hides his head in the sand is a lie, for no such ostrich exists. And yet that nonexistent ostrich is just about the only one we talk about, and it has more reality for us than the ostrich who still goes on providing man with those useless and unfashionable plumes.

If my Dumas should eventually become the real Dumas in the minds of people, dimming or even blotting out the Dumas of the facts, just as Edmond Rostand's Cyrano de Bergerac has blotted out the real Cyrano, or for that matter just as Dumas' own d'Artagnan has blotted out the real d'Artagnan (who was Cyrano's contemporary), then that will be the proof that the lie can sometimes be truer than the truth.

GUY ENDORE

ABOUT THE AUTHOR

ONE REASON that Guy Endore has been unusually successful in projecting an authentic background for *King of Paris* is that a large part of his early education took place in Europe, mostly in Austria and France. He was, however, born in Brooklyn, U.S.A., and he was graduated from Columbia College in the class of 1924. Romance languages was his major subject, and he has translated a number of books from both French and German. Previous original books of Mr. Endore's have included Casanova (a biography), *The Werewolf of Paris* (a novel), and *Methinks the Lady* (a suspense story).

Mr. Endore makes his home in Los Angeles, where he lives with his wife, who has a school for small children, and his two daughters. He has numerous credits for movie scripts.